A TIME *to* DANCE
~&~
A TIME *to* EMBRACE

KAREN KINGSBURY

THOMAS NELSON
Since 1798

NASHVILLE   DALLAS   MEXICO CITY   RIO DE JANEIRO   BEIJING

Published in Nashville, Tennessee, by Thomas Nelson. Thomas Nelson is a registered trademark of Thomas Nelson, Inc.

Published in association with the literary agency of Alive Communications, Inc., 7680 Goddard Street, Suite 200, Colorado Springs, Colorado 80920.

Thomas Nelson, Inc., titles may be purchased in bulk for educational, business, fund-raising, or sales promotional use. For information, please e-mail SpecialMarkets@ThomasNelson.com.

Scripture quotations used in this book are from the Holy Bible, New International Version (NIV). © 1973, 1978, 1984, International Bible Society. Used by permission of Zondervan Bible Publishers.

ISBN 978-1-59554-521-3

Printed in the United States of America
08 09 10 11 12 RRD 6 5 4 3 2

A Time to Dance

Dedicated to

Donald, my lover and playmate and best friend of all. With you, all of life is a dance and I can only pray the music continues for all time. Thank you for stating early on that the *d* word would not be part of our vocabulary. And thanks for modeling in Christ what it means to truly love.

Kelsey, my sweet girl, who stands on the brink of those tough and tender teenage years. Already you are old enough to understand love, to know that you're a one-in-a-million catch and to believe no one will ever love you like your daddy or your heavenly Father. You once said you wouldn't marry a boy unless he was like your daddy. Keep that, honey; believe me, your standard couldn't possibly be any higher than that.

Tyler, my dreamer and doer, who wants so much from life and whom God has chosen for great and mighty things. I will hear your voice singing to me on faraway nights when my hair is gray and our family days are but a memory. Thank you, buddy, for always making me smile.

Austin, my boy of boundless energy, better known as Michael Jordan. You defy man's wisdom each day by merely breathing. You grace our home with constant dribbling and shooting and slam-dunking, sounds that have almost made me forget those hospital machines in intensive care. Almost, but not quite. And each time your arms come around my neck, I thank God for the miracle of your life.

E.J. and Sean, our chosen sons, who have brought us all together in a common cause, a common love. Thank you for defining our family's eternal perspective and for giving us reason to celebrate God's plan. Remember, dear sons, although you did not grow under my heart you most certainly grew in it. I look forward to all that God has planned for you.

And to God Almighty,
Who has, for now, blessed me with these.

Acknowledgments

The dream of writing a book that might show love—marital love—for the glorious thing that God has intended it to be, was inspired in my heart long ago and given wings here, by the grace of our Lord. Still, it would not have been possible to write this book without the help of many people. First and foremost I'd like to thank the Women of Faith organization: everyone from Steve Arterburn to Mary Graham and all the wonderful WOF friends I've had the privilege to meet in the process of pulling this project together. What a great idea—a line of fiction for all women everywhere . . . fiction that will entertain and change lives, encourage love and inspire hope. Bravo, for giving readers an option! Also to my fellow WOF fictionettes for being excited alongside me and for helping make this and the next three books in the WOF Fiction Club a reading experience like none other.

Professionally, a special thanks to Greg Johnson who is brimming with ideas and without a doubt the world's best agent. Greg, your enthusiasm and creativity, energy and devotion to God are a constant testimony to me. You inspire me to new heights, and I'm blessed and honored to be among those writers in your care.

Also to my editor, Karen Ball, who has been with me along the entire fiction journey and who makes my work sing. God has gifted you, friend, and I am grateful to benefit from the fact. Also to Ami McConnell, Mark Sweeney, and all the wonderful folks at Word Publishing. I'm honored to be writing for you now and in the future.

Thanks, too, go to Joan Westfall for doing a read-through of this book at the last minute. You are an amazing person, Joan—always encouraging others, looking for the good, and taking the time to catch even the smallest detail in this book so that it will be that much more professional. I treasure you more than you know.

And finally, on a personal note, a special thanks to Kristy and Jeff Blake for loving my precious Austin through the process of writing . . . and to Sorena Wagner for being the most amazing nanny anyone could have. You are wonderful and I am blessed for knowing you. Also to my true friends and self-appointed publicity crew Christine Wessel, Heidi Cleary, Joan Westfall, Jan Adams, Michelle Stokes, and Debbie Kimsie . . . Thank you for being excited about the stories I tell and for bringing me such encouragement. God has used you more than you know.

A humble thanks also goes to my prayer warriors Sylvia and Ann. The two of you are the most selfless, amazing servants—listening to Christ's call and lifting me and my work to His throne room daily. I don't deserve you, but I am grateful all the same. You won't know this side of heaven how much your constant intervention and love for me has affected the lives of our readers.

Always a special thanks goes to my family for their love and support and for understanding when dinner is macaroni and cheese three nights running. And to my parents, Ted and Anne Kingsbury, and siblings, Susan, Tricia, David, and Lynne, for your love and support. Also to Shannon Kane, one of my best and most faithful readers and certainly one of my favorite nieces. One day I'll be reading your work, honey!

Finally, a special thanks to the readers who have taken the time to write me over the years. I remember each of you and pray for you often. And to the Skyview basketball team for always giving me something to cheer about—even on deadline.

There is a time for everything, and a season for every activity under heaven: . . . a time to weep and a time to laugh, a time to mourn and a time to dance.

—ECCLESIASTES 3:1, 4

One

WITHOUT QUESTION, IT WAS THE MOMENT ABBY Reynolds had waited for all her life.

Beneath the Friday-night lights in the biggest college stadium in the state of Illinois, Abby's husband was on the brink of winning his second high-school football championship. Moreover he was about to do so largely on the talents of their older son, the team's senior quarterback.

Abby pulled her blue-and-gray Marion Eagles jacket tighter to her body and wished she'd brought a thicker scarf. It was early December, after all, and though snow hadn't fallen for more than a week, the air was biting cold. "Football weather," John always said. Cold and dry, straight from heaven. She stared beyond the lights to the starry sky. *Even God is rooting for you tonight, John.*

Her gaze fell across the field, and she picked out her husband on the sidelines, headset angled just so, body bent over, hands on his knees as he waited for the play to unfold. She could remember a million afternoons when his eyes had sparkled with laughter, but here, now, they were hard and focused. His face was the picture of concentration, lined with the intensity of the moment as he barked commands in a dozen directions. Even from her place high up in the packed stands, Abby could feel the energy that emanated from John in the final minutes of this, his most prized football game.

No doubt about it, coaching was his gift.

And this was his finest hour.

If only everything else hadn't gotten so—

"Come on, Eagles. You can do it!" Abby's daughter, Nicole, clapped her hands and gritted her teeth, holding tighter to her boyfriend, Matt's, hand, every ounce of her energy focused on her younger brother.

Tears nipped at Abby's eyes, and she blinked them back. *If only I could freeze time, here and now . . .* She turned and squeezed her father's knee. "I can feel it, Dad. They're gonna win."

Her father, an old man who barely resembled the dad she'd grown up with, raised a shaky fist partway into the freezing night. "You can do it, Kade!" His hand dropped weakly back into his lap.

Abby patted her father's limp arm and then cupped her hands around her mouth. "Make it count, Kade. Come on!" Her fingers tightened into fists, and she tapped them in a fast, steady beat against her knees. *Please, Lord, let him have this.*

After tonight there were bound to be few moments of light for any of them.

"I kinda hate to see it end." Her father grinned at her through wet eyes. "All those years of football together. The boy's amazing. Plays just like his father."

Abby focused her gaze on her son and the corners of her mouth lifted. "He always has."

"Mom, isn't it weird?" Nicole leaned her head on Abby's shoulder.

"What, honey?" Abby took her daughter's free hand and resisted the urge to close her eyes. It felt so good, sitting here in the thrill of the moment, surrounded by family . . .

"This is Kade's last high-school game." Nicole's voice was thick, filled with tender indignation, as though she'd only now realized a loss she hadn't prepared for. "Just like that, it's over. Next year he'll be at Iowa, and it won't be the same."

A stinging sensation made its way across Abby's eyes again, and she struggled to swallow. *If only you knew, sweetheart . . .* "It never is."

Nicole stared down at the field. "I mean, this is it. After tonight he'll never play for Dad again." She glanced at the scoreboard. "All those practices and games, and in a few minutes it'll be over. Just a box full of memories and old newspaper articles."

The lump grew thicker. *Not now, Nicole. Let me enjoy the moment.* Tears clouded Abby's vision. *Come on, get a grip. Life is full of endings.* She squeezed her daughter's hand and uttered a short laugh. "We're supposed to be cheering, remember? They haven't won yet."

Nicole stuck her chin out and shouted as loud as she could. "Go, Eagles, come on! You can do it!"

Abby's eyes moved toward the field where Kade was at the center of the huddle, relaying his father's plays to the team. Third down and eight, twenty-five yards to go for a touchdown. There was just over a minute to play, and Marion was up by three. This touchdown—and Abby could feel in her gut that there would be a touchdown—would seal the win.

"Let's go, Eagles!" Abby clapped her mittened hands together and stared intently at the field as the play unfolded. *Come on, Kade. Nice and easy. Like a hundred times before . . .*

Her strapping son took the snap and, with practiced grace, found his place in the pocket, searching downfield until he saw his target. Then, in the fluid motion that comes from being the talented son of a storied football coach, he fired the ball, threading it through two menacing defenders to land, almost like magic, in the hands of a Marion receiver.

The home crowd was on its feet.

Over the din of ten thousand screaming fans, the announcer explained the situation: the Eagles had a first and goal on the three-yard line with less than a minute to play.

The opposing team called a time-out, and Abby breathed in slowly. If she could savor this moment, bottle it up or capture it forever, she would. Hadn't they dreamed of this time and place since Kade was born, first joking about it and then realizing with each passing year the chance of it actually happening? Dozens of yesterdays fought for her attention. The first time she saw John in a football uniform . . . the way his eyes loved her as they spoke their wedding vows and toasted to forever . . . Nicole playing in the backyard . . . the gleam in four-year-old Kade's eyes when he got his first football . . . the thrill of Sean's birth seven years later . . . years of meeting on the pier at the end of the day . . . the music that they—

A whistle blew, and the players took their positions.

Abby swallowed hard. Her family had spent a lifetime getting here—two decades of memories, many of them centered around a white-lined, hundred-yard field of mud and grass.

The crowd remained on its feet, but despite the deafening noise there was a quiet place in Abby's heart where she could hear her children's long-ago laughter, see the way John and the kids tickled and tackled on the Marion High field every day when practice was over. For years John had known instinctively how to involve their children in his role as coach, how to put the game behind him at day's end. The image and voices changed, and the stadium noise was only a distant roar.

"Dance with me, Abby . . . dance with me."

There they were, on the pier. Dancing the dance of life, swaying to the sound of crickets and creaking boards long after the kids were asleep on nights when summer seemed like it might last forever.

A gust of wind sent a chill down her arms, and she blinked back the fading visions of yesterday. No matter how he'd betrayed her, no matter what happened next, there would never be a better father for her children than John Reynolds.

Another memory rang in her mind. She and John on the lake, adrift in an old fishing boat a year after Kade was born. *"One day, Abby, one day Kade'll play for me, and we'll go to state. All the way, honey. We'll have everything we ever dreamed of and nothing will stop us. Nothing . . ."*

Now—in what seemed like the blink of an eye—they were here. Kade took the snap and raised the ball.

Come on, Kade. It's yours, honey. "Go, Eagles!" she screamed.

The ball flew from Kade's hands like a bullet, spiraling through the winter night much the way Kade himself had flown through their lives, a blur of motion. *Come on, catch it* . . . Abby watched as Kade's best friend, T. J., the team's tight end, jumped for the ball. *Fitting*, she thought. Like the perfect ending to a perfect movie. And she realized that everything about Kade and John and their football days—even this final play—had somehow been destined from the beginning.

It all seemed to be happening in slow motion . . .

T. J. wrapped his fingers around the ball, pulled it to his chest, and landed squarely in the end zone.

"Touchdown!" Abby's heart soared and she leapt up and down, her fists high in the air. "I can't *believe* it! We did it! We *won!*" She pulled her father and Nicole into a hug and high-fived ten-year-old Sean three seats down the row. "State champs! Can you believe it?"

On the field the players kicked the extra point and then lined up for the kickoff. Fifteen seconds more and the Marion Eagles would be state champs. The Reynoldses' father-and-son team would forever be part of Illinois prep football lore.

John, you did it . . . you and Kade.

In honor of everything they'd ever been—of the beacon of light that had been their love, their family—Abby felt nothing but pure, unhindered joy for her husband.

Two tears spilled from the corners of her eyes and burned their way down her freezing cheeks.

Not now, Abby. Not when it's supposed to be a celebration. The crowd was shouting in unison: "Five . . . four . . . three . . . two . . ."

As the stands emptied onto the field, a swirling blue-and-gray mass of celebration, Abby's father hooted like he hadn't since he'd been relegated to a nursing home. Sean bounced along behind Nicole and Matt as they rushed down the stairs to join the others.

Abby sat frozen in place, soaking in the moment. She searched the crowd until she found John, watched as he ripped off his headset and ran like a madman to meet Kade. Their hug put Abby over the edge, and the tears came in quiet streams. John pulled their son into a solid embrace that shut out everyone else: teammates, coaches, members of the press. Everyone but each other. Kade gripped his helmet in one hand and his father's neck with the other.

Then it happened.

While Abby was still savoring the moment, Charlene Denton came up behind John and threw her arms around his shoulders. A rock took up residence in Abby's stomach and began to grow. *Not now . . . here in front of everyone we know.* John and Charlene were easily fifty yards from Abby, but it made no difference. She could see the way the scene played out as clearly as if she were standing beside them. Her husband pulled away from Kade and turned to hug Charlene briefly. There was something about the way John brought his head close to hers and kept his hand on her shoulder that conveyed his feelings for Charlene. Feelings he had long had for her. Charlene Denton, fellow teacher at Marion High, John's greatest stumbling block.

Abby blinked, and suddenly everything good and memorable and nostalgic about the night felt cheap and artificial, like something from a bad movie. Even the tenderest thoughts couldn't stand against the reality in front of her.

Abby's father saw them, too, and he cleared his throat. "I'll be fine here by myself, honey. You go be with John."

She shook her head, but her gaze never left her husband and Charlene. "No, I'll wait."

Her eyes were dry now, and anger pulsed through her, glazing her heart with hard, empty bitterness. *Get away from him, lady. This is* our *moment, not yours.* Abby stared at Charlene, hating her. John's voice echoed in her heart once more, but this time his words had nothing to do with dancing.

And everything to do with divorce.

This was the weekend they'd agreed to tell the kids. The weekend they would shatter their family's mistaken belief that Abby and John were perhaps the most happily married people in all the world. Abby sighed. No matter how it felt to see John with Charlene, the reality was he could talk to the teacher or any other woman for that matter. In a few months, John would be single, after all. As would Abby. She hugged herself tightly, trying to will away the nausea that swirled around inside her. *Why does it still hurt, Lord?*

No magic answers came to mind, and Abby wasn't sure if she wanted to disappear or bolt down onto the field and join them so that Charlene would feel too uncomfortable to stay.

I thought I was past this, God. We've already agreed to move on. What's happening to me? Abby tapped her foot against the concrete stadium floor and shifted positions, hating the way the other woman seemed unfettered, lovely and young and without the burdens of two decades of marriage. What was this feeling assaulting her? Jealousy?

No, it felt more like regret. Abby's pulse quickened. It couldn't be, could it? What was there to regret? Hadn't they *both* realized the place they were in, the place they were headed?

Or was this how it would always feel to see John with another woman?

Her vision clouded over, and again she heard John's voice from long ago. *"Dance with me, Abby . . . dance with me."*

The silent words faded from her mind and she blinked back fresh tears. One thing was certain: if this was how being divorced was going to feel, she'd better get used to it.

No matter how much she hated it.

Two

THE STADIUM WAS EMPTY, STREWN WITH CRUSHED Gatorade cups and half-eaten hot dogs. Assorted remnants of blue and gray hung from the student section, proof that the Marion Eagles had indeed been there, that John and Kade had accomplished their lifelong dream and won a state championship together.

Abby wandered down the steps to the field and across the grass toward the locker room. John would still be inside, talking to the press, going over the game's great plays with the other coaches, picking up after his team.

Savoring the moment as long as possible.

There was a bench just outside the visitors' door and Abby sat down, gazing across the empty field. Kade, Nicole, Matt, and Sean were holding a table for them at Smokey's Pizza a block down the street from the stadium. Abby's father was waiting in the car. She studied the muddied lines and the way the goalposts stood proudly erect on either side of the field. Had it only been an hour ago that the place had been packed, an entire crowd holding its collective breath while Kade threw the final touchdown?

Abby shivered and buried her hands deep in her pockets. The

temperature had fallen, but that had little to do with the terrifying cold that reigned in her heart.

A Marion assistant coach walked out and stopped when he saw her. "Hey, Abby." A smile took up most of his face. "How 'bout them Eagles."

She chuckled softly. No matter what painful twists her life was about to take, she would remember their football days as absolutely wonderful. Every player, every coach, every season . . . all of it a mosaic of memories she would cherish forever. "Amazing. A dream come true."

The man huffed slightly and shook his head, gazing into the winter sky. He was the biggest coach on staff, a former lineman with a reputation for getting in kids' faces. But here in the quiet shadows of a stadium void of cheering fans and the guttural grunts of sixty teenagers in full warrior gear, Abby noticed his eyes glistening with unshed tears. He cleared his throat and caught her gaze.

"If I live a hundred years, I'll never forget the way John and Kade worked together tonight. They're magic, those two." He crossed his arms and stared up at the stadium lights, trying to compose himself. In a moment, he looked at her again. "What a ride, Abby, you know? I'm just glad I got to be part of it."

"Me, too, Coach." The corners of Abby's mouth lifted slightly as a layer of tears clouded her vision. She gestured toward the locker room. "Is he almost finished?"

"Yep, last reporters left a few minutes ago. He's just getting his things." The coach smiled at her again as he set off. "Well . . . see ya next year."

Abby nodded, afraid her voice would betray her if she tried to speak. *There won't be a next year for us . . . for me.*

When the coach was gone, Abby thought about John, about their wedding more than twenty-one years earlier. What had happened to the people they were back then, the people who had walked through fire together and come out stronger on the other side?

Forget it, Abby. The coach was right. It was over now; she was just glad she'd been a part of it. Abby wished with everything in her she could go back in time, even an hour back to the moments before the final touchdown when John's long-ago dreams all were coming true.

All but one.

Five minutes later, John came through the door and saw her there. Abby thought of Charlene, her arms around John after the game. *Do I hug him like she did? Do I nod politely?*

There was an uncomfortable silence while he held her gaze.

"Abby . . ." He spoke softly, but every word was coated in exhilaration. "We did it!" His eyes sparkled with an electricity that would take days, weeks to diffuse, and it beckoned her in a way she was powerless to resist. As sure as gravity, they came together, and Abby circled her arm around his neck, burying her head against his shoulder.

"I can't believe it! State champs!" She savored the comforting feel of his heart thudding inside his chest, and it occurred to her that months had passed since they'd hugged this way.

"I know." He pulled back, his eyes as full of life and hope and promise as they'd been two decades earlier.

There was a smudge of mud on his cheek, and she erased it gently with her thumb. "Best in the state, you and Kade. Amazing."

He drew her to him again and they stayed that way, their bodies close, swaying slightly. His arms securely around her waist, hers holding on more tightly than usual.

Every moment was steeped in a desperate finality.

John pulled away first, and Abby hugged herself to ward off the sudden chill. "Could you believe that last touchdown?" He grabbed his gym bag from the bench and grinned at her. "Kade was something else . . ."

Abby smiled back. "Beautiful."

John stared out at the field as if he were watching a replay in his mind. "I've pictured this day ever since Kade first learned to throw."

They started walking toward the stadium steps, their feet keeping time in a familiar rhythm. John swung the bag up onto his shoulder. "Abby, about this weekend . . ."

The rock in her stomach grew. "What?"

He studied the ground. "I don't feel right about it . . . what I mean is, the kids . . ." His eyes found hers as they kept walking. "I don't care what the counselors say; we can't tell them now." His forehead was creased with concern. "Not after tonight. They'll be celebrating right through Christmas, Abby. They have a right to that."

Abby felt her shoulders tense as a burst of nervous tension spewed into her veins. "They have a right to know the truth."

His eyelids were heavy with sorrow. "We'll tell them soon enough." His steps slowed and he stared hard at her, begging her to understand. "Come on, Abby. This is the happiest day in Kade's life. And before you know it, Christmas'll be here. Can't it wait?"

She stopped walking and stared at her husband, one hand on her hip. "What are we supposed to do, John? Pretend forever?"

His jawline hardened but he said nothing.

Stop, daughter. A kind word turns away anger.

Abby heard the still, small voice somewhere in the distant corners of her soul, but she shook her head. John had brought this on, after all. Why cover for him now?

"What good does waiting do?" She crossed her arms and huffed. "We should've told them last month." She hesitated. "You can't be the good guy forever, John." *Don't say it, Abby . . .* "Even if you are state champs."

"Here we go." John removed his Marion High baseball cap and dug his fingers through his damp, dark hair. "What do you want, Abby? A fight? Right here on the fifty-yard line?"

She thought of a dozen quick comebacks but held her tongue. "I'm just saying we should have told them by now. For goodness sake, John, we're filing in January. They won't know what hit them if we don't say something soon."

His face twisted, and she thought he might cry. He looked like a little boy who'd lost his best friend, and for a crazy instant she wanted to take him in her arms and beg him to stay, beg him to break it off with Charlene and love only her, Abby, for the rest of his life. Her heart softened. *We're both wrong, John. Isn't what we've built worth another try?* But before she could find the courage to voice the words, the feeling vanished. *I must be crazy. We're too far gone for second chances . . .*

Nothing is impossible with God, My child.

Abby closed her eyes. That time she was sure the silent voice in her heart belonged to the Lord. *We tried. You know we did . . . But even You would grant me an out in this situation . . . Your word says so, doesn't it?*

I hate divorce, daughter . . . Nothing is impossible with—

It's too late . . . Her eyes opened. "Listen, I just want to get through this."

He was still watching her, but his sadness had changed to determination. "We can file in February. We've waited this long. Let's get through Christmas."

The image of John and Charlene taunted her. "Ho ho ho," she whispered.

"What?" John's voice rose a notch.

She cocked her head. "Let's just say I'm not in the mood for the holidays."

John gritted his teeth. "I swear, Abby, all you ever think about is yourself. It's Christmas, remember? That used to mean something to you."

Don't do this to me, John. Don't pretend like it matters when it doesn't. Images came to mind of her and John wandering the hallways of their house in recent years . . . silent, tense, loveless. "Yeah, back when *I* used to mean something to *you.*"

They stood planted there, face to angry face, the chasm between them growing with each breath. Abby broke the silence first. "Don't make me the bad guy. I don't want to ruin their Christmas, either." She gestured at herself. "I'm just trying to be realistic."

"Selfish, you mean?" He was struggling to keep his voice down.

"No, *realistic!*" Her words were little more than a hiss. "I hate pretending!"

The muscles in John's jaw flinched. "You think I like it? I'm not talking about us here, Abby. I'm talking about the kids. We'll tell them after the holidays, and that settles it."

He started walking and Abby wanted to scream. "Wait!"

John stopped and after a beat, turned back to her. "What?"

She exhaled, struggling to control the emotions that rocked her heart. She couldn't imagine another moment trapped in a house with John while he was in love with another woman . . . and through Christmas?

Then it occurred to her that the holidays were apt to be busy, anyway. Her shoulders slumped. Oh, what did it matter? Maybe John was right. Maybe it wouldn't hurt if the kids had less time to get used to the idea. Maybe she could survive waiting for their sake. As long as the divorce came quickly after that. "Okay . . . fine. After Christmas." She hesitated. "But keep your hands off Charlene in public, will you? At least until after we've told the kids."

John's eyes widened and his anger became indignation. "What's that supposed to mean?"

"Come on . . ." Her mouth hung open. Why did he insist on lying to her? What was the point? "It means I have no intention of looking the other way while you run around with your *girlfriend* just so we can give the kids a happy Christmas."

John took a step toward her, his expression growing hard as flint. "You know, I'm sick of you blaming this on Charlene. Our decision to divorce is separate from my friendship with her. It's because you've changed . . . we've both changed." He sighed and stared into the moonlit sky, and she wondered if he were searching for answers—as she'd done so many times. She watched his jaw work and knew he was trying to control his temper. "We're not the same people we were, Abby."

She rolled her eyes. "Don't tell me it's not about Charlene. No matter how much we've changed we could've worked it out; we had an obligation to work it out. But when you took up with Charlene, it was time to get out." She uttered a short laugh. "I mean, come on, John. Don't tell me you aren't having an affair with her when I walked into your classroom and found her in your—"

"That was a hug!" John spat the words at her. "I told you she was upset about her . . ." His voice trailed off, and Abby felt her blood pressure rise a notch. How dare he deny it when she'd caught him in the act? When she'd been hearing about John's relationship with Charlene from a dozen different sources ever since then?

"A hug? Really?" Her voice dripped with sarcasm. "And what was she upset about tonight when she was hanging all over you in front of ten thousand people?"

John's body hunched forward, as though the fight had left him. "Forget it." He buried his hands deep in his pockets and resumed walking, his strides long and purposeful. "Believe what you want."

Abby was furious. He was lying, of course. Like he'd done a hundred times before. She jogged the few steps to catch up and fell in place beside him again. "I believe my friends, and they've seen the same thing I have."

He said nothing, his eyes straight ahead as he continued up the stadium steps toward the car.

Jerk. "Fine, don't talk to me. Just don't make a scene with her, okay? If we wait 'til after the holidays, at least give me that."

They were at the top of the stairs. John stopped and glanced at his watch. "Whatever." His voice was void of any emotion. "I'll meet you back at the hotel in a few hours."

"What?" Abby's heartbeat doubled. *Don't do this to me, John, not tonight.* "You're coming with me. The kids are waiting for us."

Even before John answered, Abby knew she'd pushed him too far. Her husband was staring down the street, lost to her and their children and all that had given them reason to celebrate an hour earlier. "The coaches are meeting at the pub down the block. Tell the kids I'll see 'em later."

Then without making eye contact, without the slightest appearance of remorse or regret, without even a single look back, John walked off into the night. Abby stood stone still, watching him go.

Turn around, John. Come back and tell me you love me; tell me this is crazy and that somehow everything's going to be okay.

He kept walking. *Make him stop, Lord; the kids need him tonight.* Silence.

She watched as John looked for traffic in both directions, jogged across the street, and headed further down the sidewalk. *Fine. Let him leave.* Turning, she blinked back tears and refused to entertain the ache in her heart. It was time she got used to seeing him walk away. This was all they had left now, all they would ever be: two people, two strangers, walking alone in separate directions into the cold, dark night of their future.

She knew it; John knew it.

And sometime after Christmas, the kids would know it, too.

Three

THE MOST WONDERFUL THING ABOUT GROWING up on a private lake, at least as far as Nicole Reynolds was concerned, was not the endless grassy hillside that spread from their back door toward the water or the old wooden pier where they gathered so often for diving contests and sing-alongs. Those things were wonderful and would always be a part of the fabric of her family's lives, of course. But the most amazing benefit was the trail that wound its way through shadowy thickets of trees and brush, then back out into the open along the water's edge. As children, Nicole and Kade would ride their bikes around the water pretending they were explorers in a foreign country or journeying across enemy territory to reach a safe place—usually the lakeside home of one of their friends.

At twenty, Nicole was too old for imaginary play and romps through the woods, but she still cherished the old trail. Nowadays it was the place where she and Matt Conley could get away from the demands of college life and walk hand in hand, sharing ever more about themselves.

Years earlier, Nicole had liked the path best in summer when the ground was warm and the leaves in full display. But now, with Matt by her side, there was something magical about walking the three-mile trail even in the heart of winter.

That afternoon, a Wednesday nearly three weeks after Christmas, Nicole got home from classes early, started a fire, and fixed lunch. Matt would be there in less than an hour with something important to tell her. Something very important. She pulled the bread from the refrigerator and ripped two paper towels from the roll. His voice came back to her, urgent and certain, telling her that no matter what else happened that day, they must meet right after classes.

Her palms were sweaty and she rubbed them on her jeans.

I'm not worried. She thought about that for a moment. What did she have to be worried about? She and Matt had been inseparable since meeting at the university's debate club two years earlier when he was a senior. Every day since then had been more wonderful than the last, and the relationship they'd started had been filled with romance and laughter. Their struggles were typical for people their age—people determined to serve God and put Him first. For that reason they'd set boundaries soon after their friendship turned to dating. But never—not once in two years—had Nicole feared Matt might break up with her.

It can't be that.

She reached for the mayonnaise, opened it, and grabbed a knife. Matt was always so thoughtful, surprising her with her favorite smoked-turkey-and-swiss-cheese lunches, bringing her wildflowers, giving her space when she had to cram for an English exam.

She thought about the bond between her and Matt, and a deep ache formed in her chest. He didn't want to see someone else, did he? *No, it isn't possible.* They were too good for each other. Matt was twenty-four, in his final year at law school, an athlete with a brilliant mind and a way of making her feel taken care of. He was strong and determined and very much in love with her. Though Nicole knew he found her physically attractive, Matt seemed most drawn to the way she made him laugh. Nicole had been a cheerleader in high school and thrived on silliness and smiley moments. She was playful and affectionate and loved closing his textbooks, pulling him outside, and having an impromptu snowball fight or a walk along the frozen trail. He was her pillar of strength; she was his reminder that life was meant to be savored.

They were perfect together. Weren't they?

Is there something wrong with our relationship, something I can't see?

Be still and know that I am God, daughter.

Nicole drew a slow, deep breath. She loved the way God spoke to her, swiftly and with loving authority, in a quiet voice that echoed from someplace in the depths of her soul. For years she and the Lord had been this way, and the certainty of His presence, His voice, brought an intimacy to their relationship that was the very rock upon which Nicole was building her life. If God wanted her to be at peace over this meeting with Matt, then deep inside she knew she had nothing to fear.

Thank You, Lord. Just keep my heart from beating out of my chest, okay? The curiosity's killing me.

Throughout lunch, Matt's eyes danced and he seemed about to burst with excitement. But he talked only about his classwork and current projects. At first Nicole played along, but when they finished their lunch she wiped her mouth and set her napkin down hard.

"Okay . . . stop."

He grinned at her. "What?"

She could feel a smile playing at the corners of her lips, but she huffed anyway. "You had something *very important* to tell me, remember? That's why we're here."

He sat back in his seat and gazed out the window, his eyes twinkling as he drew a long breath. "Let's see, something important . . ." He murmured the words under his breath, as though trying to jog his memory. "What was it . . . ?"

Nicole's exasperated grunt filled the silence and she grabbed his right arm with both hands, pulling on him like a petulant child. "Matt, this isn't funny. I'm serious, come on. I've been waiting all day."

He grinned at her but said nothing.

She huffed. "Okay fine, I'll guess. You're moving to Antarctica to take up ice fishing? Moving to Zimbabwe to be a missionary? Quitting law school and joining the circus?"

They both laughed and their foreheads came together. "You're funny—" he wiggled his nose against hers—"did you know that?"

"And you're a brat." Her voice was a whisper, their faces still touching, and in an instant the mood changed. Matt cradled the back of her neck, adjusting her head so that their mouths met in a kiss that started out sweetly but filled with urgency in very little time.

Flee!

The Lord's voice was clear, as it always was in times like this. An empty house, a warm fire, snow falling gently outside with no one expected back for more than an hour.

They pulled away and studied each other, their faces inches apart. "Let's take a walk . . ." Matt's voice was thick.

"Now? I thought you wanted to talk?" Nicole caught her breath and sat back in her chair.

He nodded, motioning toward the backyard. "Out there. On the path."

Nicole shrugged. "Okay." They moved in reverent silence into the backyard and onto the trail, each enjoying the presence of the other, remembering their kiss minutes earlier. Then as though he'd planned it, Matt stopped and kicked the snow off a fallen log. He took his scarf from around his neck, laid it over the soggy wood, and looked deeply into Nicole's eyes.

"Sit." It was not a command, but part of some sort of mesmerizing ritual Nicole couldn't recognize and had never taken part in.

She dropped slowly to the log and stared at Matt. "Okay . . ."

Moving in what seemed like slow motion, Matt reached into his coat pocket and pulled out a tiny package wrapped in gold paper. It glittered in the shadows, and suddenly Nicole had trouble feeling her arms and legs, like she was floating somehow, living out a dream she'd carried with her since she was a little girl. Tears stung at her eyes, and she moved her gaze from the package to Matt's face. "Matt?" Her voice was barely audible, but full of love and questions and disbelief.

Without hesitating he bent down and planted one knee firmly in the snow as he held out the gift for her to take. Gingerly, her gloved hands shaking, Nicole took the box and stared at it. Could it be? Had he chosen today to ask her? *Dear God, help me open the ribbon . . .*

She worked her way through the paper, pulled out a blue velvet box, and opened the lid. The diamond ring inside captured the light and sprayed brilliance in a thousand directions as Nicole's breath caught in her throat. It was a wedding set, a single solitaire engagement ring and a matching wedding band with a trail of tiny diamonds across the top. *Oh, Lord, I can't believe it.* Tears clouded her vision and she blinked, sending a steamy trail down both cheeks. "Oh, Matt . . ." She pulled him to her and held on until he gently freed himself and caught her gaze with his eyes.

"Nicole Michelle Reynolds, I love you more than life itself." He gently brought his hand to her face and brushed away her tears with his gloved thumb. "I've loved you since our first day . . . and I love you more each time we're together."

He paused, and two more tears spilled onto her cheeks. So this was it . . . he was asking her the question.

Thank You, God. Thank You for this man.

She waited while he considered his words. "All my life I've been afraid of commitment, afraid that if I promised myself to a woman I'd wind up like my father one day . . . angry and alone and . . . well, pathetic, I guess." He smoothed a tendril of hair from her eyes. "Then I met you."

There were a hundred things Nicole wanted to say, but she was silent, memorizing the moment, soaking it in because she knew she'd never forget it as long as she lived.

"I see the way your parents have built their love for . . . what, twenty-one years now?"

Nicole nodded, a smile punctuating her tears.

"Twenty-one years." Matt shook his head. "Amazing." Tenderness shone in his eyes. "What they have together, Nicole, I want that for us, too. A family and a house where traditions and memories are built, where we can make a life together that will last until God calls one of us home."

Her happiness spilled over and a gleeful laugh escaped her. "Oh, Matt . . . I love you so much!" She tried to hug him again but he put his hand up, stopping her from coming closer. Studying him, she saw that his eyes were wet. In all the days and months they'd spent together, she'd never seen him so serious.

"Nicole, I want you to be my wife." He framed her cheekbones with his fingertips, and she felt so safe in his powerful gaze. "I've asked your father, and he's given us his blessing." He paused for what seemed like an eternity. "Will you marry me?"

The tears came harder now, and she threw her arms around his neck, holding on as she would the rest of her life. How precious and perfect and beautiful were God's plans for His people. To think that her mother had prayed for her future husband hundreds of times over the years and now here he was. She was ready—pure and whole the way God intended—to cleave to Matt and become his wife. Just like her mother had prayed. She could hardly wait to tell her parents.

Oh, Lord, thank You . . . I'm overcome with gratefulness. We can tell my parents at the family meeting this week!

"Yes, Matt." She would remember this moment as long as she lived. "Yes. I would love to marry you . . ."

four

IT WAS FRIDAY NIGHT, HOURS BEFORE THE FAMILY
meeting, and Abby was exhausted beyond belief. Despite a series of
joint sessions with their counselors, she and John had refused to come
to any sort of last-minute agreement. Instead, they'd met at a restaurant outside of town and talked through the details, finally settling on
a scenario that would work well enough for the future.

Abby would stay in the house; John would find a place of his own.
The kids were old enough that custody wouldn't be an issue. Sean
would stay with Abby during the week and with John on weekends
or holidays—whenever he liked, really. Otherwise life would go on
pretty much the same. Kade would move to a dorm at the University
of Iowa sometime that summer, and Nicole would continue living at
home while she took classes at Southern Illinois University.

Abby's tiredness was understandable. For years she and John had
been merely going through the motions, pretending to be happily
married, but these last few weeks Abby had been repulsed by their
charade. She'd found herself wanting to scream at John, the kids, anyone who would listen that she was sick of her life being little more
than an act. The children had been caught up in their Christmas
excitement, what with Sean's new skis and Kade's specially made class

ring, complete with the insignia declaring him state football champion. Nicole was wrapped up in her life, working through the tougher classes that came along with being a junior and spending nearly all her free time with Matt.

As John had predicted, the excitement of a state title was still very much the buzz of family conversation. He continued to field weekly calls from reporters and other coaches wanting to congratulate him and compare plays, hoping perhaps that some of Coach Reynolds's success might rub off or spark an idea that would play out in their own lives. People seemed to think John had the answer for everything, everyone.

Everyone but her.

Abby exhaled slowly and pulled an old flannel nightie from her dresser drawer. She and John still shared a living space, but not a bed. Not for months now. She would dress in the bathroom, brush her teeth, and when she was sure the kids were asleep or too busy to notice, she'd sneak down the hall to the guest room. She'd always been the first one up in the morning, so none of them had ever caught on.

It was early and John was at a league meeting that would last until after ten o'clock. *Just as well. I'll be asleep before he gets back.*

A bitter wind howled outside as she slipped out of her clothes, donned the nightgown, and realized her feet were cold. *One of these days I'll have to buy my own socks.* But for now, this one last night anyway, she could use his. They were bigger and thicker and kept her feet warm even on the coldest nights.

After they told the kids about the divorce, John was going to talk to one of his coaching buddies about staying at his house for a while, until the whole thing was final and he could find a place of his own. Either way, he planned to be out of the house within a week. Abby slid the drawer open and dug her hands inside, looking for the thickest pair of socks she could find. Instead, her fingers felt a folded piece of paper. She pulled it out, staring at it. Hadn't she just cleaned the drawers a few weeks ago?

Her heart began pounding in her chest, shouting at her to drop the wrinkled note and avoid the message inside. She ignored the warning. Perching on the edge of her bed, Abby unfolded the piece of paper, which bore handwriting that—though not her own—clearly belonged to a woman. She began to read.

John, thanks for talking with me the other night. I don't know what I'd do without you. I mean it. You're the best friend a girl could ever have. Abby doesn't know what she's losing. Anyway, I'll meet you early Friday like usual. Can't wait to see you. Love, Charlene.

Abby stared at the note as angry feelings galloped about in her gut. Unable to stop herself, she read it a second time—then she ripped it in half and in half again, and again and again until she could no longer recognize any of the woman's words.

She couldn't decide whether to race for the bathroom or punch a hole in the wall. In the end she did neither, only stayed there on the edge of the bed, imprisoned by the hurt in her heart. *How could you, John? Can't you wait until after the divorce? Isn't what we shared worth at least that?*

Abby could hear her husband's voice, indignant and defensive whenever she'd brought up Charlene's name: *"She's just a friend . . . just a friend . . ."*

She huffed as her eyes scanned the shreds of paper. Just a friend . . . what a joke. Booster club members had reported to Abby several times that they'd seen John and Charlene together in his classroom. And at least once a person had walked in and found the two locked in an embrace. *"She was having a hard day . . . she's all alone . . . she's just a friend."* The excuses were endless.

Fine. John could be all the friend to Charlene he wanted after tomorrow. As long as he moved out and stopped the terrible lie he'd been living these past few months.

She scrunched the pieces up and moved into the bathroom, dropping them in the toilet and flushing them. On the way out she caught her reflection in the mirror. Was she not pretty enough? Had she gained weight in the past few years?

Abby studied herself and knew it wasn't a weight problem. She wore the same size-seven jeans she'd always worn, and at five-foot-eight she was thinner than most women half her age. She walked the treadmill early each morning and was careful about what she ate.

It has to be my age.

She scrutinized her skin and saw the visible pores and fine wrinkles that hadn't been there ten years ago. How old was Charlene, anyway? Thirty-two, thirty-three? Abby anchored her fingertips along her hairline and lifted up, watching as her face took on a look she was more familiar with, the look she'd had as a teenager and young woman.

Was that what their love had come to? After surviving so much, celebrating so much, after raising a family together . . . had it really come to this? To losing her husband because the skin on her face showed wear?

I gave you those years, John . . .

She took a step back and studied herself again. Her hair was a mass of short stylish layers that still turned men's heads. Old men, maybe, but men all the same. And with a little help from the salon, her hair was still blonde. Abby angled her face this way and that, trying to see herself the way John saw her. Okay, so she'd just turned forty-one, so what? Charlene would turn forty-one someday, too. That couldn't be the reason things hadn't worked between them.

Abby frowned. She was being ridiculous. Their breakup had nothing to do with looks. It was because their marriage had become an old sock years ago, threadbare in all the important places and too worn out and stained to bother saving.

She turned away from her reflection and padded through the bedroom door, down the hall to the guest room. Without turning on the light, she shut the door and climbed into bed.

She was fast asleep in a matter of minutes.

An autumn wind blew through the trees knocking leaves of every shade and color onto the walkway that surrounded an oversized stadium. Abby was inside yelling, *"Go, Blue! Come on, John, you can do it!"* He waved at her from the huddle, an impressive six-foot-four quarterback with dark hair and aqua blue eyes—by far the best-looking player on the field.

"Wait a minute, Abby . . . I have something to tell you . . . something to tell you." John drew his arm back and threw the football into the stands where it soared and dipped and finally landed in Abby's hands and became a bouquet of pink-and-white baby roses. A grin worked its way across John's face, and Abby noticed that the other players seemed frozen in time. Then, as though it were the most normal action in the world, John raced up the stadium steps toward her, his uniform clanking and jostling about as he came. He drew closer, and the crowd and bleachers and football team disappeared. In their place was a well-dressed congregation staring straight at them, smiling and motioning for her and John to move closer to each other.

"So, Abby, will you marry me . . . huh? Will you, Abby?"

She looked, and instead of his uniform, John was wearing a black tuxedo. She glanced nervously at her jeans, then shrugged and began reciting her vows.

"I, Abby Chapman, promise to love and cherish—"

But before she could finish, a doctor ran into the church waving his hands and shouting, *"It's a girl! It's a girl!"* Behind him came three nurses, the middle one carrying a tiny baby. The church crowd vanished, and they were in a hospital room. Abby was sobbing, crying as though her heart was being torn in two and she took the baby from the nurse. But it wasn't the baby at all, because now Nicole was standing at her side, and John was holding their daughter's little-girl hand. The new baby, the one in Abby's arms, wasn't moving, wasn't breathing.

"I don't know what happened. She was taking her nap just like every other day and when I went to wake her up she was—"

"A boy, Abby. Can you believe it? We got ourselves a boy!"

She looked down. The dead baby was no longer there, and Nicole was older now, dancing in her ballet costume, doing toe-raises and spins and singing a song Abby couldn't understand. Without warning Nicole's spins became a whirlwind, and the whirlwind became a tornado, angry and menacing and building with each passing moment. In the distance Abby could see her mother, smiling, waving.

"Congratulations, Abby, you've got yourself a real beaut there. Congratulations, Abby . . . Congratulations . . ."

The tornado switched directions and headed for Abby's mother, shaking the ground and filling the air with the sound of a thousand blazing freight trains.

"Mom! Help yourself . . . run! Get out before it kills you!"

Suddenly the room was empty except for a hole in the ground. John crawled out of it holding the baby boy in his arms. Kade . . . it was Kade; Abby knew it. She ran a finger over the infant's fore-head and then saw Nicole climb out of the hole as well.

"Nicole, you're okay!" She hugged her daughter, convulsing with tears and stroking her golden hair. Before Nicole could say anything the baby in John's arms let out a loud sound and Abby turned to him. Only now he was three years old, and he and John were having a burping contest in the middle of the living room. Abby looked at John, and they both laughed until tears were streaming down their faces. She glanced out the window and saw that their house was in the middle of the football field. Through the fifty-yard line ran a street where Nicole was sitting, playing in the middle of the road unaware of the car speeding straight for her . . .

"Nicole!" Abby's voice echoed into the night and she was deathly afraid, utterly alone until she felt the arms around her. Warm, strong, reassuring arms. John's arms. *He's here . . . he's come.* She turned and hugged him close. *Oh, John, I love you . . . thank God you're here . . .*

Instantly they were bathed in Friday-night-football lights, standing in the end zone at Marion High. Slowly a distance began to grow between them, leaving John on the field and her in the stands—in the back row—squinting to see what was happening. The crowd was frenzied, and the Eagles were down a touchdown in what Abby knew was the biggest game of the year. *Halftime . . . it must be halftime.*

Over the loudspeaker someone was reading a letter.

"Mr. Reynolds, I think you're the worst man who's ever coached football. Maybe our boys might win a game or two if they could get someone at the wheel who knew what he was doing . . . knew what he was doing . . . knew what he was doing . . ."

The words echoed across the field, and Abby ran down the stairs as fast as she could toward John. Only it took longer than usual, and she was forced to run for what seemed like hours until finally she closed the gap between them. Then, with everyone watching, she wrapped her arms around his neck. *"It's okay, honey . . . God has a plan in this. It'll be okay . . . you've got a gift and one day the whole world will know it . . ."*

Suddenly she was in the school weightroom, heading for John's office, finding him at his desk. *"John . . ."*

There were tears in his eyes when he turned to her. *"Don't tell me, Abby. It's been hard enough already, please don't tell me . . . don't tell me . . . don't tell me . . ."*

She came up behind him and placed her hands on his shoulders. "It's my job to do this, John . . . even if it's the worst news you'll ever hear. I have to tell you . . ."

Without warning there was the sound of a stadium exploding with the cheers of thousands of football fans. *"And now—"* the stadium announcer bellowed over the crowd—*"the state of Illinois would like to award to Coach John Reynolds and the Marion Eagles the honor of—"*

John stopped him before he could finish. *"What I really want,"* he said, *"is my dad. He's supposed to be here. Maybe if someone could find him . . . find him . . . find him."*

"*Congratulations! Here he is . . .*" Only the voice no longer belonged to the announcer, but to another doctor . . . one in a green coat and strange glasses. And Abby wasn't in the stands, she was on an operating table. "*It's a boy . . . a boy . . . a boy.*"

Sean smiled at his parents and gave them the thumbs-up sign. But before Abby could hold him or savor the downy fuzz of his newborn cheek, they were all in the car, the old sedan they'd driven back when they were newly married. At the stoplight John pointed to a building up ahead. "*What's that, Abby? I've seen it before but I can't remember . . . can't remember . . .*"

It took her a minute to recognize it. The building was their church, the place where they'd taught Sunday school together, where they'd taken their children when they were young. Only it looked different now, and John was wrinkling his brow. "*That's not what church looked like, Abby . . . Are you sure? Are you sure?*"

They stopped the car and climbed out, and she held Nicole's and Sean's hands while Kade stood with John, and suddenly a crack in the ground developed between them. It began to grow.

"*John! Quick, jump!*"

He stared strangely at her. "*You jump, Abby. I like it on this side.*"

"*But it's better over here! I like my side. Come on . . . jump!*" Her voice was shrill, filled with panic as the distance between them continued to grow at an alarming rate. Eventually she couldn't make out what he was saying, just that he was trying to talk.

"*Come on, John. Don't you care about me? Jump! Jump, John! Before it's too late!*"

Nicole started to cry, and Sean closed his eyes. "*I'm scared, Mommy. Make him come back. Make Daddy come back . . .*"

Then John grabbed a long piece of rope and though the space between them was widening more with each passing second, he heaved it with all his might and it spanned what was now a canyon. In a blink, the rope became a sturdy footbridge.

"*I've changed my mind, Abby. I'm coming . . . I'm coming!*"

Without waiting another moment, John and Kade ran as fast as they could across the bridge. They were almost there, almost to the safe place where Abby and Sean and Nicole waited, when the bridge began to give way. Kade caught his father's arm and the two jumped the remaining feet, barely landing on solid ground.

"Oh, John, you could have been killed . . ." Abby ran to them and hugged first Kade, then John. *"You should have stayed over there where it was safe."*

He caught her eyes with his and drew her close, kissing her the way he had when they had first fallen in love. *"I had to be with you, Abby. I love you! I'll always love you . . . always love you . . . always love you . . ."*

His words repeated, over and over again—*". . . always love you . . . always love you . . ."*—but his voice changed, and Abby pulled back, studying him.

No! It can't be . . .

Abby untangled herself, frantic. Instead of John holding her, it was a dummy made up to look like him. *". . . always love you . . . always love you . . ."* There was a recording playing from inside the life-sized doll, and as Abby moved backward, her heart racing, the dummy fell to the ground, eyes open. *". . . always love you . . . always love you . . ."*

Abby's scream pierced the night and she shot straight up in bed, gasping for breath, her heart racing faster than ever before. What had happened? What had she just lived through? A dream?

No, a nightmare. A terrible, terrible nightmare.

She shook her head, trying to clear the strange words and images that had consumed her night. Everything about the dream—the voices and feelings, the way her body had felt wrapped up in John's arms—all of it had been so real. She struggled to catch her breath.

In the still of the night, she glanced at the clock on the bedside table. Four-fifteen. Bits and pieces from the pictures in her head still played in her mind, and she sank back down onto the pillow. Had any other two people been through as much as she and John and then decided to throw it all away?

Abby didn't think so.

And, in the quiet hours before she and John would sit down with their children in the home where they'd been raised and tell them about the divorce, Abby grieved for all they'd been, all they'd done, all they'd never be again after today.

The grieving turned to quiet weeping. She sobbed in a way she hadn't done in years until she heard the early morning stirrings of John in the kitchen making pancakes and the kids taking showers down the hall. Feeling as though she'd aged decades overnight, Abby dragged herself from bed, wiped her tears, and drew a deep breath.

There was no point dwelling on the past. It was time to face the future.

five

ABBY PULLED ON A TURTLENECK AND MATCHING sweatshirt and slipped into a pair of jeans. Might as well be comfortable since they were bound to spend most of the day in deep conversation, wiping their children's tears and making shallow promises that somehow everything was going to be all right.

The house was colder than Abby liked, and after she made her way downstairs she rounded the corner and flipped on the heater. *At least our home will be warm, even if we can't be that way toward each other.*

John glanced up from the skillet and spotted her. "Pancakes are ready."

Abby stared at him and blinked. Didn't this day matter at all? Had it been so easy for him to come home late, sleep through the night, and pop out of bed to make pancakes like everything was fine? "I'm not hungry."

She turned her back to him and wandered into the living room where the meeting would take place in less than an hour. Everything was neat and tidy, but in the morning light she could see a layer of dust on the old photos that sat on the bookshelves— framed pictures from when they were young and just starting out.

Abby thought about getting a rag and dusting them, then shook her head. *It's fitting that they're covered in dust. Just like our lives.*

She closed her eyes for a minute and considered the enormity of the announcement they were about to make. *So this is it, huh, God? Dusty photographs, dusty lives. How did we make such a mess of things?*

Seek first My kingdom and all these things—

Abby's comeback was quick and rude. *We did seek You and look what happened.* Immediately she was seized with remorse. *I'm sorry. It's not Your fault.* She squinted and stared across the room, out the window at the front lawn she and John had landscaped themselves. It seemed like an eternity ago that they'd been able to laugh together, to love each other the way they'd once hoped to spend a lifetime loving. And now . . .

Now their lives were an unmanageable ball of knots too tangled to understand, let alone make right again.

Abby sensed someone else had entered the room and turned around.

"I think we should talk." The corners of John's eyes were lined; maybe he was more concerned than she had thought.

"About what? Haven't we been through it a hundred times with the counselors?" She crossed her arms and chided herself for finding him attractive. After all he'd put her through, all the lies he'd told . . . even now, an hour before their big announcement, she could not force herself to be unmoved by the sight of him.

John sighed and dropped into the nearest chair, anchoring his elbows on his knees as he lowered his head. After several beats he looked up and caught her gaze so powerfully she couldn't have blinked if she wanted to. *Do your eyes have to be so blue all the time?*

"Look, Abby . . . what I'm saying is . . . are you sure? Are you sure this is what we should do? Are you sure it's the right thing?"

Abby shifted her weight and released a short laugh. "I'm absolutely sure it isn't the right thing. The Bible tells us that much."

John sat perfectly still, his gaze still locked on hers. "Then why, Abby . . . why let it happen?"

She'd always hated the way her eyes stung with the initial onset of tears. This time was no different. "*I* didn't let anything happen, John, and you know it. *We* let it happen. And right now—to be perfectly honest—*you're* letting it happen. You and Miss Meet-You-Friday-Morning-Same-Time-as-Usual."

"What?"

"Don't look surprised, John. You're the one who saves her notes in your sock drawer. Did you forget I'm the one who does your laun—"

"Be quiet." He stopped her midsentence, the connection between them broken as he stared at his feet, shoulders stooped. "The kids are getting ready, and Matt'll be here any minute."

What? Abby felt like she'd been slapped in the face. "Matt? Why's he coming?" This was outrageous! The most difficult announcement they'd ever had to make and now they had to do it in front of a stranger? John must be crazy to have allowed Nicole to—

"Oh, get off your high horse, Abby. Nicole wanted him here for the first part of the meeting. I guess he's got something to ask us. Talk to *her* if you're so frustrated."

"Stop blaming me for everything." She took a chair opposite him and lowered her voice. Even in this they couldn't get along. "You make it sound like I'm crazy to want just our family here when we tell the kids we're getting a divorce. I mean, seriously, John, why not invite the whole neighborhood? We could sell tickets, pass out popcorn. I don't know, I guess I thought it was kind of a private moment."

"It will be." His voice was a tightly controlled hiss. "We can take a break after Matt talks to us, and he'll be on his way. Nicole said he has a hundred things to do today."

"Then why come to our meeting?"

John forced the air from his lungs and shook his head, chuckling in a way that was completely void of humor. "Don't you ever let up?"

"I know, I'm the bad guy, the relentless one, pushy and demanding. Fine. So be it. But why does he have to come to the meeting?"

"Forget it!" John stood up and glared at her. Gone was the intensity in his eyes, the searching and questioning heart that had moved him to wonder aloud if this decision to dissolve their marriage was really one they should be making. In place of all that was a man with whom Abby was more familiar these days, a man who seemed neither to love her nor care for her feelings. "Ask Nicole."

He turned to leave, and Abby was instantly on her feet. *Not that quick, John. You started this conversation.* "Wait!"

He spun around, his expression cold as wet cement. "What?"

Don't say it, daughter . . . A kind word turns away anger . . .

Abby narrowed her eyes. "You asked me a question earlier."

John waited, silent.

"You asked me if I was sure if this was the right decision." Fresh tears stung at her eyes, and she blinked them back. There was a tightening in her chest, and she recognized what it was: the walls of her heart were growing higher, harder.

"And . . . ?" John's look had gone from cold to impatient, and she wanted to kick him in the shin. Maybe then he'd share some of the pain she was feeling.

"It's the right thing to do, John." Her voice was measured, barely more than a whisper as she fought for control over her tears. "As long as you're sleeping around behind my back, it's the only thing we *can* do."

Fire exploded in his eyes, and he clenched his teeth. "I am not sleeping with her, Abby. She's a friend."

"How can you stand there and lie to me?" She gave a shake of her head and glared hard at him. "I mean, you're absolutely amazing. Your sock drawer has a love letter from the woman, and you're trying to tell me she's only a friend? Be real, John. And when the kids ask why, make sure you mention your weakness for sad, lonely women, will you?"

A dozen emotions flashed in John's eyes, and his jaw muscles flexed. But he said nothing, only turned around again and disappeared into the kitchen.

Abby stood there, watching him go, and a strange, sad feeling came over her. In that instant, her hardened, walled-up heart felt like an unbearable burden deep within her. *"She's a friend . . . she's a friend . . . she's a friend."* John's words beat at her relentlessly until she shut her eyes to make them stop.

He *was* sleeping with Charlene, wasn't he? He had to be.

Let he who is without guilt cast the first stone . . .

There it was again—that same voice. A piercing pang entered her consciousness, and Abby thought of her e-mail friend, a man she'd been talking with almost daily for the past two years. *That's not the same.*

Let he who is without guilt cast the first—

No! She shouted silently at the words assaulting her heart. *I've never even met the man.* Why would God want her to feel guilty now? She needed that friendship. Especially with John devoting all his attention to Charlene.

Daughter, hear Me. Let he who is without—

Abby closed her eyes and forced the words from her mind. *Okay, fine. We're both guilty. But it's John's fault, Lord. He's the one who broke faith first.*

Abby considered the number of times she'd found out from other sources that John and Charlene were together, and suddenly her mind was filled with the image of the two of them on the football field after the state game. It was amazing the kids hadn't gotten wind of their father's affair.

Like the old saying went, where there was smoke there was fire. And where Charlene and John were concerned, there had been enough smoke to indicate an outright inferno.

Lean not on your own understanding, but in all your ways acknowledge Me and I—

Why was this persistent voice rattling around in her heart lately? Ever since the football game. Certainly it had to be habit, familiarity with Scripture, and not the presence of God trying to communicate with her. After all, it had been years since they'd attended church regularly, and at least that long since she'd prayed or read her Bible with any consistency. *What would the Lord want with me now? Now that John and I have gone against everything He ever wanted for our lives?*

There was no answer, and she allowed her eyes to find the dusty photographs once more. Every time there'd been a chance to make things right somehow she and John wound up in a fight. *Just once, Abby, couldn't you have shut your mouth? Couldn't you have walked straight up to him and allowed him to hold you like old times?* She thought about that for a moment and realized the answer was no. Fighting words were all they had left.

Apparently today would be no sentimental exception.

They had no choice now but to move ahead with the divorce and pray that somehow God—if He still cared enough to listen—would forgive them and help them make new lives without each other.

Sean and Kade were already downstairs in the living room, but Nicole was reading her Bible on her bed, feeling as though she might actually float if she tried to stand up. She glanced across the room at her mirror and realized that she had never felt more beautiful. Really and truly, she was a daughter of the King, and He alone had set her apart for this moment in time. It was overwhelming.

She scanned the pages of Jeremiah 29 until she found the verse she wanted, the one she'd lived under and believed since she was a little girl: *"For I know the plans I have for you, . . . plans to prosper you and not to harm you, plans to give you hope and a future."* Nicole let her eyes read over the words several times. Never had her future looked brighter than at that moment and it had everything to do with the nature and faithfulness of God Almighty.

Leaving the Bible open to that page, she found the velvet box that had been hiding in her jewelry cupboard. With ease she placed the ring on the appropriate finger and stared at it. *Oh, Lord, I'm the happiest girl alive.* Folding up the fingers of her left hand so the ring wouldn't be obvious, she danced down the stairs and peeked into the living room where Matt, Kade, and Sean were watching an NFL pregame show. "Where's Mom and Dad?" It was already after nine, and Nicole knew she couldn't wait much longer. If they didn't start the meeting soon she might just have to jump up on the kitchen table and announce her news for all the neighborhood to hear.

Kade shrugged, his eyes fixed on the television set. "Upstairs, maybe."

Nicole caught Matt's gaze and held it, grinning at him as he spoke a hundred silent words with his eyes. He stood and crossed the room, kissing her lightly on the cheek. "You look pretty."

Sean grabbed a pillow from the sofa and threw it at Matt. "Aw, quit it, guys. No ooey-gooey stuff before noon on Saturday, okay?"

Nicole giggled as Matt linked his fingers through hers and led her into the room. He patted Sean on the top of his head. "One day you'll understand, little brother."

Everyone smiled, and Nicole's love for the man beside her swelled. Already he thought of Kade and Sean as his brothers. Her parents were going to be thrilled at—

"Okay, TV off." Mom and Dad entered the room together, and for a brief moment, Nicole felt a frown crease her forehead. Were Mom and Dad mad at each other? She had the oddest sense that there was something foreign—a tension or a wall or a wedge—something between them. Something big.

Nicole caught herself. She blinked away the image and looked at her parents again. There. Now they looked right. They were smiling and taking their seats next to each other. *Must be my imagination. Too much on my mind.*

The room was comfortably quiet. She and Matt sat on one sofa, Sean and Kade on the other, and Mom and Dad in chairs beside each other. Dad spoke first.

"Let's get started. You all know how busy football season is around here—especially this last one. And now that things have settled down there are a few things we need to discuss as a family. First, I'd like to—"

"Aren't we going to open in prayer?" Nicole looked from her father to her mother and back again. "We always start our family meetings with prayer, right?"

Nicole watched her mother cast a knowing look at her father, and a twinge of apprehension hit her again. He looked nervous . . . convicted, even. A feeling of fear came over her. *I can't believe he actually forgot, Lord . . . Wow, what's going on with them?* She shook the worry away. Everything was fine. Her parents were solid. Rock solid. Why imagine a problem where there wasn't one?

"You're right, Nicki." Dad looked at her, and the uneasiness of a moment earlier disappeared. She loved it when her father called her that. He was the only one who did. "Why don't you pray, honey?"

She shrugged and glanced at the faces around her. "Sure." She bowed her head and focused hard on the Lord, on His goodness and kindness, on the plans He was bringing to fruition in her life. "Father, we come before You as one, one unit, one family, determined that our ways and plans and decisions will be only those that You have planned for us. Bless this time of communication and let it bring us closer as a family, closer to You and to each other. Thank You, Lord. In Jesus' name, amen."

There was a pause, and Nicole couldn't fight off the sense of something fearful and foreboding in the air. *Come on, Dad, say something funny like you usually do. This is getting weird here.*

Her father cleared his throat and looked in her direction. "Matt, we'll start with you. That way you can get on with your day and leave us here to finish up."

Matt nodded and squeezed Nicole's hand, the one with the engagement ring on it.

"Well—" he looked at her, and she knew she would never forget the way his eyes sparkled—"actually Nicole and I both have something to tell you."

Nicole took in her mother's reaction, noting how her eyes changed from cool tension to wide-eyed disbelief. Her father still looked clueless, but that was typical.

Nicole drew a deep breath and looked expectantly at Matt. "Do you want to tell them?"

"Come on, guys . . . the suspense is killing us." Dad crossed one leg over his knee and settled back against his chair, his smile forced and stiff. *Why does he look nervous? Or does he?* Nicole couldn't get around her pesky suspicion that something wasn't right. *I'll find out later. Right now there's something more important to discuss.*

Matt grinned and then faced her family. "Okay, this is it—" he gently lifted Nicole's hand so that everyone could see her ring— "I've asked Nicole to marry me."

Nicole wrapped her other hand around Matt's neck and gave him a quick hug. Without turning toward her family she spoke, her eyes locked onto Matt's. "And I told him yes."

She whipped around and saw that her parents were stunned, their mouths hanging open, their eyes wide.

"Mom, Dad . . . did you hear us. We're *engaged!*" Nicole hooted out loud, and then in a blur of motion her parents were on their feet, pulling her into a three-way hug. Mom squealed as Dad stepped back and shook Matt's hand.

"Talk about a shocker . . ." He pumped Matt's hand until he realized that the moment called for something greater than a handshake. "Come here." He grabbed Matt and pulled him into a hug.

At the same time, Mom braced her hands on Nicole's shoulders and kissed her on the cheek. "Nicole! I can't believe it. When did this happen?"

All feelings of impending doom had vanished like morning fog on the lake; Nicole was overcome with joy. "Since Wednesday. Matt took me out on the trail and proposed to me with his knee in the snow."

The group shifted so that Mom could embrace Matt and congratulate him, as well. Kade moved into the circle, gently grabbing the necks of both Nicole and her fiancé, pulling them close. "You crazy guys, keeping a secret like that." He punched Matt's arm lightly. "Hey, way to go, Matt. Welcome to the family."

Gradually the hugs ceased, and they returned to their seats. Nicole beamed at her father, who was tapping his fingers in a nervous rhythm on the arms of the chair. "Now, Dad, don't tell me you're shocked. Matt said he asked you about this a long time ago, and you gave him your blessing."

Her parents exchanged an uneasy look. "Really?" Mom raised one eyebrow and cast Dad a strangely partial smile. The uneasy feeling hit Nicole again. *What's Mom's problem? Why're they acting like this?* "I didn't hear about it."

A nervous laugh came from her father's throat, and he glanced from Mom to Nicole and back. "Matt said it could be . . . years. I thought . . . well, I had no idea that's what he wanted to tell us today."

Matt reached for Nicole's hand again, and she slid up next to him. Everything was going to work out just as she'd always dreamed. She nestled her shoulder against his much larger arm and studied him. He was something else, really. The complete package. Exactly what she and her mother had prayed for.

Sitting up a bit straighter, Matt faced her parents. "Actually, I had no idea I'd be ready this soon." He glanced down and gave Nicole a smile that echoed in the core of her being. *He loves me! Thank You, God, he loves me!* Matt turned back to her parents. "The change came sometime last summer, or maybe in the fall. I started thinking that I'd be finished with law school this June, so why not get married this summer? Nicole can keep taking classes. In fact, we both think it's a good idea for her to get her education so she can teach if she wants to."

Nicole loved the way he worded that. *If she wants to . . .* The truth was, married to Matt she would have a choice. The thoughts were almost too wonderful to bear.

Mom nodded and looked from Nicole to Matt. "That's wonderful. I'm so happy for you." She hesitated, and Nicole studied her eyes. They were flat and the happiness in her voice seemed artificial. *Why aren't you glowing, Mom? This is my finest hour here.* She wanted to mention the fact that everything about this day, this news, was an answer to the prayer her mother had prayed so often when Nicole was a young girl, but somehow the timing didn't seem right.

"Have you thought of a date?" Dad looked at them curiously and his eyes, too, seemed strangely untouched by the joy of their news.

Nicole and Matt looked at each other and grinned as they turned back to Mom. "We figured it out last night. July fourteenth. Your anniversary, Mom and Dad! Isn't that great!"

Matt slipped his arm around Nicole and looked intently at her parents. "The truth is, Nicole and I want the kind of marriage you two have." He looked at Nicole again. "The kind that grows better every year."

Mom stood up and her smile was strange . . . awkward. "How nice." She looked at Dad and Nicole thought she conveyed some unspoken message. "I'm going to put the kettle on for tea. Nicole? Matt? Can I get you some?"

Kade raised his hand. "Actually get some for me, too, Mom." He worked his face into an ultraformal expression. "English tea with a dash of sweet cream would be simply smashing."

Sean burst into little-boy laughter and tackled his brother until the two landed on the floor. Nicole smiled at her mother. "Sure. Thanks, Mom."

Without another word, without crossing the room for a hug or asking Nicole to join her, Mom hurried from the room and headed for the kitchen.

Dad stood. "I'll help." He hesitated, looking at them strangely. "We'll be right back."

Kade and Sean were still wrestling on the floor, and when her parents were out of earshot, Nicole turned to Matt. "Are my parents acting weird, or is it just me?"

Matt shrugged. "I think they're happy." A concerned look crossed his face. "They are, aren't they?"

"Yeah, they seem like it." Nicole thought about her mother's reaction and worked her mouth into a smile as she snuggled closer to Matt. Of course they were happy. *It's only my imagination.* "Mom's probably just in shock. I mean, she turns forty-one last week and now I'm getting married. That's a lot to handle."

Matt laughed. "If I know your mother, once it sinks in she'll be bouncing off the walls."

"Yeah," Nicole ran her finger along Matt's face. "You're the answer to both our prayers."

Six

THE NOISE OF SEAN AND KADE WRESTLING in the next room was enough to hide Abby's convulsing whimpers as she braced herself against the kitchen sink and stared through her window at the frozen lake. Beside her, his back to the view, John stood silently, arms crossed, eyes cast downward.

Her heart was so heavy she could barely stand up under the weight. *Help me, God. I've never felt so alone in my life. What are we supposed to do now?*

What God has joined together let no one separate, My child.

Oh, quit! Abby was bone-tired of pat answers. That scripture couldn't possibly be from the Lord. Not when He knew what was happening with John and Charlene. *I need real answers, God. Please!*

Silence.

Her tears came harder, and she buried her face in her hands. Nicole was going to get married in six months—on their wedding anniversary, no less—during the exact same time as the divorce proceedings were scheduled to take place. It was like something from a terrible nightmare. Was the pain of living in a loveless marriage fated to go on indefinitely?

For two minutes neither of them said anything. Abby glanced at

John and felt the hatred rise within her. *Look at him, standing there speechless. Say something! Hug me or tell me we'll find a way to break the news to the kids despite Nicole's plans. Something. I mean, come on, John. We should be celebrating out there with them, not in here where there are no answers, no ways out.*

John shifted his weight and turned his head in her direction. "You gotta get a grip here, Abby. The kids could come in any second."

She stared at him, mouth open. Didn't he get it? Didn't he understand that Nicole and Matt's announcement changed everything? She yanked a paper towel from the roller, wiped hard at her eyes and blew her nose, reaching down to slam the wrinkled ball into the trash beneath the sink. When she looked up she caught his eyes and searched them, trying to understand.

"Get a grip? You want me to get a grip when our kids are out there celebrating Nicole's engagement?" She uttered a brief laugh and shook her head. "I mean, didn't you *hear* them? They want a marriage like ours, John. They're getting married on our anniversary, for goodness sake. You think we can go out there now and tell them we're getting a divorce?"

John clenched his teeth and stared at the ground, rubbing the back of his neck with his right hand.

Stand up and look me in the eye! Abby folded her arms and glared at him. He was always rubbing his neck about one thing or another. It was too late for that now.

"Can't you say something?"

John brought his head up slowly, and Abby was not prepared for the transparency of his eyes or the sadness she saw there. "I'm so sorry, Abby. I feel . . . I don't know, I guess I feel like I failed you, failed God. Failed everyone."

She had expected him to snap back at her, but this . . . this broken man before her was someone she hadn't seen in nearly a decade.

Don't forget about Charlene.

The taunting voice flung darts at her compassion, bursting it like a cheap balloon. *Good point. We're too far gone to feel sorry for each other. Not with—*

Don't say it, daughter. The tongue is full of evil.

"Save your confessions for Charlene."

As soon as the words were out she wished she could snatch them from the air and shove them back inside, where she could sort through and filter them. She remembered something her father had told her once after he'd given his life to the Lord. *Trying to take back unkind words is like trying to put the toothpaste back in the tube. You can't do it, and you'll only make a mess of things trying.*

Abby uncrossed her arms and tapped her fingers softly on the kitchen counter. "I'm sorry. That wasn't very nice."

John cocked his head and studied her. "No, it wasn't, but then we haven't exactly been very nice to each other for a while now."

Abby felt fresh tears in her eyes as she turned to fill the kettle and light the fire beneath it. "So what're we supposed to do?"

"We pull it together, go back in there, and act excited for our daughter, that's what." John's voice was quiet and measured, the way it sounded when there was no arguing with him.

"What about *our* announcement?" Panic rose in Abby's chest; she desperately needed fresh air. They couldn't pretend another six months, could they? In the shadows of planning a wedding for Nicole and Matt? *Help me, God, I—*

She caught herself. What point was there in asking the Lord for help when He wasn't handing out answers anyway? At least not any she could use.

"We can tell the kids after the wedding. Really, Abby." John worked his face into an incredulous frown. "You think we can go back in there, ask Matt to leave, and then tell them we're finished? Nicole would probably pack her bags and elope. She deserves more than that from us."

"Well, that's why I don't have a grip here, all right?" Pain and sarcasm oozed from every word, and Abby fought to keep from spitting at him. "You're dating another woman right under my nose, and now I get to pretend everything's fine for another six months." He rolled his eyes and she continued, her anger building with each whispered word. "Not only that, but I have to act like our marriage is this shining *beacon* of an example for our daughter and her fiancé while we shop for wedding dresses and flower arrangements. It's enough to put me over the edge, John."

"For crying out loud, Abby, I'm not dating her!" It was the loudest John had gotten during the discussion, and Abby glanced toward the kitchen entrance then back at him.

"Keep it down. Please. And quit lying." If the kids came in now, she had no idea what they'd say to explain why they were fighting in the kitchen.

John continued as if he hadn't heard her. "Okay, you want to know the truth? I kissed her. There, are you happy?"

Her world shifted wildly as she stared at him. He was finally admitting it; she had been right after all. John was having an affair. That could only mean one thing: he was in love with Charlene. Abby reeled backward until she came up against the place where the counter formed an L-shape. She had accused him often, yes, but somewhere in the recesses of her mind she had always hoped it wasn't so, that John's constant declarations of innocence were maybe, at least in part, the truth.

"You *kissed* her?" Abby's words were weak and hoarse, like the sounds that come from a dying old woman. A whistling began to build from the kettle, and without looking Abby reached over and flicked off the burner. Forget tea. Her head was spinning too hard to even think about putting something in her stomach.

John took a step closer, determination etched in his face. "Yes. You were right; are you happy? Isn't that what you wanted to hear? I did it; I kissed Charlene one night after practice because I was stupid and weak and not thinking straight." Another step in her direction. "But, Abby, I have not slept with that woman, and I'm not having an affair with her."

Abby's eyes fell to the floor, to the place where their feet now faced each other as they'd done so many times before. He was lying—she could feel it in her bones. She began shaking her head in short, jerky motions. "I don't believe you . . ." A surge of renewed anger filled her, and she found the strength to look him in the eyes again. "You kissed her? Why don't you just tell me the whole truth, John? That you're having an affair and you're in love with her."

His lips formed a straight, angry line and all trace of sadness and compassion vanished from his face. He brought the palm of his hand down hard on the countertop.

There was a beat. "Hey . . . did something break in there?" Nicole yelled her concern from the next room.

Abby forced her voice to sound cheerful, normal. "No, dear. Your father dropped a cup. Everything's fine."

She shot an accusatory look at John and he narrowed his eyes.

"Believe what you want, Abby. I've told you the truth. I don't care how you want to handle this, but we need to make a plan." He paused and the tension left his face. "Our decision to divorce isn't about Charlene any more than it is your e-mail buddy, Stan. Things have been falling apart between us for years." Some of the warmth returned to his eyes. "Let's not go out fighting like this, hating each other."

New tears filled her eyes, and she crossed her arms tightly, gazing once more at the floor. He was right, and she hated him for it. Stan was her editor and friend, nothing more. But her marriage to John had been dead long before Charlene entered the picture. How in the world had they managed to keep everyone fooled for so long? Even the kids? Habit, Abby guessed. A lifetime of loving for all the right reasons had become a pattern of going through the motions. Nights of laughter and deep conversation had given way to silent isolation, hours of meaningless television, and using old magazines to pass the time and fill the emptiness.

And now they were left with this.

She nodded, wiping at a tear before it could slide down her face.

John sighed. "I'll stay away from Charlene as much as possible. I mean, I work with her and nothing can change that fact. But I'll do my best." John reached out and gently lifted Abby's chin, and she felt even the small muscles along her spine go tense. He never touched her that way anymore. Now that they'd agreed it was over, she preferred his angry indifference to this . . . this reminder of all they'd once been.

"Can you do it, Abby? For six months?"

She held her breath, searching for another way and knowing there was none. This was Nicole's season, her time of becoming. Abby would do nothing to mar it, even if the pretending killed her. She turned her head slightly and John took the hint, allowing his hand to drop to his side. But she maintained eye contact. "We'll be busy, I guess. With wedding plans and all."

John nodded slightly. "Right. The weeks'll fly by and then later on—when they're back from their honeymoon—we can go on with our plans."

Abby considered the notion and knew it was the only way. Her thoughts landed on Charlene and her heart skipped a beat in response. "Don't make a mockery of me, John." For the first time that morning there was fear and vulnerability in her voice.

Again John brought his hand to her face and brushed a lock of hair back from her eyes. "I respect you, Abby. You have my word."

She wanted to push away his fingers, his kindness, shout at him that it was too late for that, but right then she needed his touch more than she understood. She shifted slightly, and he removed his hand once more. "So it'll be our secret, right? We tell no one?"

"Right."

She raised her eyes and studied the silk plants that lined the top of her cupboards. "I guess it won't matter, anyway. The next six months won't be about us; they'll be about Nicole and Matt."

"That's right." His hesitation drew her eyes back to his. "Besides . . . we're already basically divorced. We go our separate ways, spend time with different groups of friends, and sleep in separate rooms. The only thing we'll be waiting on is telling the kids."

Abby blinked. John's description of their lives sounded as appealing as cold oatmeal, and she willed away the wetness that returned to her eyes. It was true, wasn't it? They were separate people living separate lives. "Let's try to get through it without a lot of fighting, okay?"

"I'm all for that . . ." John chuckled lightly, and immediately Abby's ire ignited. What did he think? She caused all the fights? Before she could come back with a biting response, she stopped herself. *Deep breath, Abby.* If they weren't going to fight, then it had to start now. With her.

Abby thought of something. If he was conceding that things were separate, that meant he couldn't comment on the fact that they weren't sleeping together, weren't physically intimate. Of course, they hadn't been for six months—ever since the first time she'd caught Charlene in his classroom late one night—but that hadn't stopped John from making an occasional dig at her. Especially after sessions with their counselors. She leveled her gaze at him thoughtfully. "So for the next six months we'll be cordial roommates, nothing more. Agreed?"

John lowered his eyebrows, clearly confused by her statement. "Agreed."

"And none of this, 'Fine wife you are, sleeping down the hall' stuff, either. Right?"

A darkness fell over John's eyes and the intimacy that had been there a moment earlier faded. "Don't worry, Abby, I don't want anything from you."

His statement left a pit in her stomach. With his words sounding again and again in her heart, she excused herself and went to the bathroom where she splashed her eyes with cold water. *"Don't worry, Abby, I don't want anything from you . . . I don't want anything from you . . ."* Wasn't that the problem? That neither of them wanted the other anymore? Abby waited until her eyes had cleared and some of the redness in her face had faded. *"I don't want anything from you . . . from you . . . from you . . ."*

Abby held back any further tears and stared hard at the mirror. John's words might hurt, but they were more than appropriate.

Because at this point, she had nothing left to give.

She drew a steadying breath and went to join John in the living room with the kids. None of them seemed to notice anything different and Abby settled back into her chair, fixing her attention on Nicole and casting her an unspoken invitation.

Nicole immediately picked up on the message and joined Abby, taking a spot on the floor at her right side. "Everything okay?"

Oh, honey, if only you knew. "The steam from the kettle melted my makeup. It got in my eyes. I'm fine now."

Relief washed over Nicole's face. "That's good. I was beginning to think you weren't happy about it. You know, excited for us."

The boys had quit wrestling and flipped on the television again for the first of two NFL play-off games. In the din of activity and football noise, no one was listening to their conversation and Abby was thankful. She needed time alone with Nicole, needed to let her daughter know from the beginning how excited Abby was about her impending wedding.

She stroked Nicole's dark blonde hair. "Honey, I'm so happy for you. Matt's a wonderful young man. Really."

Nicole smiled at her. "He is wonderful, isn't he?"

Abby felt another wave of tears and she did nothing to stop them. Tears for Nicole's happiness were appropriate; tears about the death of her own marriage and the tombstone they would be keeping in the closet for the next six months would be absolutely forbidden. At least in public. "I can't believe you're all grown up." A single tear spilled over onto Abby's cheek. "My little girl, ready to make a home of her own and get married."

Nicole's eyes were suddenly brimming with tears, too, and she reached up and clasped Abby's hand. "You know what I read today?"

Abby smiled through wet eyes. "What?"

"Jeremiah 29:11 . . . 'I know the plans I have for you . . . plans to give you hope and a future' . . . Remember that one?"

The words hit Abby like falling bricks. Remember? Their pastor had recited those very words at their own wedding more than twenty-one years earlier. She swallowed hard. *How do I handle this, God? What do I tell her?*

The truth will set you free, daughter . . .

Abby wasn't sure the response had come from God, but she acted on it anyway. What would it hurt? "I remember it well. We read it at our wedding, honey. Did you know that?"

Nicole's eyes lit up. "No, way . . . really? I thought it was *my* special verse. That's amazing." She thought for a moment. "Maybe we should use it, too." She started to rise as if she might approach Matt and ask him about the scripture right in the middle of the football game, then she paused and sat down again. "I'll tell him later. Hey, Mom, I almost forgot. I bought a *Christian Bride* magazine. Wanna look at it later, after Matt leaves?"

"Sure."

Pangs of nostalgia stung at Abby's heart. She remembered going over the details of her wedding with her own mother, planning the reception, searching for the perfect dress . . .

Would she feel this way every day for the next six months? Aching and grieving every time she drifted back through yesterday and re-visited the days before she and John had taken this very step? She sighed inwardly. If she could get her perspective right, it wouldn't be so bad to walk through that time in her life. Sort of like recalling a friend who had died too young. Yes, that's exactly what their marriage was like. No amount of recall could bring it back, but certainly there would be nothing wrong with remembering the good times.

Sean interrupted her thoughts by muting the sound on the television and staring expectantly first at John, then Abby. "When do we finish the meeting?"

John glanced around the room. Abby wasn't sure what to say, so she shot him a look that said, *Think fast; it isn't going to get any easier.*

There was a momentary deep-seated fear in John's eyes as he cleared his throat and sat up straighter in his chair. Shrugging lightly, he forced a smile. "Summer plans." He looked at Abby once more. "Right, honey?"

Abby felt like a character in a poorly written play. "Yep. Summer plans."

John clapped his hands in a show of closure. "And since Nicole and Matt have given us their news, I guess the summer has enough plans already."

Sean looked satisfied, and a quick glance around the room told Abby the others believed John, too. "Then can I go to Ben's? Please?" Sean was on his feet, already heading for the coat closet. "He got the new Play Station for Christmas. You should see the NFL game, Dad."

Abby couldn't stop herself from laughing. "Okay, go. But be back before dinner."

"Right . . . and make sure you're the quarterback," John yelled after him, winking at Kade who was now stretched out on the sofa grinning. "Reynolds men are always quarterbacks."

"You got it, Dad!" Sean was gone in a blur of flying scarf ends and a half-fastened coat.

Matt stood up and after another round of congratulations, set off to take care of errands and pressing schoolwork. Abby watched him go, and someplace deep inside her she trembled at the charade she and John were living out, the way the kids were believing them and had been for months. *Just like everything's fine.* The whole family was plummeting toward a major disaster, and not one of their children had even the slightest idea what was coming. What would the kids think when they found out? Would they feel deceived? Lied to? She forced the thought from her mind. Whatever price she and John would pay, they wouldn't have to face it until after the wedding.

John and Kade were lost in the football game as soon as the door closed. Nicole studied them and then giggled at Abby. "Never changes, does it?"

"Nope." Abby's mind flashed back to a long-ago celebration—a moment in John's career for which they had waited years—a time when she and John were madly in love in every way that mattered. John's arms had been around her and everything had seemed perfectly right with their world. She could hear him, even now: "I couldn't have done it without you, Abby . . . couldn't have done it without you . . ."

Stop! The silent, harsh command forced the memory to disappear. It was one thing to remember how she and John had met, how they'd fallen in love and decided to marry. It was another to be hit by more recent memories, glimpses of their happy days together, back when they were halfway to forever.

Nicole squeezed her hand. "Did you hear me?"

Abby sat up. "Sorry, honey. I was drifting."

"I said, let's go check out my magazine."

Nicole led the way, and Abby looked to see if John would notice their departure. She should have known better. His eyes were fixed on the screen and the play about to unfold.

Up in her room, Nicole tossed the magazine on her bed, and Abby sprawled out next to her.

"I think I know what I want in a dress, but I'm not sure about the neckline, you know?"

Abby smoothed her forefinger over the images of fresh young brides in their assorted wedding gowns. "Lots to choose from."

Nicole sat up and crossed her legs, her eyes full of wonder. "Isn't it amazing, Mom? How faithful God is? Bringing Matt like this as an answer to all those years of prayers."

Abby pulled herself up and brought her knees close to her chin.

Where was Nicole going with this? There was only one right response, of course. "He's always faithful."

Indeed, God had answered Abby's prayer for Nicole to find a godly husband.

But for the life of her, as she and Nicole poured over pictures of wedding gowns, there was something Abby couldn't understand. If God could answer her prayers for Nicole, why hadn't He answered her prayers for herself?

Seven

JOHN HAD NO IDEA HOW HE WAS GOING TO pull off pretending for the next six months that he and Abby were happily married, but he did know one thing: if the problem continued to consume him, he would be useless in the classroom.

He planted his elbows on the cluttered surface of his desk in the back of the weightroom and closed his eyes. He had to handle four health classes and two sessions of weight training, do grades and tests for 152 students, and get ready for spring league coming up in ten weeks. All while trying to avoid Charlene Denton. Someone dropped a weight in the next room, and John looked up. As he did his eyes fell on his family's Christmas photo from . . . hmm . . . what year? He looked at it more closely. Sean was two, so it had to be eight years ago.

Lord, how did it all get so crazy?

It had been so long since he'd talked to God that the silent question felt foreign, and he was struck by a pang of guilt. Maybe it was his fault. He was supposed to be the spiritual leader, after all. Maybe things would be different if only he'd—

There was a knock at the door and John turned. Charlene stood there.

Ah, Charlene . . . What am I going to do with you? He kept the question to himself and smiled big as he reached for the door and opened it. "Hey, what's up?"

She swept into the room and took a seat opposite him. John studied her for a moment, enjoying the easy way they had with each other. It wasn't so much that she was beautiful, really . . . There was just something about her—a Sandra Bullock look maybe—that made him want to spend time with her, to protect her from the dangers in life.

"Wanna get coffee?" Her eyes twinkled and John wondered, as he had a hundred times before, whether down the road a year or two things might work out for the two of them. She was willing; she'd told him as much. But he wasn't sure. He'd already made a mess of one marriage.

He resisted the urge to take her hand in his. "Not today." How was he going to say this? "Listen, Char, I have something to tell you."

Her expression changed, and John could see fear in her eyes not far from the surface. "Okay."

"It's about Abby and me."

Charlene shifted in the chair. "I'm listening."

"We're postponing the divorce." John watched as she sat straighter in her seat, more formal, further back from him, as though the words had sent a knife straight through her heart. When she didn't say anything, he continued. "It wasn't anything we planned. Nicole and Matt announced their engagement Saturday. Right before we were going to tell them."

Charlene moved her head up and down in a subtle motion, and John knew she was trying to be strong. "Okay, so for a few weeks or what?"

A few weeks? Didn't she know how hard this was going to be on his kids, his family? He uttered a disbelieving laugh. "No, until the wedding is behind us. Six months at least."

She held tightly to the arms of the chair. "And you want me to wait around six months?"

Her voice wasn't angry, but it was close. John closed his eyes and wished himself a thousand miles away—there had to be a place where life was quiet and uncomplicated . . . maybe a football field, where the main thing that mattered was the way his boys played the game. When he opened his eyes, she was waiting. "What you do is your choice. I haven't promised you anything."

"I matter more to you than she does. I know I do." Charlene sounded like a petulant child, and John felt a ripple of doubt. This was a side of her John had never seen before. "Ever since Rod left last year, you've always been there for me." Her voice showed she was back in control. "You know how I feel about you, John."

Yes, he did. She was in love with him. If he hadn't been sure before, her reaction now removed any doubt. "I only wanted your friendship, Charlene. I'm sorry if I've made you think there was more between us."

This time she was the one who laughed. "Who are you kidding? That was *you* I kissed that night after practice, right? Don't tell me all you wanted was friendship then."

There it was again. As though someone else had entered the room wearing Charlene's skin. He released a troubled breath. "I don't know *what* I want anymore, but I know this. I can't face a future with you—or with anyone—until my past is behind me."

The scowl on her face faded, as though the fact that he'd admitted a possible future with her somehow calmed her concerns. "You're right. We both need time to think about things." She grinned at him and tapped his foot playfully with hers. "Besides, it's not like we won't be together."

John felt his neck muscles relax. This was the Charlene he was familiar with, the one who was his buddy, his fun friend. The one who reminded him of the way Abby used to be. John leaned forward, resting his forearms on his thighs. He hoped Charlene would still be smiling when she heard what he had to say.

"Actually . . . I promised Abby I'd stay away from you as much as possible."

Charlene's eyebrows raised. "She knows about us?" The corners of her mouth lifted slightly, and the look in her eyes grew confident as though she'd notched some kind of victory. John wasn't sure why, but her reaction bothered him.

"How could she not know, Charlene? We're together all the time. People talk." He thought a moment.

What remained of Charlene's frustration and fear faded even further, and he could see in her eyes again the carefree, youthful exuberance he so deeply appreciated about her. "So I have to stay away, huh?"

Seeing her there, dark hair falling over her shoulders, green eyes glistening even in the fluorescent lights of his cramped office, made him long to take her in his arms and . . . His mind filled with the memory of their kiss, and he gritted his teeth. *Show a little control, Reynolds.* "We *both* have to stay away. I promised Abby."

Charlene's mouth curved into a full smile and she stood to leave. "Okay, if that's the way it has to be." She quickly kissed her two fingers and then touched them to his lips. "Whatever happens, I'll be here for you. If you need to talk, anything. I live alone, remember? I can make sure no one ever finds out. That way you can keep your promise to Abby."

With that she turned and walked away, weaving her lithe body between the machines and free weights and leaving without ever looking back.

The air in John's lungs leaked out slowly as he ripped the baseball cap from his head and tossed it on his desk. Charlene's words rang in his mind: *"I can make sure no one ever finds out . . . that way you can keep your promise to Abby."*

If that's how she felt, Charlene didn't know the first thing about keeping a promise. Doubts began to nibble at the ankles of John's conscience. What sort of future did he hope to have with a woman who could lie so easily? Who could justify an affair without a second thought? He had no answers for himself.

A sudden image flooded his mind—him kissing Charlene in the

moonlight of the empty Marion High football field—and he hung his head. He had no room to judge her. He didn't know the first thing about keeping a promise, either. *At least she's gone. Maybe she'll stay away until fall, and then . . .*

Then maybe he and Charlene would find a way to make it work; maybe theirs would be a better relationship because of what he'd learned the first time around with Abby.

He turned his attention back to the stack of "Nutritional Supplements" tests that lay on top of the pile of player profiles and camp applications and advertisements for football equipment. Normally it took him less than an hour to correct tests like this— multiple choice answers and single-word fill-ins. But today he'd already been working on it for two hours and he wasn't even halfway done.

Focusing on the task at hand, he narrowed his eyes and made himself concentrate, but all he could think about was Charlene— how she'd looked and smelled and so easily presumed he'd take her up on her offer of being available and secretive.

"I can make sure no one ever finds out . . . no one ever finds out . . . no one ever finds out."

Who would have ever dreamed things would get this complicated with Charlene Denton? As if in response, he heard Abby's voice from years ago: *"I don't like the way she looks at you, like she doesn't care a bit that both of you are married."*

He set down his pencil and leaned back in his chair, lacing his hands together behind his head and closing his eyes. Forget the tests. The only way to figure out how things had gotten so complicated was to go back to the fall of 1993, the year Charlene was hired to teach at Marion High. The same year things between Abby and him went from fun-loving and unforgettable to busy and stressful.

Nicole had turned thirteen that year, and every hour the girl spent at the junior high seemed to require another two hours of Abby's time to sort through Nicole's problems and help her understand the pains of growing up. And of course there were the sports activities. That year Kade was ten and building a name for himself in youth football leagues around Southern Illinois. When there wasn't football there was baseball or basketball.

Abby always seemed to be driving Kade one place or another, and Nicole was just as busy. She needed to get to youth group and swimming lessons and piano recitals and soccer games. On top of everything else, there was Abby's father. The man lived alone, but he'd lost much of his independence since being diagnosed with Parkinson's disease. He'd sold the old house in Wisconsin in 1993, along with much of his furniture, then packed up his few belongings and moved to a retirement home ten minutes from John and Abby's. So in addition to the kids' schedules, Abby took time to stop in and see her dad several times a week. Where once he and Abby had spent Sunday afternoons watching fall football, that year she spent those hours with her father.

Most of the time Abby was so busy she'd drive three-year-old Sean over to the weightroom at Marion High and leave him with John so she could attempt the insurmountable schedule of the day.

It was so different from those early years, back when the children were young and the only thing on Abby's agenda each afternoon had been getting the kids down to the high school so they could run around the grassy hills and watch the Marion Eagles' football practice. By the fall of '93, not only was Abby too busy to watch his team practice, she was no longer interested: *It's the same thing, year after year . . . Besides, it's too cold out there on the hillside.*

He could hear her excuses and even now, years later, they still hurt. In the early days she couldn't wait to hear who went out for the team and who made it. She'd pepper him with questions about players and strategies and upcoming games until long after practice was over.

Those were the days.

John opened his eyes and reached for his water bottle, taking three long swigs before setting it back down and staring hard again at the family photo. Why had she changed? Did football lose its appeal somehow? Or was it him she'd grown tired of? Either way by the time Charlene started teaching at Marion, life at the Reynolds house was little more than a functional blur. At least four out of five nights, John and Abby would see each other only when they met back at the house long after dark to grab a quick meal before putting the kids in bed.

Late evenings—a time Abby and John once had reserved for each other—became the only opportunity to clean dishes or fold laundry or for Abby to edit a magazine piece due the next day. Each season they told themselves things would get slower, they were *bound* to get slower.

But they only got busier. And the busier they got, the more lonely life felt.

John remembered the in-service training three days before school started in 1993, when Charlene came up and introduced herself to him. She had been twenty-five then, young and fresh and bound to catch the attention of hundreds of high-school boys. John had heard about her from one of the other coaches, but even their praise hadn't prepared him for the impact she made in person.

"Hi, I'm Charlene Denton. You must be Coach Reynolds." She held out her hand and he took it, taken aback by her directness.

"I guess I just look like a Coach Reynolds . . ." He grinned at her, and she laughed in a way that Abby had long since stopped doing.

"State title, 1989; quarterfinals, 1990. I'm a big Eagles football fan, Coach. Everyone knows who you are."

John pondered her statement now. Maybe that was why he'd felt so attracted to Charlene. She was a football fan, *his* fan. The way Abby had been before the hillside grew too cold and practices became too routine.

He remembered how he'd felt lost in her wide-eyed gaze that

afternoon. "Well then, it's a privilege to meet you, Ms. Denton. We can always use an extra fan around Marion High."

That should have been the end of it, but Charlene was persistent—and he was weak. Surprisingly so. She stayed by his side, clearly enjoying his company and pumping him for dozens of details about the team and its chances that season.

"My husband's a fan, too." She casually tossed the comment his way, and he remembered feeling himself relax, relieved to discover she was married. There would be no threats for either of them that way.

Before the training session was over, he had found a way to invite her and her husband over for dinner that weekend. "Just to make you feel welcome," he'd told her.

Abby had been puzzled when John brought it up later that evening.

"We don't even know them, honey. I mean, it's the busiest time of the year. I have an article due Monday and school shopping for the kids. I wasn't exactly planning to entertain this weekend."

John had shrugged like it was no big deal. "She's new on staff, that's all. Besides, I don't think she and her husband are Christians. It'd be a good witness."

Abby thought about that and smiled that weary smile she'd picked up by then. "Oh, all right. We'll barbecue. And maybe if you help me with the cleanup . . ."

The night had been a disaster from the beginning.

Charlene and Rod arrived, and it was obvious from the way they avoided each other and spoke around each other that they were fighting. Introductions were simple, and though Charlene was polite to Abby, she stayed by John's side throughout the night, pulling football stories out of him and laughing hysterically at anything he said that was even remotely funny.

Why didn't I see it back then? Maybe none of this would have happened . . .

John's question wasn't really directed at anyone, and there was no magical answer in response. He let his thoughts drift back again. The evening had been enjoyable enough for him, but Abby had seemed tense almost from the beginning. When Charlene and her husband left, Abby shook her head and headed for the kitchen. John remembered following her and asking—innocently—whether something was wrong.

Abby slammed the dishrag on the counter, splattering soapy water across the floor. "Come on, John. Don't tell me you didn't notice."

John had been baffled. Was she jealous? Just because a beautiful young woman enjoyed his company? "Notice what?"

Abby huffed. "Charlene."

A laugh escaped before John could stop it. "I don't believe it. You're jealous of her. Come on, Abby, be realistic."

Abby seemed to struggle with whether to scream or break down and cry. Instead she pushed her hands in a controlled manner, palm down, until her arms were straight. Then she cocked her head, a gesture that meant she was forcing herself to be calm. "In case you weren't watching, the woman got all drippy around you and hung on everything you said."

"Come on, honey. She's married." John had approached Abby, but she took a step backward.

"You're married, too, and that didn't stop you from playing right into her little plan."

At the time, John honestly hadn't known what Abby meant, and her accusation roused his own anger. "Wait a minute, don't go blaming me about her actions. I can't help it if—"

"If what?" Abby's voice was louder than before. "If that woman has a crush on you? Well, for the record, John, I don't appreciate you inviting her here to parade around *my* house flirting with *my* husband eating *my* food at *my* table. Are you reading me?"

John had stormed out of the house then, refusing even to acknowledge Abby's tirade. Back then it had seemed ridiculous. Like maybe it was that time of the month or possibly Abby was frustrated about her hair or something. Looking back . . . well, he knew that she'd been more right than he could have imagined. From his current vantage point, it seemed Charlene had used the dinner to make her attraction to him known.

John leaned forward again and sifted through the papers on his desk. He'd asked Charlene about the dinner since then, and each time she'd denied having an agenda. "How could I have known things would get like this between us?"

How did *they get like this, anyway?* John had asked himself the question a hundred times if he'd asked it once. It wasn't really Charlene, was it? It was Abby. Too busy with the kids and their schedules and her father to even ask about his day let alone attend Friday night games. Basically, she had forgotten about him. Left him to live his own life while she managed the lives of everyone else around her, always complaining about something. Ever since life had gotten busier, she was constantly blaming him, accusing him of not helping enough around the house, not being involved enough with the kids' lives. He was doing everything he knew how to do, but it was never enough. She'd turned into a meanspirited shrew.

All things considered, any man would have been weak in those circumstances.

At first it had been lunch with Charlene in his classroom, and then an occasional phone call after work. Still, it wasn't until four years later that Charlene began having serious trouble with Rod.

"I have no one to talk to," she'd tell him. "Meet me here before school. I just need someone who understands."

And so—without telling Abby or the kids—he began getting up earlier and arriving at Marion High half an hour before classes. John remembered that not once that year did Abby even ask why. It wasn't every day, of course, but in time he and Charlene began meeting in the weightroom and working out together before classes began. Occasionally there'd be teasing and rib-poking between them and a rare tickling match or two. But he'd been up-front with her about his situation.

"I don't believe in affairs, Charlene."

Once when he said that, she came up behind him and started rubbing both sides of the base of his neck, seemingly concerned only about the tension in his back. "Who's having an affair?"

She was so innocent, so sweet and fun to be with. He'd convinced himself she was harmless, and there was nothing wrong with a backrub now and then after working out. He remembered laughing lightly and lowering his head, enjoying the way her fingers worked themselves into his muscles. "Okay, so it's not an affair. I just want you to know where I stand."

She ran her fingers lightly down the sides of his arms and whispered. "Don't worry, Coach. I'm not trying to seduce you."

John had done a quick check of his emotions and realized she didn't have to try. Just being near her . . . He'd reached up and caught her hands, firmly taking them from his arms as he turned around. "Look, Charlene. I care a lot about you, but I could never do anything to jeopardize my marriage. I mean it."

Charlene grinned at him then and shoved him roughly on the shoulder. "Yes *sir,* Coach. I'll just be your buddy, then. That's all I want from you, anyway."

John had risen to his feet and noticed that he towered almost a foot above her. "Let's keep it that way then, okay?" But even as he said the right thing, an intense desire began to take hold of him. He wanted to kiss her, could feel himself drawn to do so. It wasn't yet seven in the morning, after all, and the kids wouldn't come around for another half-hour.

Hypocrite! The accusation rang in his mind, as though his desire were mocking him. *Hypocrite!*

He'd nearly given in, but finally he'd stepped back and released a breath, striving to alleviate the sinful feelings assaulting him.

Before he could leave that morning, Charlene gently took hold of his arm, her green eyes piercing his, begging him to understand. "Things are so bad at home, John. Just understand one thing. You're the best friend I have. I won't do anything to lose that."

That year and the next they kept their obvious attraction for each other at bay. Sometimes, when it seemed their feelings were getting too tense, he'd take a few days off and avoid her. But they always found each other again, whether in the weightroom or at lunch or after school out on the football field. She was, in many ways, his constant companion. And though he still felt deeply committed to Abby, Charlene was quickly replacing his wife as his best friend.

It wasn't until the fall of 1999 that Charlene and Rod's divorce became final. After that, things heated up considerably. The early morning times John spent in the weightroom with Charlene were charged with sexual tension. If she was within ten feet of him, John found himself almost unable to work out. The times their bare, sweaty arms brushed against each other in passing or their fingers met in the exchange of a dumbbell, John fought against scintillating feelings he was sure would anger a righteous God.

God.

The thought snapped John back to the present. Where did God fit into the mess that his life had become?

He pushed the papers around on his desk until they formed a neat stack. He still loved God, still believed the Scriptures and God's promises. It was just that sometime back in the early 1990s, when life got more hectic and Abby was busy with the kids and her father, it seemed easier to skip Sunday service and Wednesday men's meetings. The coaches who ran the kids' football and soccer games were not respecters of the Sabbath. Why should he be?

No offense to the Lord or anything. After all, by that time John had been a believer for so long it seemed he'd heard every sermon imaginable. He knew thousands of stories and analogies and illustrations, all designed to keep him on the straight and narrow. In fact, when John turned 35 in the fall of 1991, he calculated the Sundays and Wednesdays he'd spent in church and figured them to be 3,640 days total and counting. 3,640 days! He considered his schedule and decided he needed less time at church with a bunch of people he barely knew and more with his family or alone getting renewed for another busy week. After all, there was no law saying he had to go to church. Not when he could read his Bible each day and carry on a perfectly devout relationship with the Father from the comfort of his Sunday morning easy chair. That afternoon, in the hours before his birthday dinner, he made God a promise, something he remembered to this day.

Okay, God, this is it. I've got Your message memorized; You know my attendance record better than I do. Give me my Sundays and Wednesdays back, and I promise I'll be a godly man all the days of my life.

John considered his promise now, in the light of all that had happened in the years since then. *I still love You, Lord. I still believe . . .*

Remember the height from which you have fallen . . . repent and turn back to Me.

John sat back hard in his chair. Where had *that* come from? It had been years since the Lord had spoken to him by bringing verses to mind. Maybe it wasn't God. Maybe it was just his guilty conscience.

It was true, his plan hadn't worked exactly like he'd hoped. He'd started off with early devotions each day, but when Charlene made arrangements for them to meet in the mornings, something had to go. After a year of meeting with her, he no longer even knew where his Bible was.

And prayer, well, he still prayed at family dinners and meetings and—

He pictured Nicole's startled face from a couple days ago asking how come they weren't going to open the family meeting in prayer. John sighed and rubbed the back of his neck. So maybe they didn't say family prayers as often as before. Still . . . he was definitely a praying man, even if he hadn't prayed much for the past few weeks. Months. Years . . .

Repent and turn back to—

The thought rattled around in his mind as though his conscience had no place to file it.

What about the football games? Hadn't he led a prayer before each contest as long as he'd coached at Marion High? Hadn't he stood up to the powers of political correctness and decided that his team would pray even if no others did? Hadn't he been a pillar of example for countless boys who had gone through his program?

The image of Charlene standing beside him near the locker room on the Marion High field late that one night, of her in his arms as he kissed her, came to mind.

So I'm not perfect. At least it was just once. It's not like I haven't had my chances.

He remembered the time Charlene asked him to stop by on a Saturday morning the previous summer so they could share teaching plans for the fall. Abby had been out of town with Nicole for a soccer match, and Sean and Kade were doing chores at home. Charlene and Rod had no children, and by then Rod had moved up to Michigan and taken a high-tech job with an engineering firm. So John had known Charlene would be alone.

He had knocked on the door that morning and found that it opened with little effort. "John, is that you?" Charlene's voice came from somewhere down the hall. *Her bedroom, no doubt.* John had swallowed hard and forced himself to take a seat in her living room.

"It's me. I'll wait for you out here."

Her answer was quick and lighthearted. "Come on back. My stuff's spread out on my desk."

Alert to the danger of the moment, John headed down the hallway toward the distant bedroom with mixed feelings. He and Charlene were already so close, such good friends, he knew he could trust her not to make a move. It was himself he was worried about.

He reached the doorway and poked his head inside. "Hey."

At the sound of his voice she appeared from a closet area, her hair wrapped in a damp towel, her body bare but for a loosely tied bathrobe. She gestured toward a small desk covered with several sheets of papers. "Come sit down."

Had the warnings he felt been audible, the room would have been bursting with the clamor of bells and whistles. But since they were silent, he ignored them and moved closer, avoiding contact with her as he took the chair. As though she were unaware of the effect she had on him, she placed an arm casually around his shoulders and bent over the back of him, pointing out the plans she wanted to discuss.

The smell of her shampoo and the occasional drop of water on his arm made him unable to understand even a little of what she was saying. After ten torturous seconds, he pushed his chair back. "I can't do this." He looked deep into her eyes and saw that no matter what she said next, she knew exactly what he was talking about.

"The kitchen table then?" She smiled warmly, a smile that said she would not push him, would not force him to cross a line that made him uncomfortable.

He nodded. Without another word he walked through the house to her kitchen table, where she joined him fifteen minutes later. The rest of the morning he was overwhelmed with an aching desire that had nothing to do with Charlene Denton.

It had to do with his wife.

And why he was spending Saturday morning here, in this stranger's house, instead of side by side with the one woman he still loved more than life itself.

Enough remembering. John stood up and scooped the papers from his desk into his hands. It was time to go home and find a way to get his work done there. At least then he wouldn't be in Abby's way. His presence only seemed to make her tense these days.

Maybe I should go home and pray.

Do it now, son, before another moment goes by.

There it was again, that voice. Was it the same one that had spoken so regularly to him back when he was logging in his 3,640 church days? John dismissed the thought. He'd wasted enough time for one day without sitting alone in his office trying to sort it out before God.

What was the point? He and Abby had made the decision to end their marriage. A decision they were not going to back down from.

No, this time they were choosing to go it alone, without the help of Almighty God. He pushed his chair in and before he left, he caught sight of the Christmas photo one last time. Abby was such a beautiful woman. So full of life and love. At least she had been. *Abby, girl, what happened to us? Did we just get busy and quit trying? Is that the legacy we'll leave our kids, our daughter as she starts a life of her own?*

There was only the buzz of the overhead lights in response, and John let his gaze linger a moment longer on the image of his wife. Without thinking, he brought his finger to her face and traced it tenderly. *I miss you, Abby.* For the first time in years he was tempted to go home, sweep her into his arms, and tell her so, face to face.

Crazy. He shook his head and the notion vanished. *We don't even like each other anymore. How can I be missing her? Answer me that, God, how?*

More silence.

Figures. First Abby, now God. Next thing I know the kids'll turn their backs on me. He stood still, feet planted, and ached for the happy family in the photo. *What did I ever do to turn you against me, Abby?* He gazed up trying to see through the fiberboard ceiling. *Or You, for that matter.* He flipped the light switch and headed into the cold, wintry night sure of only one very sad thing—whatever decisions he made about his future in the coming months they would not involve the two people who once upon a time had mattered more than any other.

Abby and God.

John had no idea how he and Abby had arrived at the decision to divorce, a decision that would virtually eliminate both Abby and God from his life. He only knew that they had. He thought about them— Abby, for whom he once would have laid down his life; God, who had willingly died to give him that very life in the first place. Abby, to whom he'd promised forever; God, who had promised forever to him.

I was young and foolish.

You were happy, My son . . . holy . . . set apart . . . Repent and turn back to—

The bitter wind hit him square in the face, and he pushed on toward his car, ignoring the silent whispers in his heart.

No, regardless of guilt feelings, he would not change his mind about the divorce. Abby was angry and hard and distant; she'd been that way for years. Even if they wanted to they couldn't find their way back to the people they had once been, the lives they'd once lived. It was too late; they were too far gone. And if that meant losing God in the process, then so be it.

He pulled the hood of his state championship jacket more tightly around his head and fidgeted with his keys. Besides, God probably had checked out on Coach Reynolds a long time ago. The thought took root as John climbed into his car and began driving, the entire time resisting an urge that was stronger than ever before: the urge to forget about everything waiting for him at home, to turn the wheel of his car and drive straight to Charlene Denton's house instead.

Eight

THE WOMAN WAS DRIVING ABBY CRAZY, THREATENING to ruin the whole outing.

Whose idea had it been to bring her, anyway? The afternoon was supposed to be a special time between Nicole and her, hours of gazing at wedding gowns, searching for the perfect dress.

Instead, she and Nicole barely had a spare moment to exchange glances, let alone attempt breaking into the conversation. *Be patient, Abby. Don't make a scene.* The woman—Jo Harter, a divorced, single mother and a nonbeliever—was Nicole's future mother-in-law, after all. Maybe she was one of those women who talked a lot when she was around people she didn't know well.

"So, anyway, like I was telling Margaret at the office the other day, a girl's got to wear white." She was punishing her gum as though it were guilty of a crime. "I mean it doesn't matter so much whether she's already got the goods, if you know what I mean, but still it has to be white." A quick breath. "I mean, look at Nicole's complexion. The girl would be lost in something ivory or off-color. It has to be white; I absolutely insist." She smacked her lips, rubbing in an excessive coat of lipstick, and sorted hastily through a rack of gowns.

Nicole shot Abby a look. "Actually, I like white, but I'm looking for a—"

"I found it!" The woman's bright red hair stood out in stark contrast to the white dresses hanging on the rack. Her freckled face flushed an uncomfortable pink as she jerked a dress free. It had a high neckline, but the hem stopped short just below the knee, where the dress cut away and curved into three lacy trains that dangled from the back.

It's hideous; it looks half done.

Abby resisted the urge to say so but cast a knowing look at Nicole. *Oh, honey, I hope things'll get easier for you two. There's nothing more wonderful than sharing a friendship with your mother-in-law.* Abby remembered Hattie Reynolds and wondered how the woman was doing. She was in the throes of Alzheimer's disease and had been relegated to an assisted living home. It'd been months since they'd talked or even—

"Well—" Nicole interrupted Abby's thoughts and looked at the dress thoughtfully—"it's not really what I had in mind, honestly."

Jo's face fell. "It's the absolute newest style, Nicole. Haven't you been reading the magazines?"

Abby was proud of the way her daughter handled the woman— patient, polite, but firmly determined to go with her own tastes. Nicole took the dress gently and placed it back on the rack. "Actually, I'm looking for a more traditional dress. White, yes. But also elegant, unforgettable, that sort of thing."

Jo nodded, slightly dejected, then turned her attention on Abby. "By the way, I've been meaning to tell you . . ." She paused and Abby mentally braced herself. Jo was from North Carolina, and many times that day only a lack of oxygen had stopped the woman from going on for hours on every topic they'd hit on.

Jo adjusted her head so that her eyes were level with Abby's, her eyebrows raised dramatically. "That's one fine man you've got there in that John of yours. Yes sir. Big U of M football star." She waved a hand in the air. "I remember how it was. Me and Denny'd be wasting a day, nothing to do on the weekend, and we'd tune in to college ball. And that man of yours . . . mmhhhm." She carried the sound out as long as she could and then grabbed a quick mouthful of air. "Best-looking quarterback I've seen before or since."

The ache in Abby's gut took her by surprise. So what if John was handsome? That didn't hold a marriage together any more than paint held together walls. "Yes, he's always been good looking."

Jo gave Abby a quick once-over and grinned. "'Course, you're not bad looking yourself. Must be nice, that's all I can say."

Nicole—capitalizing on the fact that she was no longer Jo's target—moved on down the rack, lost in private thought as she carefully checked out each gown in the section. Again Abby felt her frustration rise. This was supposed to be *her* time with—

"How long you say you were married?"

Abby blinked. *Here we go.* "Twenty-one years last July."

"Twenty-one years, eeeewwwhheeeee!" Jo sounded like a farm woman calling the pigs in at the end of the day. Her last, loud note lingered in the afternoon air, and Abby glanced about in hopes that they weren't attracting an audience. Jo set her hands firmly on her hips. "You know what I think? I think twenty-one years is a miracle anymore." She poked Abby roughly in the shoulder.

Abby took the slightest step back and wished desperately that the woman would leave her alone. *Don't talk to me about miracles, lady. Those kind of miracles don't happen to people like me.*

Abby worked to hide her discomfort, not that it mattered. Jo was too busy enjoying the sound of her own voice to notice much of anything else. She examined her fingernails, admiring the way the ends were perfectly rounded and painted burnt orange to match her blouse. "You know, I might even step foot in a church one of these days if I thought it'd get me my Denny back. Yes, sir, I believe I just might." Her hands fell to her side and she looked straight at Abby. "You're churchgoing folk, right? That's what Matt tells me. Ever since he went and got himself saved, that's the first thing he talks about. 'They're Christians, Mama.' 'She's a believer, Mama.' Seems like people making more and more a big deal out of spending time in a church building, but you know what I say?"

Abby opened her mouth but didn't have time to answer.

"I say more power to 'em. And you know what else? If I thought it'd get me my Denny back, I'd probably take it up, too." She refueled instantly. "Matt didn't tell me what you folks are exactly, anyway. You those Pentecostals or Presbyterians or Baptists or door-knockers or TV-watchers or what? 'Cause I don't have nothin' 'gainst any of it; I want you to know you heard it from me first. Right here. Out of the horse's mouth. Don't want no arguing about religion when it comes to the kids' wedding." She hesitated, actually giving Abby a chance to speak, but Abby wasn't sure what to say. "Well, what is it? Which one are you? 'Course you don't look like a door-knocker, and I mean that as a compliment."

"We belong to a Calvary Chapel, actually." *The woman's a lunatic. Be prepared in season and out.*

Abby was inwardly shocked at the words that filtered through her mind. *I can't even make my marriage work, God. You can forget me being prepared with this woman, especially if she's going to keep on—*

"Calvary Chapel . . ." Jo gazed at the store ceiling for a moment. "Sounds like a Christmas shop." She gasped. "Wait a minute! I think I know the kind. They the ones that get all wild and start laughin' and runnin' around in circles?"

Despite her frustration, Abby had to resist the urge to laugh out loud. That'd be great, to make her think it was true. "No, nothing like that."

Jo shifted her weight to one foot. "So what's the deal with the Calvary Chapel folks? What'd y'all believe? All that hellfire and brimstone stuff everyone's always talkin' about?" She caught herself quickly. "Not that I care, really. Never bothered me all that 'Gotta-get-your-ducks-in-a-row-Lord-might-be-comin'-back-tomorrow' stuff." Despite Jo's words, concern flashed in her eyes. "I mean it's okay for you and all, but I'm a very busy person. Sundays are my cleaning days, really."

Tell her the truth, Abby.

The voice was so strong and clear Abby wondered if Jo had heard it, too. Out of habit more than anything else, she looked tenderly at Jo. "Our church is like a lot of churches. We believe in Jesus Christ and that the Bible is the only infallible Word of God."

Jo seemed intrigued and she was silent nearly two full seconds, something of a record for the afternoon. "You really think so, huh? Smart woman like you?"

Abby nodded. She did, didn't she? She might not have been living like she believed it, but somewhere deep in her heart she knew His Word was truth.

Everything on earth will pass away but My word will remain forever.

Longer than Abby or John or the fact that they'd chosen to divorce. God's Word was eternal. "Yes, I believe it."

Jo's jaw dropped. "Huh. Well, you and me'll have to have ourselves some down-home, old-fashioned, long, drawn-out conversations on that one. Especially between now and the big weddin' day. Denny and his new wife are split up now, and don't I know he was the best thing ever happened to me. I'm gonna lose ten pounds and dye my hair between now and then just to get his attention. And he'll come all right, know why?"

Abby studied the woman's hair and realized the red wasn't natural after all. "Why?"

"'Cause ever since Matt's been into this God stuff, Denny's been into it, too. I think he's actually startin' to believe it. Nothing wild, mind you, but Matt says it's almost like there's something different in his tone. Something that wasn't there before." Jo smiled broadly and Abby noted that the woman must have had her teeth bleached. They were whiter than the wedding dresses.

If she weren't so obnoxious, Jo would almost be a pretty woman— but if she had talked like this during the years she was married, Abby could only congratulate Denny for having had the good sense to leave.

What God has joined together let no man separate, My daughter.

Fear washed over Abby, and she felt the holy admonishment as strongly as if God had appeared and spoken it to her face. What was wrong with her? When had she begun feeling so jaded and cavalier toward marriage? The situation between John and her was one thing, but to agree so easily with divorce? Just because a person talked too much?

I'm sorry, God, I don't even recognize myself anymore.

Nicole was fifteen feet away and she held up a dress. "Mom, what do you think?"

Abby cocked her head and studied it. High lace collar, fitted bodice, narrow waist, and a traditional skirt that glistened with sequins and lace. She pictured Nicole in it and smiled. "I like it."

Nicole glanced at her watch. "We still need to eat and I have to meet Matt in a few hours. Maybe I'll ask them to hold it for me."

"Good idea."

When the dress was safely put away, the threesome headed for a salad restaurant a block away. Jo was talking about Denny again, and Abby reminded herself continually that the outing was nearly over.

"I told you the story about me and Denny, right? How we decided it was too much work and threw in the towel?" Jo was walking between them. "Worst decision I ever made."

"Uh . . ." Abby caught a glimpse of Nicole's grin and she smiled at her daughter in return. *Oh, fine, little girl. Let me deal with her.* "I don't think you mentioned it." Abby kept a straight face and waited for the next chapter.

"Thing of it was, with me and Denny, we really loved each other. I mean really. Started off that way and seemed that way right on through about the seventh year or so. Then something happened and good golly if I'm just stumped to tell ya what it was."

That last part caught Abby's attention. *She could be telling my story, too . . .*

"One day we was flyin' high as a kite, spendin' time together, laughin' and lovin' and making babies and fishin'. The next—" Jo made a ripping sound with her teeth and lower lip—"the next we weren't hardly talkin' to each other. Before you could say cat-got-caught-in-the-washing-machine, we was livin' separate lives. I mean, completely separate. Him stayin' out in the trailer, and me not carin' if he did. And that wasn't the way it started out at all. Fact, if you have a minute I'll tell you about how we got started. Nothing short of a love story, tell you the truth."

Abby had the feeling there was no way around hearing it. They entered the restaurant, and Jo paused long enough to get the attention of the hostess. "Ma'am, we need a booth for three and not too busy either." Jo smiled big at Abby and then Nicole. "We got us a lot of talking to do." She pointed a finger at the reservation sheet. "And not too close to the smoky section, if you don't mind."

"Smoking section?" The hostess was a brunette not more than sixteen years old, and she seemed genuinely confused by Jo's comment. Again Abby and Nicole exchanged a look that made them both bite their lips to keep from laughing.

Jo leaned closer to the girl. "The smoky section. That's what I call it, okay? The place where the air's so thick with smoke a person could lose her voice in fifteen minutes. We don't want the smoky section 'cause like I said, we got a lot to talk about."

The girl stared blankly at Jo for a moment. "Sure. Okay."

Jo remained unmoved, obviously waiting for more information. "Well, how long a wait are we talking? 'Cause there's a Micky D's around the corner if this isn't going to work. Nothin' personal mind you, but we ladies need a quiet place to talk."

And we'd get that at McDonald's? Abby kept her comments to herself and watched the hostess sympathetically as she checked her seating chart.

"Should be about five minutes." The girl sounded uncertain, as though she'd spiraled into confusion the moment Jo walked into the building and hadn't quite recovered yet.

"All right, five minutes it is." Jo grinned conspiratorially at the girl. "I'll be timin' you, startin' now."

With quick nervous steps, the girl headed for the dining room, and Jo used her departure as a signal to resume her monologue.

"So anyway, like I was sayin', there's never been a love story like me and Denny and I'm tellin' the God's honest truth about it . . ."

She rambled throughout their five-minute wait, pausing only long enough to follow the hostess to the table and fill her plate at the salad bar. By the time they were back at the table, Jo had talked about her love story with Denny for almost half an hour, and still Abby wasn't quite sure how the two of them had met.

Nicole seemed lost in her own thoughts, content to let Jo ramble. *She's thinking about Matt and the dress and the rest of her life.* Abby pretended to be listening, but inside she was smiling at Nicole. *You're so beautiful, honey. I couldn't be happier for you.*

How would Nicole remember this, her love story with Matt, when one day her own daughter was getting married? In some ways she was thankful for the distraction Jo provided. Otherwise she was sure Nicole would have been peppering her with questions about Abby and John's love story.

Someday . . . Maybe someday I'll be able to talk about it without feeling angry and hurt and frustrated, without wanting to punch my fist through a wall at the way John ruined everything. The way he let me take over the efforts of raising the kids and got so busy with football he couldn't so much as pick up after himself.

Abby tuned in for a moment.

"But after that day at the county fishing derby, there was no turnin' back, no sir. Denny had himself the shiniest, most man-size fish you or anyone in all of Marion, Illinois, ever saw before or since. I mean to tell you, it was a big fish. Truth be told—and I'm a truthteller from way back—fish don't get any bigger than the way that one looked when . . ."

Abby's mind drifted again. Jo and Denny didn't have anything on her and John. Theirs was a love destined from childhood, like an amazing rainbow laid across the sky for everyone to marvel over. She swallowed hard and set down her fork, staring at the wilting lettuce on her plate. Of course, like all rainbows, their light had faded, and now all that remained were stormy grays and lackluster hues of beige. Very soon everyone would know that no matter how great a story it had started out to be, no matter how long it had lasted, it had long been doomed to an awful ending. The kind that made people leave movie theaters wanting their money back.

Oh . . . but once upon a time their story had been truly brilliant.

Back in their first decade of marriage, she had told the story often, referring to John as her Prince Charming and secretly savoring the way other couples tried to model what the two of them had together. Lately the tale of how they'd met as kids and eventually married seemed to belong to another time, another woman. As though maybe it had never happened at all.

Jo's voice interrupted her thoughts. "So there we were, all these belly-opened fish spread out on the kitchen counter at his mama's house when what did we see but something shiny lying in the guts of one of the little fellers . . ."

Jo didn't need an audience. If Abby and Nicole leaned their heads back and fell fast asleep, the woman would continue talking. The story would go on as long as the two of them were breathing— maybe even if they weren't. She noticed Nicole picking her fork through a scoop of tuna fish on her plate. Fish guts. Great lunch conversation.

No, Abby was fairly certain there wasn't anyone whose love story topped hers and John's. She thought back, and at first the pictures seemed hazy. But after several seconds of trying, the images came more easily, and Abby realized something. It wasn't that she'd forgotten their past or convinced herself that maybe it never happened. She simply had stopped giving herself permission to go back.

But here, with Jo Harter going on about a story that seemed to have no real plot and yet was bound to last the rest of the afternoon, Abby allowed herself to remember as she hadn't done in years.

There, in the privacy of her own mind, she journeyed to a time and place when she was just a young girl, ten years old, and living in a wonderful old house on the back side of Lake Geneva.

"Abby, come in and get cleaned up . . ." It was her mother's voice, crisp and vivid as though she were still alive, still looking at Abby from the back porch and beckoning her to come in from the water—

"You're listening to me, right, Abby?" Jo's gravelly voice cut into the memory, stopping it cold.

Abby drew a settling breath. This was not the place. But maybe it wasn't such a bad idea, after all. Nicole's wedding plans were bound to bring up much of Abby's memories of the past anyway . . .

She took out a ten-dollar bill and set it on the table. "It's a fascinating story, Jo, but I'll have to hear the rest later."

Nicole practically lurched from her seat and joined Abby near the edge of the table, grabbing money from her purse and handing it to Jo. "Me, too. Sorry . . . Matt's waiting for me."

Jo looked disappointed, but she collected the money and began calculating. "Well, now, don't you know something I never even counted on? It's been the best afternoon I can remember in a long time, spending it with you girls. I say next week we do it again, huh? Lots of shopping to do, and if there's one thing I love it's—"

"Not next weekend, Jo." Abby looked at Nicole and smiled. "I promised Nicole we'd take a couple of date days, just her and me." She shifted her gaze back to Jo. "We've done that ever since she was a little girl."

Jo's eyes lit up. "Well, then, I know. Thursday night, week from this. How 'bout say we go scrapping together?"

Get me out of here . . . "Scrapping?"

A laugh bubbled up from deep in Jo's throat. "Oh, I forgot . . . you 'Northern' types call it scrapbookin'. You know, getting together at the craft store and puttin' pictures down on paper. I'm makin' a book for Matthew for the wedding." She glanced quickly at Nicole and held a finger up to her lips. "Shhh, now, don't go tellin' him. It's a surprise. Just like when I used to bring homemade peanut-butter fudge to school after he got a good report card." She grinned proudly at Nicole. "And you, sweetie girl, are the best thing he's gotten since who knows when, and like I always say, the celebration has to fit the thing you're celebratin'."

Abby watched Nicole's eyes dance with possibilities as they turned to her, half expectantly, half apologetically. "Mom, I know you're busy with your writing." She batted her eyelashes in a gesture she'd used since she was a little girl. "Do you think you could? Find time to make me a scrapbook, I mean?" Nicole looked at Jo once more. "I think it's a great idea."

At that point, Abby was willing to do whatever she could to end the afternoon and get as far away from Jo Harter as she could. Besides, the idea wasn't bad. She'd started a scrapbook for Nicole back when her daughter was in grade school, but it was missing pages. Sometime after Nicole's tenth year, Abby had gotten too busy to work on it. If she was ever going to finish it, there was no time like the present. "A week from Thursday, then. What time?"

Jo grinned. "Six o'clock. Meet at the Crafter's Bin on Main and Sixth."

When the three of them were out in the parking lot, Nicole and Abby bid good-bye to Jo and watched her leave. Then Abby turned to her daughter and the two nearly collapsed in laughter. "I thought I was going to lose it for sure." Nicole could barely breathe she was laughing so hard.

"All I know is if I heard one more detail about fish guts and shiny objects slithering about I was going to lose my lunch." Abby caught her breath and held her sides. "I'm sorry. That wasn't very nice."

Nicole looped her arm around her mother's waist and walked alongside her to the car. "I understand, Mom. It's not like you're condemning the woman. And it could be worse. Marli's mother-in-law acts like Marli isn't even alive. At least Jo likes me."

"That's for sure." They were at the car and Abby turned to her daughter. "You go on home. It's not too cold this afternoon. I think I'll walk."

Nicole frowned. "Mother, that's two miles. You don't want to walk two miles on frozen sidewalks. You'll break your neck."

Abby tousled Nicole's bangs. "Now you sound like me." She grinned. "No, really. Don't worry. I'll take the scenic route along Willow Way. That's a gravel path. No danger of ice."

"Are you sure?" There was concern in Nicole's eyes, and Abby worked as hard as she could to appear casual about her decision.

"Yep. I need the fresh air. Tell Dad I'll be home in an hour if he asks, okay?"

Nicole smiled and pulled her mother into a close hug. "Okay. I guess I can understand wanting a little silence in light of the afternoon."

Abby laughed again and kissed her daughter on the cheek. "Drive safe."

"Walk safe." They smiled at each other again, and Nicole climbed into the car. "See you at home."

When her car was out of sight, Abby released the deep breath that had been building since they'd met up with Jo Harter. Especially over the past twenty minutes, while memories of another day, another time, beckoned her back to the hallways of yesterday. Abby could hardly think of anything else.

"Abby, come in and get cleaned up . . . The Reynoldses will be here in half an hour."

She could see the cotton sheets blowing on the line, hear the rustling of leaves in the oaks that lined the sides of their property. The smell of the lake, the feel of the sun on her tanned little girl arms . . . all of it was right there, so close she could touch it.

And now, with a two-mile walk of solitude and a future of loneliness lying just ahead of her, she was ready to go back and live the past again.

Nine

ABBY AND JOHN WOULDN'T HAVE MET AT ALL
if it hadn't been for their fathers. Abby considered that as she set out
toward home and remembered once more the stories her father had
told. Stories of the glory days, back when Joe Chapman and Allen
Reynolds had been football heroes for the University of Michigan
Wolverines. Her father had been a receiver, John's father, the quarterback. Abby stared at the cloudy sky above and held her jacket a bit
closer.

I wish I could have seen you play, Dad.

Instead she'd heard a hundred tales of game-winning touchdown
tosses and crazy anecdotes in one of the most famed locker rooms in
all of college football. Long after their playing days were over, her
father and John's remained friends, the kind who sent Christmas
cards and surprised each other with a phone call once or twice during the football season, just to be sure the other was watching a good
Michigan game. The one against Ohio State, usually.

The Chapmans settled in Lake Geneva, Wisconsin, in a hundred-
year-old cottage given to them by Abby's grandparents. The house
bordered the lake on the far end, away from the area where tourists
flocked each summer. With football rich in his blood, Abby's father

taught and coached at the local high school. So completely absorbed were the Chapmans in football that even now Abby remembered finding her father on the sidelines at halftime one cool Friday night and tugging on his jacket.

"Yes, honey . . ." Her father had always been patient, enjoying the way his family stayed involved in his passion.

"Daddy, when I grow up I'm going to play football for you, okay?"

Something about the night, the crimson and gold of the trees surrounding the stadium, the smell of burning leaves faint in the wind, caused the memory to stand out sharply in Abby's mind.

Football.

When she'd been old enough to realize that girls simply didn't play the game, she figured there was only one other option. She'd marry a football player. The realization had come when she was ten years old. The same year she first met John Reynolds.

For reasons Abby never fully understood, the summer of her tenth year her family's friendship with the Reynolds stopped being a Christmas-only correspondence and turned into something rich and personal, something the two families would continue the rest of their days. Back then Abby hadn't cared about any of that, only that Daddy's friends were coming for a visit and bringing along their kids.

Of course, she'd been bitterly disappointed when her mother explained that they had no little girls her age. Still, there was an air of excitement knowing they were coming. And that afternoon, when her mother called her in from the lake, Abby remembered running into the house, her child-blonde hair wispy in the wind, cheeks golden from the early summer days on the lake.

Abby hadn't wanted to be downstairs when they arrived, so she scurried to her room and held private watch from a bench just beneath her grand window. Maybe her mother was wrong. Maybe they did have a child her age, or at least near it. As she tried to imagine what the coming week would be like, a blue station wagon pulled up and a family climbed out.

Even now, with Abby's and John's divorce a certain thing, with the bitter cold stinging her cheeks and summer forever away, Abby could remember how her face grew hot that afternoon the moment she first laid eyes on John Reynolds.

He was tall and muscled, with hair as dark as the mane on her old mare out in the barn. Abby recalled her little girl sigh, long and hard. Still, he was just a yucky boy. How much fun could they have together? Especially when he was so much older.

The reality had been surprisingly different. With no one else for him to play with, thirteen-year-old John had taken a liking to her that week. Together they rode horses on hidden trails and built sandcastles on the beach around the lake. There was a public pier a hundred yards down the shore, and they spent hours there, tossing rocks into the lake and telling silly jokes. She taught him how to somersault off the end of the pier, and he taught her how to throw a spiral pass.

Abby realized he wasn't attracted to her. He was three and a half years older and she was only ten, after all. But as he held the football and ran his fingers over the leather laces, taking her hand in his and positioning it just so, she was overwhelmed with a feeling she had never been more sure of in all her young life.

One day, she was going to marry John Reynolds. And if he didn't know it now, that was okay. Because she wasn't going to stay a little girl forever, and when the years allowed, she had no doubt that he would feel about her the way she already felt about him.

Abby grinned as she walked, remembering the pixie she'd been and how hard she'd fallen for John that summer. She kicked a loose rock and let her eyes gaze up into the winter sky. *There was never any other boy for me, was there, Lord?*

Silence.

Abby didn't think too hard on the fact that there were no holy whispers in response to her daydreaming. *Maybe God's giving me space. After all the conversation today, I probably need it.*

She dug her hands deep into her coat pockets and kept walking. It hadn't taken long for John to come around. Not really.

Four years later, the summer she was fourteen, John and his family came back to Lake Geneva and this time spent two weeks. He remembered her, of course, and though he was going into his senior year in high school and she was only a freshman, they again found common ground. By then she could throw and catch a football better than most boys her age, and they spent hours barefoot on the beach tossing the ball back and forth.

"You're not so bad for a girl," John had teased her.

She remembered holding her head a bit higher. Older boys didn't intimidate her. After all, her father coached sixty of them every year at the high school, and oftentimes they hung out at the house, playing on the lake or eating barbecued chicken with her family. She cocked her head and stared at John, her heart dancing close to the surface. "And you're not so bad for a *boy*."

John had laughed hard that afternoon, hard enough that eventually he took off after her, tickling her and pretending she could outrun him. The truth was, he had become a great quarterback in his own right by then and was being pursued by a dozen major universities, including their fathers' alma mater—Michigan.

How strange you were back then, John . . . seventeen, star football player, yet somehow content to spend two weeks running around with a little girl.

One night the two families brought blankets down to the sandy shoreline and her father built a bonfire. There they did something Abby couldn't remember ever having done before: they sang songs about God. Not the usual silly campfire songs about chickens or trains comin' round the mountain, but sweet songs about peace and joy and love and a God who cared deeply for all of them. When the songs ended and the adults were lost in their own conversation, John moved next to her and poked her with his elbow.

"You got a boyfriend, little Miss Abby Chapman?" He grinned, and Abby still remembered the way his blue eyes shimmered with the reflection of the moon on the water.

She had been sorely thankful it was dark, because her cheeks were hot from his question. Again, years of being teased by older boys paid off, and she kept her cool. "I don't need a boyfriend." She nudged his bare foot with her own.

He nudged her back. "That so?" A grin spread across his face, and Abby hadn't been quite sure how to take him.

"Yes." Her head raised another notch, and she leveled her gaze straight at him. "Boys can be very immature." She studied him for a moment. "Let me guess . . . you've got a different girlfriend every week, right? That's how it is with Dad's quarterbacks."

John's head fell back for a moment, and he laughed out loud before he looked at her again. "I guess I'm different."

Abby's eyes grew wide in mock amazement. "What? John Reynolds has no girlfriend?"

He reached for the football then—it had never been more than an arm's length away that entire summer—and tossed it lightly in the air a few times. *"This* is my girlfriend."

Abby nodded playfully. "She'll make a great prom date, I'm sure."

He pushed her foot again and lowered his eyes in mock indignation. "Shhh. You'll offend her." He chuckled, then his smile faded. "Truth is I don't have time for girls. I wanna play football at Michigan, like my dad and your dad. Either I work out every day and get better all the time, or someone else'll beat me to it. Girls can wait." He reached over and tousled her hair, and at the contact, something changed in his eyes. "Hey, you be careful next year, okay, Abby? Big high-school girl and all."

His comment seemed to come out of nowhere. *Be careful?* Butterflies fluttered wildly in her stomach. "Of what?" She thought she understood what he meant, but still . . .

He shrugged, his brown shoulders lifting in a way that showed the muscled lines in his arms. "Of guys." There was another elbow in her ribs, and she had the impression he was trying to say something serious without letting the mood become too heavy. "Know what I mean?"

"Guys?" Abby nudged his foot again and grinned at him. "Oh, you mean like you?"

"Come on, Abby . . ." John turned so he was sitting directly across from her. "You've looked in the mirror lately, right?"

"The mirror?" The butterflies were swarming now, and everything in her wanted to believe that John Reynolds was thinking what she thought he might be. *He thinks I'm pretty . . .*

John whistled in response and casually shook his head. "You're gonna be a knockout, Abby. And the boys'll line up from here to your front door. Especially your dad's players." His smile faded and his eyes connected with hers again. "Just be careful."

It was as if someone had opened a trapdoor to her heart and released the butterflies all at once. In their place was a feeling deeper than anything she'd felt before. More than a crush, more than what she'd feel for a summer friendship on the beach. Instead, in that instant there was something deep and intimate—like a best friendship—that took up residence in her heart and set down roots.

Abby sighed, drawn back to the gravelly pathway of the present and the light snow that had begun to fall.

Roots that held firmly to this very day.

What happened to us, John? How could anything have come between us?

Abby felt tears in her eyes and she blinked them back. If she was going to remember how she and John had been, she might as well not stop now. Not with the best part, the sweetest days of all, just footsteps ahead.

John had gone back home with his family a few days later, and before Christmas he signed a letter of intent to play football at Michigan—just like his father and hers decades earlier. Three years passed, and instead of summer visits John's family sent newspaper clippings. He was easily one of the most talked about quarterbacks in the country and often the topic of conversations in the Chapman household. Once a year Abby's parents drove to Ann Arbor and took in a game, but Abby stayed home, busy with high-school life and certain that John Reynolds had forgotten about her.

Then one September afternoon in 1977 the phone rang in the Chapman house.

"Hello?" Abby was out of breath, seventeen, and busy cheering for her father's high-school team.

"Hey—" the caller's voice lingered—"long time no talk."

Abby's heart caught in her throat. Months and years had passed since they'd been together, and John had been right—the offers had been plentiful. But none of the boys had ever made her feel the way John had that long-ago summer night, their bare feet touching in the sand. And now there was no doubt in Abby's mind that the deep voice on the other end of the phone belonged to him. "John . . ."

There was a chuckle that warmed Abby's heart. "Don't tell me the cute kid from all those summers ago has grown up?"

Once again she'd been thankful he couldn't see her blush. "Yeah, I guess so."

"Okay, I have a question for you." He was teasing her, taking his time, and Abby couldn't believe it. *He remembers me . . . after college, after everything he's done since then . . .*

"I'm listening." *Do I sound older . . . more mature? More—*

"Every year your parents come all the way to Ann Arbor to see me play . . ." he interrupted her thoughts, and she could picture the way his eyes danced, just like they'd danced that night on the beach, the last time she'd seen him. "And each time I ask 'em where you are, and you know what they say?" He hesitated for effect. "They say, 'Oh, Abby . . . she's busy with her friends, busy with school.' I mean, come on, Abby. Not a single game . . . you couldn't make it out for even one?"

Abby felt her confidence growing. That fall she was just a few months shy of her eighteenth birthday, and with John on the line everything felt right with her world. "Hmmm. Let's see, now . . . If I'm remembering right, I don't recall you ever inviting me. Not that I blame you—I mean I'm just a *cute kid*. What would a big-time Michigan QB like you want with a punk little girl like me, anyway?"

John allowed a silence, and she could practically see him grinning through the phone lines. "So how old are you now, anyway, Abby?"

"Almost eighteen." She tried to sound official, mature, but as the words escaped her mouth she was struck by the fact that they sounded downright silly. He would have just turned twenty-one. *He's not interested in me. He's just playing with my—*

"So, was I right?"

At first she'd been confused. "About . . ." She let her voice trail off.

"About the guys lined up at your door."

That was the moment when it had all started feeling like a dream. *Why's he doing this? He couldn't really care, could he?* "There've been a few."

"Okay, okay . . . so who's the lucky guy?" He was still teasing, still playing with her and making it impossible for her to tell if he were even a little interested.

She giggled out loud. "You're crazy."

"No, I'm serious. I want details . . . I warned you, Abby. Don't forget that."

"No one. Just friends, that's all."

"Oh, sure . . ." His words were drawn out and playfully sarcastic. "I know your type. String along some poor fool, make him think he has a chance."

"No, really." She was laughing harder now. "There's no one. I don't have a boyfriend. Besides, you should talk. Mr. Hot Stuff on Campus. Your line probably wraps around the stadium."

"Oh-hooo. Very good." He paused a moment and his chuckling faded. "Actually, I'm still seeing the same girl, the one I was dating the last time I saw you."

Abby stifled a giggle, picturing the way he'd cradled the football that night on the beach. "Paula Pigskin, wasn't it?"

He laughed. "Yep. Me and my ball, together forever." His voice grew more serious. "Like I always say, girls can wait."

Her heart soared with hope, and she chastised herself. *Be real, Abby. He's too old for you.* "So, your motto hasn't changed much since high school, huh?"

"Not much."

Neither of them said anything for a beat, then John picked up the conversation. "So what's your answer?" He was upbeat again, having fun with her. But the teasing was gone, and Abby knew instinctively that he was serious.

"You mean it, don't you?"

He huffed in mock indignation. "Of course I mean it. You haven't seen me play once. And I know for a fact that your parents are coming out again this season—mid-November."

Mid-November. The idea was suddenly very appealing. "Serious?"

"Sure." John's tone was light. *He probably sees me as a little sister.* "I'll show you around the campus. Introduce you to the real big men on campus."

"Your offensive line?"

"You got it." They both laughed. "So, what's your answer?"

The memory of how she felt that day warmed her heart even now. "Okay, okay. I should be done cheering for football by then, and if I'm not too busy . . ."

"Oh, right. I wouldn't want to cramp your style or crowd your schedule." He was still teasing her and she decided to be serious.

"No, really. I'll come." She paused. *Should I tell him?* Abby closed her eyes and plunged ahead. "I've always wanted to see you play."

"Oh, sure." John's voice grew quieter as he continued talking. "I can tell by the effort you've made."

A giggle made its way to the surface. "I watch television, you know. You've been doing great, John."

"What? Miss Too-Busy-to-Come follows Michigan football?"

"Not like I have a choice. It's like a national holiday around here when the Wolverines are on TV. My dad gets the Ann Arbor paper delivered by mail so he can follow it each week. He's so proud of you, John."

He cleared his throat. "And you . . . ?"

Why was he acting like this? He couldn't possibly be interested in her as more than a family friend, could he? "Yes, John—" she bathed her words in a protective, teasing sarcasm—"I'm proud, too. I'm sure that makes your day."

There was a hesitation. "Actually, it does." He waited again, almost as though he wanted to say something else. Instead he wrapped up the conversation. "I'll see you in a couple months then, right?"

"Sure." She felt her eyebrows lower in confusion. "Did you want to talk to my dad or something?"

"Nope. Just you. Figured I'd never get you out here for a game if I didn't ask you myself. What with your busy schedule and all . . . well . . . I thought I better give you plenty of notice."

The months of waiting were unbearable. Everything about the high-school football season that year seemed dull and unimportant compared with the idea that John Reynolds wanted her to watch him play college ball. Better yet, he wanted to show her around campus.

A cold blast of winter wind startled Abby from her memories, and she snuggled deeper into her coat, picking up her pace. John had been bigger than life back then. A hero, really. Someone talked about in homes across the country, an athlete known for his physical talent, good looks, and high moral character. His name was mentioned in connection with college football's most prized award—the Heisman Trophy. Yet there she'd been—all of seventeen years old—believing that he really wanted to see her. Her, of all people.

Abby blinked and the past disappeared. She stared straight ahead and felt the pull of gravity on her lips, realized how it tugged her mouth downward, giving her a perpetual frown. It wasn't just the passing of time that had aged her. It was her relationship with her husband, as well. When was the last time she'd laughed at one of his jokes? The ridiculous ones that left a new batch of high-school students in stitches every semester. She forced a smile, sad that it felt so foreign on her face. A farm and a frozen pond came into view on her right, and she stopped for a moment, trying to picture the way she'd looked that November day as she and her family took their seats at Michigan Stadium.

They'd arrived two hours early with plans to meet John on the field before the game. She could see her dad, still robust and healthy back then, waving his arm at the rest of them. "Come on, I know right where he'll be."

Abby had tossed her long hair over her shoulder and followed her father, determined not to let her nervousness show. Besides, what did she have to worry about? The whole thing was probably more her imagination than anything else. But just in case, she had worn her new black jeans and a formfitting white turtleneck sweater. Her mother had commented on the drive over that Abby had never looked prettier. She had no reason to be nervous, but as they approached the entrance to the locker rooms, Abby thought she might faint from the uncertainty of it all.

John appeared almost immediately, wearing Wolverine sweats, his short dark hair combed neatly off his face. Abby sucked in a quick breath. He was gorgeous. Much better looking in person than on TV or in newspaper photos. And much more a man than he'd been the last time they were together at her house that summer.

"Hey, how're you doing?" He was breathless, his face filled with energy, and his eyes quickly moved from her father's to hers. "Abby . . ." His eyes grew wide and he moved closer so he was only a few feet away, his six-four frame towering over her. Even with her parents and younger sister standing around them, Abby could see the admiration in John's eyes. "My gosh . . . you've grown up."

She'd expected him to tease her, since that was the side of John Reynolds she knew best, but his eyes held pure admiration and not a trace of humor. Unsure of how to respond, she laughed lightly and cast him an exaggerated upward glance. *Lord, don't let my heart fall out of my chest.* "Not as much as you have."

He grinned. "Yeah, I shot up a bit."

She was still studying him when her father stepped up and put his arm around John's broad shoulders. "Perfect size for a Wolverine quarterback. And I believe it's true when I say never—not before or since—has Michigan had a quarterback like you, son. You're one of a kind."

Abby savored the chance to study John's face, his pronounced cheekbones, and she found herself agreeing completely with her father's assessment—even if all he threw were interceptions.

John's cheeks reddened slightly. "Thank you, sir. Did you find my folks?"

"Not yet." Abby's father glanced at the rest of them and nodded toward the field. "Let's take a walk around. I wanna show you the spot where the greatest play in history took place." He waved at John. "Go get suited up. Beat 'em good now, you hear?"

Abby and her sister had seen the famous spot—marked on the field only by the memory of the play—on trips to Ann Arbor when they were little. They'd heard the stories again and again. But still they turned to follow him, thriving on the memories every bit as much as their father did.

"Hey, Abby, wait." She turned around, her heart still pounding loudly.

"Yeah?"

The rest of Abby's family stopped and turned also, waiting expectantly for whatever John was about to say. He shifted his weight and hesitated, looking from Abby's father to Abby and back again. "Uh . . . can Abby and I catch up a bit? She can meet you back in the stands, maybe?"

Everything about Abby's world tilted crazily. *He wants to talk to me?* Wasn't it all just a joke? His way of trying to be nice to a family friend? Suddenly it seemed much more serious, and Abby could hardly contain her excitement. After a slight pause, Abby's mother took her father's hand and answered for him. "That's fine, John. You two go right ahead and catch up."

When her family was out of sight, John turned back to Abby. "Thanks for coming." His voice was gentle, tender, and though his eyes sparkled in the ice-cold early morning sun, there was not even a trace of teasing or silliness there.

Abby adjusted her scarf and grinned at him. "I told you I would."

John shrugged, his eyes still locked on hers. "I was afraid you'd think I was joking."

What's he mean? Where's all this going? Abby swallowed and angled her head curiously. "You . . . you weren't?"

"No, I wasn't." He hesitated and ran his thumb gently along the curve of her cheek just below her eye. "You're so beautiful, Abby. Do you know that?"

For all the times when she couldn't seem to stop talking, Abby was absolutely speechless. She stood there, soaking in the nearness of him, trying to convince herself she wasn't dreaming. When she said nothing, he continued. "Go out with me tonight after the game. We can get pizza or just walk around the campus."

Go *out* with him? Again the shock nearly knocked Abby to the ground. She felt suddenly shy with him. "Okay. If my parents don't mind."

A smile filled his face and he glanced over his shoulder. "I better go get ready. Meet you at my folks' house after the game, okay?"

"Okay."

Then without any hesitation, he hugged her the way old friends hug at a class reunion. "It's good to see you again, Abby Chapman." He pulled back and smiled at her. "Really."

In an instant he was gone, taking with him all that remained of her heart.

She laughed out loud now, remembering the innocent, carefree days of seventeen and how smitten she'd been with John Reynolds, how sure that even if the world stopped spinning nothing would ever change the way she felt about the young man who stood before her that Saturday morning.

Abby's smile faded as she saw their house a hundred yards up the road. It was more fun walking down yesterday's trails than taking this very real one. Blinking back tears Abby dug her hands deep into her pockets, imagining the cool reception she would receive from John in a few minutes. An image came to her. She and John two years into their marriage, nestled close together on a threadbare sofa watching a suspenseful movie.

"I hate this part!" she whined and buried her head in John's shoulder. Stifling a grin, he took her hands gently in his and laid them across her face so she couldn't see.

"There. That better?" She remembered feeling safe and sheltered with John's arm around her.

"Yeah. Just one more thing." Her voice was muffled, filtering through the cracks in her fingers.

"For you, love, anything . . ." He leaned down and kissed her on the cheek.

"Tell me when I can open my eyes, okay?"

"Always, Abby. Always."

What had happened to that man, the one she'd fallen in love with that Saturday morning outside the Wolverine locker room? For the first time in years, against all her better judgment or reasoning abilities, Abby missed what they'd been, ached for the loss of what they'd once shared.

"Always, Abby . . . always, Abby . . . always . . ."

She was only a dozen yards from the front door and she stopped, feet buried in a foot of snow as tears pricked at the inside of her eyelids. *I hate this part. Help me through this, God; it's more than I can bear. I'm terrified of being alone, and the scary parts haven't even started yet. But this time I have no one to turn to, no shoulder to hide my face in.*

And no one to tell me when I can open my eyes.

Ten

THERE WAS NOTHING QUITE LIKE THE RELIEF of silence echoing through a high-school classroom ten minutes after the final bell.

It wasn't that John Reynolds disliked teaching. In fact he was one of the handful of teachers on campus that truly relished arriving at school each morning, greeting his classes, and alternating between educating and entertaining them. His classroom was his personal domain where he ruled supreme, the place second only to the football field where he felt completely in charge of his destiny.

Still, there was something he cherished about the solitude that came after every student had cleared the campus. Oftentimes it was the first chance all day for John to work on lesson plans for the coming week or ponder his personal life. Especially on days like today when everything about his existence outside the classroom seemed to be caving in around him.

The image of Abby's face earlier that day flashed in his mind. She'd been on the Internet, no doubt, probably e-mailing the editor she swore she wasn't involved with. But even with all the distance between Abby and him, John knew guilt when it flashed across his wife's face. And Abby was definitely guilty of something. He closed

his eyes and remembered the exchange as though it had happened only minutes ago.

The tension between them had gotten worse since Nicole's engagement announcement, and he'd been determined to find a neutral zone, a common ground where they could set up camp and co-exist for the next six months. With ten minutes to spare before leaving for work, he'd popped his head into her office.

Immediately she moved her computer mouse across the pad and clicked twice. "You scared me." Her tone was filled with accusation, and a dark shadow of wrongdoing shrouded her features.

"Sorry." He struggled for the right words as he entered the boxy room and shut the door behind him. Why was it so hard to talk to her now? Were they really that far gone, unable even to carry on a conversation? He knew the answer as surely as he knew that divorce was the only option they had left, the only way either of them would ever find happiness again. "Can you talk for a minute?"

She had sighed loudly and closed down her America Online application. "What is it?"

Her attitude caused his entire mind-set to change. If she couldn't be civilized first thing in the morning, what hope was there that she might be willing to reach some sort of combat-free agreement? *Never mind, Abby. Who needs your moodiness anyway?* "Forget it." He spat the words and turned to leave, but she cut him short.

"Listen, don't come in here interrupting my work and think I'm going to turn somersaults about it, okay? I have a life, too, you know." She remained in her office chair but turned it to face him. John hated the contempt in her eyes, the way they seemed to belittle him and everything he might have wanted to say.

"Why do I bother?" His arms hung at his sides, fists clenched. "I came in here to see if we could maybe work out some kind of deal, some way we might actually survive the months between now and July. But like always your attitude is too big to get around."

Anger pinched her features tightly together. "*My* attitude?" She

didn't pause long enough to let him respond. "When you won't stay away from Charlene even now after I've asked you a dozen times to give it a rest. I mean really, John. Six months? Can't your teenage hormones wait that long?"

John chuckled once and shook his head. "I don't have to listen to this."

"Well, maybe you do. I'm finding notes, counting hours. Don't you think I know when you should be home? I've been married to you twenty-one years, John. I'm not completely stupid. I mean, you're either leaving early to be with her or staying late for it. Even now, when you promised me you'd back off."

"I absolutely refuse to make this a discussion about Charlene!" He was raising his voice, no longer worried about whether it might catch the kids' attention from upstairs, where they all were getting ready. "I've been keeping up my end of the deal, Abby. But you . . ." He let his voice trail off and stared at her dumbfounded. "You're so downright hateful I don't even see the point anymore."

Don't do it, My son.

He closed his eyes now, remembering the holy warnings, how they'd echoed through him . . . but they hadn't mattered. After years of ignoring them he'd become an expert at blocking them out. Besides, they were so infrequent these days he wasn't even sure anymore that they were holy warnings. *I can say what I want . . . she deserves it.*

"The point of what?" Abby stared at him as if he were a stranger demanding entrance to her house.

"If I spent more time with Charlene, at least I wouldn't have to be around here."

Abby shot him one more daggerlike glare, then spun around and anchored her gaze on the computer screen. "Get out of here, John. I have nothing to say to you."

Resignation worked its way up from John's chest. "What else is new? Isn't that where this all started? Back when you found your own little writer's life and stopped having anything to say to me?"

She refused to even shift her eyes in his direction. "Oh, here we go. Let's blame the whole thing on my writing. That's so you, John." She released a laugh that was completely devoid of humor. "You discouraged me about writing from the get-go, refused to read my work, and left me with the job of raising the kids. Now blame me for the fact that our marriage is in cardiac arrest. That's really good. Perfect."

Her sarcasm stung at his nerves like so many fire ants. "Just once why don't you get off your high horse and look at the bigger picture, Abby? I wanted you to write articles. It's a great outlet for you. But you let it take on a life of its own, and whether you want to see it or not, after you started writing I fell down the list to about fifth or sixth in importance. Somewhere after the kids and your dad and e-mailing that—" he waved at her computer—"that *editor* friend of yours."

She jerked ever so slightly at the mention of her editor, and again John was sure that the darkness in her eyes was guilt. "I didn't realize you were so needy, John. I mean, did it ever occur to you I might need a little help, that I had a lot on *my* plate? Would it have killed you to do a load of laundry or fold your own socks?" She tossed her head in mock amazement. "You expected me to fawn over you when I was too tired to spell my own name by the end of the day?"

Her words were dry and biting, and he was suddenly sure he'd had enough.

"I'm leaving. And if I'm late tonight I'm sure you'll be too busy writing to notice."

John had replayed the scene a dozen times throughout the day. Now he reached for a paper clip from the organizer on his desk and bent it mindlessly. Had it really come to this? Was it impossible for them to even get along? If so, then how in the world was he supposed to stay away from Charlene? Especially now when Abby's mandate that he keep his distance only made him think of Charlene more.

He planted his elbows on his desk and hung his head. If Abby had been this way back in their dating days, he'd have dumped her after their first night out. She was arrogant and rude and downright mean.

No wonder their physical relationship had been the first thing to go. Clearly she had no good feelings for him whatsoever and hadn't for years.

Maybe it's my fault . . . maybe I stopped loving her the way she needed to be loved . . .

Almost as if in response to his musings, Charlene opened the classroom door and peered inside. "Hi. Got a minute?"

She was dressed in navy slacks and a blazer, which she wore unbuttoned over her tight white T-shirt. John forced himself to keep his gaze from falling below her neck. "Sure." He sat up straighter and all thoughts of Abby vanished from his mind. "What's up?"

"It's the kids in fifth period again." She moved into the room and sat across from him, her forearms resting on his desk so that their hands were only inches apart. "No matter what I do they test me. Don't you ever get sick of it? The way kids have changed over the years?"

"Sure." John studied her, fairly sure she hadn't come to talk about unruly students. Her perfume filled his senses, and suddenly it was nothing short of work to keep from thinking about how good she made him feel.

Flee! What God has joined together let no one separate.

The scripture felt like a bucket of cold water, and John blinked, trying to focus on what she was saying.

"So, what's the answer? You never struggle with control in your classroom."

I'm struggling now . . . "They know I'll make 'em run laps if they act up." He was teasing her, enjoying the relief she brought from the heaviness in his life.

She pushed at his arm in mock frustration. "Come on, I'm serious. You're supposed to have all the answers." With those words something changed in her eyes and her gaze locked onto his. "Are the answers any clearer these days, John?"

Without a doubt she was no longer talking about classroom control.

He ached with the desire to walk around the desk and take her in his arms. It wasn't her fault. She cared for him, clearly. And now the two of them would be forced to wait another six months before anything could be decided.

What God has joined together—

I didn't divide us, Lord; Abby did. His silent comeback was swift and sure. Besides, it was way too late for Bible verses now. Their decision to divorce was already set.

Charlene remained motionless, waiting for his answer, her head cocked, her face full of questions about his feelings for her. John released a hiss of air through clenched teeth. "I told you, Nicole's getting married in July. I won't know anything until she's back from her honeymoon."

Her face flooded with defeat. "So you're really going to wait?"

John hated the way her innocent questions underlined the fact that he was trapped, stopped against his will from doing the one thing he wanted to do—start over again with the fun-hearted, beautiful woman sitting across from him. "I have to. We owe it to the kids."

Abby would have fought him on the issue, but not Charlene. She settled back in her chair and let the information sink in. "What if . . . what if Abby wants to work it out?"

John chuckled sadly. "The only thing Abby and I are going to try and do is not kill each other." His eyes met hers again. "Lately we can't say two sentences without it getting ugly."

Charlene angled her head in a pretty gesture that always tugged at John's heart. "I'm sorry. I . . . well, I wish there was something I could do to help."

Yeah, you could convince me to run away with you and never—

Flee, My son . . . Flee.

I'm not doing anything wrong! The voice in his heart fairly shouted at the whispered warning echoing in his soul. He tried to keep his thoughts on a more honorable level. "It's just one of those things. We'll get through it somehow."

Questions continued to flash in her eyes. "What you asked me . . . you know, about giving you space . . . is that true for the whole time, the whole six months?"

She looked so young and lovely, so lonely and in need of someone to take care of her. John tightened his fingers into fists and forced himself to answer her. "I have no choice."

For a moment she said nothing, but John was sure she was wrestling with her emotions. Clearly she wanted to be with him, and finally, after nearly a minute, she reached out and wrapped her hands around his. "I'll stay away." She paused, allowing her thumb to rub small patterns of empathy across the back of his hand. "I didn't really have to talk about fifth period today." She dropped her gaze. "I just missed you."

John tightened his grip on her hands and lowered his head so he could connect with her gaze once more. "I miss you, too. And once in a while we're bound to spend time together. But otherwise it has to wait until—"

At that moment his classroom door swung open, and Kade walked in carrying a notebook and a stack of papers. His eyes fell to the desk where John's and Charlene's hands were still linked. "Dad? What's going on?"

Charlene was immediately on her feet. "Your dad was praying for me." There was an uncomfortable silence. "I was just leaving."

Praying for her? Charlene's words hit John in the gut like a prize-fighter's fist. Charlene was not a praying woman; they'd never even discussed his faith. *What kind of witness have I been to her, Lord . . . what am I doing here?*

Kade stepped aside as Charlene hurried across the room and out the doorway. "See you later," she said, casting John a pained look before she disappeared down the hall.

"What was *that* all about?" Kade's face was still flooded with confusion. "Since when do you and Ms. Denton pray together?"

John's throat was suddenly thick, and he struggled to find his voice. "She, uh . . . she needed someone to talk to. She's having some trouble at home."

"Isn't she divorced?" Kade moved into the room, set his backpack down, and took the chair Charlene had been sitting in. The boy wasn't accusing, just curious and more than a little bothered.

"Yes, for a while now."

Kade shook his head as though the situation didn't make sense. "Weird." He reached into his backpack, pulled out his notebook, and set it on the table. "Do you think it's a good idea to pray with her like that, Dad?" He leveled his gaze at his father. "Might give her the wrong idea."

John laughed but it sounded tinny and forced even to him. "Son, Ms. Denton and I have been friends for a long time. I don't think anyone's going to get the wrong idea."

Kade studied him a moment longer. "Okay. But what would Mom think if she walked in and saw you two holding hands like that? It's kind of . . . I don't know, just weird, you know?"

God, give me the right words here.

Repent! Remember the height from which you have—

"Everything's fine between me and Ms. Denton," John interrupted the scripture flashing in his heart. "Besides, your mother knows we're friends. Don't worry about it, okay?"

"Sure . . . whatever." Kade shrugged, and John was struck by how much the boy looked like himself twenty years earlier. Almost like history repeating itself. "It just didn't look good."

John shifted positions, desperate for Kade to change the subject. "I'm sorry. She needed someone to talk to." He fingered his son's notebook. "Did you want something?"

Kade opened the book and took out a bundle of stapled papers. "I had to pick a topic for my senior project." He turned the paper so it faced his father.

John let his eyes scan the sheet. "Habits of Eagles? That's your topic?"

A grin spread across Kade's face. "Yep. You know, like kicking tail all season long, winning the big games, standing up to adversity. Habits of Eagles. Marion Eagles, get it, Dad?"

John laughed and hoped it didn't sound as hollow to Kade as it felt. The memory of Charlene's hand in his still burned deep in his belly, stirring feelings he desperately wished he could control. *She's like a drug, God . . . get her out of my system.*

Repent! Flee immorality! Remember the height . . .

It was like a broken record. Wasn't there anything more comforting God could whisper to him? Something about how he and Charlene could be together when this unbearable time with Abby was over and Nicole and Matt were married and on their own? He shut out the warnings and focused on his son's paper. "I like it, Kade. A study on eagles."

Kade eased back in his chair, confident and comfortable, all signs of his earlier concern gone. "Yeah, only not the Marion Eagles, Dad. I don't think they'd let me do a report on that. I'm gonna study real eagles. I can go on-line and read books, and then I have to put together a graphic display. Mr. Bender said someone did a report on eagles last year and the stuff he found out was amazing. Like, listen to this . . ."

He rustled through his notebook until he found a slightly crumpled sheet of paper. "The eagle is the only bird that doesn't run from trouble. Instead it uses the storms of life to take it to a higher place."

John nodded, trying to seem interested. *Is Charlene waiting for me down the hall? Has she gone for the day? When can we finish our conversation . . . ?* He forced the thoughts from his head and focused on his son.

"Isn't that tight, Dad? He uses the storms to take him higher. Just like a Marion Eagle." Kade waited for his father's response. "Remember . . . when Taylor Johnson went down with a torn ACL and everyone thought we'd fall apart. But we didn't."

John worked to see the connection. "We rose above it; is that what you mean?"

"Right!" Kade's eyes sparkled. "And know what else? Eagles are in the Bible a lot, too."

Just the sound of the word "Bible" put John's innards into knots. "The Bible?"

"Right . . ." Kade rustled through his papers once more until he found what he was looking for. "Here it is. We shall mount up on wings as eagles. See, Dad, God didn't say we'd be like chickens or crows or parakeets. He said we'd be like eagles."

John smiled at his son's enthusiasm and tried to ignore the conviction strangling his heart. "Marion Eagles, no doubt."

A look of mock humility flashed in Kade's eyes. "Well, I wasn't going to make the connection, but since you brought it up . . ."

John pushed his fist into his son's shoulder playfully. "Sounds like the report'll be a winner, son. Just like . . ."

They finished the sentence in unison. "The Marion Eagles."

Kade grabbed his dad around the neck with the crook of his elbow. "That's my dad, sharp as a whip."

"Sharp as a tack . . . quick as a whip." John rubbed his knuckles against his son's head. "That's my boy, the dumb jock."

Kade was giggling now, sounding more like the little boy he'd been ten years earlier than the full-grown man-child he'd become. "Whatever." He rubbed his father's head until they were both locked in the embrace, laughing and struggling to get free.

John pulled away first and inhaled sharply, catching his breath. "Are you on your way home?"

"Yeah, wanna join me?" Kade sat back, not even breathing hard despite their roughhousing. "Mom's making homemade pizza."

The thought of Abby made John lose his appetite and he struggled to keep his expression neutral. "Better not. Tests to correct."

Kade loaded his belongings back into his bag and swung it over his shoulder. For an instant he leveled his gaze at his father, as though there was something he wanted to say but couldn't. "Hurry, okay." His grin faded some. "Mom likes it when we're all home for dinner."

John nodded, grateful Kade couldn't read his mind. "Okay, tell her I'll be there."

When Kade was gone, John exhaled and realized he'd been holding his breath since Kade's comment about dinner. If they were going to survive the coming months, Kade was right. He should make an effort to be home once in a while. Otherwise the kids were bound to figure out something was wrong.

He pulled out the papers from sixth period and began grading them. *Don't think about Abby or Charlene or any of it. Just work. Get it done so you can go home.*

Though he successfully fended off thoughts of the women in his life, he couldn't shake his mind of one very powerful image: an eagle midflight, climbing higher and higher while storm clouds brewed in the background. The harsher the storm, the higher the eagle flew, and John couldn't help but realize that regardless of the embroidery on his coach's shirt, he was not an eagle.

Not even close.

Eleven

AS WAS OFTEN THE CASE THESE DAYS, ABBY'S father was asleep, and she sat alone in his room, no longer repulsed by the medicinal, nursing-home smell or the way the man she'd once thought bigger than life had wasted away to little more than skin and bones. She held his hand, stroking it gently with her thumb and wondering how long it would be now. Parkinson's did not keep a schedule, and the doctors had told her he could leave her this year or not for another five.

Abby's eyes fell on a wooden sign hanging near the foot of his bed: "I'm only passing through . . . this world is not my home."

Oh, but the passing through can be so painful, God. Like watching Dad disappear before my eyes . . . or seeing John with Charlene.

There was no whispered assurance or instant scripture to fill her mind, and Abby sighed, leaning back in her chair. She'd been busy most of the week, absorbed in household details, cleaning bathrooms, and folding laundry. And of course her writing assignments. She'd had three major pieces that needed finishing by Friday, and she hadn't submitted them via e-mail until after midnight the night before.

Now, for the first time since her walk in the snow, she actually had time to herself. Time when she didn't have to worry about where John was and what they might say to each other and how best to avoid him in the house they still shared. The entire week they'd done nothing but fight with each other, either about Charlene or about her writing or her editor. They hadn't said a kind word to each other, and Abby realized only now how draining it had been.

Six months of this, Lord? How am I going to survive?

What God has joined together let no one separate.

Abby sighed. God's warnings were like a broken record. They were trite and forced and lent no application whatsoever to her life today. Clearly there was nothing left between John and her. Why did God insist on bringing to mind scriptures of idealistic behavior? She and John were separating. Period. Now they had to find a way to survive the process.

Closing her eyes, Abby remembered her walk the week before and how good it had felt to spend time in the past, in the place where she and John were in love beyond anything she could have dreamed. A time when just waking each morning offered more excitement and promise than young Abby could bear.

Where had she left off . . . ? Abby concentrated, and her mind filled with the image of herself, black jeans, white turtleneck, sitting with her family watching the game—the first time she'd seen John play for Michigan. With every play she'd held her breath, desperately praying he wouldn't be hurt and at the same time mesmerized by the way his body moved. The Wolverines won handily that day with John throwing for three touchdowns and running for another.

"Show-off," she told him later as they strolled along the campus just before dusk. The temperature had dropped, and he had lent her his lettermen's jacket. Snuggled inside it, she felt like Cinderella at the ball, afraid that midnight would strike at any moment and she'd be forced to wake from the dream.

He had walked alongside her, as comfortable as if they'd spent every day for the past three years together. "Did I have a choice? You blow me off all those years and now . . . finally . . . you make it to a game. I mean, come on, Abby. The pressure was on big time."

His grin warmed her insides so that it felt like midday deep in her heart. For two hours they talked about his classes and hers, their goals and dreams. "It wouldn't surprise me if I end up coaching someday, when my playing days are over . . ."

His father was a successful banker, and Abby tilted her head thoughtfully. "Not going for the big bucks like your dad?"

She was teasing, and it was obvious he could tell. He smiled and shrugged. "There's more to life. I think if Dad had it to do over again he'd coach, too. Like your dad." John gazed at the sunset through the trees, keeping his steps in time with hers. "It's a hard game to walk away from."

Abby thought about how intricately the game had been a part of her life growing up. "I know."

They had made their way across campus to a bench under a shady, ancient oak tree and John stopped, turning so he faced her squarely. "You really do know it, don't you? You understand, Abby. Football, I mean. How important it is to guys like me and your dad."

Abby basked in his nearness. *Is this really happening? Am I here a million miles away from home and inches from John Reynolds?* She nodded shyly. "Yeah, I do."

John shook his head, his face incredulous. "And the best part is, you actually like it. A lot of girls could care less."

She grinned. "Well, now, I've only made it out for one game."

He laughed at first, then gradually his smile faded and his eyes locked onto hers. "I've thought about you a lot, Abby. Do you know that?"

Something in her wanted to bolt, wanted to protect her heart before it became too lost to ever find again. Instead she nodded, unwilling to break the connection between them. Then, with the winter wind sifting through the leaves around them, John placed his hands on her shoulders and leaned close, touching his lips to hers. He kissed her so sweetly, so simply she was certain she was floating a foot off the ground.

It was not a seductive kiss or one that demanded more of her than she was ready to give, but it was a kiss that made his intentions crystal clear. She had pulled away first, breathless, scanning his face for the answers she suddenly needed more desperately than oxygen. "John?"

His gaze never left hers as he ran his thumb tenderly over her eyebrows. "I know you're young, Abby. But there's something between us. Something I've felt ever since I met you." He hesitated, and for all his fame and glory and cocksure athletic ability, he looked utterly vulnerable. "Do you . . . can you feel it, too?"

A giggle rose from Abby's throat, and she threw her arms around his neck, allowing him to hold her close, savoring how his body warmed hers in a way she'd never known before. With his question still hanging in the air, she pulled back and angled her head, sure her eyes were sparkling with all she was feeling inside. "Yes, I feel it. I thought I was the only one who did. You know, because I was too young for you."

A grin broke out across his face. "No, it was never just you. But back then you were too little to talk about it; I even thought maybe I was imagining it. But over the years, it didn't go away. I would get home from a game and wonder where you were, what you were doing. Like . . ."

Suddenly confident in all she'd ever felt for him, she finished his sentence for him. "Like we were meant to be?"

He nodded and kissed her again. This time there was a fire between them, and when he pulled back he distanced himself from her. "Abby, I don't know how everything's going to work out. We won't even see each other much this next year. But there's one thing I've never been more sure of—I've never felt like this with anyone before."

She spread her fingers across his chest and met his gaze once more. "Me neither."

He trembled and now she knew it had been with desire. She hadn't understood back then, but she was certain of it now in light of a lifetime of experience. How many times had she known that same trembling in their first ten years of marriage, felt him that way as his limbs spread out across hers, beneath hers, up against hers.

Yes, he'd felt deeply for her back then, their first night together, and she for him. But it would not be until after their wedding that either of them would act on their feelings.

As they made their way back to his dorm that night, Abby remembered the way he held her hand, treating her like the rarest of gems, precious and unique, convincing her with every step that his words were sincere. He had never felt this way about anyone else.

Abby's father stirred in the bed beside her chair and she let go of his hand, instantly back in the present. Without warning, his eyes flashed open, frantic as he looked about the room until he found Abby. "Where's John?"

The question pierced the silence, and she felt her heart sink. "He's home, Dad. With the kids." Her words were loud and measured, the way people talked to the aged.

"He should be with you." There was wild fear in her father's face, and his hands shook uncontrollably.

"It's okay, Dad. He's with the kids." Abby took his fingers in hers and tried to still the shaking.

The sleep was wearing off. Her father's expression was less shocked and fearful. For a long moment he looked deep into Abby's eyes; then for the first time he voiced the thing that probably lay heaviest on his heart. "There's trouble, isn't there?"

Abby's first thought was to lie to him, the same way she lied to everyone else these days. But then the tears came, and she knew it was impossible. She was too close to this man, this giant-hearted father and friend, to hide from him the thing that was killing her. She nodded, squeezing his hands gently in her own. "Yes, Dad. There's trouble."

He seemed to shrink beneath the bedcovers, and his eyes grew damp. "Are you . . . have you prayed about it?"

Abby felt a gentle smile play across her lips. Her father meant well. *Dad, if only you understood how bad things were . . .* "We have."

Her father's emotions played across his face as clearly as if they were written on his forehead. Sorrow and confusion, followed by frustration and deep, boundless pain. "It's not . . . you aren't getting a . . ."

The tears spilled onto Abby's cheeks. Had it really come to this? Wasn't she the same girl who had stood beneath the oak tree with John, barely able to think while he kissed her for the first time? Wasn't she the only girl he'd ever loved? Her tears came harder and the words lodged in her throat. She opened her mouth but nothing came out.

Now it was her father's turn to comfort. He held her hands close to his heart and ran his frail fingers over the tops of them. "Oh, Abby, you can't, honey. There's gotta be a way . . ."

Abby shook her head and struggled to find her voice. "You don't understand, Dad. There's more to it."

Darkness clouded her father's eyes. "That woman? The one on the field after the state title game?"

So even her father knew the truth. John had taken up with Charlene and in the process left everyone but Abby's blindly devoted kids aware that he was cheating on her. She hung her head and a fresh wave of tears spilled from her eyes onto her father's bedsheets. "He says they're just friends, but it's a lie, Dad. I've found notes."

With all the effort he could muster, her father raised a single hand and wiped the tears from her cheeks. "Have you tried counseling? Christian counseling?"

Abby exhaled and caught her breath, lifting her gaze to her father's questioning one. "We've tried everything. It's more than a faith issue, Dad."

Her father's hand fell to his side and he stared sadly at her. "Nothing is beyond God, Abby. Maybe you've forgotten."

She met his gaze. "Maybe we have."

Questions flashed in his eyes, and he cleared his throat, probably trying to stop himself from breaking down and crying. After all, John was the son of his best friend. The news was bound to be devastating, regardless of his earlier suspicions about Charlene. "Have you . . . told the children?"

Abby leaned back in her chair. "We tried, but the morning we were going to tell them, Nicole announced her engagement. We decided to postpone it until after the wedding."

"So it's final; you've made your decision?"

Again Abby hung her head. "We've talked to each other, talked to counselors, tried everything, Dad. We don't see any other way."

There was silence for a moment as her father took in the news. When he didn't comment, she continued, desperate to fill the space between them with something that might help him understand. "Maybe it'll be better this way."

Anger flashed in her father's eyes for the first time since she was a small child. "It can *never* be better to divorce, Abby. Never. That's a lie from the pit of hell; mark my words."

The tears came harder now and Abby felt her own anger rising. It wasn't her fault after all. "Don't blame me, Dad. I'm not the one seeing someone else."

Her father raised an eyebrow enough so that she noticed. "That right? What about your writing friends, your editor?"

Alarm raced through Abby's veins. *How in the world . . . ?* "Who told you that?"

Her father waited a beat. "John. Last time he was here. I asked him how the two of you were, and he said something about you spending more time e-mailing your editor than talking to him." Her father stopped to catch his breath, and Abby realized the conversation was draining him. His arms and legs were trembling harder. "He made light of it so I didn't think it was a problem. Until now."

Abby stood up and folded her arms, staring at the ceiling. "Oh, Dad, I don't know how it all got so ugly." She lowered her gaze to him again and wiped fresh tears from her cheeks. "I need my friendship with Stan. Sometimes he's the only one who understands what's happening in my life."

Her father's anger was gone, and in its place was a sadness unlike anything Abby had seen before. "The only thing you need is faith in Christ and a dedication to each other. If you have that . . . everything else will fall in place."

He made it sound so easy. "He's having an affair, Dad. He admitted to kissing her. It isn't as simple as you think." She made her way back to the chair and sat down again, taking his hands in hers. "Go back to sleep. I didn't mean to get you so worked up."

This time the tears that filled her father's eyes spilled onto his cheeks, and he wiped at them self-consciously. "That boy's part of our family, Abby. Don't let him go. Do whatever it takes. Please. For me, for the kids. For God."

You don't understand, Dad. She hesitated, not sure how to answer him.

"Please, Abby." He looked so pained, so earnest in his request, that she knew she had no choice but to tell him what he wanted to hear.

"Okay. I'll try harder. Really, I will. Now you get some rest before they kick me out of here for good." She held tight to her father's hands, and in a matter of minutes he was asleep again, leaving her to wrestle with the knot of emotions that made up her insides.

Losing John would be like losing a part of who she was, a piece not only of her history, but of her father's as well. Abby's heart hurt as she watched her father sleep. She'd told him the truth; it wasn't her fault. She and John had let time come between them, and now he was seeing someone else. It was simply too late to undo the damage, too far into the process of breaking up to patch things together.

Her thoughts drifted back again to their first kiss, the way John made her feel like she was the most important girl in the world, the way he'd promised to write and call, and the way he surprisingly kept his word in the coming year. She would never forget the look on her friends' faces when he showed up at the prom with her. The dance took place in the spring, just weeks before her high-school graduation. There he was, a junior at U of M, a nationally known quarterback, dancing by her side in front of all her classmates.

She wore a light blue chiffon dress and he outdid every other girl's date with his black tuxedo and pale blue vest. "They're all staring at you," she whispered during one of their slow dances. Abby loved the way he held her close but not too tight, secure enough to show the world she was his girl, but respectful of her purity at the same time.

"They're not looking at me; they're looking at you. I've never seen anyone more gorgeous than you are tonight."

He was singly devoted to her throughout the year, and the following fall she enrolled at Michigan. If there was a period in her life she would never forget, a time that would never dim in its brilliance, it was the 1978–79 school year. John led the Wolverines to a championship season, and though he lost out on the Heisman, with two games to go, it still looked like he'd be drafted. She was at every game, every practice, soaking in everything about him.

Then, in his final game that season, John dropped back to pass and couldn't find an open receiver. A linebacker spotted his vulnerability and leveled a blow against his knees that buckled his legs and caused his head to ricochet off the artificial turf. He was knocked unconscious and lay there on the field for ten minutes while team doctors worked on him from every angle.

Abby still remembered how desperately she'd prayed for him from her place in the stands. "Please, God . . . please . . ." She'd been too terrified to voice the unimaginable, to consider that he could be paralyzed or that he might even die out there on the field. Suddenly everything about the game she loved became ugly and cheap. *What's the point?* she recalled thinking. *Give up your legs, your life . . . for a football game? Please, God, let him get up . . .*

Finally John moved his feet, and Abby began breathing again. *Thank You . . . oh, thank You, God.* She couldn't bring herself to imagine how different things would have been if . . .

A medical cart took John to the locker room where Abby met him after the game. The news was better than it could have been, but it wasn't good. John had suffered a serious concussion when his head hit the cementlike turf. And worse, he had torn a ligament in his knee—an injury that would require surgery and most likely end his football career.

The doctor had been brutally honest with John. "You might find a way to get that leg in playing condition again, son, but your head can't take another blow like that one. It would be a risk for you to play."

The knee surgery took place later that month, and by March John was running sprints and getting ready for NFL scouting combines. "I can do it, Abby. My head doesn't hurt. Really."

She knew there was nothing she could say, nothing that would take away his love for the game, a love that had been in his family and hers for as long as they could remember. But in the end, she hadn't needed to say anything. He never regained the speed and mobility he'd once had, and the NFL scouts wrote him off as too slow. By April it was clear that he no longer had a career in professional football.

For a week, John was devastated. He stayed in his dorm, saw little of Abby, and said even less. But at the end of that time, he took her out for pizza and walked with her to the same spot where he'd first kissed her more than a year earlier. "I've been thinking up a plan, Abby." He touched his fingers to her cheek and studied her eyes in a way that even now made her insides melt at the memory. "If I can't play the game, I have to coach it." He drew a steadying breath. "I'm going to take another year and earn my teaching credentials. Then I can go anywhere, teach, coach. Follow my dream."

As the moon made its way up in the sky, he held out a glistening diamond ring. "Marry me, Abby. This summer. That way we can live together next year and never be apart again."

Abby glanced at the ring now, still on her finger but dulled from the years. She had been stunned back then, shocked that he had asked her so soon. But she had never been more sure of anything in her life.

She closed her eyes now and remembered again what it felt like to lose herself in John Reynolds's arms and know without a doubt that it was the place she was born to be, the life she was created to live.

"Yes! I'll marry you."

She almost said it aloud again, as she'd said it back then. John had lifted her off the ground and swung her around, setting her gently on the old wooden bench. Then he sat beside her and took her face in his hands, holding her gaze in a way that no one had been able to do before or since. "I promise, Abby, I'll never let you down. We might have hard times, sad times. But I'll be by your side forever. There could never be anyone but you for me, Abby Chapman."

Yeah, me . . . and Charlene. Abby let the cynical words simmer in her mind for a moment. *Don't do this to yourself, Abby.* She heeded her own warning and banished the thoughts. No matter where time had taken them, she and John had been beautiful together back then. Their parents had been surprised and thrilled by their announcement, and that July she and John married in a church just off campus before a crowd of several hundred. The local Ann Arbor paper carried a picture of the two of them on the front page of the Society section with the caption "Dream Come True—Childhood Friends Make It Official."

Never in her wildest imagination had Abby ever thought for a moment that things would not work out with John Reynolds. They were together constantly that first year, whispering softly to each other in a crowd and strolling the campus hand in hand. When other people looked at them, it was with that jealous longing, that certainty that even if *they* lived a hundred years they would never experience the magic that existed between John and Abby Reynolds.

Six weeks after their honeymoon they were excited to learn that Abby was expecting, and while she freelanced articles for the university paper, John located a teaching and coaching position for the coming fall. Nicole Michelle was born April 16, 1980, and that summer John took a job teaching at Southridge High School outside Marion, Illinois. Both their families were happy for them, and his father set them up with enough money to buy a small house near the high school.

What happened to our storybook finish, Lord?

An image appeared in Abby's mind and burned itself into her conscience: John holding a three-month-old Nicole on the sidelines during football practice not long after they moved to Illinois. Abby remembered capturing the scene and storing it in her memory for another time, aware even back then that their days would fly all too quickly and that before either of them knew it their little girl would be grown.

John had been a wonderful father, every step of the way. When Nicole was five and rode her bike into the oncoming path of a Buick while Abby was at the market, John was the one who calmly, quickly scooped her into his arms and got her to the hospital. Nicole had escaped with a broken leg and five stitches above her forehead, but John refused to let go of her hand until Abby and Kade met them there an hour later.

Even during their darkest days of parenting, the desperate moments of unimaginable grief, he'd been a pillar of strength, a beacon of love and concern for all of them.

She thought her tears had dried up long ago, but they welled once more as her father's recent words played over in her head. *"That boy's part of the family, Abby. Don't let him go . . . don't let him go . . . don't let him go."*

Abby wished with all her heart there were some way she could fulfill her father's request. But no matter how many happy memories she had, no matter if John had long ago been the man of her dreams, and even though he'd been the most amazing father through every stage of their parenting, there was nothing she could do to keep him now.

Abby kissed her father's cheek and stood to leave. How could she hold on to John when he was already gone?

She walked through the front door twenty minutes later and saw Kade sprawled on the family sofa, NFL highlights playing on the television screen.

"Hey, honey, how was your day?" Abby did her best to sound upbeat. With a lifetime of memories rushing through the channels of her mind, she was bound to look preoccupied, even deeply depressed, unless she made a concerted effort to appear otherwise.

Kade sat up and stared curiously at her. "Come here for a minute, will you, Mom?"

Abby caught a note of concern in Kade's voice and she felt her heart skip a beat. Had John done something at school? Made a scene with Charlene maybe? She hated this life of pretending, not knowing when someone might discover their secret. *Please, God, help me say the right thing . . .* "Okay, I'm all yours." She plopped down beside him, her tone light and playful while her heart beat up in her throat.

"Mom, how did you and Dad get such a cool thing between you?"

Something inside her relaxed. "A cool thing?"

Kade smiled and for a moment looked like the young boy he'd once been, quizzical and absorbed with love for her. "Yeah, you know. The way you aren't all jealous and everything. Maybe that's why you guys have such a good marriage."

There was a lump in Abby's throat, and she swallowed, struggling as she uttered a forced laugh. "Where did all this come from?"

Kade leaned back and crossed his arms across his chest. "Well, like Ms. Denton. The other day I came into Dad's room and she and Dad were holding hands." Kade's eyes flashed with concern. "Not like anything was happening between them, you know? Dad was just praying for her, which at first I thought was kind of weird."

Abby's insides suddenly hurt and she slumped over a bit. *Act normal, Abby. Don't think about it; don't cry. Keep listening.* "Yeah, I could see that."

"Anyway, now that I've had time to think about it, maybe that's why you and Dad have such a great thing between you. There's no jealousy. I mean, the trust between you guys is something else." He shook his head. "I asked Dad what you'd think of him praying with Ms. Denton, and he said you already knew Ms. Denton was having trouble and it was no big deal that sometimes he prayed with her."

Kade's face lit up into a grin again. "The more I thought about it, the more I realized how cool it was."

Abby uttered a pinched laugh, but Kade didn't seem to notice. "I want my wife to be just like you. That way, she won't freak out every time I talk to another woman."

Her voice was missing again, and Abby struggled to find it. "Well, that's good, son. I'm glad it made a good impression on you."

She stood and stretched, desperate to find a place where she could sort through her feelings, someplace away from the curious eyes of her children. Sean entered the room and walked up to her, throwing his arms around her neck. "Hey, Mom, how's Grandpa?"

"Good. He sends his love."

Sean nodded and continued across the room to an oversize sofa chair. It wasn't yet two o'clock in the afternoon and already the sun seemed to be setting, as if the whole world was in mourning for all that Abby was going through. Her anger at John was raging just beneath the image she was trying to maintain, and she needed to be alone before she exploded in a heap of fury and tears. Her sons were caught up in the television again, and she gazed out the front window, doing all she could to appear normal. "Is Nicole home?"

Kade stretched out his feet. "No, she's out with Matt. She'll be home after dinner."

Abby nodded and held her breath. "Dad?"

"He's at the club with Joe."

Good. He'd be gone awhile. Joe was one of the assistant football coaches, and the two could spend hours working out and playing pickup basketball with the guys at the club. Abby kept herself from racing out of the room, instead making her way slowly up the stairs into the guest room. There, curled on the bed, she buried her face in a pillow and gave way to the rage that welled within her.

Waves of tears assaulted her, and she hit the mattress with her fist over and over again. He had promised not to make a scene! Swore he would stay away from Charlene for the next six months. Yet there he was, holding the woman's hand in his classroom for the whole world to see. Who else besides Kade had walked in on them that afternoon? Abby could barely breathe, but she didn't care. She dug her face deeper into the pillow and allowed another onset of sobs. Poor Kade. How would he feel when they told the kids the truth? He would know that his father had lied about praying with Charlene, lied about many things.

"Great example, John," she whispered, easing back from the pillow and reaching for a tissue on the nightstand, "way to go."

Time wound back, and she could see herself walking down the hallway of Marion High, humming a happy tune, bringing John dinner since he'd had to work late grading tests. Their relationship had been badly strained back then, too, and the dinner was Abby's way of taking her counselor's suggestion to look for ways to be kind to John. She remembered actually feeling sorry for him because he was putting in so many hours on the football field and then relegated to overtime in the classroom as well. It had been eight o'clock, long since dark, and the rest of the school was deserted. Abby finally reached the end of the corridor and opened the door to John's classroom without knocking.

Her breath had caught in her throat at the sight of them. John and Charlene, standing near his desk, locked in a full-length embrace.

They pulled apart immediately, of course, and Abby—desperately unsure how to respond—refused to run away. Instead she kept her angry feelings inside and wandered into the classroom. "Hello, Charlene. Hope I'm not interrupting." She remembered smiling intently at the woman and then at John.

"Uh, no . . . I was just saying good-bye."

Charlene tripped over a few sentences, alternately trying to explain herself and voice reasons why she needed to leave.

Abby would never forget the anger and pain she'd felt when only she and John remained in his classroom. It was exactly how she felt now. Suspicions were one thing; facts were another. Her gut ached from crying so hard, but buckets of tears wouldn't ease the rage that burned within her.

There was a sound in the hallway outside, and before Abby could prepare herself, the guest-room door opened and John walked in. She faced him like a child caught in an act of disobedience, and he stared at her strangely, his eyebrows knit together. "Abby, what's wrong? The boys said you were making dinner."

She wanted to punch him, shake him, make him wake up to the pain he was causing her. Instead she blew her nose and let her eyes bore into him, infusing him with some of the hate she felt. "Kade told me about your little . . . *prayer* meeting." Her words were barely more than a hiss, and she noticed that her arms were actually shaking from the fury that welled inside her heart.

John's face went blank. "Prayer meeting?"

Abby huffed. "Hard to keep all the lies straight, isn't it, John?"

He entered the room and shut the door behind him. "Abby, I have no idea what you're talking about. What prayer meeting? And why are you crying?"

He honestly didn't remember. How much must have been happening between Charlene and him if Kade's discovery wasn't even something he had logged in his memory. "Think back. The one with Charlene, remember? Kade walked into your classroom and found you and that . . . that woman holding hands." Every word was a dagger, but instead of diffusing her emotions, they intensified as she spoke. "And you told him the two of you were *praying*. Sound familiar?"

A tired breath escaped from John's lungs, and he lowered himself onto the foot of the bed. "I didn't know what else to tell him."

Abby clenched her fist and punched it with all her might into the headboard. Three of her knuckles started bleeding, but she didn't care. She wiped the blood on her jeans and glared at her husband. John's eyes were wide. "That's right, I'll punch the bed if I want to!"

There was a beat where John seemed frantically to search for something to say. "It wasn't like that. I was—"

"Spare me."

From downstairs came Kade's voice. "Hey, everything okay up there? I thought I heard something break."

John cleared his throat and yelled, "Everything's fine. Your mother dropped something, that's all."

Abby shook her head and stared at him in disbelief. "Is that what we're going to do for the next six months, John? Lie to the kids every time one of them sees you with Charlene?"

He was on his feet and began pacing, rubbing the back of his neck. "What do you want to do, Abby, tell them the truth? That I'm trying to stay out of a full-blown affair with Charlene, and that you're so mad at me you're punching holes in the furniture? Is that a better option?"

Abby shook her head and stared at him. *He doesn't comprehend what he's done wrong . . .* "Look at me."

John stopped pacing and met her gaze. "What do you want from me, Abby? I didn't know Kade was going to walk in on us."

"I asked you to stay away from her. Six months, John. *Six months.*"

He sighed, no longer trying to defend himself. "I'm trying, Abby. I didn't invite her in; she came on her own. So I told her I needed time, told her to give me space until after Nicole's wedding. And whether you want to believe it or not, she actually understood. She was just telling me she would do whatever she could to make it easier on me when . . . when Kade walked in."

Every word that came from John's mouth was like an assault. How *dare* Charlene even *need* to be told to stay away? Who had led her to believe John would want her help to get through the next six months?

The answer hung in the room like an executioner's sword: John, of course.

He had allowed himself to get that close to Charlene, and now Abby could picture the scene in his classroom as if she and not Kade had been the one to discover them. Charlene would have been almost inconsolable at the thought of a six-month silence between her and

John. Of course he'd taken her hands to comfort her. If Kade hadn't walked in, who knew what else might have happened?

John was waiting, staring at her, a man at the end of his rope and out of options. "I'm sorry, Abby."

Abby hated the way she felt, the way the anger ripped at her heart and made her feel like a monster inside. "John Reynolds . . . I hate you." Through gritted teeth, she fired each word with as much venom as she could muster. "Get out of here before I walk down those stairs and tell the kids the truth."

John's gaze narrowed as he studied her. "I can't believe what you've become, Abby. What we've become . . ." His expression softened. "I don't know what to . . ." He released a heavy sigh and shrugged. In all her life she'd only seen him look that sad one other time. "I'm sorry, Abby." Then without saying another word, he left the room.

As he shut the door and made his way down the stairs, she hurt in places she hadn't known existed. *Come back, John. Don't you care? Can't you tell me you'll forget about her, that she's not important to you and that you still love me?* She balled up her aching, bleeding hand again, and this time punched the pillow. Again and again and again . . . until the rage inside her subsided and gave way to an ocean of sadness.

Help me, God . . . I don't know what to do anymore. Make the time go fast, please. I can't bear to live with him, knowing he's in love with her.

Love bears all things; love never ends . . .

For most of her adult life, Abby had taken one thing for granted: if the Bible said it, she believed it. But as she lay there sobbing in a way that threatened to consume her, the scripture that came to mind made her consider that perhaps God's Word wasn't truth at all.

The verse played again in her mind. *Love bears all things . . . love never ends . . . never ends . . . never ends.*

It was a lie; it had to be. The love between John and her could not possibly bear this. While their daughter dreamed and planned about love's beginning, she and John were plotting and planning love's end.

Either they had never loved at all—and Abby knew without a doubt that they had—or this time Scripture was wrong.

Because the love they'd once shared, the love that had shone like a lighthouse among the shipwrecks of other marriages, was absolutely, undoubtedly over.

Love ended, all right.

She cradled her swollen fingers close to her chest and allowed another wave of tears. The terminal illness their bond was suffering had taken years, and in the end their love had died a predictably painful death. In a matter of months they'd have the proper documentation, the paper grave marker to prove it.

Abby sat there a long while until she began to drift off, the same words, same feelings playing over and over in her mind.

I hate you, John Reynolds . . . I hate you . . . I hate you.

I hate you.

Twelve

IT WAS SUPER BOWL SUNDAY, A HOLIDAY THAT ranked up there with Christmas and Easter in the Reynoldses' house, but Abby and Nicole had agreed to spend the morning and early afternoon looking for wedding dresses. The day out with Jo Harter had produced nothing but endless conversation, so this time Nicole was determined to find at least one gown she liked.

They were in the dressing room, and Abby was closing the zipper on the fifth dress in an hour when Nicole's mood seemed to darken. Ever since the comment from Kade, Abby had been extrasensitive to each of the children, aware that they might hear something about their dad and Charlene or pick up on the tensions between their parents. "You okay, honey?" Abby fluffed Nicole's hair over the back of the dress and stood back. "Oh, Nick, it's gorgeous."

Abby only used her pet name for her daughter once in a while anymore. Nicole tilted her head and looked intently at Abby. "Dad's been quieter than usual lately. He's happy about me getting married, right? I mean, he likes Matt, doesn't he?"

Every inch of Abby's body was on instant alert. "Yes, sweetie, of course he likes him." She paused, searching for the right words. "He's been busy with school, that's all."

Nicole studied her reflection in the mirror and tugged at the dress a few times until she was satisfied with how it fit. "The sleeves are too plain."

Abby took in the details on the sleeves of the dress and thought them simple, but lovely. But this wasn't the time to argue with Nicole. "You're right. Let's see if we can find a few more."

Nicole hesitated and stared at Abby once more. "Kade said Dad's been praying with Ms. Denton." Nicole's pained expression gave Abby the sense that her daughter was uncomfortable, as though she were opening a deep, dark topic. "That bugs me, Mom. Doesn't she know he's happily married?"

Alarms sounded in Abby's heart and soul, but she worked to keep her face from showing it. *See what you've done, John? Why couldn't you stay away from her?* Abby angled her head and crossed her arms. "Well . . . I can understand how you feel. It bugs me, too." *Pick your words here, Abby. In a few months she'll know the truth . . .* "Your dad's doing his best; that's all I know."

Nicole thought about that for a moment, then shrugged. "Yeah, I guess. There's just something about Ms. Denton I don't like. She's always flirting with Dad, giggling around him. It's obnoxious."

If only John could have seen through Charlene as easily as Nicole had. Abby uttered an appropriate laugh. "Your dad can take care of himself."

Nicole smiled and bent her neck as Abby unzipped the dress. "So everything's okay with you guys?"

Abby knew her daughter well enough to know that this was the heart of her concern, the fear that every child lives with but rarely voices. And even now, with Nicole grown and about to begin a marriage of her own, the childlike antennae were still up, her concerns still deep and frightful at the thought of her parents in trouble.

"We're fine. Don't worry about us." She helped Nicole slip out of the dress and waited while her daughter donned her skirt and sweater once more. "This is supposed to be your day, remember? We have a wedding gown to find."

By the day's end Nicole had found the perfect dress, and Abby was grateful that in her excitement her daughter had forgotten all thoughts of her parents and whether they were having trouble or not. After they were home she holed away in her room while Abby cut up vegetables and made snack trays for the game. Like always, they would have a house full—several of John's coaches and their families, a few players, and the boys' friends. Abby didn't care who came over as long as she kept busy. The busier she was, the less she needed to find ways to avoid John.

Her heart still ached from their blowup the day before, and she wanted more than anything to get through Super Bowl Sunday without a conversation or time alone with him.

Just before kickoff Nicole bounded halfway down the stairs and stopped at the landing. "Is Matt here yet?" Her voice was brimming with excitement, and Abby guessed her daughter wanted to show off her wedding gown.

"Not yet." She placed a stack of carrot sticks on the platter and ran her fingers under the water.

"He said he'd be a few minutes late." Kade's voice came from the next room. "What're you hiding on the stairs for?"

"Ta-da! Mom, come here. I have my dress on. Quick, before Matt comes."

Abby dried her hands on a towel and headed for the TV room. Although the gown had looked beautiful on Nicole in the dressing room an hour earlier, now she had taken time to fix her hair and slip on a pair of heels. The sight of her elegantly posed before her father and brothers caused Abby's breath to catch in her throat. She stopped midstep and let her mouth drop open. *Lord, she looks just like I did at her age. Have twenty-two years passed since I modeled my own dress in the weeks before marrying John?*

Before she could speak, John muted the television and stared wide-eyed at their daughter. "Nicki, it's gorgeous. You look . . . all grown up." His gaze caught Abby's, almost as if by mistake, and what she saw there mirrored all the things she was feeling. *Did we really create this woman-child? Have the years flown by as quickly for you as they have for me? And how come when our little girl is celebrating love, we're finding new ways every day to destroy ours?*

Abby looked away, refusing the subtle intimacy of the moment, and turned her attention where it belonged. To Nicole. "Sweetheart, the dress is perfect."

And it was, as right as if it'd been handmade for her. The bodice clung to her in fitted white satin, marked by sequins and fine embroidery. Sheer and subtly decorated with additional sequins, the sleeves ended with a wide cuff edged in elegant lace that lay against the backs of her hands. The layered satin skirt fell away gracefully, edged in the same lace as the sleeves and barely skimming the floor in the front. At the back it extended into a breathtaking train and a series of sequins and more embroidery that ascended to the bodice and made Nicole's waist look beyond tiny.

"I remember when my waist was that small." Abby angled her head, gazing at Nicole. *Back when I was the only one who could turn John's head.*

Abby glanced in his direction and found him staring at her again. This time she scowled, doing her best to discourage him from making contact. They had nothing to talk about. Any nostalgic glances were only bound to make things more difficult. When she looked again, he'd directed his attention completely on Nicole.

"Matt's one lucky guy." John stood up and stretched his bad leg, the one that had suffered the injury two decades earlier. It was something he did often—something most people missed—but Abby knew how badly John's knee still bothered him, how it stiffened up on cold days and caused him to limp first thing in the morning.

John took Nicole in his arms and hugged her close. "When did you get to be such a beautiful young woman, Nicki?"

The sight of John and Nicole together was too much for Abby. *If you cared about her at all, you wouldn't be holding hands with another woman in your classroom.* She kept her thoughts to herself and turned back to the kitchen. "Matt'll be here soon, Nick."

She heard her daughter gasp lightly and kiss her father on the cheek. "Gotta run. Don't say a word to Matt." And with that she was back up the stairs, completely unaware of the tension between her parents.

John was caught up in the second quarter when the phone rang. Abby had long since locked herself into her office, so he grabbed the cordless receiver and clicked the talk button.

"Hello?"

John thought he heard a rustling sound, but otherwise only silence. "Hello?" He was about to hang up when he heard her voice.

"John, it's me. Charlene."

A dozen emotions tore into John's heart. Surprise, elation, guilt, anger. He waited a beat so he wouldn't say anything he'd regret. Especially with a roomful of people seated around him watching the game. "Uh . . . hi."

She released a heavy sigh. "I know I shouldn't be calling you at home . . . I shouldn't be calling you at all. I just . . . I feel so alone, John. I didn't know what else to do."

There were times when hearing Charlene's voice sent unspeakable feelings coursing through his body. But here, in plain view of his children on a day that had always been theirs alone, John was torn between wanting to help her and knowing he should hang up on her. "We're watching the game, of course. And you?"

"You can't talk; I knew it. I'm sorry, John . . . I'll let you go."

"Is everything okay?"

Kade cast him a strange glance as soon as he asked the question, but John wasn't worried. He was willing to lie about it if he had to. If Charlene was in some sort of trouble, he wanted to be available for her.

There was silence for a moment, and he heard Charlene crying. "I feel like . . . like I'm in limbo or something, like there's no hope or promises or future for us." She paused and John's heart lurched. *Why is she doing this now? When she knows my family is around?* When he didn't speak, she continued. "I love you, John. I wasn't sure until you asked me to stay away. But now . . . now I'm sure. I love you like I've never loved anyone else. But I can't wait around forever . . ."

Careful, watch your tone. "I understand that." What did she expect him to say? Already there were bound to be questions, at least from Kade.

Charlene sighed. "Oh, I don't know . . . I never should have called in the first place. I'm sorry."

Again John was at a loss for words. He could hardly make her flowery promises now, even if the kids weren't listening to every word. "Right, well, thanks for calling."

"John, wait . . . I know I shouldn't have called you, but do me this one thing. If you think we have a chance . . . after Nicole's wedding, I mean . . . tell me. Please. Tell me you think the Rams are the best team no matter what happens in the game. That way I'll know at least that you care, that you want to be with me as much as I want to be with you."

John thought about that for a moment.

Flee immorality, son. What God has joined together—

The voice that surely belonged to God changed and became Abby's from the other day. *"I hate you, John . . . I hate you."*

"John? Did you hear me?"

He closed his eyes and massaged the bridge of his nose with his thumb and forefinger. Too many voices for a Sunday of football. How was he supposed to know what he wanted? Abby's words of hate continued to play in his mind and the image of her spewing rage took up residence in his heart. Why not make promises to Charlene? He cared about her, didn't he? And things were only going to get worse where Abby was concerned.

John cleared his throat. Charlene knew him well—knew that his favorite team was the Rams and that no matter who was in the room, the words he was about to say would not sound unusual. Especially as well as St. Louis had done in the play-offs. "I don't feel this way all the time, but right now I'd have to say the Rams had the best season all year."

There, he'd said it. It was true. If he and Charlene could make it through the next six months without spending time together, John had every reason to think he'd have his second chance at life with Charlene Denton.

"What do you mean you don't feel that way all the time?"

John clenched his teeth. Why was she pushing him? He exhaled deliberately and forced a laugh. "You know me; I've liked the Rams for a long time."

Charlene hesitated for a moment and then released a childlike shout for joy. "John Reynolds, you've made me the happiest girl in all of Illinois. I'd wait a lifetime for you now that I know how you feel."

"Okay, well I better go. The game's just heating up."

"All right, I'm sorry." Charlene was contrite, but her happiness still spilled over into her voice. "And what I said about being discreet, I still mean it . . . I'm here for you whenever you want me."

Her last words hit their mark, and John could feel his cheeks getting hot. "Right, well, I'll call you later."

He hung up and immediately Kade caught his gaze. "Who was that?"

Even though he'd expected the questions, John wasn't prepared. "A teacher."

One of the coaches turned to him. "Who?"

Way to go, Reynolds. Lie about a teacher in front of a room full of school employees. "Uh . . . Joe Jackson, track coach. Just wanted to see what I thought of the game."

Another coach joined the conversation. "Jackson called you? I thought he was in Palm Springs with his wife?"

Cold fear ran through John's veins, and he suddenly felt like everyone in the room knew he was lying. "Come to think of it, maybe he was in Palm Springs. He didn't say."

The questions stopped as the room gradually turned back to the game. Only then did John realize how desperate he'd become. He had just promised forever to a woman who was not his wife in front of a dozen family and friends, and now his heart was beating almost out of his chest as payment for his choices. *I'm a rotten excuse for a man.*

It was halftime already, and while John made small talk with his friends about the game statistics, Kade began rattling off facts about the eagle.

"Okay, listen to this." The men gave him their attention and Kade cleared his throat, glancing at the rough draft of his senior paper. "An eagle almost never eats anything dead." He raised a single finger. "But if it does, if something happens to make him sick, he flies to the highest rock he can find, spreads himself across it, and lets the sun soak out all the poison."

The analogy was so strong John wondered if Kade suspected his father of deceit. *Or is this just Your timing, Lord?*

I'm here for you, son. Remember the height from which you have fallen . . .

John banished the thought and focused on Kade, who was standing now, enjoying the attention as he carried on with more eagle information. John was still thinking about the poisoned eagle, who after getting in trouble at least had the sense to take his pain to the rock and let the sun make him strong again. He had a Rock he could go to, a Son that would certainly make him strong like before.

Repent! Remember the height from which you have—

John blinked away the warning. The trouble was, he didn't want that kind of help. Not now. Not when his wife had turned into a shrew and his closest friend, a beautiful young woman thought the sun rose and set on him alone. What would God know of trouble like that?

A pain worked its way through his chest, and he became completely unaware of the others, their conversations about eagles and whether they were or weren't involving him. *I'll probably have a heart attack and go straight to hell.* John wiped a thin layer of sweat from his forehead and tried to understand how his life had gotten so completely out of hand. And how come the love of his life, the woman he had longed for since his childhood days, not only didn't love him . . .

She hated him.

Abby had heard the phone ring and figured it was for one of the kids. Either way she wasn't coming out of the office, not today. Her job as snackmaker was over, and now she needed to send in a piece for *Woman's Day.* Her Internet connection was good on the first attempt, and the opening screen showed her she had mail. Two clicks later she was into a lengthy letter from Stan.

Everything about her editor was as surreal as the cyberworld itself. Stan was the divorced father of two and the senior editor at one of the largest magazines in the country, one she wrote for at least every other month. Though she had started her freelance career with bit pieces for small Christian publications, in time she'd worked her way up so that now the articles she wrote were read by more than a million readers and brought her thousands of dollars each.

Now and then she missed the chance to share her faith in print the way she had when she'd written for the Christian magazines, but then these days there wasn't much to share anyway. Besides, she would need the extra income once she and John were living apart.

Her eyes found the beginning of Stan's note.

Hey, Abby . . . maybe it's my imagination but something told me this weekend's been a little rough on you. John and the other woman, maybe? Just a guess. Anyway, I hope not. In fact, even though it sounds crazy, I really hope things still work out for you two. And if they don't . . . well, I can think of at least one man who will celebrate the day you're finally free.

She read his note again. Was there any doubt that this man was interested in her? At first his letters had been purely professional, but two years ago he asked about her marriage in a note that was clearly more personal than the others.

Abby had written back, "Let's just say I'm not ready to give you an article on marital bliss."

The next week Stan surprised her with a bouquet of flowers. The card inside read, "To the prettiest woman in Illinois . . . John doesn't know how lucky he is."

It had been easy to write even that off as professional flirtation, the kind of transaction that happened in the business world, a way to convince Abby to write primarily for their magazine and not another. Then his e-mails changed. There would be the usual discussion of her articles and developing ideas, but then he'd add a line or two that went far deeper, into territories of her heart that had been unexplored for years.

People who feel the most and deepest become writers . . . and inevitably they marry those who can't feel at all.

Or another time: *In the depths of my soul is a place unlocked only by the prose of a wordsmith. And you, my dear Abby, are the most accomplished wordsmith I know.*

It wasn't long before Abby began looking forward to his mail, signing on to the Internet twice a day in hopes that maybe there'd be a letter from him. Of course the timing couldn't have been more perfect because that same season Abby began getting weekly reports from her friends.

"What's up with John and Charlene Denton?" Rosemary from the booster club wanted to know. Rosemary was a blonde busybody whose very life centered around the happenings at Marion High. Her report was the first in a long line.

Next it was Betty from the school office, calling to say, "I hate to be the bearer of bad news, but rumor is that Charlene Denton has the hots for your husband. You know that, right, Abby?"

And in the football stands, Jill, one of the coaches' wives, asked her, "Doesn't it bug you that Charlene hangs out at practice each day? If she was after my husband the way she's after yours, I'd get down there and tell her off myself."

One parent to another in the school office: "Is Mr. Reynolds still married? I always see him with Ms. Denton. They sure make a cute couple."

"They're together every afternoon from what I hear . . ."

The comments continued like so many painful, pelting balls of hail until Abby would have had to be blind to miss the storm gathering in the not-so-far distance. Whenever she would bring it up, John would get frustrated and deny any wrongdoing.

"People want to see us fail, Abby," he'd say. "Let's not give 'em a reason, okay?"

After a month of knowing about Charlene and receiving more e-mails from Stan, Abby broke down and bared her heart to the man. She could still remember the letter she wrote the first time she let him see inside her soul. *It feels like all our lives John and I have been creating this intricate quilt, stitched together with a hundred colors and patterns from stormy grays to brilliant yellows. And now, when it should finally be taking shape, we're both standing by and watching it unravel.*

Suddenly life is all about him, his work, his career. He's too caught up in himself to notice that I'm balancing the house and the kids and my writing, all while picking up after everyone else. I feel like we're becoming strangers . . .

She had seen Stan's picture by then and knew him to be at least five years older than she with a full head of white hair and the average build of a professional. Certainly not the physical specimen John had always been, but then maybe that was better. Maybe beauty lasted longer when it came from inside a person.

Abby scanned the rest of Stan's note and allowed her eyes to linger on the last few lines: *I've been through it before, Ab . . . if things get really bad, don't hesitate to call. I'm here for you always.*

Here for you always . . . here for you always . . .

Where had she heard those words before? Maybe a million years ago from John, but weren't they somewhere in the Bible, too? Wasn't that one of God's promises, that He'd never leave His people, never forsake them?

"Ah, but those words are for faithful hearts," she whispered into the stillness of her office, barely aware of the enthusiastic cheers going up at the other end of the house where the game was probably heading into the fourth quarter. She closed her eyes and thought about the Lord, how sweet it had once been to meet with Him in private each morning and seek His plan, His way for her life.

She stared again at the note from Stan and her fingers began typing out a response. *It was good to hear from you, good to know that someone, somewhere, cared enough to ask how I was . . .*

Her fingers continued to dance across the keyboard, baring her heart, her soul, the deep-seated feelings she could no longer share with John. Other than their children, she shared nothing at all with the man she had once loved, the man she married. Because no matter what lies John told her there was no denying the truth—he was having an affair.

Yes, things were different now. John had made a choice to love someone else; he'd chosen on purpose to be unfaithful. She stared at the note she'd written to Stan and hit the send button.

The moment the mail was gone, she was hit square in the gut with the reality of their situation. No matter what lies she told herself, no matter how badly she wanted to blame John, the truth was suddenly clearer than water: John wasn't the only one being unfaithful.

Thirteen

THE LAST THING ABBY WANTED TO DO THAT
Thursday night was sit across the table from Jo Harter and listen to
another monologue about Denny. But the idea of getting out of the
house and finally finishing Nicole's scrapbook was too appealing to
turn down.

"This is my first time scrappin', Abby. I've cut out pictures and
done some thinkin' on it, but I haven't actually started Matt's scrapbook, so this is all brand new to me. In other words, I'm as wide open
for suggestions as a great white at breakfast time. Just fire away any
old time you have an idea, Abby . . ."

Not more fish stories, please.

Jo caught a quick breath and kept talking. It had been an hour of
monologue while Abby painstakingly laid out the photos and news
clippings and dance programs that made up Nicole's eighth-grade
year. Despite the constant rush of wind coming from Jo's direction,
Abby was grateful for a night away from John. Being near him left her
torn between detesting him and longing for some far-off yesterday
when they still loved each other.

Abby had just applied the glue to the final photo in a layout when

Jo asked the question. It was the one everyone knew was taboo, the one friends and family alike had avoided for nearly two decades.

"Matt tells me you lost a little girl; is that right?"

As soon as the words were spoken, Abby's hands felt leaden, unable to move, and her heart took an eternity to decide whether it might actually continue to beat. *Matt tells me you lost a little girl . . . lost a little girl . . . lost a little girl . . .* The words ricocheted in her heart, poking holes into a wound that had never quite healed.

Haley Ann.

Her face filled Abby's memory until all she could see was their precious second daughter. Even with all the pain their separation was causing, those were easily the darkest days of her life with John.

Haley Ann. Sweet little Haley Ann.

Abby didn't have to think about how old the child would be today if she'd lived. She knew it as surely as she knew her own name or the way home after a long vacation: Haley Ann would have been nineteen, as lovely as Nicole and more excited than any of them about her sister's wedding. She'd have been maid of honor, no doubt. Nicole's best friend.

Haley Ann.

The silence was deafening, and Abby realized Jo was waiting for an answer. She blinked back the tears that burned in her eyes and without looking up tried to think of the right words. "Yes. We did. She was . . . she was very young."

Even Jo had the sense not to rush into a monologue on the topic of young, dead children. Instead she waited nearly a minute, and when she continued, her voice was softer than before. "I'm sorry, Abby. It must be harder than the steel trap over a sewer drain."

Abby nodded, embarrassed that she was unable to control her tears. When Jo looked down at her photographs, Abby dabbed quickly at her cheeks, stopping the watery trail from landing squarely on her scrapbook and ruining pictures that would have been impossible to replace.

Haley Ann. Was that when Abby's faith had taken a turn for the worse? It hadn't seemed so at the time, back when her ties to the Lord had been her only assurance that one day she'd hold her daughter again, cradle her in her arms in a place called eternity. But really, now that she looked back, God could have given her second daughter more time on earth. What sense was there in allowing a precious angel like Haley Ann to be born into this world only to take her back four months—

"Was she older than Nicole?"

Abby wanted to curse at the woman, beg her to stop asking questions about the one place in her heart where no one trespassed. But logic told her Jo meant well. Abby summoned her strength, ignoring the way fresh tears blurred her vision, and without gazing up she searched desperately for her voice. "She was . . . she was younger. Eighteen months."

Jo squirmed in her chair. "I know you probably don't talk about her much, Abby, but since you and me's gonna be family from here on out, I hope you don't mind my questions. I never knew anyone who lost a child so young. Most people say it's the death knell for a marriage. But you and John, I mean, look at you two. Still going strong after all these years. You'd never know the two of you'd been through something awful like that."

Despite the photographs spread out before her, a different picture came into focus. She and John at the hospital emergency room saying good-bye to the lifeless body of little Haley Ann. SIDS, the doctors had said. Sudden death, a risk for any infant. And there was John, T-shirt and gym shorts, tears streaming down his rugged, handsome cheeks, cradling the baby in his arms as though he could somehow love her back to life. Abby could still see him, still feel the tears shaking his body, still hear his voice. *"Dear God, I loved her."* She remembered how he wrapped his arms more closely around their baby's lifeless little body, protecting her the way he hadn't been able to when she lay dying in her crib. "Haley Ann . . . my precious girl, Haley Ann . . ."

The image of John and their second daughter stayed in Abby's mind, burning its way into her consciousness until she couldn't take it another moment. "Excuse me." She pushed herself away from the craft table, hurried into a back bathroom, and dropped herself on the closed lid of the toilet. As real as Haley Ann been, there was no room in Abby's life for thoughts of her now.

"Why did you take her from us? Why?"

The whispered question bounced around the tiled bathroom walls and came back to her. There were no more answers today than there had been back when Haley Ann died. And though that secret place in Abby's heart kept Haley Ann alive, monitored her milestones and birthdays, she never allowed herself to drift back to the day when she found her baby girl facedown in her crib, motionless and not breathing.

Abby clenched her fists and the tears came with a force that was almost violent. *Why here, God? At the craft store?* Couldn't she have had a neutral response to Jo Harter's question? Would it take another twenty years before mention of Haley Ann didn't ignite a bonfire of emotions?

Five minutes passed, then ten, and there was a soft knocking at the door. Abby's heart rate doubled. *Don't make me explain myself, God, please.* She swallowed hard. "What?" Her throat sounded thick from the effects of her tears.

"Abby? It's me—Jo. You all right?"

If Abby had made a line of people she might choose to befriend in this, her season of letting go, Jo Harter would have most certainly been at the end. The woman was all frosting and no cake, too caught up in surface conversation to understand the workings of the heart. Still, they were about to be linked by the marriage of their children and Abby would not be responsible for doing anything that might alienate her. Even now, when all Abby wanted was to disappear through a crack in the mortar and find herself under the covers of their guest-room bed.

"I'm fine. I'll be out in a minute."

There was a beat. *Make her believe it, please . . .*

"All right. I was getting a little nervous out there by myself. Wasn't sure if you were sick or something."

Sick of your questions . . . "I'm fine. Really. I'll be right out."

When Jo had moved away from the door, Abby stood and splashed cold water on her face. There was no hiding the fact that she'd been crying, but most of the women would be too involved in their scrapbooking to notice her tear-stained face. Drawing a deep breath, she refused to think another minute about Haley Ann and the time in her life when she had needed John Reynolds just to make it through the day.

She looked at her reflection in the mirror. "Focus on the here and now, Abby." Her heart seemed to toughen some in response. She could do this, go back out there and face Jo and whatever other questions she had, finish an evening of photo layouts, and make it home. She could do it all without giving in to the pressing urge to go back in time, back to Haley Ann's birth and all that their lives had been that year.

Forget about it, Abby. Think about today.

With a resolve she hadn't known she was capable of, she drew a deep breath and returned to the craft table. The rest of the night, despite Jo's questions and well-meaning attempt to steer the conversation back to small talk, Abby hid behind her heart's iron gates and refused to let herself feel.

Not until she came home at half past ten that evening and found her entire family asleep did she do the thing she'd wanted to do since Jo first brought up the topic. Moving quietly so as not to wake them, she bundled into a parka that would protect her from even the most frigid temperatures. Then she wrapped scarves around her neck and head and donned a pair of thermal gloves. Grabbing a folding chair from the garage, she trudged outside through the snow to the pier, opened it, and sat down, gazing out at the moonlit reflection on the icy lake.

Had it really been nineteen years?

The cold made its way through a crack in her scarves and she pulled them more tightly. Whenever she needed time alone, space to think and dream and remember how to be again, Abby came here. To the pier: winter, spring, summer, or fall. The weather made no difference.

She remembered the dates like it was yesterday. Haley Ann, born October 24, 1981, an hour after the league football game against Southridge High. Dead just four months later, February 28, 1982. Nights like this it seemed as though Haley Ann had never really died at all, as though maybe she was asleep upstairs in the room next to Nicole, as much a part of their family as Kade or Sean or any of them.

Abby's body adjusted to the cold, and she relaxed. Across the backdrop of the shimmering lake she watched pictures take shape, saw scenes come to life again as though they were happening for the first time. Her pregnancy had been a dream, and more than once John had whispered to her that this child, this second baby, would certainly be a boy.

"You know, Abby . . . to carry on the tradition."

He'd been teasing of course, and as her due date neared he no longer even joked about having a boy. "I'm sure it's a girl. As precious as Nicole and as perfect as you. What could be better than being surrounded by princesses?"

And sure enough, when he arrived at the hospital after the football game in time to join her in the delivery room, they learned together that he'd been right. There was nothing difficult or remarkable about the delivery, nothing that might lend even a shadow of foreboding that this little girl was anything but the picture of health. Her skin was pink almost from the moment she was born, and her cries came in short bursts that sounded more like the tinkling of her older sister's laughter than the wailing of a lusty newborn.

"I knew it, Abby girl; she's perfect. Another precious princess for the Reynolds castle."

She could still hear him, see him holding his tiny daughter, cooing at her, welcoming her to the world. "Only the very best princesses have the good sense to be born after a football game is over . . ." He sang to her and whispered silly nothings to her while Abby fell asleep exhausted.

The next morning when Abby woke, there was John, long legs stretched across the hospital room, one hand on Haley Ann's back as she lay in the bassinet beside him. Abby remembered well the feeling of joy that grew in her heart that morning, the way she'd imagined only sunshine and rainbows for all the days that lay ahead. Her mother was down from Wisconsin watching Nicole, and later that day the group held an informal birthday party for the newborn with cake and streamers and balloons and a song that Haley Ann slept right through.

"She's *my* sister, right, Mommy?" Nicole angled her head lovingly, putting her nose so close to her baby sister's the two were almost touching.

"Yes, she's all yours, Nicole."

Abby had imagined the fun these two would have, growing up together, sharing a room and secrets and clothes and friends. They would be inseparable, not like Abby and her sister, who was four years younger and too caught up in her own life to have much of a friendship with Abby.

Nicole and Haley Ann.

Not long after Abby brought the newborn home, she stenciled the girls' names on their lavender walls and bought them matching bedding. Abby closed her eyes and let the memory become real in her mind. She could see the white, swirly letters, smell the fresh paint on the walls, hear the infant cries of Haley Ann when she was hungry or needed to be held.

Football season ended in December, and that same week they sold their two-bedroom home and moved into the house on the lake—the home where they'd lived ever since. Each day afterward brought hours of family time, leisurely evenings with John spread out on the sofa,

Haley Ann bundled in the crook of one arm while Nicole cuddled into the other. He was such a wonderful dad, gentle and loving with the innate ability to make Nicole and even Haley Ann giggle at will.

One night when the boxes were unpacked, not long after the girls had fallen asleep, John took Abby by the hand and led her outside to the pier. In the bustling activity of moving and having a newborn in the house, Abby had done little more than admire the pier from a distance. But that night, bundled in their winter coats, John wove his fingers between hers and gently turned her so she was facing him.

"Do you hear it, Abby?"

She listened intently, the winter night quiet like the moon across the water. John moved his hands along her arms, drawing her close, pulling her into a hug. "Close your eyes," he whispered.

As she did, she heard gentle sounds she hadn't noticed before. A subtle breeze in the trees that lined the lake, the simple lapping of water against the frozen shoreline. The heartbeat of the man whose arms surrounded her. "I think so."

He pulled back then and stared into her eyes, and she sensed he loved her more deeply than before, if that were possible. "It's the music of our lives, Abby." A smile played on his lips, and he leaned toward her, kissing her in a way that made her feel safe and protected and wanted. Desirable, despite the circles under her eyes from late nights with Haley Ann. "Dance with me, Abby . . . dance with me."

Taking her hand carefully in his, John led her in small circles, dancing with her alone on the pier to the melody of life, while their angel girls slept inside. Never mind the areas where ice made the wood slippery, in John's arms she was safe and secure, a ballerina being led across the grandest dance floor of all.

It was something he did often over the next two months: swept her outside and danced with her on the pier. Something that made her forget the day's diapers and feedings and sleepless nights. With all her heart Abby believed those days, those feelings between John and her, would never end. It wasn't just the dancing; it was the way Nicole became tender and gentle around Haley Ann, the way they felt together as a family. Invincible, almost. As if no bad thing in all the world could touch what they shared.

Abby blinked, trying to contain a tidal wave of sadness.

There was nothing remarkable about February 28. Nothing during Haley Ann's morning feeding to indicate it would be the last time Abby would hold her little girl close or stare into her eyes as the two of them held a conversation only mother and child could understand. When the baby was finished eating, Abby kissed her tenderly and lay her down on her side.

Two hours later, about the time when Haley Ann usually woke from her morning nap, Abby was folding a load of laundry on her bed when she was pierced with a sudden sense of panic, a warning she could not explain. "Nicole?" Abby's voice rang urgently through the house and her older daughter, nearly two that month, was quick to respond.

"Yes, Mommy?" Her voice told Abby she was where she was supposed to be. Situated in front of the television, watching *Sesame Street.* "Is it lunchtime?"

Abby tried to calm her racing heart. "No, sweetie, not yet. Mommy has to get Haley Ann up from her nap first."

She dropped the towel she'd been holding and hurried into the baby's room. "Haley, sweetie, wake up. Mommy's here."

The memory sent a shiver down Abby's spine. Haley Ann was on her stomach, a position she often wound up in, but even with Abby's singsong voice she showed no signs of movement.

Hot tears forged a trail down Abby's cheeks as she relived the moment, felt again the slight stiffness in her baby daughter as she swept her into her arms and saw the blue in her face and fingers.

"Haley Ann! Wake up!" She had shouted the words, jerking the tiny baby just enough to jump-start her breathing, to waken her from the terrible sleep she had fallen into. When there was no response, no signs of life, she grabbed the phone and dialed 9-1-1.

"Hurry, please! My baby isn't breathing."

For the next ten minutes she gave Haley Ann mouth-to-mouth resuscitation, oblivious to the way Nicole sat huddled in the doorway watching, singing the alphabet song to herself over and over again.

"A-B-C-D-E-F-G . . ."

Abby could still hear the fear in Nicole's voice, see the way she was whisked to another corner of the house when the paramedics arrived and one of them reached out his arms for Haley Ann.

"Ma'am, we'll take over now."

And in that moment she'd been forced to hand over her newborn, desperate to believe there was still hope but certain deep in her gut that Haley Ann was dead. A police officer took information from Abby, what time the baby went down, what she'd eaten that morning, how long she'd slept. Finally he asked about the baby's father. "Is there a number we can call for you, Mrs. Reynolds?"

Abby had been beside herself, barely able to breathe. But some-how she pulled the number from the recesses of her mind. Everything that happened next was a blur. The police took Nicole to a neighbor's house, then escorted Abby to the hospital behind the ambulance. As soon as they arrived, John greeted them.

"Honey, what is it? What's happened?" His face—normally ruddy and full of life—was gray and washed out. Fear screamed from his eyes.

There was nothing Abby could say. Haley Ann was gone; she was sure of it. "Haley Ann . . . she's . . . she didn't wake up from her nap . . . Oh, John, pray. Please, pray."

They were the last words Abby could say, the final moment before she collapsed against John and gave way to the sobs that tore at her heart. Together they took up their position outside the emergency room, where doctors were shooting drugs into their baby, using every possible attempt to jump-start her heart.

But it was too late. God had taken Haley Ann home, and there was nothing anyone could do to change the fact. Before the hour was up, doctors left them alone with their baby so together they could say their good-byes. It was impossible to imagine that just four months earlier they had been celebrating at this very hospital, welcoming her new life into their hearts and home.

John was the first to hold her. Moving slowly, like a man trapped in quicksand, he positioned himself near the hospital bed and carefully lifted her to his chest. It was the same image Abby had seen earlier that night at the craft store, the picture of John holding his tiny, dead daughter, trying to find a way to say good-bye.

He said little more than their baby's name, speaking it over and over again as his tears splashed onto her cool skin. But when it was Abby's turn to hold her, he broke down and wept. "Oh, Abby, it's my fault. God's punishing me. I know it."

Abby held Haley Ann tight and leaned into John's shoulder, the three of them connected as they'd been so often in the previous weeks. "No, love, it isn't anyone's fault. No one could have known . . ."

He shook his head, the sobs coming harder, almost violently. "I . . . I wanted her to be a son, Abby. I never told you, but deep inside . . . I hoped she'd be a . . . a boy."

His words caused her heart to swell with compassion, made her own tears come even harder than before. Poor John. He had loved the fact that Haley Ann was a girl, even welcomed his second daughter with open arms. But truly he'd longed for a son. And there in the hospital room . . . with Haley Ann's body locked in their embrace, he was blaming himself for her death. "No, John, don't do that. This was God's choice; He called her home. Don't you see? It has nothing to do with you wanting a son."

Somehow her words breathed strength into him, and though his tears continued to fall, he became the rock once more, the pillar of strength as they lay her down, fixed the blankets around her still body, and kissed her good-bye.

They made the decision to cremate her, and two weeks later they crept out to the pier together and spread her ashes on a breeze that blew over the lake. She and John cried silent tears that night, and when Abby was unable to say anything, John bowed his head and prayed aloud.

"Lord, we know that You are sovereign. You alone give life and You can call us home, any of us, at any time—" His voice broke, and Abby reached her arm across his shoulders. The gesture gave him the ability to continue. "Take care of our little Haley Ann, please, God. And know that our love for You, for each other, has only been strengthened because of her brief time here, her sudden passing. We dedicate our lives to You again, Lord. And beg You to bless us with more children in the years to come."

After thirty minutes had passed, when the ashes of their infant daughter had settled into the depths of the lake, John wrapped his arms around Abby and whispered words she would never forget in a million years.

"She will always be a part of us, Abby. Right here. Whenever we take the time to stop and remember."

After losing Haley Ann, the bond between Abby and John seemed stronger than ever before. Friends and family offered condolences and words of comfort, but the only real peace, the only healing to be had, was found in each other's presence. They were best friends who had survived a devastating blow and come out stronger on the other side.

Because of their faith, yes. But because of each other, most of all. They needed no words, no explanations, only the way it felt to stand at the edge of the pier, hand in hand, and look out across the lake. It was a loss that seemed possible only because each had the other. As if after losing Haley Ann they could survive anything life handed them so long as they were together.

Abby drew a deep breath that pulled her from the memory as she allowed the winter air to fill her lungs, washing away the sadness. She wiped her wet cheeks and remembered something else.

Haley Ann's death had been only the beginning.

Three months later a tornado ranking four on the Fujita scale ripped through Marion, missing the Reynoldses' house but killing 10 people and injuring 181 others. The Southridge High kicker—a lighthearted young boy responsible for a majority of locker room pranks—was among the dead, along with one of John's coworkers, a biology teacher with a wife and two young children.

As with losing Haley Ann, John and Abby needed no words that afternoon when the storm had passed. They left Nicole with the neighbor again, rolled up their sleeves, and worked side by side helping bandage victims in the temporary hospital ward set up in the Southridge gymnasium. Again that night they drew strength from each other, finding that together they could handle the unimaginable. In the wee hours of the morning, John drifted off to a private alcove, rested his head against a brick wall, and finally allowed the tears. Abby was instinctively at his side, covering his back with her body, telling him in a way that needed no words that she was there, she understood.

It was no wonder they so greatly appreciated their vacation that summer, celebrating life in the aftermath of all they'd lost. And neither of them was surprised when Abby learned early that fall that she was pregnant again.

Beauty from ashes, just like Scripture promised.

When Kade was born in April 1983, they figured that maybe, just maybe, the trials of life were behind them. Kade was their proof that life goes on, that regardless of the future, each day was precious all by itself. Nicole was three that spring, and though she still occasionally mentioned Haley Ann, her new brother quickly filled the empty places for them all.

"They'll be best friends one day, Abby; I can feel it." John had made the statement while they huddled together in the family room not long after Kade came home from the hospital. Abby appreciated the way John projected Kade's life, assuming that their son's days would not be cut short the way his sister's had.

And in the end John was right. A year later they celebrated Kade's birthday, relieved and grateful beyond words that this baby had never stopped breathing in his sleep.

"We're survivors, John, you and me." Abby had uttered the words against his chest while he held her close on the pier one evening a few weeks later. Summer had seemed to come early that year; already there were crickets singing in the background.

"The music never changes . . ." John stared wistfully out at the lake. "But it's up to us to keep dancing." Then he met her gaze, and she knew she would never feel connected to anyone the way she did with him. He was a jock, a football coach given to short sentences and barked commands, but she knew another side of him, the man who could look straight into her soul. He held her gaze. "Dance with me, Abby. Don't ever stop dancing."

Abby blinked and felt the memory fade into the winter wind. For all the times when John seemed utterly wrapped up in football, for the days and weeks and months when he seemed little more than a gridiron guy with no feelings beyond his drive to win, Abby knew differently. The heart of the man John Reynolds had been was deeper than the lake behind their house, deeper than anything Stan Jacobs might offer in an e-mail.

That was especially true on June 7, 1984.

A sigh escaped Abby, and she knew she could not truly leave the places of the past without revisiting one last memory. Along with the early summer that year came a rash of severe storms that culminated in an outbreak of tornadoes that June 7. Since most of them were developing in Wisconsin and Iowa, Abby had called her father that day, anxious for their safety.

"Everything's fine, honey. We've only had a few in our area, and they've all been small. Besides, your mother's completely out of danger. She's visiting her sister this week."

Abby remembered the surge of relief her father's words had brought. Aunt Lexie lived in Barneveld, Wisconsin, at the far west end of the state. Her father was right. None of the tornadoes that day had been near Barneveld. Abby assured her father she would keep praying and, after tucking Nicole and Kade into bed, she and John watched the news until after ten o'clock.

"Looks like it's easing up," John said. He flipped off the television, and together they turned in for the night. It wasn't until her father called the next morning that she learned the devastating news.

Just before midnight, an F-5 tornado ripped through Barneveld destroying nearly all of the small town. Nine people were killed, nearly two hundred injured. Abby's mother and aunt were among the dead.

"I'm sorry, baby, I never wanted to have to tell you something like that." Her father, longtime football coach and perennial tough guy, wept on the other end. By the end of the day, John, Abby, and the kids were at his side, helping him cope and planning a funeral for Abby's mother.

Looking back now Abby knew there was only one reason why she'd survived that time in her life. God, in all His mercy, had given her John. And with him at her side, she could survive anything. The ferocity of a tornado, the loss of her mother. Even the death of precious Haley Ann. With John there were no words needed. She felt comforted merely by being in his arms, basking in his presence.

The years had brought other hard times, but nothing like the string of tragedies they survived in the early '80s. Abby felt the tears once more and moved closer to the edge of the pier, removed her glove, and bent down so that her fingers connected with the icy water below.

Haley Ann. I miss you, baby.

John's voice echoed on the breeze. *"She will always be a part of us, Abby. Right here. Whenever we take the time to stop and remember . . ."*

John's words faded into the night and silence, icy-cold and terrifying, worked its way through Abby's veins. *What if we aren't a "we" anymore, John? Who will remember Haley Ann when we're just two people, separate and alone?*

She removed her hand from the water and dried it on her parka before slipping it once more into the glove. As she did, she realized how deep and great and overwhelming was the loss of what they shared together. How this pier, this spot where she stood, would not only be the place where Haley Ann's ashes lay, but also the ashes of their love, the burial ground of all they'd been together.

In the tender places of their hearts, the single heart they once shared, Haley Ann still lived. But now . . . without the two of them taking time to remember, everything about her would fade into the cold night.

Haley Ann, baby, we love you. No matter what happens, Mommy and Daddy love you . . .

Tears spilled onto her cheeks, and Abby reached her gloved hand out toward the water again, trying to somehow grasp their tiny daughter and everything they'd lost since then. Everything including each other.

"I can't hear it, John . . ." Her choked, whispered words hung like icicles in the air above her. "The music isn't playing anymore."

She had always known she could survive the darkness because something about being near John gave her strength to go on. But now she was just a woman in her forties with a head full of memories of a little girl that no longer existed. A woman cold and afraid and alone in the night, sitting on a pier by herself where once, a very long time ago, she was loved.

Fourteen

RUNNING WAS GOOD FOR THE SOUL, AT LEAST that's what Coach Reynolds always told his players. But it was a brisk afternoon in early February, and this time John wasn't sure he'd survive the workout. His breathing was hard and labored, as though he were jogging with the stadium bleachers fixed to his back. Even worse, there was an occasional tightening in his chest, much like the feeling he'd had on Super Bowl Sunday . . .

John wasn't really worried; he knew there was nothing wrong with his heart. Not physically, anyway. He was too fit, too careful about what he ate. No, the pains were purely stress-related, the result of being married to one woman while falling in love with another.

He rounded the corner of the Marion High track and considered using this time to pray like he'd done in his younger days, like he'd done for a while even after he stopped going to church.

You wouldn't like much of what I'm thinking about these days, God.

Repent! Flee immorality, My son . . . draw near to Me and I will draw near to you.

The verses rattled around in his heart and drifted off like birds in flight. There was truth in the Bible words; John knew it as surely as he knew his name. But nothing about them applied to his current situation. Nowhere in Scripture was there wisdom for a man who was making promises to a woman other than his wife.

A passage from Proverbs flashed across the screen of his mind. *Avoid the harlot; stay clear of her doorway.*

Ridiculous. John shook his head, trying to clear his mind of the idea. Charlene was a beautiful young woman without a friend in the world. A fun-loving woman who admired everything about him and was willing to wait patiently while he and Abby worked out the details of their divorce.

She was hardly a harlot.

John picked up his pace and in the distance, in the trees that lined the creek adjacent to the school, he saw a hawk hanging in the wind. Bits and pieces from Kade's report on the eagle came to mind and seemed to hit him for the first time.

"The eagle allows the storm to take him to a higher place . . . the eagle finds a rock when he's in trouble and lets the sun cleanse him from any poison. The eagle doesn't flap around like the chickens and crows and sparrows. It waits patiently on the rock for the thermal currents, and only then does it take flight. Not by its own effort, but by the effort of the wind beneath its wings."

Again the analogies nearly screamed at him. With Christ, he soared like an eagle, not by his efforts but by the strength of the Holy Spirit. On his own . . . well, he was barely more than a chicken. Flapping and scuffling about in the dirt and never getting off the ground.

I want to be an eagle again, Lord. Show me how. When this mess is behind me, help me be the man for Charlene that I wasn't able to be for Abby.

Stay clear of the harlot, My son.

It wasn't the answer John wanted and he shifted his gaze. Forget about the eagle. If he was doomed to the chicken pen, at least he'd be a happy chicken. The idea of fighting with Abby all his life was unimaginable. Unthinkable. Divorce was the only option left, even it meant he might never soar again. Besides, his flying days with Abby were long over. At this point they needed separate chicken coops if they were going to survive.

Together they were pecking each other to death.

John rounded another corner, appreciating the way the fresh air cooled his sweaty skin. In summer the track would be busy with people all day long. But now, months before spring, it was often just him. He cleared his mind and let his thoughts wander.

Oddly enough, the person he missed most these days wasn't Abby, but his father, Sam Reynolds. Invincible both on the field and in his faith. John drew a deep breath and kept running. *Dad, if only you were still alive, I know you could make sense of all that's happened.*

His father had been there through the tragedies of losing Haley Ann and Abby's mother in the early '80s. And again in '85 and '86 when Marion High opened and he left Southridge for the job as the Eagles' head football coach. There were days when John hadn't thought he'd survive the trials of building a program from the ground up. But his father had always been there, ready with words of wisdom, willing to lend balance to a life that seemed out of control.

Thoughts of eagles and harlots and an angry God faded as John drifted back to his first seasons as head coach at Marion —but instead of memories of his father, there was image after image of the one who had been there in an even more tangible way.

Abby.

Football reigned in Southern Illinois, where the magnetic pull of the pigskin was, for most people, greater than any other. The idea of Southridge's successful coaching staff giving up their top assistant to head the brand-new program at Marion High was at first welcomed by the townspeople. Especially since many of them still remembered him as Michigan's Miracle Man, the quarterback who could do no wrong. But when the varsity team went 0-11 its first season, a rumbling of community voices made their feelings known. Editorials appeared in the local paper questioning whether a young assistant with no head-coaching experience was the right choice for the prized new program at Marion.

The long-ago voices of discontent still rang clear in John's mind. The school board had seen to it that the students at Marion had the best of everything: science labs, computer rooms, and teachers. On top of that, the school had a half-million-dollar stadium; it was better than any in the state. Why, then—the editorials asked—had the school district hired the first guy looking for a coaching job? Why not search the state for a man who could make Marion High the winner it deserved to be? Forget this building-a-program business. The Eagle parents and boosters wanted a winning tradition. Now. Not next year or the year after.

The frustration of that season and the one that followed burned in John's gut. Didn't they know it took time to develop tradition? Couldn't they see that the moment the doors opened at Marion, every boy who didn't have a chance of playing varsity at Southridge transferred to the new school?

Up front John had predicted it would take every bit of three years to acquire talent that could match up with that at Southridge. He couldn't worry about the fact that the brand-new booster club and overanxious parents at Marion wanted results overnight—especially in games against the now rival Southridge Chieftains. He was only human, after all.

One day midsummer between his first two seasons, Abby found him at practice and waited patiently until the last player and coach had left the field. He'd been alone on the bench, unaware of her presence, when she came up behind him and eased her arms around his shoulders. "I got a baby-sitter," she whispered in his ear. "Let's take a walk."

They spent an hour strolling the track—the very one he was running on now—and in that time she told him a dozen different ways that he was a gifted coach. "The parents don't know a thing about play calling or creating a defense. They have no idea what type of dedicated athletes you need in order to compete with Southridge."

He listened, hanging on to every word. It wasn't so much that she shared any deep revelations that evening, but as she spoke he realized he'd forgotten the truth. He'd allowed the criticism of the community to tear at his confidence and heap upon him the pressure to make a better showing that fall than the previous one.

At the end of their walk, she faced him, brushing a section of hair off his forehead. "Everyone in town, everyone in the world for that matter, might overlook your talent as a coach, John Reynolds." She leaned into him, kissing him on the mouth in a promising way. "But I never will. What you have out there—" she waved her hand toward the field—"is nothing short of magic. A gift from God. Don't ever let anyone convince you otherwise."

Abby's pep talk restored his belief in himself and carried him through the off-season and into fall practice. But his second year proved to be even more disastrous than his first. Midway through the season they played Southridge and came up on the wrong end of a 48-0 beating.

The next day's headlines read "Marion High's Only Chance— Dump Reynolds?" In the article, the press blamed him for passing too much, not knowing his personnel, and not having his team prepared.

"You're playing with Southridge's bench, for goodness sake," Abby cried when she saw the newspaper. "None of your kids would have made the team if they'd stayed at Southridge. What do they want?"

It got worse before it got better. By the end of the season John found an anonymous typed note in his box warning him that the parents were circulating a petition to have him fired. Another note, signed by the overbearing father of one of the players, said, "I've never seen a more worthless coach than you, Reynolds. You might be a nice guy, but you're hopeless out on the playing field."

John's father offered advice that had helped him in the banking business: "There will always be naysayers, son. The key is to listen to God's calling. If you're doing that, then everyone else's opinion amounts to little more than hot air."

John tried to keep his focus, tried to remember the words of wisdom from Abby and his father, but the season became unbearable as the weeks wore on. One night, after another lopsided loss, John stayed in the locker room an hour later than usual. The game had been a disaster, his players were bickering, and even his assistant coaches had seemed to disagree with the plays he called. Now that they were all gone, he dropped to his knees and gave his coaching game to the Lord, begging God to show him a way out. At the end of that time, he felt there was only one option: quit. Step down and let someone else give the people of Marion the winning program they wanted.

It was after eleven o'clock when he locked up and walked out onto the field that night, but regardless of the late hour, Abby was there, waiting for him like she did after every game.

"Honey, I'm sorry. You didn't have to wait." He took her in his arms, rocked by how good it felt to be held and loved and supported on a night when it seemed the whole world had been against him.

"I'd wait a lifetime for you, John Reynolds. Remember?" Her voice was soothing, a balm to his wounded spirit. "I'm the girl who's loved you since I was ten years old."

He pulled away and looked deep into her eyes. "I'm turning in my resignation tomorrow."

John remembered the anger that flared in Abby's eyes. *"What?"* She backed up several feet and faced him squarely. "You are *not* turning in your resignation." She paced nervously, her mouth open, eyes locked on his. "You can't do it. God brought you here to do a job. You can't let those . . . those ignorant parents push you out of the very thing you were created to do. I won't let you quit. Think about the hours of . . ."

She had gone on that way for five minutes until finally she ran out of words.

"That's my Abby, shy and reserved." He tousled her hair and smiled sadly. "I still think it's time. They want someone else. Let 'em have their way."

Abby's eyes had filled with angry tears. "Those people are wrong, John. A couple of them are nothing more than frustrated, bitter old men who never amounted to anything in life. My guess is they couldn't play sports as kids and they can't coach sports as adults. So what do they do? They pretend to coach from the stands, making their sons and people like you miserable in the process." She paused and John remembered the sincerity in her voice. "They want you to quit, John. Can't you see that? They don't know the first thing about coaching, but still they've spearheaded this . . . this entire community into a frenzy to have you fired." She clenched her fists and swung at the air. "Don't let those crazy parents win like that, John. You have a gift; I've seen it. Besides, you're forgetting the first rule of being a Christian."

John could hear himself silently agreeing with her on every count. "What rule is that?" He moved closer to her, tracing his finger along her cheekbone, loving her for the way she believed in him.

She stared deep into his eyes, her voice softer than before. "The enemy doubles his efforts when a breakthrough is right around the corner." Leaning up, she kissed him long and slow before pulling back. "Don't give up, John. Please."

Indeed, the enemy attacks had doubled that year. Both he and Abby received angry, anonymous letters—some even sent to their home address. "Why do they hate us?" she had cried that afternoon, ripping one of the letters into a hundred pieces.

"They don't hate you; they hate me. Don't you get it, Abby? If they can hurt us bad enough, then maybe they'll get their way and I'll step down."

But every time he was tempted to scrap his efforts, Abby helped change his mind. In those early years she'd always known just what to say or do when he was hurting or tired or lonely for her touch. It was an art that had taken years to perfect.

He remembered how quickly the team's atmosphere had changed once that second season was behind him. That summer he could hardly wait for fall and the chance to show the town of Marion the fruits of his hard work. John hadn't thought about that summer for years . . . but it felt right to do so now as though by drifting back in time he might find some of the strength and reason and guidance that was missing in his life.

He remembered one hot afternoon when training had been going better than ever, and he'd called his dad to talk shop.

"Sounds like you're doing everything right, son." It was a ritual, talking football father to son: a part of life John had known would always be there, the same way winter followed fall. "What're your chances?"

"This is the year, Dad," he'd been quick to answer, the misery of the previous season all but forgotten. "You gotta get down here and see these guys. They're bigger than most college players."

"Just as long as I'm there when they hand you the state trophy." His dad chuckled confidently on the other end. "That's a moment I wouldn't miss for the world."

"It may not be this year, but it'll happen, Dad. You heard it here first."

The news that rocked his world came the next day. He was in the weightroom with temperatures sweltering outside at just under a hundred and the humidity not far behind. Custodians rarely ran the air conditioner in summer and John and the other coaches didn't complain. It was good for the guys to work out in a hot gym. Made them tough, ready for competition.

John was going over a player's routine, making sure the young athlete's training regimen was increasing on schedule, when Abby appeared at the door. A darkness in her eyes told him two things. First, the news was not good; second, whatever it was they would get through it together. The way they'd gotten through all the hard times they'd faced.

Without words, she used her eyes to suggest that the conversation they were about to have should take place behind closed doors. John excused himself from the player, and in seconds he and Abby were alone, face to face.

"What is it?" His heart was thudding so loud he wondered if

Abby could hear it, too. "Are the kids okay?" After losing Haley Ann he never assumed that his children would be alive and well at the end of the day just because they'd appeared that way at the breakfast table.

He held his breath while Abby nodded. "The kids are fine. It's your dad." She moved closer, placing her hands on his shoulders. "Your mother just called. He had a heart attack this morning. Oh, honey . . . he didn't make it." The news cut through him like a hot knife, but before he had time to react, he noticed tears in her eyes. It was her loss, too. Feeling as though his heart were in his shoes, he circled his arms around her, strangely comforted by that fact.

For twenty minutes she stayed there with him, holding him, assuring him that his father was with the Lord, in a better place. Promising him that the few tears that slid down his cheeks were okay, even there in the Marion High weightroom. When the news had sunk in, she left him alone and told the other coach on duty that John needed privacy, that his father and mentor had died that morning.

When John was ready to leave, there were no students hanging around, no well-meaning teachers or staff members wondering what had happened. Abby had seen to that.

He thought back now and realized how different the day might have gone. Abby could have left a "call home" message with the secretary or waited until after dinner to tell him. Instead she'd gone the extra mile, bore the brunt of the bad news, forced herself to grieve later, and immediately found a way to be with him.

He tried to picture Charlene in that situation . . . but it was impossible.

Charlene had never known his father, never loved him or respected him or looked forward to his calls. Charlene hadn't borne his father's grandchildren or lived with the knowledge that her father and John's were best friends as far back as the beginning of time.

What could Charlene possibly have said that would have touched him the way Abby's presence had that afternoon?

It's a new day, Reynolds. Give the girl a break. You'll make memories with her in time.

The thought should have comforted him, but instead he felt the oddest chill run down his spine. He shook off the feeling and remembered Abby again—Abby whose father lay ill in a nursing home . . . a man who had been his father's best friend.

"I need to see him, talk to him."

John whispered the words and slowed his pace. He'd logged in five miles that day, but the relaxing sense of euphoria that usually accompanied his workouts was missing. In its place was a sense of confusion, uncertainty.

In the end, of course, the state title had come. Less than six months after his father's death, the Marion Eagles finished their season undefeated. It was as though the terrible seasons in the mideighties were only a bad dream, for there John stood, high on the winner's platform, accepting a trophy that was half the size of six-year-old Kade.

John remembered the moment like it was yesterday. He leaned over, stretching the muscles in his legs as he closed his eyes. Everything about that night was as sweet now as it had been back then. When it was his turn to speak, his message was simple. "I wanna thank God for giving me a wife who never once stopped supporting me." He gazed into the stands, knowing she was there somewhere, crying no doubt, cherishing the moment as deeply as he was. "I love you, Abby. I wouldn't be here without you." Then he raised the trophy into the night sky and stared up toward heaven. "This is for you, Dad!"

The memory faded. John stood up, wiped his brow, and headed for the car. How could he spend the rest of his life with Charlene, a woman who'd never met his father? A woman who hadn't ridden out the Marion tornado with him, or stood beside him while the ashes of his baby daughter danced in the wind and settled across the lake he loved best. A woman who was in love with a man that Abby Reynolds helped create.

If there's another way, God, show me . . .

The silence told him there was none. They were down three touchdowns with less than a minute to play. It was simply too late in the game. But even though that was true, John couldn't deny what he'd finally come to realize: taking up with Charlene would be like allowing a part of himself to die.

The part that still belonged—would always belong—to a blonde, blue-eyed pixie who had captured his heart on the sandy shores of Lake Geneva the summer he was just seventeen.

Fifteen

THE IDEA OF A COUPLES' WEDDING SHOWER had been Matt's. He reasoned that since Abby Reynolds was daughter of the famous Coach John Reynolds, she was very nearly royalty—at least by Marion's standards. So certainly there ought to be at least a barbecue to celebrate the fact that she was getting married.

Abby wasn't about to disagree since the whole reason they'd postponed telling the kids about their divorce was to give Nicole this season of happiness.

"Absolutely!" She'd looked expectantly at Nicole the moment Matt brought it up. "We could invite half the town of Marion."

Nicole's eyes had sparkled at the thought, and Abby's heart ached for her. Regardless of how happy these six months were, they would never make up for the hurt she and John were about to cause Nicole and the boys.

"Can we really, Mom? You wouldn't mind?"

"Not at all, honey. Invite whoever you want."

"Sort of like a couples' wedding shower." Nicole nudged Matt. "Like your friend Steve had last year, remember?"

"Right. Something like this can take the place of another wedding shower later on." He grinned at Nicole, teasing her.

"Now wait a minute—" Nicole poked him harder this time, giggling—"I never said anything about that."

Abby watched them. *They look like us twenty-two years ago, Lord. Love does not fail . . . love never ends, My daughter.*

The words were dim at best, but they were there all the same. A constant reminder of how she and John had missed the mark.

Nicole cast a smile at her mother. "I can't help it if my friends throw me an all-girls' shower later on, right, Mom?"

With that the idea had taken root. They invited John's coaching staff and a dozen of Nicole's longtime friends, girls she had cheered with at Marion High and with whom she still kept in close contact. Matt asked several of his law school buddies, and Nicole insisted on inviting three families who had been closer than relatives as far back as she could remember.

John agreed to the party, but privately he didn't like the idea from the beginning. "It's hard enough pretending around the kids," he told Abby one evening. "Let alone with the world watching us."

Abby felt hatred bubbling to the surface again. "Don't talk to me about pretending. I'm not the one parading around with a lover on my arm." She disappeared into her office before he could return fire.

They got along best when they avoided each other, and in the days that led up to the party, they managed to do just that. John spent more time working out or grading papers at school, and she kept busy helping Nicole make guestlists and pick out wedding decorations. Afternoons were spent with Sean, hauling him to indoor soccer games and baseball practice and lap swimming at the club.

When Abby was absolutely forced to be home with John, she found reasons to be in her office. And in that way they survived the first two months.

It was pouring rain the evening of Nicole's and Matt's party, and Abby glanced at the table. Cheese and crackers, fruit and cookies, everything was in order. Even the wrapped family Bible from John and her.

A Bible was the standard Reynolds family wedding gift, and even though John had argued with her about buying it, Abby had decided on a leather copy engraved with the couple's names.

"That way Nicole can always look at the Bible and remember how we lied to her during her engagement." John had tossed out the comment from where he sat in the living room, flipping between ESPN and Fox Sports. "Great gift idea."

"Maybe if we'd read ours a little more often we wouldn't be in this mess."

The barbs between them were getting more frequent, and Abby had no idea how they were going to survive until July. She laid a stack of decorated napkins on the kitchen table. It was no wonder John was more irritable than before. *He wants to be with Charlene, not us.* The thought pierced Abby's heart, and she pushed it away. This was Nicole's and Matt's day, and she'd promised herself she wouldn't wallow in pity for herself.

Just get through it, Abby. Keep smiling and get through it.

John had dreaded this day since he'd first heard about it. It was one thing to honor Nicole's season of happiness. But this . . . this couples' shower idea was a joke. Let someone else throw them a party.

The doorbell rang, and John rose to greet the guests, helping them with their raincoats and stashing umbrellas in the entryway. At this point he had no choice but to put on a smile, go along with the plan, and pray he could steer clear of Abby for the next five hours.

Nicole's friends arrived first, but within a half-hour the house was full of dozens of familiar faces. As was usually the case when coaches gathered together, the Marion Eagles staff congregated in the living room not far from the television and a sports news program. But with thunder clapping outside and the banter of so many other people in the room, the coaches finally gave up and turned off the set.

John studied his buddies, guys he'd been with through long hours of training and planning and celebrating. Joe and Sal and Kenny and Bob. The best friends a man could ever hope to have. Maybe if he could keep his thoughts on football, the night would fly by and no one would notice anything different between Abby and him.

"How long's it been, guys, the five of us?" John leaned back in his easy chair, feet up, grinning at the men around him.

Joe stroked his chin and cocked his head. "You know I was just asking Alice that the other day." He gazed toward the ceiling in deep concentration. "The five of us weren't together until 1987, right?"

"Yeah, I waited until Rod Moore's kid graduated before applying." Kenny laughed hard at his own joke and patted his round stomach. "There's only so much the old ticker can take."

"I think that was it, 1987. First year we were all Eagles." John shook his head. "So it's been fourteen years. Where in the world did the time go?"

"Think about it . . . all the highs and lows." Bob grinned, his eyes glistening with a million memories. "That first state title . . . Tell ya what, there's never been nothing like it except this last one, watching you and Kade. Now that was something else."

Kenny chuckled softly and slapped John on the knee. "Yeah, the Reynolds family's always been something else. I mean, really, how many of us have wished over the years we had a marriage like John and Abby's?"

"Yeah, Abby's a kick all right. I wish my wife understood the commitment to coaching like Abby does." Bob tossed a pretzel at John and winked at him. "She's a one-in-a-million, John. If you hadn't kept her I woulda married her myself."

A tingling sensation worked its way from John's scalp down his spine. Did everyone have to put his marriage to Abby on a pedestal?

Couldn't they talk about something else? He took small, steady breaths and tried to look natural.

Bob was still going on about Abby's many merits. "And just so you know, John, Kenny's next in line after me, right, Ken?"

Kenny grinned and nodded once for emphasis. "She's a keeper."

Bob and Kenny were both divorced, and Sal had never been married. Only Joe had a wife at home, and from everything John knew they were happy together. He racked his brain trying to think of something else to talk about. "We've had our ups and downs like anyone else."

Joe laughed out loud. "That's right, like the time Abby tumbled down the stairs at Sea World." He looked at each of the faces around him. "Remember, guys?" He gestured his hand in a downward sliding motion. "Those must have been the 'down' moments."

Despite himself John smiled at the memory. He closed his eyes and shook his head slowly, still embarrassed for Abby after all these years.

"Come on, John, tell us again." Kenny leaned forward and took a swig of ice tea. "It's been a while since we've had a good laugh at Abby's expense. Besides Sal's never heard the Sea World story, have you, Sal?"

"No, I think I missed that one."

"Yeah, well we used to get stories all the time." Joe grabbed another handful of chips and waited expectantly. "You know . . . Abby's latest driving story, Abby's latest shopping story, Abby's latest run-in with the neighbors . . ."

Joe's comment struck John like a blow. When had he stopped talking about Abby with his coaches?

"Come on, John." Joe stuffed several chips in his mouth. "Wasn't she carrying an ice-cream cone or something?"

The memory became clear and vivid. Sean had been something of a surprise baby, born the fall of 1990. It was the following spring and they'd taken a drive to Ohio to visit Sea World. Nicole was ten that year and Kade, seven. The trip was a comedy of errors from the beginning.

They'd decided ahead of time that John would carry Sean in a baby carrier and Abby would tote the family's sweaters and belongings in a backpack. John glanced around the room and saw that the guys were waiting expectantly for a story. He grabbed a napkin and wiped his hands. "All right, all right. Most of you know the story. We were at the park, and Abby wanted to watch the sea lion show."

"Not the dolphins or whales, but the sea lions, right, Coach?" Joe was great for adding color whenever John told a story.

"Had to get to the sea lions . . . before we could do anything else." John hesitated for effect. "Anyway, we've got five minutes before the show starts and we see this ice-cream stand right next to the sea lion stadium. It's a hot day, the kids are hungry, so Abby decides why not? Let's get the kids cones before the show. That way they can eat them inside."

"Sounds like a plan." Joe had heard the story several times before and he knew what was coming. He leaned back in his seat and grinned.

"Right, so we get to the front of the line and order three cones. There were two teenagers working the booth so we thought we had a pretty good chance of getting waited on. But the guys just looked at each other real slow, then looked back at us, and back to each other again. 'Ice-cream cones?' the one guy says."

"These were linemen, no doubt." Joe elbowed Kenny in the gut. Kenny had been a lineman years earlier and it was his specialty as a coach.

"Hey, don't pick on us linemen. We get a little goofy around ice cream."

"Yeah, well these guys were at least one crayon short of a box because they spent the next several minutes deciding between themselves whether we had actually ordered three cones." John was smiling now, enjoying the story, caught up in the memory of that summer a decade ago. "The whole time Abby's glancing at her watch and saying things like, 'I can't miss the sea lion show, John. We've got to get these people to hurry.' So I'm like, 'Yes, dear, I'm doing my best.' Because of course there was nothing I could do to make them move faster. So then—I'm absolutely serious here—the one guy goes to the ice-cream machine, takes a cone, and pulls the lever. The ice cream piles higher and higher until it flops over onto the floor. Without missing a beat the guy stares at the mess, tosses the cone in the trash, and takes down another empty cone."

"Ended up being about three for seven, isn't that right, John?" Joe chuckled at the thought. "Forget the fact that the line's out past the sea lion stadium now."

"Right. So finally we have the three cones, and Abby realizes we need napkins. The guys point to a service counter thirty yards away and Abby takes off sprinting. I mean, Abby was quite an athlete in her day. Track, tennis. Even now she could take most of you guys in a footrace. But that day her footwork wasn't as smooth as it might have been and, with three yards to go, the ice cream toppled from the cone she was holding and landed splat on her foot."

Joe was laughing harder now, rocking slightly in his chair. "Eased right into her nice shoes. Can you see it, guys? Abby Reynolds? Dressed just so, with soft chocolate ice cream melting between her pretty toes?"

John began laughing at the picture. "People were staring at her, wondering why this woman had run so hard and fast with an ice cream cone in the first place. And there she was, a shoe full of ice cream, empty cone in her hand, the rest of us watching from the other side of the rest area and the sea lion show just about to start. So Abby grabs a stack of napkins, wipes the ice cream out of her shoe, and sticks her foot back inside."

Kenny grimaced at the thought, and Sal began laughing so hard he had to set his drink down. "What about the sea lions?"

"So she runs back to the ice-cream booth, cuts in line, and tells the guy she needs another cone, only this time put it in a bowl. The guy does it, and now the music is playing for the sea lion show. 'Come on, let's get seats,' she tells the rest of us. And she's off . . ."

"Leading the way like a woman at a Nordstrom sale." Joe's face was red from trying to contain himself.

"We followed right behind, weaving our way through the crowd, determined to get seats before the first sea lion took the stage." John took a breath and chuckled harder at the images in his head. "So there we are at the top of the stadium, and Abby spots a row halfway down the stairs. 'Follow me,' she says. And those were her last words. The stairs . . ." he tried to catch his breath and realized how good it felt. Sitting here with his friends, barely able to breathe for the laughter and the way Abby had looked that summer afternoon. "The stairs were kind of like—" he gestured—"big, small, big, small. No idea why, that's just the way they were. But Abby must've only seen one size because the first step went just fine, but the moment she tried to get her foot to land on that second step, she wound up stepping on nothing but air and she began to tumble."

All the men were laughing now, putting down their food, bent over, struggling for air. John found his voice and despite the way his body shook he continued the story. "Not just any tumble, mind you. The backpack rode up onto the back of her neck and . . . and it pushed her down further and further . . ."

"She looked like—" Joe's voice was shrill from the lack of oxygen—"she looked like a turtle, right, John? Sliding down the stairs, one after another . . . the backpack . . . on her head."

"Right." John drew a deep breath and tried to control himself. "Her head was peeking out just a little from the backpack and finally . . . finally a man put his hand out and stopped her."

Kenny was a big man, and when he laughed as hard as he was now, he began sounding like a sea lion himself. The realization made John chuckle even harder than before. Between breaths he was able to finish the story. "Of course the whole . . . the whole stadium was full of people and the show had already . . . started." He inhaled sharply. "At first the people thought it was part of the act . . ."

"A few women started clapping." Joe could still barely get the words out for the laughter that shook his body. "She actually stopped the show. Even the sea lions waited to see what was going to happen."

John nodded, the memory so funny he was starting to giggle like a girl. Abby had looked so pathetic. "Anyway, this man reaches out and stops her and . . . trying to look casual . . . she gets up all quick and waves at the people. Then she turns around and looks at me, and that's when I see the ice cream . . ."

"The bowl of ice cream she'd been holding." Joe was almost bent in half now, and the other guys were laughing so loud they were attracting the attention of everyone in the room. "Remember, the one she'd lost down her shoe the first time!"

"So there she is, knees and elbows all skinned and bleeding, back-pack caught up in her hair and ice cream smeared down the entire front of her shirt."

Sal hooted out loud. "I woulda bought tickets to that all right. Little Miss Perfectly Dressed Coach's Wife looking like that . . . with a whole stadium of people watching."

"We sat down and the show started up again." John caught his breath and forced himself to calm down. "She didn't say a word until the show was over, then she turned to me and said, 'Okay, how'd that look?' And I absolutely lost it."

"Somewhere someone probably got themselves a ten-thousand-dollar video moment." Joe slapped his own knee this time, and the group laughed hard again.

"Oooooeeee." John shook his head and exhaled long and hard. "That was something else all right."

Joe wiped a tear from his eyes. "I haven't laughed that hard in years." He shook his head. "And the thing about it is, to this day, Abby can laugh at it, too."

Kenny got control of himself. "Yeah, that's the best thing about Abby. She doesn't take herself too seriously."

"Where is she, anyway? She should have been out here to tell us how it felt." Sal exhaled, still trying to catch his breath as he looked around the room.

A stabbing feeling cut into John's gut and erased all the silliness of a moment earlier. But before he could answer, Nicole walked up and grinned at them. "Okay, what's all the commotion over here?"

Joe shoved John in the shoulder. "Your dad was telling us about the Sea World trip . . . you know, the actual 'trip.' When your mom made a splash at the sea lion show."

"Yeah, good thing Sean was on Dad's back, huh?" Nicole giggled and shook her head. "Poor Mom, we'll be telling that story until she's old and gray. At least she wasn't hurt."

Nicole wandered back across the room to her group of friends, and the guys began talking all at once. John felt suddenly sick to his stomach, Nicole's words punched around at his insides like perfectly delivered blows.

"Until she's old and gray . . . until she's old and gray."

The wife of his youth, his best friend and lifelong companion, would not grow old and gray with him. No, she would be married to someone else by then, spending the rest of her life with another man. In fact, there would be no stories about Abby in the years to come, no regaling the crowd with stories of how she'd talked herself out of a speeding ticket or burned the sweet potatoes on Thanksgiving Day. If he was honest with himself, the story he'd just told was probably the last he'd ever tell about his precious Abby girl. Once they were divorced, what sense would it make to sit around with the guys recalling the good times with Abby, the funny moments that no one in their family would ever forget.

And Charlene . . . well, John was fairly sure she wouldn't see the humor in their family memories anyway.

Abby managed to spend the first hour of the party in the kitchen, chatting with a number of Nicole's friends as they passed through. Dad had wanted to join them at the house but his nurses said the excitement would be too much for him. Instead Nicole and Matt had promised him a visit after church the next day. Abby stared out the window at

Matt and his buddies anchored around a picnic table on the covered back porch. She felt the corners of her lips lift slightly. She liked Matt. He was strong and intelligent. There was a gentleness about him when he was with Nicole that told Abby he'd make a wonderful father. *I pray it lasts. Don't ever let the years get away from you, Matt . . .*

It was the first weekend in March, and though spring hadn't officially arrived, the thunderstorm that was blowing over assured them it was coming.

It won't be long now. Four months and the charade will be over.

She was alone in the kitchen freshening up the food platters when she heard John and his friends laughing in the family room. At first the sound made Abby angry. *He's sounding a bit too happy out there, God. Isn't he hurting even a little?*

Easing herself closer to the door she caught pieces of the conversation. *Sea lion show . . . halfway down the stairs . . . tumbling . . . like a turtle.*

They were talking about the Sea World trip some ten years ago. By herself with no one to fool, tears filled Abby's eyes as a smile played on her lips. How long had it been since they'd laughed together over that story? And why was John telling it now?

She moved away, leaning against the refrigerator, eyes closed, heart thudding against her ribs. *God, how can we do this to each other? Why don't I go out there and laugh with him, sit with him. Love him again?*

Love never fails, daughter. Love never ends.

Well, it has for us, so now what, Lord? Where do we go from here?

It had been months, years even, since she'd held a discussion with God, allowed His thoughts to permeate her own, and given herself permission to respond. But now, tonight, with a house full of people she loved more than any in the world, she was desperate for answers.

I'm waiting, God. Tell me. What are we supposed to do next? I need real help here, Lord.

Silence.

Abby hesitated a beat, then wiped her tears. Fine. If God wasn't going to talk to her she'd just have to make her way alone. It wouldn't be the first time. For all intents and purposes, she'd been alone since the day Charlene Denton set her sights on John.

Let he who is without sin cast the first—

That's not the answer I want . . . Abby spun around and forced herself to think of something else. She had guests to tend to, after all. This was no time to be wading knee-deep in guilt, not while everyone else was having a good time. John was the one to blame for the mess they were in, and she wouldn't let anyone tell her differently.

Not even God Himself.

The last of the guests were gone, and Nicole was stacking their opened gifts neatly in the middle of the coffee table. The boys and Matt were in Kade's room playing Nintendo, and Dad had turned in early. Only Mom was awake, but after finishing the dishes she'd excused herself to the office to finish up an article.

The party had been a huge success, giving Nicole and Matt time with their closest friends and family. There had been laughter and shared memories and good times for everyone until well after ten o'clock. But Nicole couldn't shake the feeling that something was wrong.

Deeply wrong.

She sat on the edge of the coffee table and slipped one leg over the other. *God, what is it? What am I feeling?*

The image of her parents came to mind, and she realized she hadn't seen them together once during the evening. *Is everything okay between them, Lord? Are they in some kind of trouble?*

Pray, daughter. The prayer of a righteous one is powerful and effective.

The answer was swift and almost audible. God wanted her to pray—but for her parents? Why on earth would they need prayer? Were they having money troubles, maybe? Was the wedding costing them more than they could afford?

Oh, Lord, my heart feels troubled beyond words. Father, be with my parents and bring them to a place of togetherness. I'm afraid . . . I didn't see them near each other tonight and . . . well, maybe I'm just looking too hard, but I get the strongest feeling something's wrong. Maybe money or something. I don't know. Please, Father, surround them both with Your angels and protect them from the evil one and his terrible schemes. Where there's stress, calm them; where there's misunderstanding, clear it up. And use me, Lord, however You might, to help make things right. If they're wrong, that is.

She finished her prayer and studied the closed office door. Without hesitating she stood and made her way across the room, knocking once before turning the handle and easing herself inside. "Whatcha doing?"

Her mother looked up quickly, then stared briefly at the computer screen and clicked twice.

"Good-bye." The computer announced.

"I was . . . just checking my e-mail." Her mother smiled in a way that seemed a little too happy and turned her chair so that she faced Nicole.

Why did she look so nervous? "Hey, Mom . . . is everything okay? With you and Dad, I mean?" Nicole studied her mother, looking for signs that things might actually be worse than she imagined. Like maybe they were in a fight or something. In all her years growing up, Nicole could remember maybe three times when her parents had fought. Always it had been the most unnerving feeling she'd ever encountered. Her parents were like two rocks, the people everyone looked to when they wanted to know how a marriage was supposed to work.

The last time her parents had even raised their voices at each other was years ago, wasn't it? Nicole waited for her mother's response, aware that her own fingers were trembling.

"Yes, of course. Everything's great." Her mother angled her head, her features knotted up curiously. "What made you ask, sweetheart?"

Nicole swallowed hard, not sure if she should voice her concerns. "I didn't see you guys together all night, you know? It seemed kinda strange."

Her mother laughed once. "Honey, there were so many people here. Every time I started out to join your father, someone else came in to talk or brought me another food tray to fill. The night got away from us, that's all."

A warm feeling came over Nicole, and her whole body relaxed. It had just been her imagination after all.

The prayer of a righteous one is powerful and effective. Pray, daughter. Pray.

An alarm sounded again in Nicole's heart. Why was the Lord giving her thoughts like that if everything was okay? She cleared her mind and stared hard at her mother. "You're telling me the truth, right, Mom? This isn't about money or anything? The last thing I want to do is make things hard on you and Daddy."

Abby uttered a quiet chuckle. "Sweetheart, when your Grandpa Reynolds passed away he left us plenty of money. Believe me, getting you married is not causing us any financial worries at all."

Nicole leaned her weight on one hip and surveyed her mother's face. "Honest? Everything's okay?"

A flash of something shadowy and dark crossed her mother's eyes, then just as quickly disappeared. "I told you, honey. Everything's fine."

Nicole reached out and took hold of her mother's fingers. "Come on, I wanna show you the goods."

Her mom stood up slowly and stretched. "I looked at them once already, Nick."

"I know, but I've got it all organized. You know, blenders and toasters on one side of the table, sentimental gifts on the other side."

"Oh, all right." Mom smiled and hugged her as they walked into the living room side by side. "Lead the way."

They were only partway there when Nicole stopped and held her mother tighter. "Thanks for the Bible, Mom." She pulled away, looking deep into her mother's eyes once more. "It's my favorite gift of all."

"Good. Keep it that way and you and Matt will spend the next fifty years in love. Mark my words, honey."

Nicole smiled and linked elbows with her mother, moving happily beside her as they found the gifts in the center of the family room. They studied each item and chatted about the party and the coming wedding, Nicole knew that the prompting she'd felt from the Lord to pray for her parents was a good thing. Even the strongest couples needed prayer. But Mom and Dad were fine. Nicole felt certain that her strange feelings of concern were nothing more than an overactive imagination.

That and a good case of engagement anxiety.

Sixteen

DENNY CONLEY WAS TOO NEW AT THIS CHRISTIAN thing to know where else to go. He only knew he had a lot on his mind, and only one Person he wanted to share it with. Besides, taking his troubles to the Lord late at night like this had become something of a routine.

Denny knew one thing for sure: it beat the old routine, hopping from bar to bar and wondering every morning how in the world he'd made it home.

The church was small, not like the big chapels closer to the city. And that Monday night in late March it was almost pitch dark inside. Denny had a key because he'd been doing janitorial chores for them lately, and he kept it on his personal key ring, right next to the one that opened his apartment.

Quietly, so that even the church cat wouldn't be bothered, Denny made his way to the front row and eased himself into a pew. Like he'd done a dozen times in the past few months, he stared in awe at the life-size wooden cross.

Denny had been raised Catholic and he'd seen his share of crosses. Crucifixes, really. The kind where a pained-looking Jesus hung from shiny brass beams. Nothing wrong with crucifixes except they put the focus on the suffering.

Sometimes that was a good thing, remembering the Lord's pain. In fact, it had been after coming home drunk one night a few months earlier that Denny had spotted the crucifix on his bedroom wall and moved in for a closer look. Was it true? Had an innocent man named Jesus really hung on a cross like that and died for Denny Conley's sins? He found it hard to believe. Why in the world would someone do something like that? For a person like him, no less?

By then it had been four years since his son had gone and found this personal relationship thing with God. It was all Matt ever talked about back then. Golly, it was all he talked about still. But Denny's encounter with the crucifix happened on a night weeks after the last time he'd talked to the boy. Denny had been wobbly and ready to pass out from the whiskey, but something in the way that Jesus hung there—taking all that pain and not complaining about it—all so people like Denny and Matt could make it to heaven.

Well, something about that was almost more than Denny could bear.

The next day he looked up churches in the phone book and found him a nice community-sized one with a picture of a friendly looking man named Pastor Mark. Denny had stopped in that afternoon and met with the guy, and sure enough, Pastor Mark told him the same thing Matt had been saying from the get-go. Jesus died all on His own, regardless of whether you were a good person or a bad person or some drunk hopping bars, halfway in-between. Either way, it was up to Denny to accept the gift of heaven or walk away from it and keep living life on his own.

Denny remembered the decision better than he remembered almost any other detail of his life. He had made some awful mistakes in the past. Walked away from Jo when Matt was just a little tyke, married another woman, and spent two decades drinking his life away. That night, drunker than a skunk, he was single again and looking for offers.

Never, though, had he been offered anything like what Pastor Mark offered him that afternoon. Eternal life. Already paid for. And all he had to do was ask Jesus to forgive him of his past sins and then grab hold of the gift that was already his for the taking.

It was too much to bear, really. An offer Denny simply couldn't refuse. He asked Christ into his life that night, and the change in his heart was almost instant. First thing he did when he got home was phone Matt.

"Your old man's a believer, Matt. Just like you."

There was a pause, and Denny wasn't sure but he thought Matt was crying a little on the other end. That conversation had been only the beginning. They'd talked more in the last few months than all their years combined, but they still hadn't seen each other. Not once since Denny had walked out on him and Jo, back when the boy was four years old. Matt had wanted to see him after Denny's first phone call, but Denny hadn't wanted the boy to see him drunk. And back then there weren't many days . . . well, there weren't many *hours* when Denny wasn't stone-flat plastered.

But the day he began believin', Denny believed for something else, too. He believed that if God could raise Jesus Christ from the dead, He could certainly deliver Denny Conley from the demons of alcoholism.

Denny smiled up at the cross. It had been four months since then, twenty-four church services and fifty meetings with a Twelve-Step group designed to help break the addiction of drinking. He was gaining weight, losing the ruddy complexion he'd developed during the years of drinking. In fact, he might almost be ready to see Matt. Every day, every hour, found him clean and sober. And it was all because of Christ.

Which brought him to his current prayer, the one that had been drawing him to church late at night, the one he'd been laying directly at the foot of the cross. It was a prayer for Jo's salvation. Denny knew from Matt that his mother was cynical about the whole Jesus thing. She was probably bitter and angry and frustrated at having lived a lifetime as a single mother. It wasn't going to be easy for her to accept the truth.

That Denny Conley was a new man.

Denny sighed. Something about the coming wedding made the whole thing seem more urgent. He was going, after all. Sure as the sky was blue, he was going to be in church when his son married that young bride of his. And if God heard him good, he was going to take a few minutes and talk heart to heart with Jo.

Then maybe, just maybe . . .

Denny bowed his head and closed his eyes. "Lord, my Jo's hurting right now because of me . . . and because she doesn't know You yet. She needs to, Lord. But . . . well, I'm not really the one to tell her, know what I mean? I hurt her pretty bad all those years ago and I'm awful sorry. You know that and I know it. But Jo . . . she thinks this whole Jesus thing is just a phase. Maybe my way of connecting with Matt after so much time's gone by between us.

"Anyway, God, You know what I mean. Reach down and touch Jo's heart, Father. Make her feel uneasy so that nothing gives her peace except You. Save her, Lord. And work it out so the two of us can have a talkin' to. Together, I mean, maybe at the wedding somehow. Make her ready to see me, God. Please." He thought for a minute. "I guess what I'm askin' for, Father, is a miracle for Jo. Just like the miracle You gave me and Matt." He hesitated. "In Jesus' name, amen."

When he was finished praying, he let his eyes linger on the cross awhile longer, grateful that Jesus no longer hung there but that He lived, that He was alive forevermore. With his gaze still upward, his thoughts on his Savior, Denny did the same thing he always did after these prayer times.

He sang.

Pastor told him the song had been around for more than a hundred years, but it was brand new to Denny Conley. As far as he was concerned it could have been written for him alone. Like the hesitant notes from a dusty piano, Denny's voice rang out and lifted to an audience of One. It didn't matter if he couldn't carry a tune or if the cat woke up and thought he was crazy. All Denny cared about was the song.

The words to the song.

Great is Thy faithfulness, oh God my Father
There is no shadow of turning with Thee.
Thou changest not, Thy compassions they fail not
As Thou hast been Thou forever wilt be.

He hummed a bit then, because he didn't yet know all the words. But one day he would. Until then, he would sing the part he knew.

Great is Thy faithfulness, great is Thy faithfulness
Morning by morning new mercies I see.
All I have needed Thy hand hath provided;
Great is Thy faithfulness, Lord, unto me."

It was Thursday night again, and the craft store scrapbooking class was empty except for Abby and Jo and two other women. Abby was midway through Nicole's high-school years and making good progress, despite Jo's ongoing banter.

There were two hours left in the session when Jo took a deep breath and leveled a new line of questions in Abby's direction.

"You think you're going to heaven, Abby? I mean really . . . like there's a place called heaven that some people go to when they die?"

Abby blinked and set down the photograph in her hand. It wasn't something she'd thought about much lately, but surely it was true. She'd given her life to Christ ages ago, and even though her personal life was a mess, that didn't mean God had rejected her, right? She gulped discreetly. "Yes, I'd say I was going to heaven."

"A real place called heaven? You think you're actually going there someday?" Jo rattled off the next question without giving Abby time to answer. "Not just a fantasy place, like an idea or a dream, but a real place?"

Abby sighed. It was enough to be racked with guilt where John was concerned, but being forced to think about heaven, too . . . it was almost more than she could bear. They were halfway through the six-month prison sentence of pretending they were happily married, halfway to the day when they would file divorce papers. *What do I know about heaven?* "Yes, Jo, it's a real place. As real as anything here."

For the first time since she'd met the woman, Jo Harter had no response. She let Abby's comment sink in for nearly a minute before she thought of another question. "If you're right . . . if this heaven place is real, then that means hell's real, too. Would you say that was so, Abby?"

Abby rested her forearms on the edge of the table and looked carefully at Jo. *I'm the most imperfect example here, Lord, but use me, please. Even as far gone as I've been lately I know this much: her salvation is bigger than anything I'm dealing with.* "That's right, Jo. Hell's a real place."

"Lake of fire and the whole works? Torment and torture forever and ever?"

"Right, that's how Jesus describes it."

"But it's only for the bad guys, right. You know, murderers and people who fish without a license?"

Abby was completely caught off guard. *Help me, Lord. Give me the words.* She brought her fingers together and tried to look deep into Jo's eyes, tried to exude the compassion she suddenly felt in her heart for this woman, her daughter's future mother-in-law. "Not according to Scripture." Abby paused. "The Bible says hell's for anyone who chooses not to accept His gift of salvation."

Jo released a tired huff. "Now that's the part that always gets me. Everyone goes on about how loving their God is and then we get to this part about Him sending people to hell and I have to really wonder about that." She grabbed a quick breath. "What kind of loving God would send someone to hell?"

I'm not up to this, Lord. Speak for me here, please. Her heart filled with words that were not her own. "People get a little mixed up when they think about God. See, when a person dies, God doesn't really *send* him anywhere."

Jo's face wrinkled in confusion. "There's only one God, right? Who else might be doin' the sending?"

Abby smiled. *Lord, she really doesn't know. Thank You, God, for the privilege of telling her.* "The way I understand it from Scripture, we make the decision for ourselves. When we die, God simply honors our choice."

"Meaning?" Jo had all but forgotten her scrapbook layout, her eyes wide with fascination.

Abby was consumed by a feeling of unworthiness, but she continued on, believing God for every word. "Meaning if we've admitted our need for a Savior and accepted Christ's free gift of salvation, when we die God honors that choice by welcoming us into heaven." Abby didn't want to give her too much at once. She hesitated, letting that first part sink in. "But if we've decided not to pursue a relationship with Jesus, if we've ignored the opportunities Christ presents for us, then when we die God honors that choice as well. Without the covering of grace from a holy Savior, a person could not possibly gain entrance into heaven. In that case, hell is the only other option."

Again Jo was silent for a moment. "So you think the whole thing's true? And if I died tonight . . . I might not . . ." She didn't seem able to bring herself to finish the sentence. Instead she picked up her photograph and began cutting. Then without looking up she changed the subject. "Did I hear Nicole right that we're planning a girls' getaway the week before the wedding? I can't think of a better idea, to tell you the truth. I mean a getaway to me suggests a cabin and a lake, and if there's one thing I love to do when I'm on vacation it's take in some good old-fashioned fishing . . ."

Jo was rambling again, running as fast and far as she could from the sentence she'd been unable to finish. Abby listened only partially, but focused most of her attention on the Lord, begging Him to let the seeds of truth take root in Jo's heart.

And in the process maybe ignite something new in her own.

"You know, Abby, I think I remember when it was things got bad for me and Denny. I mean, it was his choice to leave and all, but it was my fault, too. I see that a lot clearer these days. It takes two to make a marriage work and two to make it fall apart. Those are words o' wisdom for sure."

Abby nodded. "Sometimes, but not always." She thought of John and Charlene. "Sometimes one person finds someone else to love. That happens, too."

Jo didn't seem to hear her. "You know what it was? I got busy. Busy with Matt, taking him to toddler classes and park outings and falling asleep beside him at night. I forgot about Denny pretty much, Abby. About that time the little things became big, know what I mean? Like him leaving the toothpaste lid off and forgettin' to put his dirty underwear in the laundry basket. We started fightin' about everything, and after that it didn't take long before we was only strangers walking around in a boxy little house in the heart of South Carolina."

"Hmmm. Where does he live now?"

"Boxy little apartment about an hour from here. At least that's what Matt says. I haven't talked to him in years."

The evening wore on, and Abby pondered the things Jo had said, things about heaven and hell and how it took two people to tear down what two people had built.

That night before she fell asleep, her last thoughts were of Jo Harter.

It's too late for me and John, Lord, for our marriage. But it's not too late for Jo. Tonight, Lord, please . . . let her finish that all-important sentence before she falls asleep. Let her know that without You, she would have no chance whatsoever of going to heaven.

Oh, and you do, right, Abby?

The voice hissed in her heart and Abby refused to acknowledge it. She still loved Jesus very much, and she'd never rejected Him or willfully walked away, had she? A sinking feeling worked its way through her gut. Okay, but she hadn't rejected Him often. And though the choices she and John were making were bound to grieve God, certainly they wouldn't keep her from heaven.

Abby closed her eyes shaken by the truth. They might not keep her from heaven, but they would keep her from the paradise of growing old alongside the father of her children, from loving the man who once upon a lifetime ago was her other half.

Seventeen

SPRING FOOTBALL BROUGHT JOHN ANOTHER reason to be out of the house—as well as the certainty that in three short months he and Abby could stop the charade and get on with the rest of their lives. Whatever that meant, John wasn't sure, but he found himself grateful beyond words for the hours when he stood planted on the sideline of the Marion High practice field, mindlessly barking correction and encouragement as the team walked through passing plays and prepared for a season still months away.

Brilliant afternoon sunshine beat down on the field and the temperatures were unseasonably high. No wonder the team was having a hard time focusing. John crossed his arms and stood with his legs shoulder-width apart, knees locked. It was a stance familiar to his athletes, one that always seemed to convey his absolute authority.

His quarterback—a sophomore looking to take over Kade's position—dropped back and searched frantically for an open receiver. Downfield two players tripped over each other as the ball soared high above their heads.

"Line up again," he barked. "You look like a bunch of junior high players. Start over and do it right, or we can spend the next fifteen minutes running lines. Take it slow. We're learning the plays, remember?"

Next time through was smoother, and the ball settled easily into the hands of one of the tight ends. "Better! That's the way. State championship football, guys. Keep it up!"

He had yelled the same thing every spring for almost twenty years, and by now he could almost set himself on autopilot and coach an intense practice while his mind was miles away.

Four miles, precisely. Back at the house he still shared with Abby, the place where wedding plans were constantly at the center of every conversation and where the woman he was married to had figured out a way to make avoidance an art form.

So this is how it's going to end, huh, God? In a blur of busyness and wedding plans and promises of new love. The whole family was all worked up over the celebration of Nicole and Matt, and the plans left not even half an hour for Abby and John to talk about how they were supposed to do this, how they might cut ties that ran two decades deep. Was what they had, what they'd shared just going to fade into the distance?

Love bears all things, My son. Love never ends.

John clenched his jaw. "Shift right, Parker," he shouted. "The defense lines up the same each time. Football is a game of adjustments."

It wasn't about love; it was about letting go. Love had long since left their marriage. Twenty years ago—ten even—this separation process would have been unbearable. But what he and Abby were losing now was a marriage of convenience. Two people who'd figured out a way to coexist, pay the bills on time, and celebrate their children's milestones together.

Love had nothing to do with it.

Remember the height from which you have fallen. Love as I have loved you.

John worked his worn-out gum and rubbed the back of his neck as he stared at the ground. He'd tried that, hadn't he? Back when Charlene first entered the picture, and he'd had the strength to walk out of her bedroom. Wasn't that an effort at remembering the height from which he'd fallen? He looked out at the players on the field once more.

It was Abby, really. It was her fault everything had fallen apart. She demanded so much and she wasn't . . . well, she wasn't fun anymore. Always bossing him around and giving him that look that said he'd failed to live up to her expectations. Sometimes it seemed the only thing separating John from being just one more kid under Abby's control was the fact that his to-do list was longer than theirs.

She hadn't loved him in years. "Line up and do it again," he shouted. If she did, she had a strange way of showing it. "Get your seat down next time, Sanders. Linemen draw all their strength from their legs. Do it again."

No, she didn't love him. Not like she used to back when she would drop by at spring training or find a spot in the bleachers once in a while for summer two-a-days or wait for him at the end of every game—not just the big ones. Back when the kids and the writing and her father weren't more important than he was.

John huffed. That was the latest guilt trip she was laying on him: her father.

"He won't be around forever, John. It wouldn't hurt if you visited him once in a while."

Why did she have to word it like that?

"Footwork, Johnson," his voice bellowed across the field. "Catching a pass is all in the footwork. Find your rhythm and let the ball come to you."

Couldn't she just have said that her father enjoyed spending time with him? John released a measured breath and shook his head. It wasn't her words exactly; it was her tone. Everything she said to him these days had an edge to it.

Not like the old days when she'd come up behind him and—

A delicate brush of fingers grazed the back of his neck and he spun around. "Charlene!" His players were watching, and he recovered instantly, regaining his stance and forcing an air of indifference. "I didn't hear you come up."

She wore a tight navy tank top and a jaunty skirt that clung to her in all the right places, stopping just short of her ankles. *I can't do this, God. Get her away from me.*

"I saw you out here and couldn't resist." She pouted in a way that made his insides melt. "Forgive me?"

He could feel a smile playing on his lips, but he shifted his weight and sidestepped her so that he faced the football field again. "Parker, try to hang back in the pocket five seconds this time. Under those Friday-night lights every second counts. Let's go, guys, come on. Eagle pride!"

From the corner of his eye he watched Charlene position herself next to him, standing close enough so their bare elbows touched, far enough away so as not to spark the curiosity of his players.

All her attention seemed focused on the field. "No answer, Coach?"

Why did she have to make him feel so alive, so good about himself? "Forgiven." He cast her a sideways grin. *Don't say it . . .* "You look good."

She angled her head so that her eyes were able to travel the length of him. "Yeah, you, too." When her eyes reached his, her expression grew more serious. "I've missed you."

John clenched his teeth. *Flee this, My son. Flee!* He blinked back the warning. "Abby and I aren't talking anymore. Two strangers under the same roof."

She moved an inch closer, brushing her arm against his in a way that sent fire through his veins. "I'm taking some night classes . . . but I'll be home tonight." She slid her sandal closer to his shoe and tapped at him playfully. "Come by, why don't you? Tell Abby it's a coaches' meeting. Sounds like you need someone to talk to."

John stepped forward and cupped his hands around his mouth. "Run it again! That was terrible, defense. Key on the ball." He clapped three times. "Let's look like state champs out there."

Charlene waited a beat. "You're avoiding my question, Coach."

A breeze came across them and filled his senses with the fading smell of her perfume. *God, I can't resist this . . .* The idea of spending an evening with her, getting reacquainted after three months of intentionally staying away, was more enticing than he cared to think about. "Maybe."

Flee! Avoid the harlot, son.

The whispered words echoed through his heart and cooled his blood considerably. For reasons he couldn't understand, he suddenly regained much of his control. After all, he'd asked her to wait until after Nicole's wedding. Why was she here, anyway? "Actually, maybe not. I have a stack of tests to grade tonight."

Charlene's words were slow and measured, aimed deliberately at the place where John's passions were birthed. "You can't run from me forever, John Reynolds." She let her arm drag along his as she turned to go. "I'll be around if you change your mind."

Knowing she was walking away caused sharply contrasting feelings. A part of him wanted to blow the whistle, call off practice, and follow her home, stay with her all evening. Nothing physical, just a night of conversation with someone who actually liked him. But another part of him was experiencing relief like he'd never felt before. Strong and tangible. As though he'd just been spared a tumble into the darkest, deepest abyss.

Possibly into the pit of hell itself.

Matt's apartment was walking distance from Marion High, and with the weather nicer than usual he'd taken to jogging back and forth to the campus each day after classes. His coursework was actually lighter than during any other semester, but what with studying for the upcoming bar exam and policing himself around Nicole, the stress was starting to get to him. Running did wonders to restore the peace.

That afternoon he figured he might do more than his usual three-mile jog. The Eagles would be practicing, and maybe Nicole's father could talk for a minute or two. It was strange, really. What with the wedding and all, he and Nicole needed to spend more time together than ever, but each day was more difficult than the previous one when it came to their physical relationship.

The night before was a perfect example. Nicole was at his house making plans about which songs the disc jockey would play at the reception, and before either of them knew it, they were on the sofa kissing. The hunger, the desire he felt for her was so strong that sometimes he felt like Esau—willing to sell his birthright for a single bowl of soup. Or in this case, a single night of . . .

Matt laced up his shoes and tied them with a ferocity that showed his frustration. Why couldn't he get a grip in this area? Twelve weeks. Eighty-four days, and they could love each other the way they longed to. But last night when she pulled away—her eyes clouded with a desire as intense as his—he literally had to ask her to leave.

"Not yet," she'd told him, still breathless from their kissing. "It's only nine-thirty."

He walked to the kitchen, ignoring her comment, and downed a glass of ice water. *Think of something else, Matt. Dirty fish tanks . . . bar exams . . . the ACLU.* That did it. His emotions cooled slightly.

"Did you hear me?" Nicole's tone was frustrated, and Matt realized he hadn't answered her yet.

He swallowed the last bit of water. "I don't care what time it is; you need to go. Believe me, Nicole."

Times like that had them on the verge of fighting, when all he wanted to do, all every part of his body wanted, was to love her totally and completely. *Lord, get me through these next three months without compromise.*

Honor one another above yourself . . .

Honor. That was the key. He'd read the verse earlier that morning but it only now hit him. Why hadn't he thought of the truth there earlier? Victory could only be found by seeing Nicole the way God saw her, as a child of the King; not as the gorgeous, godly girl who was about to be his wife.

Honor one another . . .

Matt set out toward the school, still thinking about the idea. That had to be it, the reason God had guided him to that verse in the first place. By the time he got to school he was determined to talk about it with Coach Reynolds. He knew from Nicole that her parents had avoided physical intimacy until after they were married. If there was one person who would understand what it meant to honor a woman, it was John Reynolds. And since Matt didn't yet have that kind of relationship with his own father, he could think of no one he'd rather talk to that afternoon than Nicole's dad.

The Marion High football field came into view. The team was spread out across the grass, and Nicole's father was on the sidelines with . . . was it Nicole's mother? The woman looked shorter, with darker hair. The closer Matt got, the easier it was to see that she wasn't Abby Reynolds, even though she stood arm to arm beside Nicole's father.

Matt studied the way Coach Reynolds seemed to be enjoying the woman's attention. The way they smiled at each other, their elbows touching . . . If he didn't know better, Matt would have been concerned. But she was probably just a girls' coach, someone he worked with.

He was still studying them, drawing closer, when the woman brushed past Nicole's father and walked purposefully across the field, back toward the school buildings. A few seconds later, Matt was at the older man's side, breathless and sweating from his run. "Hey, Mr. Reynolds."

Nicole's dad had been watching the brunette as she left, and he swung around, eyes wide. "Matt! Where'd you come from?"

Matt bent over to catch his breath. "Home. I jog by here every day. Thought I might catch you." He pointed at the kids on the field. "You whippin' these guys into shape?"

Nicole's father uttered a strange-sounding laugh and hesitated a beat. "Every year. Same routine." He took a step toward the playing field. "Get some air under the ball, Parker. Give your receivers time to get downfield!"

Waving in the direction of the woman, Matt cocked his head. "Is she one of the coaches here?"

Nicole's dad licked his lips and glanced over his shoulder. "The woman, you mean? The one I was talking to?"

Again his reactions seemed odd. *Probably preoccupied with coaching* . . . "Right. A few minutes ago."

"She's a teacher here, a friend." He barked another command at his team. "What brings you by?"

Matt took up a similar stance as the man beside him, his attention focused on the playing field. "Honor, I guess."

He glanced at Nicole's father. Was it Matt's imagination, or had the man's face gotten paler since Matt's arrival? Maybe he was sick. "Honor?"

Moving his foot in small figure eights in the grass, Matt thought about his choice of words. "Nicole and I are fighting a lot lately. I don't know, I don't think it should be like this right before our wedding."

Coach Reynolds's brow wrinkled. "Fighting? You mean you're not getting along?"

Matt exhaled through pursed lips and shook his head. "No, it's the other way around. We're getting along too well, if you know what I mean." He leveled his gaze at Nicole's father. "It's like I can't even be near her. I'm so tempted I can't see straight."

There was a flexing motion in the man's jawline. *Great, now he thinks I'm a dog. Why did I want to talk to him about this? Give me the words, God. I'm sure this man has insight . . . if only I can get him to share it with me.* Mr. Reynolds looked like he was afraid to ask the next question. "But you've . . . I mean so far you haven't . . ."

Matt was quick to answer. "No, that's just it. We've stayed away from each other. We promised God, each other for that matter, that we'd stay pure." He shook his head and stared at the ground for a moment. "It's a lot tougher than I thought it'd be. Like there's this constant tension where we want to be together, but we know there's only so much we can take."

Nicole's father nodded. "Gotcha. Wish I could tell you it'll get easier."

"Maybe I need to change my thinking, you know?" Matt shifted his position so he could see the man better. "This morning I read a scripture about honoring others, putting them above yourself. I think there's truth there, something that might help me get through this without breaking my promises."

The coach swallowed hard and seemed to struggle with his words. "Honoring others, huh?"

The cheerleaders had been working out on an adjacent field, and two of them ran up, slightly out of breath and giggling. Their entire attention was focused on Matt. "Mr. Reynolds, you've been holding out on us . . ." a tiny blonde said, tossing her ponytail.

"Yeah, who's the new coach?" The taller of the two blushed and giggled, elbowing her friend.

Matt contained a chuckle. It had been a while since he'd been on a high-school campus, but girls like these didn't affect him. There was only one girl who had power over him anymore. He held out his hand politely to one cheerleader, then the other. "Matt Conley, and I'm not a new coach."

Nicole's father cleared his throat and raised his eyebrows sarcastically at the girls. "Matt's marrying my daughter in a few months."

Both girls' eyes grew wide, and they repressed a bout of nervous laughter. "Oh . . . right. Okay." The blonde grabbed her friend's arm, and the two headed off, giggling over their shoulders. "Bye, Matt. Nice to meet you."

Coach Reynolds leveled a humorous gaze at him. "Is this a daily problem?"

Matt laughed softly and shrugged. "Sometimes, but that's true for most guys." He grew serious. "After meeting Nicole it's like they're not even there." He looked at the man beside him. "Sort of like you and Mrs. Reynolds."

Nicole's father crossed his arms more tightly in front of him, and Matt noticed that his fists were clenched. "Keep that feeling, Matt. Whatever you have to do, keep that."

"Was it, you know . . . did you and Mrs. Reynolds struggle with staying pure before you got married?"

A sigh slid out through the man's clenched teeth. He looked at Matt and angled his head as if caught up in a dozen memories. "It wasn't easy. I guess it was like you said: I honored Abby. I loved her for who she was, not what she could do for me. Not for the feeling I got when we were together." He paused. "When I had my focus right, it wasn't so bad."

He loved her for who she was, not what she could do for him. Matt played that over in his mind again and felt like someone had turned on a light. Hope filled him and he knew that next time he saw Nicole, he would see her soul and not only her body. Maybe that's why God asked couples to wait. So they could learn to love each other. Because over the years it would take that kind of love to make their relationship a beautiful thing.

"You have the best marriage, Mr. Reynolds. I want you to know how much your example has helped me." Matt shook his head, amazed at the wisdom the years had developed in Nicole's father. "I want to love Nicole the same way you've loved her mother. The last thing I want is the mess my parents made of their marriage."

Nicole's father changed his footing. "Your parents split up a while ago, huh?"

"Back when I was a little kid. Mom was busy with me, and Dad . . . well, he had a hard time telling the girls no. Same thing with the bottle. After a while he took up with someone else and left us."

Coach Reynolds swallowed hard and stared at his football team. "He's, uh . . . been in contact with you lately, that right? That's what Nicole said."

"Yeah, it's amazing. He gave his life to God, and the changes have been something else. Still, he missed out on me growing up. Missed out on a lot." Matt let his gaze fall on the tree line in the distance. "Makes me wonder how different it might have been if he'd been a believer before. You know, like you guys. Then divorce wouldn't have been an option, and they'd have found a way to make it work."

Nicole's father took a deep breath and bellowed toward the field. "All right guys, bring it in." Immediately the players stopped what they were doing and jogged toward their coach. Mr. Reynolds looked at Matt. "Don't know if I was much help, son, but I need to talk with the team. You wanna hang around?"

Matt reached out and shook the man's hand. "That's okay. I gotta get back and study. Actually, you helped me a lot." It was all Matt needed, knowing that this man had faced temptation and succeeded by learning to truly love his wife-to-be. "See ya, Coach."

And with that Matt jogged off toward home, certain between God's help and Mr. Reynolds's example he could survive the next three months.

John had been trembling inside from the moment Matt walked up, deeply afraid his daughter's fiancé had seen something between him and Charlene, a nuance or glance or flirtatious look. A sign that John Reynolds was not the man he appeared to be, but rather a cheap, two-timing hypocrite.

He talked to his team briefly and dismissed them to the weight-room, where Coach Kenny would be in charge. By the time the last player had made it off the field, John's trembling had become full-blown shakes.

Liar, John Reynolds. Liar, phony, hypocrite.

He shook off the taunting voice and began making his way around the field, collecting cones and gathering equipment.

You're a snake, a worthless excuse of a man.

John gritted his teeth and forced his body to relax. Nausea caused his lunch to well up somewhere near his throat and he gulped several times to keep from losing it. *I need to talk to someone, get this off my chest.* Maybe Abby's father. He thought about the man as he had so often lately, his father's best friend, lying ill in a nursing home without the benefits of his son-in-law's regular visits.

He wouldn't want to see me now, anyway.

An aching filled his heart, and again John knew deep in his bones it had nothing to do with his health. Suddenly his words to Matt came back loud and clear, as if someone was shouting at him.

"I honored Abby. I honored Abby . . . honored Abby. I loved her for who she was, not what she could do for me. Not for the feeling I got when we were together. I loved her for who she was . . ."

He chided himself. *How could you talk to that boy as if you understood love? You don't know real love from lust anymore.*

An oppressive feeling settled over his shoulders bringing with it a burden he could barely stand up under.

One after another, Matt's statements flashed in his mind.

"You have the best marriage, Mr. Reynolds . . . your example has helped me . . . I want to love Nicole the same way you've loved her mother. Makes me wonder how different it might have been if he'd been a believer like you guys. Then divorce wouldn't have been an option . . . wouldn't have been an option . . . wouldn't have been an option."

John hauled a bag of cones across the field. Without realizing it, everything Matt said had been wrong. All of it. *And you let him believe it was all true.* Suddenly he understood the nausea; he was making himself sick. He was so far gone he ought to get Charlene and leave town tomorrow. Forget about his family. They wouldn't want anything to do with him once they learned the truth. The burden in John's heart grew heavier until he dropped the equipment bag and eased himself onto his knees, falling forward, his face buried in the musty grass.

God, help me! I can't leave them now, not yet. Oh, Lord, how have I failed You so badly?

Hear Me, son. The voice was so strong, so real, John sat up and looked around. *Love one another . . . as I have loved you, so you must love one another.*

He glanced in a handful of directions, but there was no one else on the field and a chill ran down his arms. God still cared, still heard his cries. Otherwise He wouldn't have answered that way. *I can't do it, Lord. She hates me. It's too late for love.*

Silence.

John turned his face to heaven. *Cure me of the desire I feel for Charlene, Lord. My body wants her like . . . like . . .*

Then it hit him.

He wanted Charlene the same way he'd once wanted Abby. The exact same way. But when he thought about the advice he'd given Matt, it simply didn't apply to Charlene. He didn't love her that way, didn't love the soul and spirit deep inside her. There was only one thing he loved about her: the way she made him feel. Emotionally and physically.

But definitely not spiritually.

It hit him there on the forty-yard line, as his heart pled for God's intervention, that what he sought in Charlene Denton was a shadow, a counterfeit. Because the real thing, the love he had longed for all his life, could only be found in Abby Reynolds.

The woman who had first taught him what it was to love.

Eighteen

THE PHONE CALL ABBY HAD DREADED ALL her adult life came at 4:15 in the afternoon the first week of May. John was at practice; Nicole and Sean were playing catch outside; Kade was working on his senior project at the school library.

"Hello?"

There was a hesitation on the other end. "Mrs. Reynolds? This is Helen at Wingate Nursing Home. I'm afraid your father has had a stroke."

Abby's breath caught in her throat. *No, God. Not now. Not with Nicole's wedding so close. I need him, Lord. Please.* "Is it . . . is he okay?"

"It happened about thirty minutes ago, and he's been in and out of a coma ever since. He doesn't seem to have control of his extremities."

What? No control? The words rang like a series of alarms in Abby's mind. "I'm not sure I understand. You mean he's too tired to move?"

The woman at the other end sighed. "The stroke may have left him paralyzed, Mrs. Reynolds." She hesitated. "I'm sorry to have to tell you this over the phone."

Dear God, no. A series of images flashed on the screen in Abby's heart: her father running the sidelines at one of his games, doing sprints alongside his players, playing tennis with her the year before his diagnosis. Her father thrived on being active. If his legs were gone, his spirit to live would quickly follow. *No, Lord . . . please. Help him.*

"I'm on my way." She thanked the woman and hung up the phone. Then as if by being in control she could keep her dad from dying, she went outside and calmly explained the situation to Sean and Nicole. Next she called Kade on his cell phone.

"Grandpa's had a stroke."

Kade's voice reflected his shock. "Are you sure? I was just there last weekend. He seemed—"

"It's true." She forced herself to remain composed. "Your dad's at practice. Get him and meet me at Wingate." She swallowed back a sob. "Hurry, Kade."

There was one last phone call, to her sister on the East Coast.

"How serious is it?" Beth had not been close to their father since before her divorce twelve years earlier. Now, though, there was concern in her voice.

"It's bad, Beth. Get on a plane, quick."

Abby, Nicole, and Sean piled into the van, and the drive that usually took fifteen minutes took ten. They hurried inside and Abby saw that Kade and John had not yet arrived. *Don't blow this one, John.* He hadn't been in to see her father in more than a month.

She banished the thought. There was no time for negative feelings now, not with her dad fighting for his life down the hall. "Nicole, stay here with Sean and watch for your dad and Kade. I'll go see Grandpa first."

Nicole nodded, her eyes damp, face drawn and filled with sadness. She had always been close to her grandpa. Especially in the eight years since he'd given up his home in Wisconsin and moved closer to them. It was the same way with the boys. He'd been a part of their lives almost as far back as they could remember.

Abby hurried down the hallway and quietly opened the door to his room. What she saw brought tears to her eyes. Her father lay prone and utterly still, his face slack, hands motionless as though he'd aged twenty years overnight. A nurse stood nearby taking his vital signs.

"Should we call an ambulance?" Abby was at her father's side immediately, taking his hand, shocked at the way it hung limp in her own.

The nurse shook her head as she adjusted his intravenous needle. "He's stable now. There's nothing more they could do for him. We're giving him a medication to undo the damage done by the stroke. It'll take time, though."

"To work?"

"To know if it did any good. Sometimes a major stroke can set off a series of strokes. With someone as ill as your father, the chances of him recovering without damage are slim, Mrs. Reynolds."

She tightened her grip on her father's hand. "But it's possible, right? I mean he could come out of this and be the way he was before the stroke, right?"

The nurse looked hesitant. "Not very likely." She finished working on him and straightened, leveling a sympathetic gaze at Abby. "We think it'd be best if the family came now, Mrs. Reynolds. Another stroke could be the end for him, I'm afraid."

More tears filled Abby's eyes and she nodded, unable to speak. The nurse took the cue and left them alone. Abby waited until the woman was gone before she found her voice.

"Dad, it's me. Can you hear me? We're all here, Dad. The kids are in the other room."

Her father's eyelids fluttered and his mouth, dry and cracked, began working without sound.

"Dad, I'm here. If you wanna talk I'm right here." Tears spilled down Abby's cheeks, but her voice was stronger than before. "I'm listening, Dad."

His mouth worked some more, and this time his eyes rolled back in his head three times, as though he was trying to focus on her, trying to see her one last time.

"Oh, Dad, I'm so sorry . . ." Her voice broke and she laid her head on his chest, allowing the sobs that had built in her heart. "I love you, Dad."

"John . . ."

The word startled Abby, and she lifted her head, searching her father's face for signs of life. His eyes opened slowly and he caught Abby's gaze. Again his mouth worked and he repeated the same word he'd said a moment earlier. "John . . ."

"You want John, Daddy?" Abby didn't understand. John hadn't been to see him in weeks. Why now, when he couldn't move, could barely speak, would he want to talk to John? Especially when he knew the truth about their troubled marriage.

There was a pleading in her father's eyes that was unmistakable, as though whatever he had to tell John was, in that moment, the most important, most pressing thing in his life. Abby remembered how strong her father had looked that day at the Michigan football game when her family had greeted John outside the team locker room. The year she was just seventeen. Later that week her father had winked at her and confessed something. "John's always been like a son to me, Abby. The only son I ever had. I kinda hoped he'd wait for you to grow up."

Abby looked at her father now and squeezed his hand. "All right, Dad. I'll get him." She started backing away. "You hang on now, okay. I'll be right back."

Tears still spilling down her cheeks, Abby rushed down the hall, relieved to see John and Kade with Nicole and Sean in the waiting room. John hurried to meet her with the others close behind.

"How is he?" John's face was a mask of concern, and Abby wanted to spit at him. *Sure, care about him now . . . now that he's dying.* She hung her head and squeezed her eyes shut.

"Abby, how is he?" John's voice was more urgent.

"He's . . . he's . . ." The sobs overcame her, and her body shook with the force of her emotion. *Don't take my dad, Lord. He's all I have. My only friend. Please . . .*

Her family circled in closer, and John put his arms around her, holding her in a loose hug that probably looked more comfortable than it felt. "Honey, I'm sorry. We're here for you."

Abby reeled at the feel of his arms around her. How long had it been since she'd stood in his embrace? And how come it still felt like the most right place in the world? She thought about his words and she wasn't sure if she should hold onto him tighter or kick him in the leg. How dare he lie and call her honey at a time like this? Was it that important to look good in front of the kids? He hadn't been protective of her for years. Why would now be any different?

And why did it feel so good to have his arms around her? She cried softly, keeping her warring emotions to herself.

"He's . . . still alive right, Mom?" Nicole's expression was racked with fear.

Abby nodded, realizing that she hadn't explained the situation. "He can't move; he can barely talk. He . . . he looks like a different man."

Nicole started crying, and John circled her and Sean and Kade into their hug. The five of them hung on to each other, and Abby realized that she wasn't only losing her father. She was losing this— her family's ability to grieve together, to suffer life's dark and desperate times under the strength of her husband. In a few months she would be on her own, forced to shoulder every major setback and milestone by herself.

From where he stood near the back of the huddle, Kade began to pray. "God, we come before You as a family asking that You be with our grandpa, Mom's dad. He loves You very much, Lord, and, well . . . You already know that. But he's real sick, God. Please be with him now and help him not be afraid."

Abby tightened the hold she had on Kade's shoulder. He was such a good boy, so much like the man his father had once been. The thought of his leaving for college in the fall was enough to send another wave of sobs tearing through her gut. Then she realized that Kade had not prayed for healing.

Almost as if God were preparing them already for the inevitable.

The sobs subsided after a few minutes, and Abby remembered her father's request. She lifted her head and found John's eyes. "He asked for you."

Was it her imagination or did John's eyes cloud with fear the moment Abby told him? "Me?" The word was barely more than a whisper.

Abby nodded. "It seemed urgent."

John drew a steadying breath and nodded toward the waiting room. "You guys wait for me. I'll be back."

Without hesitating, he led the way down the hall while Abby stayed close behind him. They entered the room together, and Abby took up watch on the far side of the bed. Her father's head was moving about restlessly on the pillow, and when he heard them his eyes opened, searching until they found John.

His mouth started working again and finally the sound followed. "Come . . ."

John moved close to the bed and took her father's lifeless hand in his stronger ones. "Hi, Joe."

It broke Abby's heart to see her dad struggle so hard to speak. Clearly he couldn't move, and she realized the nurse had been right. The stroke had left him paralyzed—at least for now.

Once more he began opening and closing his mouth, but this time his eyes were more alert, more focused. Never once did they leave John's face. "Lubber . . ."

What was her father saying? Abby couldn't make it out and the expression on John's face told her he couldn't either.

"It's okay, Joe," John's voice was low and soothing. "Don't struggle. The Lord's here."

Oh, please . . . you of all—

Abby stopped herself. This wasn't the time to harbor resentment toward John. "Dad . . ." She spoke loudly so he could hear her from across the room. "Say it again, Dad."

Her father kept his gaze glued to John's face. "Lub-ber . . ." His words were slurred, running together so that it was impossible to understand. Abby closed her eyes and tried to hear beyond his broken speech. "Lub-her . . . lub-her . . ."

"Lu . . ." John tried to repeat the beginning of whatever it was her father was trying to say. "Can you say it once more, Joe. I'm sorry."

Abby willed her father the ability to speak clearly. Just this once when whatever it was he wanted to say was of such importance to him. *Please, God . . . give him the words.*

Her dad blinked twice, and his eyes filled with desperation as his voice grew louder. "Love her . . . love her."

"Love her." The words hit Abby like a tidal wave, washing away her determination to be strong. *"Love her."* In his most pained moment, when death itself might be only minutes away, his single message to his son-in-law was this: Love her. Love his daughter Abby for now, forever. Love her.

Abby looked across the room at John and saw that he, too, understood. Tears trickled down his rugged cheeks, and he seemed to struggle for the right words. When none came, he nodded, his chin quivering under the intensity of the moment.

Her father didn't let it rest. He blinked again—the only action he seemed to have left—and this time said it even more clearly. "Love her . . . John."

Guilt and remorse worked their way into John's features and he cocked his head, gazing across the bed at Abby. Then without speaking, he held up a single, shaky hand in her direction, beckoning her, begging her to come to him. Silently he mouthed the word, "please."

Two quick breaths lodged in Abby's chest, and she moved toward him. No matter that he'd fallen out of love with her, regardless of the ways in which he'd betrayed his wedding vows, despite Charlene and everything she represented, Abby came. John held his arm out to her until she was nestled underneath it, snug against him, side by side. A couple, facing her father as one.

Even if only to appease him in his dying hour.

"She's here, Joe. See . . . she's here." John's tears fell on her father's hand and bedsheets as Abby remained at his side, one arm clinging to her husband, the other stroking her father's kneecap.

Her dad's eyes moved from John to Abby and his head began to bob ever so slightly, up and down, as if approving what he was seeing between them. He nodded this way for a while then let his eyes settle on John once more. "Love her."

"I will, Dad." John had never called him that before. But since his own father had died, he hadn't had a man to fill that role. Over the years John had grown too consumed with his increasingly separate life to spend much time with her father. And now . . . by calling him *Dad*, John was conveying his regrets.

"Love her . . . always." Her father's words were getting weaker, but his message was exceptionally clear and repetitive. *Love Abby. Again and again. Love her now. Love her forever.*

Two short sobs escaped from deep in John's heart, and he blinked hard so he could see clearly. Tightening his grip on Abby he nodded again. "I'll always love her, Dad."

A peace came over Abby's father, and his entire body seemed to relax. His eyes moved slowly until they found Abby again. "Kids . . ."

John was quick to pull away, nodding to Abby. "I'll get them." He returned with all three in tow in less than a minute. They filed in, Nicole taking up her position opposite the place where Abby stood, and Kade and Sean falling in beside her.

Her father shot a questioning look at John, and in response he immediately resumed his place at Abby's side.

"Hi, Grandpa." Nicole cried unabashedly, indifferent to the way her makeup ran down her cheeks. "We're praying for you."

As if every bit of motion required the effort of a marathon, Dad turned his head so that he could find his grandchildren. "Good . . . good kids."

Sean started to cry and Kade—his own eyes wet—put an arm around his brother, pulling him close, letting him know that tears were okay in times like this. Sean leaned forward and threw his arms around his grandpa, holding on as though he could keep Abby's father from leaving them. "I love you, Grandpa."

The sounds of gentle sobs filled the room, and Abby noticed tears in her father's eyes as well. "Jesus . . ."

Sean stood up slowly and crowded close between Nicole and Kade.

Abby thought she understood, but it grieved her all the same. "Jesus . . . Dad . . . you want to go to Jesus?"

In response, another wave of peace washed over his features and the corners of his lips lifted just a fraction. "I . . . love you . . . all."

A flicker of concern flashed once more in her father's eyes, and he turned with excruciating slowness back to John and Abby. Before he could say anything, John tightened the grip he had on Abby, fresh tears spilling from his eyes. "I will, Dad."

His shoulders sank deeper into the bed and his smile grew until it filled his face. "God . . . is happy."

Abby's body convulsed with sobs, hating how they were tricking him into believing everything was okay, and yet wishing with all her heart that John meant what he said. That he actually might still love her, that he always would love her . . . that they would love each other. And that somehow by doing so they might actually make God happy again.

With the five of them holding on to him, each hoping that somehow it wasn't his time to go, he closed his eyes and breathed three more times.

Then he was gone.

It took five hours to say their good-byes, finish the paperwork, and watch while a mortuary attendant took her father's body to prepare it for burial. The funeral was set for three days later, and throughout the evening Abby felt as if she were wading through syrup, as if death had happened to somebody else's dad and not hers. As if the entire process of planning her dad's funeral was little more than a poorly acted scene from a bad movie.

John stayed by her side until they got home, then as all three kids headed for bed he went to sit in the silent living room, dropping his head in his hands. Abby stared at him. *Are you wishing for more time with him, John?*

She kept her question to herself and headed upstairs to make sure the kids were okay. One at a time she hugged each of them again and assured them that Grandpa was at home now, in heaven with Grandma where he'd longed to be for years. Each of the kids wept in her arms as she made the rounds, but Abby stayed strong.

It wasn't until she headed downstairs that she felt the finality of the situation. Her father was gone. Never again would she sit by his side, holding his hand and listening while he talked about the glory days on the gridiron. Her mentor, her protector . . . her daddy.

Gone.

Abby reached the last stair, rounded the corner, and suddenly she couldn't take another step. Her back against the wall, she collapsed, burying her face in her hands, giving way to the sobs that had been building since her father's final breath. "Why?" she cried out softly in a voice meant for no one to hear. "Daaaad. No! I can't do this!"

"Abby . . ."

John's hands were on hers before she heard him coming. Gentle, strong, protective hands that carefully removed her fingers from her face, then eased her arms around his waist as he drew her to himself. "Abby, I'm so sorry."

She knew she should pull away, should refuse his comfort in light of the lies he'd told her father earlier that evening. But she could no more do so than she could force her heart to stop beating. She laid her head on his chest and savored the feeling, allowing him to absorb the shaking of her body, the stream of tears that worked its way into his sweaty coaching shirt . . . a shirt that smelled of day-old cologne and musty grass and something sweet and innate that belonged to this man and him alone. Abby savored the scent, knowing there was no place she'd rather be.

John tightened his embrace and let his head rest on hers. Only then did Abby feel the way his body trembled. Not with desire as it had so often in their early days, but with a sadness, with a wave of sobs deeper than Abby had ever known him to cry. She thought how her husband had missed his chance, how he'd chosen to be too busy to visit with her father in his dying days.

How great his guilt had to be.

She raised her head and swallowed back her own sobs, searching John's face, so close to hers. His eyes were closed and grief filled his features. Abby allowed his forehead to rest against hers and felt his weeping ease some. His arms still locked around her waist, he opened his eyes and looked deeply into hers. "I loved him . . . you know that, right, Abby?"

Fresh tears forged a trail down her cheeks as she nodded. "I know."

"He was . . . he was like my own dad." John's words were little more than a whisper, and Abby savored the moment even as her heart shouted at her: *What are you doing, Abby? If things are over between you two, why does it feel so right to be here? Why did he come to you if he doesn't love you anymore?*

John let the side of his face graze up against hers, nuzzling her in a way that was achingly familiar. A roller-coaster feeling made its way across Abby's insides as her body instinctively reacted to John's nearness.

"My dad told me you were like a son to him . . ." Abby clung tightly to John, speaking the words inches from his ear. "He said he was glad you waited for me to grow up because you were . . . the only son he ever had."

A faint sense of hope filled John's watery eyes and he pulled back a few inches, searching Abby's face. "He said that?"

She nodded, her hands still linked at the back of his waist. "When I was seventeen. A few weeks after that first game, remember? The first time I watched you play at Michigan?"

Instantly the mood changed, and John went still as his eyes locked on hers. Without saying a word their embrace grew closer, their bodies melding together. Wasn't this how he'd looked at her all those years ago, back when he had wanted nothing more than to be by her side?

John ran his thumb over her cheek. "I remember . . ." He framed her face with both hands and wove his fingers into her hair. "I remember . . ."

She realized what was about to happen seconds before it actually did. He brought his lips closer to hers, and she saw his eyes cloud with sudden, intense desire. Abby's heart pounded against his chest.

What are these feelings, and why now? When everything is over between us?

She had no answers for herself, only one defining truth: she desperately wanted John's kiss, wanted to know that he could still feel moved in her arms, even if it made no sense whatsoever.

He kissed her, slowly, gently at first . . . but as she took his face in her hands, the act became more urgent, filled with the passion of a hundred lost moments. His mouth opened over hers and she could taste the salt from both their tears. Fresh tears, tears of passion . . . tears of regret.

The urgency within Abby built and she could feel John's body trembling again—but this time in a way that was familiar, a way that made her want to—

His hands left her face and he ran them slowly up and down her sides as he moved his lips toward her ear. "Abby . . ."

What did he mean by all this? Was this really happening? Was he comforting her the only way he knew how? Or could he be trying to tell her he was sorry, that no matter what had happened in the past, it was behind them now? She wasn't sure about anything except how good it felt to be in his arms, as though whatever mistakes their hearts and minds had made might somehow be erased by the physical feelings they apparently still had for each other.

Abby kissed him again and then slid her face along his, aware of the way his body pressed against hers. "I . . . I don't understand . . ."

John nudged her chin with his face and tenderly moved his lips along her neck as his thumbs worked in small circles against her upper ribs. He found her mouth once more and kissed her again . . .

and again. He moved his mouth closer to her ear. "I promised your father, Abby . . . I said I would love you . . ."

What? Abby felt like someone had dumped a bucket of ice water over her head. Her body went stiff. *That's* what this was about? His coming to her now, his kisses and desire . . . it was all part of some kind of guilt trip her father had placed on him minutes before dying? Her desire dissipated like water on an oil-slicked freeway. She braced her hands against him and pushed him.

"Get away from me." The tenderness in her voice was gone and she spat the words through gritted teeth.

John's eyes flew open, his face awash with shock and unrequited desire. "What . . . what're you doing?"

"I don't need your charity, John."

His expression was frozen in astonishment. "My . . . what do you mean?"

Fresh tears filled her eyes and spilled onto her cheeks as she pushed him again. "You can't love me out of . . . of . . ." She searched for the right words, her angry heart racing in her chest. "Out of some kind of obligation to my dead father."

Abby watched as a handful of emotions flashed in John's eyes. Shock gave way to understanding, then shifted to intense, burning rage. "That is *not* what I'm doing!" His face grew red and the muscles in his jaw flexed.

A wind of regret blew across the plains of Abby's barren heart. Why was he lying to her? He explained it perfectly a moment ago: he'd promised Abby's father that he'd love her, and this—*whatever* this was that had happened between them—was merely some dutiful way for John to make good on his word.

Strangely, his expression grew even more troubled, and Abby tried to make sense of it. Was that hurt in his eyes? Pain? How *could* it be? She was the one who'd been tricked into thinking he actually wanted her again . . . actually felt about her the way he had before they'd grown apart.

New tears built up in his eyes, and twice he started to open his mouth as if to speak, then once more he clenched his teeth together. The intense anger in his eyes was too much, and Abby looked away. As she did, he put his hands on her shoulders and jerked her close against him again, kissing her with a passion that was as much rage as it was desire. She kissed him back, her body acting with a will of its own.

"Stop!" She was crying harder than before, disgusted with herself for her inability to tear away from him. *How can I enjoy his kiss even now?*

In response to her own silent question she yanked her head back and snarled at him, "Get away from me!"

His hands fell to his sides and he took a step backward. His eyes were dry now, his words hard, lacking any of the emotion of the past ten minutes. "It's no use, is it, Abby?"

She shook her head. "Not if it's going to be like that . . . just a way for you to keep your promise to my dad." She fanned her fingers over her heart as another wave of tears spilled from her eyes. "You don't want me, John. You're in love with Charlene. I know that. Don't stand here and try to convince yourself you feel something for me when we both know you don't."

John sighed and his head dropped in frustration. He looked up and gazed at the ceiling. "I give up, Abby." His eyes found hers again. "I'm sorry about your dad." He paused, the anger and even the indifference replaced by a sad resignation. "I loved him, too. And about tonight . . ." He shook his head. "I'm . . . I'm sorry, Abby."

His last words were like a slap in the face. *Don't apologize, John. Tell me you meant that kiss . . . every moment of it. Tell me I'm wrong, that it wasn't because of your promise to Dad.* She wiped her hand across her cheeks and hugged herself tight. *I know you felt something with me, John. We both felt something! Tell me that . . .*

But he said nothing, and Abby exhaled as the fight left her. She didn't want to argue with John; she just wanted her dad back. "It's been a long day for both of us . . ." She was suddenly sorry she'd lost her temper with him. Even if he had kissed her for all the wrong reasons, somehow she knew he was trying to comfort her, trying to show her that despite their differences he still cared. The fact made her want to reach out and at least hug him, but there seemed no way to bridge the distance between them. She took a step toward the stairs. "Good night, John."

He stood there, not moving, watching her as something raw and vulnerable flashed in his eyes. Whatever he was feeling, he shared none of it with her. "Good night, Abby."

She forced herself up the steps to the guest room, peeled off her clothes, and slipped into a T-shirt she kept under the pillow. Then she tried desperately to remember every happy moment she'd ever shared with her father.

But it was no use.

As she drifted off to sleep there was only one troubling thought that reigned in her head . . .

How good it had felt to kiss John Reynolds again.

It was the morning of the funeral service and for John, the single feeling that prevailed in the days since Joe Chapman's death was not grief at the man's passing or the chasm of loss he felt at having missed the chance to know him better. Rather, it was the memory of Abby in his arms, wracked with tears, clinging to him, fitting next to him, beside him, the way she hadn't been in years.

The memory of their kiss.

No matter what Abby thought, his kiss hadn't been out of obligation. His feelings had been stronger than anything he'd ever felt for anyone else. Even Charlene. But obviously Abby hadn't felt the same way. As always, she'd found a reason to fight with him.

Since then John had wrestled so strongly with thoughts of Abby that the morning of the funeral service he was running on only two hours' sleep. He had been up most of the night wondering what the feelings meant. Had Abby's father prayed some miraculous prayer, uttered some powerful words of healing? Was it possible that John Chapman's death might spark new life in their dying marriage?

It didn't seem like it.

After all, she hadn't said more than five words to him since then and at night she still headed off for the guest room without so much as a good-night. But still . . . the possibility was there, wasn't it? Or maybe Abby was right. Maybe the kiss was out of some deep obligation to her father, something to make up for the fact that he'd made the man a promise he couldn't possibly keep.

Love her forever? When they were weeks away from being divorced?

John released a quiet, frustrated sigh and glanced around the church. There weren't many people, only a fraction of those who remembered the goodness of Joe Chapman. Abby's friends from school—mostly parents of the kids' friends. Matt Conley and his mother, Jo; Abby's sister, Beth; and a handful of nurses from Wingate. John's mother was too ill with Alzheimer's to leave her nursing home, otherwise she would have been there. Abby's father had been her friend, too.

In his glory days, Joe had been every bit the well-known football coach John was. Hundreds of people would have recognized him as he went about his day, greeted him in the markets, and counted themselves lucky to be among his friends. Yet here, at the end of his journey, Joe Chapman was only remembered by a handful, a remnant of the fan club that had once been his.

Is this all it amounts to, God? Live your life year in, year out, affecting the lives of hundreds of kids only to go out all alone?

This world is not your home, son . . .

The verse came to him as easily as air, and John knew it was true. But still . . . John wrestled with his feelings, not sure exactly how he felt about heaven. It sounded good, certainly. Talking about Joe Chapman being at rest, at peace, having a body that was healthy and would never wear out . . . assuring each other that he was in the presence of God and his wife and John's own father and a dozen others who'd gone on before him.

But still, he was gone. And right now that seemed like second best.

A preacher took the podium and unfolded a sheet of paper. "I didn't know a lot about Joe Chapman," he began. "So I acted on the suggestion of his daughter Abby and contacted the Christian church where Joe was a member for nearly thirty years." He paused and let his eyes fall over the small gathering of people. John liked the way the man talked, slow and friendly, as if he'd known them all for years.

"You might be surprised with what I found." The pastor shrugged his shoulders and smiled in a sad way. "I'm not sure he'd like me telling you, but I think it's okay just this once. So you might know what an amazing man Joe Chapman really was."

Peering down at his notes, he began. "Joe Chapman was a teacher, a football coach. He did not make a great deal of money. But every fall from the first year he taught until he retired, he purchased a complete Thanksgiving dinner and had the church deliver it to one of his players. A boy and his family who would otherwise have gone without."

John cringed inwardly. *What had he ever done for others? In that moment he could think of nothing . . .* Beside him, Abby cast a curious glance down the row at her sister. Abby's father had never talked about the dinners, never mentioned them at all. Obviously even Abby hadn't known about them. John focused his attention back on the pastor.

"Until Parkinson's disease got the better of him, Joe spent the early hours one Saturday each and every month raking leaves or planting flowers or doing whatever he could to keep the church grounds clean. Joe's pastor tells me even his family didn't know about those acts of service. Why? Because Joe didn't want anyone but his Lord knowing about it."

John felt his insides melting. *We wasted a lifetime talking about first downs and passing plays and missed out on the real victories. Why didn't I take the time to get to know him better, Lord?*

There was no response as the pastor looked down at his notes and shook his head once. "Here's the kicker, though. When Joe's wife died in the tornado of 1984, eight other people died, too. Among them was a man with no insurance, no worldly means but to work by the sweat of his brow. He left behind a wife and four kids destined to spend the rest of their days on welfare.

"Joe found out about the lady at his own wife's funeral and the next day he called a banker friend of his in Michigan . . ."

A banker friend? John sat up straighter in the pew. That had to be his father. What other banker friend did he have in Michigan?

"Turns out the banker friend was the one who led Joe Chapman to the Lord years earlier, and now Joe wanted to give him another chance to invest in eternity. The widowed woman and her kids needed a place to live, he told his friend. And Joe combined half the money from his wife's insurance with a donation from his banker friend and together they asked the church to buy that family a house. Maybe you don't know it, but money donated to a church for a specific cause is not tax deductible. In other words, the only reason Joe and his friend asked the church to be the middle man was because they wanted their act to be totally anonymous."

John heard Abby's breath catch in her throat. Neither of them knew anything about the woman or her orphaned children or the house that their fathers had provided. A house built with a kind of love John had all but forgotten about. The goodness of their act was too much for John to bear and his eyes grew wet. No wonder he'd made such a mess of his life. When had he ever given that way, selflessly, at the expense of his own personal ease?

The pastor was finishing his message. "Until the day he died, Joe Chapman helped that woman, arranging his pension so that a hundred dollars went through the church into her bank account every month, year in, year out." He paused. "Anything else I could say about Joe Chapman—details of his coaching career or how he is survived by two daughters or that he had hundreds of students who loved him—all of it seems like an afterthought compared to the way he loved his Lord."

John felt hollow, as though he had failed to furnish a room in his heart reserved for Joe and his father. *God, why didn't I know before?*

"I do want to read one more letter. Abby found it in a drawer by his bed when he died. It's an essay written by one of his students." The pastor looked at the paper in his hands and hesitated. "'Mr. Chapman is my favorite teacher because he never forgets what it is to be a kid. He doesn't bark at us like some teachers, and yet everyone in class listens to him and respects him. A lot of us want to be just like him when we grow up. Mr. Chapman tells us corny jokes, and in his classroom it's okay if we make a mistake. Other teachers say they care about their students but Mr. Chapman really does. If someone's sad or lonely, he asks them about it and makes sure that when they leave his classroom they're feeling better. I'm a richer person for my time in his class and no matter how long I live, I'll never forget him.'"

John felt like falling on his face, crying out that it wasn't fair, that God should have taken someone like him instead and let someone as good and generous as Abby's father live to be a hundred.

The pastor cleared his throat. "Now, just in case you're thinking that Joe was somehow robbed, that after a lifetime of giving he wasn't given a fair shake by God Almighty, let me tell you this. Some people store up treasures on earth . . . houses, cars, illicit relationships . . . and every day they wake, they move one day further from their treasure, one day closer to death." He smiled broadly. "Ah, but then there are people like Joe, people who wake every day one step closer to their treasure. One day closer to leaving this lobby and entering the main ballroom. Closer finally to being home in the place that was created for them. So don't grieve for Joe, people. Believe that, as C. S. Lewis once said, for Joe life here on earth was only the title and cover page. And now he has begun the greatest story of all, one that no one on earth has ever read in which every chapter is better than the last. Believe that, if given the chance, he would have agreed with D. L. Moody, who said in his dying days, 'In a little while you will read in the newspaper that I am dead. Do not believe a word of it, for I will be more alive than ever before.'"

John felt like the wind had been completely sucked out of him. The pastor's words, the picture he'd painted of heaven, was like none John had ever heard. It felt as though his entire perspective had shifted in a single sermon, and suddenly John grieved for the hundreds and thousands of sermons he'd missed over the years.

Jo Harter sat near the middle of the church hanging on every word the preacher said. For weeks, months really, she'd been feeling a calling, something stronger than anything earthly, stronger than her desire to fish or shop. Even stronger than her hope that someday she'd find new love with Denny.

It was the very thing Matt told her to watch for. A holy longing, he called it.

"It'll happen one day, Mom, wait and see. You'll wake up and have a feeling of want so big and bad nothing in the world'll be able to fill it. Nothing but Jesus."

Well, here she was at this funeral feeling a want every bit as big and bad as Matt had described it. Throughout the service she fidgeted in her seat this way and that until Matt leaned over and whispered at her. "You all right?"

"Fine." She reached out and patted her son's knee, grateful he'd chosen to sit by her instead of Nicole just this once. "I'll tell you later." She didn't want to talk about it yet. Not when every word the pastor uttered seemed handwritten for her alone.

At the end of the service the pastor did something Jo had never seen done at a funeral. He told them he had an invitation for them. At first Jo thought it was an invitation to the potluck at the

Reynoldses' house after the service, but then the pastor asked them to close their eyes.

Okay, God, my eyes are closed. What's happening here, anyway?

Come, daughter. Come to Me.

Jo opened her eyes and sat straight up in the pew. She poked Matt in the ribs and whispered, "Who said that?"

He looked at her like she maybe needed a little more sleep and put his finger to his lips. "Shhh. No one said anything."

Fine. Now I'm hearing things. Jo closed her eyes again and listened hard to the pastor's invitation.

"Many of you may already have the assurance that Joe did, assurance that your name is written in the Lamb's Book of Life, assurance that you are saved from your sins because of what Jesus did for you on the cross. Assurance of heaven. But I believe there may be some of you out there who have never made the decision to trust Jesus Christ for life. You have a hole in your heart only Jesus can fill and you want to know your future is safe with Him. If that's you this morning, could you please raise your hand? I'll make sure I talk with you after the service, give you a Bible, and help you get started on the right path."

He hesitated, and Jo could feel the longing grow with each passing second. There was a hole in her heart all right. No doubt about it.

"Anyone?"

It made no sense to wait. If walking with Jesus had filled the holes for Matt and Denny, then just maybe they would fill this one for her. It was time she stepped down from her high horse and did something about it. Without another moment's hesitation, her hand shot into the air.

I do want You, Jesus. I do. Show me the way, God . . .

Beside her, Matt reached over and squeezed her knee, and as the prayer ended, she hugged her only son. It was then that she noticed something she hadn't before.

For the first time since the funeral started, Matt had tears in his eyes.

Nineteen

BETWEEN THE SCENE AT HER FATHER'S DEATHBED, and the way John had kissed her later that night, Abby had moments when she wondered if maybe, just maybe, John was having second thoughts about their divorce. Could a man fake the trembling she'd felt when John had his arm around her, promising her dying father that he would love her forever? Could he manufacture tears of regret for the hours and days he might have spent with the man who had been his own father's best friend?

Could he really have kissed her that way out of some obligation?

Abby didn't think so, but for all the emotion that surrounded them that week, time passed like always and nothing changed between her and John. The proof came just one week after the funeral, when Nicole burst into Abby's office, her face stricken.

"Why's Charlene Denton hanging out with Dad at practice?" She was angry and her mouth hung open while she waited for Abby's response.

Before Abby could come up with something witty and believable, she let loose the first thing that came to mind. "Why don't you ask Dad?"

The reaction on Nicole's face made Abby sure she had said the wrong thing. Nicole's eyes grew wide, and a flicker of raw fear flashed across her face, like heat lightning in a summer sky. "What's that supposed to mean?"

In that instant, Abby had the first glimpse of the nightmare it was going to be to tell Nicole and the boys the truth. She tried to cover up with an innocent-sounding laugh. "Relax, honey. I'm kidding."

"Well, Matt wasn't. He saw them together and asked me why." She shifted her weight, her eyebrows lowered. "What am I supposed to tell him?"

Abby released a controlled sigh. "Obviously they work together, honey. Ms. Denton's been friends with your father for years."

"Yeah, and I don't like it. She flirts with him." Nicole clenched her fists. "And Dad spends more time with her than he does with you."

Abby couldn't think of anything to say. She angled her head and resisted a shudder as she thought again of how hard Coach John Reynolds—father, hero, and friend—was about to fall in the eyes of the children who loved him most. "What do you want me to tell you, honey?"

Nicole huffed in response. "Tell me it's a coincidence; tell me it's my imagination; tell me Dad's acting the same as always." She hesitated and her eyes filled with tears. "Tell me everything's okay between you guys."

Abby's heart plummeted. She stood up and pulled Nicole into her arms. "Oh, honey, I'm sorry." Nicole held on tighter than usual and Abby desperately wanted to ease her fears. "Everything's—"

Don't lie to her, daughter.

The voice rang clear in the inner places of Abby's heart, and she stopped short.

"Everything's what?" Nicole pulled away slightly, meeting Abby's eyes, searching for any sign of the security she had always taken for granted.

God, give me the words. "You know how much we love each other." Abby hugged Nicole again as her insides contorted in a wave of sadness so deep and strong it shook her to the core. "Our family's always loved each other."

Nicole drew back again as though she wanted to say something, but before she could speak, Abby bent close and kissed her on the tip of her nose. "How 'bout some tea, huh? Why don't you go start a pot of water and I'll join you in a minute."

The diversion worked, and Nicole smiled at Abby, clearly convinced that her comforting words were proof that everything was, indeed, all right.

Like enemy soldiers easing their way across a minefield, Abby and John survived the next several weeks without anyone bringing up Charlene's name. It was Monday night, the last week of school, and Abby was making brownies—part of a longstanding Reynolds family tradition. Every year just before school let out, the kids took plates of brownies to their teachers and shared them with their classmates. As they got older, the ritual became almost silly, but the kids still loved it. Even as a senior football player, Kade had asked her the night before if she was going to bake this week.

Abby pushed the wooden spoon through a bowl of wet brownie mix and thought how next year at this time the kids probably would have adapted to their new life, the one where their dad was no longer married to their mom. She dumped the batter into a buttered pan and slipped it into the oven. Abby gazed out the window across the expanse of green, rolling hillside and out over the lake.

Was it possible Kade was already graduating? Where had the time gone? Abby blinked back the tears that stung at her eyes. She was always fighting tears these days . . . and why not? She had a daughter getting married, a son graduating and moving away to college, and a husband who didn't love her anymore.

It was a wonder she didn't wake up crying.

The phone rang, and Abby inhaled sharply, switching gears. No amount of remembering could change the fact that every aspect of her life was about to change.

"Hello?" She pinned the receiver with her shoulder and wiped her hands on a paper towel.

"Uh, yes . . ." It was a woman, and she seemed nervous. Abby felt the color draining from her face. *It couldn't be . . .* The woman cleared her throat. "Is . . . is John Reynolds there?"

Abby's heart felt as though it had fallen onto the kitchen floor. Even when she tried she couldn't bring herself to breathe. "Can I . . . tell him who's calling?"

There was a heavy sigh on the other end. "It's Charlene Denton. I need to ask him a question about school."

A round of emotions exploded at strategic points throughout Abby's body, temporarily decimating her heart, soul, and gut. *Breathe, Abby. Breathe.* She felt sick to her stomach and she closed her eyes. A dozen comebacks fought for position. *You have a lot of nerve, lady. What kind of an idiot do you take me for? Something about school? Give me a break.*

In the end, Abby couldn't speak over the pounding sound of her heart. She gripped the phone tightly, covering the mouthpiece as her initial hurt and shock gave way to a burning rage. *How dare he have her call at the house!* Carrying the phone as though it were a weapon, she stormed through the living room and into the garage.

John was tinkering with a fishing pole and he looked up when she appeared. He waited for her to speak, his expression slightly baffled, as though he could feel her anger from twenty feet away and hadn't a clue what he'd done to cause it.

She thrust the receiver in his direction. "It's *Charlene.*"

The surprise on his face seemed genuine, but his eyes were immediately flooded with guilt. He took the phone, turned his back on Abby, and spoke in a muffled voice.

It was as though she were drowning at sea, and John had made the decision to let her go under for the final time. He was choosing

Charlene over Abby so blatantly she didn't know how to react, and she waited until she heard the subtle electronic tone indicating the call was over.

John held the phone but let his hand drop to his side, his back still to her.

"We need to talk." Abby's voice wasn't angry or frantic; it held none of the range of emotions that had assaulted her since the phone rang. Why be angry now? It was all over but the paperwork.

A sense of finality hugged Abby close, bringing with it an unnatural calm as John spun around and met her gaze, his back stiff, eyes narrowed and ready to fight. His voice was hot from the moment he started talking. "Look, Abby, I didn't tell her to—"

"It doesn't matter." She was businesslike, which clearly surprised him, as he stopped midsentence. "I don't want to fight, John. It's not going to change anything." She dropped down onto the garage steps and set her elbows firmly on her knees, her eyes still locked on his. Suddenly she felt too old and tired even to explain herself. "Charlene's your future. I can see it. I'm not going to scream at you and call you names because you're in love with another woman. It's too late for that."

John released a huff and rolled his eyes. "I didn't tell her to call me, Abby; you've got to believe—"

Abby held both hands up, and again John stopped short of finishing. "Don't give me excuses." Her tone was calm but resigned, and as she spoke John's posture relaxed. "I'll be honest . . . I don't want her calling here. But I'm not blind. I can read the writing on the wall and one day . . ." The last thing Abby wanted was tears, especially now when her heart no longer seemed linked to the issue at hand. But they came anyway, filling her eyes and spilling onto her cheeks before she could do anything to stop them. "One day she may be my children's stepmother. I'm tired of hating. I don't want to hate her or you or anyone else."

John hung his head for a moment and then came closer, leaning against their blue sedan and drawing a slow breath. "I'm sorry, Abby. I never meant to hurt you with any of this." He dropped his gaze once more, obviously unwilling to watch her cry.

As calm as Abby felt she was rocked deep in her heart by John's agreeing with what she was saying. *Fight for me, John. For us. Tell me you can't stand her, that you were out here thinking of how we might find a way to make it work . . .* But the truth was, at this stage of their marriage they both knew the score. There were only minutes left in the game, and there were simply no winners anywhere. Except maybe Charlene. Abby wiped away her tears. "I have a favor to ask."

He stuffed his hands in his pockets, his head still lowered so that only his eyes made contact with her. "Anything, Abby."

Don't say it, Abby. Love bears all things . . .

The voice faded and she angled her head, willing John to see that this was the only way out for either of them. "Get the paperwork done. Make an appointment with an attorney. Someone we don't know. That way we can move quickly once the kids are married." She hesitated, trying to read his expression and failing. A devastating realization struck her: *I'm no longer the expert on navigating the deep places of John Reynolds's heart.*

His gaze fell to his feet, and nearly a minute passed before he spoke. "I'll call first thing tomorrow." Without looking at her or saying another word, he walked slowly past her into the house. After a few minutes, the automatic lights clicked off and Abby peered into the black emptiness, realizing it was in some ways a sneak preview of her future without John.

Complete and utter darkness broken only by frightening shapes and vague, uncertain shadows.

The week sped by in a blur of final exams and yearbook signings and preparations for Kade's graduation. But John had kept his promise. It was Thursday, and his appointment with the attorney was set for four o'clock. He had finished entering grades into the computer and was taking down the posters from his classroom, an annual task required of all teachers. Like so often that week, as he worked he was haunted by the look on Abby's face when Charlene had called.

He rolled up a poster and sighed out loud.

Charlene.

He still wasn't sure why she'd called him at home. She'd said it was because she had a question about Marion High's computer grading policy, but John thought there might be more to it. Although she'd kept her distance as he'd asked, when their paths crossed she seemed more forward, less patient than before. The last time he'd seen her prior to the phone call, she'd asked if Abby knew about them.

"What's there to know?" John was still drawn to her, but her questions set him on edge. Whatever happened to the days when their friendship was fun and carefree? Didn't she understand how hard this was for him? How devastating it was to watch his son graduate and his daughter get married weeks before he would walk out on all of them and start his life over?

Charlene had pursed her lips in a mock pout. "I just mean in a few months we'll be together all the time. She has to know you have a life outside the family home. You're getting divorced, after all. It's not like you have to keep me a secret from everyone who matters to you."

Her words rang in his head still, and he figured they had more to do with her phone call than any excuse about grading policies or trouble with her classroom. He remembered the way Abby's face changed from anger to ice-cold indifference. *Is it that easy, Abby girl? Letting Charlene have her way? Wanting only divorce papers from me, nothing more?* He rolled the final poster and was slipping a rubber band around it when Charlene walked in.

She stopped in the doorway and grinned at him. "Do you know how gorgeous you look when you're working?" Her skirt was shorter than usual, legs tan and toned as she made her way across the classroom. She caught him looking and smiled when his eyes made their way back up to hers. "Hi . . ."

No question John was attracted to her, but her sudden appearance made him angry at her. What right did she have to violate his solitude? Besides, he wasn't in the mood for her questions. He thought about telling her to leave as he straightened and stretched his bad knee. "Hi."

"The school's a ghost town." Her eyes burned into his, the meaning of her words far from lost on John. Classes let out at one o'clock every day the last week of school, so she was right. There were no students anywhere. She crossed the room and perched herself against the edge of the desk. She was inches from him, and her perfume filled his senses. "I've stayed away as long as I can, John."

He cocked his head and thought of what he might say to hold his ground. *Give me the words, God . . . please.*

Flee, son! Return to your first love . . .

"You shouldn't be here. I asked you not to . . ." John wished he could speak with more conviction, but he didn't want to be mean. Charlene was one of his closest friends, even though she'd been getting on his nerves lately.

"I missed you . . ."

He kicked the empty poster box gently toward the edge of the room. "I'm still a married man, Charlene."

Suddenly, his frustration shifted. It was Abby's fault he was in this mess. She was the one he should be angry with, not Charlene. All Charlene had done was be his friend, listen to him, make him feel like he mattered.

Things Abby hadn't done for a long time.

He looked at Charlene, and suddenly he felt drawn to her again. He took a step toward her. "No matter how much I might wish I wasn't."

John thought about what he'd just said. *No matter how much I might wish I wasn't? Wasn't what? Wasn't married to a girl I waited years to marry?* Was that really him talking? John broke the connection between him and Charlene and let his gaze fall to the floor. Was he crazy?

Charlene seemed to sense that his thoughts had shifted. She angled her head and raised her eyebrows, her face the picture of sympathy. "It must be hard. Pretending all the time in front of the kids, I mean." She hesitated. "I wish there was something I could do . . ."

John leaned against his desk alongside her. This time Charlene's offer of help played over in his mind. When was the last time Abby cared about his feelings or wanted to help him? She hadn't been his best friend in years. Maybe the tensions with Charlene were just the result of his inability to spend time with her. After all, these days his best friend was . . . he looked up and caught Charlene's eyes again. "We need to take it slow."

As naturally as if they were the ones who had been married for years, she came to him, wedging herself between his knees as her arms went up around his neck. "I haven't waited this long because I want to rush things." Her voice was a whisper, her eyes probing his, and John was certain she could see how weak he was. Without meaning to, his knees tightened slightly, keeping her close, not wanting to let her go now or ever.

"I don't want to make the same mistakes again." Desire swept John so overpowering it was frightening. It suddenly felt as though he might sell his very soul to have the object his body so intensely craved. He brought his hand to her face and traced her cheekbone. "Tell me we won't make the same mistakes, Charlene."

She didn't answer. A smile filled her face, but instead of smiling back, John felt something deep in his gut. Something hesitant . . . even resistant. He couldn't pin it down, but there was something in her smile he didn't like . . . something wrong.

Before he could think those feelings through, she moved closer, fitting up against him . . . and he readily accepted her kiss. At first it was slow and tender, but in a matter of seconds it became filled with blazing passion, intense beyond anything John could remember.

"Come home with me, John. I need you . . ."

He was still sitting on the desk, but as the kiss continued he slid closer to the edge, closer to her, digging his fingers into her beautiful, dark hair. *Help me, Lord . . . I've lost all control . . . it's like she's cast a spell over me.*

A burst of loud, tinny feedback filled the room. "This is a reminder that Mr. Foster has asked all teachers to have their class-rooms ready for inspection by eight o'clock tomorrow morning."

The words rang loudly from the intercom at the front of the class-room, and John jerked back as though he'd been slapped.

"Also, graduation assignments have been posted on the main office door. Thank you."

Charlene's eyes were clouded with the intensity of their kiss, and the same smile that had bothered John moments ago returned. She nestled herself up against him again, framing his face with her fingers. "Where were we?"

He thought of Abby, of their brief but intense encounter after her father died, how the passion then had been far stronger than this, bet-ter somehow . . . more pure. Nausea at what he'd done racked his gut. *What kind of man have I become?*

He turned his face and squirmed free from her, moving three feet away and easing into one of the student desks. When his breathing was stable, he looked at Charlene. "I'm sorry; that was wrong." He rested his elbow on the desk and caught his forehead between his thumb and forefinger, rubbing his temples, praying that God would disperse the pent-up feelings he had for this woman. He closed his eyes as he spoke. "I'm not ready for this." He opened his eyes and peered over the edge of his hand at her.

She nodded once and moved to sit behind his desk, suddenly less the seductress and more the good-intentioned friend, and he shifted uneasily. It was as though to please him she could take on any role she wished. That thought, and her smile, set him even further on edge and he felt his body cool. She met his gaze straight on and spoke gently. "I've missed you . . . but I didn't come here for that."

John was suddenly nervous, anxious to be on his way to the appointment with the attorney. Where could this meeting with Charlene possibly go, anyway? He waited for her to continue.

She crossed her arms, her face more serious than before. "I've been given a job offer."

John's heart lurched. She wouldn't move away, would she? Charlene had finished her administrative credentials the year before and had put out feelers in local school districts. Her goal was to take an assistant principal position somewhere in Marion. "That's great." He searched her eyes, looking for clarification.

Charlene's hands came together, and she dropped her gaze. "The job's in Chicago, John. Someone at the district office told the staff up there I was looking." She brought her eyes up again, and he could see how strongly she was struggling. "It's a good offer."

The muscles in his jaw clenched, and he fought with himself. Why were his feelings for Charlene all over the board? One minute he was wishing he'd never met her, the next wishing he could . . . "Is it what you want?" If it was, he could hardly stand in her way.

She exhaled through pursed lips and a sadness filled her eyes. "I want you, John Reynolds. If I have to wash dishes for a living."

Well, there it was. So why did her words make his heart feel like it was being squeezed by a vice grip? There was something she wasn't saying. "But . . ."

"But if you don't see yourself . . . having a future with me . . ." Tears filled her eyes, and she pulled a neatly folded tissue from her purse, dabbing at the wetness before it could mar her perfect makeup job. "Then I have no choice but to go. To start life over somewhere without you."

Once, a long time ago, John had seen a movie where a man was trapped in a shrinking corridor, where both walls were moving slowly in on him. Now, with all that was looming in his life, John knew how the man felt. His shoulders slumped. "What do you want me to say?"

"Tell me you feel the same way I do, that you see us together when this mess you're going through is finally behind you." Her answer was quick, and he saw in her eyes that she cared enough for him to turn down any job, to call him at home even when it meant making him angry, to risk getting caught kissing him in his classroom—clearly a violation of school policy. The truth was simple. She thought she was in love with him, and if he were willing, she would gear the rest of her life around him.

She was young and pretty, bright and incredibly devoted to him. In her presence he felt loved and appreciated and full of life. So why didn't he jump at the chance she was offering him?

Was it the fact that he wasn't legally divorced yet that held him back? Was it his faith? Or was it the way she'd come across as manipulative and pushy lately? His feelings were so jumbled he had no answers for her. "You know how I feel about you."

"That's not what I'm asking." Her tone had gone from troubled and sincere to impatient. "Am I part of your future? *That's* what I need to know."

John thought about her question. He did care deeply for her . . . didn't he? Hadn't she been the one willing to put her life on hold while he sorted out the details of his divorce? Wasn't she the one who had been his friend, his confidante and ally, while Abby drew further away with each passing year? He thought about the pain in Abby's eyes when Charlene had called at the house the other day. Was that why Abby had stopped being his friend? Because she felt replaced by Charlene?

He suddenly wanted nothing more than to be away from her, by himself where he could sift through his emotions.

"When do you have to let them know?" He gathered his posters and felt her eyes follow him.

"The end of July."

The end of July. There wasn't any way the timing could be more perfect. *Like trading Abby's dreams in for Charlene's.* He winced inwardly and forced the thought from his mind. "Give me some time, okay? I'll let you know before the wedding."

"If you want me, John, I'm staying."

He had nothing more to say to her. Instead he glanced at the clock on the wall. "I have to run." Divorce attorneys charged by the hour. He stood and grabbed a few files and his car keys, leaving Charlene alone in his classroom without so much as a good-bye.

As John climbed into his truck he caught a glimpse of himself in the mirror and wondered at the man he'd become. His older son was graduating the next day, and a few weeks after that he would walk his only daughter down the aisle and hand her over in marriage. But here, in the hours before the milestones his family had waited a lifetime for, he'd allowed himself to be swept into a wave of passion that but for his weakly uttered prayer would have led . . . where? Would he have cancelled his appointment and followed her home? Allowed his passions to dictate his actions as though he didn't have a responsibility in the world?

He thought of his prayer again and how the blaring office message had broken the spell, changed the moment so that he could think clearly again. A shudder went over him at the thought of what might have happened.

Then it hit him.

What was the difference? Whether he gave in to Charlene now or later, he was still destroying something he'd vowed to keep forever, burying for all time the dreams of Abby and Nicole and Kade and Sean. Who was he kidding?

The image of Abby's father and his final request filled his mind: *"Love her . . . love her . . . love her."*

He pushed the gas pedal down and felt the truck pick up speed.

The plans were already in motion, too far gone to change despite distant holy whisperings or graduations or weddings or deathbed promises made about honoring his marriage. It was too late for any of it. His marriage was terminally ill, and in a few minutes he would take part in the only thing left to do.

Sit down with an attorney and draw up the death certificate.

Twenty

FOR THE MOST PART DENNY CONLEY WAS NOT a nervous man. After all he'd found the nerve to stand in front of his Twelve-Step group and tell the whole wretched story of how he'd drunk away his early years of being a father, how he'd walked out on Jo and Matt when the kid was barely old enough to remember him. Not only that, but in the past year he'd been bold enough to tell a whole congregation that he, Denny Conley, was a sinner and needed a Savior.

The boldness, he'd learned, came from God and not himself, and that was a good thing. That kind of power would never let him down.

But none of that mattered now as he followed the final directions to Nicole Reynolds's house. He was shaking like a leaf, and only the grace of God kept him from flipping a U-turn and heading back home, an hour south.

The meeting had been Matt's idea.

"Dad, don't wait 'til the wedding." His son's voice had been filled with such sincerity that this time it was Denny who'd been choked up. "Come to the graduation party. There'll be lots of people; you'll fit right in."

Denny gulped. *Calm me down, Lord. Calm me down.*

He'd seen pictures of Matt of course, but he hadn't looked into his son's eyes since the boy was four years old. Hadn't felt those young arms around his neck or wrestled with his son or brushed his fingers against the boy's hair. Hadn't loved him the way a father should. A gust of shame blew through his beat-up Ford, and he shook his head.

"Kid must be crazy," Denny mumbled out loud as he changed lanes. "Shouldn't be givin' me the time of day."

It was another one of the benefits of following after Jesus, the rewards Pastor Mark had talked about back when Denny first made his decision. The idea that he might actually have a second chance with his boy, a chance to know him and love him like he should have done at the start, was almost more than Denny could imagine.

No doubt it was the reason he was fighting the shakes. After nearly twenty years he was about to be a father again. Not only that, but he was going to meet the pretty little thing who was marrying his boy. She was a smart one, just like Matt, and she came from good people—parents who'd loved each other since the beginning of time.

Parents like he and Jo might have been if he'd done things differently.

Denny eased up on the gas pedal at the thought of Jo. With all the excitement of seeing Matt again, he'd done everything he could to keep from thinking about the woman to whom he'd once promised forever. He glanced at the directions. Right turn at the light, four blocks to the lake. Left, and the Reynoldses' house was third on the right. He'd be there in two minutes.

The best news of all, of course, was that Jo had actually given her heart to God, too. Two decades after scattering into the world, the members of the Denny Conley family had each found their way home to the Savior. That fact alone was proof that God was real and that He listened to the prayers of His people—even those in the off-key voices of one like himself, those with so little to offer.

Denny was more nervous than ever before, if that were possible, but nothing could replace the deep-rooted joy that grew in his gut like an everlasting flame. He was going to see his wife and son again! Going to hold them, feel them snug in his arms. Denny's heart pounded so hard he was surprised he couldn't see it pushing its way out of his chest with every beat. He made the final turn and saw twenty or so cars gathered around one of the driveways.

The Reynoldses' home. *Here I go, Lord. Walk before me.*

He ran a hand over his slicked-back hair and moved quickly now, as though he were leaving everything about his old life behind and moving into some new, brighter existence with every step.

Jo Harter had been anchored in a chair by the front window, glancing out every minute or so and searching the street for the old beater Denny drove. Matt had described it, and then fiddlesticks if he wasn't able to let it go at that. None of this hanging-around-the-window routine for Matt.

The party was in full swing, people gathered in pockets throughout the house, celebrating young Kade Reynolds's graduation. That boy had a real good future set before him for sure, and Jo'd made a point of telling him so when she first arrived. After that she'd found Matt and asked for the tenth time when Denny was set to arrive.

"Mom, he said he wasn't sure." Matt grinned at her as though somehow their roles had reversed, making him the patient adult and her the pesky child.

Come on, get here, Denny . . .

She'd no sooner thought the words than she saw a car like the one Matt described move slowly past, turn around, and stop not far from the house. Jo held her breath as he climbed out and headed for the house. He looked just like she remembered him. Not much taller than herself, dark hair—what was left of it—and just enough bowlegged that she could pick him out in a crowd. A catch if ever she saw one.

Without another moment's hesitation, Jo nearly danced across the living room to the front door and swung it open. "Denny!"

He stopped in his tracks, his eyes locked onto hers while a full-bore grin spread across his face. It punctuated his cheeks with the cutest dimples Jo had ever seen, and suddenly she was in his arms, certain beyond words that the marvelous God they served had pulled off nothing less than a miracle.

He put his hands along either side of her face and studied her like a winning lottery ticket. "Jo . . . I've missed you, sweetie. I can't believe I'm here."

There were a hundred things Jo had hoped to say but none of them was right at hand except a few simple words: "Welcome home, Denny Conley."

Once again his smile lit up the late afternoon. "Thank you, Jo. And now I believe I have a son to see."

Abby surveyed the dwindling party guests from the doorway of the kitchen and her gaze fell on Jo and Denny, deep in conversation with Matt and Nicole. They looked awfully cozy. Was it possible that life was going to turn out right for Jo and her beloved Denny after so many years? She remembered Jo's monologue about her ex-husband and how she'd hoped to lose ten pounds in order to catch his eye at the wedding.

She watched Jo's eyes sparkle and saw the way she spoke to the man she clearly still loved. The woman might have lost weight in the past few months, but it wasn't what she'd lost that had Denny Conley hanging on her every word.

It was what she'd gained.

Abby sighed and turned back into the kitchen. *How come Jo's faith seems more real than mine, God? She's only believed for a few months.*

Silence.

Abby grabbed a stack of empty platters and began wiping them down in the sink. It wasn't fair. She and John had been faithful all their lives, teaching their children about walking with God, building a relationship with Him, worshiping Him. But now, when it mattered most, their faith was like a corroded, dead battery. Incapable of giving off any power at all.

Washing dishes was mindless enough, and she listened to conversations in the adjacent room as she worked.

"So, Kade, tell me it isn't true about your sister." Abby recognized the voice of Dennis Steinman, one of Kade's football buddies. "She isn't really marrying someone else, is she?"

"Yeah, in four weeks." Kade's tone was light and full of laughter. The party was already a huge success, graced by the presence of friends, teachers, and townspeople who had been a part of Kade's life since he was a young child.

"Come on, I thought she was waiting for me. She loved me, man."

"No, Steiner, that wasn't love. It was pity."

Laughter erupted among the friends, and Abby thought back to earlier that afternoon and the graduation ceremony. John had been one of the teachers asked to stay near the student section, so Abby and the others sat together without him. She had glanced at him every now and then and knew his attention couldn't have been farther from the students. It was all focused on Kade, his older son, his star quarterback . . . and Abby's gut had ached at the loss John must have been feeling that afternoon. There was always pain in bidding good-bye to a senior player, someone John had worked with three, sometimes four years straight.

But losing Kade . . .

Abby pictured their son the way he'd looked a few hours earlier, decked in his cap and gown and ready to tackle the world. No matter what the future brought she would never forget the image of him walking proudly across the football field to receive his diploma—the same field where he and John had built a lifetime of memories, a bond that would remain through all time. It filled her heart with misty, watercolored yesterdays and pictures of a happier time when Kade was just starting school and everything looked like it would go on forever.

She finished washing the last platter and began drying. This should have been a day when John would pour out his feelings to her, a day when they might have taken a walk or wound up on the pier, reminding each other of the times when they'd predicted this very thing. How Kade's school years would fly by, just like Nicole's had. No one, not even Charlene Denton, could know exactly how John's heart felt watching Kade graduate.

No one but Abby.

She stacked the dried platters and wiped her hands on the dishtowel as her ear picked up Matt's voice.

"Yep, we're completely ready. Flowers, bridesmaids, color schemes, matching plates and napkins, little minty things so the guests can spoil their dinner . . ."

Nicole laughed at that. "Matt's right. I can't believe the planning."

"Of course the planning's half the fun." It was Jo, and she sounded as though she were keeping a secret. Denny had been there little more than three hours and already the two of them were brushing shoulders and making eye contact like newlyweds. Jo was going on about the trouble and cost of big weddings when she paused just long enough to catch her breath.

"Okay, kids," Jo said. "Don't you want to know the news?" Abby would have loved to move into the room and fall in place alongside Nicole, but she stayed in the kitchen. Something about Jo's tone told Abby she didn't really want to be there, anyway. Not if the news was as good as it sounded.

"I'm moving here." Denny sounded as though he was about to burst. "Packing up my things and getting a new job quick as I can." Abby could hear Denny's smile and a strange pang worked its way across her heart. It wasn't right. How come two people like Matt's parents could work things out and she and John—the couple everyone had always looked to as an example—couldn't find enough common ground to hold a conversation?

No answers ricocheted in Abby's heart.

"Dad, my gosh, are you serious?" Matt's voice rang with hope.

"Yep, and something else, too . . ."

"Wait a minute," Jo interrupted. "Nicole, where's your mother? I want her to hear this firsthand." Jo's voice came closer, and Abby spun around expectantly as Jo and Denny entered the kitchen holding hands, with Nicole and Matt giggling close behind.

"Abby, I simply can't tell the kids what me and Denny decided without telling you at the same time." She glanced at the man beside her and shrugged her shoulders up and down like a high-school girl.

The towel in Abby's hand hung limp. "Okay . . ." She chided herself silently for not sounding more enthusiastic. The fact that Abby's life was a mess wasn't Jo's fault. The least she could do was be happy for the woman. She forced a smile.

Jo leaned forward, beyond excited. "We're getting married!" The words spilled out as though Jo couldn't hold them in a moment longer. A quick squeal escaped her lips. "Can you *believe* it? Me and Denny, after all these years?"

"My goodness, congratula—" Abby's voice was drowned in the celebratory shouts and exclamations from Matt and Nicole, both of whom now had their arms wrapped around the older couple.

Abby stood on the outside, awkwardly looking in, waiting for the moment to pass. When it did, Jo drew a steadying breath, a smile taking up her entire face. To describe her as beaming would have been a vast understatement.

"You know what it was, don't you, Abby?" Jo reached out and placed her hand on Abby's shoulder.

Fate playing games with me? "Not really . . ." She smiled again, hoping not to raise Nicole's suspicions by acting less than enthusiastic.

Jo slapped Abby on the arm playfully. "Come on, Abby. You're the one who told me about Him."

"Him?" The woman was loony. Abby had never seen Denny until tonight.

Jo released an exaggerated sigh. "God. The Lord, God, Abby. Remember?" Jo shook her head and let out a hearty laugh. "I declare, you have the driest sense of humor this side of Arizona." She poked Denny in the ribs and drew a small laugh from him, as well. "This here's Abby who told me about heaven and God and all the rest." Jo looked at Matt and Nicole. "Then at your granddaddy's funeral . . . well, that's when I first gave Jesus my heart. After that I knew He was gonna give me something, too. Not just eternity with Him, but my own sweet Denny back where he belongs."

That said, Jo planted a lingering kiss square on Denny's lips, causing a crimson glow to spread quickly from the man's neckline right on up to his balding head. "Uh, honey, let's say you and me take a walk outside where it's quiet."

Abby hadn't thought it possible, but Jo's smile spread even farther around her face at the suggestion. She bid the others good-bye, and in an instant they were gone. Matt and Nicole hugged in celebration of the moment, and then Matt excused himself, leaving Nicole behind, her face glowing, eyes full of hope for the future.

"Can you believe it, Mom? Isn't God amazing?"

Abby's gaze fell to the dishrag still in her hand and she began absently polishing the tiles on the counter. "Amazing."

Nicole hesitated for a beat, her smile suddenly faded. "You don't sound sure."

Recover, Abby. Don't give her a reason to doubt you . . . She looked up, feigning ignorance. "About what?"

Nicole crossed her arms and moved her weight to one hip. "About God. I said isn't He amazing and when you answered . . . you didn't sound sure."

Abby laughed as lightly as she could manage. "I'm sorry, honey. I guess I'm tired. It's been a long weekend. Watching Kade graduate, throwing the party, getting ready for your wedding."

A look of concern danced in Nicole's eyes. "You're not sick or anything, are you?"

Abby shook her head quickly. "Not at all, sweetheart. Just a little caught up in what's happening around here."

"But you're happy for Jo and Denny, right?" Nicole's voice still had an edge, and Abby was desperate to change the direction of the conversation.

Pour it on, Abby. "Oh, absolutely. They're just wonderful together. I mean, if that's not how God loves to work, I don't know what is."

Nicole's shoulders eased and the lines on her forehead smoothed. "Exactly. That's what I was trying to say in the first place. I mean, those two back together is like . . . I don't know, it's like more than Matt and I ever imagined."

Abby felt herself relax as she folded the towel and set it on the edge of the counter. She moved closer to Nicole and hugged her gently, pulling back enough to see Nicole's eyes. "You and Matt have been praying for them, haven't you?"

Nicole's eyes danced like they had earlier. "Every day."

This time Abby's smile was genuine. "Then that, my dear, is absolutely amazing."

They were still standing that way, face to face, Abby's wrists balanced on Nicole's shoulders when John walked in and stopped short. "Oh . . . I thought Nicole was with Matt."

Nicole twisted around and smiled at John. "Hi, Dad. Why, where's Matt?"

"Outside with his parents. I thought . . ." He looked preoccupied.

What is it now? Abby felt her insides tighten, and she released the hold she had on Nicole. "Go on out and join him, honey. You should be together at a moment like this."

Abby was grateful that this time Nicole didn't scrutinize their faces or look deeply into the reasons why John might want to talk to Abby alone. Instead she grinned and bounced off in the direction of the backyard. "They're probably down at the pier. Matt knows that's where we celebrate everything."

Abby felt her daughter's comment as strongly as if it were a physical blow to her gut. *"That's where we celebrate everything . . . that's where we celebrate everything . . ."* Abby turned and met John's gaze. "Is everyone gone?"

He swallowed and had trouble making eye contact with her. "Yeah. Everyone but Jo and Denny." He was quiet for a beat but Abby refused to rescue him. *You have something to say, say it. I can wait all night.*

John cleared his throat. "We need to talk."

Abby shrugged. "Yeah, for about five years now."

"Look—" John's tone was suddenly impatient, tired and impatient—"I don't need your sarcasm, Abby. I'm serious. The wedding will be here before you know it and we need to . . . there are a few things we have to discuss."

Abby stared hard at him. "I'm listening." Her voice gave away nothing.

He let his gaze drop for a moment and then pulled it back up again. "The papers are ready. I talked to the lawyer again yesterday." There was defeat in his voice—but something else, too. Something more determined and set that hadn't been there before. "He wants you to stop in sometime this week and take a look before we sign."

The corners of her eyes began to sting. "You've seen them?"

John nodded. "It's just like we discussed. Everything's split. You get the house. I get the savings and the truck. Child support until Sean's eighteen. I keep adding to their college funds. It's all spelled out."

Listening to him was like hearing an autopsy report of their marriage. Abby tried to fight the sick feeling that welled up inside her but it was a losing battle. She let her head drop some. "Fine. Whatever gets us out of this mess."

There was a distant sound of laughter, and Abby knew that Nicole and the others would be outside for a while. The evening was too nice to waste it inside.

Unless, of course, you had divorce details to work out.

John was staring hard at her. "The reason we're in this mess is because sometime . . . a long time ago . . . we stopped loving each other. It wasn't just me who stopped, Abby. It was both of us. You were busy with the kids, and I was—"

"Busy with Charlene."

He angled his head in frustration. "No. I was busy with work. And before we knew it we stopped talking to each other. Maybe we were too tired or maybe we just ran out of things to say. But I can guarantee you one thing, Abby. This mess isn't because of me alone." He studied her, and for a moment she thought she saw a flicker of regret in his eyes. "I've made arrangements to stay with one of the PE teachers after the wedding. I'll have my things packed so I can leave when the reception's over."

The stinging was back. Abby blinked twice and struggled to make her voice sound normal. "When do we tell the kids?"

"After Matt and Nicole get back from their honeymoon."

Abby nodded slowly and walked over to the kitchen sink, staring out across the dark yard toward the lake and the pier and the happy voices that still rang out from that direction. "Okay."

For a moment neither of them said anything, and Abby wondered if John had left the room. Her breath caught in her throat when he came up behind her and let his hands settle on her shoulders. "I'm sorry, Abby. This isn't . . . I never thought . . ."

She was torn between jerking her body from his grasp and turning into his embrace. Instead she remained utterly still. "I know. I'm sorry, too."

He withdrew his hands and cleared his throat. "I'll keep my promise about Charlene, though. Nothing until after the divorce is final. You have my word."

"You have my word . . . have my word . . . have my word." A silent, sad laugh started up Abby's throat and died. She kept her back to him and blinked her tears away. "I'd like to be alone now, John, if you don't mind."

Without saying good-bye, without touching her again or asking if she was all right, John simply turned around and retreated. After a minute she heard the bedroom door close behind him, and she thought of the hundreds of times when that sound would have pulled her from a late-night task, beckoning her to the quiet intimacy of making love or whispering side by side under the covers or laying her head on his shoulder and merely listening to him breathe.

But tonight . . . tonight the sound marked the end of a business meeting between two coworkers who had gathered to discuss funeral arrangements for an associate. An associate whose imminent death was bound to be something of a relief.

Twenty-One

IN ALL HER LIFE NICOLE HAD NEVER FELT closer to God than she did during those weeks leading up to her wedding. Everything her parents had ever taught her about love, all that they had prayed for her and modeled in their own marriage, was finally about to culminate in the single, most glorious moment of her life.

It was Monday, an unforgettable summer morning, mere days from her wedding, and Nicole could barely wait another minute.

She opened a suitcase and set it on her bed. Maybe the camping trip would make the time pass more quickly. Nicole didn't know if it would, but she was glad she was going all the same. It was something she'd always dreamed of: a chance to spend a few days with the women closest to her and glean all she could from them and from God about what it really meant to love a man, to be partners for life in a bond that would last as long as life itself.

A gentle breeze sifted through the screened window, and Nicole gazed outside across the lake. She had always loved the fact that her room faced the back of the house. How many mornings had she sat in her window seat and written down the feelings in her heart while gazing outside? Something about the way the sun threw diamonds across the water always made her emotions rise to the surface, and today was no different.

Nicole stopped and stared, breathing in the summer air. There was nothing like summer in southern Illinois, and she and Matt had talked often about having a house much like her parents', a modest home with a lake view and plenty of room for . . . well, for children one day. Just last week they'd received news that Matt had passed his bar exam, and already he was receiving offers from two local firms and several in the Chicago area.

The thought of their future made Nicole feel all lit up inside.

She pictured her parents one day not too many years off having the chance to be grandparents, and she smiled . . . but just as the image took root, it changed, and Nicole remembered Matt's concerns about Charlene Denton.

There's nothing to be worried about. The woman's a floozy.

Her mood cooled considerably. Nicole crossed over to her dresser and pulled out two pairs of shorts she'd need for the campout. Charlene wasn't a threat to her parents' marriage. No way. Her father was deeply devoted to her mother and would be forever. They were in love. Busy maybe, but in love all the same.

Still, the more Nicole tried to shake the idea, the more threatened she felt by thoughts of the other woman. Finally she released a loud sigh and dropped to her knees near the foot of her bed.

"Fine." She hung her head and began praying out loud, in a whisper only she and the Lord could hear. "Okay, God, I don't like my thoughts, but maybe I'm having them for a reason. Maybe there's something about that woman that's causing my dad and mom some trouble." She struggled for a moment. "I mean, I don't think so, really. But still. Whatever this feeling is, I want You to take it, Lord. If Charlene's a problem, make her go away." She hesitated, allowing God's Spirit to lead the prayer. It was something she'd learned years ago when she first realized her habit of rushing ahead of Him. As she waited, she felt led in a specific direction. "What I'm really trying to

say, God, is be with my parents. They've had a lot on their minds and
. . . well . . . make their love new again. Use me and Matt if it'll help.
Whatever it takes, just make sure they love each other forever. And
help me not to waste any more time thinking about my dad and that
. . . that woman. Love is from You, Father. And love is always what
we've had in this family. Make it grow so that it's greater than ever
before."

A peace came over her and calmed her anxious heart. Nicole
smiled, relieved and grateful at the same time. "I can always count on
You, God. Thank You ahead of time for what You're going to do on
this camping trip." She was about to stand up when she thought of
one last thing. "Oh, and make the hours fly, Lord. Please."

Abby lugged her suitcase into the hallway and leaned it against the
others as she looked around for John. He had promised to load up
the van, but as usual lately he had busied himself in the garage—his
most common hiding place in the hours when he absolutely had to
be home.

The others were already in the living room, talking in unison and
swapping stories of earlier camping trips. Originally there were to be
six of them, but Nicole's friends were both sick with the flu. That left
Abby, Nicole, Jo, and Abby's sister, Beth, who had flown in for both
the campout and the wedding and who was in an uncharacteristically
upbeat mood.

Abby walked down the hallway and opened the door to the
garage. "We're ready."

She didn't wait for John's reply, but let the door shut and turned
to join the others in the living room. In seconds she could hear him
moving luggage outside, and in no time he found them in the living
room, slightly out of breath. "You're all loaded up."

He refused to make eye contact with her, but his tone was cheerful and she was sure the others hadn't picked up on it. Jo was on her

feet first. "I declare John Reynolds—" she walked up to him and patted his cheek much the way a favorite aunt might—"you haven't aged a bit since your playing days in Ann Arbor, Michigan." She winked at Abby and then turned back to John. "Oughta be against the law to look that good at your age."

The others laughed at Jo's directness. For the briefest moment John caught Abby's gaze and she looked away. *Get me out of here, God. What am I supposed to do, stand around and agree with her?* So what if he was good looking? She and John were counting down the days until the divorce.

Abby led the way out to the car with the other women trailing behind. The foursome piled into the van and bid good-bye to John. Abby was grateful that Nicole didn't comment on the fact that John hadn't kissed her as they left. In five minutes Abby merged onto the highway, and Jo seized an almost imperceptible break in the conversation.

"Well, girls, I think I need to tell you about the miracle of God." She was sitting next to Beth in the backseat, with Nicole in the passenger seat up front. Jo tapped Abby on the back. "You girls already know about this, but Beth here hasn't heard, and besides—" she giggled loudly—"I can't stop talking about it. I mean really and truly. It's worse than my fish stories. Everywhere I go it just sort of leaks out all over the place—"

Beth broke in. "What leaks out?"

"Well, my love for God and Denny and being together and marriage, and all the things I'd given up on long before I . . ."

This should be good. Abby leaned back in her seat and focused on the road. There couldn't possibly be anyone more cynical about the virtues of marriage than her sister. Beth had been married at twenty-one, had two baby girls at twenty-three, and been deserted at twenty-five. Beth liked to say joining someone for life was less marriage and more psychological warfare, and that if she were ever tempted to make a mistake like that again she hoped someone would have her committed for insanity. Beth was one of those If-I-get-lonely-I'll-get-a-dog women, and so far she hadn't even done that. Every time the topic came up she'd explain that being married three years cured her of loneliness for a lifetime.

Not until just now had Abby considered the sparks that might fly if Jo and Beth chose to get into the faith issue that weekend. *Well, God, whatever happens work it out for us . . . this is Nicole's campout.*

The prayer came easily, as though she'd been in conversation with the Father for months on end.

The appointed time is for you, daughter.

Abby's breath caught in her throat and she tightened her grip on the wheel. It was one thing to let loose an incidental prayer, but to sense what seemed like an answer so quickly and surely in the depth of her heart . . . Abby blinked hard and pushed the words from her mind. She must be imagining things. The campout had nothing to do with her. Abby tuned out the Lord and honed back in on Jo's conversation.

"And so I just kinda leak all over about the Lord and His goodness and how He done worked a mighty miracle for me and Denny, and how He could do the same thing for anybody willing to take Him at His word."

Abby glanced in the rearview mirror and saw Jo grab a mouthful of air. Beth used the opportunity to clear her throat. "Well, I hate to be a kill-joy, especially when we're getting together for Nicole's wedding, but I for one found my miracle in being divorced. Something about making dinner night after night for a man who can't keep his pants zipped around other girls just doesn't smack with the feel of a miraculous God, if you get my drift."

Nicole shifted uneasily in the front seat and shot Abby a glance. Abby nodded. *Great.* She'd probably be playing referee all weekend at this rate. "Anyone want to stop for coffee before we head out toward the cabin?"

The drive to the cabin took two hours, but the last thirty miles were so remote Abby didn't think there was another person within fifty miles of them. The cabin belonged to a friend of her father's, and at least once a year the Reynolds family had use of it, even if only for a weekend of fishing. Abby knew the spot represented quiet and utter solitude to Nicole and the boys, and when Nicole requested it in lieu of a bridal shower, Abby hadn't been surprised. After all, they'd already had the couples' barbecue.

After they arrived, the four of them unpacked, after which Abby stood up and surveyed the group. "Okay, who wants to go for a walk?"

Beth was on her feet almost instantly. "Me."

Jo waved toward the door. "You go ahead." She patted the cover of her Bible. "Me and the Lord have some catchin' up to do."

Nicole looked at Abby as she spread out on the now-empty bottom bunk. "Mom, why don't you and Aunt Beth go this time. Jo had a few verses she wanted to share with me, okay?"

Abby felt a pit form in her stomach. If she and Beth were going to be alone, then maybe it was time to tell her the news. She nodded. "Sounds good, we'll take the path around the lake and be back in an hour."

They headed north on the gravelly trail that circled the water, walking in silence until the cabin was out of sight.

"Sure is beautiful." Beth was trim like Abby but more rugged, earthy almost. She spent her days as an advertising executive, but she'd worked her way to a position of seniority so that getting time off was not a problem. Although Beth could be cunning and brilliant in a business meeting, she was far more at home with hiking boots and walking shorts, taking in a few days on Silver Moon Lake.

"Hmmm. I love the trees. Especially this time of year." Abby fell in place easily beside Beth and in no time the cabin was out of sight. "Like they're shouting the fact that summer is here."

Beth chuckled. "That's my sister. Always the writer."

They walked in silence for a moment, stopping to spy on a family of deer drinking at the lake's edge. The evening was cooling quickly, nightfall descending like a quiet blanket over the woods.

Abby's heart beat so loud she was sure Beth could hear it. *Do I tell her now? Should I wait?*

"Beth, I—"

"So what's the—"

They laughed because it was something they'd done since they were children, rushed into conversation at the exact same moment. Abby nodded toward her sister. "You go."

Beth's smile faded. "What's the deal with you and John?"

An alarm sounded near the surface of Abby's heart. If Beth could sense a problem, what had the kids been feeling? Had she and John been that obvious? "What do you mean?"

Beth raised one eyebrow sardonically. "Look, big sister, I've been around the block a few times myself. Back at the house you and John were the only people still stuck in winter, like you were afraid you'd catch something if you exchanged so much as a passing glance."

Abby was silent, horrified that Beth had seen through what she and John thought was a perfect act. "We . . . we have a lot on our minds."

Beth said nothing, just cast Abby the look of a younger sister waiting for the whole story. She resumed walking and Abby joined in beside her. They went on that way for another five minutes while Abby's stomach churned with the truth. When she could take it no more, she stopped and hung her head. The tears weren't something she thought about, just an overflow of emotion that had gotten too great to contain.

Beth saw the first teardrops splash against the gravel below and she reached out, wrapping Abby in a hug that felt safe and warm and familiar. It made her miss the fact that she and Beth hadn't been closer over the years, and with a suddenly sure realization she understood that the distance had been her fault. When Beth and her husband divorced, Abby had basically written her off. What kind of Christian woman couldn't make things work with her husband? Abby had wondered. And there had been nothing in the past decades to indicate Beth was drawing closer to God, so Abby had chosen to let the relationship wither.

The truth of her own judgmental spirit was almost more than she could bear, and in Beth's arms Abby's tears became heart-wrenching sobs that tore at her and uprooted all that remained of her belief that things worked out for the best.

"Tell me, Abby, it's okay . . . what's wrong?" Beth, normally tough and flippant, was now—in their own private world on the backside of the lake—as kind and caring as their mother would have been.

"You're . . . you're right about me and John." Abby kept her face hidden in Beth's shoulder. "Beth, we're getting a divorce."

As many times as she would have to say the words in the months and years to come, this was perhaps the only time when her statement needed no explanation whatsoever.

"Oh, Abby, I'm so sorry." Beth stroked Abby's hair and, thankfully, refrained from saying anything even remotely sarcastic. "Do the kids know?"

Abby shook her head. "We're waiting until after the wedding."

Beth exhaled through pursed lips. "Boy, Abby, I don't envy you." She paused and shook her head. "I mean who'd have thought . . ."

After a few minutes, Abby's tears subsided and she pulled away, wiping at her wet cheeks, unwilling to make eye contact with Beth. Was this how she would always feel when someone asked her about her failed marriage? Like she had let the entire world down?

Love is patient and kind . . . love never ends.

The words from 1 Corinthians 13 ran through her head as they had so often these past months, and Abby shook them off. No matter how she had prayed about her marriage in years past, this time love was ending. Her husband wanted to be with someone else. It was over and there was no turning back, nothing to do but figure out a way to go on.

"Is there someone else?" Beth angled her head so she could make eye contact with Abby. "For either of you, I mean?"

Abby shrugged. "John's been seeing someone at work, but honestly our marriage died before she came into the picture."

Beth shuffled her feet absently in the gravel along the path. "You, too? Seeing someone, I mean?"

Abby thought about her editor. "No, nothing like John's situation."

They moved on in silence, more slowly than before. "Men can be such scum." Beth's statement wasn't meant to belittle Abby or the marriage that she and John had shared over the years. She was merely sharing her heart on the matter. "Still . . . you and John? I mean, I could sense something was wrong but I had no idea . . ."A sigh eased from Beth's lips, and she stared up through the trees as she walked. "Makes you want to warn Nicole, doesn't it?"

Abby's defenses reared up at Beth's suggestion. No, she didn't want to warn Nicole! Marriage was still a good thing, the right thing for most people. What had happened to Beth and her husband, what was happening now with Abby and John, was still the exception. It had to be. Abby couldn't imagine a world where all hope for lasting love was nonexistent. "Nicole and Matt'll be fine." There was certainty in Abby's voice, and Beth raised an eyebrow.

"I thought you and John would be fine, too."

"For a lot of years we were." Abby picked up her pace. She was suddenly anxious to be back with Nicole, to a place where new love still seemed full of promise and the reality of her divorce was weeks away.

"What happened, if you don't mind me asking?"

Abby sighed and stared out at the lake, her feet finding their own way as they rounded a bend. She'd had months, years to think about that question but still the answer did not come easily. "I think it was the year Nicole made the Select soccer team. John was busy with football and the boys, and Nicole and I were gone almost every weekend."

Beth nodded but said nothing.

"We were so busy with the kids, so caught up in our separate lives, that when we were together . . . I don't know, it was like we were strangers or something. I'd get frustrated when he didn't ask about the kids' games or the articles I was writing; he'd feel the same way when I didn't ask him about practice or Friday night football games." She paused. "I don't know. He'd leave clothes lying around, and I'd forget to make dinner every night. We started getting on each other's nerves. Like too much had happened since the last time we were together and there was no real way to catch up. Things I used to rush home and tell him seemed not so important anymore and . . . our conversations became more functional small talk than anything else."

Abby felt the tears again and blinked so she could see clearly. "I can't really put my finger on it, Beth. It was like overnight all the things we used to laugh at weren't funny anymore. The details he used to share with me about football went unsaid. Our time together on the pier—where we used to talk just the two of us—was forgotten. Things like that. I knew it at the time and I guess that made it worse. I didn't want to hear about his players or the training routine; I was tired of caring about which sophomore might make varsity and which senior had the best shot at a blowout year. It just didn't matter. I wanted him to ask me about *my* day, act a little interested in what I was writing and which magazine was buying."

There was quiet for a moment as they kept walking. Finally Beth drew a deep breath. "You and John had something most people never get in a lifetime."

A wave of overwhelming sadness washed over Abby, and she stopped in her tracks, wiping her eyes and trying to get a handle on her feelings. "When I think back to the man he was, the man I fell in love with . . . I can't believe we're going through with this."

"But the truth is you're not the same people you were back then, even I can see that." Beth made it sound so matter-of-fact, as though people like she and John simply changed and marriages like theirs died every day of the week. It made Abby want to scream, made her want to stop the madness, race home, and shake John until both of them realized the mistake they were about to make.

But was it a mistake?

He was in love with Charlene now and he hadn't so much as asked about Abby's day in more than a year. The truth that Beth was right made Abby even angrier. "Let's get back." Abby felt like she was carrying John and Nicole and Kade and Sean squarely on her shoulders, knowing that the burden would only get heavier, not lighter in the days to come. She wiped away the last of her tears and began moving forward once more. "Nicole'll be wondering where we are."

"I won't say anything. Obviously." Beth reached out and squeezed Abby's hand once. "I'm here for you."

Abby managed a smile. Beth meant well, and though Abby had spent a lifetime convincing herself she had little or nothing in common with her independent, cynical little sister, the days were quickly coming when they would share more similarities than Abby cared to think about. "Thanks."

They walked the remainder of the trail in silence and soon were back at the cabin. Abby opened the door, then stopped cold at what she saw. Jo and Nicole were sitting cross-legged on the same bottom bunk, facing each other and holding hands as they bowed in prayer. Beth caught a glimpse of them and moved back outside to a distant chair on the front porch.

But Abby couldn't bring herself to turn away. Here was her only daughter, the girl she herself had taught to pray, the one she had prayed over on countless nights year after year, now joined in prayer with a virtual stranger. A woman who until a few months ago was a divorcée who didn't know the first thing about having a relationship with the Lord. Yet here was Nicole praying with that very woman.

Probably the kind of prayer she might have prayed with Nicole back before . . . well, if things were different. Abby realized then that she had lost something of herself, the part that years earlier would have been sitting where Jo was. *Another casualty of our dying marriage.* Through her tears she wondered how—by what awful, miserable twist of fate—she had switched roles with the woman before her. And whether there was any way she could ever rise again from the pit she occupied to that graceful, peaceful place Jo Harter had somehow found.

The moment the van was out of sight, John set aside the bicycle gearshift he'd been working on, washed his hands, and wandered into the family room to his old easy chair. Sean had ridden his bike halfway around the lake to a friend's house, and Kade was working out at school, trying to gain another ten pounds before college.

The house was quieter than it had been in days.

How had none of them noticed? Wasn't it obvious that he and Abby hadn't so much as touched in front of the kids in months? John let the question hang in the rafters of his mind and it occurred to him that he was thirsty. He made his way through the dining room into the kitchen and poured himself a glass of water. As he filled it, his eyes fell on the phone.

"I'll be home . . . call me if you want . . . call me if you want . . . call me if you want . . ."

Charlene's words played in his ears until he could feel himself being pulled toward the receiver. *Help me out of this, God . . . Please. I promised Abby . . .*

Love bears all things, My son . . . love never ends.

The thought rattled around in his tinny heart and set his feet in motion, moving back through the dining room, away from the phone. Halfway to his chair he spotted a paper on the table and stopped to read the cover.

"Merits of the Eagle—A Senior Class Project by Kade Reynolds."

Kade had aced the paper and for days now he'd been harping on John to read it. He reached down and picked it up, opening the first page and scanning the table of contents. "Traits of an eagle . . . What makes the eagle different . . . The eagle takes a mate . . ." The paper was ten pages long and looked tedious.

Read it, son . . . read it.

He was drawn to the report by something he couldn't see . . . couldn't explain. A silent voice almost like God's had once been, back when they had spent their days in conversation . . . but why would God want him to look at Kade's report?

Then another voice echoed through him.

Don't waste your time. Who cares about the eagle? You're a week away from moving out and you have the house to yourself. Make the most of it.

As the thought slithered across his conscious, John pulled his eyes away from the paper in his hand and stared hard at the telephone.

"I'll be here . . . call me, John . . . I'll be here."

Without giving it another thought, he dropped the paper on the table once more. Refusing to think about promises to Abby or what kind of man he'd become, John lifted the receiver. But just as he was about to dial her number, the phone rang. John drew back as quickly as if Abby had walked into the room. He pushed a button and held the phone to his ear, his heart beating wildly. "Hello?"

"Dad?" It was Nicole, her voice dripping with tender nostalgia. "It's me. I'm on the cell phone at our old campsite. Can you believe it reaches from way out here?"

John's desire to call Charlene disappeared instantly. He forced his voice to sound normal, as though he'd been sitting around the living room watching ESPN. "Hi, honey. You having fun?"

"Yeah, we're gonna play Scrabble and stay up all night talking." She paused, and John could almost see the sparkle in her eyes. "Mom said I could call real quick and tell you good night."

A thin layer of sweat broke out across John's forehead and he gulped back his anxiety. "I'm glad you're having a good time, sweetheart." *Should I say it?* "And, uh, tell Mom I said hi."

Nicole sighed at the mention of her mother, and John had the feeling she was debating whether to speak. "Dad, I'm praying for you and Mom."

John's anxiety level doubled. "For . . . for us?" What had Abby told her? And why now, with her wedding days away?

Nicole giggled. "Parents need prayers, too, Dad. I figure as long as we're gone for a few days talking about love and stuff, I might as well pray for you guys. Maybe watching me and Matt get married on your anniversary will make you feel like newlyweds again. I figured it couldn't hurt."

There were a hundred things John wanted to say, but he wasn't sure he should voice any of them. To defend their marriage was to lie to her, but to say nothing was to admit there was a problem. John drew a deep breath. "It never hurts to pray."

"Well, I gotta run. I just can't believe that a week from now I'll be on my honeymoon. It feels like my days of being a little girl are ending, you know?"

John's heart felt as if someone had ripped it from his chest and stomped on it. Dozens of snapshots of Nicole raced through his mind: toothless on her first day of kindergarten, decked out in blue and gray at one of his football games and cheering alongside the big girls, booting a soccer ball over the heads of three defenders in a tournament game her eighth grade year, playing the piano in her cap and gown hours before her high-school graduation. Where had the time gone? And what would happen to Nicole's smile in two weeks when the news was out?

There was a lump in John's throat, and again he had no idea what to say.

"Dad? You still there?" The connection was breaking up and Nicole sounded concerned.

"I'm here, honey. Try to remember it isn't so much an ending as . . . a new beginning."

"Right . . . that's what Mom said, too." Thank goodness she was too excited about being married to spend much time reminiscing. "Well, I'll see you in a few days, Dad. I love you."

John closed his eyes and dropped into the nearest dining room chair. "Love you, too, Nick."

He disconnected the call and left the receiver on the table, imagining the fallout that lay ahead. Before he could decide what to do next, the phone rang again. *What'd you forget this time, Nicole?* "Hello, honey, I'm all ears . . ."

There was a pause, then Charlene's voice sounded coolly on the other end. "That's nice . . . expecting me or someone else?"

John's head began to spin. He hated the crazy, confused web that his life had become. "I . . . I thought it was Nicole."

"Nicole." Charlene's voice was flat. "Not Abby, though, right?"

That was it. "Look, get off my back. I don't have to defend myself to you, Charlene."

He sighed and massaged his temples, his eyes closed. Nearly a minute passed in silence. "I'm sorry for snapping at you. I just don't want to talk to you right now . . . I need time."

There was a pause, and then he heard a sniffling sound. *Great, now I'm making two women cry.* Strangely Charlene's tears only frustrated him more. "I've gotta go."

She cleared her throat. "Call me when you're ready . . . and not until then, okay?"

An odd sense of relief flooded John's soul. "Okay."

When he'd hung up, John planted his forearms on the kitchen table and stared out the window into the dark night. What had he almost done? Why was he going to call her in the first place? And how could he feel so strongly for her one minute and barely able to tolerate her the next?

It had never been that way with Abby, not in the beginning at least. Not after ten years, for that matter. With Abby he'd always looked forward to their time together. They'd shared a chemistry that had not let up with time. *So why'd you stop loving me, Abby? Why'd you lose interest in everything about me?*

His eyes fell on Kade's report still lying on the table, and he could hear his son's voice. *"Take a look at it, Dad. I'm leaving it right here until you read it."*

Fine. Charlene wouldn't be calling again; he was alone for the night. Why not? He picked up the report and moved across the kitchen to his easy chair in the next room. When he was comfortable he turned to the first page. The report was well-written and informative, and despite every other emotion that warred inside him, John felt a surge of pride. Kade would do well at the University of Iowa, and not just on the playing field.

He read through the introduction and into the body of the report, remembering again how the Lord called His people to be like eagles. *Mount up on wings as eagles . . .* not crows or chickens or pheasants. Eagles. Key phrases from the report jumped out at him, information Kade had shared with him months ago. "The eagle eats only life-giving food. When he eats something that makes him sick, he flies to the highest rock he can find and lays spread eagle with his wings out against the surface of the rock. He stays there until the sun draws out the poison, freeing him to fly with the other eagles."

John let the image sink in again. The next section was about the eagle's mating habits.

"Female eagles like to test their male counterpart." *Counterpart?* Where did Kade come up with a word like that? John kept reading:

When the female knows a male is interested, she leads him on a chase through the skies, swooping and diving and soaring high above the hills. When the chase is nearly over, she flies as high as she can and flips onto her back, free-falling toward the ground. It is the male's job to place his body over hers and grasp her talons, flapping his wings with all his might to keep her from certain death. Moments before they hit the ground, the female pulls out of the dive and circles the male. Because he had been willing to stay even unto death, he will have proven himself as a mate. The eagles are joined for life from that point on.

John closed the report and set it down on the table beside him. He felt sick to his stomach, laboring under a mantle of guilt as heavy as any brick wall.

The comparisons were obvious. Of course he and Abby were destined for divorce—he had let go of her years ago, and now they were just two lonely eagles, free-falling hopelessly toward the ground. And as he pondered their plight he began to have a revelation unlike anything before in his entire life.

A revelation that could have come only from God Almighty Himself.

Twenty-Two

IMAGES OF EAGLES FALLING FROM THE SKY kept John awake long into the night, so the next morning he was not only deeply troubled, but tired as well. He waited until nine o'clock to call Charlene.

"Hello?" Her voice was chipper and upbeat; she seemed unaffected by the phone call from the previous night. Didn't she know how upset he'd been? Wasn't she concerned by his reaction, his decision to avoid conversation with her? A brief thought occurred to John . . . maybe he was just a passing interest in Charlene's life. A conquest of some kind.

No . . . he and Charlene had known each other too long for that. "Hi. It's me."

"John! You called!" The excitement in her tone was instant. The last thing he'd done was agree to call her when he was ready, when he'd had enough time. His hand came up along the back of his neck and he massaged it idly. She had no idea what had happened since then.

"We need to talk. Can you . . . would you mind coming by this afternoon. Sometime after lunch?" He was trying to sound friendly but not suggestive. The last thing he wanted was Charlene showing up in a bathing suit ready to spend an afternoon along the lake.

"Our conversation last night didn't . . . well . . . it didn't work out so well. Are you sure you're ready to see me?"

John released a measured breath and flexed his jaw. "Yes. One o'clock."

"Perfect." She sounded upbeat and . . . triumphant. How well could she know him if she thought he could change his mind that easily?

As the morning passed, John read more of Kade's report. The eagle had two natural enemies: storms and serpents. He embraced the storm, waiting on the rock for the right thermal current and then using that to carry him higher. While other birds were taking cover, the eagle was soaring. An eagle would never fight against the storms of life.

He saved his fighting for the serpent. Especially when the snake threatened the eagle's young.

John put the report aside again. Did Kade know he'd been writing specifically for his own father? Could God have found any better example to show him how he'd fallen short?

He didn't think so. And though his marriage was over, though he'd messed up over the last few years, he felt the seeds of change taking root in his soul. If only he could get his life with God right again . . . maybe, just maybe he could remember what it was to be an eagle. The type of eagle he'd always wanted to be. The type that would embrace the storms of life.

And fight the serpent at all costs.

Charlene was right on time, wearing white shorts and a formfitting tank top. Her makeup was simple, and she looked twenty-five when John opened the door and invited her in. *Give me strength here, God. I don't have the words . . .*

I will tell you what to say and when to say it, My son. Wait on Me. Wait on Me . . . wait on Me. The words rang in his heart, reminding him of another verse. The one in Isaiah that talked about waiting on the Lord . . . what was it? *"Those who hope in the Lord will renew their strength. They will soar on wings like eagles; they will run and not grow weary . . ."*

Eagles again. Okay, God, I'll wait on You.

He opened the door and motioned for her to follow him. "Thanks for coming."

John sat on the edge of his easy chair, and Charlene took the sofa seat closest to him. "I thought you needed more time." Her voice was confident—clearly she was expecting him to tell her it was time, maybe even take her in his arms and show her exactly how he felt about her.

Instead—in light of all God had showed John through Kade's report —he looked at her the way he might look at an old friend, one for whom he felt nothing but platonic concern. "Charlene, you have your whole life ahead of you. You're . . . you're young and beautiful and . . . I guess what I'm trying to say is I want you to take the job in Chicago."

She laughed nervously and adjusted her legs in a way that made them beyond attractive. John noticed, but was not in the least bit tempted. "You mean both of us, right? You've decided to apply for a coaching job there, is that it?"

John slid back in the chair and leaned over his knees. *Help me, God. Give me the words.* "No . . . I mean it could take months, years, Charlene. Abby and I might be through, but I can't just walk into another relationship with you. Not now anyway."

Momentary impatience flashed in Charlene's eyes. "I told you I'd wait. Why the big speech?"

John knew that on his own strength he'd lose a battle of words with Charlene. She had a way of finishing every conversation in complete control. He waited for God's wisdom. "You've allowed me to tie up your life long enough." He looked into her eyes and willed her to understand. "This'll sound funny to you, but next year when I'm living alone, I want to get things right with God. It's important to me."

Charlene raised a single eyebrow and seemed to stop just short of laughing out loud. "Right with *God?* You think you can divorce your wife and then spend the next year getting religious?" She dropped slowly to her knees and came to him, wrapping her arms around his bare legs and laying her head across his thighs. "It's not God you want; it's me."

A tingling sensation made its way through his body.

No! God, get me out of this. I've messed up one relationship; I won't do it again. Help me!

Gently, and with power that was not his own, he nudged Charlene off his legs so that she fell reluctantly into a cross-legged heap at his feet. "I can't. Understand?"

"Why?" Charlene's eyes filled with tears. "You've wanted to . . . we've both wanted to since the day we met. You're just scared, John. Let me love you. Please . . ."

He clenched his jaw. "Charlene, I'm telling you it's over between us."

Her face grew pale and she retreated back a few feet. "What's that supposed to mean? I thought you just needed time."

"I need time alone with God." As difficult as this was, he was absolutely sure it was the right thing. And nothing Charlene could do would change his mind.

"With God? Come on, John. Like that mattered to you the other day in your classroom or that night on the football field."

He remembered the breakthrough from the night before and silenced her with an icy glare. How dare she throw that at him now? "I've made up my mind, Charlene. Do what you want about the job in Chicago. It's over between us."

Just as Charlene was about to say something there was a knock at the door.

John's heart rate tripled. Were they home early? How would he explain Charlene being there? He stood on suddenly shaky legs and motioned for her to move up onto the sofa again. She did so, and he ordered himself to be calm as he opened the door.

The sight of Matt Conley was both a relief and a source of concern. "Uh, hey, Matt. What's up?"

Matt looked beyond him and saw Charlene in the next room. "Oh, I'm sorry, I didn't know you had company."

Charlene took the cue and stood up, grabbing her purse and making her way to the front door. She laughed lightly. "Don't mind me, gentlemen. I was just leaving."

She breezed up alongside them and, with Matt watching, she looked John squarely in the eyes. "About your suggestion, I think you're right. I can't pass up a job like that." She hesitated, and he could read in her face the things she wasn't saying: the pain and anger and resignation. "I'll probably find a place in Chicago before the end of the month."

John hadn't pictured ending it this way, talking in cryptic phrases while his future son-in-law hung on every word. He managed a smile, taking a step backward to keep the distance between them. "You'll do great." He patted her on the shoulder the way he might congratulate one of his players after a good performance. "Thanks for stopping by."

There were fresh tears in her eyes as she left, but John was fairly sure Matt hadn't noticed them. When she was gone, the two men moved into the living room. Matt fidgeted. "I didn't mean to run her off . . . I just thought . . ."

"Don't worry about it. She needed a little advice, and it was a good time to talk to her. She's taking a position in Chicago."

"I gathered." Matt wrung his hands and chuckled. "Nothing personal, but Nicole can't stand that woman."

"Charlene?" John's heart skipped a beat. He hadn't realized Nicole had an opinion on her, one way or the other.

"Yeah, Nicole thinks she has designs on you."

John's laugh sounded forced, but again Matt didn't seem to notice. "There's nothing to worry about where Charlene's concerned. We've been friends for a while, but she's moving on now."

John willed his heart to beat normally, stunned at the timing of Matt's visit and how his presence had caused Charlene to leave. He thought about Nicole's phone call the night before and the classroom announcement the other day. How close he'd come to . . .

God, You're so faithful! I've done nothing but live life on my own for so long, and yet here You are giving me all the help I need. Help me be an eagle, Lord . . . Help me learn to fly again.

"That's sort of why I'm here, I guess. I mean, you're amazing, Mr. Reynolds. Women like Charlene breathing down your back and still—after all these years—you and Mrs. Reynolds have this perfect marriage."

Okay, switch gears, John. Matt wasn't there to spy on him; he was there for advice. "Well, no marriage is perfect."

Matt stood up and walked from one end of the living room to the other and back again. "It's not that I'm getting cold feet." He stopped and stared earnestly at John. "I love Nicole more than I ever thought possible."

A flashback lit up in the corners of John's mind. He and Abby under the big oak tree on the University of Michigan campus: *"I'll never love anyone like I love you, Abby . . . like I love you . . . like I love you."* "I remember the feeling."

"But that's just it. You and Mrs. Reynolds never *lost* that feeling, you know? I mean how can I keep what's bottled up inside here—" he cupped his hand over his heart—"and make sure it never goes away?" His arm fell back to his side. "Like it did for my parents."

John started to open his mouth but the hissing voices were back. *Hypocrite, hypocrite, hypocrite! How dare you give this godly young man advice when you can't even keep a simple promise to Abby?* "I don't have the answers, Matt."

The young man before him was so serious, so intent on finding the secret to lasting love, that John wanted to crawl into a hole and never come out. How would Matt feel about him in two weeks?

Tell him about the eagle, My son.

The thought echoed through the place in his heart reserved for holy whispers.

Give me the words, God . . . one more time.

Matt moved back to the sofa and sat down, crossing his legs. "I know there's no set formula, but I want at least a clue." He ran his hand across his brow. "I should have asked you a long time ago. I just wasn't sure how to bring it up without you thinking I was having doubts. I mean, you're not just this great man I admire and look up to . . . you're Nicole's father. That made it tricky."

John was almost desperate to come clean with Matt, to stop the farce and let him know what a terrible husband he really was, how he and Abby had stopped trying years ago.

Remember My grace, son. Tell him about the eagle . . .

There it was again. He wasn't up to this, couldn't look Matt in the eyes and tell him anything that might—

"Maybe a scripture or something. I mean, I've studied all the verses about God hating divorce and how the two shall be one . . ."

John felt a knife of regret slice through his midsection. *I can't do this, God . . . make him leave.* "Have you ever studied the eagle?"

Matt grinned. "You mean like, Marion Eagles . . . the winningest football program in southern Illinois?"

John was suddenly bolstered by a strength he hadn't known in years. "In Isaiah, God says we'll soar on wings like eagles." He reached over and grabbed Kade's report from the nearby end table. "Kade did his senior project on the eagle, and I think there's a lot there."

Matt's expression twisted curiously. "About marriage?"

For the next ten minutes John talked about the eagle and its ability to embrace the storms of life, how the eagle fought the serpent, keeping the snake from destroying its baby eaglets or the great eagle nest. He told Matt how, when it was sick, the eagle knew enough to get alone on the rock and let the sun soak the poison from its system. And most of all how the male eagle was born to cling to the female regardless of the fall, even unto death.

When he was finished, Matt no longer seemed concerned. From where he stood, on the doorstep of new love and commitment, the idea of clinging to Nicole for life seemed easy and exciting. John prayed it would always feel that way.

"That's perfect, just what I needed." They chatted awhile longer about the wedding and how quickly everything would take place that week. Finally, after nearly an hour, Matt stood to leave.

Though John still felt like a hypocrite, though he was certain the strength to talk to Matt had been supernatural, he walked Matt to the door and bid him good-bye.

"Four days, Mr. Reynolds. I can't wait." Matt was tall and handsome, and with his ability to reason, John was sure he would make a good attorney one day soon. But more than being an ample provider, John hoped his future son-in-law would be able to grasp the lesson of the eagle and the importance of never letting go.

A lesson John only wished he'd understood years earlier when he and Abby had first started to fall.

Abby stood alone in her driveway, tired and satisfied, as she waved good-bye to Beth and Jo. Nicole had already taken her suitcase inside the house, and if her outlook was any indication, the girls' campout had been a complete success. They'd laughed and talked and even prayed together—now Abby wandered around the side of the house toward the backyard and spotted John, adrift in their aluminum rowboat in the middle of the lake.

Probably feeling guilty. Didn't want to face us when we got in. She allowed her gaze to linger, and a dozen memories of happier times danced into view. The boat didn't seat more than three people, but there had been times when it seemed like a yacht, times when she and John could spend an afternoon in it, floating on the lake, soaking up the sun and sharing laughter and conversations. It was out in that very boat that they'd dreamed about Kade's football career and that she'd told him she was pregnant with Sean.

John wasn't rowing, and since his back was to her, she figured he didn't know they were home yet. And it occurred to Abby that this might be the last time she'd come home and find him out on the lake like this.

There was something peaceful and timeless about being on the lake, and John knew with the craziness of both the dress rehearsal and the wedding over the next few days there would be little time for anything resembling quiet. Besides he needed to think, needed to imagine how different life might have been if he'd seen the split coming and done something, anything, to stop it.

Of course, it was too late now. Abby didn't love him, and no effort at holding on to her would make a difference at this point. In the free fall of life, they'd both crashed and burned. Now she was moving on to other territories.

He leaned into the boat, his back to their home and all the joy and sorrow that would take place there over the next few weeks. As he stared into the sky, he watched a bird soar effortlessly into the air, crisscrossing over the water in search of evening fish. John stared at it more closely. It couldn't be. Not here and now, when so much was going through his mind, when Kade's report had been the trigger for the greatest change of heart he'd had in all his life.

But it was. It was an eagle. And as he watched it, he felt washed in God's grace and forgiveness, filled with a hope that had no reason for being.

John stared at the eagle as tears burned his eyes. Something about seeing the majestic bird in flight gave him strength. As though God wanted him to know it was possible to fly again, even after a lifetime of poison. And that was good because nothing was going to poison his system more than going before a judge and divorcing the woman he'd fallen in love with more than two decades earlier.

John watched the eagle until the sun set and then, with a strange new sense of forgiveness and purpose, a sense of grace that had nothing to do with himself, he rowed back to shore where there were still no answers for the most important questions of all.

Tell me how, God . . . how do I find my way back to the Rock so the Son can rid me of all those years of poison? And how with broken wings will I ever learn to catch the thermal currents in life and fly again?

Twenty-Three

THE NEXT THREE DAYS PASSED IN A BLUR OF preparation. Party coordinators worked to make the backyard perfect. Florists called to double-check the order for the church and the back porch. The DJ needed to set up a wooden platform and hadn't realized the yard was sloped. A carpenter was called in to make the platform level and to lay out a small dance floor, and by the time the rehearsal was underway, Abby was almost too tired to feel anything but drained.

Drained and cheated.

This should have been a time when all her energy was focused on Nicole. Instead Abby felt almost as though she was only going through the motions: the wedding, the divorce, Kade's move to the university—all of it. Like she was delaying her feelings in the here and now because to experience them might actually kill her.

For days she and John had passed like enemy ships in the night, speaking only when necessary, yet still somehow avoiding the notice of the kids. Kade was getting ready to leave for Iowa, and Sean was busy with his friends, looking forward to a summer of fun. Everyone had his or her own life to worry about, including John—who no doubt already had plans with Charlene for the moment Nicole and Matt were gone from the wedding reception.

Well, she wasn't going to sit there and watch them. Abby had realized she needed to get away as soon after the wedding as she could. She made arrangements for Sean to stay with one of his friends and booked a flight to New York. She'd stay in a hotel downtown and catch a few shows with her editor. It was time they finally met, time to see if they would share anything lasting beyond their e-mail friendship. The days away would be good. Better than sitting around the house wondering what John and Charlene were doing.

Her flight was set to leave Monday morning and return Friday. The kids would be back from their honeymoon the following Sunday, and on Monday she and John had agreed to break the news. It still seemed unrealistic, like the scary part of a horror movie. Only this time there would be no turning the channel, no getting up and walking away. The reality was upon them and together—perhaps for the last time—she and John would have to help the kids understand.

The boys thought their dad was going fishing with some friends from work right after the wedding and that Abby had a business meeting in New York. The idea of their parents heading in different directions for the week didn't raise even a bit of concern among them. Nicole was too busy to think about it or she probably would have had questions.

That night, with the wedding set to take place in less than twenty-four hours, Abby delayed her office time and made her way across the house to Nicole's room. Her daughter was beaming, completely packed, and writing a letter. The moment Abby walked into the room, Nicole hid the paper under her pillow. "It's a surprise for Matt."

"Oh. That's nice." Abby wandered across Nicole's bedroom floor and kissed her. "I'm so happy for you, honey. I want you to know that."

The joy in Nicole's eyes was not something that could be contrived. It was the most real and satisfying thing Abby could have hoped to see the night before Nicole's wedding. "He's the one we prayed for, Mom. I love him so much."

Abby sat on the edge of Nicole's bed and smoothed a hand over her daughter's golden hair. "No matter what life brings, no matter what happens all around you, don't forget how you feel tonight. Keep that. Make your marriage first in your life."

Nicole nodded and some of the sparkle faded from her eyes. "God first, then my marriage. That's what you mean, right?"

Abby felt her face growing hot. Why hadn't she thought of that? Was she so far removed from God? So far away from—

"Are you okay, Mom. You've been kind of quiet these past few days."

Focus, Abby. She smiled, holding back tears. "I've had a lot on my mind." She put her arms around Nicole and pulled her close. "My baby girl is getting married tomorrow."

"Ah, Mom, but it's not like that with you and me. You know that, right? This will always feel like home. I mean, Matt and I will come over for dinner and hang out playing cards with you and Dad, and one day we'll bring the grandkids here for you guys to baby-sit." Nicole's face was beaming again, caught up in the certainty of God's blessings and goodness.

Abby folded her hands in her lap and forced herself not to weep. Hadn't she felt the exact same way the night before her own wedding? Certain of their happy-ever-after? Yet the truth was none of Nicole's pictures of home would ever be the same after she and John were divorced.

The tears came of their own volition and Abby leaned over, kissed Nicole once more, and bid her good night. "See you in the morning, sweetheart. You're going to be absolutely beautiful."

Nicole dabbed her finger under Abby's eyes. "Mom . . . you're crying."

Abby smiled, her vision blurred as another round of tears waited their turn. "Happy tears, sweetheart. That's all."

And when she left the room, sure that everyone else was asleep, Abby scurried toward the office where she could let loose and cry all night if she wanted to. She was almost there when she heard John's voice.

"Abby . . ."

She turned and saw him standing in the kitchen doorway. He still wore his dress slacks and white button-down from the rehearsal dinner, and Abby realized how little she'd looked at him that night. Though they'd sat next to each other all evening, they'd managed to carry on conversations with other people. Until now he hadn't said more than what was absolutely necessary to pull off their charade.

"What?" She was not up to a verbal battle. Not when it was all over but the walking away. Not when in twenty-four hours they would reside at different addresses.

"We haven't had a moment alone in a long time and . . . I don't know, I thought we could talk."

Abby sighed. "It's too late, John. There's nothing to talk about."

There was a depth to John's eyes that hadn't been there in months. Years, maybe. *It's my imagination; nostalgia coming up against the finality of it all.* "Okay. Never mind." He hesitated. "Are you . . . will you be around this week?"

Abby sighed and felt her frustration level rising. How dare he ask about *her* plans when he'd be with Charlene? Of all the things he might want to talk about, why on earth would John want to know her plans for the coming week?

Don't say it, daughter—

"Let me guess, you and Charlene want to make dinner plans with me?"

John flinched as though he'd been slapped, and his eyes took on the hard look she was more familiar with. "Forget it, Abby." He studied her for a moment. "Someday I'd like to know what happened to the girl I fell in love with . . ."

"I—"

He put his hand up, cutting her off. "Never mind. I know it's my fault. It's all my fault, and I'm sorrier than you'll ever know. But years from now when this is behind us, take a minute and look in the mirror. And see if *you* even know who you've become." His tone wasn't hateful like she'd heard it before. It was more dumbfounded. And sad. And that only made Abby angrier.

She could live with the idea that he was finally taking credit for the train wreck of their marriage, but how *dare* he accuse her of changing. She hadn't changed; she'd survived. Back in the beginning, when their schedules had first taken precedence over their relationship, the woman he'd fallen in love with had been there just beneath the icy surface. She spread her hand across her chest and kept her voice low so the kids couldn't hear her. "That same girl is still in here somewhere, John. But a long time ago you stopped looking for her." New tears filled her eyes and she blinked so she could see more clearly. "And now that you've fallen in love with someone else, maybe she'll stay hiding in there forever."

"I'm not in . . ." His voice trailed off, and his look of protest faded as he shrugged. "I'm going to bed."

With that he turned and trudged up the stairs toward the bedroom. When he was out of earshot, Abby stepped into her office and clenched her fist, leaning her back against the oak cabinet and sliding slowly down it until she was in a heap on the floor.

"I hate this, God . . . what's happened to me?"

John was right. The girl he'd married had become hard and angry and bitter. She smiled so rarely that when she did her face felt strange, like the muscles at the corners of her mouth had forgotten what it was to work on their own. With no one around to hear her, she allowed her tears to come, crying for all that she would be losing the following day.

Her sides ached, but her heart hurt worse. It was really happening. John and Abby Reynolds were getting a divorce, breaking their greatest promise to each other, to her father, to Haley Ann, to the others. To God Almighty. Suddenly she longed to forget about the whole thing, follow John up the stairs, and crawl in bed beside him.

She could feel the warmth of his skin against hers, hear herself telling him she was sorry, begging him for one more chance.

The idea fled as quickly as it came.

John had been seeing Charlene for years, no matter when the two of them had first become physical. Abby was a fool to have allowed the pretense of their marriage to last as long as it had. Rage built within her at the role he'd played in destroying their lives. *I hate you, John. I hate you for what you've done to us, to me.* "It isn't fair, God," she wailed out loud in a whispered voice. "Help me . . ."

Come to Me, daughter. The truth will set you free.

She shook her head and struggled to her feet to find a tissue. How could the truth set her free? If she knew the reality of how close John and Charlene were, it'd probably send her over the edge . . . Another wave of quiet tears came and she was overwhelmed with the feeling of loss that welled up inside her. Loss of her marriage and her family. But mostly the loss of that young girl, the one John had fallen in love with.

The one Abby feared might not be hiding at all, but rather too far gone to ever find again.

The morning of Saturday, July 14, dawned more beautiful than any Nicole could remember. She had more than enough time to get ready, since the ceremony wasn't until three o'clock that afternoon. But she wanted to savor the day and that meant rising before anyone in the house and watching the morning come to life across the lake.

She'd been reading the Epistles lately, trying to understand the message Paul had for the church, especially his desire that they live in love and grace the way God would have them live. Nicole situated herself in her window seat and gazed across the lake. *Thank You, Father . . . the day is finally here.* Her heart felt as though it had been created for this time in her life, and she eased open the cover of her Bible, flipping to the thirteenth chapter in First Corinthians. She had read the verses a dozen times since getting engaged, and each time the Lord had showed her something new and revealing about true love, the kind she and Matt would share for a lifetime.

She read down to the fourth verse. *"Love is patient, love is kind. It does not envy, it does not boast, it is not proud . . . "* The words flowed from the pages straight into her heart and she could feel them building her up, preparing her to love Matt the way God wanted her to. Nicole thought about the fact that sometime late that night, when the celebrating was finished, she and Matt would have their first opportunity to love each other with their bodies. She closed her eyes and felt a smile make its way across her face.

We actually managed to wait, Lord. We stayed within Your plan, and I know with all my heart that tonight will be only the beginning.

She thought about the times when they'd been tempted and knew that God's strength alone had brought them to this point, to a place where they could pledge their love to each other on their wedding day, knowing that they had kept themselves pure. Nicole could think of no greater gift to give Matt, no greater way to please the One who had brought them together.

God, You're so good. Just like Mom always told me, You've had a plan for me all my life and today it's actually going to happen. She opened her eyes and found the place in Scripture where she'd left off. *"Love always protects, always trusts, always hopes, always perseveres. Love never fails."*

Nicole let her gaze roam about the backyard of the house where she'd grown up. That was the trouble with too many couples. They didn't understand what it really meant to love. Oh, sure, it was the butterfly feeling that happened when two people first met, but it was so much more than that. She thought over the verses again. *"Love always hopes, always perseveres. Love never fails."*

It was an entire marriage manual in less than ten words.

She thought of her parents and how long they'd stayed together, and a strange cloud of concern blocked the sunshine of the morning.

What is it, Lord? How come I feel this way whenever I think of their marriage?

Pray, daughter.

Her heart rate quickened, and Nicole felt the rumblings of fear deep in her gut. Pray? For her parents? Again? The insistent urging was the same one she'd felt before the camping trip, and it was beginning to make her wonder if her parents were hiding something. Today wasn't the right time, but when she and Matt returned from their honeymoon, she would take an afternoon and talk to Mom. Ask her straight out if she and Dad were having trouble.

Whatever it might be, it couldn't be serious enough to spend time dwelling on now, on her wedding day. Right?

Pray. Pray hard, dear one.

Okay, Lord, I hear You. The feeling was so urgent, Nicole's hesitation dissolved. Whatever the situation, her parents needed prayer. And for the next thirty minutes she lay aside all thoughts of her wedding and the things she needed to do to get ready, and poured out her heart on behalf of the two people she admired most in all the world.

The excitement was so great in the minutes before the ceremony that for the first time in six months Abby wasn't consumed with thoughts of their divorce. Instead she was swept up in what felt like a dream scene, one she'd dreamed decades earlier when Nicole Michelle was still a newborn. Nicole was radiant, of course—the waist and bodice of her dress fit perfectly, the skirt and train billowed about her like a satin cloud trimmed in lace.

Abby and Jo had already lit the candles at the front of the church, and now Abby made her way through the tuxedoed men and stunning bridesmaids and sidled up next to Nicole. "You could've worn rags today and you'd have looked every bit as beautiful."

Nicole cocked her head and grinned, meeting Abby's gaze and holding it. "I'm so happy, Mom."

A light chuckle came from Abby. "It's obvious, sweetheart." She leaned forward and kissed Nicole, patting her gently on the cheek. "Kade's walking me down now. Next time I see you you'll be a married woman."

"Can you believe it, Mom? It's finally here!" Nicole squeezed Abby's hands. "You and Dad look so good. No one'll believe you're old enough to be my parents."

Yes, Abby had noticed. John looked more handsome than the groom in his black tux and baby-blue cummerbund. She smiled, hiding the way Nicole's comment pierced her heart. "I've got to go. Love you, honey."

"Love you, too . . . and Mom?"

Abby waited. "Yes?"

"Happy anniversary!" The words poked daggers at Abby's heart, but she smiled at her daughter.

"Thanks, honey. Love you . . ." Tears welled up in Abby's eyes as she turned to find Kade. Happy anniversary? She'd almost forgotten that this day marked twenty-two years of marriage for her and John.

Maybe everyone else will forget . . . I can't get through it otherwise . . .

She spotted Kade a few feet off, chattering with one of Nicole's bridesmaids. As Abby walked up to him, she felt someone looking at her and she glanced over her shoulder. John was there, ten feet away, standing by himself near the church window. Was he smiling at her? Why? Why work so hard to pretend when the charade was only hours from being over? Abby turned away and linked arms with Kade as he promised the bridesmaid a dance at the reception.

"Flirting with the girls already, Kade?" Abby was desperate to preserve the lighthearted feeling she'd had moments earlier, before Nicole's happy anniversary wish . . . before she'd spotted John.

"Always, Mom. You know me." His grin faded and he studied Abby. "You're the best-looking mom a guy could have."

Abby bowed her head. "Thank you, kind sir."

"Oh, and happy anniversary." He grinned and the hurt in Abby's stomach was so great she wondered if she'd make it down the aisle. *I can't do this, God . . . help me . . .*

Kade was waiting for her. "You ready?"

She nodded, forcing herself to move ahead as the wedding coordinator opened the church doors. As Abby took in the church setting, her breath caught in her throat. It was like something from a movie, white satin ribbons adorned the ends of each pew and huge sprays of pink roses fanned out across the altar. And so many familiar people, most of whom had known the Reynolds family since they moved to Marion. In fact, the church looked almost identical to the one she had entered twenty-two years earlier back when . . .

And the song. Was it the same one that had drifted down from the balcony all those years ago? Abby had to blink hard to remind herself where she was and who she was and that this was her daughter's wedding, not a flashback of her own. They arrived at the front row where Kade kissed her cheek and winked at her. Abby took her seat and sat alone to watch the attendants make their entrance.

The bridesmaids wore light blue, the exact shade as the cummerbunds worn by the men. Sean was the youngest groomsman, and when the wedding party was lined up, Abby was struck by how beautiful they were. Suddenly the music changed and every head turned toward the back of the church. As the crowd rose to its feet, Abby peered around them and was among the first to see Nicole and John as they made their way down the aisle. Halfway there, John leaned toward their daughter and whispered something that made them both smile. Abby felt the sting of tears in her eyes as she watched them.

Who are you, John Reynolds? I don't even know you anymore. The man who'd stood beside her mere months ago making promises to her dying father . . . the man who had kissed her so passionately that night, and who years ago had asked to her to listen to the music of their lives, who had begged her not to ever stop dancing with him . . . the man who shared with her the only memories of little Haley Ann . . . Was that the same man walking their little girl down the aisle? Or was he an impostor, going through the motions, biding his time until he could be free from them all?

Abby no longer knew.

She glanced at Matt. His eyes shone as he saw Nicole in her wedding gown for the first time. Surely any man who could look at his bride with that type of adoration would be faithful to her for a lifetime. But then, John's eyes had looked that way, hadn't they?

Abby wasn't sure anymore.

The minister cleared his throat. "Who gives this woman to be married?"

John smiled at Nicole in a moment shared between them alone, regardless of the nearly two hundred family and friends who watched. "Her mother and I do." Keeping his eyes trained on Nicole even after his words were said, John lifted her veil and kissed her on the cheek. A hundred images flashed in Abby's mind. John kissing Nicole's infant cheek and that same cheek again when she was hit by the car that awful afternoon. Always Daddy's little girl. Nicole had cherished the role, and as Abby watched them she was struck by a realization: the John Reynolds she remembered would have struggled greatly with this moment. In fact, it would have torn his heart wide open. For the past days and weeks and months, Abby had wondered if John was looking forward to the wedding. She figured he was, since it signaled the end of his attempt at staying clear of Charlene. But the truth—at least in part—had to be that John was dying inside. He'd dreaded the coming of this day since Nicole first made her way into his heart the morning of her birth.

Are you sad, John? Does it hurt the way you thought it would, or have you already moved on, even from a moment like this?

Almost in response, she caught John's glance as he made his way next to her. His eyes were watery with tears and the ceremony hadn't even begun. The fact reminded Abby that if things had been different, she and John would have had ample opportunity to grow close over the past six months. Sharing their thoughts on Nicole's wedding and reminiscing about their own love. Remarking at how fast her childhood had disappeared and wondering where the time had gone.

Abby sighed and stared at her hands, at the wedding band she still wore. John said nothing but positioned himself so that his shoulder was nearly touching hers. She could feel the heat from his body and she tried to imagine what Beth must be thinking, sitting back a few rows. Probably the same thing they'd all think by the end of the next week.

That Abby and John Reynolds were world-class hypocrites.

John clenched his jaw as Pastor Joe commanded the attention of the crowd and began speaking about commitment and God's plan for marriage. The preacher was a man the Reynolds family knew well. He was the associate minister at the church, the man who had led the high-school youth group when Nicole was a teenager.

Had Nicole and Matt met with him to plan all this? And why hadn't John been more involved? He could have at least had a conversation with one of them about what scriptures they wanted read at the ceremony or what direction the message might take. Had he fallen that far from his daily walk with the Lord? John felt himself being suffocated in a blanket of shame and he silently begged God to take it from him. *I'm so sorry, Father . . . never again will I let You go. I don't care what else happens; I can't make it without You.* He thought about Abby, how they had been unable to have even a pleasant conversation in weeks. *Lord, is there a way? Someday, down the road a year or two? Is it possible that she might forgive me and maybe even . . .*

"When two people marry, the commitment is lifelong." Pastor Joe smiled at the congregation. "No matter what else happens along the way, they will be tied to that promise forever . . ."

John remembered a distant friend of his father's who had gotten divorced in his thirties and remarried his wife again twenty years later.

And of course there were Matt's parents, Jo and Denny. If they could find a way back together after so many years then . . .

Maybe that'll be us one day, Lord. John considered the idea. *You're the only One who could make it happen, God.* He pictured the way Abby's eyes had grown hard, how she never smiled or laughed or allowed her feelings to show around him anymore.

Reconciliation seemed about as likely as snow in July.

With Me all things are possible . . .

John reveled in the return of the inner voice. God was beyond faithful, prodding him, encouraging him, bathing him in grace every moment since the night he'd read Kade's paper on the eagle. The deepest regret in all his life was that his restored relationship with the Lord was—for him and Abby—too late. He'd even started writing his feelings down in a journal, confessing his shortcomings, analyzing all that he'd done that had hurt their marriage. *Maybe someday when she's not so mad . . . maybe she'll read it, Lord. It's all my fault . . .*

Confess your sins to one another; talk to her; tell her.

For just a moment, he let his imagination take him down such a path—but he knew there was no way. *Abby's mind is made up, Lord. She has . . . other plans.* John's fingers tightened into a fist and relaxed again as a pang of jealousy gripped him. Kade had mentioned earlier that morning that the house was going to be quiet with Nicole and Mom gone. A few questions later and John knew the truth. Abby was going to New York on business, which could mean only one thing. She was seeing her on-line friend, her editor.

Not that he could blame her. It was simply over.

Pastor Joe had moved from commitment to honor and he seemed to be winding up. "I'd like to close by talking about the eagle for a moment." He grinned in John's direction, and John felt the blood draining from his face. Had someone told the pastor? His breathing seemed to slow to a stop as the man continued. "The bride's family has spent a lifetime calling themselves Eagles. Marion Eagles." A friendly chorus of chuckles sounded across the church. "But God also calls us to be eagles. Why? Well, lots of reasons, really."

Kade shot John a curious glance and raised an eyebrow. Obviously Kade hadn't told Pastor Joe about his report. He glanced at Abby and could tell from her unchanged expression that the message wasn't hitting a personal chord with her. *You're really trying to tell me something here, aren't You, God?*

Anyone who hears these words of mine and puts them into practice is like a wise man who built his house on the rock.

A hollow pit formed in John's gut. He was familiar with the scripture that wove its way through his mind, but it was too late to put anything into practice. At least where Abby was concerned.

The pastor smiled at Nicole and Matt. "But the main reason I want to talk about the eagle is because of something Matt shared with me. Something he learned from his future father-in-law, John Reynolds."

Abby looked skeptically at John, and he turned his attention back to the pastor. *That's okay. She doesn't know what's happened in my heart.*

"Before eagles choose a mate—" Pastor Joe paused, making sure he had the attention of everyone in the building—"the male eagle will lock talons with the female as she falls upside down toward the ground. At that point the male must pull her out of the tumble or die trying. In other words he grabs on to her and refuses to let go—even unto death." He smiled again at the couple. "And that's why—Nicole and Matt—God calls you to be like the eagle. Because the commitment that you make here today is one you make in the same way. Unto death. Let's pray."

John wasn't sure when the tears had filled his eyes, but sometime near the end of the message, he felt them on his cheeks. As he wiped them, he noticed Abby do the same thing. What was she thinking? Did she realize that they'd failed the eagle test? That they had done everything *but* stick together in the past years? That when life got busy and the kids' schedules even busier, they hadn't locked talons but simply set out on totally different flying patterns? And if she felt the sting of the message, what direction were her thoughts headed? Did she still hate him as she'd told him the night after Kade found Charlene in his classroom?

It was time for the vows. Pastor Joe asked Matt to repeat after him, and John realized how grateful he was that Nicole was marrying him. Matt was a good kid—a good man. He'd make a wonderful husband for Nicole. Matt finished his part and it was Nicole's turn.

"I, Nicole Reynolds, take you, Matt Conley, to be my husband." John was struck by how calm Nicole seemed, and his mind diverted to the hazy memory of Abby saying similar words to him on a day not so different from this one. *Were we that way twenty-two years ago? Sure beyond any doubts that what we had would last forever?*

Pastor Joe was moving on to the ring part of the ceremony, and John shot a look at his gold band. How many times had he taken it off so he could work out in the morning with Charlene? Oh sure he'd told himself it was for safety reasons. Wouldn't want to crack the ring or hurt his finger on the free weights. But the truth—and he wasn't up to anything less at this point—was that he wanted to feel single. Even just for an hour.

It was something else he could write in the journal. *Lord, I have so much to be sorry for . . .*

And a promise to keep.

A promise? What promise?

"And now, by the power vested in me by the state of Illinois, I am honored to present to you, Mr. and Mrs. Matt Conley—" the pastor grinned at the couple and waved a hand toward the congregation— "whose promise before all of you today is the beginning of a lifetime of love." He looked back at Nicole and Matt. "You may kiss the bride."

It was during the kiss that John remembered the promise, and the realization cut like a dagger through his heart. It was the promise he'd made to Abby's father. A promise not too different from the one Nicole and Matt had just made.

That he would love Abby Reynolds as long as he lived.

As terrifying as the coming weeks seemed to Abby, nothing could have marred the joy in her heart as Nicole's wedding reception came to life. The house had been decked out in flowers and folding chairs, and the caterer had set up a series of white canopies for the buffet line. From the moment the wedding party arrived back at the house, the disc jockey seemed to have the perfect music playing in the background. The fading sun sent a glistening spray of light across the lake, and though the evening was warm, it was not humid. A faint breeze stirred the tops of the trees, and the sunset promised to be something out of a painting. Nicole and Matt sat closest to the house with the rest of the wedding party while their friends and family found places at tables situated about the yard on either side of the constructed dance floor.

Abby surveyed the gathering and noticed that many couples seemed happier than usual, as though they were touched, as people often are at weddings, by the reminder that they, too, had once shone as brightly as the bride and groom. And even though the memories were sad beyond words for Abby, she refused to let her sorrow win tonight.

Throughout dinner Abby sat next to John, talking mostly to Jo and Denny who were bursting with excitement over the next week's events.

"If it were up to me, I tell you, we'd stop the music, take our place up there on the dance floor, and say our vows right now." Jo pointed at the lake. "Then me and Denny would get out there and do what we always did best."

Jo jabbed her elbow gently at Denny's side, and he broke into a grin. When he noticed the odd looks from the others at the table, he cleared his throat. "Fishing. We'd go fishing; that's what we've always done best."

"Something the Lord Himself liked to do, I might add!" Jo nodded at Abby. "I've been doing what you said. Reading the book of John and learning all sorts of things about the Lord. When I got to that fishing part, I had to stop and clap my hands. I mean, I just knew I liked God from the get-go. Just wish I hadn't taken so long to figure it out. In fact what was it I was reading the other day, Denny, you remember . . . about that—"

The conversation showed no signs of slowing. And while it might have been nice to talk to some of the other guests at the table, Jo and Denny's streaming dialogue took the spotlight off Abby and John so that no one at the table seemed to remember it was their anniversary or that they hadn't said a single word to each other since back at the church.

Dinner was winding down, and the DJ called the wedding party forward for a dance. Abby watched the young people laughing and swaying together, caught up in the joy of the moment. As the song ended, Abby heard the beginning notes to "Sunrise, Sunset" and she knew it was time for John to dance with Nicole.

"I'll be back." John made the general announcement to the table and eased onto the floor as the music began asking the same questions that rattled around in Abby's empty heart. What happened to the little girl Nicole had been? When did she get so old and grown-up? Wasn't it yesterday when she was just a child? Just skipping in from the lake, asking for a towel and a glass of juice?

Tears built up in Abby's eyes as she watched her football player husband dance the age-old number with their daughter.

And suddenly all Abby could hear was John's voice as he'd said it dozens of times before, as he'd never say it again. *Dance with me, Abby. Dance with me. Dance with me.*

As the reception wound down Abby found herself comparing this evening to the one six months earlier when John and Kade had won the state title football game. All the while she kept reminding herself that this was the last time she and John would entertain and socialize as a married couple. After all the years of frustration and pain and buildup over their divorce, they had finally arrived at this place and now every minute brought them closer to the end. Abby knew that like the night of the big game, even the smallest memories made that evening would be savored in their minds forever. There was one difference, of course.

This time there were no winners.

"Beautiful wedding, Abby, tell Nicole she looked gorgeous . . ."

"Happy anniversary, you two . . . you look every bit in love as always . . ."

"Matt's going to make her happy; I can feel it my bones. Thanks for a great evening . . ."

"Wonderful party, Abby, give me a call sometime . . ."

One at a time friends and family left until it was Beth's turn. She and her daughters would stay at a hotel in Chicago that night and catch a flight out tomorrow for the East Coast. Abby had already said good-bye to Beth's girls, and now Beth pulled Abby to a place on the back porch where no one could hear them. "Well, big sister, I don't envy you telling those great kids of yours the truth. But you've got to do it; there's no other way. I watched you and John today." Beth angled her head sadly and brushed a stray lock of hair off Abby's forehead. "It's gone between you, Abby. You're doing the right thing."

Abby wished she could feel some sense of victory in Beth's words, but there was none whatsoever. The fact that Beth was right brought little consolation to the reality of all that lay ahead for Abby, living life as the divorced mother of three grown children. The sound of it so chilled her heart that goose bumps appeared on her arms as she hugged Beth and wished her a safe flight home.

"I'll give you a call next week when I'm in New York." Other than the children, Beth was the only person Abby had told about her trip.

Beth nodded. "I know we haven't always been close, but I'm here if you need me." She squeezed Abby's hand and then found her daughters. "We'll be getting our things in the car. Tell Nicole and Matt I'll be ready to leave in five minutes."

Abby glanced at a clock on the wall inside. Quarter past ten and only the wedding party and Jo and Denny remained. Nicole and Matt disappeared into the house and came back dressed in sporty outfits.

"Okay, everyone," Nicole announced from the porch. "We're off to the airport." Abby had helped Matt and Nicole with the logistics of their honeymoon. Beth would drive them to a hotel near the Chicago airport where the bride and groom had reservations for the honeymoon suite. Like Beth, they would board a plane in the morning, but theirs would take them to an all-inclusive resort on the island of Jamaica.

John had been chatting with Denny down near the pier, but at Nicole's announcement both men made their way up to the porch.

"Bring home a tan for me." Kade pulled Nicole into a hug and kissed her on the cheek. "Love you."

Nicole's eyes glistened with tears. "Love you, too, Kade."

Abby's full-grown son turned to Matt and pushed him playfully in the arm. "Take care of my sister, okay, buddy?"

There was a smile on Matt's face, but his eyes were more serious than Abby had ever seen them. "Always."

One by one Matt and Nicole shared similar words with Sean and the others and eventually with Matt's parents.

"Don't know about you, sweetheart, but right next to that Bible of yours I'd pack myself a fine fishin' pole; wouldn't you, Denny?" Jo was completely serious, and despite the sadness at saying good-bye to Nicole and Matt and the impending doom of what was set to happen when everyone was gone, Abby had to stifle a giggle.

"Well, Jo, I thought about it and . . ." Nicole gazed into Matt's eyes, her entire face lit up with her feelings for him. "I decided we probably wouldn't have enough time to fish. Not on this trip anyway."

Abby watched a pretty blush fan across Nicole's cheeks and then noticed that Jo was astonished. "Not enough time to fish? When you'll be stuck out there in the middle of that warm Atlantic Ocean. Now listen, you two, if you change your mind you could always rent the—"

Denny gently placed his hand over Jo's mouth and nodded toward the bride and groom. "What she's trying to say is have a wonderful trip and we'll see you when you get back."

Jo conceded and laughed lightly as Denny circled her waist with his arm and brought her close to him. "Okay, okay. Go. We'll fish later."

Watching them, seeing how Denny loved Jo, how Matt loved Nicole, Abby felt more alone than ever, drowning in an ocean of separateness and solitude. *Get me through this, God, please.*

Seek first My kingdom and all these things will be added to you . . .

Abby sighed quietly. *Later, God. Let me get through this nightmare and then I promise I'll come back around. After next week I'll need You more than ever. Okay, Lord?*

There was nothing in response, and Abby's lonely feeling worsened. Even God was against her these days.

John was next. He took the initiative and stepped up, placing one hand on Nicole's shoulder and the other on Matt's. That deep something or other was back in his eyes as he began to speak. "If it's okay, I'd like to pray before you leave."

Pray? An unnerving feeling worked its way down Abby's spine. Was this part of his act, his way of making sure Nicole and Matt would think things were fine back home while they celebrated their new marriage in Jamaica? Other than before football games, Abby couldn't remember how long it'd been since John had offered to pray.

"Lord, grant Matt and Nicole safe travel this week, but above all else, give them time to realize the beauty of the commitment they've made to each other. Help them be like eagles, Lord . . . now and forever, amen."

"The beauty of the commitment they've made?" Abby played John's words over and over in her mind and felt baffled by them. Was he so out of touch with the fact that he'd broken his own commitments to her? How could he pray for Nicole and Matt to be like eagles, to hold on forever, when he had determined years earlier to let go of Abby and all they had?

She pushed the thoughts from her mind. What difference did it make? Their fate had been sealed for months, years. They had been helpless to keep their marriage together. Even counseling hadn't helped. Why begrudge John the chance to pray for a different path for Nicole and Matt?

It was Abby's turn then, and she hugged first Nicole, then Matt, smiling through tears on the verge of spilling over. "It was a beautiful wedding, you two."

Nicole took Abby's hand and bent her head close, her eyes glowing with sincerity. "Thank you so much for everything, Mom. We couldn't have pulled it off without you and Dad."

Abby nodded. "You two go. Have a great time."

Nicole hugged Abby once more. "Love you, Mom. You're the best."

"Love you, too."

Nicole leaned forward and whispered into Abby's ear. "Remind me to tell you what God's had on my heart lately. We'll talk about it when I get back, okay?"

When they got back . . . That would be when the meeting would take place, when she and John would finally tell the kids the truth about their marriage. Whatever Nicole wanted to talk about would probably be forgotten in the aftermath.

"Okay, sweetheart. We'll talk then."

In a flurry of motion, Nicole and Matt left the house and climbed into Beth's car, waving out the window as they drove away. Sean had already gone home with his best friend, Corey, since he'd be staying with his family that week. With the bride and groom gone, the others said their good-byes and Kade set out with some friends. Jo and Denny were the last to leave.

"Abby, thanks for everything." Jo had tears in her eyes as she hugged Abby longer than usual. "Without you and John, your marriage and faith, I wouldn't have known what real love was."

The lump in Abby's throat was too thick for her to do more than nod her head. John reached for Denny's hand. "It's your turn next. When's the big day?"

"Two weeks. It'll be a small wedding, nothing like this, but we'd like you and Abby to be there."

Tension began gnawing at Abby's insides and she swallowed hard.

"And happy anniversary, guys." Jo reached out and pinched first her cheeks then John's.

Denny nudged his bride-to-be. "If we'd let 'em have a minute alone, they might actually get to celebrate. Come on, Jo, I'm taking you home."

"Bye! Thanks for everything . . ." Jo was still talking as Denny linked arms with her and headed for their car, leaving Abby and John standing in the doorway.

When they were gone, the house was silent, echoes of laughter and conversation from moments earlier still fading in the foyer. Abby took a step back and leaned against the wall for support. An overwhelming sense of dread settled over her, their home, the air between them.

John cleared his throat as he turned to face her. "I guess it's time."

The sadness in his eyes was too much for her and she let her gaze fall to the floor. "Go, John. Don't make a long ordeal out of it. Just go."

His suitcase was already in the car, and Abby was sure his keys were in his pocket. But instead of leaving, John stepped a few feet closer. "Abby, I know you're mad at me and I don't blame you." He came closer still and gently lifted her chin so that their eyes met. The tears that had been brimming spilled onto her cheeks and she gulped back a torrent of sobs. "I'm sorry, Abby." His voice was tender, barely more than a whisper. "Sorrier than I've ever been in all my life."

Abby had no fight left in her. She looked down again and nodded her understanding as she managed to speak. "Me, too."

"You don't have to believe me, but the other day—while you were on the campout with Nicole—I told Charlene to move on with her life." He hesitated. "The enemy of my soul wanted me to get sucked up in that mess, but God and I, well . . . we've been doing some talking. I ended it with Charlene, Abby. She's moving to Chicago in a few weeks."

Abby kept her eyes trained on the ground, not sure what to say. Not sure whether she believed him. When she found the strength to look at him again, she saw tears on his cheeks as well. "Abby, I made some awful mistakes and I'm sorry. I kissed Charlene twice when I never should have . . ."

Abby huffed under her breath. This wasn't true confession time. Abby didn't want to hear about Charlene now. *Go, John, get it over with.*

Instead he slid his fingers up the side of her face and continued. "There was never anything more between us, Abby. Never."

"John, this isn't the—"

"Wait . . . let me finish." His voice rang with sincerity, and again Abby was confused. *Why is he doing this? Breaking things off with Charlene—if he really had—and talking so tenderly to me? Why now when it's too late?*

He drew a deep breath and continued. "Look, Abby, I know you don't believe me, and that's something you have to work out, but it's important for me to tell you anyway. I made mistakes but I was not having an affair with Charlene and I was never in love with her." He sighed, his hand still framing her face. "For what it's worth, I think God wanted me to tell you."

Her soul felt like it was being strangled within her and she remained motionless. *How much can I take here, God? What's he doing to me?*

He's lying to you, Abby. Taking you for a fool.

The answer came quickly, angrily, from some dark recess of Abby's being and her back stiffened as she silently agreed with it. Of course he was lying. All those mornings and afternoons together and time alone when she was busy on the weekends? He must think she was incredibly gullible to believe there'd been nothing but a few kisses between him and Charlene.

"I'll always love you." He brought her chin up again and looked directly into her soul. "You know that, right?"

If he loved her, would he have taken up with Charlene in the first place? Her tears were falling onto the floor now and her lack of response to his question caused fresh pain in John's eyes.

He captured a tear from her cheek and mingled it with one of his own. "We were supposed to be one; that's what we promised each other twenty-two years ago. And just because we stopped being one doesn't mean I stopped loving you."

A sob escaped from Abby's throat as she nodded again. "G-g-go, John. Please."

"Okay." He backed up toward the front door, his eyes still locked on hers. "I'll never forget the years we had together. No matter what the future brings."

See, there it was! The reference to Charlene and the future they'd have together. She hung her head and let the sobs come. They stood there, not speaking to each other for nearly a minute. When she finally found control again, she opened the screen door and held it that way. "Good-bye, John."

He nodded his understanding, his voice thick. "Good-bye."

With that he walked out of their home, out of the life they'd shared together. In years to come he would be little more than a stranger, someone she used to love a long, long time ago.

Feeling as though her arms were being ripped from her sides, Abby watched him go, watched him climb into his truck and drive away. She stayed there until his taillights disappeared and she could no longer hear his engine. Then she shut the door, locked it, and wandered back into the house like a child orphaned in battle, wounded and cut to the core. Her eyes fell on the back door, and she knew where she needed to be: on the pier. Even if she was all by herself, she needed to be there.

The air had cooled some, so she ran upstairs to find a sweater. Tears still streamed down her face as she made her way through their closet. It was emptier now, missing the items John had taken with him. It would all be gone soon, everything that might remind her of John's place in their home. His former place.

Her eyes fell on John's zip-up Marion Eagles sweatshirt. Gathering it to her, she buried her face in the soft fleece and felt another wave of sobs wash over her. It still smelled like him. She eased it off the hanger and slipped it on over her dress, relishing the way she felt small and protected inside it, as though John's arms covered her shoulders.

"Dear God . . ." She could barely speak for the force of her tears. "I can't believe he's gone . . ."

Again the pier beckoned her. Hugging herself tightly, she moved from the closet into their bedroom . . . then paused. A brown notebook sat on John's dresser. She blinked twice, clearing the tears so she could see more clearly. What was that? Abby had never seen it before

Don't let it be from Charlene . . . please, God . . .

Abby almost walked past it, but something halted her, nudged her, and she went to take it gingerly in her fingers and open the cover.

It was John's writing. She turned a few pages and saw that there were several entries. Was it a journal? Could it be that her husband had kept notes she was completely unaware of? She flipped back to the first page and began reading:

July 9, 2001: I have made the most terrible mistake in all my life and I—

Abby closed her eyes. Was it a confession about what John had done with Charlene? If so she couldn't bear to read it, not now. She opened her eyes, terrified at what she was about to see. Unable to stop herself, she continued down the page.

. . . and I have no one to talk to, no place to share my feelings. That's why I'm writing now. Oh, God, what You've shown me in Kade's report. About the eagle and how he will hold onto his mate to the end. Even to death. My mistake is this: I let go of Abby. I loved her with all my being but someday, sometime, I let go. I'm sorry, God . . . if You're listening, let Abby know how sorry I am.

Her heart fluttered strangely. What was this? What had he done that caused him to be so sorry? And why hadn't he told her in person? Suddenly her mind filled with the image of John trying to talk to her the night before, and she bit her lip. He *had* tried to talk to her, but she was too weary, too sure he was lying to listen. She swallowed a series of sobs and dried her face on the sleeve of John's sweatshirt. The next entry was on the same page.

July 10, 2001: There's nothing I can do to make Abby believe me. I've made mistakes, God. You know that. But I haven't lied to her about me and Charlene. The memory of every moment with Charlene makes me sick to my stomach . . .

The room was spinning, and Abby had to sit on the foot of the bed to keep from falling on the floor. Was it possible? Had John been telling the truth all along?

A dozen times when she had ridiculed him, shouted at him, called him a liar played again in her head. What if she'd been wrong? What if he *had* been telling the truth?

She read the other entries, struck by John's humility, his transparency. Had he left the journal on his dresser intentionally, hoping she'd find it? The final entry answered her question:

July 13, 2001: Nicole is getting married tomorrow, the same day that I'll lose everything that ever mattered to me. One day . . . maybe ten years from now . . . I'll find the right moment to share these feelings with Abby. For now . . . there's nothing I can do. It's over between us and it's all my fault.

Abby closed the book and set it down. A different kind of sorrow gripped her heart, suffocated her with the reality that she'd been wrong about John. Yes, he'd made mistakes. They both had. But clearly he wasn't in love with Charlene and he hadn't lied about his relationship with her. Just the opposite. He'd tried to tell Abby every detail, to confide in her the feelings in his heart . . . but she had refused to listen.

Tears still pouring down her face, the sobs having their way with her, she followed the familiar path outside and down the damp grassy hill, past the deserted tables and empty dance floor to the old wooden pier. There were two chairs there, and Abby took one of them, doing her best to get control of herself. No wonder he had left. She hadn't really listened to him in years, hadn't been the friend he needed to confide in.

Okay, Abby, let it go. He's gone. It's all over; you can open your eyes.

She was cold and alone and the ache in her chest felt like it would kill her. John Reynolds, the man she had fallen in love with when she was barely more than a girl, was gone from her life. In part, at least, because she had refused to hear him, to believe him. *Lord, what have I done?*

Trust Me, daughter . . . look to Me. All things are possible with God.

But it's too late . . . I've pushed him away and now we have nothing left.

The wind in the trees made it sound as though God Himself were holding a finger to His mouth. *"Shhhhhh,"* He seemed to say. *"It's okay. Trust Me, daughter . . . come home to Me . . ."*

I want to, God, I do . . . But I've made such a mess of things.

Abby had no idea how long she sat there, sobbing quietly, not sure she would survive the losses in her life. Finally, when she didn't think she had tears left to cry, her mind moved back to the wedding and the lovely bride Nicole had been.

Dear God, let her and Matt stay together forever; don't let her happiness be dimmed because of John and me.

Abby stared out at the water and imagined how Haley Ann might have looked if she'd been Nicole's maid of honor. Abby looked intently across the water. "Haley Ann, baby, we missed you today. I missed you."

There was a rustling of bushes and grass behind her, far up on the hillside, and Abby spun around. She had never felt nervous here, in this place where she had lived nearly all her married life. But now that she was alone, every sound seemed magnified. Nothing caught her eye, so Abby decided it must have been a deer making its way across the field.

She turned back to the water and stood up, her pale blue dress flowing in the breeze beneath John's sweatshirt. She moved to the edge of the pier, then reached down and moved her fingers across the water. *Mommy loves you, baby girl.* Haley Ann wasn't there of course, but something about dipping her hand in the place where her baby's ashes lay gave Abby a sense of connection with her.

It was the closest she could come this side of heaven to holding Haley Ann, and right now it was the only thing that brought even a fraction of peace to Abby's heart. As she stayed there, the lake water moving between her fingers, her mind returned to John's final words in the hallway. So, he hadn't lied after all . . .

The reality left a sick feeling Abby knew would never quite go away. The death of their marriage was no longer something she could blame on John alone. It was her fault, too. *Why didn't I see it sooner, Lord?*

Love covers a multitude of sins, My daughter.

If only it weren't too late . . .

Abby gazed into the starry summer sky and there, alone in the night, she was overwhelmed by the presence of God.

As I have loved you, so you must love one another . . . love deeply, Abby.

The unspoken words came at her again and again, and she ached for the chance to tell John about finding the journal. To think that everything he said had been the truth. That he hadn't wanted an affair, hadn't been sleeping with her. That Abby's mocking comments had probably driven him into Charlene's arms in the first place. That it had been both their faults . . . refusing to talk, watching love die . . .

Year after year after year.

The realization was suffocating, and she pulled her hand from the water, frozen in that stooped position at the end of the pier. *God, forgive me. What have I done? I could have believed him. Instead I convinced myself he was a cheater, a liar. And I treated him that way for years. Dear God . . . what kind of woman am I?*

Return to your first love, Abby. Love as I have loved you . . .

But how could she return to God now when she deserved nothing but condemnation? As if in response, Abby felt an overwhelming sense of grace wash over her. Grace precious and undeserved. *I'm sorry, Lord. How much of what happened was my fault and I didn't see it until now? And why couldn't I have heard You this way before it was too late? Oh, God, please forgive me . . .*

A strong voice full of love and peace echoed in her being. *I died for you, child, and I have loved you with an everlasting love . . . All is forgotten, all is forgiven . . . Now, go . . . return to your first love.*

Return to my . . . ? Abby had thought the words in her heart referred to the Lord. But maybe . . . could it be? Could God want her to talk to John, to make peace with him somehow, to tell him she was sorry for doubting him?

Sadness and regret filled her to overflowing, but Abby recognized that in those sacred moments she'd been blessed with some sort of miracle, a private encounter with the Lord Almighty. Abby opened her eyes and gazed across the lake once more. Whatever God had done to her soul, her entire perspective was different now, changed in a divine instant.

"Haley Ann would have loved the wedding, don't you think?"

Abby gasped and spun around, rising to her feet at the sound of John's voice. He was on the pier, walking toward her, and Abby had to blink to convince herself she wasn't seeing things. "John? What are you . . . why . . . ?"

A million questions came at her, but she couldn't find the strength to voice any of them. He moved closer still until his feet were nearly touching hers. His eyes shone with tears, but there was a calm in his features now, a certainty that Abby couldn't explain, and it filled her with hope.

Could it be that the same holy realization that had dawned in her heart had dawned in his as well?

"Abby, give me your hands."

Her shock was so great she could think of no response but to do as he asked. Tentatively, she reached out, surprised at her body's reaction to his touch as he turned them palms up and linked his fingers over hers.

He blinked back tears as he started to speak. "I was two miles down the road when I realized that if I kept moving in that direction, away from all this, from my life here with you, then something inside me would die forever." He studied her eyes intently. "I couldn't have that, Abby. So I pulled over and started walking back."

Abby had to remind herself to breathe as she listened. "You . . . you walked back?"

He nodded, his gaze never leaving hers. "The whole way. I wasn't sure at first what I wanted to say, but I knew I had to say it."

Somewhere in the newly illuminated alleys of Abby's bruised and broken heart the seed of hope began to take root. "I don't understand . . ."

The lines in John's jaw hardened and then relaxed again. "I need to tell you about the eagle."

"The eagle?" Abby's heart rate doubled. What was he getting at? Was this a confession or another apology?

"Yes." He spoke slowly, every word steeped in sincerity. "A long time ago I made the mistake of letting go of you, Abby." He tightened his grip on her fingers. "I was crazy, and I don't blame you if you never forgive me. I started spending time with Charlene and . . . it was like everything fell apart between us. Like we were free-falling toward the death of our marriage and neither of us could do anything to stop it."

He massaged her fingers, never taking his eyes from hers. "It wasn't until you were gone on the campout with Nicole that I had a chance to read Kade's report."

Abby blinked and tried to make the connection. "Kade's report?"

"On the eagle, Abby. Remember?" He paused. "As I read it God spoke to me like I haven't heard Him speak in . . . well, in too long. And I knew then I could never be with a woman like Charlene. Or any other woman for that matter."

Fresh tears burned in Abby's eyes. "I found your journal."

John's eyebrows lifted. "What? I packed it . . . it's in the car with my clothes . . ."

Abby shook her head. "It's on your dresser. Right on top."

"That's impossible, Abby. I know I packed it . . ."

"It doesn't matter—" Her voice broke as still more tears filled her eyes. "I read it, John. How could I have thought you were lying . . . ?" She let her head fall against his chest. "I'm so sorry." Her eyes found him again. "Everything I accused you of . . . you were telling the truth, weren't you?"

"Yes." He studied her intently as a single tear slid down his cheek. "I did a lot of things I'm not proud of, I broke promises I should have kept," he looked at her again, "but I never lied to you, Abby."

"I'm sorry I didn't believe you. Sorry I . . ." Abby's throat was too thick to speak.

John shook his head. "It's okay, Abby. It was my fault, and that's why I'm here now. The truth is . . . I still love you." He came closer to her, their hands still linked. "I couldn't seem to find the right time or the right way to tell you these past few days, but . . ." He stroked Abby's palms with his fingertips. "I don't ever want to let go again, Abby. Never. I don't care if it kills me; I want to love you like an eagle loves his mate. Like the Lord *wants* me to love you. Holding on until death makes me finally let go."

Abby's head was spinning, her heart racing so fast she could barely breathe. "What're you saying, John . . ."

"I'm saying I can't divorce you, Abby. I love you too much. I love the history I have with you and the way you are with our children, the way you brighten a room just by walking into it. I love that you share every important memory of my entire life and that you loved my father and I loved yours . . ." Two more tears made their way down his cheeks, but he ignored them. When he spoke again his voice was only a broken whisper. "And I love . . . the way only you understand how I feel about Haley Ann."

He cocked his head, pleading with her. "Please, Abby, stay with me. Love me forever the way I want to love you. Take time away with me and talk to me. Laugh with me and grow old with me. Please."

John's words unlocked something in Abby that sent what remained of the walls around her heart tumbling down. She came to him slowly, fitting her body against his and laying her head on his chest as she sobbed tears of unabashed joy. "You're . . . you're serious?"

He pulled back and stared at her once more. "I've never been more serious about anything in my life. God's worked on my heart, Abby. I want to go to church with you again and read the Bible with you and pray with you. Forever." He looked deeper into her eyes. "I love you, Abby. Please don't hide from me anymore. You're the most beautiful woman I know, inside and out." He hesitated. "Do you think . . . could you forgive me, start over with me here and now and never let go again?"

A sound that was part-laugh, part-sob came from Abby as she clung to John. "Yes, I can do that. I love you, too. I realized tonight that I never stopped loving you, even when I . . . even when I said I hated you."

"I'm so sorry, Abby." John whispered the words into her hair, clinging to her the way a dying person clings to life. "Why did we do this to each other?"

Abby was suddenly confused as well. Why hadn't they had this talk months ago, years ago, back when they'd first grown apart?

A shiver of terror ran through Abby's body as she nestled deeper into John's chest. What if she hadn't found his journal? What if he'd kept driving and never looked back? What if they hadn't embraced the grace of God, swallowed their pride, and admitted that divorce was the most wrong thing they could ever do?

Thank You, God . . . thank You. Abby's tears were those of gratitude now, and she felt humbly awed at the power of Christ's love, the power to turn them from certain destruction and send them back into each other's arms.

She would cancel her trip, he would bring home his suitcase, and the kids wouldn't know how close they'd come. Not now, anyway. Someday, when the time was right, they would share some of what they'd gone through. So the kids would know that no marriage is perfect, and that only by God's grace did two people—no matter how right they seemed for each other—ever stay together.

Abby and John talked about that and other aspects of what had happened for nearly an hour, acknowledging their mistakes and pronouncing their love for each other as they never thought they'd do again.

Finally they were quiet and slowly, gradually, his arms still around her, John began to sway.

"Do you hear it, Abby?" His voice was low, filled with a love that would bear all things, forgive all things. A love that would never end.

She closed her eyes and listened to the subtle creak of the pier in the water, savored the sound of crickets around them, and the steady thud of John's heartbeat against her chest. In the trees a gentle wind carried with it echoes of long-ago memories. The announcer saying, *"Ladies and gentlemen, your 2000 state champions, the Marion Eagles!* The precious jingle of Haley Ann's cry . . . Nicole's sweet, clear voice promising a lifetime of love to her young man . . . her father using the last of his breath to pass the baton to John. *Love her . . . love her . . . love her.*

It was music. The same music John had asked her to listen to all those years ago. "I hear it."

John eased back and kissed her then, tenderly, sweetly, with a longing that was undeniable. The same way he had kissed her twenty-two years earlier, and Abby was filled with certainty that somehow, miraculously, they had again gone through the fire and come out stronger on the other side.

They were caught in the moment, and as John led her across the pier in time with the music of their lives, he whispered to her soul the words she had never expected to hear again.

"Dance with me, Abby." He brought his lips to hers once more and their tears met and mingled somewhere in between. "Please, Abby . . . for the rest of my life, dance with me."

Nicole and Matt were at the hotel counter checking in as Mr. and Mrs. Conley for the first time when Nicole's breath caught in her throat. "Did you hear that?"

They were waiting for the attendant to get their room key and Matt glanced at her, his expression blank. "Hear what?"

"Wow." Nicole grinned. "I guess it was God, maybe. It was so loud I thought everyone heard it. Like a voice told me my prayers had been answered."

Matt slipped an arm around her. "Of course they have, honey," he teased. "Look who you married."

She laughed, but shook her head. "No, I think it was my prayers for my parents."

"Your parents? You weren't really worried about them, were you?"

Nicole remembered the burden she'd felt, the heavenly insistence that had preceded her prayers for her mom and dad those past months. "Yeah, I guess I was. God kept putting them on my heart, and I kept praying."

"Then you did the right thing." Matt smiled. "Better safe than sorry."

"You think it was God then, telling me my prayers were answered?"

"Probably." He shrugged. "But, it couldn't have been anything serious. Not with your parents."

Nicole grinned, her heart and soul bathed in peace. "You're probably right. Whatever it was, God's got it under control."

A man approached them from the other side of the hotel check-in counter. "Here you go, sir. Room 852, the honeymoon suite." He handed Matt a set of key cards. "Enjoy your stay."

Matt took her hand and led her toward their room—and into the beginning of a marriage that Nicole knew had been destined by God Himself. A marriage she prayed would always feel this wonderful and amazing, one that with the Lord's help would survive whatever life gave them and somehow wind up stronger, more beautiful on the other side.

A marriage just like her parents'.

Author's Note

When I think of the divorce situation in society today I am and always will be deeply grieved. In the dance of life, the casualties of our instant, self-serving, self-indulgent society abound among us. Brokenhearted men and women who struggle through life alone; toddlers whose lives are built around two houses, two bedrooms, and two sets of parents; teenage boys and girls who have no idea how to honor one another or keep commitments.

None of this is how God intended love to be.

If nothing else, I pray that *A Time to Dance* made you compassionate. Compassionate for people suffering through divorce, for children whose parents have separated. Compassionate toward the spouse you might—even now—be walking away from.

There are obvious exceptions—abuse or infidelity or abandonment, for instance—and for those of you hurting in such a situation, I pray miraculous intervention and healing. But even still divorce is deeply displeasing to our Lord. Scripture tells us God hates it, that what He brings together no one should separate. Strong words, really. Strong enough to make us consider how greatly the enemy of our souls wants to destroy our relationships.

But for every marriage that dies a painful death, there are others like Abby's and John's. Marriages that we are too quick to throw away, marriages where a joyous, boundless, restored and renewed love might be discovered if only we would be willing to dig deep enough to find it. Willing to humble ourselves and hear our God on this issue that is so close to His heart.

If you or someone you love is in the throes of divorce, please do not hear condemnation in this letter. Hear compassion and hope and, above all else, love. Because where there is God, there is faith, there is hope, and there is always love.

Love that perseveres. Love that never ends.

Fight for your marriages, friends. Pray for wisdom and godly counsel; seek God and find a way back to the place where love began, a place where love can begin again.

For some of you that might mean renewing a relationship with the Creator and Savior. For others it might mean starting such a relationship where one never existed. The process is fairly simple. In the most definitive example of love ever, Christ died to pay the price for your sins, for mine. In doing so, He gave us the choice of abundant eternal life now and forever as an alternative to hell. Perhaps it's time that you admit your need for a Savior and commit your life to Him. Find a Bible-believing church and study what the Scriptures say about having a relationship with Jesus Christ.

Once you understand that kind of love and grace, it'll be easier to love others around you. Easier to let them love you.

Finally, know that I have prayed for each of you, begging the Lord to meet you where you are, dry your tears, and bring beauty from ashes. That He might help you and your spouse find a place of love greater than anything you've known before. Let us all love deeply, friends. No matter how impossible it feels, God is pulling for you, waiting, watching. Ready to help if only together you will let Him.

If you or someone you love is divorced or separated from a spouse who has been unwilling to try, then know God is there for you, also. Keep praying. As God was faithful to answer Nicole's prayers for her parents, so He will be faithful to answer yours. His grace and mercy know no bounds, and with your hand in His, He will one day lead you to that place you long for.

A place of magnificent, boundless, unimaginable love.

Thanks for journeying with me through the pages of *A Time to Dance*. May God bless you and yours until our next time together.

Humbly in Christ,
Karen Kingsbury

P.S. As always, I would love to hear from you. Please write me at my e-mail address: rtnbykk@aol.com.

Reading Group Guide

The following questions may be used as part of a Book Club, Bible Study, or Group Discussion.

Relationships do not change overnight. What were some of the signs that Abby and John were having trouble? Why is it easy to miss such signs?

Name three things that caused a strain in the Reynoldses' relationship. What can people do to safeguard against the common problems of busyness, distractions, and judgmental attitudes?

Many of the Reynoldses' problems stemmed from a lack of trust. What could John have done differently so that Abby might have believed him from the beginning? What could Abby have done differently to keep the lines of communication open between the two of them?

Share what you feel about your spouse's friendships with members of the opposite sex? What guidelines should a married person follow when it comes to such friendships?

When was it clear that John and Abby were crossing into dangerous territory with their outside friends? How can married people avoid reaching out to strangers to have their needs met?

What did you learn about the eagle in *A Time to Dance*? In what ways can we learn from the eagle's example?

How was it apparent that Nicole's prayers for her parents were being answered?

What were the individual breakthroughs John and Abby needed to experience? What lessons did they have in common?

What role does our memories play when we're faced with the temptation to walk away from our spouse? How does attending a conference like "Women of Faith" help us remember what's important?

Marriages—like all relationships—are tapestries woven with an assortment of colors and fabrics. The dark colors and brilliant hues make up the beauty of our lives together. Think of three moments of sorrow and three moments of celebration in your own marriage. Recall a time when you knew you would love your spouse forever. If you don't feel that way still, what has changed? What can you do, with God's help, to take the first step toward healing?

A Time to Embrace

DEDICATED TO . . .

My husband, in honor of his fourteen years as a varsity basketball coach. You have suffered much this past season, but always you held your head high and believed. "God has a plan," you would say, leaving me and everyone else awe-struck at your faithfulness. Without a doubt you are the most honest, most loyal man I've ever known. How blessed I am to be your wife . . . truly. Your character stands as a shining beacon for all who have had the privilege of even the briefest contact with you. Yes, my love, God has a plan. And one day in the not so distant future, the name Coach will ring once more, and you'll wear the whistle again.

I have two prayers for you. First, that we savor every minute of this season of rest. For the basketball program's loss is most certainly our gain. And second, that the loving legacy of your coaching days will change forever the lives of those boys who called you Coach.

Kelsey, my precious little teenager, whose heart is so close to my own. I watch you on the soccer field, giving everything you've got, and I am grateful for the young woman you're becoming. Nothing pushes you around, sweetheart. Not boys or friends or the trends of the day. Instead you stand at the front of the pack, a one-in-a-million sweetheart with a future so bright it shines. Wasn't it just yesterday when you were teetering across our kitchen floor, trying to give your pacifier to the cat so he wouldn't be lonely? I can hear the ticking of time, my daughter. The clock moves faster every year . . . but believe me, I'm savoring every minute. I am blessed beyond words for the joy of being your mother.

Tyler, my strong and determined oldest son. Since the day you could walk, you wanted to entertain us. Singing, dancing, doing silly tricks. Whatever it took to make us laugh. And now here you are, tall and handsome, writing books, and learning to sing and play the piano, putting together dramas in a way that glorifies our Lord. All that and you're only ten years old! I've always believed God has a special plan for your life, Tyler, and I believe it more all the time. Keep listening for His lead, son. That way the dance will always be just what He wants it to be.

Sean, my tender boy. I knew when we brought you home from Haiti that you loved God. But it wasn't until I saw your eyes fill with tears during worship time that I realized how very much you loved Him. "What's wrong, Sean?" I would whisper to you. But you would only shake your head, "Nothing, Mom. I just love Jesus so much." I pray you always hold that special love in your heart, and that you allow God to guide you to all the glorious plans He has for you.

Joshua, my can-do child. From the moment I met you I knew you were special, set apart from the other kids at the orphanage. Now that you've been home a year I can see that all the more clearly. God has placed within you a root of determination stronger than any I've seen. Whether you're drawing or writing, coloring or singing, playing basketball or soccer, you steel your mind to be the best, and then you do just that. I couldn't be prouder of the strides you've made, son. Always remember where your talent comes from, Joshua . . . and use it to glorify Him.

EJ, our chosen son. Yours was the first face we saw on the Internet photolisting that day when we first considered adopting from Haiti. Since then I've been convinced of one thing: God brought you into our lives. Sometimes I think maybe you'll be a doctor or a lawyer, or maybe the president of a company. Because the things God has done in the one year since you've been home are so amazing, nothing would surprise me. Keep your eyes on Jesus, son. Your hope will always only be found there.

Austin (MJ), my miracle boy, my precious heart. Is it possible you are already five? A big strapping boy who no longer sees the need for a nap, and who has just one more year home with me before starting school? I love being your mommy, Austin. I love when you bring me dandelions in the middle of the day or wrap your chubby arms around my neck and smother my face in kisses. I love playing give-and-go with you every morning. And wearing my Burger King crown so I can be the Kings and you can be the Bulls in our living room one-on-one battles. What joy you bring me, my littlest son. You call yourself MJ because you wanna be like Michael Jordan, and truly, I don't doubt that you will be one day. But when I see you, I'll always remember how close we came to losing you. And how grateful I am that God gave you back to us.

And to God Almighty, the Author of life, who has, for now, blessed me with these.

One

THE KID MADE COACH JOHN REYNOLDS NERVOUS.

He was tall and gangly, and he'd been doodling on his notebook since sixth period health class began. Now the hour was almost up, and John could see what the boy was drawing.

A skull and crossbones.

The design was similar to the one stenciled on the kid's black T-shirt. Similar, also, to the patch sewn on his baggy dark jeans. His hair was dyed jet black and he wore spiked black leather collars around his neck and wrists.

There was no question Nathan Pike was fascinated with darkness. He was a gothic, one of a handful of kids at Marion High School who followed a cultic adherence to the things of doom.

That wasn't what bothered John.

What bothered him was a little something the boy had scribbled *beneath* the dark symbolism. One of the words looked like it read *death*. John couldn't quite make it out from the front of the class-room, so he paced.

Like he did every Friday night along the stadium sidelines as the school's varsity football coach, John wandered up and down the rows of students checking their work, handing out bits of instruction or critique where it was needed.

As he made his way toward Nathan's desk, he glanced at the boy's notebook again. The words scribbled there made John's blood run cold. Was Nathan serious? These days John could do nothing but assume the student meant what he'd written. John squinted, just to make sure he'd read the words correctly.

He had.

Beneath the skull and crossbones, Nathan had written this sentiment: *Death to jocks.*

John was still staring when Nathan looked up and their eyes met. The boy's were icy and dead, unblinking. Intended to intimidate. Nathan was probably used to people taking one glance and looking away, but John had spent his career around kids like Nathan. Instead of turning, he hesitated, using his eyes to tell Nathan what he could not possibly say at that moment. That the boy was lost, that he was a follower, that the things he'd drawn and the words he'd written were not appropriate and would not be tolerated.

But most important, John hoped his eyes conveyed that he was there for Nathan Pike. The same way he had been there for others like him, the way he would always be there for his students.

Nathan looked away first, shifting his eyes back to his notebook.

John tried to still his racing heart. Doing his best to look unaffected, he returned to the front of the classroom. His students had another ten minutes of seatwork before he would resume his lecture.

He sat down at his desk, picked up a pen, and grabbed the closest notepad.

Death to jocks?

Obviously he would have to report what he'd seen to the administration, but as a teacher, what was he supposed to do with that? What if Nathan was serious?

Ever since the shooting tragedies at a handful of schools around the country, most districts had instituted a "red-flag" plan of some sort.

Marion High School was no exception. The plan had every teacher and employee keeping an eye on the classrooms in their care. If any student or situation seemed troublesome or unusual, the teacher or employee was supposed to make a report immediately. Meetings were held once a month to discuss which students might be slipping through the cracks. The telltale signs were obvious: a student bullied by others, despondent, dejected, outcast, angry, or fascinated with death. And particularly students who made threats of violence.

Nathan Pike qualified in every category.

But then, so did 5 percent of the school's enrollment. Without a specific bit of evidence, there wasn't much a teacher or administrator could do. The handbook on troubled kids advised teachers to ease the teasing or involve students in school life.

"Talk to them, find out more about them, ask about their hobbies and pastimes," the principal had told John and the other faculty when they discussed the handbook. "Perhaps even recommend them for counseling."

That was all fine and good. The problem was, boys like Nathan Pike didn't always advertise their plans. Nathan was a senior. John remembered when Nathan first came to Marion High. His freshman and sophomore years Nathan had worn conservative clothes and kept to himself.

The change in his image didn't happen until last year.

The same year the Marion High Eagles won their second state football championship.

John cast a quick glance at Nathan. The boy was doodling again. *He doesn't know I saw the notebook.* Otherwise wouldn't he have sat back in his chair, covered the skull and crossbones, and hidden the horrible words? This wasn't the first time John had suspected Nathan might be a problem. Given the boy's changed image, John had kept a close eye on him since the school year began. He strolled by Nathan's desk at least once each day and made a point of calling on him, talking to him, or locking eyes with him throughout the hour. John suspected a deep anger burned in the boy's heart, but today was the first time there'd ever been proof.

John remained still but allowed his gaze to rove around the room. What was different about today? Why would Nathan choose now to write something so hateful?

Then it hit him.

Jake Daniels wasn't in class.

Suddenly the entire scenario made sense. When Jake was there—no matter where he sat—he found a way to turn his classmates against Nathan.

Freak . . . queer . . . death doctor . . . nerd . . . loser.

All names whispered and loosely tossed in Nathan's direction. When the whispers carried to the front of the classroom, John would raise his eyebrows toward Jake and a handful of other football players in the class.

"That's enough." The warning was usually all John had to say. And for a little while, the teasing would stop. But always the careless taunting and cruel words hit their mark. John was sure of it.

Not that Nathan ever let Jake and the others see his pain. The boy ignored all jocks, treated them as though they didn't exist. Which was probably the best way to get back at the student athletes who picked on him. Nothing bothered John's current football players more than being looked over.

That was especially true for Jake Daniels.

No matter that this year's team hadn't *earned* the accolades that came their way. The fact that the team's record was worse than any season in recent history mattered little to Jake and his teammates. They believed they were special and they intended to make everyone at school treat them accordingly.

John thought about this year's team. It was strange, really. They were talented, maybe more so than any other group of kids to come through Marion High. Talk around school was that they had even more going for them than last year's team when John's own son Kade led the Eagles to a state championship. But they were arrogant and cocky, with no care for protocol or character. In all his years of coaching, John had never had a more difficult group.

No wonder they weren't winning. Their talent was useless in light of their attitudes.

And many of the boys' parents were worse. Especially since Marion had lost two of its first four games.

Parents constantly complained about playing time, practice routines, and, of course, the losses. They were often rude and condescending, threatening to get John fired if his record didn't improve.

"What happened to Marion High's undefeated record?" they would ask him. "A good coach would've kept the streak going."

"Maybe Coach Reynolds doesn't know what he's doing," they would say. "Anyone could coach the talent at Marion High and come up with an undefeated season. But losses?"

They wondered out loud what type of colossal failure John Reynolds was to take a team of Eagles football players onto the field and actually lose. It was unthinkable to the Marion High parents. Unconscionable. How dare Coach Reynolds drop two games so early in the season!

And sometimes the wins were worse.

"That was a cream puff opponent last week, Reynolds," the parents would say. If they had a two-touchdown win, the parents would harp that it should have been four at least. And then John's favorite line of all: "Why, if *my* son had gotten more playing time . . ."

Parents gossiped behind his back and undermined the authority he had on the field. Never mind the fact that the Eagles were coming off a championship season. Never mind that John was one of the winningest coaches in the state. Never mind that more than half of last year's championship squad had graduated, placing John in what was obviously a rebuilding year.

The thing that mattered was whether the sons of John's detractors were being used at what they believed were the proper positions and for enough minutes each game. Whether their numbers were being called at the appropriate times for the big plays, and how strong their individual statistics appeared in the paper.

It was just a rotten break that the biggest controversy on the team had, in a roundabout way, made Nathan's life miserable. Two quarterbacks had come into summer practices, each ready for the starting position: Casey Parker and Jake Daniels.

Casey was the shoo-in, the senior, the one who had ridden the bench behind Kade up until last year. All his high-school football career had come down to this, his final season with the Eagles. He reported in August expecting to own the starting position.

What the boy hadn't expected was that Jake Daniels would show up with the same mind-set.

Jake was a junior, a usually good kid from a family who once lived down the street from John and his wife, Abby. But two years ago, the Danielses split up. Jake's mother took Jake and moved into an apartment. His father took a job in New Jersey hosting a sports radio program. The divorce was nasty.

Jake was one of the casualties.

John shuddered. How close had he and Abby come to doing the same thing? Those days were behind them, thank God. But they were still very real for Jake Daniels.

At first Jake had turned to John, a father figure who wasn't half a country away. John would never forget something Jake asked him.

"You think my dad still loves me?"

The kid was well over six feet tall, nearly a man. But in that instant he was seven years old again, desperate for some proof that the father he'd counted on all his life, the man who had moved away and left him, still cared.

John did everything he could to assure Jake, but as time passed, the boy grew quiet and sullen. He spent more hours alone in the weight-room and out on the field, honing his throwing skills.

When summer practices came around, there was no question who would be the starting quarterback. Jake won the contest easily. The moment that happened, Casey Parker's father, Chuck, called a meeting with John.

"Listen, Coach—" the veins on his temple popped out as he spoke— "I heard my son lost the starting position."

John had to stifle a sigh. "That's true."

The man spouted several expletives and demanded an explanation. John's answer was simple. Casey was a good quarterback with a bad attitude. Jake was younger, but more talented and coachable, and therefore the better choice.

"My son cannot be second string." Casey's father was loud, his face flushed. "We've been planning for this all his life! He's a senior and he will not be sitting the bench. If he has a bad attitude, that's only because of his intensity. Live with it."

Fortunately, John had brought one of his assistants to the meeting. The way accusations and hearsay were flying about, he'd figured he couldn't be too careful. So he and his assistant had sat there, waiting for Parker to continue.

"What I'm saying is—" Chuck Parker leaned forward, his eyes intent—"I've got three coaches breathing down my neck. We're thinking of transferring. Going where my kid'll get a fair shake."

John resisted the urge to roll his eyes. "Your son has an attitude problem, Chuck. A big one. If other high-school coaches in the area are recruiting him, it's because they haven't worked with him." John leveled his gaze at the man. "What exactly are your concerns?"

"I'll *tell* you my concern, Coach." Chuck pointed a rigid finger at John. "You're not loyal to your players. That's what. Loyalty is everything in sports."

This from a man whose son wanted to toss his letterman's jacket and transfer schools. As it turned out, Casey Parker stayed. He took snaps at running back and tight end and spelled Jake at quarterback. But the criticism from Casey's father had continued each week, embarrassing Casey and causing the boy to work harder to get along with Jake, his on-field rival. Jake seemed grateful to be accepted by a senior like Casey, and the two of them began spending most of their free time together. It didn't take long to see the changes in Jake. Gone was the shy, earnest kid who popped into John's classroom twice a week just to connect. Gone was the boy who had once been kind to Nathan Pike. Now Jake was no different from the majority of players who strutted across Marion High's campus.

And in that way, the quarterback controversy had only made Nathan's life more miserable. Whereas once Nathan was respected by at least one of the football players, now he didn't have a single ally on the team.

John had overheard two teachers talking recently.

"How many Marion football players does it take to screw in a light bulb?"

"I give up."

"One—he holds it while the world revolves around him."

There were nights when John wondered why he was wasting his time. Especially when his athletes' elitist attitudes divided the school campus and alienated students like Nathan Pike. Students who sometimes snapped and made an entire school pay for their low place in the social pecking order.

So what if John's athletes could throw a ball or run the length of a field? If they left the football program at Marion High without a breath of compassion or character, what was the point?

John drew a salary of $3,100 a season for coaching football. One year he'd figured it came out to less than two bucks an hour. Obviously he didn't do the job for the money.

He glanced at the clock. Three minutes of seatwork left.

Images from a dozen different seasons flashed in his mind. Why was he in it, then? It wasn't for his ego. He'd had more strokes in his days as a quarterback for University of Michigan than most men received in a lifetime. No, he didn't coach for pride's sake.

It was, very simply, because there were two things he seemed born to do: play football . . . and teach teens.

Coaching was the purest way he'd known to bring those two together. Season after season after season, it had worked. Until now. Now it didn't feel pure at all. It felt ridiculous. Like the whole sports world had gone haywire.

John drew a deep breath and stood, working the tendons in his bum knee—the one with the old football injury. He walked to the chalkboard where, for the next ten minutes, he diagramed a series of nutritional food values and meticulously explained them. Then he assigned homework.

But the whole time there was only one thing on his mind: Nathan Pike.

How had a clean-cut student like Nathan once was become so angry and hateful? Was it all because of Jake Daniels? Were Jake's and the other players' egos so inflated that they couldn't coexist with anyone different from them? And what about the words Nathan had scribbled on his notebook? *Death to jocks.* Did he mean it?

If so, what could be done?

Schools like Marion High grew from the safe soil of Middle America. Most did not have metal detectors or mesh backpacks or video cameras that might catch a disturbed student before he took action. Yes, they had the red-flag program. Nathan had already been red-flagged. Everyone who knew him was watching.

But what if that wasn't enough?

John's stomach tightened, and he swallowed hard. He had no answers. Only that today, in addition to grading papers, inputting student test results in the computer, holding afternoon practice, and meeting with a handful of irritated parents along the sidelines, he would also have to talk to the principal about Nathan Pike's scribbled declaration.

It was eight o'clock by the time he climbed into his car and opened an envelope he'd found in his school mailbox just before practice.

"To whom it may concern," the letter began. "We are calling for the resignation of Coach Reynolds . . ."

John sucked in a sharp breath. *What in the world?* His gut ached as he kept reading.

"Coach Reynolds is not the moral example we need for our young men. He is aware that several of his players are drinking and taking part in illegal road races. Coach Reynolds knows about this but does nothing. Therefore we are demanding he resign or be let go. If nothing is done about this, we will inform the media of our request."

John remembered to exhale. The letter wasn't signed, but it was copied to his athletic director, his principal, and three school district officials.

Who could have written such a thing? And what were they referring to? John gripped the steering wheel with both hands and sat back hard. Then he remembered. There had been rumors in August when practice first started up . . . rumors that a few players had drunk and raced their cars. But that's all they'd been: rumors. John couldn't do anything about them . . .

He leaned his head against the car window. He'd been furious when he'd heard the report. He'd asked the players straight out, but each of them had denied any wrongdoing. Beyond that there wasn't a thing John could do. Protocol was that rumors not be given credence unless there was proof of a rule violation.

Not a moral example for the players?

John's hands began to tremble and he stared over his right shoulder at the doors of the school. Surely his athletic director wouldn't acknowledge a cowardly, unsigned letter like this one. But then . . .

The athletic director was new. An angry man with a chip on his shoulder and what seemed like a vendetta against Christians. He'd been hired a year ago to replace Ray Lemming, a formidable man whose heart and soul had been given over to coaches and athletes.

Ray was so involved in school athletics he was a fixture at the school, but last year, at the ripe age of sixty-three, he retired to spend more time with his family. The way most coaches saw it, much of the true heart of Marion sports retired right alongside him.

That was especially true after the school hired Herman Lutz as athletic director.

John drew a weary breath. He'd done everything possible to support the man, but he'd already fired the boys' swim coach after a parent complaint. What if he took this absurd letter seriously? The other coaches saw Lutz as a person drowning in the complexities of the job.

"It just takes one parent," one of the coaches had said at a meeting that summer. "One parent threatens to go to Lutz's boss, and he'll give them what they want."

Even if it meant firing a coach.

John let his head fall slowly against the steering wheel. Nathan Pike . . . the death threat against jocks . . . the change in Jake Daniels . . . the attitude of his players . . . the complaining parents . . . the inexplicable losses this season . . .

And now this.

John felt eighty years old. How had Abby's father survived a lifetime of coaching? The question shifted his thoughts and he let everything about the day fade for a moment. Thirteen hours ago he'd arrived at school, and only now could he do what he wanted more than anything else. The thing he looked forward to more with each passing day.

He would drive home, open the door of the house he'd almost lost, and take the woman he loved more than life itself into his arms. The woman whose blue eyes danced more these days, and whose every warm embrace erased a bit more of their painful past. The woman who cheered him on each morning, and filled his heart when he couldn't take another minute of coaching and teaching.

The woman he had almost walked away from.

His precious Abby.

Two

ABBY WAS WRITING THE OPENING PARAGRAPH FOR HER latest magazine article when it happened.

There, between the third and fourth sentences, her fingers suddenly froze at the keyboard and the questions began to come. Was it true? Were they really back together? Had they actually dodged the bullet of divorce without even their kids knowing how close they'd come?

Slowly, Abby's eyes moved up away from the computer screen toward a shelf on her desk, to a recent photograph of her and John. Their newly married daughter, Nicole, had snapped the picture at a family softball game that past Labor Day weekend. There they were, Abby and John, side by side on the bleachers behind home plate, arms around each other. Looking like they'd never been anything but happily in love.

"You guys are so cute," Nicole had said at the time. "More in love every year."

Abby stared at the photo, her daughter's voice ringing like wind chimes in the corners of her mind. There was no obvious sign, really, no way of seeing how close they'd come to losing it. How very nearly they had thrown away twenty-two years of marriage.

But when Abby looked at the picture, she knew.

It was there in the eyes, too deep for anyone but she and John to notice. A glistening of survivor love, a love tested and tried and so much stronger because of it all. A love that had placed its toes over the edge of a cold, dark abyss, steeled itself against the pain, and jumped. A love that had only at the last moment been caught by the nape of the neck and snatched back to safe pasture.

Nicole had no idea, of course. None of their kids did, really. Not Kade—now eighteen and in his first year at college. And certainly not their youngest, Sean. At eleven he had no idea how close she and John had come to walking away from each other.

She glanced at the calendar. Last year at this time they were making plans to divorce. Then Nicole and Matt announced their engagement, which delayed their timetable. But Abby and John planned to tell the kids after Nicole and Matt got home from their honeymoon.

Abby shuddered. If she and John had divorced, the kids might never have recovered. Especially Nicole, who was so idealistic and trusting in love.

Baby, if you only knew . . .

And yet here they were . . . she and John, exactly the way Nicole believed them to be.

Abby often had to pinch herself to believe it was true, that she and John weren't filing for divorce and looking for a way to tell the kids. They weren't fighting or ignoring each other or on the verge of having affairs.

They had survived. Not only that, but they were actually happy. Happier than they'd been since they'd said their vows. The things that tore so many couples apart had—through God's grace—made them stronger. One day, when the time was right, they would tell the kids what had almost happened. Maybe it would make them stronger, too.

Abby turned her attention back to the computer screen.

The article was one that grew from the roots of her heart: "Youth Coaches in America—a Dying Breed." She had a new editor at the national magazine that bought most of her work. A woman with a keen sense for the pulse and conscience of American families. In September she and Abby had discussed possible articles. An exposé on coaching had actually been the editor's idea.

"The whole country's sports crazy," the woman said. "But everywhere I turn it seems another quality coach is calling it quits. Maybe it's time we took a look at why."

Abby almost laughed out loud. If anyone could write honestly about the pain and passion of coaching youth sports, she could. She was a coach's daughter, after all. Her father and John's had been teammates at the University of Michigan, the school where John played before getting his degree and doing the only thing that seemed natural— coaching football.

Her entire life had taken place around the seasons of the game.

But after sharing the past two decades with John Reynolds, Abby could do more than write a magazine article about coaching. She could write a book. And she'd include it all: parents complaining about playing time, players ignoring character and responsibility, unrealistic expectations, second-guessing, and catcalling from the stands.

Fabricated accusations spouted in behind-the-scenes gossip circles designed to pressure a coach to step down. Never mind the team barbecues in the backyard or the way John used his own money to buy the guys breakfast a dozen times after a Saturday practice.

It always came down to the bottom line: win more games or else.

Was it any wonder coaches were quitting?

Abby's heart softened. There were still players who made the game a joy, still parents who thanked John after a hard-fought contest or dropped him a card in the mail expressing their gratitude. Otherwise there wouldn't be a man like John left in the coaching ranks. A handful of players at Marion High still tried hard in the classroom and on the field, still showed respect and earned it by their hard work and diligence. Players who appreciated the barbecues at the Reynoldses' house and the time and love John put into every season, every player. Young men who would go on to get college degrees and good jobs, and who years after graduating would still call the Reynoldses' house and ask, "Is Coach there?"

Those players used to be the norm. Why was it that now—for coaches across America—they were the exception?

"Yes," Abby had told her editor. "I'd love to write the story."

She'd spent the past few weeks interviewing coaches of longtime, successful programs. Coaches who had stepped down in recent years because of the same troubles that plagued John, the same reasons he came home tired and dejected more often.

The front door opened, and Abby heard her husband sigh as he closed the door. His footsteps sounded across the tiled entryway. Not the firm, crisp steps of spring or summer, but the sad, shuffling steps of a football season gone awry.

"I'm in here." She pushed back from her computer and waited.

John slumped into the room and leaned against the doorframe. His eyes found hers, and he held a folded piece of paper out to her.

She stood and took it from him. "Long day?"

"Read it."

Abby sat back down, opened the note, and began to read. Her heart sank. They wanted John's resignation. Were they crazy? Wasn't it enough that they harassed him daily? What did the parents want? She folded the note and tossed it on her desk. Then she went to John and slipped her arms around his waist. "I'm sorry."

He pulled her close, hugging her the way he'd done back when they were first married. Abby relished the sensation. John's strong arms, the smell of his cologne, the way they drew strength from each other . . .

This was the man she'd fallen in love with, the one she'd almost let get away.

John straightened and studied her. "It's nothing to worry about." He leaned close and kissed her.

A ripple of doubt sliced through the waters of Abby's soul. "It says a copy was sent to Herman Lutz. Athletic directors fire coaches when parents complain."

"Not this time." John shrugged. "Lutz knows me better than that."

"Ray Lemming knew you best of all." Abby kept her tone gentle. "I get a bad feeling about Herman Lutz."

"Lutz'll support me." He uttered a heavy chuckle. "Everyone knows I'd never let my players drink or have . . . what was it?"

"Street races."

"Right. Street races. I mean, come on." He angled his head. "One or two parents will always complain. Even when we win every game."

Abby didn't want to push the issue. "God's in control."

John blinked. "What's that supposed to mean?"

"It means God'll back you. No matter who else does or doesn't."

"You sound worried."

"Not worried. Just concerned about the letter."

John leaned against the wall, took off his baseball cap, and tossed it on the couch. "Where's Sean?"

"In his room." Their youngest son was in sixth grade. In the past few weeks, girls had begun to call. "His social life's left him a little behind at school. He'll be doing good to finish by ten."

"No wonder it's so quiet." He released the hold he had on Abby's waist and brought his fingertips up along her face, tracing the outline of her cheekbones. "It isn't supposed to be like this."

The feel of his hands against her face sent a shiver down her back. "Coaching?"

He nodded. "We won state last year." His tone was tired, his eyes darker than she'd seen them in a while. "What do they want from me?"

"I'm not sure." Abby studied him for a moment, then lowered her chin. "I know what you need, though."

John's expression softened. "What?"

"Dancing lessons." Abby could almost feel the sparkle in her eyes.

"Dancing lessons? So we can fox-trot over Jefferson next Friday night?"

"No, silly." She gave him a light push. "Stop thinking football." Her fingers linked with his and she waltzed him one step away from the wall and back. "I'm talking about *us.*"

A quiet moan rumbled up from John's chest. "Come on, Abby. Not dance lessons. I'm tone-deaf, remember? And not a stitch of rhythm."

She led him into the room a few more steps, her body close to his. "You dance with me on the pier." Her tone was pleading, and she did an intentional pout. She sounded like Nicole when she wanted her own way.

"Oh, Abby . . . no." His shoulders slumped forward a bit, but there was a light in his eyes that hadn't been there before. "Dancing on the pier is different. Crickets and creaking boards . . . the wind on the lake. I can dance to *that* kind of music." He arched his arm and twirled her beneath it. "Please, Abby. Don't make me take dance lessons."

She'd already won. Still, she grinned at him and held up a single finger. "Wait." In a flash she darted to her desk and snatched the piece of newspaper she'd clipped earlier that day. "Look. They're at the high school." She held up the article.

With a slight roll of his eyes he squinted at the headline. "Ballroom Dancing for *Mature* Couples?" He planted his hands on his hips and raised his eyebrows at her. "Great. Not only will I be sashaying for the first time in my life, I'll be doing it in the company of people twice my age." His head fell back a notch. "Abby . . . please."

She pointed to the smaller print. "Forty and older, John. That's what the article says."

"We're not that old." He was playing with her now, teasing her the way he'd done back when she was a high-school senior, surprised beyond words that this college-age star quarterback who'd been a family friend forever, wanted to date her. Her, of all people.

A giggle slipped from her lips and she drew close to him once more. "Yes, we are that old."

"No." His mouth hung open for a moment and he pointed first to her, then to himself. "How old are we?"

"I'm forty-one and you're forty-five."

"Forty-five?" He mouthed the words, his expression a twist of mock horror.

"Yes, forty-five."

"Really?" He took the news clipping from her and studied it again.

"Really."

"Well, then . . ." The article drifted to the floor. This time he took her hand in his and waltzed her toward the doorway. "I guess it's time for dancing lessons."

John led them from the center of her office into the entryway. "Mature, huh?"

"Yep." She loved moments like this, when it felt like she and John shared one heartbeat. They waltzed down the hall toward the kitchen.

"You don't think I'm mature, though, do you?" As he said the words, his feet became tangled with hers, and he fell backward, pulling Abby down with him. They smacked the wall as they landed, one on top of the other.

The shock lasted only a few seconds.

When it was clear they were both okay, a ripple of laughter burst from both of them. "No, John . . ." Deep waves of giggles sent Abby rolling onto the floor beside him. "No worries. I don't think you're mature."

"That's good." He was laughing harder than her, even. So hard there were tears in his eyes. "I wouldn't want that."

"But you *do* need dance lessons."

"Apparently." His laughter grew. "It reminds me . . . of the time you . . ." He tried to catch his breath. "The time you fell down the stairs at Sea World."

"That's right." Her ribs hurt from laughing so hard. "I had to get that seat."

"I'll never forget the sea lions." John imitated how the animals had swung their heads in Abby's direction that day.

"Don't . . ." Abby sucked in a breath. "You're killing me."

"People sticking out arms and legs trying to stop you." John sat up and rested his elbows on his knees.

She exhaled, finally catching her breath. "We're . . . quite a pair."

John struggled to his feet and leaned against the wall. "It worked." He stuck his hand out and helped Abby to her feet.

"What?" Abby's heart felt lighter than a summer breeze. How good it was to laugh like this, rolling around on the floor, being silly with John.

"I know you don't think I'm mature now." They linked arms and entered the kitchen.

"Definitely not."

"Starving, maybe." He rubbed his backside. "But never mature."

Three

DINNER WAS IN FULL SWING. IT WAS WEDNESDAY, AND every seat at the table was taken. John and Abby and Sean filled out one side, while Nicole and Matt and Matt's parents, Jo and Denny Conley, took up the other.

Abby loved nights like this, when the gang gathered at the Reynoldses' house, laughing and sharing updates about their lives. Across from her, Abby admired the glow on Nicole's face. *Thank You, God, for bringing Matt into her life. Don't ever let them go through what John and I did . . .*

The group was giggling about something Denny had said, something about a fishing hook getting caught in the pastor's hairpiece the previous weekend.

"Thing is—" Jo set her fork down, her face red from laughing— "none of us knew about the hair thingy. I mean Pastor stands up there every Sunday as honest as a trout in summertime." She gestured around the table. "You know what I mean . . . the man's not one of those big-hair types you see on TV. He's the real deal. Gen-u-ine."

Abby didn't know the man, but she felt for him all the same. "He must've been mortified."

Denny shrugged, but before he could respond, Jo leaned forward and held up her finger. "Know what he told me. He says, 'Jo, don't you go tellin' no one at church about this. The good Lord took my hair, but that don't mean I can't wear a hat.'" Jo slapped the table and the water in her glass jostled over the rim. "A hat! Isn't that the funniest thing y'all ever heard?"

Abby studied the red-headed woman, tiny and full of fire, a woman Abby never would have chosen for her daughter's mother-in-law. But Jo had grown on Abby and Nicole, and now they found her charming. A bit talkative, and maybe a little too interested in fishing, but wonderfully real and full of love. Their family get-togethers weren't the same without her.

Nicole wiped her mouth and looked at John. "Heard anything from Kade?"

"Nothing new." John shrugged. "School's going well, football, too."

"He's a redshirt this year, isn't he?" Denny anchored his elbows on the table.

"He is. It'll give him an extra year of eligibility."

"The whole redshirt thing doesn't sit well with me." Jo made a face. "Like a bad bucket o' bait."

Abby smiled. "It's a coach's call. There's a lot of talent ahead of Kade on the depth chart. He's okay with redshirting."

"I don't care." Jo's tone grew loud, more passionate. "Young Kade's good enough to start, after all, and I'd tell 'em so myself if I had the coach's number." She cocked her head in John's direction. "You don't have it, do you?"

Everyone laughed except Jo, who glanced about the table as though they'd all taken leave of their senses. "I'm serious as a thunderstorm on Lake Michigan. The boy's good."

"It's okay, Jo." John grinned at the woman, and Abby savored the effect. Lately, John's smile did wonderful things to Abby's heart. His voice was kind as he helped Jo understand. "Kade *agreed* to redshirt. He has a lot to learn before he takes the field."

"Yes—" Nicole looked at Abby—"and he's coming home soon, right?"

Abby admired the way her daughter handled herself around Jo. In the few months since marrying Matt, Nicole had become expert at dealing with her mother-in-law, knowing when to steer the conversation and how to distract Jo when she became too excited.

"That's right." Abby nodded. "Iowa plays at Indiana, October 20. It's only a four-hour drive from here. The school has that Monday off, so Kade'll come home with us, stay Sunday, and fly back to school Monday."

"Yep." Sean looked up from his dinner. "Ten days and counting."

"Well, don't you know I want in on that surer than a flea on a billy goat. Me and Denny, here, why we'll be tagging along right behind you down the turnp—" Jo gasped. "Wait." She jabbed her elbow into Denny's ribs, and the man jumped. "That's the weekend we have the mission thing, isn't it?"

Denny thought for a moment. "I think it is."

Matt looked up, his fork hanging in the air. "Mission thing?" He loved Abby's cooking and usually spent dinner letting the others talk while he worked on cleaning his plate. Abby had made stuffed pork chops and glazed potatoes, and Matt was already on his third serving. His eyes twinkled as he met his mother's gaze. "What mission thing?"

"Aw, shucks." Jo exchanged a look with Denny, and then exhaled hard. "We weren't going to tell you young folks yet. Wanted it to be a surprise."

Nicole leaned forward so she could see her in-laws more clearly. "You're taking a mission trip?"

"Actually—" Denny reached for Jo's hand—"it's a little more involved than that."

Abby could feel the anticipation building around the table. After all, Matt's parents had divorced when Matt was a small child. They'd lived separate lives until Matt and Nicole's engagement. Then—in a series of events that was nothing short of miraculous—first Denny, then Jo became believers. Two months ago they remarried and got involved at church. Now they spent Saturdays fishing with their pastor.

"Mom—" Matt set his fork down and leaned on the table—"what're you guys talking about?"

"Dag-nabbit." Jo shot an apologetic look at Denny. "I must have the biggest mouth this side of a steelhead." Then she turned and faced her son. "The truth is, your dad and I are thinking about spending a year in Mexico. Working at an orphanage down there and . . ."

For maybe the first time since Abby had known Jo, the woman was silent. The news was so amazing, so unlike anything Jo had ever done, even she could think of nothing to add.

Nicole squealed. "That's *amazing!*" She bounced up from her chair and positioned herself behind Jo and Denny, placing an arm around each of them. "You'll love every minute of it."

Jo shrugged, her cheeks suddenly red. "Well, it's not like we can do much for 'em, you know. But we're willin'. Pastor says that's what matters."

Denny cleared his throat. "We'll help build a second room for babies and do general maintenance. Sort of act as caretakers for the place."

"Dad, that's great." Matt reached out and shook his father's hand. "I guess I can't believe it. I never thought my parents would spend a year in mission work."

John flashed Abby a quick look. "We serve a God of miracles—that's for sure."

Abby let her eyes fall to her plate. She understood the secret meaning in John's words, and at times like this, she wanted desperately to tell the kids about their own miracle. How they'd almost divorced and then somehow, found the way to the old pier in their backyard. How, there and then, in the hours after Nicole's wedding, God had opened their ears to hear the music once more—the music of their lives—and they'd remembered again how to dance.

The miracle was this: they'd stayed together and made something beautiful of their marriage. It wouldn't have happened without God's divine hand, and as such, it was a miracle worth sharing.

But they couldn't. Abby and John had never told any of them

about what had almost happened. The kids would have been too shaken, especially Nicole. No, the kids had no idea. She doubted they ever would.

Abby looked up and let the thought go. Congratulations continued around the table, and Jo and Denny answered a host of questions. If all went well, they would leave for Mexico in July and return a year later.

"They asked us if we could teach the children anything while we were there." Jo winked at Denny. "I told 'em I'd have those kids baitin' a hook in no time."

Matt gave his mother a warm smile, his tone light and teasing. "If I know you, you'll probably bring back a couple of little fishermen."

"Right." The tips of Jo's smile faded and her laugh sounded suddenly forced.

The change wasn't enough for everyone at the table to notice, but Abby caught it. Something about Matt's mention of the orphans had caused Jo's heart to stumble. Abby would have to look for opportunities in the coming months when she and Jo could talk. She was almost sure the woman harbored deep feelings on the topic, feelings she maybe hadn't shared with Matt or Nicole.

"Wait a minute—" Denny nodded his head in Matt's direction— "your mother and I aren't looking to be parents again."

"What he means is, I wanna be a grandma. Sooner the better."

"A grandma?" Nicole's mouth hung open in pretend shock. "Sorry, Jo. We're years away from granting that wish."

"I'd say." Matt slipped an arm around Nicole's shoulders. "I think the game plan is four years, isn't it?"

"Exactly."

Abby had to bite her lip to keep from laughing out loud. "If only it worked that way."

"Yeah." John narrowed his eyes. "We got married July 14, 1979. And what was our plan on children?"

"Five years, I believe."

"And when was Nicole born?"

"April 16, 1980." Abby gave Nicole a quick smile. "But that's okay, honey. You can pretend you have a plan. Less stress that way."

On the other side of the table, Jo was still working out the math. Her fingers moved one across the others, then came to an abrupt stop. She gasped and stared at Abby. "You mean Nicole was born nine months and two days after the weddin'?" The light in her eyes was full strength once more. She leaned across Matt's plate and patted Nicole on the hand. "No wonder you're so sweet, darlin'. I always thought it was your upbringing." She sent a quick look John's way. "And it's that, too, of course." She looked back at Nicole. "But I had no idea you were a honeymoon baby. Honeymoon babies are better than a week on the lake. All gushy and drippy and believin' in happily ever after."

Jo sucked in a quick breath and shifted her eyes to Matt. "You better take good care o' her, son. She ain't no ordinary girl. She's a honeymoon baby." She lowered her voice, and the others had to strain to hear it. "Good for you, son. You got yourself a catch better'n anything a rod and reel will ever land you. Besides, honeymoon babies beget honeymoon babies. That's what I always heard, anyway."

"Excuse me." Nicole held up her hand, her smile sincere. *"This* honeymoon baby will not be begetting anytime short of four years." She leaned against Matt and gazed at his eyes. "My brilliant husband has a law career to launch first."

It was only then that Abby noticed John's eyes. They'd grown distant in the past few minutes, like he'd already left them and headed up for bed, leaving his body behind as a means of being polite.

Abby looked harder. No, it wasn't distance. It was depth . . . depth and pain. Then it hit her. He was thinking about football again. The topic hadn't come up all night, and Abby was glad. They'd both spent most of their recent days battling the questions all people in coaching have to ask themselves if they stay in long enough: What's it all for? Why are we involved with this? Isn't there more to life?

The dinner wound down, and Nicole and Matt left with Denny

and Jo behind them. Sean turned in with promises to finish his math homework. Abby followed John up to their bedroom.

"What's on your mind?"

Only then, when they were finally alone, did his feelings find words. They were words she hadn't ever expected John Reynolds to say. He simply rubbed the back of his head and studied her. Then in a voice filled with conviction and fatigue, he said it.

"I'm quitting football, Abby. This is my last year."

The statement knocked around in her mind and rattled its way down to her gut. She had always known the day would come. But she had never expected it to come now. Not on the tails of a championship season. Oh, sure this season was harder than others. But John had dealt with complaining parents before, handled bad attitudes and unexplainable losses. Those things happened to every coach. But the idea that he might hang up his whistle now, with so many years of teaching left, was more surprising than anything John could have said.

Almost as surprising as the feelings rising within her.

All her life, in the cellar of her heart, Abby had dreaded the day when football would no longer be part of her routine. But here, now . . . with her eyes locked on John's, she felt no dread whatsoever.

She felt relief.

Four

EVEN PARKED, THE CAR LOOKED FAST.

Jake Daniels and a handful of his teammates were leaving practice Saturday morning when they spotted it. A red Acura Integra NSX. Maybe a '91 or '92.

Unable to keep from gawking, the group stopped. Casey Parker was the first to recover. It was the nicest car Jake had ever seen.

"Tight, man." Casey slung his gym bag over his shoulder. "I'll bet that baby can run."

The car was so shiny Jake almost had to squint. It had two doors, a spoiler in the front, and a riser across the back. The body hugged the ground, snug against a hot set of Momo wheels.

Suddenly the black-tinted passenger window lowered, and a man waved in their direction. Jake narrowed his eyes even more. *What the . . . ?*

"Hey, Daniels, isn't that your dad?" Casey punched Jake in the arm. "Where's the blonde?"

Jake gulped. It was his dad, all right. He'd showed up at last night's football game—the first he'd attended since moving to New Jersey. Beside him had been some blonde girl in a spandex shirt, leather pants, and spiked heels. She couldn't have been more than twenty-five. Big-time bimbo, working a wad of gum and batting her eyelashes.

The other guys razzed Jake about her all morning at Saturday's practice.

"She available, man . . . or does your dad have first dibs?"

"Your dad into sharing, Daniels? That's the hottest stepmom I've *ever* seen."

"She's not his stepmom . . . she's his girlfriend. He and his dad take turns."

The comments had gotten old after the first hour, but the guys kept at it. Still, whoever the blonde was, she wasn't in the Integra. Jake nodded to his teammates, shouldered his bag, and headed for the car. Normally his mother met him after practice in their old van, faithful and sure, always on time.

But not today.

"Hey . . ." His father waited until Jake was closer before he said anything. "Climb in."

Jake did as he was told. The car must be a rental. Apparently his dad was making big bucks at the radio station. Back when he worked for the Marion paper, before the divorce, his father never would have rented an Acura NSX. But then, he wouldn't have had an airhead for a girlfriend either. A lot had changed.

"Well . . . what do you think?" His father's smile was practically bursting through his skin.

"Where is she?"

His expression went blank. "Who?"

"The girl. Bambi. Bimby . . . whatever her name was."

"Bonnie." A shadow fell across his eyes, and he looked older than Mom. They were the same age, but there were more lines on Dad's forehead now. He worked them with his thumb and forefinger and cleared his throat. "She's getting a massage."

"Oh." Jake wasn't sure what to say. "Thanks for picking me up." He patted the dashboard. "Nice rental."

His dad leaned forward, sunglasses in one hand, his arm resting on the steering wheel. He looked like one of those guys in a *Sports Illustrated* ad. "What if I told you it wasn't a rental?"

It took a moment for Jake to remember to breathe. "Not a rental?"

The grin was back on his father's face. "Remember last summer, that conversation we had about cars?"

"Cars?"

"That's right." An unfamiliar chuckle slipped from his dad's mouth. Something about it made Jake feel like he didn't know the man. Almost like he was trying too hard to be cool.

"Uh . . ." Jake tried not to be bugged. Where were these questions going, anyway? "You asked me which cars were hot right now, right? That conversation?"

"Exactly. You told me the hottest car would be a used Acura NSX . . . maybe a '91. Remember?"

"Okay . . ." Jake's heart rate doubled. It wasn't possible, was it? After all, he would be seventeen next week. But would his dad really come all the way from New Jersey to bring him a—

He swallowed hard. "Dad . . . whose car is it?"

Moving his arm off the wheel with more flare than usual, his father turned off the engine, pulled out the key, and handed it to Jake. "It's yours, son. Happy birthday."

Jake's mouth hung open a moment. "No way."

"Yes, way." His dad grinned again and slipped on the sunglasses. "I'm busy next weekend so I brought it down now. That way you'll have it for your big day."

A million thoughts crowded Jake's ability to think. Was his father serious? A car like this had to cost forty grand! And what about Jeni and Kindra and Julieanne? For that matter what about Kelsey? The superbabes would all be after him once they got a look at this thing. Man, she could probably do zero to sixty in five flat. Probably reach one-thirty, one-forty in a street race.

Jake gulped. What would Mom think? She didn't want him owning *any* car yet—let alone the hottest street racer this side of the Illinois state line.

His father was staring at him, the grin still in place. "Well . . ."

"Dad, it's awesome. I'm in shock."

"Yeah, well . . . it's the least I can do." He removed the sunglasses again, his eyes serious. "I've missed a lot, being gone, son. Maybe this'll make it up to you. At least a little."

"A little? How 'bout a lot." Jake's fingers and toes tingled; the flesh on his arms and legs all but buzzed with excitement. He wanted to stand on the roof and shout it to the world. *I own an Acura NSX!* His dad might have changed, but the man did love him, after all. He must. And Jake loved him, too. Especially now.

His father was watching him again, waiting. But what could Jake say? How did a kid thank his dad for something like this? He lifted his shoulders a few times. "I don't know what to say, Dad. Thanks. It's perfect. I . . . I can't believe it's mine."

His dad laughed again, the kind of polished laugh he probably did often on his radio program. "I think you're in my seat, son." His father released the hood latch and climbed out. Jake did the same. They met near the front of the car, and Jake couldn't resist. He slipped his fingers beneath the hood and popped it open. Jake pulled in a sharp breath. No way! He cast a quick glance over his shoulder. Did his dad know this wasn't a stock engine? *Act normal*, he told himself. *Don't give it away.*

The engine block was raised, with a reshaped combustion chamber and a custom intake manifold. Forget fast. This car was going to fly.

"Good stuff, huh?" His dad patted his shoulder and left his hand there. The feel of it made Jake miss the old days. Back when there wasn't this . . . this awkwardness between them.

"Yeah . . . nice."

His dad did a little cough. "It's a fast car, son."

Jake twisted around and met his father's eyes. He probably had plans to take the engine back to stock first thing next week. "Yes, sir."

"Let's keep that little detail from your mother, okay?"

"Really?" Jake's mouth was dry. What would the guys say about this? They'd want to hang with him every weekend, for sure. He'd be the most sought-after kid at Marion High. Mom would be furious if she knew how fast it was . . . or how much it cost. But Dad was right. No point bothering her with the details. "I won't say a word."

Dad raised a finger and pointed it close to Jake's face. "But no tickets, now, you hear?"

"Not a one." Jake nodded, serious and certain. This was a car he could have fun with, but he'd be careful. No risk taking. No street racing. Well . . . maybe a little street racing, but nothing dangerous. A few of the guys on the team had started racing lately. But even if he did, it wouldn't be much. Once a month, maybe. Besides, he had a reputation for being one of the safest drivers at school. "You can trust me, Dad."

"Good." His father dropped the sunglasses back in place and glanced at his watch. "Better get you home. Your mom'll wonder what took us so long."

Besides, Bunny—or whatever her name is—is waiting. Jake let the thought go. He moved to pass his father en route to the driver's seat. It was a moment when, in years past, Jake would have hugged his dad hard, or crooked his elbow around his neck and given him a few light, playful punches in the gut.

But not now.

Since his parents' divorce, everything had changed. First his father's address and job title, then his clothes and the ways he spent his Saturday nights. Girls like what's-her-name were a dime a dozen for his dad. And why not? His dad was a looker. Handsome, strong, former jock, smooth voice . . .

Girls liked men like his dad.

What Jake didn't get, though, was what his dad saw in the girls. Especially with someone as wonderful as Mom living at home alone.

With each passing second, the moment grew more awkward, and finally Jake thrust his hand forward. His dad did the same, and the two shook hard. "Thanks again, Dad. It's awesome."

Jake made his way around the car, climbed in, and started the engine. As he drove back home, careful to keep to the speed limit, the car felt like one of those racehorses chomping at the bit in the moments before the big event. Something told him his Integra wouldn't hit stride until it was cruising well over a hundred.

Of course, he didn't share that thought with his dad. In fact, he doubted he'd share it with the guys. This car would blow away anything they drove, so what was the point? Racing would only get him in trouble. It was enough merely owning a car like this. He smiled. His father had nothing to worry about. He would be the most careful Integra NSX driver ever.

The moment his mother walked out of the house, her feelings were obvious. First shock, then awe, then a fierce and pointed anger aimed directly at his father. She barely shot a look at Jake as the two of them climbed out and anchored themselves on either side of the car.

"What's this?" She gestured at the car the same way she gestured at his math papers when he fell short of a C.

"This?" Dad looked from the car back to Mom. "A birthday present for Jake. I'm out of town next week, so I brought it a few days early."

"You mean the cruise you and *Bonnie* are taking?" His mother's smile made Jake's skin crawl . . . it was practically evil. "Your girlfriend talked, Tim. Word gets around."

Jake winced at the pain that cut him deep in his gut. *It's because of Mom's tone,* he insisted to himself. Not because his father would rather take a cruise with some blonde than be there for his own son's birthday. He lifted his eyes in his father's direction.

Dad's mouth hung open, and he seemed to search for something to say. "How'd you . . ." He crossed his arms. "Look, what I do on my own time is my business, okay?"

"So that's what this is."

"What?"

"The fancy sports car." Jake's mother laughed once, but there was nothing funny in her voice. The pain in Jake's gut worsened, and he thought he might be sick. He hated when she acted like this. His mother waved at the car and continued. "I get it, Tim. It's some kind of atonement for everything you're not doing for Jake this year. A makeup for all the hours you're spending with the girlfriend."

"You have no right saying that in front of—"

"In front of who? Jake? Like you care." She huffed. "No boy Jake's age should be driving a car like that."

Wait a minute . . . Jake wanted to interject but one look at his mom's rage-filled face and he decided against it.

"You're crazy, Tara. The car's perfect."

"What do you take me for, a fool? That's an *Integra.*" Her voice grew louder. Jake clutched his stomach. His parents were acting like kids fighting over some stupid toy. Only *he* was the toy—and it wasn't so much that they wanted him, really, but that they each wanted to win.

"So what?"

"It's too fast, that's what." She paced a few steps back toward the apartment and then spun around. "If you want him to have transportation, Tim, buy him a Bronco or a truck." Her eyes narrowed. "But an Integra?"

Jake had heard enough. He swung his bag over his shoulder and slipped past his parents without either of them seeming to notice. This was why they'd divorced. The fighting and yelling. The name-calling. Jake hated it, especially today. Hated the way it shot darts at his good feelings.

He flopped on his bed and buried his face in the pillow. Why couldn't they love each other like they used to? And why'd they have to fight all the time? Didn't they know how much it hurt him? Other kids had divorced parents, but at least they tried to get along. Not his parents, though. Every time they were together it was like they hated each other.

Jake rolled over and stared at the ceiling. Why was he letting their problems ruin the day? Nothing would change the thrill of what had just happened. The car was his, and it was a dream. Tons better than the heap of rust that dork Nathan Pike drove.

His parents' fights were their problem. No matter how determined they were to ruin the weekend, Monday would be the greatest day of Jake's life for one simple reason.

He was the proud owner of a shiny red Integra NSX, a car faster than just about anything in Illinois.

five

MATURITY HAD NOTHING TO DO WITH IT.

Thirty minutes into the dance lessons at the Marion High gymnasium, John felt like a freshmen struggling through gym class, bumbling about on two left feet and not sure of his next step.

The instructor was a white-haired woman in her late fifties named Paula. She wore a microphone headpiece and was dressed in thick tights and a leotard. Her tone was condescending, with a forced cheerfulness that made John feel anything but mature. On top of that, she clapped her hands often. "Okay, class." She let her eyes drift down the line of fifteen couples.

Two, maybe three cups of coffee too many. John grimaced.

Paula clapped her hands again. "Line up." Her eyebrows seemed permanently raised. "Let's try that again."

Abby was holding her own, except when he stepped on her foot. Trouble was, he'd been doing that often enough to make it part of the dance routine. He gave Abby a quick grin. "Here we go again. Hope your feet can take it."

"Stop it, John." She giggled. "The teacher will hear you."

"Perky Paula, you mean." The music had started, and already they were struggling to keep up with the other couples. John kept his voice to a whisper. "She's too busy counting out the beat."

John twirled Abby, and she nodded once in his direction. "Very nice."

"Sure, next thing you know I'll be up there with Paula." John danced a bit straighter and tried the next series of steps without looking. As he did, he came down on Abby's foot, sending her shoe skittering across the gym floor.

Paula shot them a stern look—the type usually reserved for students who shot spit wads. She clucked her tongue. "Please . . . hurry back in line."

Abby's lips were tight, the last line of defense before she burst into laughter. She ran after her shoe with tiptoe steps, ducking down as though that might help make the two of them less of a distraction. When the shoe was back on her foot, she returned to John's side, and they did their best to blend back into line with the others.

It was no wonder John couldn't concentrate on the dance steps. Abby looked simply radiant. She could easily have been a decade younger, and the sparkle in her eyes made him feel as giddy as it had back when they first started dating. Why hadn't he seen her beauty last year or the year before? Or the year before that? How could he possibly have allowed himself to be distracted by another woman?

What could have made him think anyone might fill that place in his heart the way his precious Abby did?

"What are you thinking?" She whispered the words, and they found their way straight to his heart.

It no longer mattered that their dance steps weren't perfectly in time with the other couples around them. "That you're beautiful. That you've always been the most beautiful woman in the world."

A blush fell across Abby's cheeks. "I love you, John Reynolds."

His feet stopped, and Abby danced her way up against him. As she did, he leaned down and kissed her. "Thank you, Abby . . . for loving me."

The couple back one spot in the line bumped into them and then danced their way around.

"Keep moving, people." Paula clapped her hands, her eyes fixed on John and Abby. "This is dance class . . . not the prom."

They fell back into line with the others once more. But no reprimand from the instructor could stop Abby and him from locking eyes, from allowing the rest of the world to fade as they danced in a way they'd always meant to. But for the grace of God, where would they be right now? For that matter, where would God be in the mix of things? And who would John be sharing his bed with?

A shudder gripped his gut.

God . . . thank You that I didn't fall the way I could have. Let me always love Abby like I do right now. Don't ever let us wander from each other again. Or from You . . . please.

A chord of three strands is not quickly broken, my son.

The silent whisper in his soul, the reminder of a Scripture he and Abby had used at their wedding, was enough to break John's concentration. Almost in perfect time to the music, he stepped on Abby's foot again.

This time she let out a quick squeak and jumped. Behind them in line, two other women did the same sort of jump, apparently thinking it was part of the dance. When Abby realized what was happening, she lost it.

Her laughter was silent, but relentless. And John was helpless to do anything but join her. Several times Paula shot them a look of pure frustration, shaking her head as if to say Abby and John would never be mature dancers. Not in a hundred years.

By the time the lesson was over, Abby was limping.

They were halfway to the car when John hunched down in front of her. "Your chariot, my dear."

Her laugh sounded like the wind chimes on their backyard deck in spring. John savored the sound, reveling in her nearness. She played out a gentle beat on his back. "You don't have to do that, John. I can walk."

"No, come on. I damaged your toes. I can give you a ride." He reached back for her legs, and as he did, she hopped onto his back. At first he walked, but the harder she laughed the faster he went until he was galloping. He went past the car and did a small circle around the parking lot. Everything about the moment felt free and undefined and alive. As though time had stopped for them to celebrate the joy of being together. He let out a shout that echoed against the wall of the school. "Yeeee-haw!"

"I wonder—" Abby's words were broken up by the bumpiness of the ride—"what old Paula would think of *this* dance move?"

Finally he ran back to their car and set Abby down near the passenger door. The parking lot was empty, all the mature dancers having gone home to chamomile tea and early sleep. Abby leaned against the car door, breathless from the ride and the laughter. "What a night."

John grew quiet and he moved up against her, leaning close so their bodies were molded in all the right places. Passion colored the moment, and he studied her in silence. The only sounds were the occasional drone of a car on the distant road and the intoxicating whisper of Abby's heartbeat against his. He traced her chin, the delicate line of her jaw. "I feel like a teenager in love."

"Well . . ." She tilted her head back, her throat slim and curved in the moonlight. There was a raspy sound of desire in her voice, the way John had heard it often these past months. "Maybe that's because we're in a high-school parking lot."

"No." He angled his head so he wouldn't block any of the light. He wanted to see her face . . . all of it . . . wanted to memorize everything about her. "That's not why."

"It isn't?"

"Nope." He ran his fingers lightly down the length of her arms. "It's you, Abby. You make me feel this way."

They were quiet a minute, their bodies moving subtly until they were even closer than before. John nuzzled her face, breathing in the scent of her perfume as he dusted his lips along the side of her neck.

When he looked up, he saw her eyes were watery. Fear stabbed at him—he'd sworn to never make her cry again. "What're you thinking, baby?"

A single tear made its way down her cheek. "It's a miracle, John. What I feel . . . what we feel for each other. Six months ago . . ."

She didn't finish the sentence, and John was glad. He held his finger to her lips. "Have I told you lately how beautiful you are?"

"Yes." She lowered her chin and gave a few slow blinks. It was a look of both shyness and flirtation, a look that had driven him mad since he was a college boy.

"When did I tell you?"

"During the dance lesson, remember?" The corners of Abby's mouth lifted and her eyes twinkled.

"That was a long time ago." He placed a soft kiss, one at a time, on each of her eyes. "I mean lately. Have I told you *lately* how beautiful you are?"

Another tear fell, and she uttered a sound that was more laugh than cry. "I guess not."

"Well . . . you're more beautiful than a sunrise, Abby Reynolds. More beautiful than spring. In case I don't tell you often enough, I want you to know. I couldn't think about anything else in that dance lesson." He gave her a lopsided grin. "Not when all I wanted to do was . . ."

He was suddenly out of words. In their place, he moved toward her in a dance step he was far more familiar with. Then he kissed her as he'd been longing to do for an hour.

When they came up for air, both their heartbeats had quickened. "Hey . . ." He kissed her twice more and then held her gaze. "Wanna come back to my place?"

"Not for dancing, I hope." One of her eyebrows lifted just a bit, the way it always did when she teased him. "My feet are sore enough."

"No—" he framed her face with his fingertips, letting a slow smile ease across his mouth—"not ballroom dancing, anyway."

"Hmmm." She gently brushed her lips against his, then put her hands on his shoulders and pushed him back a few inches. "Lead the way, Mr. Reynolds. Lead the way."

They crept into the house like a couple of delinquents breaking curfew. Not that it mattered. Sean was spending the night at a friend's, so they had the house to themselves.

Abby felt better than she'd felt in years as she followed John into the living room. "Okay, so where's the ballroom for this dance?"

"I'll show you, Mrs. Reynolds." He took her hand and led her up the stairs toward their room. "Follow me."

The hour that came next was more wonderful than Abby dared dream. She had heard from other women that after rocky times in their marriages, physical intimacy was never quite the same. Especially if another woman had been in the picture.

But from the moment she and John stood on their backyard pier in the hours after Nicole's wedding and recognized the impossibility of walking away from each other, Abby had fallen in love with her husband all over again. It really was a miracle. Their relationship now was like an intense, passionate release of all the feelings they'd buried for those three awful years.

Now they spent their intimate moments making it up to each other. Celebrating the joy of having rediscovered something that was almost lost for good. Never mind that conventional wisdom would have them struggling in this part of their relationship, taking a year or more to build back what those bad years had cost them.

Abby trusted John completely. And he trusted her.

Before they fell asleep, John rolled on his side and studied her. "Have I told you lately . . ."

The moonlight played across his face, and she smiled. "Yes . . . you've told me."

"You know what I liked best about tonight?"

She inched onto her side so they were facing each other. "The dance?"

He chuckled soft and low. "Always that. But you know what else?"

"What?"

"It made me forget about coaching. Even just for a night."

A pain sliced through her heart. "It's that bad?"

"Worse." His smile faded. In its place was a look that was more sad than frustrated. "Know what I read in the paper yesterday?"

"What?"

"Some high-school basketball player's parents are suing his coach for seven million dollars."

"Seven million?" Abby propped her elbow up on the pillow. "For *what?*"

"For costing the kid his chance at an NBA career."

"What?" The story didn't make sense. "How is that the coach's fault?"

"Because—" John drew a slow breath—"the coach put the kid on JV instead of varsity."

Abby gasped. "You're kidding, right?"

"No." John's chuckle was so sad it almost broke Abby's heart. "I'm serious. That's what it's come to, Abby. Sometimes I don't think I'll survive the season."

"I'm sorry." She moved her elbow and let the side of her face rest on the pillow. "I wish there was something I could do."

"I keep thinking about that note. How one of my player's parents wants me fired badly enough to go to the district level to see it happen." He rolled onto his back again. "Me? Letting players drink and race their cars? Don't they know me at all? Don't they appreciate what I've done for that school since I've been there?"

The pain in Abby's heart spread to her soul. How could they possibly attack this man's character? If she could, she would walk into the school, take over the public address system, and tell the entire school population that Coach Reynolds did not and never would have done anything unethical where his players were concerned. She would demand they recognize his efforts and treat him with the respect and gratitude he deserved.

But she couldn't do that.

She couldn't even write a letter on his behalf, though she wanted to. Badly. "There's only one thing I can do, John. But it's the most important thing of all."

"Pray?" He turned his head so he could see her again.

"Exactly." She ran her fingertips lightly through his hair. "Pray that God shows you how much the kids still love you, the kids who wouldn't play ball for any other coach."

"Okay." He smiled, and for the first time since he'd brought up the topic, his features relaxed. "You pray. It's only because of your prayers that I've coached there this long."

"You know what I think?" She laid her head on John's shoulder and snuggled close to him.

"My season's falling apart?"

"No." She rested her hand above his heart. "I think something very big's about to happen."

"Like we win three games straight?"

"No, again." Abby gave a muffled laugh. "Something spiritual. Like God's got something major going on. Maybe that's why the season's starting so rough. We may not see how all the pieces fit right now. But maybe we'll see it soon. You know?"

John was quiet.

"You awake?"

"Yeah. Just thinking." His chest rose as he inhaled. "I'd forgotten about that."

"About God having a plan?"

"Mmmhmm." He hesitated. "It must be that."

"Yep. And whatever it is, it's going to be huge."

"How do you know?"

"It's something I feel."

"Oh. Okay." John's breathing was slower, his words running together the way they did just before he fell asleep. "I'm sorry."

"For what?"

"For stepping on your feet tonight."

"That's okay. We have another lesson next week."

"I love you, Abby. G'night."

"Goodnight . . . I love you, too."

She drifted off to sleep, her head still on John's shoulder, her mind filled with a dozen happy memories from the evening.

And with the increasing sense that somehow, someway, God was up to something very big at Marion High School. Something that involved football and parents and most especially her wonderful husband.

Coach John Reynolds.

Six

NICOLE WAS AFRAID.

There was no other way to say it. After the whirlwind weekend with Kade home, she wasn't merely tired; she was exhausted. Too exhausted. Now it was Wednesday, and she and Matt had plans to eat dinner out. But as Nicole slipped into a pair of jeans and a sweater, her arms and legs felt like they were made of lead. Every movement was a colossal effort.

It couldn't be the flu. She didn't have a fever or a cough or an upset stomach. She raised the zipper and studied her reflection in their bathroom mirror. Pale . . . ashen, even. True her summer tan had faded, but Nicole couldn't remember her face ever looking this white.

She sighed. Maybe the events of the past few months had finally caught up to her. After the honeymoon they'd come home and immediately helped Matt put together his résumé for a position with the district attorney's office. Now that he was hired, Nicole was knee-deep in studies, trying to balance running their home with the demands of being a college senior.

On top of that, there were constant discussions with Matt about his parents' impending yearlong missionary trip. And then there was her younger brother Kade.

Last week, when he was home, something about him had been different. Older maybe, quieter. He was anxious to get playing time at the University of Iowa and he had a lot on his mind. On Sunday night he stopped by Matt and Nicole's apartment. They talked until 3 A.M. about whether he'd made a mistake taking the scholarship at Iowa when he'd rather be playing closer to home at Illinois.

"It's too far away," Kade said an hour into the conversation. Matt had gone to bed back at the beginning, leaving Nicole and Kade in the living room. Kade had tossed his hands in the air. "I feel like I'm on another planet." He sat on the floor, his back against the wall.

"It's only a day's drive from here." Nicole didn't want him pulling out of Iowa just because he was homesick. "It's always hard the first semester."

"Yeah, but Dad's been my coach forever, Nic." His knees were up, legs wide apart the way he always sat when they'd had these conversations over the years. "I'd at least like to see him in the stands, you know?" He rested his forearms on his knees. "This was the first weekend he and Mom have been to a game."

Nicole could see his point. "Why didn't you consider Illinois before? They sent you a letter didn't they?"

"Yeah." Kade frowned. "A bunch of letters. I thought being away from home would be fun."

"Maybe it will be. You've only been there two months."

"I know . . . but now I want to be here. Does that make sense?"

The discussion went in circles that way until the only thing Nicole could tell him was what he wanted to hear. "Transfer, then." She muttered a tired laugh. "We'd love to have you closer, bud. Then we could have these talks every weekend."

Kade grinned. "Just like the old days."

"Right. Just like the old days."

Memories of the discussion faded and Nicole checked the mirror once more. The morning after their late talk, she'd had class at eight o'clock. Every hour of the day and night had been booked since then. No wonder she was tired. Her body was merely trying to catch up.

Unless . . .

Nicole swallowed hard and turned from the mirror. She put a quick spritz of perfume on her neck. *Don't think about it . . . it's impossible.* But her mind refused to change the topic. Especially in light of the one memory that wouldn't go away.

It had happened three weeks after their honeymoon. They'd agreed to wait three or four years before having children, so birth control was a must. By waiting, Nicole could finish school and find a teaching job. She would teach two years and then take a decade off to have babies. When the kids were in school, she'd resume teaching. That way she could be with them after school and miss almost none of their at-home family time.

That was the ten-year plan, anyway. And they'd intended to follow it to the letter. All of which meant being very careful. Not only because of the ten-year plan, but because of something else. Something she hadn't wanted to share with anyone. Something she couldn't voice even to herself.

They'd talked about birth control pills, but Nicole was concerned about the side effects. In the end they decided to use condoms instead.

"You probably learned about condoms in school," the doctor told Nicole when she was in for a checkup just before her wedding day.

"We did. They're one of the safest ways to prevent pregnancy, right?"

The doctor chuckled. "Not hardly." He gave her a crooked grin. "Every month someone whose husband used a condom comes into my office pregnant."

Nicole had been surprised, but also fairly certain the doctor was exaggerating. Obviously condoms worked or they wouldn't sell them.

Still, there was that one time . . .

Late that night, just weeks after their honeymoon, in the moments after being physically intimate, Matt had come out of the bathroom with a strange look on his face.

"What's wrong?" Nicole had sat up in bed, holding the sheet to herself.

"I think it broke." Matt ran his fingers through his hair and shook his head. "I thought that only happened in the movies."

A wave of alarm came over Nicole and then passed. There was no way it broke. "Maybe it just looked that way."

Matt climbed back into bed. "Let's hope so."

Now, ten weeks later, the conversation came back to Nicole every few hours. Not just because she was more tired than usual, but because she hadn't had a period since before her wedding.

She'd heard her mother talk about being pregnant before, how she'd known from the moment of conception—known without a doubt—that a new life had begun to grow within her.

Nicole had searched for such signs, but there'd been nothing. Her period had always been irregular. Sometimes she'd missed three months in a row before it showed up again. So there wasn't any real reason to think she might be pregnant.

Was there . . . ?

The bedroom door opened and Nicole jumped. Matt stuck his head inside. "Ready?"

"Sure." She forced a smile. "I'll be right down."

She was quiet through dinner, and finally when Matt was finished eating, he pushed his plate away and looked at her. "Okay, Nic. What's wrong?"

"Nothing." Her answer was too quick. She stared at her food. More than half her cheeseburger was still untouched. Her eyes lifted and found his again. "I'm fine."

"You're not fine. You've been sleeping late and going to bed early. You yawn all the time and hardly have any appetite." Matt's voice was gentle, but concerned. "I'm worried about you."

Her gaze fell again. She pushed a fork through the small dish of beans beside the burger. The food looked old and uninteresting. A sigh slipped from her lips. It was time. If they were going to build a marriage of closeness and trust, she couldn't keep her fears from him another minute.

"Okay." Drawing a quick breath, she looked at him once more. "I think I might be pregnant."

She had expected him to look shocked, even upset by her statement. After all, a baby now would mean their plan was out the window.

Instead, Matt's face lit up like a Christmas tree. "Nicole? Are you serious?"

"Matt—" she lowered her head so people at the other tables wouldn't hear her—"it's too soon. You *can't* be excited about this."

His face went blank for a moment, then he let loose a single, quiet laugh. "Yes, I can. Babies are a miracle, honey. Whenever they come."

Her heart dropped to her socks. His enthusiasm made the entire possibility seem more real. What if she really was pregnant? How could she be a mother when she hadn't finished college? And what about her worst fears, the ones she couldn't admit even to herself? Question after question assaulted her until she felt Matt's hands on hers.

"Sweetheart, I don't get it. You're upset because you think you might be pregnant?"

"Yes!" Nicole felt the sting of tears in her eyes. "We wanted to wait four years, remember?"

"Sure." He sat back a bit and blinked. "But if you're pregnant now, there's no point being upset. God will work out the details." He took her fingers in his. "Besides, maybe you're not. We've been careful."

"Yeah, but what about that one night? When you thought it broke?"

A knowing look filled Matt's eyes. "You think that's when it . . ."

"Maybe. The doctor told me it happens all the time." She dropped her head back for a moment and then found his eyes again. As she did, two tears slid down her cheeks. "I didn't believe him."

"Okay." Matt took her hand. "But, honey, you've always said you can't wait to be a mother. So why . . . are you crying? I mean, our plan can be adjusted, can't it?"

"I guess."

"Then . . . why the tears, honey? I don't get it."

Nicole wanted to climb across the table and hug him. He was such a good guy, so full of love for her and the future family they would one day raise. She steadied herself and decided to tell him her fears. The ones that had kept her up at night even when she desperately needed to sleep. "I guess I'm afraid."

Empathy filled in the lines on Matt's worried face. "Of what?"

Nicole sat back and took a sip of water. "Remember last year? When we were planning the wedding?"

"Of course." Matt studied her, his body halfway across the table as he leaned toward her.

"Something was wrong with my parents' marriage." Nicole gave Matt's fingers a gentle squeeze. "I think I told you I was worried about them."

"Right. You prayed for them, and as we checked into the hotel the night of our wedding, you felt the Lord had answered your prayers. That everything was going to be okay."

Nicole nodded. "I've thought about it a lot since then and I've decided maybe . . . just maybe their marriage isn't all it seems to be. You know?"

"Okay." Matt looked as lost as a child alone at the zoo. "So . . ."

"So I think I've figured it out."

"Figured it out?"

"Yes." Nicole stared at him. "The reason why my parents aren't really happy like I thought they were."

Matt blinked again. "Just a month or so ago you told them they looked like newlyweds."

"That was before I put the pieces together. It was something your mother said at dinner one night." Nicole released his fingers and sat back. If only he could understand. "Now I think I know the problem."

"Which is . . ."

"I was a honeymoon baby, remember?" Couldn't Matt see it? She worked to make her tone patient. "They had kids too early."

"Sorry, Nic." This time Matt sat back and crossed his arms. "I don't get it."

"How can you not get it?" Nicole held her hands out palms up. "My parents never got those crucial years, the years when the two of them could have bonded and built their love."

Matt looked at her for a moment. Then he stood and eased himself around the table and slid onto the bench seat beside her. He placed his arm over her shoulders and pulled her up against him. "I have the surest sense that you're wrong, Nicole. Your parents love each other very much. Having children early in their marriage hasn't hurt that. Not then or now."

Her husband's nearness, the warm shelter of his arm around her, made everything somehow better. Her defenses fell like autumn leaves. Maybe Matt was right, but this was something Nicole had thought about ever since they'd been back from the honeymoon. "You don't think it hurt them?"

"No." He kissed the side of her face and smoothed her hair back behind her ears. "But if it worries you, why don't you ask your mother? She'll tell you the truth."

Ask her mother? Why hadn't Nicole thought of that? Rather than imagining the reasons her parents had struggled last year, it couldn't hurt to come out and ask. She shifted her position so she could see Matt more clearly. "Okay. I'll do that."

"Now, how 'bout we pay this bill and do some shopping before we go home. I think there's a little something we have to get before another day goes by."

Nicole's heart was lighter than it had been in weeks. With God on her side and a husband like Matt, everything was going to be okay. "What's that?"

He grinned. "A pregnancy test."

Seven

THE INFORMATION WAS ALL THERE, ON THE INTERNET.
Whatever research Abby had done for her article could easily be supplemented with information from the Web. She signed on and waited for the connection. She'd been so busy catching up from the weekend with Kade that she hadn't had time to work on her coaching article until late that evening. Last night she might have had a few hours, but John needed the computer. He had to look up some new Internet site that gave coach's tips and defensive tricks. John had heard about it from one of the other coaches.

Abby hadn't minded. She had plenty of time to pull the article together.

The screen danced to life and a digital voice announced, "You've got mail."

For the briefest instant she remembered how badly she'd looked forward to those words a year ago. Back when she and John were speeding in opposite directions, headed straight for divorce. She'd been E-mailing an editor almost daily, a man who wanted to spend time with her.

If she hadn't found John's journal after Nicole's wedding, hadn't read it and learned the real way he felt about their marriage and the mistakes he'd made, she might never have forgiven him. In fact right now she might be in the midst of a full-blown relationship with the editor.

The thought turned Abby's stomach. She let it pass as quickly as it had come. These days her E-mail was almost all business related. She was working with several new magazines and keeping her relationships with editors at a strictly functional level. Occasionally there'd be an E-mail from a friend or a forward from one of the women at church.

But that was about it.

And even though John was spending more time on the computer, he never got E-mail. He merely surfed the Web for football strategies and plays he hadn't thought of before. Once in a while he'd check out a site with ranch property for sale and report to Abby that they should buy a hundred-acre piece in northern Montana. But he was only kidding, only looking for a way to ease the tension brought on by the football season.

Abby clicked the mailbox and immediately a list of mail appeared. There was more than usual, and it took a moment for her to scan the list. Something from a new magazine, three from her current editors, then . . .

Her heart stopped.

The next E-mail on the list had a subject line that read, *"More excitement than you can imagine!"* It was from someone named *Candy* at a Web site called *Sexyfun.*

Abby's heart thudded hard and resumed beating, twice as fast as before. Her eyes did a quick check down the rest of the list and there were five more E-mails like it. All from girls at Web sites with similar names as the first.

Her mind screamed it wasn't so. It couldn't be. Everywhere she turned someone was talking about Internet pornography. She and John had talked about the phenomenon, but neither of them had really understood the fascination. There was no way John had been accessing pornographic sites, was there? He'd been on the Internet, yes. But only to look at coaching sites, right?

There was one way to find out.

Abby maneuvered her mouse through a series of clicks until a list of Web sites appeared on her screen. The last fifty sites that had been accessed by their computer. The most recent were three that were clearly football related. But beyond that the list was horrendous.

Names of Web sites Abby could barely read let alone utter out loud. She closed her eyes. *God, no . . . don't let this be happening. Please.* After all she and John had been through, as much as he seemed to be in love with her . . . he couldn't be turning to pornography. It was impossible.

Yet, what other explanation was there? They were the only two people who used the Internet on this computer, other than Sean. And he only used it for homework. Abby thought back. It had been at least a month since Sean had been anywhere near the computer.

So that meant . . .

"No, God! I can't take it." She covered her face with her hands. Dealing with her husband's fascination with another woman had been one thing. But this?

You pulled us through that time, God . . . so why this? Why now?

She waited, but there were no reassuring utterances in her soul, no verses that came to mind. Only an awful empty pit in her stomach, a pit that grew larger with each passing moment.

She opened her eyes and looked at the list. Maybe they weren't porn sites. Maybe they were coaching sites with stupid names. Yes, that had to be it. A thin veil of perspiration broke out across Abby's nose and forehead. She felt faint, desperate, terrified. Her heart couldn't take the shock, couldn't believe the list of Web site names staring back at her.

There was only one way to find out.

She picked the first one, something about naked girls, and clicked the link. *Let it be coaching information . . . defensive plays . . . anything but—*

A picture began to take shape and Abby gasped. Immediately she found the *X* in the upper right corner and closed the window. It wasn't coaching plays; it was exactly what one would expect to see on a Web site with that name.

Pornography.

Somehow in the midst of his distress and discouragement, John had used his late-night hours on the Internet to click his way into a seedy underworld of sin. Anger bubbled up from Abby's gut and filled her with a burning rage. *How dare he . . .*

She shut down the computer and spun her computer chair toward the dark window. The moon was only a sliver that night, but Abby stared outside anyway. What was he thinking? They'd been doing so well, enjoying each other both as friends and lovers. How could he—

Then another thought hit her.

Maybe that's why he had enjoyed their physical love so much lately . . . maybe he wasn't thinking about Abby at all, but these . . . these . . .

Nausea welled within her and she wondered if she would be sick to her stomach. How dare he sleep upstairs like nothing was wrong, when all the while he was keeping this terrible secret from her? And how could her body, her love ever compare with the images on his computer screen?

The array of emotions assaulting her was almost too much to bear. Sorrow . . . fury . . . regret. She'd trusted him, after all. Believed him that he wanted to be like the eagle—strong by her side until death parted them. Why in the world, then, would he begin experimenting with pornographic Web sites? Especially when he knew from friends of theirs how addictive and destructive they could be?

For more than an hour Abby sat there, her stomach in knots, until finally she went upstairs and studied her husband. Last year she'd had no trouble knowing John was interested in another woman. His distance, the hours he was gone from home, the strange phone calls. The signs had all been there. But this . . . this pornographic thing? He'd been masterful at hiding this. Abby blinked in the dark, sickened by the innocence on his face.

She lay down on the far edge of their bed, turned her back to him, and fell asleep. But not before two simple thoughts filled her mind . . .

How could they possibly stay together now?

And most of all, why hadn't she been enough for him?

The game that Friday was away, and John's Eagles won with a last-minute field goal. Rumors were spreading about the players who drank and took part in the street races. It was so bad John could almost hear the parents whispering about him.

"Coach Reynolds isn't the man we thought he was . . ."

"We need a man with better moral character than that . . ."

Of course the real reasons were as obvious as his record. The Eagles had only won three games. A dismal feat considering the hopes everyone had once held for this team. Winning had a way of shutting up the critics. Lose and a coach immediately became fair game.

The stands were rife with parents who would have run on fourth down or passed the ball on first. People whose sons didn't play much were the worst. Most of them figured the team would win if only their boys were in the mix. Those whose sons did play had another answer: poor coaching.

Either way the bad start this season fell on John's head.

As John boarded the team bus back to Marion that night, he felt only a small amount of relief from the victory. Jake Daniels's head hadn't been in the game no matter what John tried to do to inspire him. John had seen Jake's new Integra NSX. The entire school was talking about it.

Rumor had it Jake was looking to race it as soon as football season was finished.

John stared out the dirty window of the bus and gritted his teeth. What was Jake's father thinking, getting the boy a car like that? How was a teenager supposed to focus on his studies and his role as quarterback with a racecar sitting in the parking lot?

Not only that, but Jake and Casey and a handful of players had stepped up their teasing against Nathan Pike and his gothic friends.

John had told the administration about Nathan's awful, scribbled words—*death to jocks*. Apparently the principal had pulled Nathan into the office and questioned him. Nathan acted calm and casual.

"It's a song, man." He shook his head at the principal. "You people are so out of touch."

The principal could do nothing but believe Nathan and issue him a warning. Song or not, he wasn't to be writing death threats on his notebook. Nathan agreed, and the incident passed. At least as far as the administration was concerned.

The reality was something else altogether. Nathan and his dark friends had gotten more hateful, more distant. At the same time, the cruel, arrogant remarks from Jake and Casey and the others had only come with more frequency. At times there was so much tension between the two groups, John felt certain the situation was about to erupt.

Several times he'd pulled Jake and Casey aside and said something, but always their answer was the same: "We're just playin' around, Coach."

Their parents didn't seem to care whether their sons were bullying kids like Nathan Pike. They were too worried about the Eagles win-loss record, too concerned with whispering and rumoring and getting John fired, filling the stands with enough negative energy to kill the rest of the season.

No wonder Abby hadn't wanted to go tonight.

Until this one, she hadn't missed a game since the season began. John had been in a hurry when he breezed home, grabbed his coaching bag, and headed back out for the game.

"You're going, right?" He went to plant a quick kiss on her lips, but at the last second she turned and it landed on her cheek instead. The gesture had seemed odd, but John hadn't had time to dwell on it. He had a bus to catch.

"Not tonight." She'd seemed distracted. In fact, she'd seemed that way since Thursday morning. Not angry, exactly. Just . . . distant.

The bus ride seemed longer than usual, and John settled back in his seat. What was eating her anyway? He thought for a moment, then it hit him. It must have been her magazine article. Sometimes she got quiet right before deadline on a big piece. The best solution, he'd found, was to let her be. Give her as much time and space as possible to get her work done, then she'd be fine.

Still, he'd missed her tonight. It was always better coaching from the sidelines knowing Abby was there somewhere behind him in the stands. Everyone else might complain about him, but Abby would have cheered. Especially tonight, since they pulled out a win.

John stretched. Enough of the negative thoughts. Jake Daniels . . . Nathan Pike . . . the complaining parents. All of it was only part of a passing season. He would pray for the kids and look for opportunities to reach them. But everything about Marion High was something he was learning to leave behind when he finished up for the day.

Life was too short to bring his troubles home. Especially when things with Abby were so unbelievably wonderful.

It was nearly eleven when he walked in the house. The lights were out. Abby must have finished writing and gone to bed. John shut the door behind him and took three steps. Then he heard her voice.

"John . . . I'm in here."

He squinted into the dark and flipped on the light in the entryway. "Abby? What are you doing?"

"Praying." She paused. "Come here, will you? We need to talk."

He wasn't sure if he should feel honored or concerned. She'd obviously waited up for him to come home, intent on talking to him. But there was nothing light about her tone. He set down his bag and took the chair opposite her. "What's up?"

"This." Moving like an old woman, Abby reached down and picked up a piece of paper from the floor. "I found it a few days ago, but it took me a while to know how to bring it up."

Bring it up? What was she talking about? He took the paper, and in the half-light from the foyer, he stared at its contents. In no time he could see what it was, and it turned his stomach.

"Where'd this come from?" He brought the page closer to his face so he could read it clearly.

It was a list of pornographic-type sites. One after another after another. Probably twenty of them in all. John glanced up the page and saw their E-mail address listed at the top. Suddenly he understood. Abby was here, waiting in the dark, because she'd found this list on their computer Internet log and wanted an explanation.

The whole time he'd been looking at the list, Abby had said nothing. Now John lifted his eyes to her, his heart racing. "You got this off *our* computer?"

"Yes." Her arms were folded tight against her waist. "You're the only other person who uses the computer besides me, John." Her voice broke. "Obviously we need to talk."

He wanted to scream at her. Did she honestly think he was visiting porn sites in his spare time? That with everything going on at school and with the team, he could possibly be crazy enough to get involved with Internet smut? When he was married to the only woman he'd ever loved?

The idea was outrageous.

"You think *I* looked up these sites?" He planted his fingertips on his chest.

"What am I supposed to think?"

John wadded the paper up and threw it against the wall. Then he stood and paced a few steps in either direction. "Abby, are you out of your *mind?* I've never looked at a pornographic Web site in my life." His tone was sharper than his words. "How could you think such a thing?"

"Don't lie to me, John." Clearly she was as angry as he, but she stayed in her chair. "You've been on the Internet more often than usual and always at night. Why?"

He stared at her, stunned. "You really doubt me, don't you? After all we've been through, you still don't trust me."

"I *did* trust you." She lowered her voice, but her intensity remained. "But I trusted you three years ago, too. Back when you and Charlene were spending every morning together."

He felt the blood drain from his face. "That's not fair, Abby, and you know it." John bent at the waist, firing his words at her. "We were *both* wrong back then, but those days are behind us. Remember?"

"I thought so, too." The fight left her voice. "Until I found that list."

She might as well have slapped his face. Wounded and furious and not sure what to say, John fell back into the chair and buried his head in his hands. "You don't know me any better than the parents of my players."

Abby was silent, and for a moment neither of them said anything.

There had to be an explanation for the sites. Abby obviously hadn't looked them up, but neither had he. And how dare she accuse him even after he'd denied having anything to do with them.

God, give me the words here . . . how can Abby doubt me on this?

Love is not easily angered . . .

The holy response flashed across the scoreboard of his mind and took the edge off his temper. His shoulders slumped, and he shook his head. Of course Abby didn't believe him. After the times he'd spent with Charlene . . . the lies he'd told Abby when their marriage was unraveling . . .

For the first time since their reconciliation, John realized something he hadn't before.

It would take years before either of them would feel completely secure again. No matter how good things were between them. Sin always had consequences. Abby's doubts about him now were one of those.

She broke the silence first. "Aren't you going to say anything? I've been carrying this around for two days wondering why I'm not enough for you." She was crying now. Not angry sobs or out-of-control weeping, but small, soundless cries that strangled his heart.

John dropped to the ground and crawled on his knees until he was up against her legs. "Abby . . ." His words were calm, quieter than before. He lifted her chin so she'd have to look at him. "I promise you with everything I have, I didn't do this. I've never looked at a porn site. Not ever."

She sniffed and wiped the back of her hand across her cheeks. Nothing came from her mouth, but John could see it in her eyes. Doubt . . . fear . . . concern. Thoughts that somehow it was happening again, that their marriage was falling apart.

God . . . please give me wisdom. There has to be an answer.

Two seconds passed, then a third, and suddenly he knew the answer. The realization brought him as much pain as it did relief. The explanation was bound to satisfy Abby, but it left them with a problem neither of them had anticipated.

"Did you forget?" Their eyes were still locked. "Kade was here last weekend. He stayed with us through Monday afternoon."

It took a moment for the information to register.

As it did, John could see his wife's expression shift. Like melting wax, her face softened and her anger fell away. In its place was a sadness and guilt so raw it was painful to look at. Nearly a minute passed before Abby opened her mouth. "Kade?"

"He was here. I'm not sure if he was on the computer, but he must've been. Because—" he met her eyes squarely—"the only thing I looked at were coaching sites. I . . . found three of them."

Abby stared into the night, her eyes distant. After a long while, she lifted her gaze back to John's. "Sunday night he was with Nicole. But Saturday . . . Saturday he was here. He didn't get to sleep until after one o'clock because I got up and . . ."

John caught her hands in his. "And what?"

"I came down for a drink of water." Tears flooded her eyes. "He was on the computer. I . . . I didn't realize it until I was halfway up the stairs and heard the clicking sounds. I completely forgot about that."

There was nothing for John to say. Abby's doubts cut to his core, but he couldn't deny they were deserved. Thankfully, Internet pornography was not something he'd ever even considered. Still, he could hardly be upset with Abby for thinking it possible.

"John . . ." She took his face in her hands and searched his eyes. "I'm so sorry. How could I have thought—?"

"Shh, Abby. Don't." He lay his head against hers and stroked her hair. "It's my fault. If I hadn't let you down in the past, you never would've wondered."

"But I'm such a jerk." Her tears became sobs, and she clung to John as though her next breath depended on his being there. "Why didn't I *ask* you first? Instead of accusing you?"

"It's okay." Peace flooded his heart. This was his Abby, fighting for their marriage, determined to let go of the past. What he'd seen when he came home was merely a momentary lapse in trust, the kind of thing that was bound to happen in light of the trials they'd weathered. "Of course you're going to have doubts, honey. It's over with. Let it go."

Abby struggled to sit up, her eyes bloodshot, her breaths quick and jerky. "I never want to doubt you again, John Reynolds." She sniffed and shook her head. Her voice was little more than a whisper. "It's not okay. What we have is too precious to waste it doubting each other."

She was right. There was no way they could build on the love and joy of the past few months without trust. Suddenly he wondered if this was the first time. "Have you had doubts before this? About me, I mean?"

"No, I—" She started to shake her head but she stopped herself. "Well . . . sometimes." She took a quick breath. For a long time she said nothing. "I guess I wonder if someday another Charlene will move into the picture, or if I'll be enough for you. Pretty enough . . . smart enough. Young enough."

If he hadn't already been on his knees, her admission would have sent him there. "You were *always* enough. It wasn't you; it was life. Time. Busyness. We let too much come between us."

"I know." Her voice was calmer, more controlled. "But the Charlenes of this world will always be there."

"Never again, Abby. Remember the eagle?"

Abby tilted her head. "Kade's English paper. He wrote how the eagle mates for life . . . clings to its mate, even falling with her to his death rather than letting go."

"Right." John worked his fingers up her arms to the sides of her face. "I'm clinging like I never did before." He leaned forward and kissed her forehead. "Nothing could make me let go of you. Nothing."

She slid to the edge of the chair and hugged him. "I believe you. I've believed you since Nicole's wedding. The doubts are just . . . I don't know, stupid I guess."

He searched his heart and knew there was something else. If he was going to be completely honest, he had to tell her his thoughts as well. "You're not the only one."

She pulled back enough to see his eyes. "Not the only one?"

"With stupid doubts."

A softness settled over her eyes. "Really?"

"Really." John let his gaze drop for a moment before looking up again. Things had been going so well between him and Abby, he hadn't wanted to admit his fleeting thoughts. Not even to himself. "I wonder sometimes what would've happened if I hadn't come back the night of Nicole's wedding. I mean, there I was, packed to leave for good. Only God could have made me stop the car and come back." He bit his lip. "But what if I hadn't come? Would you be dating that editor or having some sort of Internet relationship with him?"

"I never should have let you go." She slipped her fingers through his hair, her eyes shining. "Then you wouldn't have to wonder."

"I don't worry about you now. Just the past and where we might be if I hadn't come back."

Abby rested her head against his once more, and they held each other. A long while later, Abby fell back into the chair again. "We still have a problem, though, don't we?"

John could read her soul as easily now as he had back when she was a teenager. "Kade?"

"Kade." Her eyes narrowed, less in anger than confusion. "Why would he do that, John? That's not how we raised him. That garbage will strangle the life out of him."

"I'll talk to him."

"On the phone? What if he denies it?"

She was right. This called for more than a phone call. "They have a bye coming up the second week in November. Let's fly him home. I'll talk to him then."

"What if he's addicted? It happens all the time." Abby hesitated. "I wish we didn't have to wait."

"We don't have to." John took her hands in his again. This time he folded them within his. "We can do something right now."

Then with hearts and hands linked in a way that filled John's being, they bowed their heads and prayed for their older son. That he would be honest about the Internet sites he'd looked into. That he would be willing to discuss the issue with John.

And that together they could eliminate the problem. Before it was too late.

Eight

PERKY PAULA WAS GOING TO KICK THEM OUT FOR SURE.

Abby could tell the moment she saw Jo and Denny at the gymnasium door. It was the first Saturday in November, and Abby had invited Nicole's in-laws—as if John dancing on her feet wasn't enough humor for the hour. They'd agreed to meet at the entrance.

Abby wore a dress, and John, nice pants and a khaki button-down. Church clothes. It was *ballroom* dancing, after all. In Abby's mind that connoted elegance and taste. Even with her husband stepping on her toes.

Jo and Denny, on the other hand, looked ready for a country hoedown.

Abby would have felt sorry for them, except neither of Matt's parents seemed to care how they were dressed. *Maybe they've never seen ballroom dancing.* For that matter it was quite possible they'd never seen a ballroom.

Denny wore pointed cowboy boots and a tall black hat. Jo was squeezed into a pink-and-black miniskirt with a matching pink-fringed shirt and pink boots.

As they approached, John bent down and whispered in Abby's ear, "Didn't you tell them what to wear?"

Abby waved at Jo as she whispered back, "I thought they'd know."

Both couples signed in and took their places.

Jo fell in place next to Abby. "You sure the teacher won't mind us buttin' in and all?"

"Positive." John and Denny led the way. "The class is an ongoing thing."

John shot a quick look at Denny. "Aren't you glad?"

Denny gave a lopsided grin and twirled his finger in the air. "Barrel of fun, I'm sure."

"Oh, stop." Jo whacked her husband in the arm. "You love dancin' with me and you know it."

Paula had been flitting about, connecting with various couples. Now she approached Abby and John with a hurried smile. "Welcome back, I see you've brought your—" Instantly the smile became a frown as Paula scrutinized Jo and Denny. "My goodness—" the muttered comment was just loud enough for them to hear—"completely inappropriate." She shook her head and turned to the front of the gym.

Abby could feel Jo's ire from five feet away. *Here we go.* Abby took John's hand and waited.

Jo spun around, her eyebrows furrowed. "That woman has a lot of nerve! What's her problem?"

"Nothing." John patted Jo on the back. "She takes her dancing very seriously."

Abby could almost see the hairs rise on Jo's neck as she planted her hands on her hips. "I take my fishin' seriously, but you won't see me sticking fishhooks in the first-timers over it."

The couples lined up while Paula worked the tape player. Abby and John positioned themselves next to Jo and Denny. Jo hissed in Abby's direction.

"Besides, *look* at her! Dressed in tights and a lee-tard at her age!"

Denny gave her a discreet nudge. "Jo . . ."

"What? She looks ridiculous."

Jo shot a laserlike glare at Paula's back. "She better not look at me like that again or I'll . . . well . . ." Jo caught Denny's look and relaxed some. "Never mind. Sorry." She shot Abby and John a weak smile. "I get a little carried away."

"Right." Denny used his eyes to apologize for his wife. "And water gets a little wet."

Abby grinned and squeezed John's hand once more. "Don't worry about it, Jo." She gave the woman a tender smile and tried to imagine what Nicole would do in this situation. Abby drew a deep breath. "Hey, how's the mission thing going? You guys still thinking about a year in Mexico?"

"Absolutely." The scowl fell from Jo's face. "Can't wait. Those little babies need people to love 'em, and me and Denny are just the folks." She winked at her husband. "Besides, the fishin' down there'll be heavenly. Just like if I died and the Lord met me at the pearly gates with a brand new rod and reel."

One of the couples was talking to Paula so they still had a moment before class began. John poked his elbow at Denny. "Watch her feet. I had to carry Abby out after our first lesson."

"No!" Jo gave John a slap on the arm. "The graceful star quarterback from Michigan University? I don't believe it."

"It's true." Abby winced and laughed at the same time. "My toes are still bruised."

"Hey, you seen the kids lately?" Jo gave her shoulders an exaggerated shrug and reached her hands over her head in a full-body stretch. The kind usually reserved for aerobic classes. Two of the couples near the front of the line noticed her and began whispering.

"Uh . . ." Abby tried to remember Jo's question. "Yes. Nicole stopped by yesterday."

"Well . . . what'd you think?"

Denny exchanged a bewildered look with John, as if to say he had no idea what his wife was talking about. Again.

"Think?"

Jo huffed lightly. "About Nicole. Isn't she glowing?"

Abby thought for a moment. "I guess I haven't noticed."

"Okay, class." Paula clapped her hands. "Everyone in position, please. Let's do a quick run-through of the steps we learned last week. Ready? And one and two and . . ." The music started.

Abby and John lurched into action, getting halfway across the gym floor before John waltzed across her foot. "Ouch!" Abby tripped a bit and then fell back into step. This time they circled the room without incident. "Not bad." She smiled at him. "You're maturing quite nicely."

John nodded at something behind her. "That's more than I can say for Jo and Denny."

Abby glanced over her shoulder and nearly tripped.

Jo and Denny were completely ignoring Paula's lead. Instead they had linked arms and were doing a side-by-side, high-stepping country line dance, oblivious to the waltzing couples around them.

Abby spun back around to face John, eyes wide. "Paula's going to kick them out!"

"I don't think so." John's eyes sparkled. "She's been watching them the whole time. She's too shocked to say anything."

As it turned out, Paula didn't say a word until midway through the lesson. That's when Jo let loose a loud "Yeeee-*haaaw!*" in the middle of a subdued classical piece.

With that, Paula adjusted her headset and clapped her hands again. "There will be no shouting out from the students. Just follow the couple in front of you or I'll have to ask you to leave."

Jo gave Paula an angry look, opened her mouth, and did it again. "Yeeee-ha—"

Denny placed his hand firmly over Jo's mouth before she could complete the sound.

Abby peered over John's shoulder for a better view. "Wow." She worked hard to keep her laughter quiet. "The woman's unbelievable."

"You invited her." John did a playful roll of his eyes. "I could have predicted this."

"Come on . . . she's just more intense than most people."

"The way a tornado is more intense than a gust of wind."

Jo and Denny were two-stepping now, and Denny whispered to her midstep. Something close to remorse filled Jo's eyes, and after that she seemed more sedate. Abby was awed. Clearly Denny's influence over Jo was considerable.

For the rest of the hour, every time Abby looked at them, they were lost in their own world of two-stepping and line dancing. Not once during the session did either of them even attempt a ballroom step.

When the lesson was over, the couples stood outside the gym catching their breath. "I think that teacher had something against me."

"No . . . Do you think so?" Denny looped his arm around Jo's neck and pulled her close. He flashed a grin at Abby and John.

"And why was she teachin' us that old-folk style dance? Someone oughta take her to a country dance hall and show her how to lighten up a little before she gets too caught up in herself and—"

Denny placed his hand over Jo's mouth once again. "What she means is, thanks for asking us to come. We had a great time."

Abby stifled a giggle. As she did, she remembered something. "Hey, what was that you were saying about Nicole earlier?"

Jo started to talk but Denny's fingers muffled the sound. He chuckled and let his hand fall. She raised her eyebrows at him. "Thank you." Then she turned to Abby. "Just that she's glowing brighter than a rainbow trout if you haven't noticed."

Glowing? What was that supposed to mean? "That newlywed look?" John and Denny exchanged another curious look.

"No . . ." Jo leaned in as if she had top-secret information. "That *glowing* look."

"Meaning . . ." Abby was desperate for Jo to explain herself. She couldn't be suggesting . . .

"Okay." Jo straightened up again. "Nicole's a honeymoon baby, right?"

John shifted his weight and glanced at his watch. Abby's signal that the conversation could wait.

"Right, so?" Abby willed the woman to make herself clear.

"So—" Jo grinned—"honeymoon babies beget honeymoon babies. That's the way it works."

"Jo, come on." John chuckled. "You don't think Nicole's pregnant?"

"Now, now." Jo held up her hand and lifted her chin. "You didn't hear that from me."

A pit formed in Abby's stomach. Certainly if Nicole *was* pregnant, she wouldn't have told Jo and Denny first. Would she? But then, maybe Nicole hadn't said a word. Maybe—"Did Matt tell you?"

"Nope. Nothing like that. The kids haven't said a word." Jo tapped a finger against her temple. "It's just a hunch. That and the way Nicole's been glowing."

John gave a gentle tug on Abby's arm. She responded with a few subtle steps backward. "Well, we need to run. I wouldn't think too much about Nicole being pregnant. The kids are planning to wait awhile."

"I think we all know how plans like that work out, don't we?" Jo looked at Denny. But this time there was nothing funny about her tone. In fact, if Abby wasn't in such a hurry she would've taken more time with Jo. Because the look she and Denny shared was almost sad.

The couples bid each other good-bye, but later that night Abby couldn't shake what Jo had said. She and John helped Sean with a Native American flathouse he had to complete by Monday. When they were done, she motioned for John to follow her out back.

Without saying a word, they strolled hand-in-hand to the pier. When one of them had something on their heart, knowing what to do was as instinctive as drawing breath.

When they reached the end of the pier, they sat on a small bench John had placed there a month ago. Abby waited a minute before saying anything, gazing instead at the ribbon of light across the water. She loved this lake, loved the fact that they'd lived there since the children were young. Way back since their tiny baby daughter Haley Ann died suddenly in her sleep.

There was never a time when they sat here together that Abby didn't remember their second daughter, the one whose ashes they'd sprinkled across this very water. Over the years they'd come to this spot to share the highs and lows of life. When Abby's mother was killed by the Barneveld tornado . . . when John's father died of a heart attack . . . when John led the Eagles to their first state title—and when the parent complaints got to him.

They would sit until words came. Then, when they were done talking, John would take her by the hand and sway with her, back and forth. Not the kind of dancing that required lessons. Rather the kind that required listening. Leaves rustling in the trees beyond the pier, crickets and creaking boards. The whisper of the wind. The faint refrains of distant memories.

"Can you hear it?" he would ask.

"Mmmm." She would rest her head against his chest. "The music of our lives."

"Dance with me, Abby . . . don't ever stop."

Abby drew in a long, slow mouthful of the cool night air. It tasted of the coming winter, cool and damp. It wouldn't be long before they'd have to bundle up on evenings like these. And Abby had a feeling there would be several of them, between John's coaching troubles and their concerns about Kade.

She turned to John and reached for his hand. He was looking at her, watching her. Abby held his gaze for a moment. "I wonder if he'll admit it."

"Probably." John stared out at the water. "He doesn't usually keep secrets from me."

"Yeah, but . . ."

"I think he'll tell me."

"I'm nervous about it."

Their fingers were still linked, and John soothed his thumb over the top of her hand. "I'm not. He's a good kid, Abby. Whatever he's doing on the Internet . . . I doubt he's addicted to it."

"I know. But what if he gets angry that we know?" She tried to will away the knots in her stomach. "Things like this could cause a rift between him and us. A rift that could take him away from God, even."

"Abby . . ." John faced her again and gave her the same look he gave the children whenever a bad thunderstorm came up. Calm and confident, gently understanding. "We've prayed for that boy since he was born. God's not going to let him go that easily."

She nodded and something in her stomach relaxed. "You're right."

"What else?"

"You know me too well."

"Yep." He flashed her the grin she loved best. "So what else?"

"Remember that kid you told me about? Nathan Pike?" Her thoughts were all over the board tonight, but John wouldn't mind. He was used to conversation like this. Random neural firings, he called them.

"How could I forget him? He's in my class every day."

"I don't like it." Abby's heart rate quickened. "He worries me, John. What if he does something crazy?"

"He won't. Kids like that aren't the ones who buy a gun and go ballistic." John released her hand and laced his fingers behind his head. "Nathan wants attention, that's all. The gothic look, the casual threats—those are his way of getting someone to finally notice him."

"I don't like it."

They were quiet again, and overhead an eagle swooped low over the water, snagged a fish, and soared over a thicket of trees. John watched it disappear. "He must be taking food back to the nest."

"Probably." Abby leaned her head back. The moon was full tonight, dimming the brightness of the stars. Abby felt herself relax. John was right. Everything was going to be okay with Kade . . . and with Nathan Pike. Even with the football team. God would work it out somehow.

"You don't think Nicole's pregnant, do you?"

John stood and stretched, twisting first to the right, then to the left. When he was finished, he exhaled hard and held a hand out to Abby. "No, I don't think Nicole's pregnant. They want to wait awhile before having kids, remember?"

"I know." Abby clutched tightly to his fingers as he pulled her to her feet. "But what if Jo's right? Now that I think about it, she has had a kind of glow about her."

"Believe me, Abby—" John eased her into his arms—"if our daughter was pregnant, she'd tell Matt first, and you second. She's just happy, that's all. Who wouldn't be glowing?"

"You're right." Abby hesitated. "But if she was . . . wouldn't that be something? You and me, *grandparents?*"

John chuckled. "I guess I'd *have* to be mature then."

Abby studied John's features, the subtle lines across his forehead, the hint of gray at his sideburns. "It's weird to think we're getting old."

"Weird?" John drew her closer. "I don't know; I think it's nice."

"Yes." Abby pictured them together this way, dancing on the pier, laughing and loving and finding strength from each other. "It'll be fun to grow old with you, John Reynolds."

"One day we'll put our rocking chairs out here."

"So when we're too tired to dance, we can rock?"

"Right." The corners of his lips raised, and Abby felt tingles along her spine. "Remember our first date?"

"You came with your family for a Michigan football game." He raised his eyebrows. "Finally."

"I was seventeen, John." She lowered her chin, remembering the shy girl she'd been. Their families had known each other forever, but John was older than her. Abby hadn't thought she stood a chance until that pivotal football game. "How could I believe that John Reynolds, star quarterback for the Wolverines, wanted to date me?"

"I'd been planning it for two years." He traced her jaw line, his eyes locked on hers. "I was just waiting for you to grow up."

"Now the tables have turned."

"Is that so?"

"Mmhhmm. Now I'm waiting for you to grow up." Abby sent a playful kick at John's foot. "At least on the dance floor."

"I can dance when it matters." He glanced up and out at the lake, taking in the beauty of this favorite spot. Then, ever so slowly, he began to sway. His gaze fell to hers, as it had so often over the years. "Dance with me, Abby."

His tender words melted her heart. "Always, John." She moved with him. "Forever and always."

She nestled her head against his shoulder, drawing strength from each beat of his heart. They moved together to the far-off cry of a hawk and the lapping of lake water against their private shore. Abby closed her eyes. What would life be like without her husband? A life where they couldn't come to this place, this pier they both loved, the spot where their daughter's ashes lay and where they'd shared so much of each other? A life where they wouldn't have nights like this one?

It was impossible to imagine.

Yet there was no denying they were getting older. And one day—when their years of being grandparents and great-grandparents were finished—the music would stop. The dance would be over. It was inevitable.

Abby pressed her cheek against John's chest once more, savoring his closeness. *Thank You, God . . . thank You for saving us from ourselves.*

Later that night, before she fell asleep, Abby uttered another prayer. One she'd said more often in the past few months.

God, I've never been more in love with John. Please . . . let us have a thousand more nights like this one. Please.

Nine

THE CONFRONTATION WAS SET FOR SATURDAY AFTERNOON.
Kade didn't know it, of course, but John had long since had the day planned out. The Eagles had won their football game the night before, so it was a light practice that Saturday morning. Kade had come along, enjoying the chance to catch up with dozens of his former teammates.

"Hey, Dad, I think I'll go throw a few balls for the freshmen." Kade motioned to the adjacent field, where the younger Eagles were practicing.

John watched from his place near the varsity squad. The moment Kade appeared in their midst, the freshmen gathered around him, shaking his hand, looking awe-struck at his presence. Big college quarterback Kade Reynolds back from school. It was enough to make their week.

John's gaze shifted to his older players. "Okay. Line up; let's do it again. This time I want you linemen shoulder to shoulder. You're a wall, not a picket fence. Let's remember that!"

When the drill was underway, John glanced once more to the other field. Kade was throwing passes for the young receivers, airing them out in a way that made even John's mouth hang open. The boy had potential, for sure. John couldn't be prouder of him.

Later that day, though, Kade wouldn't be Mr. Big-time Athlete. He would simply be John Reynolds's boy. And the father-son conversation wouldn't be about Kade's talents.

Give me the words, God . . . how I handle this could affect his life forever.

Two hours later they were at home and finished with lunch. Sean needed new soccer cleats, and Abby had arranged to take him to the store. That way John and Kade could be alone.

When they were by themselves, Kade headed for the television. "Ahhh . . . Saturday football. Time to check out the competition."

Before he could grab the remote control, John cleared his throat. "Let's take the boat out instead. You and me."

Kade hesitated for a moment and then shrugged. "Sure. Why not? I can catch the highlights on *SportsCenter.*"

The day was unseasonably warm, as though fall was doing its absolute best to steal a few hours from the impending winter. A light cloud layer kept the sun's glare down, but there was no rain in the forecast. It was the perfect afternoon for a few hours on the lake.

They made idle chitchat at first, joking about the time when Sean was four years old. Abby had been at the supermarket, and John was in charge of the children. He, Nicole, and Kade were playing Frisbee on the grassy hill behind their house, when Sean snuck off, donned a life jacket, climbed into their family rowboat, and loosed the moorings. By the time John realized Sean was missing, the child had drifted a hundred yards out onto the lake. He was standing up in the boat screaming at them for help.

"I was scared to death." John worked the boat's oars as he laughed at the memory.

"You thought Sean would drown?"

"Are you kidding?" John huffed. "He had a life jacket. Besides, he knew how to swim." He winked at Kade. "I was scared of your mother. She would've killed me if she'd gotten home and found Sean out in the middle of the water by himself!"

The lake was a private one, frequented mainly by the homeowners whose houses sat along the three-mile shoreline. Today, the water had only a few other boats on the far side. John rowed out a bit further and then pulled in the paddles.

Kade leaned back and positioned his face toward the thinly veiled sun. "I forget how good it feels. Quiet. Peaceful." He sent John a quick grin. "Good idea, Dad."

"I can think out here." John hesitated. "Or have a real conversation."

It took a moment, but Kade sat forward again and met John's gaze. "Something you wanna talk about, Dad?"

"Actually, there is."

"Okay, shoot."

John searched his son's features for a sign . . . some flicker of apprehension or guilt. But Kade's expression was the picture of trusting innocence. John's heart tightened. Was Kade so far into this thing that he didn't feel even a hint of guilt?

Here I go, Lord . . . give me the words. John rested his elbows on his knees and looked deep into Kade's eyes. "After your visit last time, your mother and I found some questionable Web site addresses on her Internet history page."

Kade's face was blank. "Questionable?"

"Well, worse than questionable, really." John resisted the urge to squirm. "What I'm saying is, we found a list of pornography sites, Kade."

"Pornography?" His eyebrows lowered into a baffled *V.* "Are you . . . accusing me of checking out porn sites?"

Doubts assaulted John. "Look, son. Your mother thought *I'd* looked them up. And I know it wasn't me. Obviously it wasn't your mother. Sean hadn't been on the computer for a month, and even then he has his own screen name that wouldn't allow those types of sites." John motioned to himself. "What am I supposed to think?"

For a beat or two, Kade's mouth hung open. John could see the battle in the boy's eyes. He wanted to deny it, wanted to yell at John to stay out of his business and quit nosing around. But with each passing second, the anger fell from his face. In its place was a hodge-podge of emotions, led by a strong and undeniable shadow of guilt. It was easy to recognize because John had looked that way, himself, not long ago.

When Kade said nothing, John dropped his voice back to normal. "I'm right, aren't I?"

A tired sigh slipped from Kade's throat. His gaze fell to his feet.

"We need to talk about it, son. When did you start doing this?"

The boy's shoulders slumped and he brought his head up. "I'm not the only one." He crossed his arms. "All the guys are into it."

There was a hardness in Kade's features, a defiance almost. It was something John had never seen on any of his children, and it frightened him. "That might be true, but it's wrong, Kade. You know that better than anyone on your team."

Kade tossed his hands in the air. "It's like a virtual girlfriend, Dad. Don't you get it?" His tone was strained, and he glanced around as though he was searching for a way to make John understand. "No strings, no ties, no sex." His cheeks looked hot. "Well . . . not really, anyway."

"It's still immoral, son. And for a lot of people it becomes an obsession."

"Okay, then you tell me what I'm supposed to do? I'm a Christian, so I'm not allowed to have sex until I'm married—however many years away *that* is. I'm a football player, so I don't have time for a girlfriend. And I don't have any money, even if I did have time." He huffed. "Don't you get it? The Internet solves all those problems with a few clicks. It's there whenever I feel like it. Besides, it's better than getting some girl pregnant."

John wanted to scream. "There's nothing better about it." Did Kade really think pornography was no big deal? Had the college culture so quickly undermined everything they'd taught him? "In God's eyes pornography is every bit as wrong as illicit sex, Kade. It's the same thing."

"It's *not* the same." Kade was angry. "There's no people involved, Dad. Just pictures."

"Yeah." John leaned back, his heart thudding hard within him. "Pictures of people."

Kade was quiet. The twists in his expression eased some. "They're getting paid for what they do. It's their choice."

"Listen to yourself, son. You think those women *like* making money that way? Some of them are slaves to the business, handcuffed, threatened, forced at gunpoint to do horrific things. Others are runaways, teenagers barely old enough to drive, desperate for a way to live on the streets. Some are drug users, needing that next hit so badly they'd do anything for it." John paused, his tone softer than before. Sadder. "Is that the kind of industry you want to support?"

"The guys talk about it like it's okay, like there's nothing wrong with it." Kade wrung his hands and stared at the floor of the boat again. "Most of the time . . . it seemed like they were right."

"Of course it seemed that way." John studied his son, willing him to understand. "That's what the devil wants you to think. Oh, it's just a bunch of pictures, no big deal. But pictures like that lead somewhere, Kade. Have you thought about that?"

He looked up. "What do you mean?"

"Still pictures lead to videos . . . and pretty soon, even that's not enough." Kade flinched, and John's heart fell to his knees. "You're into videos, too?"

Kade looked from one side of the lake to the other, and then at John. "Just a few times. After practice the guys sometimes get together at one of the dorms. They have a bunch of movies, and well . . ."

The boat might as well have disappeared. John felt like a drowning man, buried in a kind of water he could not escape. "It's not long before videos aren't enough, either. Then it becomes prostitution."

"No!" Kade's answer was quick. "I've never done that."

"The guys?"

Kade hesitated. "A few of them . . . once or twice. Before the season started." Sweat beaded up across Kade's forehead. "But not me, Dad. I swear!"

The problem was worse than John had dared imagine. *Come on, God . . . give me something profound here.* "Pornography is a lie, son."

"A lie?" Despite Kade's humbled tone, his expression told John he still didn't see the severity of the problem.

"Yes, a lie. It makes women look like nothing more than sexual objects with no purpose except to please men." John cocked his head. "That's a lie, isn't it?"

"Yeah, I guess."

"You guess?" John worked the muscles in his jaw. "Think about your sister . . . or the girls you've dated. How would you feel if you ran through a series of computer clicks and found *their* naked pictures on the Internet?"

"Dad!" Kade narrowed his eyes. "How can you say something like that?"

"Well . . . the girls you're looking at belong to someone, too. They're someone's sister, someone's daughter. Someone's mother, in many cases. Someone's future wife. Why is it okay to treat them that way?" John grabbed a quick breath. "That's the first lie: that a woman is merely a body."

Kade looked up. Was he listening more closely, or was John merely imagining it?

"The second lie is this: true sexual satisfaction can come from sinful behavior." John stared at the sky for a moment. The clouds were clearing, and suddenly he knew exactly what to say. He met Kade's eyes once more. "It might feel good to your body, but not to your soul. And it can never come without intimacy."

"You mean like actually having sex?"

"No. Intimacy and sex are totally different things, son. Intimacy . . . is the bond that God brings about between two married people. It comes from years of commitment, of sharing and talking and working through problems. Years of getting to know that person better than anyone else in life. A physical relationship with someone like that—that's intimacy. And anything less is a lie."

Kade leveled his gaze at John. "You mean like you and Ms. Denton?"

It took several seconds for John to breathe again. Was it possible . . . ?

Did Kade know John had nearly gotten involved with Charlene Denton? She'd taught at the school with John. For years, though they were both married, Charlene would flirt mercilessly with him. After she divorced her husband, Charlene found her way to John's classroom often.

In the year before she moved away, Kade had walked into his father's classroom and found him with her more than once, but always John had talked his way out of the situation. One time Kade had found them holding hands . . . John had lied and said he was praying with the woman. As wrong as that had been at the time, John always thought Kade had believed him.

At least until now.

"What about me and Ms. Denton?" John was desperate, buying time. The look on Kade's face told John his son had doubted his father's wrong relationship from the start.

"Come on, Dad. She was with you all the time. The guys on the team even talked about it. Ms. Denton would come out to practice and stand next to you, she hung out in your classroom . . . I'm not stupid."

John felt like a dying man. "How come you never said anything before this?"

"You told me she was just a friend. That she needed your prayers." Kade shrugged. "I guess I wanted to believe it."

A breeze drifted over the lake and washed away any pretense John had left. "Everything about my friendship with Ms. Denton was wrong. It was a lie, just like pornography's a lie."

"So you slept with her?" Kade looked like he was about to cry.

"No." John considered telling Kade about the two times when he and Charlene kissed. But there was no point. That was behind him now. "I did things I'm not proud of, son. But I never crossed that line."

"So, it's true." Kade shook his head. His shoulders slumped forward, and John couldn't tell whether the shadows on his face were disgust or despair. "The guys used to razz me all the time and I'd tell 'em to get lost. My parents were different. They loved each other. And now . . . all the time . . . what a joke."

"Wait a minute, Kade. That's not fair."

"Yes, it is. Porn stuff isn't the only lie. You and Mom are, too. It's all a lie. So, what's the point of—"

"Stop!" John leaned forward until his knees were touching Kade's. "What your mother and I share is not a lie. We struggled, yes. And we came back together stronger than before." He looked straight into Kade's eyes, trying to see into his soul. "You know why we drifted apart?"

Kade said nothing, his lips tight and pinched.

"Because we forgot about being intimate. We stopped talking and sharing our hearts with each other. We let life and busy schedules rule our relationship, and because of that we almost walked away from a love that, other than God's, is greater than any I know." He uttered a single laugh. "No, son, what your mom and I share is as honest as anything I'll ever have. Charlene Denton—now that was a lie. And every day I thank God for letting me recognize the fact before it was too late. For helping your mom and me remember the importance of intimacy."

Kade straightened some, his eyebrows still knit together with doubt. "So . . . you're fine? You and Mom?"

"We're much better than fine. I think we love each other more now than ever before." John took hold of Kade's shoulder with a light grip. "But we're worried about you."

"I'm okay."

"No, you're not. If you believe the lie now, if you convince yourself that satisfaction can be found in visual unrealities, how will you ever share intimacy with a real woman?"

"That's different."

"You'll meet someone one day, and she'll want to know about you. Everything about you. If she finds out you've had a fascination with porn sites, my guess is she'll drop you like a bad pass. What girl wants to measure up to those kinds of images? Besides she wouldn't respect you, not if you see women as nothing more than objects, sex slaves."

Kade's expression changed. This time John was sure about it. The boy was finally listening.

"Relationships take work, son. Hours and days and years of getting close to that person. That's real love, real intimacy. If you train your mind to believe that the work isn't important, you'll not only be going against every plan God has for your life . . . you'll lose out on a chance to experience the greatest gift He's given us. The gift of true love."

"So you really think it's a sin?"

"Yes." John kept his tone calm, reasonable. "Absolutely."

Kade looked away. "We talked about that, a few of the guys and me. They told me it wasn't a problem because the girls agreed to have the pictures taken, and we weren't really doing anything wrong." Kade's face clouded. "But inside . . . I guess I always knew it couldn't be right."

"And the other thing is the temptation to get involved with it again anytime you feel frustrated with the real thing."

Kade sighed.

"The question is this—" John leaned back against the edge of the boat—"how hard will it be to stop?"

Kade squinted at a line of trees in the distance. "Hard."

The word hit John like a rock. "Have . . . have you tried to quit before?"

"Once." Kade looked eight years old again. "But my computer's right there in the dorm, and . . . I don't know . . . you get used to it."

For the first time, John caught a glimpse of why Internet pornography was so addictive. Computers were everywhere, access to the Web as easy as finding a telephone. If a person got on those sites once and experienced pleasure, the body would cry out for more.

"There are filters you can buy. That might help."

"Yeah. One of the guys did that. He had to get counseling, too. Maybe he and I could help each other."

"We can get you help, son. Whatever it takes. You have to believe me that this is bad stuff. If you let it continue, it'll destroy you."

Kade nodded slowly. "I guess I never thought of it that way. You know, like where it could lead."

"That time . . . when you tried to quit . . ." John let his hand fall back to his knees. "Did you ask God for help?"

"Not really. I didn't think it'd be that hard to stop."

"It's something you need to walk away from, son, and never look back. Not ever."

"I know." Kade fidgeted, his eyes glued to his hands. "I bought a book about stopping. Before I came here. It's in my bag."

"A book?" Relief flooded John's soul. "Then how come you fought me, Kade? You acted like porn sites were a good thing."

"I guess I felt cornered. Everywhere I turn someone's telling me it's bad." He looked up, and his eyes were wet. "What if . . . what if I can't stop?"

John slid his way closer to Kade and hugged him. "You'll stop, buddy. God'll give you the strength." He thought of Charlene again. "He can give you the strength to walk away from anything bad, no matter how trapped you feel."

Kade sniffled and gripped John's neck with the crook of his elbow. There were tears in his voice. "Pray for me, Dad. Will ya, please?"

It took a moment for the lump in John's throat to subside.

When it did, he let his forehead fall against Kade's, and there in the rowboat, in the middle of the lake, he prayed for his son with an intensity he'd never known before. He asked that Kade would have the strength to walk away from the seedy, sinful world of pornography. That he would find the right friendships and counseling and support to help his eyes be opened to the horror of that world. That God would erase the images captured by Kade's mind, and replace them with a true understanding of a woman's beauty. And that Kade would grasp the reality of real intimacy in the example John and Abby provided. That as the two of them had learned from their mistakes, so would Kade.

And in the end, that he'd be a stronger, more godly man because of it.

Ten

THE ANONYMOUS LETTERS WERE COMING MORE FREQUENTLY now.

Not only did they accuse John of being a poor ethical example for the young men of Marion High, but they blatantly marked him as "a coach whose time has passed." The administration, which at first had assured John that they were completely behind him, now was waffling.

"People are worried about the program," Herman Lutz told him that week. "As the school's athletic director, that concerns me. I think you can understand my position."

Though a year ago it would have been unfathomable to think so, John now carried around the sinking feeling that before he could quit the job, he was going to be fired. That Lutz was going to let the parents bully him into a decision that would be easiest for him. John tried not to think about it. If he lasted long enough, he would resign after the season's final whistle.

Thing was, the team's performance had turned around.

John packed his duffle bag and headed for the team bus. They'd won their last four games and a win tonight over the hapless Bulldogs up in North County would send the Eagles to districts.

All of which meant the season wasn't nearly over.

But that afternoon, football and fanatical parents didn't even make the list of John's greatest concerns. He was about to do something he hadn't done since he'd started coaching. The boys' athletics office was open and John stepped inside. He only had a few minutes before the bus left.

The phone rang three times before she picked up. "Hello?"

"Abby, it's me."

"John?" She hesitated. "Aren't you supposed to be on the bus?"

"Yeah. Hey, real quick. Don't go to the game tonight."

There was another pause and John prayed she'd understand. He didn't have enough time to go into lengthy details. She finally recovered. "Why not?"

"A threat came into the office today. Something about the game." John steadied himself against the office desk. "The police think it's a hoax, but you never know . . . I don't want you there. Just in case."

"Was it Nathan Pike?"

"They're not sure. It might be." He glanced at his watch. "Look, I gotta run. Just know that I love you. And please . . . don't come to the game."

"But John—"

"Don't come, Abby. I gotta go."

"Okay." There was concern in Abby's voice. "I won't. I love you, too."

"See you in a few hours."

"Wait . . ." She hesitated. "Be careful, John."

"I will."

He hung up and jogged to the bus. He was the last one on. The ride to North County took fifteen minutes, and though the team was in high spirits, John stared out the window at the countryside wondering how it had come to this. He hadn't told Abby all the details. They would have terrified her.

Apparently the phone call came into the office about one o'clock that afternoon. A raspy voice told the school secretary that a suicide bomber would be in attendance at that night's game.

"It's gonna be big, lady." The caller had chuckled. "Ya hear me."

The secretary motioned for the principal to pick up the line, but he was busy talking with a parent at the front counter. "Who . . . who is this?"

"Right!" The caller laughed again. "You'll know soon enough. Just tell Coach it's too late to help me now. Tonight's the big night."

"If this is a prank, you better say so." The secretary scrambled for a piece of paper and a pen. "It's a felony to make these kinds of threats."

"This is no threat, lady. People are going to die tonight. You heard it here first."

Then he hung up.

Pale and shaken, the secretary pulled the principal into a private office and told him what happened. Police were on campus asking questions within fifteen minutes. Had anyone made death threats at the school before? How were such incidents handled? Did anyone have knowledge of a student with access to explosives? Where was that night's game being held? And how many entrances to the place were there? Did anyone have something against the football team?

Time and again the answers pointed to Nathan Pike, but there wasn't a thing the police could do. They couldn't even talk to the boy about the phone call.

Nathan Pike was out sick that day.

Determined to question him, police had gone to Nathan's house. Apparently his mother had answered the door, a bewildered look on her face. Her son was at school as far as she knew. She hadn't seen him since that morning.

All of it turned John's stomach. Okay, so police would be at the game, posted at every entrance and scattered throughout the crowd. What good would that do? Suicide bombers didn't advertise. They merely walked into a crowded setting and blew themselves and every-one around them to the moon. By the time the police spotted Nathan Pike, he'd be just another body in a line of corpses.

It was no comfort that John and the team were a safe distance from the stands out on the field. Hundreds of teens would be at the game that night. Thousands, even. If a bomb went off amid that crowd—

John couldn't bring himself to think about it. Of course the person could wait until after the game when the stands emptied onto the field. Then there'd be nothing the police could do to stop a kid from—

"Coach?"

His fears dissipated as he turned around. It was Jake Daniels.

The boy had been one of the bright spots in the past few weeks. He'd let up quite a bit on Nathan. Three times he'd even stopped in to talk to John about the pressures of high school and his concerns for his mother. Apparently she was furious with his father. The two fought whenever they were forced to talk, and Jake felt caught in the middle. Jake always seemed more relaxed after a half hour of sharing life with John.

This was why John still coached, to help young men like Jake. And since they'd started talking again, Jake seemed happier, more at ease. Less likely to join in with Casey Parker and the others who thought they ran the school.

John had even wondered if that's why they were doing better on the field. There was no question Jake's numbers had led them to their recent victories. Now, though, Jake looked troubled.

John managed a smile. "Hey, Jake."

"Uh—" the boy glanced around as though he wanted to make sure no one saw the two of them talking—"can I sit here for a minute?"

"Sure." John slid over. "What's on your mind?"

"There's a rumor going around that . . . well, that Nathan Pike's going to shoot people at the game tonight."

John held his breath. If the media ever had to compete with teenagers for getting a news flash to the public, the teenagers would win every time. He exhaled hard. "A threat came into the office. Yes. Police have checked it out. They're not worried about it."

"Serious? There was really a threat?" Jake's eyes grew wide. "Coach, what if the police are wrong? Nathan Pike's a freak; don't they know that?"

"The police are aware of Nathan." John worked to appear calm, but inside he was as anxious as Jake. What business did they have showing up at a game where there were threats of murder and mayhem? What football game could ever be that important?

"So no one's doing anything about it?"

"The police'll be at the game."

"Yeah, but that won't stop him. I mean, what if he doesn't care about dying?"

"The police are pretty sure it's not a serious threat, Jake. If it was, they'd call off the game."

"I doubt it." Jake held his helmet in his lap and now he hugged it to his middle. "All everyone cares about is winning this game. You know, so we can go to districts."

Jake was closer to the truth than he knew. "You have a point."

"Coach—" Jake lifted his eyes to John's, but only briefly—"I know who's writing the letters."

"Letters?"

"Yeah, the ones that talk about getting you fired."

John's heart sank. It was enough that *he* knew about the angry swarm of parental protests against him without his players knowing. Especially kids like Jake, who had always looked up to John. He wanted to know what the boy knew, but he wouldn't ask. He patted Jake on the knee. "A coach will always have his critics."

"Casey Parker was talking in the locker room the other day. He said his dad had it out for you, bad. They've had meetings."

"His dad and him?"

"His dad and some other parents. At first the other people didn't want to come but . . . well, after we lost. More people came. They've talked to Mr. Lutz."

"That's their right, I guess." John worked his mouth into a smile. "All I can do is my best."

"You're not leaving, though, are you?" Jake's eyes were wide, and John wished he could say something to encourage the boy. "I mean, you won't quit on us, will you? I still have one more year."

"I'd love to be here next year, Jake."

"So you will, right?"

"We'll see." John didn't want to share too much information, but he didn't want to lie either. The odds of him coaching another season at Marion High were growing slimmer all the time.

"You mean you might quit?"

John sighed. "I might not have to quit if Mr. Lutz fires me first."

"He won't fire you! Look at everything you've done for football at Marion High."

"People don't see it that way. They see their sons not getting playing time, the team not winning enough games. If you get the wrong parent upset with you, well . . . sometimes there's nothing anyone can do."

John refrained from saying anything more about Herman Lutz. It wasn't his place to undermine the man's authority in front of a student. But ultimately John's professional fate lay in Lutz's hands, and he was notorious for letting parents have their way. If Casey Parker's father wanted him out, Lutz would likely oblige.

If John didn't quit first.

"If it matters any, Coach, I'll win the game big for you tonight."

John smiled. If only it were that simple. "Thanks, Jake. That means a lot."

Jake fiddled with the chin strap on his helmet. "What can I do about Nathan Pike and the whole threat thing?"

"Pray about it."

Jake's eyes grew wide and his mouth hung open for a moment. "Me?"

"Not just you—the whole team." John lowered his brow but kept his eyes on Jake's. "You guys haven't exactly been kind to Nathan this year. The threat isn't a surprise, really."

Jake swallowed hard and stared at the seat in front of him. "So you want me to pray with the guys about it?"

"You asked."

For a moment, Jake was quiet. "Coach, I think he's jealous of my car."

"The Integra?"

"Yeah. A few days after I got it, I saw Nathan's mom drop him off at school. She has this, like, beat-up old station wagon with a dent on the side. Right then he looked at my car and then at me. Usually he looks at me like he hates me, but that time it was more like he wanted to *be* me. Like he would've given anything to trade places with me."

"Is that why you've let up on him these past few weeks?"

Jake nodded. "It wasn't right. I was such a jerk before."

"You were."

"But now . . . what if it's too late? What if he really does do something?"

John searched the boy's eyes. "I told you what I'd do."

"Okay, Coach." Jake tightened his grip on the helmet. "We'll pray. I'll make it happen."

Nothing in the world could have kept Abby from the game that night.

Yes, John would be upset with her. She'd have to deal with that later. But if someone was going to harm students or players or even her husband, Abby wanted to be there. What if there was something she could do, a student she could help, or a life she could save? What if it was the last time she saw her husband alive?

These thoughts went through her head in an instant, the moment John told her what had happened at school that day. He was late for the bus, so she couldn't argue with him. But there was no way she was staying home.

She filed into the stands and took her place at the far end, near parents from the other school. Bomb threat or not, she didn't enjoy sitting with the parents of John's players. Not this year, at least. Rarely ever, in fact. It simply didn't work to be involved that way.

After John took the job at Marion High, Abby had reveled in her role as the head coach's wife. She had the idyllic sense that she would sit with the parents, chat with them, befriend them. And at first, she did just that. Those were the years when she invited parents over for Thanksgiving dinner and Saturday night socials.

"Be careful, Abby," John would warn her. "You think they're your friends now, but wait and see. Sometimes people have an agenda."

Abby had hated his insinuation that the wonderful people she sat with at games were merely being kind to get their sons in good with Coach Reynolds. She disagreed with him time and again, insisting that people weren't that shallow; football wasn't that important.

But in the end John had been completely right.

One couple—people who were Christians and had shared many meals with the Reynolds—was the first in the office complaining about John's coaching when their son didn't get enough playing time. Other parents turned out to be phony as well, talking about Abby behind her back and then presenting big smiles and happy hellos when she came around.

They weren't all that way, of course, but she'd learned her lesson about players' parents, and she no longer took chances. For years now she sat by herself or with one of the other coaches' wives.

Tonight, though, she had no intention of sitting with anyone. She would camp out in the far side of the stands and watch. Not the game, but the stands, searching the students for any sign of unusual behavior, any sign of Nathan Pike. She had seen Nathan enough times on campus to recognize him. Of course, Nathan and his cronies were easy to spot, dressed as they were in black clothes and spiked collars. Tonight Abby wanted to be the first to notice them, the first to recognize any indication that one of them might be about to blow the stadium to pieces.

The minutes ticked off the clock and halftime came, all without incident. Police were stationed throughout the stadium, some—Abby guessed—in plain clothes. But so far the most remarkable thing that had happened all game was Jake Daniels's five touchdown passes.

Abby was fairly certain that was a league record. Kade had been one of the best quarterbacks to come out of that area, and he'd never come close to throwing five TDs in one half.

The second half was uneventful as well. Jake was pulled in the third quarter and replaced by Casey Parker, who had two passes intercepted. Despite that, the Eagles went on to win by thirty points. As the final buzzer sounded, the crowd spilled onto the field, embracing the Eagles as though it hadn't been a season wrought with controversy and parental complaints.

What did it matter now? The Eagles were going to districts.

Abby stood and made her way down to the field. *Where is he, Lord? Where's Nathan Pike? If he's here, please, Father, show me.* She scanned the crowd . . . and then hesitated. Had something moved along the far fence of the stadium? Cornfields surrounded the huge structure on three sides. A parking lot was on the fourth side.

Abby stared, eyes narrowed . . . Yes. There amid the tall corn . . . Abby could swear she saw movement.

Taking the stairs in an almost trancelike manner, Abby walked along the bleachers, drawing closer to the place where John and his players were receiving congratulations from hundreds of students and the entire marching band. The whole time she kept her eyes locked on the place in the cornfield.

Suddenly a figure emerged—a figure dressed in black.

Before Abby could do anything—before she could get close enough to be heard by John and the others, to run or duck or grab a police officer—the figure slipped through a hole in the fence and jogged through the crowd toward her husband.

"John, look out!" Abby shouted the words, and around her, a handful of parents stopped their conversations and stared at her.

Abby ignored them and set out in a full run, bounding down the stairs as fast as she could. *Please, God . . . save them from this. Please, God. In Jesus' name, I beg you . . .*

She was on the field now, but the figure's face was closing in quickly on John, placing himself in the center of the crowd of students and players. Even from fifty yards away, Abby could see the boy's face.

It was Nathan Pike.

He was dressed in his usual black, but this time he had on a new garment. A bulky jacket.

"John . . . run!" Abby screamed the warning and drew the stares of dozens of students. "All of you, run! Quick!"

Some of the students did as she said, but most of them only stood planted in place, motionless, staring at Abby as though she'd lost her mind.

She was ten yards away from John when Nathan walked up to him and put his hand on John's shoulder. At the same time, four officers darted through the crowd and gang-tackled Nathan to the ground.

"John!" Abby was faint by the time she reached her husband's side. Her stomach was in knots and she couldn't breathe. "Come on." She grabbed his arm. "Let's get out of here."

"What in the world . . . ?" John's face was white, his eyes wide.

The circle of students had grown and tightened around the place where the police had Nathan pinned to the ground. The boy appeared to be cooperating. A slew of officers came from every direction and in a matter of minutes directed the students away from the action and out into the parking lot. John directed his assistants to accompany the team bus back to school.

"He's clean," an officer announced. "No bombs."

Every muscle in Abby's body felt weak with relief. She gripped the sleeves of John's jacket and buried her face in his chest. "I thought he was going to kill you, John. I . . . I was so scared."

She whispered the words, so the other coaches couldn't hear. The entire staff was privy to the bomb threat, so none of them was surprised at what was happening.

"It's okay, Abby. It's all over." John ran his hand over her back and took her fingers in his. Then they walked to the place where Nathan still lay on the ground in handcuffs.

The police nodded their okay, and John walked up to the boy's side. "Did you do it, Nathan? Did you make the call?"

Nathan shook his head, his eyes wide and frightened. "They keep asking me that." He gulped, his words sticking in his throat. "I don't know what they're talking about."

Abby clung to John's arm, her body shaking from the adrenaline rush. The kid was lying. He had to be.

John tried again. "You weren't in class today."

Nathan blinked. "I . . . I went to the library. I had an English paper due and I needed some place quiet. I swear, Mr. Reynolds. I don't know what they're talking about."

An officer stood near Nathan's head. "Why'd you sneak in through the hole in the fence?"

"I was coming back from . . . from the library and thought I'd swing by. I saw the score and wanted to . . . to congratulate Mr. Reynolds. It was a big game."

The story had more holes than a sieve, but that wasn't Abby's problem. All that mattered was that John was okay. John and the students and players. She closed her eyes and rested her head against John. *God, thank You . . . thank You so much.*

The police pulled Nathan to his feet and led him to a waiting police car. Before they left, an officer approached John. "You think he could be telling the truth?"

"It's hard to tell with Nathan." John thought for a moment. "I'll say one thing though. In all the time I've known that boy, I've never seen him afraid until today. If I didn't know his past, I'd swear he was being straight with you."

The officer jotted something on his notepad. "Thanks. We'll take that into consideration."

Before long, John and Abby were the only people left in the stadium. He folded his arms around her and held her close. "You're shaking."

"I thought . . . I thought he was going to blow you up right there. Before I could do anything to help you."

"I told you not to come." Despite the reprimand, his voice was gentle, and Abby was glad. He wasn't mad at her.

"Right. Like I could sit home while someone might be out here trying to hurt you." She pulled back and looked him straight in the eye. "I had to come, John. Nothing could have kept me away."

"Why doesn't that surprise me?"

She grinned. "Guess what?"

"What?"

"You won!"

"We did."

"Congratulations."

"Thanks." The scoreboard was still lit, as were the stadium lights. Groundskeepers would clean up for another few hours before shutting the place down. "Now we get to go to districts."

"You don't sound thrilled." She worked her hands up the side of his face.

"I'm not. The parents hate me, remember?"

"Not if you're winning." Abby ran her finger lightly over his brow.

"These parents are different. Jake Daniels told me who's writing the letters. It's Casey Parker's father."

"No surprise there."

"Hey." He brought his face close to hers and kissed her. "Thanks for being here tonight. Even though I asked you not to. It means a lot to me."

"You're welcome." She kissed him back, breathing in the scent of him, trying not to imagine how different the night might have played out if . . .

She couldn't finish the thought.

"You look tired."

"I am. I've never been so scared in my life."

"Ahhh, Abby." He brushed his face against hers, clinging to her the way she clung to him. "Sweet, Abby. I'm sorry. I hate thinking of you afraid like that. Why don't you go home and get some rest?"

"What about you?"

"I'm a little wired for that." He pulled his gym bag over his shoulder and led her toward the parking lot. "I think I'll go back to school and correct papers. I'm about two weeks behind. Can you give me a ride?"

She grinned. "I'd love to."

"My car's at the school."

They talked about the game on the ride home, and when Abby pulled up in front of the school, she turned to John and yawned. "Will you be late?"

"Maybe. Could take me until one or two if I have enough energy."

"Don't forget about our dancing lesson tomorrow." She gave him a quick peck on the cheek as he climbed out.

"I won't be that late, don't worry."

"Yeah, but I want you to have enough energy. Paula's pretty demanding, you know."

John laughed. "See ya later, Abby. Love you."

"Love you, too."

Abby drove away knowing it was never more true.

Eleven

THE PARTY WAS PACKED WITH TEENAGERS AND JAKE Daniels was on top of the world. All except one thing.

He couldn't stop thinking about Nathan Pike and Casey Parker.

Nathan, because Jake had watched the whole arrest thing go down. In fact, he had the best view of anyone, since he'd been standing a few feet from Coach Reynolds when it happened. At first he'd been terrified, certain Nathan was going to whip out a gun and they'd all be dead.

But then he saw Nathan's eyes.

Jake and Nathan had never been good friends, but back a few years ago they'd been acquaintances. They'd known each other enough that they'd say hi and help each other with an occasional homework assignment. As Jake had risen in athleticism and popularity, Nathan had spiraled in the opposite direction.

Jake had been honest when he told Coach Reynolds Nathan was a freak. That's what the guy had become. But that night on the field when he saw Nathan's eyes, he knew deep in his gut that Nathan had nothing to do with the threat that day. He was scared as a guy could get.

And that bothered Jake for two reasons. First, because it wasn't right that Nathan was arrested over something he may not have done.

And second, because if Nathan didn't do it, who did? Whoever it was, he was very likely still walking around, making plans.

Then there was Casey Parker.

Jake had entered the locker room before the game that night and told everyone first off that the rumors were true. Someone had called the school and threatened to kill people at the game that night.

When the commotion settled down, Jake told the guys there was only one thing they could do about the threats. They could pray. Two and three at a time, the guys had dropped their gear and made their way over to Jake. In less than a minute, the whole team was gathered in a huddle—everyone except Casey Parker.

"This is a public school," Casey snapped at them. "It's against the law to pray."

In the past three weeks—since Jake had been meeting with Coach Reynolds again and being kinder to kids like Nathan Pike—the friendship with Casey had cooled. In the locker room earlier, Jake would have refuted Casey, but one of the other players did it first. "A kid can pray anywhere he wants."

Several others reiterated this truth with grunts and "Yeah, that's right" and other such things.

Casey sat off to the side while the rest of them prayed for God's protection over not just the game but every person in attendance. When the prayer was over, the team formed a tight circle and did their usual chanting and cheering to get fired up for the game.

Casey didn't join in any of it.

He sat by himself all night. Coach didn't call his number until Jake had six touchdowns. It was no surprise to the other Eagles when Casey took the field and promptly threw four incompletes and two interceptions. After that the coaches went to a running game to kill the clock.

On the bus ride back to school, Casey didn't say a word to the rest of them. When talk about the party came up, he split without a good-bye or anything. Jake tried to forget about it. After all, this was *his* night. His team had survived some sort of weird death threat *and* won the game. Big time. They were even going to districts.

It was time to celebrate. Big time.

He looked around. The party was at some girl's place, a freshman cheerleader, Jake thought. The girl had a huge house, lots of food, and parents who didn't mind them gathering there. Most of the team had showed up, but not Casey. A group of guys Jake didn't know that well walked up to him.

"Nice game, Jake . . . way to throw it."

"Yeah, was that like a record or something? Six touchdowns?"

Jake had been asked a hundred times so far, but he was polite as he answered. "A school record. Tied with a league record."

"That's so cool. Way to go."

The guys left, and Jake leaned against the kitchen counter. Some of the kids had beer in their cars outside. They drifted in and out, downing a few beers and then returning to the house. The girl's parents didn't mind the kids drinking as long as it wasn't on their property.

That was fine for them, but not Jake. Not tonight. He'd promised his dad that he wouldn't drink and drive, and since getting the new car, he'd kept his word. He grabbed a plastic cup and filled it with ice water. Besides, he wanted to savor the night, not lose it in a haze of drinking. He'd done that too many times over the summer. He was smarter now.

The party had been going on for two hours already, and it was after midnight. Jake wanted to be fresh for practice in the morning. A few more minutes and he'd call it a night.

At that moment, the front door opened and Jake stared. Casey Parker walked in, his arm around Darla Brubaker—the girl Jake was planning to ask to prom. Jake set his cup down and gritted his teeth. Whatever sort of stunt Casey was trying to pull, it wasn't going to work. Casey searched the room until his eyes landed on Jake. Then he turned to Darla and kissed her on the cheek.

Jake looked away. What was Casey's problem, anyway? He was

acting like a total loser. If Darla wanted to hang out with a jerk like that, let her. Still, he couldn't help but look back at the couple, still standing near the front door.

Casey whispered something in Darla's ear, and the girl giggled and took a seat in the corner of the room. When she was gone, Casey sauntered into the kitchen. Something about his expression looked almost hateful.

"Jake." He nodded once and leaned against the opposite counter. "Nice game tonight."

"Thanks." Jake grabbed his cup again and took another swig of water. "Hey, what's eatin' you, man? You weren't yourself out there."

"Let's just say the praying thing freaked me out, okay?"

Jake uttered a single laugh. "It worked, didn't it? No one shot us while we played the game."

Casey slammed his fist onto the counter. "Enough about prayer, okay? If you weren't a junior, I'd take you out for pulling a stunt like that before the game."

"Stunt?" Jake frowned. He didn't like Casey's insinuation.

"I saw you . . . talking to Coach the whole ride up to North County." Casey crossed his arms. "The thing I don't get is this: You're already his favorite little go-to guy. Did you really have to let him talk you into praying? I mean, haven't you sucked up enough these past few weeks? Dropping into Coach's room and acting all buddy-buddy."

Jake set his cup down and took three steps closer to Casey. "What's that supposed to mean?"

"Oh, come on. You're part of Coach's C-squad. Guys like me don't have a chance."

"C-squad?" Jake's mind reeled. What was Casey talking about? What the heck was a C-squad?

"You know, Jake. The *Christian* squad. Coach always gives the best spots to the Christian kids. Everyone knows that."

Jake felt his face go hot, then ice cold. "You're crazy, Parker. That's a lie and anyone on the team'll tell you so."

Casey grabbed a handful of Jake's T-shirt and jerked him close so their faces were only inches apart. "I'm the best quarterback on the team." He hissed the words, giving Jake another jerk for emphasis. "So tell me why I'm sitting the bench and you're getting all the p.t."

"Playing time is *earned.*" Jake placed his hands squarely on Casey Parker's shoulders and shoved him. "Anyone who's played for Coach Reynolds knows that."

"That right?" Casey shoved Jake, this time into the kitchen counter.

Before Jake could retaliate, a group of girls rushed into the kitchen squealing at them.

"Break it up, guys."

"Yeah, come on . . . let it go."

Jake straightened his shirt and glared at Casey. When the girls left, Casey shot an angry look at Jake, his expression pinched. "It's time we got to the bottom of this thing."

"Let's take it outside."

"Fine. But not on the grass."

"Where then?"

"The streets." He sneered at Jake. "You think you're the only one with speed?" Casey spat at him. "Well, you're wrong."

"You're talking about a race?" Jake's spine tingled. No one was listening to their conversation. It wouldn't be a big deal. Just a simple race between the two of them. Then Casey would know once and for all not to mess with Jake Daniels. "Any time, Parker. Your car'll look parked next to mine."

"Only one way to find out."

"Where do you want to do it?"

Casey narrowed his eyes, his voice strained with anger. "Haynes Street . . . the milelong stretch in front of the high school."

"Done."

"Meet me at Haynes and Jefferson in thirty minutes." Casey turned and headed back to Darla.

Jake had just one more thing to say, and he said it loud enough for Darla to hear. "Don't forget to bring the winner's trophy."

Late-night hours after a game were John's favorite times to catch up on his classroom work. He taught six health classes each day, and it was easy to fall behind. Especially during the season. Good thing he had more energy than usual tonight.

Generally, he'd get into his office, go through a day's worth of papers, and start feeling tired. Then he'd head home and crawl into bed with Abby sometime around eleven o'clock. But tonight he had enough stamina to work until morning. Not that he would. He'd promised Abby he wouldn't stay out too late. Besides, she was right. He needed his energy for their Saturday night dance lessons.

John scanned a series of papers and entered the tests in his grade book.

He'd never been one of those coaches who watched game films on Friday nights. As much energy as it took to coach a football game, he needed to fill his mind with something completely different. Grading was just the thing. So far that night he'd breezed through three days' worth of papers.

All the while he couldn't stop thinking about Nathan Pike.

Something deep in his gut told him Nathan hadn't come to the stadium for any reason other than the one he'd given—to congratulate John on coaching the team to a victory. He paused and thought about the scenario that had unfolded after the game. No doubt there were troubling pieces to the way it played out. Why hadn't Nathan entered the stadium through the main gates like everyone else? And why would he spend the entire day at the library only to drive ten miles out of the way to a football game? John couldn't remember seeing him at any other game so far that season.

Still, John was an expert at looking into kids' eyes and finding the truth. And something about Nathan's story rang truer than anything the kid had ever said before.

John corrected another batch of papers and then stretched. The framed picture near the edge of his desk caught his attention. He and Abby, at Nicole's wedding. Abby had thought it a strange choice. After all, there was nearly two feet of space between them, and even a stranger could see the tension on their faces. It was hardly a happy picture.

But it was honest.

They had made their decision to divorce, and that night, when the kids had gone on their honeymoon, John had planned to take his things and move in with a fellow teacher—a guy who had divorced his wife a year earlier. In fact, when the picture was snapped, John's car was already packed with his belongings.

The deal was all but done.

Kade and Sean had been spending the week with friends, and Abby had plans to fly to New York and meet with her editor. Their entire lives were falling apart, and the children had known nothing about any of it.

That night, after the wedding, John was only halfway down the road when he stopped and parked the car. He didn't know how to turn it around, didn't know how to erase the mistakes they'd made . . . but he knew he couldn't drive another inch away from the only woman he'd ever loved. The woman God intended for him to love forever. At that point, the divorce plans were all very neat and tidy, the arrangements they'd made about how to tell the kids and how they'd split time . . . everything was set. Everything but one troubling detail.

He still loved Abby. Loved her with all his heart and soul.

So he climbed out of the car and walked back home. He found her outside, where he had known he'd find her. On the pier, in their private spot. And in the hour that followed the walls they'd built around their hearts came crashing down until all that remained were two people who had created a life and a family and a love that could not be thrown away.

John sighed.

How he loved Abby . . . more so now than ever before.

He could hear her voice the last time she'd visited his classroom. "Take the picture down, John." She'd stared at it, her face filled with disgust. "It's awful. I look like an old, bitter woman."

"No. It makes me remember."

"Remember what?"

"How close we came to losing it all."

Besides, that wasn't the only picture on his desk. There was the other one right beside it. A smaller photo of John and Abby laughing at some family function a few months ago. Abby was right. She looked a decade younger in the later photo. It was amazing what happiness could do for a person's face.

He looked up at the clock on his classroom wall. Twelve-thirty. Abby would be asleep by now. The thought made him suddenly tired. He shot a look at the papers on his desk. The pile was half finished, but the rest could wait. If he had to, he could stay late Monday night, too.

The restlessness he'd felt earlier had worn off. If he went home now, he wouldn't lie awake wondering about this play or that one. He'd cuddle up to Abby, breathe in the fragrance of her sleeping beside him, and drift off to sleep in a matter of minutes.

That settled it.

He gathered his papers, stacked them neatly, and slipped them in the appropriate folders. Then he grabbed his keys, closed up his classroom, and headed for the parking lot.

As he pulled out of the school entrance, he worked the muscles in his legs. He was more tired than he'd thought. The streets were long since deserted, and because John and Abby only lived a few minutes from the school, he could almost count on being home in bed with Abby in five minutes flat.

He looked both ways, began to buckle his seat belt, and swung his car right onto Haynes Street.

A sound came up behind him, almost like an approaching freight train. All within an instant's time, John reminded himself that there were no train tracks in that part of Marion. He glanced in his rearview mirror just as a series of lights blinded him from behind.

What in the world? He was going to be hit. *Dear God . . . help me!*

There was no time to react . . . no time to think about whether he should hit the brake or the gas. The roaring noise behind him became deafening and then there was a terrible jolt. Screeching tires and breaking glass filled John's senses—along with something else.

A blinding pain burned through John's back, an indescribable hurt like nothing he'd ever felt in his life.

His vision blurred, leaving him gasping for air in complete darkness. He found his voice and screamed the only thing that filled his mind, the only thing he could put into words.

"Aaaabby!"

His voice echoed for what felt like forever. It was impossible to draw another breath.

Then there was nothing but silence.

Twelve

THE AIR BAG INFLATED IMMEDIATELY.

One minute Jake was barreling down Haynes Street, stunned at the speed Casey Parker had gotten out of his Honda. The next, there was the most horrific crash Jake had ever imagined possible.

His car was still now, but the bag smothered his face. He punched at it, gasping for air. What had happened? Had he blown a tire or lost control? Jake tried to shake off the dizzy feeling. No, that wasn't it. He'd been racing . . . racing Casey Parker.

Jake had the lead, but just barely. He'd stepped on the gas and watched the speedometer climb toward the one hundred mark. It was faster than he'd ever intended to drive, but the race would be over in half a mile. Then he'd seen movement, a truck or a car turning onto the road just ahead of him.

Was that what had happened? Had he hit someone? His mouth was dry; he couldn't catch his breath. *Oh, God . . . not that.* Jake kicked at the air bag, fighting free from it enough to open his door. He set his feet on the pavement, his chest heaving. Why couldn't he grab a mouthful of air?

Stand up, you idiot! But his body wouldn't cooperate. His muscles were like limp noodles, unable to move. A few seconds passed until, slowly, his lungs began to fill. Then it hit him. He'd had the wind knocked out of him.

Breathe . . . come on, breathe.

Finally he felt the oxygen make its way through his system. As it did, his legs jerked into action. He stood and looked around. Casey Parker was gone. "God, no . . ."

His heart thumped wildly against the wall of his chest as he turned and looked at the roadway in front of his car. There, about twenty yards ahead, was the crumpled remains of what looked like a pickup truck. It was impossible to tell what color it was. Jake wanted to throw up but instead he began to cry. He had no cell phone, no way to call for help. The entire school was surrounded by open fields, so no residents would have heard the crash.

He stared at the twisted metal and knew without a doubt that the driver was dead. Passengers, too, if there were any. In driver's ed they'd taught them to wear seat belts because usually, almost always, there was room to live in a smashed-up vehicle.

But not this one. The front end was all that was left. The back was crumpled like tinfoil, and the cab . . . well, the cab seemed to have been swallowed up by the other pieces.

Something inside him told him to run, flee as fast as he could. If he'd just killed someone, he would spend years in prison. He glanced back at his car. The front end was totaled, but there was a chance it might still run.

He shook his head, and the thought vanished.

What was he thinking? However impossible it looked, someone might be alive in the wreckage! He walked closer. Whatever . . . whoever lay inside the totaled pickup, he didn't really want to see it.

His heart raced so fast now, he thought he might pass out. The trembling he'd felt earlier had become full-blown shaking. The sound of his teeth chattering filled the night air as he approached the back of the other vehicle.

Suddenly something caught his eyes.

He looked down at the ground and there, in the ten feet that separated him from the destroyed pickup, was a license plate. Jake inched toward it and his heart stopped.

GO EAGLES

Go Eagles? No, God . . . please . . . it can't be. Only one person had a license plate like that. And he drove a pickup truck.

"Coach!" Jake felt his eyes grow wide, his heart stop as he ran the remaining steps to the side of the wreckage.

From inside there was a moaning sound, but the doors were so mangled, Jake couldn't see anything, let alone find a way in to help him. "Coach, is that you?"

Of course it was. Jake gripped the sides of his face and made jerky turns in a dozen different directions. Why hadn't anyone else come by? Where was Casey Parker? He pulled his hair and shouted again. "Coach! I'll get help. Hang on!"

With every bit of strength Jake had ever mustered, he pulled on what looked like part of the door. *Open, you stupid door . . . open. Come on.*

"Coach, hang in there."

Panic came upon him like a tidal wave. What had he done? He'd taken his car past a hundred miles an hour and hit Coach Reynolds . . . How could that possibly have happened? Coach should have been home hours ago. And now what? Coach was lying inside the twisted metal dying, and there was nothing he could do about it. "Coach . . . can you hear me?"

Nothing.

"God . . ." Jake threw his head back and tossed his arms in the air. He wept, shouting like a crazy person. "Please, God, help me! Don't let Coach die!"

At that moment, Jake heard a car coming up behind him. *Thank You, God . . . whatever happens to me, let Coach live. Please.*

He positioned himself in the middle of the road, waving his arms frantically. Almost immediately he recognized the car. Casey Parker. The Honda came to a screeching halt and Casey jumped out.

"I think it was Coach's truck." Casey looked as bad as Jake felt. Shaking, pale-faced, deeply in shock. "I . . . had to come back." He held up a cell phone. "I already called 9-1-1."

"He's . . . he's . . ." Jake was jerking violently, too frightened to speak.

Casey ran up to the wreckage. "Help me, Jake. We have to get him out."

The two boys worked with frantic determination, trying to find a way inside the pickup truck. But there was none. They didn't give up, not even when they heard sirens—not until the emergency vehicles pulled up and EMTs ordered them away from the vehicle.

"That's . . . that's my coach in there!" Jake couldn't think straight, couldn't make his mouth work. *"Help* him!"

Casey took over. "Our coach is trapped inside. We're sure it's him."

One of the paramedics hesitated. "Coach John Reynolds?"

"Yeah." Casey nodded, licking his lips. He looked like he might faint at any moment, but at least he could talk. Jake thrust his hands in his pocket and stared at the ground. He wanted to crawl into a manhole and never come out, or fall asleep and have his mother beside him, waking him, promising him it was all just a bad dream.

Instead, a police car pulled up.

Jake and Casey stood ten feet from the wreckage, alternately watching the rescue effort and staring at the asphalt. Jake hadn't given the police much thought. He was too concerned with whether the paramedics would be able to reach Coach Reynolds and, when they did, whether they could save him or not.

He was so distracted that when the officers positioned themselves in front of him and Casey, Jake stepped to the side for a better view.

"You the driver of the red Integra?" The officer shone a flashlight at his face.

Jake's heart skipped a beat and he squinted. *Oh God . . . help . . .* "Yes . . . yes, sir."

"You injured?"

"No, sir." Jake's throat was so tight he had to force the words out. "I had an air bag."

The other officer shone a flashlight in Casey's face. "You the driver of the Honda?"

Casey's teeth were clattering. "Yeah."

"We had a tip from a driver a mile down the road, said she saw a yellow Honda and a red Integra racing like a couple of speed demons down Haynes Street." The first officer took a step closer to Jake. "That true?"

Jake shot a look at Casey. This was a nightmare. What were they doing here? Why had he ever agreed to race Casey? Wasn't he going to go home? Just a few more minutes and then he'd call it a night, wasn't that what he'd told himself?

"Get your license." The officer pointed to Jake's car. Then he gestured to Casey's Honda. "You, too."

Jake and Casey did as they were told. The first officer handed the laminated cards to the second. "Run a check on them, will ya?" Then he turned back to Jake. "Listen, pal. Make it easier on yourself here. Forensics teams will tell us how fast you were going—down to the mile. You don't cooperate now, and we'll make the process miserable for you *and* your parents."

The sound of a power tool filled the air. *Please, God . . . let them get him out of there.*

Jake tried to swallow, but he couldn't. His tongue was stuck to the roof of his mouth. This time he didn't look at Casey. "Yes, sir . . . we . . . we were racing, sir."

"You aware there's a law against that?"

Jake and Casey nodded in unison. The other officer joined them again. "Clean records for both."

"Not after tonight." He nodded to his partner. "Cuff 'em. Then call their parents."

Jake's blood ran cold—not because he was going to jail but because they were taking him away from Coach. He wanted to scream, shout at everyone to back off and let him stay until he knew everything was okay. His heart felt heavier than cement as the realization set in. Coach might die . . . he might already be dead. And even if he wasn't, nothing would ever be okay again. Jake was the worst, most awful sort of person, and whatever happened to him after this, he deserved every minute of it.

The first officer grabbed Jake's wrists and held them tightly together behind his back. The metal pinched his skin, and Jake was almost glad. In seconds the handcuffs were on, and the officer walked back to his car. The other officer did the same to Casey, and then left, so the two of them were alone on the road, cuffed and staring at Coach Reynolds's destroyed vehicle.

The medics were still working frantically around what was left of Coach's truck, still desperate to get him out. Jake closed his eyes and willed them to hurry up. *God, how could You let this happen? It should be me in there, not Coach. He didn't do anything wrong. Get him out, please . . .*

"I got it!" A paramedic shouted from amid the workers. He tossed a mangled truck door behind him. It landed on the neatly manicured grass that bordered the Marion High parking lot. "I need a backboard, stat. And an airlift. The guy's not going to make it by ground."

They were going to get him out! Jake's knees shook, and again he couldn't catch his breath. A wild splash of hope colored the moment, and Jake fought the urge to shout Coach's name above the chaos.

The paramedic began barking out orders, shouting words Jake had never heard before. The one thing he did pick up was this: Coach Reynolds was still alive! That meant there was a chance . . . a prayer that maybe he might make it! Jake's legs could no longer hold him, and he fell to his knees, his heart thudding hard against the surface of his chest. *Hang in there, Coach . . . come on. God, don't let him die.*

Jake had no idea how long he and Casey stayed there, stone still, watching the rescue. Finally, a helicopter appeared overhead and landed on the empty street. About the same time, one of the paramedics waved his hand at the others. "I'm losing him."

"No!" No one heard Jake above the sound of the chopper. He struggled to his feet, took three steps toward the huddle of medics, and then returned to his place.

Beside him, Casey began to sob.

There was a rush of motion and someone began doing CPR. "Let's get him out of here!"

A team of paramedics lifted a board, and for the first time, Jake could see the man they were working on. There was no question it was Coach Reynolds. He still had on his Marion Eagles jacket.

A wave of sobs strangled Jake's heart. What sort of monster *was* he, to race that way on a city street? And what about Coach, the man who had been more of a father to him than his own dad these past years.

"Please don't let him die!" Once more Jake's agonized cry drowned in the whirring helicopter blades and engine noise.

They loaded Coach Reynolds into the chopper, and it lifted off the ground, disappearing into the sky. Jake watched it go until he could no longer hear the whirring of the engine. When it was gone, an eerie, deathly silence fell over the street. He looked around, suddenly aware of the action taking place near the damaged cars. Other police had arrived and were taking measurements, marking the spot from Jake's car to the wreckage of Coach's truck. As the paramedics left the scene, two tow trucks pulled up. The drivers climbed out and waited by their rigs.

Jake began to shake again, and his arms ached from being cuffed behind his back. "We're going down," Casey whispered beside him. "In flames, Jake. You know that, right? The season's over."

The season? Jake wanted to vomit. What kind of a person was Casey anyway? The *season?* Who cared about the stinkin' season? He turned to Casey, his eyes so swollen from crying he could barely see. "Is that all you can think about?"

Casey wasn't crying anymore, but he shook like someone having a seizure. "Of . . . of course not. I'm worried about Coach. It's just . . . this'll stay with us the . . . the rest of our lives."

Jake's anger blazed, cutting off his tears. "Yeah, and we *deserve* it."

Casey opened his mouth, and at first it looked like he was about to disagree. Then he hung his head and finally, the tears came again for him, as well. "I . . . I know it."

Jake was disgusted with both of them. The officers were right. Coupla rich kids driving cars that were way too fast. He gritted his teeth until his jaw ached. It didn't matter what kind of trouble they faced. The police could toss him in jail and throw out the key for all he cared. In fact, Jake would have gladly given his life for the only thing that still mattered.

That Coach Reynolds survive the night.

Because if Coach didn't live, Jake was pretty sure he wouldn't be able to either.

Thirteen

IT WAS A NIGHTMARE.

It had to be. Abby squinted at the clock and saw it was just after two in the morning. There was no way John would have been out this late. Car accidents didn't happen to men like him . . . men who should have been home asleep by now.

Yes, it was just a nightmare. Abby almost had herself convinced, except for one troubling detail: John's place in bed beside her was empty, untouched. She tried to swallow, but her throat was too thick. Why was she trying to scare herself? It wasn't so unusual that John be missing from bed at this hour. Not after a football game. He could be downstairs watching television or eating a bowl of cereal. He did that lots of times.

Still, as convinced as she was, she had to tell the caller something.

"Did you hear me, Mrs. Reynolds? Are you awake?" The voice was calm, gentle. But the urgency was undeniable. "I said we need you down here at the hospital. Your husband's been in an accident."

The man was relentless. "Yes." Abby huffed out her answer. "I'm awake. I'll be there in ten minutes."

She hung up, then called Nicole. If the dream was going to be persistent, she might as well work it out, and that meant playing the role expected of her.

"Your father's been in an accident."

"What?" Nicole's voice was half shriek, half cry. "Is he hurt?"

Abby forced herself to be calm. If she lost it now, she'd never make it to the hospital. And only by going through the motions would she ever break free from the awful nightmare. "They didn't tell me. Just that we need to come." Her eyes closed, and she knew she was right. It had to be a nightmare. And no wonder, especially after the bomb threat earlier. Her dreams were bound to be bad.

"Mom, are you there?"

"Yes." She forced herself to concentrate. "Is Matt home?"

"Of course."

"Have him drive you. I don't want you going out at night alone."

"What about you? Maybe we should pick you up."

"Sean's already dressed and waiting for me."

"Is he okay?"

"He'll be fine as soon as this nightmare is over."

The entire ride to the hospital, Abby was shocked at how real everything felt. The cool breeze on her face, the steering wheel in her hands, the road beneath the wheels. Never in her life had a dream felt like this.

But that's what it had to be.

John hadn't been doing anything dangerous tonight. The danger had been back at the football stadium, when he could have been blown to bits. But driving home from school? There couldn't have been a soul on the road.

Abby whipped the car into the hospital parking lot and saw Matt and Nicole just ahead of her. They entered the emergency room together and were immediately led to a small room behind the double doors, out of sight from the rest of the public.

"What's going on?" Nicole started to cry, and Matt put his arm around her. "Why'd they bring us in here?"

Abby clenched her fist as a realization slammed into her. She had no information whatsoever. Not about the type of accident or whether another car was involved. Not about the extent of John's injuries or how he got to the hospital. She was completely in the dark, and in some ways that brought her comfort. Dreams were like that—strange, missing details, disconnected . . .

Beside her, Sean began to cry, too.

"Shhh." Abby hugged him to her side and stroked his back. "It's okay."

A doctor entered the room and shut the door behind him. The first thing Abby noticed was his face. It was marked with tension and sadness. *No, God . . . don't let this be happening. Not really. Make me wake up. I can't take another minute . . .*

Lean not on your own understanding, daughter . . . I am here with you even now.

The words seemed to come from nowhere and speak straight to her soul. They gave Abby the strength to look up, to meet the doctor's eyes straight on, and ask the hardest question in her life. "How is he?"

"He's alive."

The four of them straightened some at the doctor's words. "Can we see him?" Abby started to stand, but the doctor shook his head.

"We have him on life support in the intensive care unit." The doctor lowered his brow. "It'll be touch and go for the next few days. There's still a significant chance we could lose him."

"No!" Nicole screamed the word and then buried her face in Matt's chest. "No, God . . . not my daddy. No!"

Abby closed her eyes and held more tightly to Sean. She remembered then that she hadn't called Kade. There he was five hundred miles away and he didn't know his father was fighting for his life. It was one more disconnected piece, a part of the nightmare.

But the dream was growing more terrifyingly real by the moment.

Nicole finally quieted down, her face still smothered in Matt's plaid, flannel shirt.

There was sanity in staying calm. Abby looked down and saw that her hands were trembling, but she managed to meet the doctor's gaze. "What . . . what are his injuries?"

"He suffered a severed trachea, Mrs. Reynolds. That type of injury is fatal in most cases. My guess is that the way his body wound up after the accident somehow held the trachea in place long enough to save his life. As soon as they moved him, he stopped breathing. They kept him on life support until he arrived here by helicopter."

"Helicopter?" Abby was seeing spots before her eyes, circling spots that threatened to take up her entire field of vision. She shook her head. No, she couldn't faint. Not now. "What . . . what happened?"

The doctor's eyes fell to his clipboard, and he grimaced. "Apparently he was the victim of a couple street racers—high-school kids."

"Street . . ." Abby's world began to spin around her. "Street racing?"

No doubt about it, it was just a nightmare. Real life didn't have that kind of coincidence. John Reynolds, the coach accused of looking the other way while his players participated in street races . . . hit by teenagers doing that very thing? It was so ridiculous, it couldn't possibly be real.

"The boys were probably going about a hundred miles an hour when your husband pulled out of the school parking lot. He was hit from behind."

"So . . ." Abby pushed her fingers hard against both sides of her head. Again her body wanted to faint, but she wouldn't let it. Not until she heard it all. "So his trachea? That's the problem?"

The doctor's expression grew even darker than before. "That's the most critical problem at this point."

"There's more?"

Nicole moaned and clung to Matt. Abby glanced at Sean and realized he was sobbing into her sleeve. Poor babies. They shouldn't have to hear this. Still, if it was only a bad dream, it wouldn't hurt anything. Besides, the sooner she worked through it, the quicker she'd wake up.

The doctor checked his notes again. "It looks like he broke his neck, Mrs. Reynolds. We can't really be certain at this point, but we think he's paralyzed. From the waist down, at least."

"Noooo!" Nicole screamed again and this time Matt shot Abby a pleading look.

But there was nothing she could do. The word was still making its way into her conscious. Paralyzed? *Paralyzed!* It was completely impossible. John Reynolds had just coached the Eagles to victory. He had walked her to the car and climbed the school stairs to his office. Later that night they had dance lessons to attend.

Paralyzed?

"I'm sorry." The doctor shook his head. "I know this must be very hard for you. Is there anyone I can call?"

Abby wanted to tell him to call Kade. Instead she stood and gathered Sean to her side. "Where is he? We need to see him."

The doctor studied the group and nodded. He opened the door and motioned to them. "Follow me."

They looked like a trail of walking wounded as they moved along behind the doctor down one hallway and then another. The clicking of the man's heels against the tile floor reminded Abby of some macabre clock, counting down the hours John had left. She wanted to shout at him to walk more quietly, but it wouldn't have made sense. Even in a dream.

Finally the doctor stopped and opened the door. "The group of you can only stay for a few minutes." He looked at Abby. "Mrs. Reynolds, you can stay beside him all night if you wish."

Abby led the way as they crept inside, and only then did her veneer of shock and disbelief give way. As it did, she collapsed in a heap near the foot of his bed, her head spinning.

It was real. *Dear God . . . it's really happening.*

Light narrowed, darkness swept in, overflowing her. "I'm fainti—"

That was the last thing Abby remembered.

When Abby came to, she was sitting in a chair beside John's bed. Nicole, Matt, and Sean were gathered around her. At her feet was a nurse with smelling salts. "I'm sorry, Mrs. Reynolds. You passed out."

Abby looked beyond them to the bed, to her precious John lying there. Tubing ran in and out of his body from his mouth, his neck, his arms and legs. A full brace was fixated to his head and neck, making John looked trapped. Abby wanted to throw it off him, free him and take him away.

But she couldn't.

All she could do for the rest of the night was stay beside John and try not to cry too loudly. Because if he was here, then he wasn't at home. He wasn't watching television or eating cereal or grading papers into the wee hours of the morning. He was strapped to a hospital bed, clinging to life.

And that could only mean one thing.

She wasn't dreaming after all.

Her dear husband, the man who had run like the wind across the football field at the University of Michigan . . . the man who played tennis with her and jogged with her and ran patterns for his players when a diagram wasn't enough . . . the man who danced with her on the pier behind their home a hundred different times . . . might never dance again.

This wasn't the kind of nightmare a person woke up from.

It was the kind that lasted a lifetime.

The hours became little more than a blur.

By Saturday afternoon Kade had joined them at the hospital. He arrived sometime between lunch and dinner, Abby wasn't sure. But they were all there, gathered around John's bed. Praying for him. Jo and Denny had come, and with them a dozen people from church and the high school.

Word was getting out.

Coach Reynolds was in an accident; he might never walk again. Teary-eyed football players kept vigil in the waiting room with the others. Only immediate family was allowed in the room, which meant Abby and the kids and Matt. Abby never left John's side except to use his private rest room. She completely avoided any conversation in the waiting room about who had been arrested and what penalty they might face for hitting John's car. She didn't care about that right now. All that mattered was John's survival.

So far he hadn't regained consciousness, although doctors thought it could happen anytime.

Abby had long since let go of the idea that what was happening was merely a dream. It was reality. But a reality she prayed would turn out differently than the doctors imagined it would. John would wake up sometime that evening, look around the room, and flash that silly grin of his.

Then he'd wiggle his fingers and toes and ask the first passing nurse to take off the neck brace. His throat would be sore, of course—any time a person had a severed trachea that was bound to happen—but other than that he'd be fine. A few days in the hospital and they could walk away from the scare of the accident and get on with the business of living and loving and taking dance lessons with Perky Paula.

That's how it would happen. Abby was sure of it.

For now, the group of them was quiet. Kade stood anchored against one wall, his gaze locked on his father. Eyes dry, face pale, Kade hadn't moved from his spot for two hours. Beside him on the floor was Sean, his knees pulled up to his chin, his face in his hands. Most of the time, Sean cried quietly to himself. At times when he would stop crying, Abby could see it wasn't because the sadness had passed. It was because he was too scared even for tears.

Matt and Nicole had taken up their position on the opposite wall, Nicole in a chair, and Matt standing beside her. The doctor had encouraged them to talk, explaining that John was more likely to wake up if he heard their voices. Occasionally Abby and the boys would say a few words, but Nicole was the most verbal of them. Every ten minutes or so she would cross the room and stand near the head of John's bed.

"Daddy, it's me." Her tears would come harder then. "Wake up,

Daddy. We're all here waiting for you and praying for you. You're going to be okay; I just know it."

After a few sentences, her tears would be too strong to speak through, and she would walk around the bed and hug Abby for a long while. Then she would return to her place next to Matt. Occasionally one or more of them would leave the room for something to eat or drink.

The only good news of the day had come that morning when the doctor upgraded John's condition from critical to serious. "He's had a great night. I'd say his chances of surviving are very strong."

Abby had no idea how long ago that was or whether night had come again or not. She knew only that she didn't dare leave, didn't consider being gone from the room when John first opened his eyes and told them all the truth: that he wasn't that bad off after all.

Finally, as the nurses were pushing dinner carts down the hallway, John let out a quiet moan.

"John!" Abby moved closer to the bed and took hold of his hand, the one without the wires and tubing. "We're all here, honey. Can you hear me?"

The kids gathered closer, waiting for his response. But there was none. Abby studied his face. It was bruised and swollen, but she was almost certain his eyes were twitching beneath the lids. That hadn't happened since Abby arrived at the hospital.

Nicole ran her fingers lightly over John's other hand, careful not to bump the various lines attached to him. "Daddy, it's me . . ." She sucked in two quick breaths and fought to keep her tears at bay. "Are you awake?"

John gave the slightest nod of his head, enough that Sean muttered a soft *"Yes!"* under his breath. It was one thing to have John injured and facing a life that might never be the same again. But to lose him . . . that was something none of them could bear to think about.

Even the subtlest movement now was like a sign from God that no matter what else might happen, John was going to live.

Another moan escaped his throat and his lips moved. A nurse

entered the room and saw what was happening. "Move back. Please. He can't be too stimulated right now, not while he's intubated."

She checked his monitors and brought her head near his face. "John, we need you to stay very still. Can you understand me?"

Again his head moved up and down, no more than half an inch in either direction, but enough to show that he'd heard the nurse. Abby's heart soared. She was right all along. He was going to be fine. They merely had to help him get past his injuries, and then everything would be okay.

The nurse held her hand behind her, indicating that the rest of them needed to keep their distance until she was finished with him. "Are you in pain, John?"

This time he moved his head side to side. Once more the motion was barely detectable, but it was there all the same.

"John, you've been in an accident. Do you know that?"

His head was still. From where Abby stood, she could see him working his eyes again, struggling to make them open. Finally, almost painfully, the lids lifted and he squinted. At almost the same time his arms twitched, and he brought one hand toward his throat.

There! See? Abby wanted to shout. He could move! If he could lift his hands, then he wasn't paralyzed, right? She blinked, and her heart sank. Even if he wasn't paralyzed, he must feel miserable. Tubing stuck down his throat, his head and neck stuck in a brace, unable to speak. John hated having his temperature taken, let alone this. Before he could pull out the lines, the nurse caught his hand and returned it to his side. "I need you to leave your throat alone, John. You've had an injury and we need to keep the tubes in place. Do you understand?"

The nurse's voice was loud and measured, as though he were a dim-witted child. Kade glared at the nurse from his spot against the wall, but Abby was glad for her directness. Otherwise her husband might do something to harm himself, and they couldn't have that.

"Do you understand, John? You mustn't make any sudden movements and don't try to remove your tubing. None of it. Okay?"

John blinked, and his eyes opened a bit wider. For the first time, it looked like he could see. He met the nurse's gaze and gave a more definite nod. Then, without waiting for the nurse to speak again, John turned his head and, using mainly his eyes, found each of them around the room. First Kade, then Sean, Nicole, and Matt. And finally Abby.

She had no idea what the kids read in John's searching eyes, but what she saw said more than any words could. His eyes told her to hang in there, that he was okay, and everything was going to be fine. But there was something else there, too. A love so deep and strong and true it couldn't have been put into words even if John could speak.

The nurse took a step backward. "I'm going to let your family visit with you for a few minutes, John, but after that you have to sleep. You must lie very still. We're working as hard as we can to get you better."

She didn't ask him about his legs, whether he could move them or feel them. Was that because the staff no longer thought he had a problem? Or because there was no point giving him that type of emotional jolt moments after he'd regained consciousness? Abby tried not to think about it.

Instead she made her way closer to the bed, her eyes still locked on his. *Don't lose it, Abby; don't let him see your tears. Not now.* She held her breath and urged the corners of her lips up, where they belonged. "John . . ."

He lifted his fingers off the hospital sheet, and she took them in her own. He couldn't speak, but he squeezed her fingers. Abby refused to notice the way his feet and legs still had not moved.

She let out a small bit of air, caught a quick half breath, and held it again. It was the only way to keep from sobbing. "God is so good to us, John. You're going to be just fine."

His expression changed, and she knew instinctively what was going through his mind. What had happened? Who had hit him? Where was the other driver and was he okay? Abby knew few details herself, so she shook her head. "It doesn't matter what happened. It wasn't your fault, John. The important thing is you're awake and you're here with us now. You're getting the very best possible care, okay?"

The muscles in his face relaxed a bit and he nodded.

At the foot of the bed, Nicole gripped John's toes. But it wasn't until she called his name that he looked at her. "Daddy, Matt and I have something to tell you."

Matt placed his hand on Nicole's shoulder. "Hi." His cheerfulness sounded forced. "It's good to see you awake."

Nicole put her fingers to her throat, and Abby knew it was probably too thick to speak. After several painful seconds, she swallowed and shook her head. "We wanted to tell you tonight, before you and Mom took your dancing—" Her voice broke and for a moment she hung her head.

Matt took over. "We had some news we wanted to share with the family. When we found out about your accident, we were going to wait, but Nicole . . ."

"I want you to know, Daddy. Because you have to do everything you can to get better." She stroked his foot, her eyes never leaving John's. "We're going to have a baby, Daddy. It wasn't something we planned, but it's a miracle all the same." She sniffed twice. "We . . . we wanted you to be the first to know, because we need you, Dad. I need you. Our baby needs you."

Tears filled John's eyes and spilled onto his cheeks. Then he gave a very deliberate nod and the corners of his mouth lifted just enough so they knew what he was feeling. No matter that he was strapped to a hospital bed . . . no matter what lay ahead on his journey to recovery, John was going to be a grandfather. And he was thrilled with the news.

Abby didn't know whether to laugh or cry. Jo had been right, after all. Nicole's glowing look was exactly what her mother-in-law had guessed it to be. She was pregnant! Here, in the midst of Abby's greatest nightmare, was a ray of hope, a reason to celebrate.

The conflicting emotions warred within her. She left John's side and put her arms around Matt and Nicole. "I can't believe it. How long have you known?"

"A few weeks. We wanted to make sure before we told anyone."

Congratulations came from Sean and Kade, though their voices were hardly enthusiastic. Abby let her head rest on Nicole's shoulder. She was too drained to do anything but stand there, motionless. She and John were going to be grandparents. It was something they'd talked about since they got married, only always it had seemed like some far-off stage. An event that happened to other people, old people. When Nicole got married, they knew the possibility was closer than ever, but still . . .

No one had expected Nicole to get pregnant so soon. No one except Jo.

An ocean of sorrow choked Abby as terrible thoughts assaulted her. Would John ever get to run and play with this first grandchild? Would he be able to walk the child around the block or bounce Nicole's baby on his knee?

Please, God . . . let the doctors be wrong about his legs. Please . . .

In this world you will have trouble. But take heart! I have overcome the world.

The verse was one she and John had looked at a month ago, when the troubles at Marion High had intensified. There had been many times in life when the words from the book of John had not comforted her, but caused her fear. "In this world you will have trouble"? What peace could be gained from that?

But over the years she'd come to understand it better.

Troubles were a part of life . . . even events like losing their precious second daughter to sudden infant death syndrome or having her mother killed by the Barneveld tornado. Some troubles were brought on by a person's own actions—like the years she and John lost because of their own selfishness. Other troubles were part of a spiritual attack—like what had happened this year at the high school.

But sometimes you simply stayed late at school correcting papers, pulled out of the parking lot for home, and found your life changed in an instant.

Troubles would come. After more than two decades together, this much Abby and John knew. The point of the verse wasn't to dwell on the certainty of hard times, but rather to be assured of God's victory through it all. If the Lord walked through the door of John's hospital room right now, He would cry with them and feel for them.

But before He left, He would give them a certain, knowing smile, and these parting words: "Cheer up! I have overcome all of it!"

It was true.

The new life growing within her daughter was proof.

Fourteen

THE JAIL CELL WAS FREEZING COLD.

Jake huddled in the corner on a cot. He had one roommate, a strung-out kid who he gathered had been picked up for attempted robbery. Jake peered at the guy when he was first brought into the cell, but neither of them had said a word since.

The past twenty-four hours had been like something from a scary movie.

Paramedics had given him and Casey a quick check, and then police had brought the two of them to the station. From there they were sent in different directions. Casey was already eighteen, an adult. Jake, at seventeen, was still a minor. That meant he had to spend the first night in a cell full of teenagers, all with attitudes.

The booking officer told Jake his mother was in the lobby, but he was being charged with a felony. He couldn't have visitors until he was properly booked and placed in his own cell, all of which happened Saturday afternoon.

He still hadn't been able to see his mother.

Everything she had warned him about had happened. He could hear her voice each of the dozens of times he'd gone out with friends since getting the car.

"Stay home, Jake. You'll be too tempted. A car like that could kill someone . . ."

It had been the primary source of his parents' recent arguments. Mom thought the car was only his father's way of making up for lost time, an apology for taking off to another state and living the life of an unfettered single man.

On more than one occasion, his mother had yelled at his father over the phone, trying to convince him that Jake was too young to handle a car like the red Integra. "You're a poor excuse for a father. If you loved him, you'd be here in Illinois. Not gallivanting around with some . . . some floozy on the East Coast."

The last thing Jake had wanted to do was prove his mother right, deepen the rift between his parents. Yeah, well . . . no question he'd done just that.

He rolled onto his side and pulled his legs up. He was lonely and scared and sick to his stomach. What if Coach had died? And if he was still alive, where was he and how was he doing? What were his injuries? Though Jake dreaded facing his mother, at least she would know what was happening with Coach.

For that reason, when the booking officer rattled the bars on his cell, Jake jerked himself upright.

"Jake Daniels." The man used a key to unlock the cell door. Across from Jake, the ratty teenager fixed his gaze on the barren wall once more. The man with the key barked at him. "You have a visitor."

Jake felt like a mess. He'd been stripped of his street clothes and wore a plain blue cotton jumpsuit—the kind you saw on criminals when they testified in court and their pictures ran in the newspaper.

"This way." The man's voice was terse. He led Jake down a hallway of small cells into a half room. There were a dozen chairs facing a solid glass wall, each with dividers that formed a series of small cubicles. At each chair was a telephone. The officer pointed to the last one at the far end of the line. "Down there."

Jake's steps sounded hollow as he made his way to the last chair and sat down. Only then did he see her. His mother sat on the other side of the glass, a telephone in her hand. Her face was swollen, her eyes bloodshot. *Look what I've done to her.* Jake gripped his sides, his heart beating out a strange, fearful rhythm he didn't recognize.

I've ruined her life. I've ruined everyone's life.

His mother motioned to the telephone, and Jake picked up the receiver. Sweat beaded up on his forehead and his palms were wet. His jailhouse breakfast lodged somewhere at the base of his throat. "Hello?"

She started to speak, then she dropped her head in her free hand and cried instead.

"Mom . . . I'm sorry." Jake wanted to put his arms around her and hug her, but the glass was in his way. Could he burst through it? If so, maybe the glass would slit his wrists and he would die the way he deserved to. He stilled his thoughts and cleared his throat. "I . . . I'm so sorry."

Finally she looked up and ran her fingertips beneath her eyes. There were black smudges there, remnants of yesterday's mascara. "What happened, Jake? The police say you were racing."

The running feeling was back. Maybe he could slip out a door somewhere and leave everything about Jake Daniels behind . . .

But the doors on every side were locked, and the mountain of misery standing before him was not going away. Jake massaged his temples. "That's right. We were racing."

His mother's expression changed, and Jake felt his breath catch in his throat. In all his life, he would never forget the shock and sadness, the disappointment that marked his mother's face in that instant. She opened her mouth, but for a long time nothing came out. Then she said just one agonized word. *"Why?"*

Jake hung his head. There was no good answer, none at all. He looked up and saw his mother was waiting. "I . . . uh . . . Casey challenged me." He was suddenly desperate to explain himself. "No one shoulda been on the road at that hour, Mom. When Coach pulled out, there wasn't time to . . ." His voice trailed off.

Through the smudged glass, his mother's eyelids closed in what looked like slow motion. "Oh, Jake . . . it's more than I can stand."

"Is . . . is Dad coming?"

She bit her lip and nodded. "He'll be here tomorrow afternoon."

The question was gnawing a hole through his gut. All day he'd wanted to ask about Coach, but now that his mother was here, Jake was terrified to do so. Finally he had no choice but to put his thoughts into words. "How's Coach?"

"He . . ." His mother sniffed, her eyes full of new tears. "He made it through the night."

A wild relief exploded in Jake's soul, a relief like nothing he'd ever known. It made him glad he was sitting down, because otherwise his knees would have certainly buckled. Coach was alive! They could lock Jake up forever and he wouldn't mind now. Not as long as Coach Reynolds was okay. He met his mother's eyes again, then frowned.

She looked upset, like there was something she hadn't yet told him.

"Jake, I talked to Mrs. Parker. She knows a family from the Reynoldses' church." His mother hung her head for a moment before looking up. "Coach is in bad shape, son. If he survives . . . he will almost certainly be paralyzed from the waist down."

Paralyzed? Coach? Paralyzed . . . from the waist down? No way . . . not Coach! Jake felt like he'd wallowed into quicksand. Coach couldn't be paralyzed. He was strong as an ox. The guys teased him that he was in better shape than anyone on the team. "Maybe Mrs. Parker's wrong. What's the news saying?"

"It hasn't hit yet. The accident happened too late to make yesterday's paper."

Jake was shaking again. He ran his hand over the top of his head and down the back of his neck. "Mom, you can't leave me in here like this. I gotta know what's happening to him. It's all my fault!"

She squeezed her eyes shut and sat perfectly still. He'd only seen her do that one other time—when his dad left home a few years earlier. Jake wasn't sure, but he thought it probably meant she was having a breakdown. Once more he wanted to punch a hole in the glass, climb through, and give her a hug, but he couldn't even do that. So many lives had fallen apart in one single moment, and it was all because of him.

"Mom, stop. I need you. The guy's watching me and any minute he'll take me back to the cell." Jake's urgent tone caused his mother to open her eyes once more. "I have to know what's going on with Coach."

"The officer told me you'll stay here until Monday, maybe Tuesday. Whenever they can get you before a judge. They're charging you with—" her voice broke, and fresh tears spilled onto her cheeks, "with felony assault and gross vehicular negligence. Also something about street racing and using a car as a deadly weapon. They want to try you as an adult, Jake. That could mean . . ." Her voice faded.

"Staying here a while." Jake gripped the phone. "That's okay, Mom. I deserve it."

"More than a while, Jake. The officer said you'll be lucky if you get out in five years."

His mother didn't understand. She could have told him he was in for thirty years and it wouldn't have mattered. What was he going to do? His football days were over, so were his days behind the wheel. He could hardly go back to Marion High where everyone would know he was the one who'd ruined Coach Reynolds's life. Yet he was only a junior, without a degree or training or any idea of how to support himself. He could hardly move to another town and start over.

No, he was trapped, and for now that suited him fine. This was where he belonged. And even here he could still walk down the hallway or pace across his cell.

If what his mother said was true, that was more than Coach Reynolds could do.

Hanging up the phone and walking away from Jake that afternoon was the hardest thing Tara Daniels had ever endured. But seeing Tim in the lobby of the city jailhouse the next afternoon was pretty close.

He walked in, his tie askew, eyes wide and bewildered, and immediately found her. After hearing the news, he'd taken the first flight he could find. This was the soonest he could get here.

Tara could think of a hundred things she'd wanted to tell him. When the phone call came from the police department telling her they'd arrested Jake for felony vehicular assault and that he'd been racing at the time of the accident, she wished they'd arrest Tim, too. Hadn't she told him? Hadn't she warned them both that a car that fast was dangerous for a teenage boy? Just like she'd told Tim their marriage was worth fighting for, that by leaving for New Jersey he'd only lose everything that mattered most: the love they once shared, the son they'd raised, and the closeness in faith that had once been so important to them.

She'd been right then, and she was right now.

But when Tim approached her, his face a mask of agony and regret, it didn't matter that she was right or that Tim was wrong. All that mattered was their son had nearly killed someone, possibly paralyzed him. And life would never be the same again.

It was hardly the time to point fingers. In all the world at that moment, only one other person could understand the pain of what Tara Daniels was going through. And that person was the man standing before her. A man she still loved, even if it had been years since she'd liked him.

"Tim . . ." She held out her arms, and he came to her, slowly, like a man stretching out his dying moments. His arms came around her waist, and hers moved around his neck. There—amid meandering petty criminals and empty-eyed drifters, with an assorted number of officers and jail clerks going about their business—Tara and Tim did something they hadn't done in years.

They held tight to each other and cried.

Fifteen

THE SWELLING ALONG JOHN'S SPINE STARTED TO RECEDE two days later.

His doctor explained that until the swelling went down, it was impossible to know if John's paralysis was permanent. So far, John was unaware of the possibility. Though he'd had visitors streaming in and out of his room around the clock since Saturday, he was mostly sedated. Too much awake time meant too much movement, and that could interfere with the respirator and trachea tube.

It was early Monday afternoon, and Nicole and Abby were alone in a quiet alcove at the back of the waiting room. John was napping, so they'd planned to catch some sleep themselves. Instead they sat together, exhausted but wide awake, staring out the hospital window at the changing leaves in the trees that lined the parking lot.

They hadn't been there ten minutes when Dr. Robert Furin appeared. Abby and Nicole sat up straighter. Abby's heart soared within her. The doctor's smile could only mean one thing. John had moved his feet!

She felt the corners of her mouth lift some, despite the exhaustion that hung on her like double gravity. "He's got movement in his legs?"

"Uh . . ." The doctor's expression shifted. "No, Mrs. Reynolds. We're still waiting to determine that. Could be sometime in the next hour." He tapped the side of his pen against his pant leg. "I do have good news, though."

Beside her, Abby felt Nicole's body react to the letdown. She must have been thinking the same thing about John's legs. "Okay. We could use some."

"It looks like the trachea wasn't severed like we thought originally. We were able to get a better picture this morning, and it seems to be intact. That happens sometimes when a person receives a severe blow to the throat." The doctor paused. "The good news is we can take him off the respirator. In fact, they're doing that right now. So the next time you see him he should be able to talk." He shook his head. "It's a miracle really. Anyone hit by a car traveling that fast shouldn't be alive."

Abby was glad for the good news. It wasn't what she'd been hoping to hear, but the doctor was right. God had delivered John from what otherwise might have been certain death. They had much to be thankful for.

"When will we know about his legs?"

"We're taking him in for more X rays before the sedatives wear off." The doctor gave a single shake of his head. "I'd say we should know something within the hour."

Within the hour.

News that would alter their lives one way or the other would come like every other piece of information that had shattered their existence these past few days. By a single sentence, delivered as a matter of fact.

"Thank you, doctor." Abby smiled, but the action felt odd. "We'll be here. Please let us know as soon as you have any information."

Nicole was quiet until the doctor left. "Did you bring the article?"

"Yes. I'm not sure when I'll show him, but at some point he'll want to know."

Matt had brought the newspaper yesterday morning and showed them the story. It had a photograph of John's truck, but not a bit of it was recognizable. Abby had covered her mouth with her hands when she saw it.

The doctor was right. Truly, it was a miracle John was alive.

The article said two teenagers had been arrested for street racing, including one who hit John's car as he pulled out of the high-school parking lot. That information hadn't come as a shock to Abby. She'd heard from the beginning that John had been the victim of an illegal street race. It was the names of the teenagers that took her breath away.

Jake Daniels and Casey Parker.

John's quarterbacks. Good kids who had made a series of poor choices and would pay the price for the rest of their lives. According to the article, Casey was being charged with reckless driving, participation in an illegal street race, and being an accomplice to vehicular assault. He had been released on his own recognizance and was expected to plead guilty to several of the charges at a hearing sometime in the next month.

Jake's charges were far more serious.

First, the district attorney's office was determined to try him as an adult. If they succeeded—and chances were strong that they would—Jake would most likely wind up with a jury trial facing a handful of charges, including felony assault with a deadly weapon. The combination of crimes could send Jake to the state penitentiary for as many as ten years.

"This town is tired of illegal street races," the district attorney was quoted as saying. "If the people choose to make an example out of this young man, he could receive the maximum sentence."

Another quote came from Jake's mother, Tara, who apparently was holding vigil for her son at the county jail. "Jake is horrified at what's happened. He's ready to accept any punishment given him." The article went on to say that Mrs. Daniels hoped the district attorney's office would be lenient with her son since he had no prior record.

Abby didn't know what to think about that. If the driver of the speeding car had been a different teenager, one she didn't know, Abby could've ridden the district attorney's bandwagon, hoping for the toughest penalty ever.

But . . . Jake Daniels?

The kid had eaten dinner at their house a dozen times, swam in their lake, and jumped off their pier. How could she hope for a boy like Jake to spend the next decade of his life in prison? Abby couldn't picture him spending ten days there, let alone ten years.

She glanced at Nicole. "Have you thought about Jake's mother? How awful she must feel?"

"She wants leniency for her son." Nicole crossed her arms. "That's the only part that stands out in my mind."

The bitterness in Nicole's voice broke Abby's heart. Nicole was never bitter, never jaded. All her life Nicole had been the first one to pray about a situation, the one who always had a bit of wisdom or Scripture or hope for a person in need.

Bitterness did not become her.

"Jake's a nice boy, Nic."

Her daughter said nothing, and Abby let it go. She couldn't imagine how awful the ordeal had to be from Jake's mother's perspective. How strange it was that just a few weeks ago, Abby and Tara Daniels had been talking about the very car that had nearly killed John.

"What was Tim thinking, giving Jake a car like that?" Tara had said. "Do you know what that thing *cost?* Nearly forty thousand dollars. That's outrageous! He could have bought him four years of college for that. And all it does is tempt a kid like Jake to do something wrong."

Prophetic words, indeed. Jake, who had only recently made the decision to spend less time with the likes of Casey Parker . . . who had stopped teasing the Nathan Pikes at Marion High and started talking more frequently with John about his future. Jake, who might have earned a college scholarship in football . . . had made a decision that had altered all their lives. Forever.

Rather than be there to love and support Tara in her most dire hour, Abby was living a nightmare of her own, and reading the details of the story from the newspaper, just like everyone else in Marion.

Beneath a smaller headline at the back of the paper was a brief article about the bomb threat at Marion High. It mentioned that a student had been questioned after the football game and released to his parents.

Abby clipped the article about the accident, folded it, and stuck it in her purse. One day soon, John would want to see it. So far, they'd had no discussions about the accident because John couldn't talk. Now that the tubes were coming out of his throat, he would have questions.

Abby prayed he would survive her answers.

Nicole turned to her, her body tense. "Can I talk to you about something? Not about the accident, but something else?"

"Sure." Abby reached over and took Nicole's hand. "What's on your mind?"

There were delicate lines on Nicole's forehead. Abby could feel her daughter's tension as strongly as if it were her own. "It's about the baby."

"Everything's okay, right?"

Nicole nodded. "It's just . . . well, I wanted to tell you I was pregnant a few weeks ago, but I couldn't." She hesitated and her eyes lifted to Abby's. "I wasn't happy about it at first."

Poor Nicole. As if she didn't have enough to worry about with John's condition, she had her own to consider as well. "That's very normal, sweetheart." Abby shifted so she faced Nicole. "Especially when you weren't planning on having babies for another few years."

"Four years."

"Right." Abby waited, giving her daughter time to voice her thoughts.

"I love children; it isn't that." Nicole's face mirrored the struggle going on within her. "It's just . . . I didn't want them to come between me and Matt." She stopped. "The way I came between you and Dad."

Abby sat back a little. What in the world was Nicole talking about? "Honey, you never came between your dad and me."

Nicole blew at a wisp of her bangs and leaned back against the vinyl hospital sofa. "Yes, I did. You might not see it that way, but it's true. That's why . . . why your marriage hasn't always been what it could be."

"Nic, that's not—" Abby couldn't put her thoughts into words. Obviously her daughter was more aware of what had almost happened last year than Abby gave her credit for. But what was Nicole thinking? Their struggles had never had anything to do with the children.

"Mom, I know it sounds crazy, but it's been stuck in my head since Matt and I got married. I've always wanted to believe you and Dad had the best relationship in the world. But last year there were lots of times I knew that wasn't true. Sure, I say you look like newlyweds, but that's only because it's what I *want* to believe." She spread her fingers across her chest. "Deep inside I know you guys aren't always happy. And I think it must be because you never had those years alone together. Without kids."

A small laugh slipped from Abby's throat, and she covered her mouth. Nicole was perceptive, but her reasoning was completely wrong. So wrong it was almost funny.

"Mom—" Nicole lowered her brow—"how can you laugh?"

"Honey, I'm not laughing at you. It's just . . . that wasn't the problem with your dad and me. Not at all."

Nicole was quiet for a moment. "Ever since I found out I was pregnant, I've been scared to death. Deep inside. Because there hasn't been enough time for Matt and me to bond, to build the kind of marriage that will last."

"Oh, Nic." Abby slipped her arms around Nicole's neck and hugged her. "Having children will only strengthen what you and Matt share. It did for your dad and me."

Nicole drew back and her eyes met Abby's. "Then what happened? I know you and Dad have struggled. You try to hide it, but sometimes it's obvious."

"Have you noticed any problems lately? Say, since your wedding?"

"Since my wedding?" Nicole worked free of Abby's embrace and stared out the full-length window. "I guess not." She spun around. "How come?"

Abby stood and joined Nicole near the window. What exactly should she tell this precious daughter? How much should she say? "Because having you nine months into our marriage was never the cause of our problems."

"What was?"

"In a nutshell, we forgot to dance."

Nicole squinted. "Meaning what?"

A tired laugh slipped from Abby's throat. "Meaning ever since your dad and I moved to the house we live in, we would go out back and dance on the pier. Not real dancing. Just a sort of swaying back and forth, listening to the sounds around us and remembering what was important."

"Really?"

"Mmmhm." Abby felt a lump in her throat. Had they shared their last dance? Was John really lying in a hospital room down the hall paralyzed? She banished the thoughts and found her voice again. "We . . . we would talk about you and your brothers, about the good and bad times with your dad's job as coach, about the victories and tragedies life dealt us over the years."

"Did you talk about Haley Ann?"

"Always." The lightness was gone from Abby's voice. "But about three years ago we stopped meeting out there, stopped taking time to talk about life and our place together in it."

"Was that when Dad started being friends with Ms. Denton?"

Abby nodded. "He wasn't the only one making mistakes, though. I spent more time talking with an editor friend of mine than with your dad. That didn't help. Pretty soon we felt like strangers."

"I didn't know it was that bad."

"It was worse." Abby paused. If she told Nicole the whole story now, she might forever be jaded toward their marriage. But if she didn't, Nicole might not grow.

"You never considered . . ." Nicole's voice faded.

"We did. Last year in fact." Abby stared out the window. A pair of birds were sitting in the tree outside. "Remember the day you and Matt announced your engagement?"

"Yes." Nicole let her head fall back a bit. "We were supposed to have a family meeting, but Matt showed up and we surprised everyone."

"Us, most of all." Abby turned and met Nicole's eyes. "We had picked that day to tell you kids it was over. We were going to get a divorce."

"Mom!" Nicole backed up a step, her eyes wide. "No way!"

"It's true. When you made your announcement, your dad and I met in the kitchen and decided we had to wait. We couldn't go through with it until you were back from your honeymoon."

Nicole grabbed her head and took slow steps back to the sofa. "It all makes sense now."

"What?" Abby turned and leaned against the window.

"Every time I prayed, no matter what I was praying about, you and Dad were on my heart. I told Matt about it. He thought it was probably because you guys were under a lot of stress what with us getting married." Nicole uttered a sad chuckle. "I always thought it was something bigger. But not this big."

"We were at the end of our rope, Nicole. All I can tell you is we felt your prayers."

"So you mean, when Grandpa was dying that day and we were all gathered around his hospital bed . . . you and Daddy were planning to divorce?"

Abby nodded.

"That's unbelievable. I had no idea." A sudden look of alarm filled Nicole's features. "Did Daddy have an affair?"

For months she had worked to keep this information from Nicole and the boys. Now . . . now she knew that hiding the truth had been wrong. *God . . . You want her to know, don't You?*

The truth will set you free . . .

Abby let the verse roll around in the basement of her heart. Of course! The truth wouldn't only set Abby free . . . it would set Nicole free, as well. After all, Nicole was a married woman. She might have to face something similar herself one day. It was crucial that she see the truth here—that any marriage could be saved so long as both people were willing to hear God's voice above their own.

She drew a calming breath. *God, help me say this so she can understand* . . . "He came close. We both did."

Nicole stood and paced to the window and back. "I don't believe it." She stopped in midstep, her voice angry. "What happened? How come you never made the announcement?"

"The night of your wedding . . . Dad had his things packed. He was going to move in with a friend after you and Matt took off for your honeymoon."

"Ms. *Denton?*" Nicole's cheeks were pale, the dark circles under her eyes more pronounced.

"No, nothing like that. By then Ms. Denton had moved away. Her friendship with your father was over."

"Then who?"

"A divorced man, a teacher from the school."

"That's terrible." Nicole sank back onto the sofa once more. "So what happened?"

"Sean and Kade went to friends' houses, and after you left, your dad did, too. Or he started to. He got halfway down the road before he turned around and came back. God wouldn't let him leave."

"What about you?" There were doubts in Nicole's tone, but she looked less panicked than before.

"I was angry and upset. Devastated, really. But too stubborn to stop him from leaving. I went upstairs and slipped on one of his sweatshirts. When I did, I found his journal." Abby could still picture the moment as clearly as if it had just happened. "I didn't even know he kept a journal until then."

"What'd it say?"

"It talked about how sorry your father was for letting our marriage grow cold, how wrong he'd been to befriend Ms. Denton. How badly he wished things would work with me, but how certain he was that I'd never be willing to try again."

"Was that when Dad came home?"

"No." Abby's vision grew dim and tears filled her eyes as she remembered. "I finished reading and went out to the pier, past the tables still set up from your wedding, past the empty glasses and crepe paper and streamers, out to the place where your dad and I had always connected." Abby glanced at Nicole. "A few minutes later, your dad came up behind me. He told me something I'll never forget."

"What?" There was the hint of hope in Nicole's eyes, and Abby knew she'd done the right thing. Her daughter needed to hear this story. Especially in light of all the years she and Matt had ahead of them.

Abby closed her eyes for a moment. "He said he needed to tell me about the eagle."

"The eagle?"

"When the eagle mates, he mates for life." Abby gazed into the distance again, seeing John the way he'd looked that night as he walked onto the pier, hands outstretched. "At some point in the eagles' courtship, the female eagle will fly to the highest heights and then free-fall to the ground. The male eagle will then swoop down and lock talons with her. In doing so, he conveys a simple message: he is committed to her."

"I didn't know that." Nicole's features were softer than they'd been all afternoon. "That's beautiful."

"Your father took my hands and told me he didn't ever want to let go again. Never. That if it killed him, he wanted to love me like an eagle loves his mate. Like the Lord wanted him to love me. Holding on until death made him finally let go."

Abby blinked and the memory faded. She looked at Nicole and saw tears in her eyes.

"So . . . that was a turning point for you?"

"Yes, very much so." Abby stroked Nicole's hand. "We're happier than ever, now. It was a miracle really. So, you see, honey. Don't be afraid about the baby. God will use this—and every other season of your life, even the hard ones—to bring you closer to each other, and to Him."

Nicole gave a sudden gasp. "Wait a minute. I just remembered something." She stared at Abby. "That night, when Matt and I were checking into our hotel, I had the strangest sense that God had talked to me."

"About what?"

"About you and Dad. Like He reached down, tapped me on the shoulder, and told me my prayers for you had been heard." Nicole thought for a moment. "I even told Matt about it."

A chill ran down Abby's spine. *It really was You, Lord . . . thank You . . . thank You.* "God's so much bigger than we give Him credit for. We see something like this accident and we think, 'If only God would make it all better.' But nothing gets by God, absolutely nothing. He has it all figured out, and one way or another, everything He does happens for a reason."

Someone was approaching them, and Abby turned. It was Dr. Furin. This time he wasn't smiling. His steps were slow and measured, and he looked at both Abby and Nicole before taking a seat across from them.

"Mrs. Reynolds, I'm afraid I don't have very good news."

Nicole slid closer to Abby and linked hands with her. *Calm, Abby . . . be calm. Remember the words you just spoke . . . God is in control.* She found her voice. "Did you . . . do the tests?"

"Yes." He frowned. "We did several. They all point to the same thing. The accident injured your husband's spinal cord in a very delicate area. The result is something we've been concerned about since the beginning." He paused. "Mrs. Reynolds, your husband is paralyzed from his waist down. I'm sorry."

As bad as the accident had been, as close as they'd come to losing John, Abby never for a minute believed this would be the final diagnosis. Not for John Reynolds. The doctor was saying something about how if the injury had been a centimeter lower, he might have walked away from it . . . but if it'd been a centimeter higher, it could have killed him. And something about rehabilitation and special wheelchairs.

Nicole was crying softly, nodding as though everything the doctor said made perfect sense.

But Abby barely heard any of it. No longer was she sitting in a stuffy hospital waiting room getting the worst news of her life.

She was fourteen again, stretched out on a blanket near the lakeside bonfire, with a young John beside her, tossing a football in the air, grinning at her, his blue eyes shimmering with the reflection of the moon on the water. *You got a boyfriend, little Miss Abby Chapman?* Then she was seventeen, seeing him for the first time in three years, just before he played in the Michigan football game. *You're beautiful, Abby. Do you know that? Go out with me tonight, after the game . . .* And suddenly he was on the field, reeling back and throwing a football like he was born to do so, running with it, bigger than life, the wind beneath his feet. The image disappeared and she was in a church, John gazing at her with all the love he could muster. *I, John Reynolds, take you, Abby Chapman, to be my lawfully wedded wife.* Then they were dancing, but the image changed and they were in the Marion High gymnasium and Paula was telling them to keep the beat.

"Mrs. Reynolds?"

Abby blinked, and the memories vanished. "Yes?"

"I said you two could go see him now. He knows about the diagnosis. He asked, and, well . . . we thought he should know."

"I don't want to go." Nicole's expression was etched with fear. She shook her head at Abby. "I can't see him. Not yet."

"Now?" Abby looked at Dr. Furin. She felt like she was underwater, like everything around her was happening in slow motion at a level she couldn't quite understand.

"Yes. He asked for you." The doctor stood. "I'm sorry, Mrs. Reynolds."

Abby nodded, but her mind was numb, desperate for the chance to go back in time even a few minutes. Back to the place where there was still a chance John might walk again. They'd lost so many years . . . was this really God's plan? That just when everything was better than ever, John would be paralyzed?

Abby's heart raced. How could she face him? What would she say? John had spent his life using his legs. Even now, in his midforties, he still ran as easily as he breathed. In the classroom he was the most active teacher on campus, spinning off impromptu comedy routines or outjumping the basketball players in his class to see whether they'd have a pop quiz that day.

Once they'd gone to Chicago to see Riverdance. The next day John entered every class by Irish-dancing his way to the front of the room. No wonder the kids loved him. Deep in his heart, he was still one of them. And that was especially true now that he and Abby were happy again. It was as though a decade had slipped off the aging process for both of them.

And now . . . *this?*

What would they do now that John would never walk again? Maybe never make love to her again? Her heart sank like an anchor. She hadn't thought about that before, the idea of never knowing John in that way again. It was unimaginable that their physical love might be a thing of the past. What in the world was she supposed to say about that?

Abby had no answers for herself. She was too terrified to cry, too shocked to feel anything except the certainty of one thing: John needed her. And because of that, she would go to him. Even if she had nothing to offer, no comforting words or bits of hope.

She would hug him and love him and cling to him, talon to talon, even if life would never, ever be the same again.

She entered his room without a sound, but his eyes found hers immediately. She made her way across the room and sat on the edge of the bed.

"John . . ." Only then did the tears come. "I'm so sorry."

There was a fresh bandage on his neck, where they'd pulled the tube. His body looked older somehow, smaller. Like he'd lost three inches off his six-foot-four frame. Then, for the first time since the accident, he looked deep in her eyes and spoke.

His voice was the only thing that hadn't changed.

"Tell me what happened, Abby." The words were painfully slow. His throat must have been raw after having tubes there for the past few days. "Tell me. I have to know."

And for the next half hour, she did.

He said nothing while she shared the article and carefully told him every detail she was aware of. When she was finished, when the facts were laid out for him to accept or rage against, he spoke. What he said told Abby that the John she loved was still in there, that an accident could take his legs, but not his heart and soul. "How . . ." He hesitated, his eyes searching hers. "How in the world is Jake?"

Sixteen

CHUCK PARKER COULDN'T SLEEP.

Sure, his son was facing hundreds of dollars in fines and who knew how many hours of community service for being involved in that stupid accident. And yeah, the boy had blown any chance of an athletic scholarship or even acceptance to one of the better schools.

But that wasn't Chuck's trouble. Coach Reynolds was.

The man was going to live, and Chuck supposed that was good—but there was one detail about the accident that troubled him. What was Coach doing at the school after midnight?

That detail—combined with others that had come out in yesterday's paper—kept him up most of the night. And that never happened to Chuck. Never.

In fact before the accident he'd slept even better, mostly because he was so tired. The smear campaign he'd orchestrated against Coach since the season began was a tough job.

For the past few months Chuck had worked the stands like a car salesman, sidling up to parents and subtly swaying them to his way of thinking: Coach Reynolds needed to go.

"He's a nice guy," Chuck would say to whomever he was seated beside. "Don't get me wrong. But we have the most talented boys in all the state right here at Marion High. Our kids need a visionary, a coach with fire in his blood. Someone who understands today's kids. Besides, Coach Reynolds needs a break. He should concentrate on his younger son, spend more time with his family."

Chuck smiled often in the course of such a statement, and before long—it almost never failed—the parent would be nodding and agreeing and making promises to attend one of Chuck's meetings.

That was where the gloves came off. In those meetings, letters were formulated, plans were made. Coach Reynolds would be fired. He had to be. It was the parents' prerogative. They'd held three such meetings so far, and after each, Chuck Parker made sure the athletic director got a report.

"Herman, the parents want him out. The Eagles need a new direction."

Most of the time Lutz would sit back in his office chair, mouth shut. Then, just to seal his plan, Chuck would remind Lutz of the drinking and street racing the players had done during summer training . . .

"Is that the kind of coach you want at Marion High?" Chuck would raise his voice just enough to make Herman nervous. "Someone who looks the other way while the kids break every rule in the book? We need a coach with courage, a man who'll demand the best from our boys without compromising moral character."

The plan was working, too.

Lutz had assured him the last time that he was taking notes, making arrangements. Finally the man admitted the one thing Parker had longed to hear: "I'm not planning on renewing his contract, if that helps."

Chuck could hardly believe it. Lutz was totally and utterly spineless. But that was the beauty of the situation. Herman Lutz was putty in his hands, and Coach Reynolds was all but fired. A few more games and it would be a done deal.

Of course, Chuck didn't really believe Coach Reynolds knew about the drinking and street racing. Shoot, he wasn't even a bad coach.

But Reynolds had made a fatal mistake: he'd chosen to sit Chuck's son.

Casey was one of the best quarterbacks in the state. Okay, so he had a few Fs on his report card. And yes, he got in trouble sometimes for mouthing off to a teacher. So what? Casey was an intense kid, as driven as they came, one of those superathletes who—and Chuck was convinced of this—would one day lead an NCAA Division I team to a national championship.

Or he *would* have, if Coach Reynolds hadn't been so particular about his players' attitudes. Jake Daniels wasn't a better QB. Just a better kiss-up. And now it was too late for Casey. His entire high school and college football careers had been ruined by Coach Reynolds's ridiculously high standards.

But it wasn't too late for Billy.

Chuck's younger son had an even better arm than Casey. The kid was a freshman this year, tearing up on the ninth-grade team. A full-ride college scholarship was a given for a kid like Billy, and that would only be the beginning. Chuck believed fully that one day Billy would wear a Super Bowl ring. He could picture him, accepting the award of NFL Most Valuable Player.

Too bad Billy's attitude was worse than Casey's.

Not a problem to Chuck. But to a man like Coach Reynolds? If Chuck didn't do something, Billy would wind up riding the bench just like his older brother. And Chuck simply could not have that.

For that reason, the campaign against Coach Reynolds would've come regardless of the Eagles' wins and losses that year. The fact that they'd lost far more games than they should have only made Chuck's job that much easier. Especially with Herman Lutz in charge. What the man knew about scheduling and practices and sports in general could fit in an ashtray. But one thing Lutz knew: what it took to keep his job. And since the man was already making a poor showing, he absolutely insisted that his coaches win.

All of it—the evenings spent working player parents, the after-hours meetings, the discussions with Herman Lutz—was going exactly as Parker planned, and not once had he had trouble sleeping.

Until the accident.

There had been two articles in the paper since then. The first was factual. It told the story of the street racing and the seriousness of Coach Reynolds's injuries. There had been a chance the man would die. Of course, like everyone else, Chuck Parker prayed Coach would live. And like everyone else, he was relieved when Monday's article said his condition had improved.

But that wasn't all Monday's article had said.

The reporter had gone into the hospital waiting room and interviewed as many kids as he could find. It was *their* story—along with Coach being at school so late that night—that Chuck found most troubling.

According to the article, the kids at Marion High loved Coach Reynolds as much as they loved football. One player said that football and Coach were one and the same, and would forever be for anyone who called himself an Eagle.

Their quotes told the story.

"Some Saturday mornings he shows up with bags of breakfast burgers, enough for the whole team."

"Coach cares about more than football. He's someone you can talk to and he'll always have the right advice. A lot of us think of him like a second dad."

"Every season we go to Coach's house for his famous Backyard Barbecue the night before one of the home games. He treats every one of us like sons. The thing with Coach is he loves us."

The kids' statements felt like they were written in permanent ink across the stone tablet of Chuck Parker's heart. If Coach Reynolds was so wonderful, why hadn't Casey done better?

Coach's answer never changed on the matter: Casey had an attitude problem. Chuck had always dismissed that. His son was just intense and competitive.

But ever since the accident, Chuck wondered if maybe . . . just maybe . . . Coach was right.

After all, what was Casey doing racing in the first place? The way the story went, Casey and Jake exchanged words at a party, and Casey challenged Jake to take it to the streets. The boy had been honest with the police, at least. It was his idea to race, his idea to beat Jake Daniels in at least one thing. And if it meant breaking the law, then so be it.

Talk about a bad attitude! A defiant, privileged attitude that couldn't possibly help Casey succeed in life.

All of which left Chuck wondering if maybe he'd been wrong about Coach Reynolds. There was only one reason Chuck could think of to be at the high school after midnight on game day. Reynolds must have been catching up on whatever it was teachers do when they're not coaching. Writing assignments . . . planning class time . . . correcting papers. Something like that.

It was something Chuck hadn't ever considered. Coach Reynolds was just a hardworking, honest, devoted guy . . . and Chuck had spent all season trying to undo him. He knew there wasn't one stitch of truth in what he'd wanted people to believe about Reynolds. The truth was there in the article.

No wonder he couldn't sleep.

It was Tuesday morning, and after another sleepless night, Chuck was so tired he felt drugged. He stumbled out of bed, splashed cold water on his face, and found his way down the stairs to the front porch. The newspaper was his window to the world these days. Casey was back at school, but he'd been kicked off the football team and couldn't drive. He was useless at providing Chuck with information about the case.

But the paper would have something. The story had played on the front page each of the past two days. There was bound to be another update that morning. He picked up the paper, shuffled into the kitchen, and spread it out on the counter.

The headline at the top of the page caught him cold, stopped his heart for more than a beat, and turned his stomach: *Marion High Coach Paralyzed in Street Racing Accident.*

There had to be a mistake. Reynolds was in great physical shape. The guy was tall and built, probably as strong now as he'd been in his college heyday. A man like that couldn't be paralyzed.

Chuck read the article.

Doctors announced Monday that Marion High Coach John Reynolds sustained a permanent spinal injury when his car was hit by a teenage street racer early Saturday morning. The injury has left Reynolds paralyzed from the waist down.

Chuck pushed the newspaper away. His stomach lurched and he bolted for the bathroom. There he fell to his knees and retched. Again and again his insides convulsed until he felt like his gut was turning inside out.

He fell back with a groan. What kind of creep was he, leading a charge against a man like John Reynolds? Coach had only done what was best for the kids at every turn. Even Chuck's own son.

His stomach heaved again.

He leaned his head on his arm, drawing in deep breaths. Coach Reynolds wasn't the problem. Casey was. Casey and Billy . . . and most of all himself. He had used his charm and influence among the parents to convince them of lies, to sway their thinking and basically ruin a man who had given sixteen years of service to the Marion High football team. A man who had built the program with nothing but hard work and determination.

The spasms in his belly finally stopped, and Chuck Parker struggled to his feet. As he stooped to wash his hands and face, he was certain a mountain had sprung up between his shoulder blades.

How much of what had happened to Coach Reynolds was his fault?

If he'd listened to Coach, if he'd done something about his son's attitude a few years ago, maybe Casey wouldn't have challenged Jake to a race. Maybe today they would merely be another high school about to enter the district play-offs, instead of front-page news, with a coach who could no longer walk.

It was all his fault.

Not only that, but he'd been responsible for making Coach Reynolds's last season with the Eagles nothing but a nightmare.

Chuck dried his hands and turned away from the mirror. He couldn't look, couldn't face the man he'd become. But there was one thing he could do, something he should have done at the beginning of the season. And in that instant he made the decision to do it.

He would call in sick and spend the day making sure it happened. If he hurried, it might not be too late.

Jake Daniels was arraigned before a judge in juvenile court. He still wore the jailhouse blues, and because the hearing required a public appearance, the escorting officer made certain he was cuffed.

The moment Jake stepped into the courtroom he knew something was wrong. His mother and father sat almost together on one of the benches, but as he entered, they barely looked at him. His dad had paid for an attorney, some slick dresser named A. W. Bennington, who had an office downtown and a reputation for getting bad guys off easy. The kind of man Jake wouldn't have associated with—until now.

"The judge will read your charges and ask you how you plead," A. W. had explained when the two of them met on Monday afternoon. "You'll plead not guilty. I'll do the rest."

"Will they keep me here?" Jake didn't know why he asked. He didn't really care. Where would he go if they let him out? Not to the hospital with his other teammates, who'd been holding vigil there. Not to Coach Reynolds's room. Hardly. And not back to school. He'd be a freak, someone the other kids whispered about and mocked and downright hated. Coach Reynolds was easily the favorite teacher on campus. Loyalty for him might have been shaky among the Eagle parents, but it was stronger than cement among the kids on campus.

Besides, Jake belonged in jail.

But A. W. had shaken his head. "You'll be out as soon as the hearing's over."

His mother and father had taken turns visiting him after the attorney left yesterday. They knew he'd be coming home, so why did they both look like they'd been handed a death sentence?

Jake was led into the courtroom and took a seat at a long table. A. W. was already seated, looking far more dressed up than any of the other adults. No telling what his father had paid the man. Anything to keep Jake from spending a decade in prison.

A. W. frowned at Jake and leaned close. "The coach is paralyzed. Your parents said it was in the paper this morning. Could make things a little tricky."

Jake spun around and found his mother. She was watching him, and as their eyes met, he saw she was crying. Slowly, firmly, she nodded her head and mouthed something Jake couldn't understand. He shifted his glance to his dad, who only bit his lip and looked down.

The muscles in Jake's neck unwound, and his eyes found their way back to the front of the courtroom. He wanted to die, to simply hold his breath and let God take him away from the horror of living.

Coach Reynolds was paralyzed. No, that wasn't it at all. He'd paralyzed Coach. That was the truth of the matter. He'd seen the pickup truck turn in front of him that night, hadn't he? He could have jerked his steering wheel and flipped his car. Sure, he might have died, but Coach would be fine. He'd been a selfish jerk, driving the car smack into the pickup. Now a man's life was ruined. A man Jake looked up to and respected, a man who was a hero to a thousand kids at least.

Coach would never again take a lap with them or run plays with them or lead them in drills. The guys would never see Coach—his equipment bag slung over his shoulder, baseball cap low over his eyes—walking across the field toward practice. Never again.

And it was all Jake's fault. He dropped his head in his hands. What had A. W. said a moment ago? It could make things a little tricky? He gritted his teeth. Was that all that mattered to these people? Didn't they understand what he'd done? What he'd stolen from Coach Reynolds?

"All rise."

The judge was a formidable looking woman with white hair and a pinched face. *Good. Maybe she'll lock me up forever.*

A. W. was on his feet. He motioned for Jake to do the same.

"Jake Daniels, you are being charged with a series of crimes that include the following." She read the list, but there was nothing new. Same things the officer had told him and his mother, the things A. W. had gone over with him yesterday. "At this point we are treating you as a minor. How do you plead to the charges?"

Jake said the first words that came to mind. "Guilty, ma'am."

"Just a minute, Your Honor." A. W. took a giant step in front of Jake and held up his hand. "May I have a word with my client in private?"

The judge's forehead lifted. "Hurry. This is a busy place, counselor. Your client should have been prepped before coming here this morning."

"Yes, Your Honor." A. W. sat and took a firm hold of Jake's blue cotton sleeve, pulling him down as well. He moved his lip almost on top of Jake's ear and hissed at him, "What're you doing?"

Jake wasn't as careful about being quiet. "She asked me how I wanted to plead."

"Keep your voice down." A. W. glared at him. He was so close it looked like he had one giant eyeball. "You're supposed to tell her, 'Not guilty.' Remember? Like we talked about."

"But I *am* guilty. I did it. I hit Coach's car, so why lie about it?"

Jake was pretty sure A.W. was going to have a nervous breakdown. Sweat was beading on his upper lip. "We aren't talking about whether you hit the guy. We're talking about what sort of crime you should be charged with." A. W.'s hands were shaking. "What we're saying today is that we don't think you're guilty of felony assault with a deadly weapon."

The words swam around in Jake's head in no certain order. It felt like everyone in the room was staring at him, including his parents. Whatever the hearing meant, he had no choice but to cooperate. He sat back in his chair, his arms crossed. "Whatever."

A. W. stared at him a bit longer as though he wasn't quite sure Jake was ready to speak the right answer. Then he gave a slow turn to the judge. "We're ready now, Your Honor."

"Very well." The judge looked bored. "Will the defendant please rise?" She paused for effect. "Again."

Jake stood.

"How do you plead to the charges leveled against you?"

He cast a quick glance at A. W. The man was staring at his notepad, refusing to watch. Jake looked at the judge once more. "Not guilty, Your Honor."

"Very well. You may be seated."

Immediately the other guy, the district attorney, rose and approached the judge. "The state would like to request that Jake Daniels be tried as an adult, Your Honor. He is seventeen years old, mere months away from the legal age of adulthood." For a brief moment, the state's lawyer hung his head. When he looked at the judge again, he almost looked like he was going to cry. "We learned this morning that the victim in this case was paralyzed in the accident. His condition is permanent, Your Honor. Therefore, because of the severity of the crime, we are convinced Mr. Daniels should be tried as an adult."

Jake wasn't sure what the difference was, exactly, only that A. W. didn't want him tried as an adult. Jake didn't care. The other lawyer was right. He wasn't a little kid. He'd known exactly how dangerous street racing was, but he'd done it anyway.

The judge said something about making a decision in two weeks as to whether Jake would be tried as an adult or not. Then it was A. W.'s turn again. He asked that Jake be released to his parents because he was really, basically, a good kid. No prior record, no alcohol in his system the night of the accident. Just a stupid mistake with tragic consequences.

"I want his license revoked immediately." The judge made a notation on a pad of paper. "Also, I want him enrolled in a continuation school so that he isn't attending classes with the other young man involved in the case. With those stipulations, your motion is granted, counselor. Mr. Daniels may be released to his parents pending the outcome of his trial."

The hearing was over as quickly as it had begun, and a uniformed man approached Jake. "Turn around."

He did as he was told, and the man removed the handcuffs from Jake's wrist.

A. W. smiled at Jake. "You're going home, Jake. You're a free man."

But it was a lie.

Coach Reynolds was paralyzed.

And as long as Jake lived, he would never, ever be free again.

Seventeen

IT WAS LIKE DRAGGING AROUND A HUNDRED POUNDS of dead weight.

Four weeks had passed since the accident, and doctors had moved John to a room in the rehabilitation unit. They had certain goals, certain benchmarks for him to attain: transferring himself from a bed to a wheelchair, and from a wheelchair to the toilet and back again. They wanted him to dress himself and know how to look for sores on his legs and torso.

Today's lesson was about knowing when an open wound needed medical treatment.

"Sores represent an insidious threat, Mr. Reynolds." The physical therapist was slender, in his late thirties. Clearly he was passionate about his job, intent on bringing independence to those like John, who had recently joined the ranks of paraplegia.

John hoped the man would forgive him for being less than enthusiastic.

"Mr. Reynolds, are you listening?"

"Hmmm?" John hadn't realized how many people called him *Coach* until he'd been admitted to the hospital. Even after four weeks it didn't sound right . . . *Mr.* Reynolds, not *Coach* Reynolds. It was as though the doctors and nurses and rehab technicians were talking about someone altogether different than the man he'd once been.

But then that was exactly right, wasn't it? He wasn't the man he'd been before the accident. "I'm sorry. Say it again."

"Sores . . . see, they develop on areas where your body gets rubbed on a regular basis. The problem is, with paralysis you can't feel the rubbing. The situation becomes especially dangerous after you've been in a state of paralysis for several months or more. That's when your body begins to show signs of muscle atrophy. Without the muscle barrier, bones have been known to rub clear through the skin. So you can see the problem, Mr. Reynolds."

John wanted to knock the man over with his wheelchair. Better yet he wanted to yell, "Cut!" at the top of his lungs and watch a dozen stagehands rush onto the scene to tell him he could get up now. The filming was over.

Of course, he could actually do neither of those things. If he wanted to get home before Christmas, he could only sit here and listen to some stranger tell him how his legs were going to waste away and that sores were going to appear on his body in the process. John settled against the back of the wheelchair, his eyes on the man's mouth. It was still moving, still explaining the reality of John's situation in meticulously vivid detail.

But John was no longer listening. His body might be a prisoner, but his mind could go wherever it wanted. And right now he wanted to think back over the past month.

From the moment he'd come to that Saturday after the accident, John had known he was in trouble. He had no memory of the accident, nothing at all. One moment he was pulling out of the Marion High parking lot, the next he was waking up in a hospital bed, feeling like he was choking to death. And something else, something even worse.

At first he'd been too distracted to notice.

Abby was there, and Kade and Sean and Nicole and Matt. He'd known whatever was happening, it had to be serious if everyone was gathered around him. He'd reached for his throat, and then the nurse had stepped in and warned him to stay still. The stiller the better.

Calm me down, God. And in seconds he felt his body relax. The tubes weren't choking him; it only felt that way. The more he relaxed, the easier it was to breathe.

It was only then, when he was able to draw a breath more normally, that John realized it. Something was terribly wrong. His body ached from lying in one place and he wanted to stretch. His brain sent down a series of instantaneous commands. Toes—curl back . . . feet—point forward . . . ankles—roll around . . . legs—shift positions.

But his body wouldn't obey a single one.

Alarm shattered John's peacefulness, but he refused to let it show. His family was watching, looking to him for strength. Besides, at first he hoped maybe he was wrong. Maybe it was part of the medication they'd given him, something to make him tired and lethargic. A painkiller maybe. Perhaps his legs had been hurt in the accident and they were still under some kind of deep anesthesia.

By Sunday he still slept most of the time, but he was aware enough to know that none of those things should have taken away the feeling in his legs. That evening he began experimenting whenever he was awake. During the few minutes when no one was in the room, he'd slip his hand beneath the sheet and feel around. First his stomach, then his hips and thighs.

Above his bellybutton he could feel his hand quite normally. He could sense the coolness of his fingers and feel pain when he pinched himself. But below that, nothing. No sensation whatsoever. It felt like he was touching someone else, as though someone had taken his lower half and replaced it with that of a stranger.

Then he'd glance around the room, and if no one was coming, he would stare at a part of his body and order it to move. His pelvis or his legs. Even his toes.

It was always the same: nothing. No movement.

So when they pulled the tubes from his throat and performed a series of X rays and tests on his back, John knew what they were looking for. He could have saved them the time. Finally John asked what was going on, what had happened to him. When Dr. Furin entered the room, closed the door, and announced that he had bad news, John beat him to the punch.

"I'm paralyzed, aren't I?"

"Yes." The doctor looked pained. As though he wished he'd become a plumber or a lawyer or an accountant. Anything but a doctor forced to tell a healthy man like John Reynolds that he'd never walk again. "I'm afraid so. We were hoping once the swelling went down that . . ." The doctor struggled to find the right words. "We were hoping the paralysis might be temporary."

The moment John knew the truth, he had only one concern. How would Abby take the news? In those early hours, he'd refused to be devastated. He was up to the challenge, wasn't he? He would take to a wheelchair and do all the things he'd done before. And one day he'd learn to walk again, no matter what the doctors said. Not just walk, but run. Yes, he'd be running again in a few months or a few years. Whatever it took. He'd show the doctors how it could be done.

The only thing that mattered was whether Abby could stand the shock.

As soon as he saw her, he knew he needn't have worried. Her face was a direct reflection of her heart and the love she felt for him. A love that couldn't possibly be affected by something like paralysis. In her eyes was a strength that reflected his own. They would fight this thing, battle it. And one day, together, they would overcome it.

Then, when she'd told him about the accident, that he'd been hit by none other than Jake Daniels, his concerns shifted completely to the boy. Jake would be devastated by the news, distraught beyond his ability to carry on. For the next two weeks John survived by praying for Jake, begging God to bring good out of what had happened, asking Him to give Jake the courage to visit John. That way the boy could see for himself that John wasn't about to check out on life just because of a lack of feeling in his legs.

Hardly.

One of his visitors that first week had been Nathan Pike. The boy looked uncomfortable, dressed in his usual black garb. But something was different . . . It took John a few minutes to figure it out, but then it was clear. The defiance was gone.

"I heard what happened." Nathan scuffed his feet around, his hands stuffed in his pockets. "I had to come. Health class's no fun without you."

John chuckled. "Health's not much fun, anyway."

"Yeah." Nathan shrugged. "You know what I mean."

There was a silence, and Nathan looked uncomfortable.

"You okay, Nathan?"

"Actually . . . about what happened at the game . . . I was gonna call you up the next day, but then . . . well . . ." He stared at his feet. "You know. You got hurt."

"What'd you want to talk about?"

"The threat . . . whatever it was." He lifted his head, his eyes more earnest than John had ever seen them. "Mr. Reynolds, I didn't do it. I swear. I've done a lot of stupid things, but I didn't do that. I was at the library all day. Really."

"Okay." It went against all reason, but John believed him. "Whatever you say."

"You believe me, right?"

John made a fist and brought his knuckles up against Nathan's. "I believe you."

"You know something, Coach?"

"What?"

"You're the only one who does."

There were other visitors after that, dozens of students and players. All of them helped distract John from the gravity of his situation. But when John started rehabilitation, the reality came crashing in on him.

John had told Abby that after a few days of therapy, he was certain he would have movement in his toes again. At least that.

Instead, a therapist spent the better parts of two days teaching him how to slide from the bed to his wheelchair. Movement in his toes or anywhere else beneath his waist was as impossible as willing a body part on another person to move.

"How much rehabilitation before I'll be able to move my feet?" John asked Dr. Furin the question on the evening of the second day of therapy.

The doctor had been on his way out of the room and he stopped, frozen in his tracks. "Mr. Reynolds, paralysis is a permanent condition. Some people have made miraculous strides, depending on their situation. But at this point we don't expect you to have feeling in your legs ever again. No matter how much time we spend on rehab."

It was the first time since his accident that John had felt anger. "Then why bother?"

"Because—" Dr. Furin's voice was kind—"if we don't, you'll never get out of bed."

The answer infuriated John, and he told Abby as much that night. "They could at least give me a reason to hope."

Abby had been strong as steel, rarely crying—at least not in front of him. He knew her well enough to know she was crying somewhere, sometime. But he appreciated the fact that she kept her chin up around him.

She had worked her way onto the hospital bed and soothed her fingers over his weary forehead. "Since when do you find your hope in what doctors tell you, John Reynolds?"

His anger had faded. "I hadn't thought of that."

"Yep." A smile filled her face. "That's why you have me. To remind you of the truth."

"That my hope can only be found in God, is that it?"

"Exactly."

"Okay, then, Abby . . . you gotta do something for me."

"What's that?"

"Pray for a miracle." His eyes were wet, and he blinked twice to see her more clearly. "Don't ever stop praying."

In the days since then, the Marion Eagles finished their football season with a second-round play-off loss. John's assistant coaches had taken over since his accident, and a quarterback from the junior varsity squad was brought up to lead the team. Nearly all the players and coaches had been by, most of them making only a brief appearance to bring John a signed football or a card or a bouquet of balloons.

When the season ended, the visits tapered off and John put his energies entirely into rehabilitation.

Day by day, he learned the things his therapists asked of him. He could balance his torso with the strength of his arms and swing himself into a wheelchair. His efforts at getting on a toilet were trickier, but he could do so unassisted now. In fact, Dr. Furin had assured him that he was maybe one week away from going home.

"Definitely before Christmas." Dr. Furin had grinned at him the other day. "I'll bet that's the best news you've heard in a while."

It should have been, but somehow it wasn't. After a month in the hospital, a month of not coming a single centimeter closer to moving his feet or legs, John's usually fiery determination was cooling fast.

Christmas? From a wheelchair?

The past few days he still prayed for a miracle, but not with any real sense of it actually happening. He was no longer thinking about fighting his diagnosis or beating the odds or somehow gaining the ability to walk again.

Rather, he was thinking of all that he'd lost.

Last night was the first time Abby had noticed it. She gave him the update about Jake. The judge had delayed making a decision about whether to try the boy as an adult, and at the same time, the district attorney was refusing any sort of plea bargain. The hearing on how he would be tried was set to take place in ten days. But either way, it looked like Jake would have to stand trial.

When Abby was finished talking, she planted her hands on her hips. "John Reynolds, you're not even listening."

John blinked. "I'm listening. That's too bad. About Jake, I mean."

"Too bad?" Abby huffed. "When you first got hurt, you couldn't stand the thought of Jake going to jail. Now it's just, 'too bad'?"

"I'm sorry."

"Don't be sorry, John, be *mad.* Be furious. Be upset. But don't lie there with that monotone and say you're sorry. That's not the man I married."

John's voice remained the same. "You're right."

"What's that mean?"

"I'm not the man you married, Abby. I've lost the fight."

"You've *what?*" Abby seethed, pacing from one side of his hospital room to the other. "Don't tell me about losing the fight, John. The fight hasn't even begun! You can't ask me to pray for a miracle if you've already given up. I mean, come on . . ."

The conversation went on that way for an hour until finally Abby broke down and wept. She apologized for expecting so much and assured him he had the right to be discouraged. Before she left, she admitted he wasn't the only one. She was discouraged, too.

No wonder he couldn't concentrate on the therapist and bedsores. For entire hours of the day—even in the midst of rehabilitation—John could do nothing but remember. How the earth felt beneath his feet as he flew down the football field; how easily he'd strolled in front of his classroom day in, day out for the past twenty years. How his children had bounced on his knee as babies, and how he'd carried them on his back when they walked through the zoo.

How Abby's legs felt near his when they danced at the end of the pier. How her body felt beneath him when they—

"Mr. Reynolds, I'd like you to explain it back to me now." The slender therapist tapped his clipboard, his expression one of scant tolerance.

"How often should you check your body for sores, especially after atrophy sets in? Have you heard anything I've told you? Mr. Reynolds?"

John looked at the man, but he couldn't bring himself to answer. The miracles he'd expected weren't happening, and he'd reached the next stage in what would be the rest of his life. The life without dancing or running or making love to Abby. It was a stage he hadn't anticipated, hadn't planned for. And for one reason alone it was more painful than even the first days after learning he'd been paralyzed.

Reality was setting in.

Eighteen

ABBY HAD NEVER FELT MORE STRESSED IN ALL HER LIFE.

In part, she wanted a glorious homecoming. It was Christmastime, after all. They should have had the tree up and decorated, their home looking festive like it always did. She pictured a houseful of guests there to greet John as he arrived, and sweet conversation throughout the evening.

But John wanted nothing of the sort.

"Just get me home and let me sit in the living room with my family, Abby. Nothing else."

She spent every waking hour trying to be whatever John needed at the moment. When he was subdued, she was the quiet supporter. When he was angry, the patient listener. And when he showed signs of determination, of a willingness to fight the terrible curse that had come upon him, she cheered him on. If she couldn't read his mood, she maintained a false sense of euphoria—her way of convincing him that she was okay with his paralysis, that the changes in their life were not enough to take away her joy.

But it was all a lie.

She wasn't happy. Hadn't been since John's accident. But she owed it to John to appear happy and positive. He needed that from her. The trouble was, she had nowhere to let her guard down, nowhere to weep and wail against the twists life had taken.

And so she kept it bottled deep inside her heart, where the only thing it did was make her a basket case. Anxious and uptight and alone.

In the end, Abby did as John asked and kept his homecoming celebration to a minimum. Kade, who had gone back to school to finish the football season and the semester, was home for a month on Christmas break. He and Sean had picked out a tree and brought it home before John's arrival. Nicole and Matt and Jo and Denny had helped decorate it.

Dr. Furin released John at one that afternoon, and an hour later Abby and he pulled up in front of their house. She turned off the engine, and for a moment neither of them moved.

"Can you imagine, Abby?" John stared at the front door of their home. "I'll never drive again. Have you thought about that? I mean never again."

"You'll drive, John. They have hand-operated vehicles set up for people with—"

"Abby, can you just let me accept the truth for a minute?" His tone was sharp, but immediately he let his head fall back against the seat. "Ugggh. I'm sorry." He looked at her, and she could see the heavy fatigue in his eyes, his features. "I didn't mean to snap at you."

"I was trying to help. They have special cars . . . lifts . . . that kind of thing." Abby's hands trembled and she couldn't draw a full breath. How was it going to feel, pushing John into their house? Knowing he would never walk up to the door beside her again? She clenched her teeth. She'd keep her sadness at bay if it killed her. John deserved at least that.

"Do you know how much we take for granted? The little things in life? Like jumping in a car, and driving, and running up the sidewalk to your front door?"

Abby held her breath. "I know." Did he want her to cry with him, or play the role of encourager? And what about *her* feelings? The loss she was suffering? She blew out a shaky breath and filled her lungs again. "Let's go in. The kids are waiting."

John nodded and opened the door. Looking like the athlete he still was, he swung his legs out of the car. Abby tried not to notice the grotesque way they hung limp and fell onto the curb. He did his best to straighten them, but it didn't help.

He looked back at her, and she jerked into action. "I'll get the chair."

John hung his head while she hurried around, popped the trunk, and heaved his wheelchair onto the road. Abby tightened her jacket. It was cold but at least it wasn't snowing. For nearly a minute she struggled with the latch, ripping a fingernail off in the process. "Yikes." She shook her hand to stave off the pain.

"What's wrong?" John craned his head but he couldn't see her bloody nail base.

"Nothing." Abby blinked back tears. How strange it felt to be struggling this way and not have John's help. He was ten feet away. Just ten lousy feet. But he couldn't stand up and help her. "I'm . . . I'm trying to open the chair, but it's stuck."

"The latches are on both sides. Can you see them?" John was trying, doing his best to help her, but she needed more than his suggestions. She needed his strength.

"They won't budge." She pulled at it again, this time with more force. *Don't let him hear me crying, God . . .* "It doesn't work."

Abby struggled a moment more, and then in a flurry of angry frustration, she tossed the wheelchair on the grass beside the curb. "I *hate* that thing!" She fell against the side of the car and hid her face in her arms. "I hate it!"

"Abby, come here." John's voice was gentle.

She wanted to turn and run a hundred thousand miles away, off to some place where John didn't need a wheelchair to get into the house. But that wouldn't do any good.

God, I'm falling apart. Catch me, Lord . . . please, catch me.
Lean not on your own understanding . . .

It was the same Scripture that had come to her the last time she felt this way. What could it mean, though? Lean not on her own understanding? Was there a different way to understand the things that had happened in their lives? Could there be a *good* aspect to John's paralysis . . . ?

Abby didn't see it.

"Did you hear me, Abby? You're killing me." John's tone was louder now. "You're crying, and there's nothing I can do about it. Not a single thing. At least come here so I can hold you."

A quick pain sliced into her, cutting her to the quick. She hadn't thought of that before. How helpless he would feel. Always before if she was upset, he could come to her. Now he couldn't even do that. She dried her face and went to him, falling to her knees before him. His legs were in the way, so she put her hands on his thighs and pushed them apart. It wasn't the first time she'd moved them on his behalf, but she still wasn't used to the sensation. They didn't move easily, but slow and heavy, like the legs of a dead person.

When the space between his knees was big enough, she moved closer, pressing her body against his and laying her head on his shoulder. "I'm sorry for crying. This was supposed to be a happy moment."

"Aahhh, Abby." John nuzzled his face alongside hers. "There's nothing happy about it."

"Yes, there is." She spoke near his ear. "You're *alive*, John. And you're home in time for Christmas. That's plenty to be happy about."

"So those are tears of joy?" He ran his lips lightly along the side of her neck.

"I hate your chair."

"It's my only source of freedom. My only way to get around anymore, Abby."

"I know. I'm sorry."

"It's okay." He brought his lips to hers and kissed her, soft and tender.

When he came up for a breath, he caught her eyes. "I hate it, too."

There was a sound behind Abby and she looked over her shoulder. It was Kade, bounding down the walkway.

"Hey, what's taking so long? We're in there waiting, and you two are out here hugging or something."

Abby studied their older son. The pain in his eyes was a mile deep, but his smile was genuine.

Abby stood and wiped her hands on her jeans. Her finger still throbbed where the nail ripped. "I can't open the chair."

"Is that all?" Kade reached for the wheelchair, checked the latches on both sides, and then with the toe of his shoe, he flipped a third near the base. With a single flick of his wrist, the chair opened, and Kade snapped it into position. He did a sweeping bow. "Your chariot, sir."

Abby stepped back, awed. "I fought with that stupid chair forever." She shook her head. "How'd you know how to work it?"

"I practiced at the hospital." Kade shrugged one shoulder. "Too much time on my hands, I guess."

Abby watched as Kade positioned the chair in front of John, then slid his forearms beneath his father's armpits and eased him onto the padded seat. The scene made Abby's heart catch. How must John feel? John who had always been stronger than Kade . . . John the mentor and teacher and coach . . . now having to be lifted onto a wheelchair? By his son? And what about Kade? The boy was only eighteen, yet he gave the impression that helping John this way was a routine event.

When John was buckled into his chair, Kade took the handles and pushed him up the walk. "Well, Dad . . ." Kade opened the front door and wheeled John inside. "Welcome home."

And with that, a new chapter of their lives began.

The black cloud that had settled in around John was darker than ever.

He appreciated the reception and was grateful to be home and surrounded by his family. But no matter where his mind settled, it always wound up in the same sorry place: deep in self-pity and regret. A place from which he simply couldn't escape.

Sure, he went through the motions. He accepted his family's cards and well-wishes and encouraging statements about how good he looked and how wonderful it was that he'd survived.

But all the while he could only think of one thing: *Why me, Lord? Why now, when Abby and I had just worked things out? When we were just learning to dance again?* Since coming home, he'd been short with Abby, short with anyone who had an answer for his poor attitude. He didn't want a wheelchair van, or an invitation to the Special Olympics.

He wanted to walk. Just once more . . . so he could savor every step and appreciate the feel of his shoes on his feet, wonder at the balance in his legs and the graceful way it felt when he jogged around the track at Marion High.

Just one more day to say good-bye to the legs that had gotten him through every major event in his life. Not that it would help, really. One day wouldn't be enough. But if he could only move his feet and legs again now, he'd appreciate them every day for the rest of his life.

Too bad that wasn't going to happen. And neither was any other good thing until he could find in God the strength to will away the black cloud.

Two hours after getting home, the kids had returned to their activities. Abby was in the kitchen, but John still sat in the chair, facing out the front window.

God, I know You're still there, watching me, loving me. You have a plan for my life, even now . . .

"But what could it possibly be?" His ragged whisper tore through the silence around him. "What good am I?"

Another hour passed. At least three times John thought of something he wanted to get or look at or check somewhere in the house. Each time he would grab hold of the chair's armrests and make an attempt to stand.

And each time his body would jerk up against the safety belt and snap back into place. He realized what the problem was. He didn't yet think like a paralyzed person. His brain still gave him reasons to move and stand and walk, but his legs no longer heard the discussion. He wondered if it was this way for everyone who suffered from sudden paralysis. And if so, how long would it be until his mind gave up, too? Until his brain no longer thought of his legs as anything more than dead weight?

John had always loved the view out the front window of his house. Trees and a winding drive that looked like something out of a painting. But right then he couldn't take another moment of sitting in one place. He worked the muscles in his jaw and slipped his hands around the wheels on either side of his chair.

Specially designed for paraplegics—people who still had the use of their arms—the wheelchair maneuvered more easily than most. John gave the wheels two hard shoves—and zipped backward so fast he crashed into the coffee table.

"John?" Abby's voice was filled with alarm. She appeared at the doorway, drying her hands on a towel. "Are you okay?"

He glanced at her, then let his gaze fall to his knees. "I'm fine, Abby. Every time I crash the chair into something doesn't mean there's a crisis."

The moment he said the words he was sorry. Why did he have to take out his frustration on her?

She came to him, slowly, tentatively. "I'm not worried about the table." He could smell her perfume, feel her presence beside him. Normally on a day like this he would tickle her or pin her playfully against the wall until she begged for mercy. Then, if the kids were busy, they might wind up in their bedroom for the better part of an hour.

His longing for her was still as strong, but how spontaneous could he possibly be now? Even if they were able to find a way to be physically intimate—which the therapist insisted was possible—it would require the type of planning that had never marked their lovemaking.

She rested her hand on his shoulder. "Is there anything I can do?"

"Nothing." He reached up and held her hand, savoring her skin against his, hoping she could feel how badly he wanted her. "I'm sorry, Abby. I've been a jerk lately. You don't deserve it."

"It'll take time. Dr. Furin . . . the therapists . . . everyone says so." She bent down and kissed his cheek. "Life won't always feel like this."

"I know." He caught her face between his fingers and brought his lips to hers. They kissed again, longer than they had outside a few hours earlier. "Pray that we find a way to live again, okay?"

"I am, John." Her eyes glistened, and he knew her heart. She had probably been praying for him constantly. More than he'd prayed for himself.

He realized then where he wanted to be. "Abby, take me outside. To the pier, could you do that?"

"The pier?" She hesitated. "It's a little cold, don't you think?"

Abby was right. Temperatures were in the low thirties that day. But John didn't care. He wanted to sit out there in that familiar spot and watch the lake, look for signs that God was listening, that He hadn't walked away and left John to live out his days suffocating beneath a sad, dark cloud.

"I'll wear my jacket. Please, Abby. I need to be out there."

"Okay." She breathed out a little louder than usual. Loud enough to tell John that she didn't think it a good idea. People with paralysis rarely got enough exercise to fully expand their lungs. Diminished lung function meant a greater risk of pneumonia. Knowing Abby, she would have preferred John stay indoors all winter.

She found his jacket, the one with the Marion Eagles insignia across the back and over the front left pocket. After she helped him slide into it, she wheeled him out the patio door and into the backyard.

Abby had hired a handyman to build a wheelchair ramp up and over the sliding door tracks, and down from the deck to the yard below. Once they reached the grass, the ride was bumpy, but John didn't mind.

There was another ramp from the ground to the pier, and Abby struggled to get him up and onto the flat surface. "Good?"

"Closer to the water."

"John, think about your safety." She positioned herself in front of him where he could see her. "The pier has a slope to it. If your brake fails . . ."

If his brake failed, the wheelchair would roll forward and fall into the water, taking John with it. The lake was deep enough at the end of the pier that unless someone saw it happen, John wouldn't have a chance.

"It won't fail." He looked straight at her. "Come on, Abby. I can't watch the lake from back here."

"Fine." She released the brake with her foot and pushed him almost to the edge. He could hear her jam the lever down and give it a test push. "Is that better?"

He twisted around so he could see her. She was angry. "Thank you."

She planted her hands on her hips. "When do you want to come in?"

If it weren't for the brake, he would've made his way inside by himself. But when the back brake was in place, John couldn't move without someone releasing it. "An hour."

Her hands fell to her sides again. "I'm sorry, John. We'll have to find our way through this. I just . . . I wouldn't know what to do if you fell in, and . . ." She hung her head for a moment before finding his eyes once more. "I can't lose you, John. I need you too much."

His neck burned from craning toward her, but he nodded. "I'm okay, Abby. I promise."

She held his gaze a few seconds longer, then turned and went back in the house.

John relaxed his neck and stared out over the lake. His other injuries were healed now, his throat and a few cuts and bruises on his face and arms. The accident had thrown him onto the truck's floorboard, breaking his neck in the sudden jolt.

Other than that, he'd fared miraculously well. But why? What could God have left for him now? The next several months would be focused on rehabilitation, which meant he was unable to teach. He could go back in the fall if he wanted, but it would be tough. The constant pity he was bound to receive would get old after a few days, let alone another ten years.

John watched a couple row out toward the middle of the lake and cast a line. All his life he'd made his mark through sports. What good was he now, like *this?* And what sense did it make that Jake Daniels would spend the rest of his life paying for it? Yes, Jake shouldn't have agreed to race. But what about his father, Tim? Wasn't he partially to blame for buying the boy a car that cried to be driven at high speeds?

John had no idea how the boy was doing. Jake and his family had sent John a card, apologizing and wishing him a quick recovery. None of them had been by to see him.

"So, what am I going to do with the rest of my life, Lord?" The words dissipated in the cool breeze that blew up from the lake.

He remembered a verse he'd loved as a boy, one that had helped him last year when it seemed he and Abby would divorce: Jeremiah 29:11. *"I know the plans I have for you . . . plans to give you hope and a future, and not to harm you."*

Okay, so if that was true, what were the plans . . . and how was he supposed to get through the next several decades feeling anything but harmed? Most of all, where was the hope?

His thoughts were interrupted by the back door opening. The muscles in his neck still hurt from the way he'd craned around to see her earlier. He waited until she was standing in front of him.

"That was the district attorney on the phone. The hearing to determine whether Jake will be tried as an adult is tomorrow morning." Abby's voice was flat. "He said the judge might be more likely to decide in our favor if you're there in person."

John cocked his head to one side. "What's in our favor?"

"Obviously the D.A. assumes we want Jake tried as an adult." Abby sighed. "The penalties are much tougher that way."

John's head was spinning. Seeing Jake sentenced to prison as an adult would be as devastating a blow as the accident. "You sound like you agree."

She squatted down, resting her knees on the pier and sitting back on her heels. "I don't know what I think." Her eyes fell to his wheelchair. "People shouldn't race their cars on city streets."

"Putting Jake in prison will change that?"

Abby's voice was barely audible. "I don't know."

John leaned forward and took gentle hold of Abby's shoulder. "Don't you think Jake's learned his lesson?"

"I'm not sure." She looked up at him again. "I suppose."

"I'm serious, Abby. Do you think a day will ever come when Jake Daniels agrees to race like that again?"

"No." She shook her head, her eyes never leaving his. "He won't. I'm sure of it."

"So why send the kid to prison?" John was surprised at the sudden passion in his voice, his heart. "Send him to a dozen high schools where he can tell other kids not to race. Send him to college and pray that he grows up to teach or coach or pass the joy of playing football on to hundreds of kids like himself." He shook his head and glanced away before meeting Abby's eyes again. "The district attorney is doing what he thinks is best. That's his job. But I know Jake Daniels. Prison won't help him or me or anyone else. And it won't stop the next kid from saying yes to a street race."

A hint of fire sparked in Abby's eyes, something he hadn't seen since his accident. In a flash of realization, John understood. Hearing determination in his voice was a victory, a milestone. The corners of her mouth lifted just a bit. "What should I tell the D.A.?"

John clenched his fingers around the wheels of his chair. For the first time in weeks, he had a purpose.

"Tell him I'll be there."

Nineteen

JAKE DANIELS WAS SITTING BETWEEN HIS PARENTS AND his attorney when he saw something that made his stomach turn.

The glimpse of a wheelchair.

Before he could do anything to stop the moment, before he could hide or cover his eyes or turn and run, the rest of the wheelchair appeared. In it was Coach Reynolds, being pushed by his wife.

The adults around Jake turned to see what he was looking at, and A. W. muttered an expletive under his breath. "We don't have a chance if he testifies."

Jake's parents were quick to turn back toward the front of the courtroom. But Jake couldn't stop looking, couldn't take his eyes off his coach. If it wasn't for the Marion Eagles baseball cap he wore, Jake would barely have recognized him. He'd lost weight—a lot of weight. And he looked smaller, older somehow.

For a moment, Coach didn't see him, but then he turned before Jake could look away, and their eyes met. Jake was spellbound, unable to blink or breathe or move. He'd spent hours imagining what Coach looked like in a wheelchair, how sad it would be to see such a tall, strong man condemned to spend the rest of his life sitting down.

But Jake had never expected this.

From across the courtroom, Coach Reynolds smiled at him. Not the big, full-faced smile he had in the locker room after an Eagles victory, or the silly smile he wore when he was pulling some crazy stunt for his health class. But a sad sort of smile that told Jake's stunned heart that his coach didn't hate him.

Coach nodded once at Jake, then Mrs. Reynolds wheeled him to the corner of the courtroom at the end of one of the spectator benches. She sat beside him, and the two began to whisper.

"Jake, you need to know how serious this is." A. W. seemed irritated at the exchange that had just taken place between Jake and the coach. "If Mr. Reynolds testifies, the judge will almost certainly decide to try you as an adult."

"Coach."

"What?" A. W. pushed his glasses back up the bridge of his nose.

Jake turned to look his attorney straight in the eyes. *"Coach* Reynolds. Not *Mr.* Reynolds. Okay?"

"Jake, your attorney is only trying to help." Jake's father put an arm around his shoulders and looked at A. W. "This is the first time he's seen Coach Reynolds since the accident."

The attorney waved his hand near his face as though his father's information was trivial. "The point is, Jake's in trouble. If the judge decides to try him as an adult, we'll have to ask for a significant continuance. We're looking at three to ten if he's convicted."

"You don't really think that'll happen, do you?" His mother was rubbing her hands together. A habit she'd picked up in the past six weeks. "Even if he's tried as an adult he could be acquitted, right?"

"It's very complicated." A. W. took out a pad of paper and a pen and began diagraming. "There are several ways a jury could look at it, starting with the felony assault charge and . . ."

Jake tuned out and positioned his head just far enough to the side so he could see Coach Reynolds and his wife. They were still talking, their heads bowed together. After a few seconds, the district attorney joined them. The conversation between the three didn't last long, and then the attorney took his seat on the other side of the table.

Jake was being rude; he knew it. But he couldn't force himself to look away. Seeing Coach in a wheelchair was the most horrible thing he could imagine. *Get up, Coach . . . run around the room and tell us it's all a big joke. Something you'd pull in one of your health classes. Please!*

But the man didn't move a bit.

The hearing would start any minute, and for the first time since hitting Coach's pickup truck, Jake didn't want to run away. He wanted to get up and go to Coach, tell him how much he'd missed him and how sorry he was. How sorry he would always be.

Then Jake saw something even worse. Coach's foot slipped off the chair and hung loose and limp to one side. And this was the awful part—Coach didn't even notice! It was his wife who saw it first. She stooped down and *lifted* his foot—like it was a book or a plant or something—and set it back on the chair.

Jake felt tears well up. *Coach, no!* How was it possible? Coach couldn't even feel his own feet? Was it that bad? Jake brushed a single tear off his cheek. Since his parents' divorce, he'd spent little time praying. But he had prayed once. When he'd desperately needed help, in the moments after hitting Coach's truck. Back then Jake had screamed out for God's help.

And God had brought it.

So, why not do the same thing here and now? Jake closed his eyes.

God, it's me—Jake Daniels. I'm sure You know I've ruined everything. My whole life's shot but the sad thing is, my coach's life is shot, too. And it wasn't his fault, not at all. So You see, God, I have this favor to ask. I believe You can do anything, God. You can make blind people see and deaf people hear—at least that's what my Sunday school teacher used to say.

Tears streamed down his face, but none of the adults around him seemed to notice. *God, I remember a story about a paralyzed man. He had a mat with him, I think. And a bunch of friends. And Lord, I know*

You made him walk again. I'm pretty sure one minute he was lying there and the next he was walking around.

Jake opened his eyes and snuck another quick look at Coach.

So, please, God . . . could You do the same thing for Coach Reynolds? Could You make him walk again and run again? Just do whatever You did to that other guy and let him have his legs back. Please, God.

How long had it been since he'd prayed that way? Jake wasn't sure, but it felt wonderful. And even though his parents told him Coach would always be paralyzed, Jake was sure God could change that if He wanted to.

Coach caught his eye, and Jake made a quick turn toward his parents. He dried his cheeks and stared at his mom and dad, hating the way they listened to everything A. W. said. The attorney saw Coach as the enemy . . . but his parents didn't feel that way, did they? Not that many years ago his parents had been friends with the Reynoldses.

Jake sniffed and studied his parents.

What was going on with them, anyway? Now that the trial was coming up, his father had taken a personal leave from work. He was staying at a hotel not far from where Jake and his mother lived. Jake spent the days at continuation school, wondering why he wasn't in jail where he belonged.

But what about his dad? Where was he spending the days lately? At his mother's house? If so, were they getting along or just trying to figure out what to do if Jake went to prison? They still sat with space between them, so there couldn't be anything that good happening.

The space between them was the first sign there'd been problems between them, back before their fighting overtook the house. Lately, though, they hadn't fought once. Not since this whole mess with the accident.

The judge walked in and the hearing began. The woman had already heard from Jake's parents on why he should be tried as a minor, but now she glanced around the courtroom and asked A. W. a question. "Is there any new evidence the court should consider before making a decision in this matter?"

Jake's attorney stood for a moment. "None, Your Honor."

The judge turned to the district attorney. "Counselor?"

The man stood and looked toward the back of the room. "Yes. The state would like to call Mr. John Reynolds to the stand."

Jake could hardly breathe as Mrs. Reynolds wheeled Coach to the front of the courtroom. This was the part where Coach would say how wrong it was to street race, and how Jake must have known what he was doing.

But Jake didn't care. He deserved whatever happened next. The only thing that mattered was Coach's legs, and whether this would be the moment God would choose to heal him.

Or if that would come sometime later.

Twenty

EVERY EYE WAS ON JOHN.

Abby knew they were staring at him, thinking him painfully thin with useless legs strapped to a prison of metal and wheels—but it didn't matter. She couldn't have been more proud of him. His back was still sore, and this morning the pain had been so bad he could hardly sit up. But still he'd come.

The district attorney didn't know what he was in for.

Abby parked the wheelchair near the witness stand. She took a seat in the front row, not far from John. When he had stated his name for the record and explained his role in the hearing, the judge turned the floor over to the state. "Proceed with your witness."

"Thank you, Your Honor." The district attorney was a plain-looking man whose square jaw was his most prominent feature. He wore a short-sleeved shirt and inexpensive dress pants, but he looked kind. Abby hoped he would understand what John was about to do.

The attorney walked John through a series of quick questions, designed to put him at the scene and verify for the court that his paralysis was, in fact, the result of Jake Daniels's street racing.

"Mr. Reynolds, let's talk about the defendant for a moment." The attorney kept his distance. Probably so he wouldn't block the judge's view of John in his wheelchair. "You know Jake Daniels, don't you?"

Abby's heart raced. Here it was.

"Yes, I do." John cast a look at Jake. Abby followed his gaze, but Jake was studying his folded hands. John turned back to the district attorney. "I've known him for several years."

"You've seen him grow up; would you say that, Mr. Reynolds?"

"Yes." John rested his hands on his lap. "I've seen him grow up."

"Now, Mr. Reynolds, you're aware that this court is about to decide whether the defendant should be tried as an adult, is that correct?"

"Yes, I'm aware."

"Is it your understanding that the defendant is only months away from his eighteenth birthday, an age that would make him legally an adult?"

"It is."

"Very well then, Mr. Reynolds, is it your opinion that a young man almost eighteen years old, who agrees to participate in an illegal street race, should be tried as an adult?"

Abby caught a glimpse of Jake's parents. They were both grimacing, holding their breath while they waited for John's condemnation.

It never came.

"No, sir, I don't believe Jake Daniels should be tried as an adult." John looked at Jake while he spoke. "Jake is one of the good kids, actually. In the months before the accident, he had shown significant maturity, choosing to go his own way instead of following his peers."

John paused, and the district attorney pounced. "Now, let me see if I'm understanding this correctly, Mr. Reynolds. You saw significant maturity in the defendant in the months leading up to the accident, but you *don't* think he should be tried as an adult. Is that right?"

"Exactly." John smiled at the D.A. "See, the fact that someone like Jake could be at a party, refusing to drink and in general being a good example for the others seems proof that he is capable of standing trial as an adult."

Abby shifted her gaze to Jake's parents. Tara was quietly crying, her hand over her mouth. Tim had his arm around Jake. Their faces were shrouded in disbelief.

John continued. "But anytime a good kid like Jake agrees to something as terribly wrong as street racing, I can only surmise one thing." John hesitated. "He's still a kid. A kid who used poor judgment to make a bad choice."

He looked at Jake, and this time the boy lifted his eyes. He was crying, and in that moment, everyone in the courtroom must've seen the truth. Jake wasn't a man; he was a boy. A frightened, shame-filled, guilty boy who would have given his life to take back the consequences of his decisions that awful Friday night.

The district attorney deflated like a worn-out tire. "Is that all, Mr. Reynolds?"

"Not really." John rotated his chair so he could better see the judge. "Your Honor, I'd like to go on record saying that I don't believe jail time is best for a boy like Jake. If he was a repeat offender, that would be different. But Jake isn't a defiant kid. He's not anxious to get his license back so he can go out and race again. He doesn't need prison time; he needs to take his story back into the schools, to talk to kids and tell them the truth about street racing. I'm willing to bet everyone who hears him will feel what *he's* feeling. And maybe then we'll stop this from happening to someone else." He nodded once. "That's all, Your Honor."

John wheeled himself back to Abby. In his eyes she saw hope. A hope she'd been afraid was gone forever.

"You did good."

"Thanks."

In the background, Abby vaguely heard the D.A. call for a meeting with the judge. Before she had time to give it much thought, the hearing was over and Jake's attorney was at their side. He kept his chin low, his hands clasped behind his back, a properly meek stance in light of John's condition. But the exuberance in his face was undeniable.

It made Abby's stomach turn. John hadn't given his speech to make a defense attorney look good. He had given it to save Jake, a boy he knew and trusted and still believed in.

The attorney effused on about John's graciousness, his act of kindness. But before John could respond, the judge called the hearing back to order.

"In light of the testimony given today by the victim in this case—" the judge glanced in Jake's direction—"I have decided to hand the defendant over to be tried as a juvenile."

Behind them, Abby heard Jake's mother contain a cry. The hum of whispering overshadowed the judge's words, and she rapped her gavel on the bench. "That will be enough of that." The room fell quiet once more, and the judge looked at the D.A. "The attorney for the state has asked for time to talk with the defendant's attorney about a plea bargain. They will set that meeting up, and we will convene again in three weeks to determine if this case will require a trial or not."

Abby flashed a look at Jake's attorney. The man was grinning, shaking Tara's hand and then Tim's, and finally Jake's. Again, the windows in Abby's soul shook with frustration, until she caught the expressions on the Danielses' faces. Jake and his family were not smiling. Their attorney might have seen today's outcome as merely a legal victory, but not the Daniels family. They were as painfully aware as she that John was still paralyzed.

Whatever penalty the courts meted out to Jake, in many ways they were all losers.

The hearing was over, and Jake's attorney pulled Jake aside. Abby stood and wheeled John around. As she did, her gaze landed squarely on Tara and Tim Daniels. Tara was gathering her things when her eyes met Abby's. The two of them hadn't spoken since the accident. Other than their sympathy card, they'd kept their distance. Abby understood. It was as tumultuous a time for the Daniels family as it was for hers.

Abby wheeled John closer, maneuvering him between the defense table and the first row of spectator benches. Her heart beat faster than it had all day.

The moment grew more awkward until finally John broke the silence. "Tara . . . how's it going?"

"I'm—" Tara's voice cracked. She and Tim moved closer, and the four of them formed a small circle. Tara's eyes filled, and she took one more step toward John. As she did, John reached up his hand, and she took it, her fingers trembling. "I'm so sorry. We would've been by but . . . I didn't know what to say." She lifted her eyes. "I'm sorry, Abby."

The tears came in streams. Abby moved around John's chair and took Tara in her arms. "Jake didn't want this any more than we did." She kept her voice soft, her sobs muted. Their hug ended, and they stood there, each planted in the awkward soil of unfortunate circumstances.

Tim cleared his throat and met John's gaze. "It's been a long time."

"It has." John shook the man's hand. "You never said good-bye."

"The situation wasn't—" Tim glanced at Tara. "It wasn't good, John. I'm sorry."

He pressed on. "You remarried now?"

"No." Tim's cheeks grew red. "I took a leave from work. I've been staying at a hotel in town." Again he looked at Tara, and something curious washed over Abby's heart. Were Tara and Tim having feelings for each other? After years of being divorced? Tim shifted his gaze back to John. "We've been talking about a lot of things. Why I left, for instance. And why we couldn't make it work."

John glanced back at Abby, then leaned forward slightly. "Would it shock you to know that Abby and I nearly made a decision to divorce this past summer?"

Tara's eyes flew open. "Abby? You and John?"

"We'd been talking about it for three years." Abby wanted to stand on the judge's bench and shout John's praises. He was the one whose life had been forever changed because of the accident, yet here he was getting to the heart of an issue that—for him—would always be even closer to his heart than his legs: the dissolution of marriages. Especially Christian marriages.

Tim stuffed his hands in his pants pocket. "So . . . what happened? I mean . . . you're still together."

"We remembered why we got married and all the memories we'd made along the way. And most of all how dismal the future looked if we didn't have us anymore." John craned his neck again until his eyes found Abby's. Then he returned his attention to Tim. "Things are better than they've ever been."

Tara wiped at a tear and sniffed. "Tim wants us to talk about taking another try at being married." She shook her head. "But I can't do it. The divorce about killed us the first time. A second failure would do me in."

"I tell you what . . ." John reached back for Abby's hand, and she came up alongside him. Sincerity rang from his voice. "As long as you're in town, how about you and Tara come by the house a few nights a week? Just to talk things through."

Abby caught John's vision, and her heart leaped. "Maybe we can share something from our story that'll help you."

Tara looked doubtful. "I don't know."

They were quiet for a while, then Tim looked at the ground, his feet restless. When he looked up, there were tears in his eyes. "I'm sorry, John. About your legs."

John shrugged, his expression more at peace than it had been in weeks. "It wasn't your fault."

"I bought the car." Tim's face was ashen. "Tara was right. It was the wrong thing for a teenage boy. I'll . . . live with that the rest of my life."

Ten feet away, the defense attorney patted Jake on the shoulder and made a quick exit. When he was gone, Jake stared at the four of them, then approached with clearly hesitant feet. Abby studied the boy. She wasn't sure what she felt. Sometimes she hated him. Jake's decision had cost John his ability to walk, and changed their lives forever. But other times . . .

She simply didn't know.

This was one of those times.

When Jake reached them, he looked at his parents. "Can I have a minute with Coach?"

"Of course." Tara collected her things and she and Tim moved toward the door. "We'll be out here when you're done."

Abby gave John's shoulder a light squeeze. "Want me to leave?"

"No." Jake answered before John could speak. "Please, Mrs. Reynolds . . . I want you to hear what I'm going to say."

Abby pulled a chair from the defense table and positioned it near John. When she was seated, Jake crossed his arms and inhaled. Abby tried to read the boy's eyes. Was this a thank-you speech concocted by his attorney? Or was there something real on Jake's heart? Even before he spoke, Abby knew it was the latter.

"Coach, my attorney just got done telling me I was lucky." Jake huffed and the air left his body in a single burst. "Can you believe that?"

John said nothing, just kept his gaze on Jake and waited.

"I want you and Mrs. Reynolds to know that no matter what happens with the hearing in a few weeks, I am *not* lucky." Jake's eyes welled, but he didn't cry. "I made a stupid decision, and it . . . it . . ."

He bit his lip and hung his head. For a long time he stayed that way, and Abby understood. His emotions were too near the surface to let go now. Not when he had more to say. Jake held his breath and looked at John again. "It was my fault, Coach. I never should've raced him. Never." The boy's knees shook. "I saw your truck pull out that night, but I was going too fast. I couldn't stop."

Abby's heart fell. *God . . . couldn't You have held John back an extra minute? Enough time to spare him this?*

Lean not on your own understanding, daughter . . .

She blinked. The strange words that played across her soul felt almost like a direct response from God. And with the same Scripture that had come to mind again and again.

Is that You, God?

I have told you these things, so that in Me you may have peace. In the world you will have trouble. But take heart! I have overcome the world.

Jake was going on, explaining how quickly the accident had happened, but Abby wasn't listening. Chills had gone down her spine the moment the Scripture flashed in her heart. It was a verse she'd read that morning in her devotion time. In fact, she and John had looked at it a little while ago . . . after Nicole's wedding, when they first began reading the Bible together again.

It was the perfect verse, the one that described their situation exactly. She understood that now even more than she had back in the hospital in the days after John's accident. The Word of God, His promises, these things God had spoken to them so that they would have peace. In the world they would have trouble—most definitely. First on the football field with parents and the administration. And then with John's accident.

But in the end, though they didn't see it now, God would win. God would always win. He would win over deceitful parents and spineless administrators; He would win over John's car accident, and even his paralysis.

He would win even if John spent the rest of his life in a wheelchair.

Jake was saying something about Casey Parker leaving the scene and then coming back to call for help. "We were so scared, Coach. We thought you were gonna die." The boy squirmed, his tears finally splashing onto his tennis shoes. "I'm so sorry." Jake sank into a chair across from John and let his head fall into hands. "I'd give anything to take back those few minutes."

Casey Parker hadn't been to see John, either. Ever since finding out that the boy's father had written the notes about John, Abby wondered if the man was maybe glad about what had happened to John. Not that he'd been injured, of course, but that he wouldn't be coaching. It was an awful thing to think, but Abby couldn't help herself. She was a coach's wife, after all. And people tended to reserve some of their greatest disdain and poorest behavior for coaches. It was a fact of American life.

If John was thinking those things, he never mentioned them.

He leaned forward now as far as he could and gripped Jake's knees. "Jake, look at me." John's voice was kind, but stern. The same tone Abby had heard him use with their own children when they were down on themselves.

Jake barely lifted his head and then let his fingers cover his face once more.

"I'm serious, Jake. Drop the hands and look at me."

Abby was quiet, watching from her place at his side. This was the John she knew and loved, the one who would see something wrong and right it with a passion that couldn't be contrived—or resisted.

This time Jake's hands fell to his lap, and he met John's gaze. Tears ran down both sides of his face. "Coach, don't make me look at you. It's too hard."

The sorrow in Jake's eyes softened Abby's heart. He really *was* just a kid, a boy drowning in a river of guilt, with no way of reaching the other side.

John leaned closer still. "Jake, I forgive you. It was an accident."

"It was *stupid!*" Jake's features twisted and he uttered a soundless cry. "You're in a chair, Coach. Because of me! I can't take that." A single sob slipped from Jake's throat. "I *want* them to put me in prison. That way I don't have to pretend my life is fine when I'm the one who wrecked yours."

"You didn't wreck my life. There's nothing I can't do if I work hard enough, and I'm going to work, Jake; you better believe it. I never let you boys settle for second, and I'm certainly not going to settle for second, now."

Abby's heart skipped a beat. This from the man who sat alone on their pier the day before, isolated and discouraged? She wanted to raise both hands and scream in victory, but she resisted.

Jake rubbed his knuckles into his forehead and shook his head. "It isn't right, Coach. What you did for me today. I don't deserve it."

"It *is* right. You do no one any good sitting in a prison cell, Jake.

You made a bad decision, and your life changed in a few seconds. Mine, too. But you won't save anyone by sitting behind bars. Not the next street-race victim, not yourself. And definitely not me. You need to be out there sharing that message, telling kids to say no if someone challenges them to a race. That way you'll save lives."

"Coach—" torment wracked Jake's face again—"that's not enough punishment. How can I look in the mirror? I mean . . . it's crazy. You and your family . . . you could never really forgive me for what I did. You *shouldn't* forgive me."

"Jake . . ." John's tone was quieter than before. "I already have."

"Don't say that."

Abby closed her eyes. She could sense what was coming. *Don't make me forgive him, too, God. Not yet . . .*

John settled back in his chair some. "The minute Abby told me what happened . . . that it was you driving the other car . . . I made a decision deep inside to forgive you." John gave a single sad sort of laugh. "How could I hold it against you? It was an accident, Jake. Besides, you're like a son to me. I forgive you completely."

Abby shifted in her chair.

Speak, daughter . . . forgive as I forgave you . . .

The prompting in Abby's soul was undeniable. *Lord . . . please. Don't make me say it now. He doesn't need my forgiveness.*

"Abby does, too." John turned to her, his eyes so transparent she could see straight to his heart. Whatever other feelings John might wrestle with in the coming months and years, she doubted a lack of forgiveness would be one of them. He was being honest with Jake. He harbored no resentment or ill will toward the boy. None at all. John was still looking at her, waiting. "Tell him, Abby. You forgive him, right?"

"Of course." She had to say it for John; she could sort out her feelings later. "We all do."

Jake hung his head again. "I hate myself."

"Then *there's* the real problem. Forgiving yourself." John dug his

KAREN KINGSBURY

elbows into his knees, and Abby was struck by a thought. *He can't feel it . . . like he's resting his arms on a table or a desk.*

Jake was silent.

"Then that's what I'll pray for—" John bit the corner of his lip— "that God will give you the grace to forgive yourself. The way *He* forgives you."

"God?" Jake's eyes lifted once more. "Someone like God isn't about to forgive me. Coach, it was my fault!"

"Have you told Him you're sorry?"

"Yes!" The pain intensified. "A dozen times that first night. But still . . . I need to pay my penalty. I wouldn't expect God or you or . . . or Mrs. Reynolds . . . or anyone else to forgive me until I've gone to prison for a long, long time."

"Why?"

"So I can make up for it."

"Make up for taking away my legs?" John's eyes showed the hint of a sparkle, and the corners of his mouth lifted. "You'd have to be in there an awful long time if that were true. Because I had some mighty fast legs, Daniels. Mighty fast."

Again, Abby wanted to clap or shout out loud. John was joking! Playing up on an old bit of banter he and Jake had exchanged since Jake was a middle-school boy. Back in the days when his parents would come over for the occasional Sunday dinner.

Abby could still hear them, still see them the way they'd been five years earlier. Jake's family would enter the house and John would welcome them. Jake would put himself toe-to-toe with John, his eyes wide.

You gotta race me, Coach; I'm getting faster! And John—whom Jake had always called *Coach*—would give a soft laugh. *I don't know, Jake. I have some mighty fast legs.* To which Jake would raise an eyebrow and pretend to punch John's shoulder. *Come on, Coach, they're not that fast. Nothing like mine!*

Chills danced across Abby's arms as she understood. John was tossing Jake a life rope, a chance to be rescued from the waters of guilt.

Abby stood stone still, her eyes on the weeping boy. Suddenly the lines around his eyes and forehead eased.

"Come on, Coach—" his voice cracked, and a tear slid onto his cheek—"they weren't that fast. Nothing . . . nothing like mine."

"Thatta boy, Jake." John gave him a light smack on the knee. "I may be paralyzed, but I'm not dead. I don't want you hanging your head every time we see each other. Because then I lose twice."

"Twice?"

"My legs . . . and then you." John paused. "Don't do that to me, Jake. It'll be hard enough getting my routine down without wondering whether you're okay or not."

Once again Jake let the tears come. As he did, he looked twelve, and Abby felt her heart grow still softer toward him. Maybe she could forgive him, after all.

"But I'm so sorry. I gotta do something, Coach. Something to make it right."

"Listen, Jake . . . every time you walk into an auditorium packed with teenagers and tell them your story, I want you to remember something." His voice dropped a notch. "I'm with you, Daniels. Right there beside you, step by step. And that'll make everything right."

Twenty-one

NICOLE WAS NAUSEOUS NEARLY EVERY DAY.

Not because of morning sickness. That had passed weeks ago. Now that she was almost halfway through her pregnancy, the sick feeling came from one thing: it was almost Christmas, and her dad still couldn't feel anything in his legs or feet.

The moment she'd heard the news about his paralysis that terrible afternoon in the hospital waiting room, Nicole prayed. Since then she'd spent hours pleading with God, believing He would work a miracle in her father. She had no idea how it would come about, just that it would. It *had* to. Every time she prayed about something and had this feeling, things went the way they were supposed to.

But as the days passed, her prayers slowed and finally stopped. In the process she'd come to grips with something that turned her stomach.

Things didn't always go the way they were supposed to.

If they did, she wouldn't have gotten pregnant for another three years, her parents would never have argued, never considered divorce. More to the point, Christians wouldn't lose loved ones to illnesses and accidents. They'd never suffer from depression or pain or money troubles.

They'd certainly never be paralyzed.

No, if things always went the way they were supposed to, they'd never have anything but blue skies until the day—as a very old person—they would lie down at night and wake up in the arms of Jesus.

But that wasn't how it worked. And the truth of that left her with a sort of sick feeling about her faith, a feeling as new as marriage and loss and disappointment.

Maybe God intended to use her father's injuries as a way to change the kids at Marion High School. Nicole didn't like that option, but it was a possibility. She'd heard rumors from Kade—who still kept in touch with a few kids at Marion High. Talk around school was that since her dad's accident attitudes had improved and kids were kinder than they'd been before. There was even talk of some sort of "Coach Reynolds town meeting," though neither Nicole nor Kade had mentioned that to their father.

He had enough on his mind, what with learning to get around in a wheelchair and coming to grips with his injury.

If that's why God had allowed her father's injury, Nicole should have felt some sort of quiet peace, a sense that the Scripture in Romans was right, that all things really did work to the good for those who loved God.

But she didn't feel that way at all.

She just felt nauseous.

Her doctor had warned her that constant anxiety wasn't good for the baby. After that she'd made a promise to Matt and herself to spend more time reading Scripture and praying, trying to ease the stress.

But every time she tried to read a favorite verse or talk to God, she found herself thinking about the accident. Why had God allowed it? Couldn't her father have left the office five minutes earlier? Seconds later? After all her parents had been through, after their hearts and souls had finally come back together? After Dad had been going to church with them again?

The questions Nicole had for God outweighed the things she wanted to pray about, so her anxiety remained. It wasn't that she was angry at God, exactly. She just wasn't sure she could trust Him. The truth about these feelings was something she didn't share with anyone. Even herself.

Because the Nicole Reynolds she'd been until her dad's accident would never have doubted God. That old Nicole had been more aware of God's whispered voice, more reliant on Bible verses and prayer, than anyone in her family.

Only lately had Nicole finally understood the reason for her deep faith. It had nothing to do with believing she was better than the others, or somehow having a greater need than the others for God's peace and presence. No, that wasn't the reason at all.

The reason was Haley Ann.

Which was something else she hadn't shared with anyone.

No one knew she remembered losing her little sister. She might have been not quite two years old, but there were scenes from that sad day that stayed with her still, written with the indelible ink of a little girl's tears. Haley Ann had been sleeping in her crib, taking a nap, Nicole understood now. Most of the details were fuzzy, but Nicole could still close her eyes and see big men rushing into Haley Ann's room, working over her, trying to get her to breathe.

Everyone assumed that because Nicole was young, she didn't grieve back then. But Haley Ann was her sister! Her only sister. Nicole remembered one conversation she'd had with her mother about losing Haley Ann.

"She's in heaven now, darling." Her mother had been crying the way she did a lot back then. "But as long as you love God, you'll always be only a whisper away from her. Understand?"

Nicole had understood better than Abby could have imagined. If loving God was the way to be closer to Haley Ann's memory, she would do so with all her heart. And she had. Every month, every year . . . until now.

Now everything had changed, and the reason was obvious. She simply wasn't sure she could trust God anymore. Not with her deepest prayers and concerns. After all, she had prayed for the safety of everyone in her family. The very morning of the accident in fact. But that night, there she was, in the hospital beside her mother, wondering what had gone wrong.

Wondering where God had been when they'd needed Him most.

The feelings she had about the entire matter only added to her anxiety. Even worse, Matt talked constantly about God's will this and God's best that and God's miraculous hand in saving her dad's life. He would find her at the most inopportune times—when she was working on a homework assignment or folding laundry or getting ready for school.

Two nights ago they'd had their first real fight over the issue. She'd been on the Internet looking for bargains on eBay.com when he came up behind her and massaged her shoulders. His tone was even gentler than his fingertips.

"Nicole, get off the computer."

She gave him a quick glance over her shoulder. "Why?"

"Because you're running."

"From what?" Her attention was back on the computer screen and the list of items there.

Matt breathed out in a sudden burst. "From everything. From talking to me . . . from your dad's situation . . . from your pregnancy." He hesitated. "From God."

Even now Nicole wasn't sure why his comments made her so angry. Words began tumbling out of her mouth before she could stop them. "Who are you to tell me what I'm running from?" She spun the chair around and glared at him. "Just because I don't want to delve into the deeper meaning on every topic doesn't mean I'm running."

"Praying with your husband isn't exactly delving into the deeper meaning, Nicole."

"Okay, fine. You want me to pray, I'll pray. But don't ask me to put my heart into it because I can't. Right now I need a little time before I go calling on God."

Matt had looked at her, clearly dumbfounded. "You don't sound anything like the girl I married."

"Thanks a lot."

"I'm serious. You used to talk about God constantly. Now you'd rather pretend He doesn't exist."

"That isn't it." She huffed. "It's just that there isn't a lot left for me to ask Him. Let my dad's legs be okay? Too late. Let us wait and have babies in a few years. Done deal. I'm not running, Matt. I guess I just don't see the point in praying."

Matt motioned to the computer. "And playing on eBay will help you work through that?"

"It's better than wasting every moment praying when in the end God will do whatever He wants."

Matt had stared at her for a long time after that. When he spoke, his voice was quieter than before. "As long as one of us still believes in prayer, I want you to know something."

Nicole was silent, her cheeks burning.

"I'll be praying for you, Nicole. That God will help you remember who you are."

Since then his words had played in her head, easing their way across her heart. What was wrong with her anyway? She still believed in prayer, didn't she? After a lifetime of seeing God's answers, her life's situations now couldn't be enough to actually shake her faith, could they?

She slipped into a black stretch skirt and a white silk blouse. Her belly was protruding now, but not so much that she needed maternity clothes. She was grateful. It was Christmas Eve, and they were invited, along with Jo and Denny, to her parents for dinner. Matt's parents were already downstairs with Matt, waiting for her.

Nicole grabbed a pair of black hose, and as she slipped them on, her eyes fell on a Scripture plaque near their bed. It was a verse from Hebrews, one that had always been a favorite of Matt's.

"Let us fix our eyes on Jesus, the author and perfecter of our faith . . ."

The pantyhose fell still in Nicole's hands. Maybe *that* was her problem. She hadn't had her eyes fixed on Jesus much. Not since her father's accident. They'd been fixed on his injury, her pregnancy, and the sorrow and frustrations that went along with both.

But not on Jesus.

Wasn't there another Bible verse about God being the author . . . of something? Nicole closed her eyes for a moment, and it came to her. The author of life. That was it. God was called the author of life. And if He was the author, it was His decision whether some characters would go through life unscathed or whether they'd fall victim to a car wreck.

The idea didn't ease Nicole's burden. And it certainly didn't increase her desire to pray. If God was the author, then the book was already written. They could love God, and He could love them. But prayer wasn't going to change anything. Not if the pages had already been written.

"Nicole, are you ready?" Matt's voice carried up the stairs. They'd both apologized since the fight the other day, but nothing had been the same between them. Matt thought she'd changed, and she thought he'd become insensitive. It was one more thing to add to the list.

She stuck her head out the door. "In a minute."

"Hurry." He shot a look at the clock on the wall. "We're already late."

Nicole began working on her pantyhose again. "Merry Christmas to you, too." She hissed the words quietly, so Matt wouldn't hear her. As she did, she sat on the edge of the bed and raised one foot. She was pulling the hose up past her ankles when it happened.

Deep within her she felt a fluttering.

As though someone was tickling her from the inside. Nicole's heartbeat quickened, and she stayed still. Was that what she thought it was? Nearly a minute passed and it happened again. It felt like the paws of a sleepy kitten, tapping at her from somewhere behind her lower abdomen.

When it happened a third time, Nicole knew. It wasn't a kitten.

It was her baby. The baby she had never quite accepted, never quite been happy about. But now here this little child was, moving and stretching and becoming. The beautiful sunrise of vibrant joy exploded in Nicole's heart. God was knitting a new life within her! How could she be anything but thrilled with that truth?

She hugged herself, wondering for the first time what the baby would be like. A boy or girl? Tall like Kade or bigger-boned like Matt? With her mother's intensity or her father's determination? Tears stung at her eyes, but she refused to cry. Whatever other problems she needed to work through, Nicole was suddenly ready to love this child within her.

And maybe one of these days she'd be ready to talk to God again, too.

The door burst open and Matt stared at her. "It's been five minutes, Nic. What're you doing?"

A single laugh bubbled up from Nicole's throat. "The baby . . ."

Matt entered the room and took a few steps closer, his expression blank. "What about the baby?"

"I felt the baby move, Matt." Another breathy chuckle slipped from her mouth. "Just a few little flutterings, but I'm sure that's what it was."

"Really?" The tension around Matt's eyes eased. He moved onto the bed beside her and lay his hand on her tummy.

"You won't be able to feel it." She covered his hand with hers. "It was soft. I would've missed it if I hadn't been sitting here."

Matt's eyes met hers. "You sound happy about it."

Had her disappointment been that obvious? Nicole's heart grieved at the thought. "Of course I'm happy." She leaned over and kissed him.

For a moment he looked at her, his eyes full of questions. But just when she thought he was going to ask her about prayer and God and her attitude, he smiled. "Let's get to your parents' house and tell them."

Nicole's love for Matt swelled as it hadn't in months. He wanted so badly to fix her, to make her feel and think and act the way she used to. But here, when he could have used this moment as a way of convincing her that God was working in her life, he'd been willing to wait. "Thanks, Matt. For not pushing it."

"I love you, Nic. No matter what you feel or think or believe." He reached for her hand. "When you're ready to talk, I'm here."

Abby was struggling.

It was Christmas Eve and the kids would be there in five minutes, but nothing felt right. She took one last look in the mirror and sucked in a steadying breath. John's good days had outnumbered the bad this past week, and Abby thought she knew why. It had everything to do with seeing Jake Daniels. John's time in court that day to talk with the boy, laugh with him, offer him hope, had done more for John than any amount of therapy so far.

If only it had helped her. She just couldn't get past her anger, couldn't seem to download it so it didn't stay bottled up inside her, eating at the lining in her stomach.

Friends from church would call, but she'd tell them all the same thing: "We're doing great . . . thanks for praying . . . John's feeling better . . . getting used to the wheelchair."

If only she had the courage to tell it like it was: "I'm furious . . . disappointed . . . heartbroken. And not sure I like the idea of spending the rest of my life watching John pine away in a wheelchair."

She was supposed to be strong, determined, positive. That had always been her role, even when she and John had been facing a divorce. Now, it felt as though every person who called—whether they were a longtime friend or a student of John's—was looking for her to encourage and uplift them.

Why did everyone in her world depend on *her* to have a good attitude about John's injury? John . . . the kids . . . their family and friends . . . it was as though they'd all gotten together and decided, "Hey, if Abby's okay, everything's all right. We can breathe a sigh of relief and move on with life."

Being positive, at peace, was the right thing to do. The expected thing. No one would know how to act if Abby wept every time someone asked her about John. Or if she threw her hands in the air and told the truth about how she was struggling inside.

She studied her reflection once more.

Whatever was brewing in the basement of her heart, she'd have to hide it a while longer. It was Christmas, after all. And the entire family would expect her to be full of good cheer and pleasant conversation. Of course, last year she'd silenced her feelings about the trouble in their marriage, and it had only made things worse . . .

But this was different. She had to keep quiet now or none of them would survive.

She held her breath as she made her way out of the bedroom. Holding her breath was one way to keep from crying. *Let it go, Abby . . . don't think about your own feelings. Think of something else . . .* She blinked hard. Kade. That was it: she could think about Kade. At least things were going better with him. He had been meeting with a counselor from church ever since he'd been home on Christmas break. The other night Kade told Abby and John that he hadn't looked at any pornography, Internet or otherwise, since his discussion with John that day on the lake. Kade's counselor had asked Kade to study a couple who seemed to best illustrate true intimacy.

Kade had chosen Abby and John.

She reached the bottom of the stairs and could hear a chorus of voices in the next room. She turned the corner into the living room and was immediately greeted by Jo and Denny.

"Now, Abby, don't you just look like a Christmas angel." Jo took three giant steps and circled her arms around Abby in a quick hug. "I'm always telling Denny you look like an angel. You know . . . that blonde halo and all. But now I have to say I've never been more right about it." She elbowed Denny. "Isn't that right, Denny?"

The man had his hands in his pockets and he gave a shy nod. "She's a pretty one; that's for sure."

"Thanks, guys. You look nice, too." Abby smiled. Compliments were wonderful. Too bad they didn't make her feel better. "Dinner's ready in the kitchen. Let's go find everyone else."

The meal was cheery and upbeat. Cinnamon candles burned on either end of the table and Abby had cooked a turkey for the occasion. John sat at the head of the table—not because he'd always sat there in the past, but because it was the only spot that would accommodate his wheelchair. Abby tried not to think about it.

"You know, Dad—" Kade finished a bite of mashed potatoes— "one of the guys at school told me his football coach spent the last five years of his career in a wheelchair. A muscle disorder or something."

Abby flashed a quick look at John, but he was nodding thoughtfully, his eyes on Kade. "I know. It wouldn't be impossible."

"So, you should do it." Kade set his fork down and leaned his elbows on the table.

"If things were different, I might."

Nicole wiped her mouth. "You mean the kids?"

"Yep. That and the parents." John shook his head. "My injury hasn't changed anything at school. Parents wanted my head, remember? I was about to be fired when the accident happened."

"Aw, Dad." Kade shook his head. "They never woulda fired you. You're too good for that."

"Doesn't matter." John took a long drink of water. "If the administration doesn't support what you're doing, it's not worth the effort."

"So you're quitting?" Kade's voice fell.

A sad smile lifted the corners of John's mouth. "I'll write the resignation letter sometime next month."

"Well, all I can say is whoever's at the top o' the heap at that school needs their head examined." Jo had finished her first plateful and was helping herself to more of everything. "Lettin' you get away'd be like hooking the biggest steelhead that side of the Mississippi and cuttin' it free before a single picture was snapped." She looked around the table. "Know what I mean?"

Sean paused, his fork midbite. "What's a steelhead?"

Even Abby laughed, though Jo launched into an explanation of the kinds of lakes where steelhead might be found and what sort of bait was best for catching them.

When they were finished eating, they exchanged gifts around the tree in the living room. One gift each on Christmas Eve. That was the family rule. And no sorting beneath the tree, either. First gift with your name on it was the one you opened.

Keeping with tradition, John was last. He chose a small package that happened to be from Jo and Denny. Wads of wrapping paper dotted the floor, and each of them sat beside a newly opened gift while they watched John open his.

At first, Abby couldn't make out what it was. Then as John opened the wrapper, she could see it clearly. It was a pair of gloves. The fingerless kind worn by serious bicyclists.

Or men in wheelchairs.

John slipped them on his hands and fastened the Velcro straps around his wrists. "These are great, guys. Thanks."

But even as he was thanking Matt's parents, Abby saw tears gathering in Nicole's eyes. Jo seemed to sense that somehow her gift was causing sadness around the previously happy circle. "See—" she waved her hands in the air—"Denny and I always think of John as active. Going here and there and making the rest of us look pretty lazy, if you know what I mean." She laughed once, but it rang hollow across the room.

Denny tried to rescue her. "What Jo's trying to say is that we figured John would be getting around more in the weeks to come. Maybe taking the chair around the track at school . . . something like that."

"Right, and the gloves . . . well, it's obvious what they're for. Otherwise John's hands would get plum tore up. All callused and blistered and banged up." She looked at Abby. "And we can't have that. Not on a man as nice-looking as John Reynolds, right, Abby?"

It was happening again. Everyone was looking to her to save the moment, to speak something encouraging and upbeat that would give the rest of them permission to cheer up. But this time she wasn't sure what to say. It wasn't Jo's fault. She and Denny had meant well with the gloves. One day very soon they'd probably come in handy.

But right now—with Christmas knocking on the door—Abby didn't want a reminder of John's handicap. She wanted packages of sweaters and scarves and cologne. Favorite books and CDs and candy.

Not gloves that would make it more comfortable to get around in a wheelchair.

When she couldn't think of anything to say, Nicole spoke up. "Jo, they're perfect." She sniffed and wiped at a tear. "I think we're all a little sad that Daddy needs them. But still . . . they were very thoughtful."

"Definitely." John held up his hands, admiring them.

"Well, I didn't mean nothin' by it." Jo's chin dropped a bit. "Just wanted to keep his hands nice."

Sean stood and moved next to John. "They're cool, Dad. Can I wear them when I ride my bike?"

The group laughed and the tension dissipated as quickly as it had built. Abby exhaled softly. She was grateful. Her bank account of ways to look at John's situation in a positive light was running frightfully low.

And come spring, when John should be out on the football field running laps with his players, she was pretty sure she wouldn't have anything positive left to say at all.

Even if everyone she knew was counting on her.

John was the only one awake. He was staring out the front window thinking of Christmases past, when he heard a sound.

"Dad?" It was Sean. The boy's quiet footsteps approached from behind.

John turned and found his son's eyes in the dark. "I thought you were sleeping." He held an arm out, and Sean came to him.

"I can't."

Only then did John realize his younger son was crying. "Hey, buddy, what's wrong? You're not supposed to cry on Christmas Eve."

"I . . . I feel like everything's a mess."

John's heart broke for the boy. How little time they'd spent together since the accident . . . yet certainly the changes in their lives were affecting him, too. Obviously more than John had realized. "You mean because of my legs?"

Sean hung his head, his lips pursed. Even in the shadowy moonlight John could see anger in the young boy's eyes. "It isn't *fair,* Dad!"

John waited. Sean had always needed more time than their other children to share his feelings. Whatever torment the boy had gone through since the accident, John was grateful he was finally sharing his heart. "I'm listening."

"I know I shouldn't be thinking about myself." He shrugged and wiped at his eyes. "You're the one hurt. But still . . .'"

"Still what?"

Sean lifted his eyes and met John's straight on. "What about *my* dreams, Dad? Have you thought about that?"

John wasn't sure what his son meant. "Your dreams?"

"Yeah." The boy crossed his arms, and it looked like he was barely containing the struggle within. "You coached Kade until he was a senior, but what about me? I'll be at Marion High in two years, remember? How can I play football for someone else?"

Realization washed over John's soul. Of course . . . why hadn't he thought about this before? In his busyness with rehabilitation and coming to grips with his altered life, John hadn't thought once about how his injury might affect Sean. They'd always talked about how John would coach Sean, too, the same way he'd coached Kade. But John hadn't known until now how much the boy had counted on the arrangement. Sean was only in sixth grade. To John, his younger son's football days seemed light-years away.

But to an eleven-year-old boy . . . they were right around the corner.

"Sean—" John tightened his hand around Sean's waist and hugged him closer—"I'm so sorry, buddy."

Looking more like a child than he had in years, Sean hung his head and wept. They were tears John understood, tears of sorrow and frustration and guilt at what he obviously thought were selfish feelings. This time when he looked up, his eyes pleaded with John. "Didn't you hear Kade tonight? You can coach in a wheelchair, Dad. There's no rule against it or anything."

John gave the boy a sad smile. The situation was so much more complicated than that. But right now his son didn't need to hear a list of specifics and details. He needed a reason to believe things were going to be okay, that life would somehow, someway be good again even if he had to let go of this boyhood dream of his. *Give me something to say, God . . . something that'll restore the peace in his heart . . .*

Then it hit him. He cleared his throat. "I'll always be your coach, Sean. Whether I'm out there on the field or not."

Something changed in his son's expression. The anger and sadness wasn't gone exactly, but his gaze held the beginning of hope. "Really?"

"Of course. We'll work out together . . . learn plays together." John felt his enthusiasm building. It was true. He might hang up his Marion High whistle, but he'd never stop coaching his boys. Especially Sean, who had so many years of football ahead. "I'll teach you everything I taught Kade."

Sean stood a little straighter. The worry lines across his forehead relaxed some. "Even in a wheelchair?"

"Even in a wheelchair."

For a moment neither of them said anything, then Sean put his hand on John's shoulder and sucked in a quick breath. "Can I tell you something, Dad?"

John reached up and tousled the boy's sandy blond hair. "Anything."

"I'm so glad you didn't die."

Tears stung at John's eyes. Again he was struck by how little he and Sean had talked lately. They needed this . . . this and many more times like it. He grinned. "Me, too, buddy."

Sean leaned down and hugged him, and they held each other for a long while. Finally Sean stood up and yawned. "Well . . . I guess I'll go back to bed."

"Yeah . . . don't wanna catch Santa Claus sneaking around the living room."

The boy's giggle was like an infusion in John's soul. *Thank You, God . . . thank You for this time with my son.*

"G'night, Dad. I love you."

"Love you, too. See you in the morning."

Sean left, and for a long while John sat there, pondering their conversation. Sean would be a joy to coach, as quick and easy to teach as Kade had been. And John would most certainly make good on his promise, working with the boy whenever they had a chance. Not just because Sean had always wanted to learn from him, but because he finally understood.

Even though he was about to resign from coaching the Eagles, as long as he had Sean, he would still be a coach.

And that, all by itself, was the greatest Christmas present anyone could have given him.

Twenty-two

JOHN HAD BEEN DREADING THE MOMENT ALL WINTER.

By the first week of March, when grass began poking through the melting snow, he knew it was time. He hadn't heard from Herman Lutz or any of the other school administrators, but there was no point waiting another day. This was the beginning of the academic hiring period, and the school officials deserved to know. They weren't going to fire him—he'd guessed that much after a few conversations with other teachers. Not this year, anyway.

"They're worried about how it would look," one of the math teachers had told him. The man had overheard Herman Lutz talking with the principal in the office one day in January. "They said the public would come unglued if the school fired you now. Just a few months after you'd been paralyzed."

So the administration was willing to wait a year, but they still wanted him gone. Still didn't trust his character enough to believe he never would have allowed his players to drink or race cars if he'd known it was happening. And they still were willing to bow to the complaints of a few parents, rather than support him and the work he'd done at Marion High.

Yes, it was time to resign.

John asked Abby to help him dress warmly that day, two pairs of sweats and an extra sweatshirt. Then he bundled into his warmest jacket and grabbed his laptop computer.

"I've got a letter to write." He winked at Abby.

She waited a moment before answering him. "Okay. I'll be here if you need me."

He smiled, but it didn't fool her. By the time he moved out the door and into the backyard, they both had tears in their eyes. John stopped and surveyed the path ahead of him. Before the first snow, they'd hired a contractor to pour a cement pathway to the pier. Now it was cleared and salted, surrounded by remnants of ice on either side.

John filled his lungs with the sweet air of early spring. His therapy still hadn't yielded the results he prayed for, but he'd learned to be more independent. He could get to the pier by himself now. The doctor had prescribed a new chair for him, one with a firm brake in hand's reach. And his upper body was stronger than before, strong enough to propel himself up hills and ramp-ways.

Carrying his laptop on his knees, he made his way almost to the end of the pier where he set the brake firmly in place. As he opened the computer, he caught sight of his legs. They'd wasted away, just like the therapist had said. Before the accident they'd been twice the size of Kade's. Now they were smaller, thinner, and John knew it wouldn't be long until they were little more than skin and bones.

He flipped the computer screen up, hit the start button, and stared at the keyboard. When the program was ready, he opened a new document and waited, his fingers poised over the keys. What was he supposed to say? How could he put into words that he was ready to give up his lifelong passion?

He began to type.

To whom it may concern: This is to inform you that I am hereby resigning as varsity football coach at Marion High. As you know, I've been the Eagles coach since the school opened in 1985. In that time, I . . .

His fingers stopped.

In that time . . .

So much had happened since he'd taken the job at Marion. And even before that. When had he fallen in love with the game anyway? His eyes drifted up from the screen and gazed out across the lake. Wasn't it when he was just a baby? There were pictures of him holding a football before he could crawl.

Images flooded his mind, memories he hadn't walked through in more than a decade.

His dad's life had revolved around the game, much like Abby's father's always had. The two men had played at University of Michigan, where they'd become best friends.

John's father had gone into banking after college, but not Abby's. He'd coached the game, too.

"It's in my blood." He always grinned when he said that. "I wouldn't know what to do with myself if I wasn't around football."

That's how it had been for John. It didn't matter that his father rarely talked about his prowess on the field. When John was old enough to wear a uniform, he begged his parents to sign him up. From the moment he took his first down as a player, John knew he'd play the game as long as he lived.

An image came to him then . . . him and his family visiting Abby and her parents at their lakeside home in Lake Geneva, Wisconsin. He'd met Abby before, but that year he was seventeen and a senior in high school. She was a freshman, just fourteen.

But she was a football coach's daughter, and it showed in everything she did. She could throw and catch a ball better than most boys her age, and the two of them spent hours barefoot on the beach tossing the pigskin back and forth.

"You're not so bad for a girl," John had teased her.

She had held her head a bit higher. Older boys hadn't intimidated her, not when her father coached sixty of them every year at the high school. John knew the team often hung out at Coach

Chapman's house, playing on the lake or eating barbecued chicken with her family.

Abby's response that afternoon was something that rang clear in his memory. She had stared at John, her eyes dancing. "And you're not so bad for a *boy.*"

John had laughed hard, hard enough that eventually he took off after her, tickling her and letting her believe she could outrun him. The truth was he could run like the wind back then. Like his father, John had become a great quarterback and was being pursued by a dozen major universities—including their fathers' alma mater, Michigan.

One night that summer, the two families brought blankets down to the sandy shoreline and Abby's father built a bonfire. They sang songs about God. Not the usual silly campfire songs about chickens or trains comin' round the mountain, but sweet songs about peace and joy and love and a God who cared deeply for all of them. When the songs ended and the adults were lost in their own conversation, John moved next to Abby and poked her with his elbow.

"You got a boyfriend, little Miss Abby Chapman?" He grinned at her, imagining her in five years or ten. When she'd grown up some.

Again she kept her cool. "I don't need a boyfriend." She bumped his bare foot with her own.

He nudged her back. "That so?" A grin spread across his face.

"Yes." Her head raised another notch and she leveled her gaze straight at him. "Boys can be very immature." She studied him for a moment. "Let me guess . . . you've got a different girlfriend every week, right? That's how it is with Dad's quarterbacks."

John laughed out loud before he looked at her again and answered her question. "I guess I'm different."

Abby's eyes grew wide in mock amazement. "What? John Reynolds has no girlfriend?"

He reached for the football—one was seldom more than an arm's length away that entire summer—and tossed it lightly in the air a few times. "*This* is my girlfriend."

Abby nodded, eyes twinkling. "She'll make a great prom date, I'm sure."

He pushed her foot again and lowered his eyes with a wink. "Shhh. You'll offend her."

John blinked, and the memory disappeared.

After that summer, John was certain he would marry Abby Chapman one day. It wasn't something he made a conscious decision about, like deciding what college to attend or what discipline to major in. Rather it was something that grew from his heart, a truth that simply was.

But since that had been a long way off, John had poured his heart and soul into his first love—football. Especially the following year when he accepted a scholarship to the University of Michigan.

John lifted his chin a bit and scanned the tops of the trees. How far could he throw the ball back then? Sixty yards? Seventy? He closed his eyes and remembered the feel of the earth beneath his feet, the explosive push with every step, as he flew out of the pocket, looking for a receiver downfield.

His parents never missed a game, but one contest would always stand out in his mind. It was at the end of his junior season, a game against Michigan's chief rival, Ohio State. Michigan won by three touchdowns that afternoon, and after the game John and his father had walked through one of the neighborhoods and found an old bench at Allmendinger Park.

"It feels so good seeing you out there, son. Watching you lead that team the way I did all those years ago."

John's father was rarely in a pensive mood, but that afternoon was different. John kept quiet and let his father talk.

"Sometimes watching you is like watching myself, every step, every throw . . . as though I'm down there doing it all over again, living it all over again."

"There's nothing like it."

"No." His father had teared up then, something John had seen only a handful of times in his life. "Definitely not. Out there on the field . . . it's you and your team and the ball, living out a drama, a battle, so rich and powerful that only another player could understand."

"Yes, sir."

"And time's a thief, son. You only get so many downs, so many whistles. So many games. Before you know it, you'll be grown up and watching your own son play. Then you'll know what I mean."

Of course in the end, his father had been right. John's years of Michigan football flew by, and late in his last game as a senior, he snapped the ligaments in his knee. Though he'd had pro scouts calling earlier that year, they disappeared after his injury and no one had to tell him to look at the clock. The truth was as real as his impending graduation.

His football playing days were over.

John kept the tape of his last game handy in the file cabinet of his mind. He remembered suiting up in the locker room, bantering back and forth with his teammates and swapping barbs as though they had forever.

Four quarters later, John was huddled on the bench, his knee swathed in three rolls of Ace bandaging, when the final whistle blew. Even now he remembered how strange it felt. How right up until that whistle, he and his teammates had just one thought in mind: beat Illinois.

They'd needed a victory in order to get a bowl bid that year. But after John's injury, Illinois ran a punt back for a touchdown and Michigan never regained the lead. Only then, in the sad silence that followed, did the reality sink in.

It was over. The game, the season . . . and John Reynolds's career.

John had glanced up at the stands, at the people filing out, and wondered what they were thinking. Better luck next year, maybe? Or what's wrong with the Wolverines? Whatever their thoughts, only one man knew how John was feeling that afternoon . . . how it felt to play a game for sixteen straight seasons and then have it be over in as much time as it took a referee to blow a whistle. Only one man knew how John's heart had ached that day, the man who hugged him an hour later after he'd turned in his uniform and showered and changed. A man who said nothing while he quietly grieved the fact that it was all finally and suddenly over.

His father.

John swallowed and remembered how proud his dad had been when he called him that afternoon in 1985 and told him the news.

"They hired me, Dad! I'm the head coach at Marion High."

"Marion, huh?"

"Yep. It's a brand-new school, and I've got a truckload of ideas. I'm going to build a program here, Dad. Something new and different and better than anything in the state."

"New programs are hard, son. Have you talked to Abby's father?"

"Not yet. And you're right." John had been barely able to contain his enthusiasm. "I know it'll be hard. But I can't let that bother me. We have good kids in this town, good teachers. A good administration. We'll start at the bottom, and in a few years we'll be league contenders. After that, who knows?"

"Is Abby excited?"

"She's happier than I am. She said she'll write press releases about the team for the paper and start a booster club. And when Kade's old enough, I'll take him with me to practice."

His father had chuckled. "Kade's only two, son."

"But he's already walking. I'll let him come to practice with Abby even this year."

"Okay, but don't forget what I told you."

"About what?"

"About how it feels to watch your son play. I hope I'm there to see it happen." His dad laughed again. "Your day's coming."

And so it had . . . but not in time for his father to see it. Four years after John took the job at Marion, his father died of a heart attack. Only Abby knew the extent of John's loss—how he'd lost not just a father, but a mentor and coach. And most of all, a friend.

Coaching football was the cure for John's grief. It turned out to be almost as great a thrill as playing the game. But there was one very wonderful difference. A player's days were numbered. A few years in high school, a few years in college for the talented ones.

Not so for a coach.

Every year a group of teary-eyed seniors would play their last football game for Marion High. Then, come fall, John and his staff would be back, welcoming in a new crop of freshmen and making plans for another season. John planned to coach until he retired. At least.

That was true even through the hard years at Marion, the years when parents grumbled that he wasn't winning games fast enough and that maybe a different man should have been hired for the job. But those seasons led to John's first state title in 1989.

By then everyone in Marion loved John. And in 1997, Kade joined the team. Only then did John get a true sense of what his father had been talking about that day at Allmendinger Park.

Watching Kade play football left John just one regret—that his father hadn't lived to see it. Kade was everything his father and grandfather had been, and then some. He was taller, quicker, and lightning fast on his release of the ball. John couldn't count the times he'd stopped in his tracks as he watched Kade line up, watched him bark out an audible and then speed to the back of the pocket, his arm ready to fire the ball at a receiver.

His father had been right.

Watching Kade, he could almost feel the pads sliding against his shoulders, smell the rich grass beneath his feet. It was a heady experience, one that was second only to being out there and playing the game himself.

The current problems at Marion hadn't started until that past summer, a few months after Kade's graduation.

John shifted his gaze back to the water.

What would his father have thought about the attitudes among his players and parents this year? Would it have jaded him? Made the

game seem less somehow? And then there was the thing John liked to think about least of all.

How would his father have handled John's resignation?

The man would have been crushed to see John in a wheelchair, to know that John would never walk or run again. And certainly he would have been saddened to know that parents were trying to get John fired. But how would he have felt knowing John was going to step down as varsity coach? Walk away without looking back?

John drew a deep breath and let his eyes fall to the computer keyboard once more. His father would have understood. Because he would have known John would have given up coaching only for one reason: if the game had changed.

And it had.

Yes, his father would've supported him completely. In fact, somewhere in heaven, his dad would most certainly know how hard the letter of resignation was to write. And as John returned his fingers to the keyboard, as he found the strength to do what he never thought he'd do, he felt convinced of one thing.

His father must be aware of all that had happened and even now, in the most difficult moment of John's football career, his dad was sitting on the fifty-yard line of heaven, cheering for him the way he'd done as far back as John could remember.

Twenty-three

JOHN WAS JUST FINISHING UP THE LETTER WHEN ABBY joined him on the pier.

Her eyes were bloodshot and pensive, like she'd been crying. She sauntered out toward him and pulled a bench up next to his wheelchair. "Finished?"

"Yep." He typed his name. "Just now."

She stared out at the lake. "It's the end of a chapter."

"It is." He reached for her hand and laced his fingers between hers. "You okay?"

Her teeth stayed clenched, but a tired sigh eased through her lips anyway. She turned to him, and he saw something that hadn't been there for months: sheer, undeniable anger. Her mouth opened, and for a while, nothing came out. Then she narrowed her eyes. "No, I'm not okay."

For a long time he'd suspected things weren't as well with Abby as she tried to make it seem. He asked her about her feelings now and then, but always she said the same thing. She was fine . . . she was grateful . . . she was happier than ever. So glad that he'd lived . . . so glad their marriage was back to what it had been when they were younger.

All of it sounded good, just not exactly real. Not that John didn't believe her. Somewhere in her soul, Abby meant every positive thing she said. But she had always been intense, and it had seemed strange to John that in this—their greatest physical challenge as a couple—she would be passive and accepting. He waited for her to continue.

"John, I've done everything I can to make this easy for you and the kids and . . . well, easy for everyone we know." She shrugged and leaned forward, digging her elbows into her thighs. "But I'm not sure I can do it anymore."

Panic flashed across the horizon of John's heart. She couldn't do it anymore? Where was this going? "Okay. You wanna explain?"

Abby clenched her fists and gritted her teeth as she continued. "I'm so mad, John! I'm so mad I can't even stand it." She opened her hands and made circles with them. "It's like a tornado building up inside of me. Every day I'm madder than the day before."

John chose his words carefully. "Who are you mad at?"

"I don't know!" Abby's tone was loud, seething. "I'm mad at you for staying at school that night when you should've been home." She stood and paced to the end of the pier and back, her arms crossed tight in front of her. "I'm mad at Jake for hitting you, and at the doctors for not being able to make you better. I'm mad that no one thinks I might be mad about this whole thing." She let her hands fall to her sides. "And I'm mad at God for letting it happen."

John bit his lip. "You're mad at me?"

Something in his question caught her off guard, and though she tried to contain it, a single ripple of laughter spilled through her teeth. Immediately, she regained her composure. "John, don't."

"Don't what?"

"You're supposed to ask me about the last part . . . about being mad at God."

"I don't know." John lifted one shoulder and leaned back in his chair. "I can understand about being mad at God. I mean, I get mad at God sometimes." He angled his head, his eyes narrow. "But me? Come on, Abby, what'd *I* do?"

She exhaled hard. "You should've come home with me, that's what." She gave him a light push on his shoulder. "Then none of this would've happened."

"Oh . . . well . . . I guess that makes sense."

"Never mind, you big jerk. This is supposed to be *my* time to get angry." Abby made a sound that was more laugh than cry, and she pushed him again. This time he caught her hand and pulled her onto his legs. She slid the laptop computer out from beneath her and set it on the pier. At the same time he released the brake on his wheelchair.

"John!" She let loose a scream. "What're you doing? We'll both fall in the lake."

He gripped the wheels and whirled the chair around just before they went over the edge of the pier. "What's this? No trust from my fair maiden?"

She grabbed a handful of his shirt and he grinned. "John, stop! You've lost your mind."

Instead, he wheeled the two of them to the far end of the pier, turned once more and let gravity pull the chair back down the wooden slats toward the water. Abby screamed again and tried to break free, but John held her firmly in place, one hand around her waist, one hand on the wheel of his chair. "Take it back."

They were halfway down the pier and moving fast. "What?" Abby's voice was a shrill mix of terror and exhilaration.

"Tell me you're not mad at me."

"Fine!" The water was closing in on them. "I'm not mad at you."

In a single, fluid motion, as gracefully as he'd once thrown a football, John grabbed both wheels and slowed the chair into a controlled spin. When they'd come full circle, he set the hand brake and wrapped both hands around Abby. Her eyes were wide, her body heaving to catch her breath.

"That was the craziest thing you've ever done, John Reynolds." She pushed his shoulder once more, this time harder than before. "What if you hadn't stopped in time?"

"It was under control, Abby." His tone was soft, the teasing gone. "Just like your emotions these past few months."

She froze and he could see the tears form across the surface of her eyes. "It was that obvious?"

"Of course."

A tired sigh worked its way up from somewhere deep within her. "I was afraid to tell you how I felt."

"Why? You've never been afraid before. Even when we weren't getting along."

"Because—" she let her head fall against his chest—"I was afraid you'd never recover if you knew how upset I was."

"No." He waited, choosing his words with careful precision. "I'll never recover if you can't be yourself, Abby. We can't pretend everything's okay, don't you see? There'll be days when you can't take another minute of helping me get dressed . . . days when you want to scream you're so angry. But there'll be days when I feel the same way. No matter how upbeat we pretend to be. The only way we'll survive this is if we're honest. Do you understand?"

"John . . ." The tears spilled onto her cheeks. "I'm so mad this happened to you. It's not fair. It's just not fair."

"I know, honey." He cradled her close, stroking her back. "I know."

She brought her face up against his and dried her tears on his cheeks. "I want to dance again. Don't you ever feel that way?"

"All the time." He released the hand brake again and wheeled her once more to the far end of the pier.

"John . . . what're you doing?" Her body grew taut in his arms. "Not another trip down! We'll fall in for sure this time."

"No, Abby—" they reached the top of the pier and he turned so the wheelchair was facing the water—"just lean back against me and relax."

She hesitated and for a minute he thought she might jump off. "You're serious?"

"Yes." He patted his chest. "Come on, lean back."

"What're we doing?"

"It's sort of a tango dance step. Something I've been practicing." He eased Abby back against him so they were both facing forward. "Okay . . . now you've gotta let everything go . . . your anger, your frustration . . . all of it. The dance doesn't work otherwise."

She giggled and the sound did wonders for his soul. "Okay. I'm ready."

John released the hand brake and the chair began rolling down the pier toward the water. Abby's laughter grew louder and she pressed her back against him. "It's kinda fun when you're not scared."

"The tango always is."

"Perky Paula would be proud."

The chair picked up speed, and their laughter built until, a few yards from the water, John slowed the chair and turned it for one final spin. After that he wove the chair back and forth, his voice a gentle whisper in Abby's ear. "Do you hear it?"

"Mmmmm." Her soft moan sounded deep against his chest. "I think so."

"The dance steps might change, Abby—" he kissed her earlobe— "but the music's still playing."

They stayed that way, swaying to the distant breeze and the rustling of still bare branches, until finally Abby shifted herself onto one of his knees and kissed him, long and slow. "You know what?"

"What?"

"I'm not angry anymore. At least for now."

"See . . . the tango, Abby." He brushed his nose against hers. "Works every time."

"No—" their lips met again and again—"your love works every time."

John was about to kiss her once more when it happened. It was so brief, so fleeting, John knew it might be nothing. But then . . . he paused, going stone still. What else could cause it to happen?

Abby drew back a few inches. "What is it, John? You're scaring me."

He gulped and concentrated on the place where he'd felt it. Then, as though God wanted him to know it wasn't a fluke or some figment of his imagination, he felt it again. Sort of a twinge or a burning sensation in his big toe. A place where he hadn't felt anything since the accident.

"Abby, you're not going to believe this." He looked straight at her, seeing past the surface to the heart of this woman he loved.

"What? Tell me." Abby leaned back further, looking down the length of him. "Is something wrong?"

"No." He pointed to his feet, his heart thudding hard against the wall of his chest. "Just now, just a few seconds ago . . . something happened. Something I can't explain."

"What was it?" She climbed off him and stood, studying his legs.

Suddenly he realized that what he was about to say would sound ludicrous. Maybe it was only phantom pain, something he'd read about where months or even years after paralysis a person might have the memory of sensation.

He couldn't say something that would build false hope only to destroy it when they found it wasn't so. He'd tell her soon, but not yet. Abby was staring at him, waiting. *Think, John . . . come on . . . make something up.*

"Well . . ." He smiled big at her. "I think we invented a new dance step."

The wind left Abby's lungs in a rush. "John, I thought you were hurt . . . like maybe you couldn't breathe or something."

He chuckled, hiding the excitement welling in his soul. "Nope. Don't you know, Abby? Dancing is good for the lungs." He patted his chest. "After a routine like the one we just did, I'll be breathing good for days."

"You're such a teaser." Abby reached for his hand, and together they made their way up the pier and toward the house. "You shouldn't do that. I really thought something was wrong."

They were halfway up the yard when it happened again. This time John had no doubt about what he was feeling. This was no phantom pain, no memory of previous sensation. He felt a burning twinge in his toe. And this time something else happened. Something he could barely keep to himself.

His toe moved!

John had no idea what that meant or why it was happening. But he had the strangest sense that something—or Someone—was working on his spine. It didn't feel like the hands of a doctor or a therapist.

It felt like the very fingers of God.

Twenty-four

CHUCK PARKER HAD JUST WALKED IN THE DOOR WHEN the call came in.

He was an insurance broker, and this past winter had been busy—busier than any in his life. Not only was business booming, but with Casey's driver's license suspended for a year, Chuck or his wife had to drive the boy everywhere he went.

The worst part about being so busy was that Chuck hadn't had time to stage the meeting. Ever since finding out about Coach's paralysis, Chuck had wanted a group discussion at school about the way they'd handled Coach Reynolds this past season. He'd made a handful of phone calls, but no meeting had materialized. The trouble was time. With so much on his plate, the idea had simply gotten away from him.

But no worries. As long as he and the other parents had backed off from pressuring Herman Lutz, Coach Reynolds's job was safe. Maybe they didn't actually need a meeting. When Coach returned next fall, certainly he'd see that everyone had changed after what had happened. The players, the students. Even the parents.

The phone rang three times before Chuck grabbed it. "Hello?"

"Mr. Parker? This is Sue Diver down at Marion High."

Sue Diver . . . Chuck wracked his brain. Oh, right. Sue. The secretary at school. Carried a whole-life policy he'd written up for her back in '98. He glanced at his watch. He had three evening appointments starting in thirty minutes. "Hey, Sue . . . what's up?"

"A letter came into the office today." Her voice was low, troubled.

"Okay . . ."

"I don't know if I'm supposed to be telling you this."

"I'm sure it's fine, Sue. Otherwise you wouldn't have felt the need to call."

His words seemed to work. He could hear her take a quick breath. "It's a resignation letter from Coach Reynolds. He's resigning effective immediately. Says that the game has passed him by . . . and that the parents no longer respect him."

What? Chuck felt as though the floor beneath him had given way. Why hadn't he scheduled the meeting sooner? Now it was too late. If Herman Lutz read the letter, he'd have Coach Reynolds's job posted on the state listing in twenty-four hours. Probably believing it was what everyone wanted.

Only that wasn't true at all. Not anymore.

He closed his eyes and pinched the bridge of his nose between his thumb and forefinger. "I'm gonna need some phone numbers, Sue. Can you get me the names and numbers of all the guys on the team?"

"I think so."

"Good." He looked at his stack of appointment files. "I'll make the calls tonight. What's the next available time on the school calendar?"

The sound of rustling paper filled the background. "Today's Monday, let's see . . ." More muffled paper sounds. "How about Thursday night?"

Chuck looked at his calendar. He had four appointments scheduled for that night. "Perfect. Let's set it for seven o'clock. In the auditorium."

"Okay. I'll run it by the administration, but it shouldn't be a problem. Parents are allowed to use the building for school-related meetings."

Sue sounded worried, like she was trying to convince herself. But it didn't matter. After months of procrastinating, Chuck had the meeting scheduled. Now all he needed were the phone numbers. "You have those numbers nearby?"

"Uh . . . can I fax you the list?"

"Absolutely." Chuck rattled off his fax number. "I'll be waiting. And, Sue, thanks for the tip. We'll have to get together one of these days and see if we can't upgrade your policy."

"Sure, Mr. Parker. Listen, I have to go."

The moment Chuck hung up, his fax line began to ring. Chuck made three quick calls to cancel his appointments. Then, when he had the phone list in hand, he took a deep breath and began to call.

John refused to get Abby's hopes up.

But that night, before they went to bed, he casually mentioned that he needed to see the doctor. Soon, if possible.

"Why?" Abby had helped him into bed, and now she was getting ready.

"I'm just concerned about my legs." John forced himself to look relaxed. "They're too thin."

"Honey . . ." Abby stopped and gave him a sad look. "The doctor said that would happen. It's normal."

John searched for a way to convince her. "Not this thin . . . and not this fast." He pressed the blankets down against his legs. As he did, his right toe moved just a bit. "I'm wasting away, Abby. The doctor needs to hear about it."

"Really?" A puzzled look came over her face. "Well, if you think so. I'll call Dr. Furin in the morning."

The next day after breakfast John was drinking coffee in the kitchen when Abby found him. "He can see you at eleven today."

"Good." He blew at the steam rising from his cup. "I'm sure there's something he can do."

"Mind if I drop you off?" Abby was a blur of motion, straightening the kitchen and sorting through a stack of papers on the counter. "We need a few things at the store."

"Sure. Fine . . . I'll be in the waiting room whenever you get back." John couldn't believe his good fortune. The last thing he wanted to do was talk about his toes moving in front of Abby. As hard as the past few months had been on her, there was no point getting her hopes up now.

Two hours later, John was in the examination room when Dr. Furin walked in. "John . . . I understand you're worried about the wasting process in your legs."

John gave a short laugh. "Actually, that's not it at all. I just . . ." He reined in his enthusiasm so he could think more clearly. "I couldn't tell Abby the real reason I wanted to see you. I didn't want to get her hopes up."

"Okay." Dr. Furin set his clipboard down near the sink. "What's the real reason?"

"Doc—" John's smile worked its way up his cheeks—"I'm feeling something in my right toe." John held up one hand. "Not constantly and not a lot. But several times yesterday and again today. Sort of like a burning feeling, a flash of pain, maybe. And a few times I've felt the toe move."

Dr. Furin's mouth hung open. "You're serious?"

"Completely. You're the only one I've told."

The doctor stood and paced to the window and back, taking slow, deliberate steps. "When we checked your X rays the first time, it looked almost as though you were one of the lucky ones. Your break was in an area where people sometimes regain feeling. But usually that happens within a few days, after the swelling goes down."

He paced a bit more, stroking his chin and staring vacantly at the floor. "Your feeling didn't come back, so we took more pictures, did more tests. And after that it looked like I was wrong. Like the break was just a hair into the area where paralysis is permanent."

John studied the doctor, trying to understand. "So, why am I feeling something in my right toe?"

"In all my years working with people who've injured their spinal cords, I've never treated a patient whose break fell so close to the dividing line. A fraction higher, you walk again. A fraction lower, you're in a chair for the rest of your life. But maybe . . ."

John waited until he couldn't stand it another minute. "What?"

"Recent research has shown that in a few rare cases, a break is so close to the separating line that surgery can be done to wire the spinal cord back together. Sometimes, after surgery, feeling can be restored. Even when it appeared that a person was paralyzed for life."

The news was more than John had hoped for. His hands shook as he stared at Dr. Furin. "And you think maybe I might be one of those people?"

"We'll have to do tests, but if I remember right, the first symptom is feeling in one or more toes. And I'm already certain your break happened in the area where research is being done."

John wanted to shout, to raise a fist in the air and holler at the good news. Instead he stayed quiet and turned his thoughts heavenward. *God . . . thank You. Thank You for this second chance.* He couldn't wait to begin the tests. Whatever needed to be done, he wanted to do it. Because if a surgery might restore feeling to his legs, he was ready to go under the knife that afternoon.

"Can you stay awhile?"

John laughed. "Operate on me now, Doc! I'm ready."

"You need to know something." Dr. Furin frowned. "Even if you're a candidate for the surgery, there's no guarantee it'll work. The research is too new. So far it looks like only about half the people who undergo surgery ever regain feeling in their extremities."

"Look, Doctor, those odds are a whole lot better than what I had before I came in here. When can we start testing?"

"I'd like to take more pictures and run a few more specific tests—tests that must be done in the hospital. Normally it takes weeks to schedule these types of pictures, but I had a cancellation today." He hesitated. "I do think you need to tell your wife what's going on. The tests will take most of the afternoon, and she'll need to drive you to the hospital so you can take them."

John nodded. How would she react? Would she be afraid of being disappointed? Anxious? Excited? Either way, the doctor was right. It was time for her to know.

Dr. Furin took a set of X rays, and thirty minutes later, John was in the examination room when Abby walked in. "Sorry." She leaned over and kissed his cheek. "It took longer than I thought."

"Abby . . . sit down." He motioned to a folding chair against one wall. "We need to talk."

Her face went slack, and he knew it was from fear. But she did as he asked, and when their knees were nearly touching, she swallowed hard. "What's wrong? Don't tell me there's something else."

He couldn't keep her waiting another minute. "Abby, yesterday . . . when I told you something strange was happening . . ."

She thought back and then remembered. "When you invented that new dance step?"

"Right." He reached out and she took his hand in hers. "Well, that wasn't exactly what was going on."

Her chin fell a little, but she said nothing.

"The truth is, I was getting pains in my right toe." His voice grew soft. "I was feeling it, Abby. I really was. Then when we walked into the house, my toe moved." He glanced around the room, looking for a way to describe how it had felt. "I thought maybe I was imagining it . . . like maybe it hadn't really happened. But then I felt it again before we went to sleep and again this morning."

"That's why you wanted to come today?"

John nodded. "I had to tell Dr. Furin. Because everyone had told me I'd never have feeling like that again. Phantom pain, maybe. But not real feeling. And there was no doubt this was real pain . . . real movement."

"So—" Abby ran her tongue over her bottom lip—"what'd Dr. Furin say?"

John did his best to explain the situation, how once in a rare while a certain type of broken neck could be operated on and feeling, possibly restored. "It's still a long shot, Abby. He wants to do more tests this afternoon. If I'm a candidate for surgery, he'll know after that."

Abby's mouth hung open, her eyes wide as she took in the news. She leaned forward, grabbing his chair with both hands. "You're *serious?*"

"Completely." John loved the hope in Abby's eyes. *Please, Lord . . . get us through this. Give us a miracle.* There was no audible answer, not even a still, silent whisper in his soul, but John was suddenly overwhelmed with an indescribable peace.

"Okay, then. Let's get you over to the hospital."

The tests took five hours and were as exhausting as they were long. Abby contacted Nicole midway through the day and asked her to pick up Sean when school was out.

"What's going on?"

"I'll tell you later." Abby hurried through the conversation, anxious to rejoin John. "I promise."

Dr. Furin arrived near the end of the day and began reading the results with a team of spinal cord specialists. Finally, at six o'clock that evening John's doctor met them in the hospital lobby.

John prided himself on being able to read a person's expression, but Dr. Furin could've made his living playing poker. It was impossible to tell the results from the look on his face. He motioned for them to follow him to a quieter corner where they wouldn't be distracted.

Abby held tight to John's hand, so tight he could feel the pulse in her fingertips. "What'd you find out?"

Dr. Furin allowed just the hint of a smile. "John's a candidate for surgery. His injury is almost textbook perfect, the kind they've done research on."

For a moment, John let his head fall. He'd been granted a second chance! An opportunity, no matter how slim, to have his legs again. It was more than he could imagine, more than he could bear.

When he looked up, he saw that Abby had covered her mouth with her free hand. Small soblike sounds were coming from her throat, but her eyes were dry. She was probably in shock, like him. Who'd have ever thought it possible? After so many months of being paralyzed?

John had never heard of such a thing. "When can we do the surgery?"

"No time soon." Dr. Furin folded his hands and leaned forward. "I'll want the nation's top experts to perform the operation. I'll assist, but since it's their research, they should do the surgery."

"They'll come here?" John still couldn't believe he was having this conversation. "I thought with specialists you have to go wherever they're based."

"They do most of their work in Arizona, but they're willing to travel for an extraordinary case. I'd say yours fits that description."

"So when, Doctor?" Abby's palms were damp. "How soon?"

"It's March now. I'd say four weeks. Sometime in mid-April. It'd probably take that long to pull the team together."

"Is there anything we can do between now and then?" John eased his arm around Abby's shoulders and hugged her close. The feeling of hope was so strong it was almost a physical assault. If the doctor hadn't been there, John would've pulled Abby onto his lap and held her until they were ready to talk about the possibilities.

"Yes." Abby's teeth chattered. "Anything we can do so the surgery will be more successful. A special diet or exercises? Anything?"

"Yes." Dr. Furin looked from Abby to John, and back again. "In a situation like this, there's one thing I'd recommend." He paused and his eyes shifted to John's once more. "Go home and pray. Have your kids and your friends and your family pray. Get the whole town praying. Pray for us . . . pray for yourself . . . pray for a miracle. After that we'll put you under the knife and do our best. It's the only chance you have."

Dr. Furin explained a bit more about the operation, and then he left. The moment he was gone, John turned to Abby and held out his arms. She climbed on his lap like a child who'd been lost for a week. Then, unconcerned with whoever else might be in the waiting room or passing by in the hallways, John and Abby brought their heads together and prayed. Not just because it was doctor's orders, but because a miracle was standing on the front porch of their lives. And John intended to beg God night and day to open the door and let it in.

Jake Daniels had a funny feeling about his mom and dad.

His hearing was in one week, the one where he and his attorney would agree to plead guilty to a list of charges, things A. W. and the district attorney had agreed on. His dad had extended his leave of absence from work and was still staying at the hotel in town. But Jake wondered if sometimes he might be really sleeping on the sofa downstairs.

There were nights when his dad was there, talking to his mother, long after Jake turned in. And in the mornings, his father would be in the kitchen making coffee. The whole situation felt strange. After all, his folks were divorced. But sometimes—when Jake wandered downstairs before breakfast and found his dad in the kitchen—it was sort of nice to pretend that his family had never really split up. Or that they'd somehow gotten back together.

It was possible, wasn't it? After all, they were out together tonight.

Jake flopped down on his bed just as the phone rang. He caught a glimpse of the alarm clock on his dresser. Nearly nine o'clock. Only a few people could be calling this late. His attorney, or his mother.

In fact, Jake was almost positive it was his mom. Lots of times when his mother was out late with his dad, she'd call and give him some kind of explanation. Dinner was served late . . . or they'd gotten into a long conversation.

Jake didn't care.

As long as they were together, there was a chance they'd work things out. He stretched across his bed and grabbed the receiver.

"Hello?"

"Jake . . . Casey Parker."

Casey Parker? "Hey." Jake sat straight up and dropped his face in his hands. He hadn't talked to Casey since the accident. "What's up?"

"I shoulda called you sooner." There was a hitch in Casey's voice, like he was trying not to cry. "Listen, Jake. I'm sorry. About asking you to race and all. Really, man. I'm . . . I don't know what to say."

Jake searched his mind, trying to imagine why Casey would call now. "We need to move on, I guess."

"You're out at that continuation school, right?"

"Right. It's okay. I've got straight As."

"You gonna get to come back to Marion in the fall?"

It was the question his mother asked him at least once a week. The counselor had said it was okay, as long as he wasn't in a juvenile detention center. By then Jake would be finished with his mandatory house arrest—a time when he wasn't allowed to go anywhere but to continuation school and home again. If he wasn't locked up, he'd be involved in community service, telling teens at other schools why they needed to avoid street racing.

Everyone seemed to think he'd be better off at Marion in the fall, spending his senior year at his own school, being a living reminder to his peers that racing could have tragic consequences. But Jake wasn't sure. It was one thing to talk with Coach Reynolds in a courtroom. It would be another entirely to watch him wheeling his way around Marion High.

"I'm not sure."

"Yeah, well. I don't blame you. It's tough being at school." Casey hesitated. "Coach is still at home. Everyone says he'll be back in the fall."

"Yep." Jake felt sick to his stomach. Where was the conversation going? "Hey, thanks for calling. I gotta get some rest before—"

"Wait." Casey's voice was urgent. "That's not why I called."

"Okay."

"We're having a meeting for Coach Reynolds."

"A meeting?" Jake's heart skipped a beat. "What kind of meeting?"

"I guess Coach sent in a resignation letter, saying he was done with football because he didn't have—" Casey's voice cracked some and it was a while before he could speak again. "He didn't have the support he needed."

Jake's heart broke at the news. Not only did Coach have to deal with his injury, but he had to live with the fact that right before he'd gotten hurt, the parents had ganged up against him. "What's the meeting for?"

"A lot's changed since Coach got hurt, Jake. We've had a chance to . . . I don't know, maybe look at ourselves a little closer. I think we realized—even the parents—that it wasn't Coach after all. It was us. You know what I mean?"

"I do. So it's a good meeting?"

"Absolutely. Anyone who wants Coach to stay with the Eagles next year is supposed to come and talk. The guys'll start spreading the word tomorrow at school. I think a lot of kids are gonna go. A lot of parents, too."

Jake was certain he could get permission from the judge to attend. He had just one question. "Has anyone invited Coach Reynolds?"

"Well . . ." Casey paused. "We were kind of hoping you could do that."

After all that had happened, Jake felt nothing but honor at the chance to call Coach Reynolds and invite him to the meeting. "I'll do it as soon as I hang up."

"Okay. The meeting's Thursday night at seven."

"See ya there."

Jake hung up and imagined Coach Reynolds surrounded by a huge room full of people who loved him. The thought gave Jake more peace than anything had in months. He smiled to himself, thinking of what he'd like to say if he could get up the courage. Then he did something he never expected to do again as long as he lived.

He dialed Coach Reynolds's phone number and waited.

Twenty-five

THE MARION HIGH AUDITORIUM WAS FILLED WITH police officers.

Chuck Parker took the microphone and started to talk, but the officers threw things at him and shouted for John. Slowly, uncertainty in his eyes, John wheeled himself up onto the stage, but the entire auditorium booed him. The moment he reached for the microphone, a dozen officers rushed the stage and handcuffed him. One of them looked at the crowd and said, "Coach Reynolds knew his players were drinking . . . he knew they were street racing. Now it's time for him to pay."

They pushed John off the stage, and not once did he speak up for himself.

"John . . . tell them what really happened!" Abby stood and yelled at him from the back of the room. "Tell them you didn't know about those things."

But John only turned around and waved at her. "It's my fault, Abby . . . it's my fault . . ."

She tried to run after him, but an officer grabbed her arm and began telling her something about having a right to remain silent.

"Don't *touch* me! My husband did nothing wrong . . . nothing! This whole meeting is a setup and—"

Something caught her attention. A buzzing or a hum of some kind. It grew louder and louder . . .

Abby sat straight up in bed, gasping for breath. She glanced at John. He hadn't been taken away by police. He was asleep beside her. The sound came again and suddenly she realized what it was.

John was snoring.

She fell back against the pillow. The week's emotional chain of events was almost more than Abby could bear.

First, the doctor's determination that they could operate on John's back, and the knowledge that maybe—just maybe—he might regain use of his legs. Then the call from Jake Daniels. The team, the parents . . . nearly the entire school planned to turn out for a meeting on John's behalf.

But what exactly did they want to say? Abby felt her heart rate return to normal. Obviously she was worried about it. Whatever it was, the idea of meeting with the very people who had tried to ruin John did not sit well with her.

The day passed in a blur of housework and other errands until finally it was six o'clock and the meeting was in just one hour. John was shaving upstairs, and Abby stared at the telephone. There was time for a quick call to Nicole. The poor girl had wanted desperately to go to the meeting, but she'd already made plans to have Matt's parents over for dinner. Besides, she was seven months pregnant and more tired than usual.

Neither Nicole nor the other kids knew about John's impending surgery. Abby and John wanted to tell them on the weekend, when everyone was at the house. Then as soon as the details were out, they could place a speakerphone call to Kade and share the news together.

Nicole answered on the first ring. "Hello?"

"Hi, honey. It's Mom."

"Oh, hi. Aren't you supposed to be at the meeting?"

"It's not till seven." Abby poured a bit of lotion on the palm of her hand and worked it into her fingers. "How are you, dear? It worries me that you're so tired. Usually the seventh and eighth month aren't like that."

"I don't know, Mom." Nicole lowered her voice. "I don't want Matt to worry, but this afternoon while I was making spaghetti sauce, I had some of those false contractions. Only this time they were pretty strong."

"Is the baby moving around okay?"

"Not so much this evening. But earlier it felt like she was doing backflips."

"She?" There was teasing in Abby's voice. Matt and Nicole had decided not to find out whether they were having a boy or girl. They wanted to be surprised. "Are you trying to tell me something?"

"It's just a guess. I have a hunch it's a girl. Matt thinks it's a boy. So I guess one of us'll be—" Nicole groaned.

"Nic, what is it?"

"Ugggh." Nicole grabbed a few quick breaths. "Just another false contraction. See what I mean? They're getting harder all the time."

Abby worked to keep the concern from her voice. "Honey, you need to write down the time and keep track of them. If they get stronger or start coming more regularly, have Matt take you in. Please, sweetie. That's nothing to mess with."

Nicole promised she'd keep track of the pains, and then she asked Abby to pass a message on to John. "Tell Daddy Matt's been praying for him. That whatever's said at this meeting will be an encouragement."

"*Matt's* been praying? What about y—"

"Don't start, Mom." A sigh sounded across the phone lines. "You know how I feel about it."

Abby did know, and she still couldn't believe it was happening. Life was tragic enough when having her husband lose his ability to walk. But watching Nicole lose her ability to pray? They chatted a bit more and Abby was careful not to be critical of Nicole. She needed Abby's love, not her condemnation. The phone call ended, and Abby closed her eyes.

God . . . work on her heart. Please . . .

Have peace, daughter . . . no one can snatch her out of My hand . . .

The words were like a balm to her soul, filling in the worn-out places of her assurance with a peace that was beyond description. *No one can snatch them out of My hand.* It was a Scripture from Abby's college days. She had memorized it after having a discussion with a youth pastor about salvation.

Nicole wasn't rejecting her faith. She was merely struggling. She thought about her daughter's contractions. Certainly God would meet her where she was, one way or another, and see her through this season of doubt. And someday very soon, Abby believed with all her heart that Nicole would pray again.

Maybe even yet that night.

The meeting was already underway when John and Abby snuck in through a back door in the auditorium. The lights were low, and John had been certain the action would come to a complete halt the minute they arrived.

Instead, Abby opened the door and slipped in first, while John wheeled in behind her without a sound. Abby found a chair against the back wall and John positioned himself beside her. They stayed there in the shadows near the back while Herman Lutz took the podium.

"You're gathered here tonight for a parent-staged meeting. As you know, our district makes school buildings available for such discussion times." He held up a piece of paper and read its contents in a slow, unpracticed manner. "As athletic director at Marion High, I wanted to make sure you're all clear on the boundaries. Please keep your comments as positive as possible, and let's avoid any name-calling. In addition, you should know that the opinions expressed here tonight are not those of the administration or staff."

The man seemed bored and condescending. The same way he

acted around the coaches and students at Marion. John tried not to let his attitude bother him.

Lutz shaded his eyes and gazed at the front row of seats. "Mr. Chuck Parker, you called this meeting, so please get the discussion started."

So it was true. Chuck Parker had called the meeting. The very man who had argued with John before the season about whether his son should play quarterback, and—according to Jake, anyway—the one who had spearheaded the attack against his character. John leaned back in his wheelchair. As he did, he felt Abby's hand alongside his. He held it, glad for her presence, and even more glad that they hadn't been spotted.

Now that his eyes had adjusted to the light, he could see the auditorium more clearly. It was packed. Hundreds of people had turned out. What in the world could all those people have to say?

Chuck Parker made his way to the microphone and, for a long while, said nothing at all. He cleared his throat and glanced at his shoes. When he looked up, his cheeks were deep red. "I called this meeting for one reason. To apologize publicly to Coach John Reynolds."

Abby squeezed his hand, her voice barely audible. "It's about time."

John strained to hear. He didn't want to miss a word.

"Many of you remember how I acted last season. To satisfy my own agenda, I tried to convince you Coach Reynolds was not the man our Eagles needed on the football field." He glanced down once more. "But I've done a lot of thinking since then."

Chuck looked up and paced a few steps in either direction. "What happened with our boys this past season was *my* fault." He pointed at the audience. "And the fault of any of you parents who tried to turn your kid against Coach Reynolds." He hesitated. "What hope did my boy have as an Eagle when all he heard from me were cuts against his coach? The more I attacked the man, the more Casey lost respect for him. Once players lose respect for the coach, it doesn't matter what the man might do or what kind of talent the team might have.

Everyone loses. It's that simple." He paused. "But it took a tragedy for me to sort it out and see it for myself."

John wondered if he were dreaming. Never in his wildest imagination had he thought Chuck Parker would face the Marion faithful and admit he'd undermined John's coaching authority. He shot a quick look at Abby. There were tears on her cheeks, but she was quiet, soaking in the things being said.

"I tried to get Coach Reynolds fired. But I was wrong." Parker shrugged and seemed at a loss for words. "Coach sent in his resignation letter this week. I guess if there's another reason I called this meeting, it's to convince Coach we want him back at Marion High. The program won't be the same without him."

Chuck opened the meeting up to whoever wanted to speak. Several parents went first, and John's astonishment only grew. These were people he'd always assumed had supported him. Yet one at a time they apologized for siding with a handful of parents who'd had an agenda against him.

One parent said, "What we did to Coach Reynolds last year made us losers, and it made our sons losers. I'm ashamed of myself, and I'm glad for the chance to tell the rest of you how I feel."

John shifted in his chair. No wonder he'd felt such pressure. Even parents who smiled at his face had talked behind his back. He and Abby exchanged a look. It was easy to see she was thinking the same thing.

Next at the podium was a wave of parents who had publicly opposed John. They, too, expressed sorrow at what they'd done.

"Not just because he's hurt now," one father said. "The reason we're here today isn't because we pity Coach Reynolds. It's because we're ashamed of ourselves and the way we treated him."

Thirty minutes into the meeting, the first of several players stood to speak. He was a lineman, a soft-spoken athlete named Buck, whose intensity came out only on the field.

Until now.

"Coach Reynolds was not a regular coach, not the kind of man you take for granted." Buck looked uncomfortable at the small podium, but he continued, passion ringing in his voice. "Coach had us to his home for movies and dinners. One time he told us if we ever needed a place to go so we wouldn't drink at a party, we could come to his house." Buck's voice lifted louder. "He loved us that much. See, that's the thing I want you parents to know. You took a stand against a man who cared about us more than any coach I've ever heard of. We were the luckiest athletes in the state of Illinois. Because Coach loved us." He hung his head for a moment. "All I'm saying is, now it's time to get the message back to Coach . . . that we love him, too."

A lump formed in John's throat and refused to budge. He blinked back tears and listened as, one after another, his players took the podium and echoed Buck's thoughts. So they did care, after all. It was worth more than John could have imagined. He brought Abby's hand to his lips and gave it a tender kiss.

She smiled at him and mouthed, "They love you, John."

Finally there was a lull in the action and a ripple of whispers fanned across the spectator section. All eyes were on someone, but John couldn't make out who it was. Finally the boy came into view.

Jake Daniels.

John hadn't seen him since that day in court, and he looked different now. Older, more grown up. He was no longer the carefree star athlete he'd been back in November.

Abby leaned closer. "What's the commotion about?"

"Jake hasn't been back at Marion High since the accident."

"Oh." Her eyes grew wide. "I didn't know."

"This must be hard for him."

Jake was neither shy nor awkward. Instead he handled the microphone like a professional, making eye contact with different sections of the audience.

"I'm here to tell you the truth regarding some rumors that went around about Coach Reynolds last year." He paused, his eyes intense.

"First of all, yes, some of us guys on the team drank during summer camp last August. I was one of them. And a few guys raced."

John exchanged a look with Abby. So, Jake had been one of the drinkers. John was fairly sure the boy hadn't raced, though. At least not back then. It wasn't until his father bought him the Integra that he'd been tempted to do that. And even then he'd done it just one tragic time. Still, he didn't claim innocence, nor did he point out which players had violated rules.

Jake slipped one hand in his pocket. "I look at our team last year, and I know what one of you said earlier was true. We were losers. Not just on the field, but off the field. Most of us were rule-breakers. Drinking, racing, getting into pornography."

Abby flashed John a look of alarm. She kept to a whisper. "In high school?"

"I guess."

"Was Kade involved last year, too?"

"No." John was careful to keep his voice low. His conversation with Kade that day on the fishing boat was still fresh. "Not until he got to college."

"It's that rampant?"

John nodded. "And getting worse." He had a thought then . . . Why not ask Kade to talk to the team about how pornography progresses and becomes addicting, about breaking free from it and getting help? It could have a real imp—

Then he remembered. He wouldn't be coaching next year. The new coach might not be interested in having the boys stay clear of pornographic material. And it would be up to him to plan speakers for the team.

Jake was still talking. "If that wasn't bad enough, we walked around campus thinking we ruled the school, treating other people like dirt. Making Marion High a miserable place for anyone who didn't play ball." Jake stopped and squared up to the edge of the stage, his eyes searching the audience. "We thought we were better than everyone. Even Coach Reynolds."

Jake paused. Even from the back of the room John could tell he was trying not to cry. Finally he cleared his throat and found voice enough to speak. "Coach wanted us to be upstanding, moral young men. Men of character. Anyone who's played for him has heard him say that a hundred times. He led by example."

The image of Charlene came to mind, and an arrow of guilt sliced through John's gut. He hadn't always been moral. But because of his faith, because of God's strength and not his own, he'd walked away from that situation, and steered clear of others that would have led him down the wrong path. Only by God's grace did Jake and the others see in him the type of character they now wanted to imitate.

"We had the best coach in the state. Like Buck said, a coach who loved us. And we let him get away." Jake sniffed and again seemed to be trying to get hold of his emotions. "I'm still believing that somehow God will heal Coach Reynolds, but maybe not. What I did by racing that day might have ruined Coach's legs forever." A single sob caught in Jake's throat, and he placed his fist over his mouth until he had control again. "But I think what our team did by going against him last season is worse, because we ruined his desire to coach." Jake shook his head, his voice strained. "I can only pray that someday Coach will come back and some lucky group of guys will be smart enough to know how good they've got it. Smart enough to listen to him, act like him, and play for him with all their hearts. The way I wish we would have."

John blinked back a layer of tears and looked at Abby.

"He's grown up." She had tears in her eyes.

"Yes." John turned and watched Jake leave the stage. "He has."

For several seconds there was a lull, and finally Chuck Parker took the podium. "I had hoped Coach Reynolds might be here tonight, but I think it's understandable why he isn't. Not just because of his injury, but because of the way we treated him last season. Why would he come?"

Abby nudged him. "Say something."

"Not yet." John felt awkward shouting out while Chuck was at the microphone. "Wait till he's finished."

Chuck shaded his eyes again and scanned the front of the auditorium. "So if no one else wants to say anything, I've brought a petition asking Coach Reynolds to reconsider and come back as coach for the Eagles. If each of you could sign it before you—"

"Wait!" A tall figure entered the auditorium from one of the side doors and strode toward the front of the room.

Chuck looked surprised and more than a little nervous. The student ambled onto the stage and approached the podium, and then John understood.

The boy was Nathan Pike.

John stared. It *was* Nathan, but he wasn't dressed in black and his arms and neck were free from spiked collars and leather bands. He looked like any other kid at Marion High, and there was something else. His expression was softer. So soft John almost didn't recognize him.

Nathan looked at Parker and extended his hand. "Sorry, I'm late. I have something to say. Would it be all right?"

Relief flooded Chuck's face. John was pretty sure most everyone at school had heard the rumors about Nathan. How could they not, after the football game where the boy was arrested? School officials later caught a boy from the opposing team for making the threat, but the incident hadn't helped Nathan's image, and John had heard that some still feared he might do something crazy.

But Chuck didn't hesitate. He handed over the microphone and stepped back, giving Nathan the floor. "First of all—" Nathan looked toward the back of the auditorium—"Coach Reynolds *is* here. He and his wife are in the back. I saw them when I came in."

A jumble of voices started talking at once as people craned their necks and pointed toward where John and Abby sat.

"So much for anonymity." Abby sank lower in her seat.

"Coach?" Nathan peered into the darkness. "Could you come down here?"

John's stomach fluttered and his hands felt damp.

"I'll be praying," Abby whispered.

"Thanks." John wheeled himself along the back wall and up the aisle toward the front of the room. He could feel every eye on him as he crossed the front and made his way up a ramp onto the stage.

At first the parents and players could only stare. The last time they'd seen him, he'd stood six-foot-four, bigger and stronger than life, a walking illustration of the physical power necessary for the game of football.

Now he was reduced to a wheelchair, forty pounds lighter, his legs strangely thin.

After several seconds, Jake Daniels stood and began clapping. Not polite applause, but loud, single claps that ignited the room. Before Nathan could say another word, Casey Parker stood, then Buck. Finally the entire audience rose to its feet and clapped for John in a way they'd never done before.

It was an applause that in sixty seconds made John forget an entire season of criticism and complaints. An applause that told him, yes, his players and their parents had done him wrong, but they knew they'd made a mistake and they were sorry. Not sorry for him—though certainly they were that, too. But sorry they hadn't supported him and given him a chance that past season.

When they'd taken their seats and the room was quiet again, Nathan spoke. "I think we've learned something about forgiveness tonight. Kids like me have to forgive kids like you." He looked at the place where the players sat. "And kids like you have to forgive kids like me. Those are lessons Coach taught me, things I'll remember forever." He paused. "But mostly, Coach Reynolds has to forgive us all."

John was too stunned to do anything but listen.

"Right now—" Nathan moved closer and took hold of John's wheelchair—"I'd like everyone to come up and gather round Coach while we pray for two miracles."

What was this? Nathan wanted people to pray? The entire scene was so strange it was unbelievable. Yet, it was actually happening. John stilled his mind enough to listen.

"The first miracle we need here is obvious—that Coach will walk again. The second one is just as hard to imagine. That Coach'll change his mind about resigning from the Eagles. Because we need him. We all need him."

One at a time they came—players and parents and students, many who hadn't spoken, but wanted to show their support all the same. The cluster of people on the stage grew until everyone was circled around John. Everyone except Herman Lutz and a janitor in the back of the room.

John saw Abby work her way up the aisle to the middle of the stage. She placed her hands on John's shoulders, and as the voices around him began lifting prayers to heaven, John felt movement in his feet. This time from both his big toes.

Then and there, in the quietest corner of his heart, he could almost hear God whisper to him.

Lean not on your own understanding . . .

As John closed his eyes and joined his silent voice with those of the others, as he realized the good God was indeed working out of the disaster of his past year, he knew something for certain.

He would never lean that way again.

Twenty-six

AT ELEVEN O'CLOCK THAT NIGHT, NICOLE REMEMBERED
how to pray.

By then she'd been charting contractions for most of the night, and
though they hadn't been regular, they were definitely getting stronger.

She'd played them down to Matt and his parents, not wanting to
bother anyone if they were only false contractions. She'd done the
same at nine o'clock when her mother called to update her on the
meeting at school.

"How're the pains, Nic?" There was worry in her voice.

"Fine. Nothing out of the ordinary."

Now two hours had passed, and she was in so much pain she'd
moved to the downstairs sofa, both to keep from waking Matt and to
chart the contractions. But something else bothered her—almost
more than the pain. Something her mother had asked earlier that
night on the phone.

Was the baby still moving?

At first, Nicole had said yes. There had still been movement, even
if it was less than before. But since then she'd paid more careful attention. And now, an hour after Matt's parents had gone for the night,

she was starting to panic. She hadn't felt the baby move since after dinner. Not once.

And that's what had led Nicole—for the first time since her father's accident—to pray again.

At eleven o'clock, as a pain worse than any of the others seized her and knocked her off the sofa onto her knees, she prayed as instinctively as she breathed.

God, what's happening to me? Help me, Lord . . . It's too early for the baby to come!

Silence.

When the pain ended, Nicole began to cry. There was no way to describe how she felt—both horrible and wonderful at the same time. Horrible because of the contractions, but wonderfully at peace because for the first time in far too long she'd spoken to God.

What had she been thinking these past months? Why had she convinced herself that prayer was useless? Look how faithfully God had answered her prayers about her parents. And about a thousand other things every day of her life.

Then it hit her. The reason why she'd stopped praying.

She had only seen God as faithful when her prayers were answered the way *she* wanted them answered. What did the Bible say about making requests to God? That He heard them, and that He would be faithful to answer.

Not necessarily faithful to grant the request, but faithful to move in the situation as He saw best.

She remembered something else. All prayers were not answered immediately. Otherwise there would be no need to pray without ceasing, as Scripture said to do.

Nicole climbed back onto the sofa, her abdomen still tight from the last contraction. Why hadn't she remembered those things sooner? And how could she have gone all these months without talking to God?

What a fool she'd been . . .

Tears nipped at the corners of her eyes and sorrow overwhelmed her. Had she really thought she could get through life without a relationship with her Creator? A relationship so vital she'd built her life around it? The answer resounded in her soul. No, she could never have walked away from God forever. She was merely mad at Him for allowing her father to be paralyzed.

But God never promised life would be problem-free. Nicole had always known that, had heard it all her life, but she'd never had to face it before. Never had to wrestle with the dichotomy of an all-loving, compassionate God who didn't stop terrible things from happening.

And yet . . . as she lay there, she thought back over all the years, all her life, all the ways God had touched and blessed and moved. He'd proven Himself over and over. And His Word proved even more. It told her the truth: God promised peace amid pain, and He promised life everlasting. Wasn't that more than anyone could hope for? Especially since this life was so fleeting, so unpredictable.

Another cramp gripped her stomach and this time she cried out. "Matt! Help me."

Even while the contraction was gaining strength, she glanced at the piece of paper on the arm of the sofa. The last pain had been at 10:58. She checked her watch, pursing her lips and pushing air out the way they'd taught her at the childbirth classes.

It was 11:04. Only six minutes had passed, and just seven minutes between that one and the one before it. They were getting stronger and closer together. *God . . . what should I do?*

In response she had an overwhelming sense to call Matt again. And as the pain eased she did so, this time louder than before. "Matt . . . I need you!"

She heard his feet hit the floor above her. The stairs shook as he took them two at a time. He was breathless when he turned the corner and saw her, huddled in a corner on the sofa, tears on her cheeks.

"Honey, what's wrong?"

"The baby's coming, Matt." She sobbed, still exhausted from the last contraction. "I'm having pains every six or seven minutes, and they keep getting worse."

Matt's face went pale, and he took a step back toward the stairs. "I'll get dressed and we'll go to the hospital. Wait there, okay?"

Though it only took Matt a few minutes, and despite the fact that he sped all the way to the hospital, it was nearly midnight when they admitted her. By then they'd given her a shot of something to stop the contractions, but all it had done was make her jittery and weepy.

"I need to call my parents." She reached for Matt's hand. "What if the baby comes tonight?"

"I'll call them as soon as they get you into a room."

A doctor wheeled her out of the emergency room and into an elevator, up two floors to a delivery area. "We're doing everything we can to stop your labor, Nicole, but your cervix is dilated to five centimeters and the contractions are still coming."

Five centimeters? Everything Nicole had read about having a baby agreed on one thing: rarely did labor stop once a woman was dilated that far. The doctor wheeled her into a room with bright lights and a shiny steel table. "We're still trying to stop the contractions, but you need to know the truth. You could deliver within the hour."

Nicole opened her mouth to speak, but another pain came. She rode it out, while Matt asked the questions. "My wife's only seven months pregnant, Doctor. What's that mean for the baby?"

The doctor frowned. "We'll have to wait and see. Babies born that prematurely can survive. The problem is the lungs on a child that little don't work on their own. Survival is a case-by-case situation."

A case-by-case situation? The words pelted Nicole's heart like so many rocks. This was *her* child they were talking about! The baby whose reality she had refused to embrace until that Christmas Eve in her bedroom when she'd first felt the child moving inside her. Since then she'd formed a bond with this little one, a bond deeper and stronger than anything she could have imagined possible.

"Nicole—" the doctor was trying to get her attention, and she blinked, meeting his gaze—"when's the last time you felt the baby move?"

"It's . . . it's been a while. Usually she's more active."

"Hmmm." The doctor moved a stethoscope over Nicole's belly. It took a minute before he spoke again. "The baby's showing signs of distress. It looks like we may have to let the birth happen if we're going to have a chance at saving the child."

The doctor hooked her up to another monitor. "I'll be back in a few minutes. Stay as still as possible."

He was gone and Nicole grabbed Matt's hand again. Her heart raced within her. *Please God . . . save my baby. Please.* "Matt . . . call my parents. We need everyone praying."

Matt moved toward the phone on the table near her bed. But then he stopped. "Did you say . . . ?"

"Of course." She locked eyes with him, knowing he could see her fear. "I was just mad before. I started praying a few hours ago and I haven't stopped since." A sob caught in her throat. "Now, please . . . call my parents."

Matt nodded and grabbed the phone. As he dialed, she could see another emotion join fear and worry and helplessness, those already working his features.

Relief.

Abby awoke to the shrill jangle of the phone ringing.

She jolted upright and caught her breath. Who would be calling at this hour? She reached for the phone. "Hello?"

"Mom, it's Matt." He paused long enough for her to recognize panic in his voice. A rush of adrenaline surged through her veins. Was something wrong with Nicole? She sat up straighter as Matt hurried on. "We're at the hospital and . . . the doctors can't stop Nicole's contractions. It looks like the baby's going to be born anytime. She wanted you to pray."

Abby's heart slammed against the wall of her chest. Nicole was only seven months along. That meant the baby couldn't weigh more than a few pounds at best. Suddenly she remembered Haley Ann. Would Nicole have to lose a child, also? *God, no . . . don't let it happen.*

"Mom, are you there?" Matt's voice was so tense, Abby barely recognized it.

"We're on our way."

When she hung up, she woke John. Twenty minutes later, they pulled into the hospital parking lot and made their way up to labor and delivery. Matt met them in the hallway. He was dressed in a hospital gown and paper face mask.

"They've tried everything, but they can't stop her labor." His eyes were red. "They say the baby's in distress."

Abby took another two steps toward the room where Matt had just exited. "Where is she?"

"The delivery room. The doctor said it could be any minute."

John wheeled himself closer. "Can we see her?"

"Not yet. I'm allowed back in, but the doctor wants you to wait across the hall. It's a private room. I'll come get you as soon as I know anything."

Matt hugged them both. "Nicole wanted you to pray for the baby, but pray for her, too. She's bleeding internally. Her blood pressure is way too low."

Abby had to force herself not to run down the hall and find Nicole. It was one thing that the baby was in danger . . . but Nicole? Abby hadn't even considered that possibility. Certainly God wouldn't allow something to happen to Nicole. Not now, when so much had happened. They'd already lost one daughter.

God wouldn't take a second one, would He?

Matt took off down the hall, and John reached for her fingers. "Come on." He led her to an armchair in the private waiting room and positioned himself as close to her as possible. With careful hands, he framed her face and forced her to look at him. "I know what you're thinking, Abby. But you need to stop. We have to believe God's here with us, that He'll help Nicole and the baby get through this."

Abby was too afraid to do anything but nod. "Pray, John. Please."

He bowed his head close to hers and placed Nicole and the baby in God's hands. "We trust You, God. No matter how the situation looks, no matter what else has happened before, we trust You. And we believe You'll work a miracle for our daughter and her baby."

As John prayed, Abby realized how strongly she still believed. Despite everything that had happened, God's fingerprints were everywhere. John had survived the accident, hadn't he? The two of them loved each other again, didn't they? And she'd finally been able to be honest with her feelings.

A wave of panic overshadowed her peace, but only for a moment. There was no time to fear. Not with Nicole and the baby fighting for their lives down the hallway. Even now, in the midst of a crisis, God was at work somehow.

Abby had to believe that.

Otherwise, she wasn't sure she'd make it through the night. Without her faith, another loss now would certainly send her over the edge.

A full hour passed before Matt appeared in the waiting room. He looked ten years older, but Abby felt a surge of elation. He was smiling!

"Nicole's okay. The bleeding was because of a tear in the placenta, something that can be fatal." He sucked in a slow breath, his eyes red and bleary. "I waited with her until her blood pressure came back up. She's tired, but the doctors say she's not in danger."

Abby exhaled hard. "Thank God . . . I knew He'd save her."

"What about the baby?" John put his hand on Abby's knee, his features taut.

Matt's smile faded. "It's a girl. But it doesn't look good. She's barely two pounds and she's having trouble breathing. They put her in intensive care."

So Nicole had been right. A baby girl . . . but now it looked as though none of them would even get to meet her. Poor little thing, alone in an incubator, struggling for every breath. Abby's arms ached for the chance to hold her. "Can we see either of them?"

"Nicole's back in her room. She might be asleep, but I know she'd want you to come in." Matt's gaze dropped to the floor for a moment. "I'm not sure about our little girl." His eyes met theirs again. "She's so small. I've never seen a baby that little."

They followed Matt to Nicole's room, and as they went, John tapped Abby's leg. She turned to him and he pointed to his feet. "Let's tell her."

Of course! The news about John's surgery, the chance he might walk again! It was bound to encourage her. "You tell her."

They entered the room, and Nicole opened her eyes. "Hi." Her voice was groggy. "How's the baby?"

"They're working on her, honey." Matt was at her side instantly, soothing his hand over her forehead.

Nicole looked past him to Abby and John. "She's absolutely wonderful. The littlest bit of dark hair and perfect tiny features. Have you seen her?"

"Not yet." Abby bit her lip. "She's very small, Nic."

"I know, but she's going to be okay. I feel it in my bones."

John glanced at Abby, and she nodded. A distraction would be good. Especially the type of distraction John wanted to share. He moved his wheelchair to the foot of her bed and took hold of her toes. "There's something I need to tell you, Nic."

"Okay." She blinked, her lids heavy, a smile lifting the corners of her mouth. "Sounds serious."

"It is." He looked at Abby once more. "This week I saw the doctor. He ran some tests and decided they could operate on my neck. The surgery's set to take place in about a month."

Nicole's eyes grew wide, and Matt turned an open mouth toward John. Nicole sat up straighter in bed, wincing at her soreness. "What for?"

"Well . . . I've been having feeling in my toes. Once in a while they even move a little." John's eyes twinkled. Abby doubted she'd ever been happier for him. "I guess in rare cases this kind of operation can repair the break."

"But what about your legs?" Matt's tone was gentle, awed.

John's chin quivered, and he struggled to find the words. Abby cleared her throat and finished for him. "He could regain full function."

Nicole hooted out loud. "Dad! That's amazing!"

"It's just a chance, but we're praying." John sat back in his chair and chuckled. "A while ago your mom thought God was up to something big in our lives. It looks like she was right."

"She is. I know it. Your legs and our little girl's survival." Nicole folded her arms. "You have to see her, Mom. She's so beautiful."

Sorrow circled Abby's heart, but she forced herself to smile. "I'm sure she is, honey."

"You guys are grandparents!" Nicole's voice was tired again, but her enthusiasm hadn't waned. "Can you believe it?"

Abby hadn't given the idea a single thought. The only thing that mattered was the safety of Nicole and the baby. Now that the little girl was born, she hadn't yet acknowledged the truth: she and John were grandparents. It was unbelievable, and for the briefest moment she wondered how this scene would've played out if they'd gone ahead with their divorce plans. Most likely he wouldn't have been here for this event. It would have been too awkward, too difficult.

How good God had been to them! She slipped her arm around John's shoulders and studied Nicole, the peace in her eyes. "Have you named her?"

Nicole and Matt had gone through dozens of names, never really settling on one for either a boy or a girl. But now they gave each other a subtle grin, and Nicole looked at Abby. "Yes. Haley Jo. After my sister . . . and Matt's mother."

"Oh, Nic." Abby could do nothing to stop the tears. "That's beautiful."

There was silence between them then, silence and the soft sound of tears. Abby guessed they all were thinking the same thing. The first Haley hadn't survived, and now this Haley might not either.

Before anyone could speak, the doctor came in. "Nicole, your baby's in serious distress. I know you're tired, but I'd like to get you in a wheelchair and take you down to the neonatal intensive care unit. I think it might help if she felt your touch, heard your voice."

In a blur, Nicole was lifted from the bed into a chair, and she and Matt left the room with the doctor in tow. Only Abby and John were left in the room. "What if she dies before we get a chance to see her?" Abby fell into John's lap and circled his neck with her arms.

"Then she and Haley Ann will have a party in heaven." John kissed her forehead. "And one day when it's our turn, they'll be there to greet us."

At three o'clock that morning, Matt found them again in the waiting room. This time his voice was thick with tears. "The doctor says you can go in." Matt folded his arms. "She might not make it. Nicole wanted you to see her before . . ."

He didn't finish his thought. John wheeled himself toward Matt, and Abby kept in step behind him. "We'll follow you."

Matt showed them into a sterilization area, where they were both given hospital gowns and directed to wash their hands. Afterward, a nurse met them at the entrance to the special unit. "It'll have to be quick. We're working very hard to save her."

The nurse led the way, followed by John and Abby, and finally Matt. Abby couldn't speak as they stopped at an incubator. The nurse laid her hand on top of the clear cover. "This is Haley."

Matt stayed a few feet back so Abby and John could get a clear look. Nicole had been right. The child was gorgeous, a miniature of Nicole at that age and even . . . yes . . . a strong resemblance to—"Do you see it, John?"

His eyes glistened with tears as he nodded, never taking his gaze off the tiny infant. "She looks like Haley Ann."

"Really?" Matt poked his head between them, staring at the tiny child. "Nicole and I couldn't figure out who she looked like."

Abby studied the baby again. Her tiny fingers were no thicker than spaghetti noodles, and her entire body would've fit comfortably in one of John's hands. There were hairlike wires attached to her at several places, and she was nearly covered with monitoring patches and bands. Her skin that did show was pale and translucent. Clearly not the normal skin of a newborn.

Abby placed her palm against the warm glass. "Come on, little Haley, keep breathing. We're pulling for you, baby."

John squeezed her knee, but said nothing. Her quiet words had spoken for both of them. Suddenly Abby realized that Matt's parents weren't there. She looked over her shoulder at him. "Have you called your mom and dad?"

"Their phone's off the hook or something. Every time I call it's busy."

"We'll go by and tell them on the way home." John wheeled himself back a bit. "You and Nicole need your time. But we'll be praying for Haley. And we're only a phone call away if anything changes."

John was right, but Abby wanted nothing more than to sit beside the baby's incubator, willing her to breathe. The entire scene reminded her of that final morning with Haley Ann, when Abby had laid her down for a nap and found her two hours later, dead in her crib.

If only she'd stayed with her, watched her breathe . . . jolted her into catching her breath the moment her body stopped drawing air. Then Haley Ann would've lived. And maybe the same was true for this Haley, also. This precious granddaughter.

John was waiting for her, but Abby studied little Haley one more time. *I'm giving her to You, God . . . watch over her. Keep her breathing, please.*

An image filled Abby's mind, that of a smiling, youthful Jesus cradling Haley Jo in His arms and holding her close to His chest. Convinced of that, Abby was finally able to pull herself away. The message she'd gotten from the image was clear as air. There was nothing Abby could do for Haley that Jesus wasn't already doing.

Her life, her future . . . her next breath . . . were all in His hands.

Twenty-seven

WHEN THE DOORBELL RANG JUST BEFORE NOON, Abby was certain it would be Jo and Denny. Nicole had called that morning to say that Haley had survived the night. After Abby and John had alerted Matt's parents, they went straight to the hospital. Now, Abby figured, they were coming by to share their fears. Certainly to join Abby and John in their concern for the tiny baby.

But when Abby opened the door, it wasn't Matt's parents.

It was Jake Daniels's.

Tara and Tim stood on the front mat, looking at each other like awkward teenagers, and then at Abby. Tara spoke first. "Can we come in?"

"Sure." Abby stepped back, surprised. Since that day at court, neither of them had made contact with Abby or John. "I was expecting someone else."

The Danielses moved into the entryway, but Tim stopped. "If you're having company, we can come back."

Abby waved her hand. "No, nothing like that." She hesitated. "Nicole had her baby early this morning. I sort of expected her husband's parents to stop by."

"Is the baby okay?" Concern flashed in Tim's eyes.

"No. Not really." Abby's voice was suddenly thick. "She's two months early. We're praying for her."

John must have heard their voices. He came wheeling down the hallway and waved. "Come on in."

They moved into the living room. John positioned himself close to Abby's chair. "Still on leave from work, Tim?"

"Yes." He exchanged a look with Tara. "Jake's hearing is Thursday."

"He might get a year at a juvenile detention center." Tara slid a little closer to Tim. "But that'd be the worst of it."

Abby squirmed in her chair. Was this why they'd come? To talk about Jake's sentence?

"We didn't come to talk about that." Tim folded his hands and planted his forearms on his knees. "Remember in court that day . . . you told us the two of you almost divorced last year?"

John nodded.

Tara raised an eyebrow. "We've wanted to come ever since, but . . . I couldn't." She crossed her legs and leaned closer to Tim. "Now the hearing's next week, and after that Tim needs to get back to work. That means our time together is almost over, and we still haven't talked about what we're feeling. Or whether we should get back together."

Abby understood. "You're afraid."

"Tim and I fought so much before he left. Then, when he was gone, all I could think about was what we'd thrown away. The love and laughter and memories. All of it was gone."

"I felt that way, too, but Tara doesn't believe me." Tim tossed his hands in the air. "There's no question we want to be together, but we can't get beyond the past."

Tim and Tara's words could have been their own a year ago, when Abby's father died. Without a doubt Abby and John knew that day that they still cared for each other, still wanted each other, but the mountain of hurt was simply too high to scale.

"After Tim moved away, he began dating." The pain showed in

Tara's eyes. "Here I was grieving all we'd lost, and he's out in New Jersey getting a new haircut, a new job, and a new girlfriend. Sometimes every few weeks. How could I compete with that?"

Tim turned his hands palm up. "Those girls meant nothing. I was running from the pain. Everything I did was my way of running. Even buying Jake the Integra."

There was silence between them for a moment, and Abby drew a quiet breath. "May I say something?"

"Please." Tim was quick to answer. "That's why we came."

Abby looked at John, silently asking him if it was okay to share the details of their situation. The peace in his eyes told her that he would have it no other way. She smiled and then shifted her gaze to Tara.

"When John and I were having trouble, he spent time with one of the teachers at school. She doesn't work there anymore, and her name isn't important. The thing is, it made me mad. Jealous, really. She was younger than I was, more professional. I figured I couldn't compete with her, didn't *want* to compete with her. I still felt angry and jealous even after John began doing everything he could to make things right between us."

Tara nodded. "Exactly."

"The thing I had to learn was this: Sometimes love makes a mistake. Even a series of mistakes. When I married John, I promised to love him in good times and bad. No matter what happened." Abby kept her voice tender, but let her passion show, too. A passion she hoped Tara would hear. "John wanted to make things right between us, but I wasn't willing to forgive him. And you know what? At that point he wasn't the one breaking our wedding vows—I was. I refused to trust him, even after he'd told me time and again that he hadn't had an affair. I wanted to punish him for even finding another woman attractive, for befriending her and being tempted by her. And because of that I could justify treating him—" she searched for the right word—"cruelly. Because my feelings had been hurt and I thought he deserved it."

A quiet settled over them again. John looked at Tim. "Of course, I

didn't understand any of that. I just figured she wasn't capable of forgiving me."

There were tears in Tara's eyes and she dabbed at them discretely.
"How . . . how did you get past it?"

"Memories." John sat back, his eyes only semifocused. "Our
divorce plans ran right along the same time frame as Nicole's engagement. It was wedding dresses this, and churches that, and what about
our vows, Daddy . . ." He shook his head. "What else could we do but
remember how it had been for us twenty years earlier."

"How we fell in love as kids and how magical it was when we first
got married." Abby smiled. "Even then it wasn't easy."

"The memories came at us separately." John gave a sad chuckle.
"Neither of us knew how to approach the other about them, and
because of that, we were ready to go ahead with our plans."

"What stopped you?" Another tear spilled onto Tara's cheek.

"God." John and Abby said the answer at the same time and then
looked at each other and grinned. John shot a pointed look at Tim.
"God might as well have sent us a telegram." John deepened his voice.
"'John and Abby Reynolds . . . do NOT get divorced. I made you for
each other . . . forgive and forget . . . and move on in the joyful life I
have for you.'"

Abby met Tara's eyes. "Do you ever feel that way, Tara? Like God
wants you to let go of the hurt and anger and simply love each other?"

"All the time."

"Then why haven't you done it?"

"Because. I'm afraid it'll happen again." She looked at Tim. "You're
the only man I've ever loved, but when you left me, I hated you.
And . . . and I swore you'd never break my heart like you did before.
Even if you begged me to come back."

"The problem—" John's voice was gentle once more—"is one
that's gotten mankind into trouble since the beginning."

"*Which* problem?" Tim wrung his hands.

"Pride." John smiled. "It's why Adam and Eve took the apple—

because they thought they were smarter than God. They wanted to be like God. And it's why good couples—loving couples like the two of you or Abby and me—start going in different directions and wind up believing divorce is the only solution." He took Abby's hand. "When really, the only solution is to grab tight to each other, forgive, and go on."

For a while none of them said anything. Then John made one final point. "Remember, the devil has always been behind the sin of pride. He wants us to think we can't forgive, can't live humbly with each other. But the devil has an agenda. He wants us to be miserable."

Tim stared at John. "And you think that's all divorce is? Two people listening to the devil's lies?"

"Most of the time, yes. When we say those wedding vows, the last thing on our mind is divorce. Isn't that right?"

Tara and Tim nodded.

"For me, I was up there knowing Abby was the only woman I'd ever loved, the only one I wanted to spend the rest of my life with."

"That's exactly how I felt." Tim set his hand on Tara's knee, and she let it stay there.

"So only a lie could change that, right? Otherwise the love I shared with Abby should've gotten better with each year." There was regret in John's voice. The regret Abby knew they both carried. A regret that realized the value of all those years they lost back when they were living separate lives under one roof.

"Instead—" Abby finished John's thought—"we began thinking badly of each other. Pretty soon we were listening to the lie, believing we deserved something better than a life together."

"When we really needed to stop running, forgive each other, and remember all the reasons we got married in the first place."

Tara sniffed, her eyes dry now. "It's all about forgiveness."

"Yes." Abby's heart went out to the woman. "It is." She felt a pang of regret. How awful it had been living on the other side of forgiveness. Holding on to bitterness and working to hate the man she'd pledged her life to.

John leaned back, more relaxed now. "The Bible tells a story about a man who was forgiven a great debt by the king. The moment he was free, he ran through the streets looking for his fellow servant. When he found him, he grabbed the man by the cloak. 'You owe me, buddy,' the guy said. 'Pay up or I'll throw you into debtor's prison!'

"When the king found out what happened, he called for the man. 'The debt I forgave you was far greater than the debt your fellow servant owed. Now, since you couldn't find it in your heart to forgive the smaller amount, neither will I forgive you the large amount.' And with that he threw the man into prison."

Abby loved the way John could come up with an illustration from Scripture like that. He had always been a storyteller. It was what made him a good teacher, a strong communicator. But now that he was back at church with Abby every week, he constantly came up with stories like the one he'd just told.

Abby searched Tim's and Tara's faces and saw that they understood.

"God's forgiven us—" Tara sniffed—"much more than we could ever need to forgive someone else."

"Exactly." John's tone rang with compassion.

Tara moved to the edge of her seat. "Pray for me, will you? That I'll find a way to forgive."

Without hesitating, John did just that. When they were done, he looked at Abby. "Honey, take off my shoes, will you?"

She wasn't sure what he was up to, but she liked his grin. With a light heart, she stooped down in front of him and slipped his shoes off. Then she returned to her chair and waited.

Tim and Tara looked at his feet, their faces a twist of curiosity.

"Watch." John pointed to his toes. "There's something I want you to pass on to that son of yours."

Whatever he was about to do, even Abby had no idea. It was one thing that John's toes had occasionally moved in some involuntary manner. But this . . . what was he up to?

Then, with all of their eyes glued to his two big toes, Abby saw it. The toes moved! Both of them. Just a little wiggle, but there was no denying the fact. Abby let out a cry and threw her arms around John's neck. "It's happening, John. I can't believe it."

Across the room, Tim and Tara looked stunned, like they'd just seen John levitate. Tim was the first to recover. "What . . . how did . . . John, does your doctor know about that?"

"Yes." John pulled Abby over onto his lap. "It's a form of spinal shock. Really rare. They're operating on me next month. There's a chance I'll get full use of my legs back."

"Oh my goodness." Tara's hands flew to her mouth. "Jake told me he asked God for a miracle. That you'd . . . you'd walk again someday."

Tim looked at her. "He didn't tell me."

"It's true." Her eyes were still wide, still focused on John's two big toes. "He thought God had told him that's exactly what would happen. Coach Reynolds would get better. But as the months went by, nothing happened. Jake . . . he stopped talking about it."

"Well, tell him to keep praying." John grinned, his arm tight around Abby's waist. "Miracles happen to those who believe."

Long after Tim and Tara had gone, after John had gone into their new first-floor bedroom for a nap, Abby sat at the dining room table and stared out at the lake. John was right. Miracles did happen to those who believed. After all, Nicole had prayed for Abby and John. And Jake had prayed about John's damaged legs. And now the boy had a sense everything was going to work out for John.

She sat there a long time, praying for baby Haley, talking to God and marveling at His plan for their lives. The more she thought about the discussion with Tim and Tara, the more convinced she became that whatever was happening with John's legs, it was only part of the miracle Jake was about to receive.

The other part, Abby was almost certain, would happen any day now, when a certain couple just might walk through the door and announce that by God's grace and forgiveness, Jake's father was never moving back to New Jersey.

By Sunday afternoon, the baby had survived three days, which was more than the doctors had thought possible. She still struggled for every breath, but Nicole had recovered quickly and spent nearly every waking moment anchored beside the baby's incubator. She was allowed to reach inside and run her finger along Haley's small leg or arm. The opening was just large enough so Nicole could see her baby respond to not only her touch, but her voice.

There was a tap on her shoulder, and Nicole turned around. It was Jo, her eyes red and swollen. "Hi."

"Jo, hi . . . sit down."

Jo nodded and slid a chair over next to Nicole's. "How is she?"

"Holding on." Nicole studied the woman. Jo defined intensity. Whatever her mood, she played it to the furthest degree. But here, now, she was quiet, pensive. Defeated, even. "You okay?"

"Sure." Jo's eyes grew watery. "Where's Matt?"

"At home getting some sleep. He's barely closed his eyes since the baby was born."

For a while they sat that way, watching little Haley, willing her small chest to continue it's up-and-down struggle. After five minutes had passed, Jo drew a sharp breath. "Nicole, I have something to tell you."

She turned her head enough to glance at Jo. "I'm listening."

"Oh, brother." Jo rolled her eyes and dabbed at her nose. "Never in a million years did I think I'd ever tell anyone about this. Least of all you or Matt."

Nicole studied the woman. Whatever it was, the burden of it weighed on her like a diesel truck. "You can tell me, Jo."

She cast Nicole a wary eye. "Don't hate me, okay?"

"Okay."

"See . . ." She huffed hard, searching for the words. "It happened a long time back, back when me and Denny were first married." Jo wiped her hands on her pant legs and stared at baby Haley. "We were young and stupid, and just a few weeks after the weddin' we found out I was pregnant."

Pregnant? Nicole tried not to act surprised. Jo was right. Neither she nor Matt had ever heard this story. She waited for Jo to continue.

"We were scared, I mean really scared." Jo shook her head. "Like a coupla fish at the end of a line. No matter which way we turned, didn't seem to be no way out. You know?"

"I do." Nicole hoped her face reflected the empathy she was feeling. It was exactly how she'd felt when she found out she was pregnant. The way she probably still would feel if God hadn't changed her attitude.

"Back then . . . well, me and Denny didn't have God. No one around us did, either. So . . ." Her voice cracked, and she hung her head. "I'm sorry. I don't know if I can finish."

A dawning of understanding shone across the landscape of Nicole's heart. Had the woman done something to end her pregnancy? Nicole reached out and took Jo's weathered hand in her own. "Nothing you could tell me would make me love you less, Jo. You don't have to share this . . . but I want you to know that."

Jo struggled to regain control. When she could speak again, she cast a quick look at Nicole. "I got an abortion, Nicole." She nodded, giving a single loud sniff. "Denny drove me to the clinic and waited in the lobby. And back in one of them dingy rooms, this handsome man came to me and told me it was all going to be okay. All I had to do was lay real still and tell him if I felt any pain. The pregnancy would be gone in no time."

Tears spilled onto Nicole's cheeks, and her heart broke for Jo. She wasn't sure what she should say, so she kept quiet.

"Isn't that something? The pregnancy would be gone . . . as if there wasn't any baby involved." Jo wiped her eyes. "But it was more than a pregnancy. I was five months along by the time I went in and one of the nurses told me." The words caught in Jo's throat for a moment. "It was a girl, Nicole. A little girl like your Haley. Only instead of helping her live, I helped her die."

Jo dropped her head in her hands and stifled a sob.

"Oh, Jo . . ." Nicole rubbed small gentle circles on her back and searched for something to say. But she could think of nothing.

Finally, Jo found her voice again. "A year later I got pregnant with Matt. We were going to have another abortion, but something stopped me. I can't remember what it was, but somehow I knew it wasn't right. It didn't matter if we were young and poor. It wasn't the baby's fault, and I wasn't going to go back to that awful place again."

Nicole's heart skipped a beat. If Jo had aborted Matt . . . She couldn't think about it. There was enough pain, knowing about Jo's first abortion. "Matt doesn't know?"

"How could I tell him? How do you look your son in the face and let him know you killed his sister?"

"Come on, Jo . . . don't." Nicole put her arm around Jo's neck and brought her own younger face against Jo's older one. "You didn't know what you were doing."

"But I know now." Jo's tears came harder, and Nicole saw a few nurses glancing over at them. Jo seemed to notice, too, and she lowered her voice. "Ever since Matt was born, I've regretted what I did. I'd a done anything to get that little sweetheart back, to have it to do over again."

Nicole released the hold she had on Jo and settled back in her chair. "God forgives you, Jo. You know that, right?"

Jo nodded and sniffed again. "After I gave my life to Jesus last year, I had a chat with Denny. I told him what we'd done was wrong and he agreed. We went to church that night all by ourselves and had a little service for the baby. We got down on our knees and told God how sorry we were." She lifted her chin a bit. "I never seen a grown man cry like that, Nicole. And I knew then that I wasn't the only one who missed that baby girl."

Nicole was struck by the image Jo painted. Both parents taking responsibility for what they'd done and asking God's forgiveness. "What a wonderful thing, remembering her together that way."

"Well, it wasn't wonderful. It was painful. Hurt more than anything in my life, if you wanna know the truth. After we told God we was sorry, we asked Him to take care of our baby up there in heaven. You know, give her little hugs and kisses and pick wildflowers with her on a summer day. Teach her how to fish and laugh and love. Watch over her until one day we could be up there to do it ourselves."

Jo was quiet again, studying baby Haley. "We sort of pictured our little girl like an orphan. A heavenly orphan." Jo gave Nicole a sideways look. "And that night we promised God if He'd take care of our little orphan girl in heaven, we'd take care of His orphans down here on earth."

Suddenly it was all coming together. "Your trip to Mexico?"

"Yes." There was a quivering in Jo's lip. "That's why we're going."

"Wow . . ." Nicole inhaled sharply. "That's beautiful, Jo."

"Yeah, well, the rest of what I have to say isn't so pretty."

Nicole's heart rate quickened, but she stayed silent.

"Ever since I heard about little Haley, me and Denny have prayed till I thought our teeth would fall out." Jo placed her hand alongside the incubator. "But every time I pray, God gives me a picture that scares me."

Nicole wasn't sure she wanted to know, but she couldn't help herself. "What's the picture?"

"It's a picture of three little girls, running through the fields of heaven, arm in arm." Jo paused and Nicole wanted to cover her ears. "One of them is your sister, Haley Ann; the other is our little girl; and the third one . . . the third one is your little Haley Jo."

It took a moment before Nicole could breathe again. When she could, she forced a quiet chuckle. "Now, Jo . . . is that what's bothering you?"

"Of course." She cast a surprised look at Nicole. "I want little

Haley to live more than anything in the world. More than I've wanted something for a very long time. But if God knows my heart, why do I keep getting that picture?"

Nicole sounded stronger than she felt. "Maybe because I got pregnant early, too. Maybe because you know that if Haley . . . if she doesn't make it, she'll be happy in heaven with her two aunts." Nicole tossed her hands a few inches in the air. "I don't know, but it doesn't mean God's going to take Haley home. You can't think that, Jo."

Something in Nicole's words or maybe the tone of her voice, caused Jo to relax. The fear and torment left her face, and in its place there was only a distant sorrow. "You're right. God's going to save little Haley. I have to believe that."

After a while Jo left, and Nicole stayed there by herself for nearly an hour, watching Haley, silently urging her to keep breathing, keep living. And praying that when Haley was old enough to run through fields of flowers, they would be the ones in their very own backyard.

And not the ones in heaven.

Twenty-eight

IT WAS THE DAY OF HIS HEARING, AND JAKE FELT HE'D aged ten years in the past four months.

Not a bad kind of aging, but a good kind. The kind that made him feel more sure about his faith and his future and his plans to help other teenagers avoid the mistakes he'd made.

If he didn't get sent to a juvenile detention center, Jake planned to return to Marion High in the fall. Everyone he talked to agreed it was the best choice, the way he could most impact his peers about the dangers of street racing. Besides, that way he could be around Coach Reynolds again. And after four months away, Jake had no intention of finishing his high-school education any place except the campus where Coach could teach him. If not on the football field, then certainly in the classroom. If the court let him, that was.

He'd decided something else, too. He wanted another shot at football. Not so he could show up the underclassmen or put himself on a pedestal among his peers, but so he could play the game the way Coach had taught him to play. With heart and class and honor.

Of course, A. W. had been straight with him. He might not get the chance. The judge could easily sentence him to a year in juvenile hall, and if that happened, he'd spend his senior year in confinement.

Jake had prayed about the outcome of today's hearing, and if that's where God wanted him, that's where he'd go. There was no question, he deserved whatever punishment he was given.

The courtroom was filling up, and Jake glanced at his parents. They were talking near the back door, looking friendlier than they'd looked at any time since the accident. He had asked his mother on occasion if anything was happening between them, but she was always evasive.

"We have a lot to talk about, Jake. Your father's only helping me through this."

Jake would raise an eyebrow, but leave it alone. Still, they spent enough time together now that he'd added it to his list of God topics—things he talked about with the Lord.

The judge entered the room and immediately his parents left their conversation and took their places on either side of him. A. W. straightened a stack of papers and whispered, "Here goes."

When the judge was seated, she called the court to order. Jake's case was first on her docket. "I understand the defendant in *State v. Daniels* would like to enter a plea; is that right?"

A. W. was on his feet. "Yes, Your Honor. We've reached an agreement with the state on the correct charges."

"Very well. Will the defendant please rise?"

Jake stood up, awed at the strange calm that had come over him. *Your call, God . . . whatever You want . . .*

The judge glanced at a sheet of paper on the bench. "Mr. Daniels, you are being charged with the gross negligent use of a vehicle, reckless driving, and illegal street racing—all misdemeanors." She looked at him. "How do you plead?"

"Guilty, Your Honor. On all charges." The words felt wonderful. He *was* guilty. There was no sense playing games about it. Whatever the judge did next was fine with him.

"Mr. Daniels, you're aware that each of these charges carry with them a maximum of six months in a juvenile detention facility?"

"Yes, Your Honor."

"And that the combination of charges means you could serve up to eighteen months in such a facility?"

"Yes, Your Honor."

The judge sorted through a file of papers. "I see that your attorney has provided me with letters on your behalf. I'll recess this court for twenty minutes while I read through the file." She looked at A. W. "At that point I'll return and hand your client his sentence; is that understood?"

"Yes, Your Honor." He barely paused. "I'd like you to also consider the fact that my client has already signed up for community service events. He plans to speak to students at four high schools a year for the next five years as a way of helping kids avoid the mistakes he made."

The judge was quiet for a moment. "Very well. I'll consider that along with the letters."

Court was adjourned, and Jake's parents hugged him from either side.

"You aren't nervous, are you, son?" His father searched his face, clearly surprised.

"No. Me and God already talked it out. Whatever happens, that's what He wants. I'm not afraid."

A. W. gave a nervous laugh. "Well, I am. If that makes you feel any better." He nodded toward the judge's chamber door. "She's a tough one, that judge. No matter what the letters say, she could make an example out of you."

Jake saw his mother wince at the thought, and he patted her back. "Mom, you gotta trust God on this one. If He wants me at a detention center, that's where I'll go. And everything will work out fine."

"I know. I just . . . I'd like to see you back at Marion. Your ideas . . . about football and helping your friends . . . they seem so good."

"How many letters were you able to get?" Jake's father directed his attention to A. W.

"Five. That's more than enough." The attorney gazed up, trying to remember. "One each from you and Tara, one from Jake's parole officer, one from the person at community service he's been working with. And the best one of all—from John Reynolds."

Coach Reynolds? Jake's stomach flip-flopped inside him. "You asked Coach Reynolds for a letter?"

"Yeah, why?"

"I can't believe you did that . . . he's gone through enough without having to write a letter for me. I mean, whoever told you to do something like that, when . . ."

A. W. held up a hand, and Jake stopped his sentence short. Though he was quiet, he was fuming. He hadn't been this angry in a while. The nerve of asking Coach for a letter that would help him get a lighter sentence.

"I didn't ask Mr. Reynolds for a letter." A. W. tilted his head, a look of vindication on his face. "Mr. Reynolds offered."

Jake's stomach stopped flipping and sank to his knees. What? Coach Reynolds—in the midst of dealing with his sick granddaughter and an upcoming surgery—had taken time to write a letter on his behalf?

Jake looked at his parents and saw they were feeling the same thing. They had all known Coach Reynolds was a great man. But this great? This concerned about a kid who had put him in a wheelchair? For the first time that day, Jake felt a lump in his throat.

The judge appeared and once more called the court to order.

"In the matter of *State v. Daniels,* I have reached a decision, one that even I am not certain is fair."

She's sending me to juvie . . . Jake blinked and tried not to feel afraid. *Help me here, God . . . help me.*

The judge continued. "Will the defendant please rise?"

Jake stood, his knees knocking ever so slightly.

"As I mentioned, it is within my right to sentence you, Mr. Daniels, to eighteen months in a juvenile detention center." She paused and glanced at the district attorney. "But in this case, I have been inundated with requests to act otherwise."

Jake saw his parents link hands.

"The letter that most affected me was the one written by the victim—Mr. John Reynolds." She held up a piece of paper. "Mr. Reynolds writes, 'I beg you to let Jake work off his sentence while attending Marion High in the fall. For you see, that is when I will return to school, and if the accident had never happened, it would have been Jake's senior year. Being on campus without Jake will be a daily reminder of what happened that awful November night. Locking Jake up won't make him a better driver or a wiser young man, nor will it lessen the impact of my injuries. But seeing Jake on campus at Marion High would be almost as good as walking again.'" She paused and looked at Jake before finishing. "'Please, Your Honor, I ask you to help my recovery by punishing Jake some other way. He's changed since the accident, and Marion High needs more kids like him on campus.'"

Throughout the courtroom the only sound was the faint sniff of his mother's tears and the thud of his own heartbeat. Had Coach really said that? Seeing him on campus would be as good as walking again?

The judge set the letter down and glanced around the room. "For that reason, and because the defendant is pulling straight As at the continuation school, I am hereby waiving all juvenile detention center time. Instead, I will agree to the community service plan, where the defendant will speak to high-school groups four times a year for the next five years."

Jake was so happy he could've floated out of the courtroom. Not because he'd dodged a bullet, but because he was going back to Marion High, back to the same campus as Coach Reynolds! And because he'd have one more chance to play football the way he should have played it all along. *God . . . I'll make it up to You . . . I promise . . .*

Beside him, his parents looked suddenly a decade younger, and Jake realized something. They'd been more worried about his being sentenced to a detention center than they'd let on.

The judge rapped her gavel on the bench. "Order." When it was quiet, she continued. "In addition, the defendant's driver's license shall remain revoked, and he shall not be permitted to apply for a new license until his twenty-first birthday. Between now and then, he will attend a ten-week driver's safety course, this year and every year until he is twenty-one." She looked at Jake. "Most often when I hand down a sentence, I have a sense as to whether justice was served." She angled her head. "This time I'm not sure."

"Yes, Your Honor."

"You're getting off very easy, son. I don't want to see your face in this court or any other ever again. Is that understood?"

Jake nodded. "You don't have to worry, Your Honor. I won't be back."

Just like that, the hearing was over and Jake was being congratulated by A. W. and his parents, and a few Marion High football players who had stayed in the back of the courtroom.

"Jake, man, this is good. We need you back next year at QB." It was Al Hoosey, a wide receiver. He slapped Jake on the shoulder. "Way to go."

Jake met the eyes of the boy. "It'll be different next year, Hoosey. Much different."

The boy blinked. "That's a good thing, right?"

This time Jake couldn't contain his smile. "A *very* good thing."

Other people milled around him, and he felt someone tug his elbow. He turned and found himself looking into the face of the district attorney. "Listen, about the judge's comment . . . that she wasn't sure if justice had been served?"

"Yes, sir?" Jake pivoted so the man had his full attention.

"I have a sense about those things, too. And this time I'm sure. Justice *was* served." The attorney's face was serious, somber. "Now go out there and make sure those friends of yours stay away from street races, okay? That'll make my job a lot easier. Deal?"

Jake swallowed hard. "Deal."

The crowd thinned out and his own attorney gathered his things and left. Finally it was just Jake and his parents.

"Amazing, huh, son?" His mom and dad were still holding hands. They seemed in no hurry to leave.

"God must have big things for me next year at Marion." Jake shot a look at the clock on the courthouse wall. "Let's get home. I have a thank-you call to make."

His mother smiled and brushed her fingertips across his forehead, straightening his bangs the way she'd done back when he was a little boy. "Coach?"

"Yep. Can't wait to tell him."

"Son . . ." His father sat up a bit straighter, and Jake had the sense he was about to say something important. "Before we go, your mom and I have something we want to tell you."

Abby never expected it to take place in a restaurant parking lot.

She had known there would be a time when her family would come together to pray for John. But with Haley still fighting for her life, the days got away from them. Finally, it was Sunday, the day before John's surgery.

Kade was home for an extended spring break, and John and Abby took the family to brunch after church. Before the group broke up, Abby looked around the circle. "We wanted everyone to pray together . . . before John goes in tomorrow."

"Great idea." Jo held her hands out to either side, closed her eyes, and hung her head. "Who's gonna start?"

A few of them shared quiet smiles. Then they did the same, joining hands and bowing their heads there in the parking lot. Kade was the first to pray, and Jo and Denny added their sentiments before Nicole and Matt and Sean took turns.

Abby struggled to speak. All she could manage was a quick thanks to God for giving them even a glimmer of hope.

Then it was John's turn.

He opened his mouth to pray, but nothing came out. Then, after several seconds, he began to sing.

"Great is Thy faithfulness . . . oh God, my Father. There is no shadow of turning with Thee . . . "

The hymn had been John's father's favorite, long before John was even born. One at a time the others added their voices, unconcerned with the looks they got from passersby. When they reached the chorus, they sang about the greatness of God's faithfulness and the truth from Lamentations that His mercies were new every morning.

No matter what.

Abby found her voice and sang clear, her heart caught up in every word. She'd never forget this. When the song ended, John looked at the faces around him. "Thank you. God is faithful; I believe that. No matter what happens."

Several of them blinked back tears as the group exchanged hugs and talked about their plans for the next day. Jo and Denny would meet the others at the hospital sometime after the surgery. Sean and Kade would be there all day, as would Nicole and Matt—who would primarily be with Haley, but would check in often to see how John was doing.

"Haley's on the third floor and you'll be on the fifth, Daddy." Nicole hugged him tight. "Isn't that something?"

Abby watched John. The strain of what the next day's events held was finally starting to get to him. He kissed Nicole on the cheek. "You just take care of my little granddaughter for me, okay?"

"Okay." She wiped a tear. "We'll be praying."

Sean rode home with Kade, so once John was strapped in and Abby took the driver's seat, they were by themselves. "Notice how no one said anything about you walking again?"

It was a beautiful April day, the kind that shouted of the coming summer. John stared out the window. "I think they're afraid to hope for it."

They were quiet the rest of the way home, but once they got out of the car, Abby had no doubts where they'd wind up. Without saying a word, she followed John into the backyard, down the cement path, and up onto the pier. They moved toward the water. Abby sat in the chair, with John beside her.

"What're you thinking, Miss Abby?" He turned so his eyes met hers.

"Miss Abby . . . you haven't called me that since we were kids."

"Really?"

"Really."

John chuckled. "Well, not because I haven't thought it. You'll always be my little Miss Abby." He waited a moment, allowing the breeze from the lake to wash over them before he tried again. "You didn't answer me."

"Hmmm." The sun was directly overhead, and it caused an explosion of light on the lake. She stared out at the water. "I guess not."

"So . . . you aren't thinking anything special, or you don't want to tell me."

"Neither." A lazy grin spread across her face.

He pursed his lips, trying to figure her out. "I'm not sure I get it."

"I *am* thinking something special—" she lowered her chin, enjoying the easy banter between them—"and I *do* want to tell you."

"Okay." He crossed his arms. "So tell me."

"I was waiting for the right time. Because what I have to say is important. I want you to hear it straight to your soul, John Reynolds."

He maneuvered his chair so he could see her better. Their knees were touching, though Abby knew John couldn't feel the sensation. Not yet, anyway. "I'm listening, Abby. Heart, soul, and mind."

"Good." Abby drew a deep breath and her eyes settled on his. "I've given your surgery a lot of thought, John. I've dreamed about what it would be like to have you healed." She paused.

"I do the same thing." His eyes narrowed. "I think of all the ways I'd use my legs if I had even one more hour, one more day."

"What would you do?" Her words were slow, easy. A hawk circled overhead.

"I'd run a mile in the morning, play football with Sean and Kade, and make love to you all afternoon, Miss Abby."

"Nice." She smiled, feeling the hint of warmth in her cheeks. "My thoughts are pretty much the same."

"That's what you wanted to tell me?" He leaned over and gripped her legs, rubbing his thumbs gently along the inside of her knees.

"No." She looked deeper, to the center of his soul. "I wanted to tell you that it doesn't matter."

John waited for her to finish, his head angled.

"It doesn't matter if you get your legs back, John. There was a time when I would've told you anything other than a complete recovery would be tragic, hard on our lives and hard on our relationship." She shook her head. "But not anymore. Over the past five months I've learned how to love you just like this. I love helping you in and out of bed; I love being there to pull your pants up for you. I even love the way you wheel me down the pier at twenty-miles-per-hour in some newfangled version of the tango."

She studied him, her eyes unblinking. "What I'm trying to say is, I want your legs back as badly as you do, but if you come out of the surgery tomorrow the same as you are today, that's okay, too. I couldn't love you more than I do right now."

For a long while, John said nothing. Just stared at Abby while the two of them soaked in everything about the moment. "What if we hadn't talked that night after Nicole's wedding?"

"I can't imagine." Abby's voice was tight, her throat thick with emotion.

"I love you so much, Abby. Thank God we were smart enough to hear His voice, smart enough to find each other again." His eyes reflected the lake. Abby felt herself drowning in them, unaware of the world around her. "You're everything to me, Abby. Everything."

"I believe with all my heart that God will be there tomorrow, in the operating room, guiding the surgeon's knife and bringing healing to your back. But remember something, will you, John?"

"Anything."

"I'll be there, too." She pressed her fingers over his heart. "Right here . . . the whole time."

"You know what we need to do first?" John's expression lightened and his eyes shone the way their sons' eyes shone when they were up to no good.

"First? Before the surgery, you mean?"

"Yep."

"Okay . . . I give up. What do we need to do first?"

He patted his lap.

"Oh, no. Not the tango."

"Yes, Abby . . . come on. We're just getting good at it."

Laughter formed in her heart and found its way out of her mouth. She stood and dropped herself unceremoniously onto his lap. "I won't be able to do this after tomorrow, you know."

He turned the wheelchair and began heading toward the far end of the pier. "Why not?"

"Because after tomorrow you'll *feel* me, silly. I'll be too heavy for you."

"You? Too heavy?" He reached the top and spun the chair around, using the hand brake to stop it. "Never, Abby. We'll save the chair and do this once a week for old time's sake."

"Oh, quit." She pushed at his shoulder. As she did, John's elbow released the hand brake, and the chair began rolling down the pier.

"Here we go." He guided the chair with one hand and grabbed hers with the other, holding it straight out in front of them, tango-style.

She pressed her cheek against his as they passed the midway point, plummeting faster and faster toward the water. Her voice was loud, breathless. "Have I mentioned that this dance terrifies me?"

"Ah, Abby . . . so little faith . . . we'll have to do it again until you're not afraid anymore."

Just before they reached the end, John spun the chair in a graceful circle. But this time the wheels skidded and the chair flipped over, spilling John onto his back near the end of the pier, and Abby on top of him.

Abby muffled a scream that was more laughter than fear. She lifted her face and held it inches from his. "Nice move, Reynolds."

"I practiced that for weeks. I thought you'd love it." He ran his hands along her back, pressing her against him. They kissed then, their lips meeting each other first briefly, then in a way that spoke the things too deep for words.

Abby started laughing.

"Hey, wait a minute." John grabbed a quick breath. "You're not supposed to laugh. This is part of the dance."

"I can't help it." Abby rested her forehead on his shoulder until she could breathe again. She raised up a bit and looked at him. "Remember that day in the hallway? How you fell backward trying to lead me into the kitchen?"

John chuckled, still stroking her back. "One of my finest moments."

"You said you'd never be mature, remember?"

The laughter came more loudly for John. "Even Paula's dance classes couldn't help me."

"Apparently not."

They laughed and kissed, and laughed some more, until the sounds of their happiness drifted across the lake and mingled with the afternoon winds. Only then, when they were tired from laughing, did Abby pick herself up and right the wheelchair. She helped John back into it and pushed him slowly up the pier.

As long as she lived, she'd never forget this afternoon. The depth of love and laughter, peace and acceptance. She had told John the truth. She could never love him more in all her life, and that would be true tomorrow, too.

No matter what else the day might bring.

Twenty-nine

JAKE WOKE UP THE NEXT MORNING AT SEVEN O'CLOCK and looked at his calendar.

This was the day. He could feel it as surely as he could feel his own heartbeat. He'd been praying, not just for Coach Reynolds, but for the man's little granddaughter as well. And God had practically told him that sometime that morning there would be drastic miracles for both of them.

His job was to keep praying.

So before he climbed out of bed, before he got dressed or ate breakfast or did anything else, he rolled onto his stomach, buried his face in his pillow, and prayed. Not the way he used to pray back when he was a kid, before the accident.

But like a man.

As though his very life depended on it.

There was a flurry of activity around Haley's incubator.

Nicole had slept down the hall in the same room where she and sometimes Matt had stayed since Haley was born. The little girl had survived four weeks, longer than the doctors had dared hope. But still her lung activity was weak. If the situation didn't improve, she was a prime candidate for pneumonia, which in her frail state would almost certainly prove fatal.

As always, Nicole had asked the nurses to get her if anything about Haley's condition changed. But no one had come for her, and now her heart raced as she saw half a dozen nurses gathered around her baby. She moved quickly down the aisle, past several incubators until she was as close as she could get to Haley's.

"Excuse me . . ." Nicole peered around the nurses. "What's going on? That's my baby in there."

A nurse Nicole recognized spun around and hugged her. "It's a miracle!" She pulled Nicole back a few feet away from the commotion. "This morning your baby's numbers looked worse than before. We were going to wake you up and have you come see her, but then at a little past seven o'clock, everything changed."

Nicole's mind raced almost as fast as her heart. "Changed? What do you mean?"

"Her lungs. It's like they opened up for the first time and actually sucked in a complete breath. Right away her blood oxygen level soared into the healthy range."

"So . . . so she's doing better?" Nicole strained to see Haley, glad that the other nurses were going about their business again.

"Not just doing better." The nurse positively beamed. "She's turned a corner. The doctor was just in and he upgraded her condition from critical to serious. If things stay this good, she can go home as soon as she's gained enough weight. No one can believe it. That's why the other nurses are here. Things like this don't just happen. Not to sick babies like yours."

There was finally an open spot alongside the incubator, and Nicole pressed in as close as she could. "Can I touch her?"

The nurse grinned. "Definitely."

Nicole worked her hand through the sterile opening and soothed a finger over Haley's legs and arms. "Honey, it's me. Mommy." Tears spilled onto her cheeks, and Nicole uttered a single laugh. "God saved you, Haley. He's going to let you live."

She remembered the image Jo had seen so often. Three little girls running and skipping through the fields of heaven. Nicole shuddered. How close they'd come to having that be true.

Haley stretched her legs, her hands flailing at the touch of Nicole's skin. Nicole glanced back at the nurse. "She wants me to hold her."

"She does?" The nurse raised an eyebrow. "We'll weigh her later today, and if her breathing is still this good, you should be able to hold her this afternoon."

Nicole wanted to shout out loud. Haley was going to live! Her mind raced, thinking of what to do next. She needed to tell Matt and his parents, needed to tell her parents—

Her parents!

It was just after eight o'clock, and her father would be wheeled into surgery any minute. He couldn't go without hearing the news. Nicole whispered near the hole in the incubator. "Haley, baby, get some sleep. I'll be back." Then she turned to the nurse. "Watch her for me. I have to tell the others."

Nicole hadn't run this fast since before the baby was born. She bounded down the hall and into the elevator, and darted back out the moment it reached the fifth floor. Quick as her feet would carry her, she made her way to the nurses' station. "I'm looking for my dad, John Reynolds."

The nurse pointed. "He's on his way to surgery."

"Thanks." Nicole took off down the hall. *Oh, not yet . . . please, God, let me catch him in time.*

She rounded a corner near the elevator and ran smack into Kade, who tripped, toppling both of them onto the floor, their legs and arms tangled. From her position on the hospital floor, she shouted at her father. "Don't go anywhere, Dad. I have to tell you something."

Her mother helped her to her feet, while Kade flopped onto his backside and struggled to get up. "Nice tackle." He straightened his baseball cap. "You missed your calling, Nicole. You shoulda been a lineman, not a teacher."

"Sorry." Nicole brushed the dust off Kade's jeans and then her own. "I had to reach Dad before he went into surgery."

Her father was lying on the stretcher, just outside the elevator doors. He was quietly laughing, his eyebrows raised. "Whatever it is, it must be good."

Nicole nodded to Sean and moved closer to her father. A technician stood at the foot of the stretcher, watching her like she was a crazy woman. She waved at him. "Hello . . . sorry about the excitement."

The elevator door opened, and Nicole shook her head at the man. "Not yet. Give me a minute, okay?"

"Nicole, whatever is going on?" Her mother came up beside her, searching her face.

"Just a minute. Dad—" she turned her attention back to her father—"Haley's turned a corner. She's breathing like a regular baby and . . ." Nicole could barely catch her breath, first from the hospital sprint, but also from the sheer exhilaration of the miracle that had occurred. She exhaled, struggling to compose herself. "The doctor said she's turned a corner. She's out of danger, Dad. Isn't that *amazing?*"

Now it was Kade's turn to tackle her. He lifted her in a bear hug while Sean and her mother circled their arms around her. Her father reached for her hand and squeezed it. "Are you serious, sweetheart?"

Nicole worked herself free from the group hug. "Yes, Daddy." She bent over him, searching his eyes. "And God's not finished yet. I couldn't let you go into surgery without knowing what God was doing. What He's still going to do for you before the day is up."

"So, honey, what happened? She just breathed on her own for no reason?"

The elevator doors opened again, and Nicole flashed the technician a smile. "One more minute? Please?"

He shrugged. "They can't start without your father."

Nicole looked at her mother. "No one knows what happened. Sometime around seven o'clock she sucked in a full breath of air. The monitors all went off, telling the staff that she was finally breathing on her own. She's been breathing great ever since."

"Yes!" Sean raised his fist in the air. "My little niece is gonna live!"

Nicole's voice grew softer. "So, Dad . . . now it's your turn, okay?"

Her father smiled, his eyes dry. "You tell that little girl of yours that one day soon, her grandpa's going to take her for a walk."

"Okay." Nicole stepped back and nodded to the technician just as the elevator doors opened one more time. "Go get 'em."

She linked arms with Sean and Kade and Mom. The last thing any of them saw as John was wheeled into the elevator was a smile that stretched across his face. That and his raised fist as he flashed them the thumbs-up sign.

Seeing it made Nicole's eyes fill with tears. It was the sign her father had always flashed from the football field, but not before every game.

Just those he was sure they were going to win.

Abby had never paced in all her life, but she was pacing now. Not the slow, musing type of pace reserved for pensive moments. Rather a quick one. Fast steps across the waiting room to the wall of windows, and then faster steps back again.

Nicole and Matt were downstairs with Haley, the boys had gone to the cafeteria for something to eat, and Jo and Denny weren't there yet. So, Abby was alone. The operation had been underway for nearly an hour, and Abby had more energy than she knew what to do with.

Yes, she would love John the same if the surgery didn't restore feeling to his legs. But what if it did? What if he could actually walk and run and drive a car again? How amazing would that be? Not only would they have found a deeper love because of the accident, but they would have a second chance to enjoy it.

The possibilities made Abby's heart race, and the only way she knew to work through it was to pace. Hard and fast, in a way that gave her nervous energy an escape.

Dr. Furin had told them the operation could take four hours. They had to identify each strand of John's damaged spinal cord and painstakingly repair it. If they were right, if he was to have any chance of walking again, they would find a few strands still intact. That would explain the feeling and movement in his toes.

But that was only half the battle.

The other half was making sure the repair went perfectly well. Strand by strand, hour after painstaking hour.

Abby paced faster.

She was still pacing when Jo and Denny came down the hall and stopped at the entrance to the waiting room. "My land, Abby, what in tarnation are you doing?" Jo came up beside her and took hold of her arm. "Trying to wear a hole in the floor?"

For the first time in half an hour, Abby stopped. "I don't know what else to do."

"Well, that's easy as fly bait." Jo led Abby to the nearest sofa, with Denny still watching from the doorway. "You sit yourself right down here and pray." She motioned for Denny to join them.

As he did, he pulled a newspaper section from behind his back and handed it to Abby.

Jo beamed at her. "Then, when you're finished praying, you can read this. After that I don't think you'll feel much like pacing."

Abby took the newspaper and nodded, closing her eyes while Denny prayed for the surgeons' hands to be guided by God's mighty grip. When they were finished, Abby held the paper up and stared at it. For a moment, she wasn't sure what she was seeing. The entire page was filled with column after column of names. Then her eyes shot to the top of the page. What she saw made her gasp out loud.

It was a full-page ad, and the headline read, "We're praying for you, Coach!"

Beneath that was a smaller section that said, "We, the students and teachers at Marion High, wish to publicly thank Coach John Reynolds for everything he's done to make us winners. Today, as he goes into surgery, we will be praying for his complete recovery. And that next year he might still be head coach of the mighty Eagles."

The sentiment was followed by a list of names too great to read through in one sitting. Hundreds of names, names of teachers and students and players—many Abby didn't even recognize.

"See." Jo gave a firm nod. "I knew that'd stop your pacing."

The newspaper shook in Abby's hand. "John won't believe it."

Jo was right about her nervous energy. After seeing the full-page ad from the community at Marion High, Abby felt strangely peaceful. She passed the next three hours either praying or playing cards with Jo and Denny.

When they weren't in the cafeteria eating, Kade and Sean kept busy with Sean's NFL Game Boy. Occasionally Nicole and Matt found their way up to the waiting room anxious for a report.

But there was none.

Abby tried not to see that as a bad sign. Dr. Furin had said he'd do his best to give the family updates throughout the surgery. Almost four hours had passed, and still they'd heard nothing.

"Shouldn't we know by now?" Denny peered over the cards in his hand and sent Abby a quick look.

"I thought so." She drew a steady breath. *Come on, heart. Stay steady.* "I guess we'll just have to wait."

"A good fisherman knows all about waiting." Jo played a card. She looked completely unfazed, as though they were passing the afternoon in a sunny parlor and not the waiting room of a hospital. "Only instead of casting a line, today we're casting our cares." She grinned at Abby. "Beats pacing, don't it?"

Another thirty minutes passed, and Abby didn't care if Jo was right. She had cast her cares on God a hundred times in the past hour, and the anxiety was back. "Okay, guys—" she looked at Jo and Denny and motioned for the boys to join them—"it's time to pray again."

But before they could utter a single word, Dr. Furin appeared. Abby squinted to make out his expression. She had seen the hint of a grin play on the man's face before, but she'd never seen his face fully taken up with a smile.

Until now.

Abby was on her feet immediately. "How is he?" The others stayed perfectly still, staring at the doctor, waiting for the news.

"He came through the surgery beautifully." Dr. Furin took a seat across from them. "His break was just as we hoped it might be. We had barely enough cord to work with."

Abby was frantic for the news. Her entire body trembled. "Can you tell yet? Whether it worked?"

The doctor's smile got even bigger. "He's already coming out of anesthesia and we've gotten reaction from all of his major reflexes." He held his hands out to his sides. "The operation was a complete success. He'll need therapy, of course, to regain the strength in his legs. But I expect him to make a full recovery."

Jo stood up and stared down at the doctor, her hands on her hips. "I'm a lot simpler than most folk, Doctor. I don't want this full recovery or therapy business. The question is: Will the man walk again?"

"Yes." Dr. Furin laughed out loud. "He'll beat you in a footrace before summer."

"Yahoo!" Jo raised her fist straight into the air. "Thank You, Jesus!"

Kade and Sean slid onto the sofa on either side of Abby and hugged her. They were both crying. "I didn't think—" Kade was too choked up to say more.

"What he means is—" Sean wiped his tears—"neither of us thought it would really happen. We thought . . . we thought you grownups were crazy to think an operation could help Dad walk again."

"I feel so bad." Kade sniffed, his face still buried in Abby's shoulder.

Dr. Furin nodded at her and quietly stood to leave. They could talk about the details later. For now she had two boys to comfort.

Jo took Denny by the hand and whispered to Abby, "I'll go tell Nicole."

Abby nodded and waited until they were gone. Then she soothed her hands over the backs of her boys. "It's okay . . . you don't have to feel bad. Daddy's going to be fine." They might be teenagers, but inside they were still children, still desperately in need of consoling. Especially with all that had happened in their lives this past year.

Kade coughed and lifted his face enough so Abby could see his swollen eyes. "I didn't believe, Mom. I've been a Christian all these years, and . . . and Matt's parents had more faith." He twisted his face in anger. "What does that say about me?"

"Me, too." Sean sniffed. "I knew everyone was praying for a miracle. I mean, I prayed for Dad to be okay. But I never really thought he'd walk again."

"You're not the only ones, boys. There were times when I felt the same way. I had to believe the operation wouldn't work and imagine my life that way. Even today I had trouble believing it would actually happen."

"Really?" Kade sat up a bit straighter. He dragged the back of his hand beneath his eyes. "I thought that kind of thing didn't happen to people your age."

Abby chuckled, giving Kade a soft punch in the gut. "People my age?" She raised her eyebrows. "I think it happens more to people my age." She thought of Haley Ann and her laughter dimmed a bit. "Because we've had a chance to see the truth that sometimes God doesn't give us the answer we want."

"So, Dad's really going to walk again?" The reality of what had happened was sinking in, and Sean couldn't contain himself. He bounced up and down on the seat. "Maybe he and I can go jogging this summer. Like, every day for a mile or two."

Kade laughed. "Give him time, buddy. First he has to get his legs strong enough to move them."

They were discussing the process of muscle atrophy, when Nicole and Matt came tearing around the corner. "Is it true?" Nicole grabbed Abby's hands. Her eyes were wide and filled with tears.

"My parents told me the operation was a success. They're taking a turn with Haley, but we had to come up and ask for ourselves. Is that really what the doctor said?" Matt blurted out.

Abby grinned and the feeling seemed to come from the depths of her soul. "To quote the man, he said your father will beat people at footraces before summer hits."

"*Yes!*" Nicole flew into Matt's arms, and then moved around the room, hugging Abby and her brothers. "I knew it was going to be a day of miracles. I just *knew* it."

As her children began talking all at once, laughing and smiling, filled with a hope they hadn't had before, Abby felt the nervous energy come over her again. Not because she was worried or anxious, but because there was something she had to do. Something no amount of pacing would satisfy.

"I'll be right back." Abby stood and headed down the hallway.

"Wait." Nicole called after her. "Where're you going?"

Abby only grinned, this time bigger than before.

"That's not fair. I want to see him, too."

"Me first. If he's awake, I'll come get the rest of you." Abby sent them a look that said they better not follow her. Then she practically ran toward John's room to do the one thing she'd wanted to do since his operation began.

Walk up to him, kiss him on the lips, and challenge him to a June footrace.

She slowed her pace as she neared his room. She didn't want to wake him if he was asleep. He was probably exhausted, and definitely still sedated. There were no sounds coming from his bed as she leaned her head inside the room, and then crept up alongside him.

"John, you did it, baby!" Her voice was a tender whisper, the kind she hoped he could hear in his dreams.

For a while he stayed still, but then he let out a weak moan. His neck was stabilized, so he couldn't turn his head. But his eyes began to move beneath the lids. After a few seconds he blinked, and Abby saw panic fill his expression.

"Honey, it's okay. The surgery's over."

He shifted his eyes toward her voice. The moment he saw her, the panic faded. "Hi."

She ran her fingers over his arm and bent down, kissing him on his forehead. "Hi."

"How long've I been here?" He winced, straining against the neck brace.

"Not long. An hour maybe."

The fog of medication seemed to clear, and his look became more intense. "Tell me, Abby . . . did it work?"

"Oh, honey, yes!" A single laugh escaped Abby's mouth, and she smothered it with her hand. She couldn't stop the tears that gathered in her eyes. "It worked perfectly. Dr. Furin says your leg reflexes are all normal."

"So . . ." He swallowed hard, and she could hear how dry his mouth was. "So . . . I'll be able to walk again?"

Abby nodded. "Try, John. Try to move your legs."

His head was strapped to the bed, but he stared down the length of his body. Abby watched as both his legs trembled beneath the sheets. If it had been any other time, if he hadn't just come out of surgery, Abby would have thought the movement an involuntary shivering.

But not this time.

John met her eyes again. "Did you see that?"

"Yes!" She brought her face close to his, not sure if she wanted to laugh or cry. "Did you feel it?"

"I did."

Abby stood again and this time she saw something she hadn't seen since John had been injured. He was crying. Not the way their sons had cried earlier, but in a quiet way that didn't seem like crying at all. Rather, it looked as though John had sprung a leak on either side of his face.

She kissed one of his cheeks, tasting the salt of his tears. "It's a miracle, John."

He sniffed and laughed at the same time. "How long before I can walk?"

"The doctor said you'd be winning footraces by summer." She kissed him again. "But I told the guy he was crazy. I'm a faster runner. I'd beat you. No contest."

"Oh, yeah?" John's voice was tired again, and a sleepy smile drifted across his face. "Is that a challenge?"

"Absolutely." She giggled, anxious for the days and weeks to pass. Desperate to see him fully recovered.

"Okay, you're on." His lids grew heavy and finally closed altogether. "June it is."

Abby stepped back and leaned against the wall. "Goodnight, John."

He was already asleep, the smile still on his face. She knew the others were waiting for a chance to see him, but she couldn't tear herself away, couldn't stop staring at him, reminding herself that it had really happened. The surgery had fixed John's legs!

She closed her eyes and lifted her face toward heaven.

God . . . thank You doesn't come close to telling You how I feel. First Haley . . . now John. You are so good, God. No matter what happens, there You are. Giving us peace . . . teaching us how to love . . . restoring us to a life bursting with hope. Thank You, God.

She remembered some of the verses that had pulled her through the dark days of John's paralysis: *"In this world you will have trouble. But take heart! I have overcome the world" . . . "Lean not on your own understanding, in all your ways acknowledge Him, and He will make your paths straight . . ."*

Abby marveled at the promises. God had definitely delivered—and long before John's successful surgery.

A dozen moments flashed in her mind. The day when John would take his first steps, the morning when he could finally come home, the time when he would first push little Haley in her stroller . . . the moment when he would run again.

And on some far-off June afternoon, the time when they would line up along one end of their backyard and race to the other. Of all the athletic feats John had accomplished, that single run would be the greatest of his life.

Thirty

AS MOVEMENT WENT, IT WASN'T MUCH.

They had to gather close around John's bed, their faces inches from his covered legs, just to see it. But Abby couldn't have been happier if John had jumped on top of the bed and danced a jig on the hospital sheets.

"See—" John pointed to his legs—"watch, I'll do it again."

Kade and Sean and Nicole and Matt closed in and stared at John's legs. His left knee rose half an inch, then his right, followed by the faintest rustling of all ten toes beneath the blankets. "It's amazing, Dad." Nicole took his hand. "You and Haley . . . on the same day. Only God could've worked that out."

It was Wednesday night, three days after the surgery, and Dr. Furin's reports had been nothing but glowing. John had surface and muscular sensation in nearly all sections of his lower extremities. The skin on the back of his calves was still somewhat numb, but the doctor wasn't worried. Rarely, in the few incidents where spinal cord injuries had been reversed, did complete sensation return just days after surgery.

"You're an exceptional case," Dr. Furin told him earlier that day. "You must have taken my advice."

John winked at the doctor. "Absolutely." He pointed to the full-page ad hanging on his hospital wall. "Most of Marion was praying for me."

Abby stepped back and let the kids ooh and aah over John's ability to move his legs. Everything about the past few days had been unforgettable. Seeing John that first day, watching their kids' faces when they were able to see for themselves that, yes, John had feeling in his legs once again.

And especially handing him the newspaper ad.

She'd given it to him the morning after the surgery, and at first he'd had as much trouble as Abby trying to make sense of it. Then he read the headline and the copy beneath it and stared at her, unable to speak.

"They love you, John." She shrugged, her voice tight. "I guess they always did."

"So they were . . ." He looked at the list of hundreds of names. "They were all praying for me?"

Abby nodded. "Apparently Kade told some of the guys on the team that Dr. Furin wanted everyone praying." She smiled. "A few of them took the order literally and began getting signatures. Anyone who would promise to pray, anyone who wanted to thank you for what you've done for that school, got their name on the list."

John had stared at it for a long time, scanning the names. "It's unbelievable."

"Not just that, but you had our prayers and those of Jo and Denny."

A chuckle worked its way through John's stiff neck and slid through his teeth. "Jo's someone I'd always want praying for me."

"She doesn't so much ask God, as she demands. Almost like she already knows it's going to work out, so let's get it worked out already."

"Exactly."

In the days since his surgery, they had shared many precious hours. So far only family had been in to see him. Family and Jake Daniels. Nothing could've kept the boy away. Abby guessed he'd be back again later that night. But now John was ready for other visitors as well.

John was feeling so good that Abby had given the green light to several people who wanted to come by. Already three players and their parents had stopped in, and now the kids were here. John never got tired of moving his legs on command—even a little. The atmosphere was as festive as Christmas Day.

"Hey, Dad. How come you can't lift your knees up or get out of bed yet?" Sean ran a finger over John's knee, staring at it. "I thought your legs were better."

"Dork." Kade elbowed his younger brother. "His leg muscles are gone. I told you, remember? He doesn't have any strength. He'll have to work to get them moving again."

John grinned at the exchange. "Yep, your dad's about as weak as little Haley."

Abby looked at Nicole. "How's she doing, sweetheart?"

"Wonderful. I get to hold her whenever I want." Nicole looked better than she had since she'd had the baby. Happy, content, and well-rested. "She weighs three pounds and she's gaining a few ounces every day. Her breathing is normal and she has no cerebral palsy from the early delivery." Nicole clasped Matt's hand. "She could come home in just three weeks if everything goes well."

The hospital door opened and Jo and Denny walked in. Jo was carrying a big wrapped box with a giant fish balloon floating from it. The fish read, "What a Catch!" Jo smiled big as she handed it to John.

He stared at it and bit his lip. "Thanks, Jo . . . Denny. You didn't have to do this."

"Ain't that the best balloon you ever saw?" Jo looked straight up at the green-and-gold mylar fish dancing above John's bed. "Denny told me it wasn't appropriate for a get-well gift, but I think it works." She looked at John, her face earnest. "See, once you're up and runnin' around again, you'll wanna get out in that boat of yours and do some fishin'. At least that's what I'd wanna do. And the minute you're back behind the rod, I know it in my bones you'll catch the fish of your life. So, see, the balloon works. 'What a Catch!'"

Abby and the others struggled to keep from laughing.

Denny rolled his eyes and shook his head in Jo's direction. "The woman's delusional."

Jo spun around and gave Denny a light kick in the shins. "I am *not.*" She turned back to John. "It works another way, too. When you're up and feeling better, those strappin' sons o' yours will have you on the football field in no time. Now I know your legs might take a bit gettin' used to, but not that arm you got." Jo brought her hand up and back behind her head, like she was about to throw a ball. "There you'll be, winding back, throwing for all you're worth . . . and one of these here boys will catch the ball. And you'll say—"

"What a catch!" John winked at Denny. "Makes perfect sense to me."

John was able to sit up now, and he positioned himself a little higher on the bed. He still wore the neck brace, and would for several weeks. But it didn't keep him from enjoying the celebration. He slid the paper off the gift box, opened it, and pulled out a pair of well-worn Nikes.

They were dirty, with barely any sole left, and two large holes near the tips.

"Okay." Jo motioned to the old shoes. "Let me explain."

A few giggles rose from Sean and Kade, but Jo waved her finger at them. "Hey, there . . . don't laugh. There's a story behind them shoes."

"Here we go." Denny shook his head. "I told her to give you flowers or candy like a normal person, but . . . well, you know."

"Stop." Jo snapped her fingers. She looked at Abby, then back to John. Abby could only guess what sort of story she was about to tell. "I hear tell you and Abby's gonna have a footrace sometime this June." She flashed a quick glance at Abby. "Ain't that so?"

Abby lowered her chin, doing her best to keep a serious face. "It is."

"Okay, then." She looked at John again. "I got the idea the other day when I was lookin' at your feet. I said to myself, 'Jo . . . why those feet look almost the same size as my Denny's feet.'" She cupped her hands around her mouth and whispered the next part. "Denny has big feet for a small man."

"Thank you, honey."

"You're welcome." Jo smiled and resumed the story. "So I started thinkin' about the time when Denny had the darndest run o' great fishin' days. I mean one day he'd catch three prize babies and the next he'd catch four. Went like that for weeks on end. And these—" she snatched the old shoes from John's hands and held them up for everyone to admire—"these were the shoes Denny wore back then." Her head jerked in a quick nod. "Saved 'em all these years in case we ever needed a pair of lucky shoes."

"So . . ." John reached for the shoes again and grinned at them. "You want me to wear these when I race Abby. Is that it?"

"O' course." She shook her head and shot a look at Abby and Nicole. "Men aren't the quickest study, are they?"

Abby opened her mouth to answer, but Jo beat her to it. "Okay, everyone, listen up. Denny and I got an announcement."

Abby and Nicole exchanged a quick giggle, before covering their mouths and giving Jo their attention again.

"Jo . . . we already told 'em." Denny's cheeks were pink, and he wore an apologetic look on his face. "Her memory's a little dim these days."

Her hands flew to her hips. "It is not. Besides, I never told 'em the facts." She turned to the others once more. "Me and Denny bought our tickets to Mexico." Jo winked at Nicole, and a knowing look filled Nicole's face. Whatever Jo was about to say, she'd obviously already shared it with Nicole. Abby made a mental note to ask Nicole about it later.

Jo whipped two small folders from her purse and held them up. "These are stamped and dated. Good for two one-way flights to Mexico the third of June."

"One-way?" Matt took a step closer and scrutinized the tickets. "You're coming back aren't you."

"Yes. Six months . . . a year maybe." Jo slipped the tickets back in her purse. "Don't worry, I can't miss little Haley growin' up."

"We'll come back to the States every few months for a visit."

Denny slipped his arm around Jo. "But we have to go." He and Jo swapped a tender look. "It's something we promised God."

"By the way—" Jo tapped Kade on the shoulder—"Denny says you've been talkin' to the pastor at church."

Kade looked startled. "Uh . . . yes." The look he shot at John and Abby was uncertain. "We've gotten together a few times."

"Well, that's not the point." Jo waved her hand in the air. "The point is, maybe you're thinkin' about being a pastor. Are ya?"

"No . . ." Kade's eyes grew wide. "Not really."

"A missionary, then?"

"Not so far."

"Well, that don't matter." Jo flicked her fingers over her head as though she were shooing away a fly. "Point is, we could use a strappin' young lad like you down in Mexico for a few weeks in July." She glanced at Denny. "Ain't that so, honey?"

Denny nodded, clearly embarrassed by Jo's approach. "That's what the pastor said. They want a team of volunteers to put a new roof on the orphanage."

Abby studied Kade and watched his confusion turn to curiosity. "Really?"

"Yes." Jo slapped Kade on the back. "And it's just a few weeks. Your football team won't miss you for a few weeks in July."

Kade asked several questions about the trip. When it was exactly . . . and whether some of his football buddies could come.

Abby watched in silent awe. A year ago Kade was heart-deep in the stench of pornography . . . and now he was considering a stay in Mexico to build a roof for orphan children. He'd been meeting with their pastor whenever he was home, and the change that had come about was amazing. Kade was tender and kind, more aware of spiritual issues. Walking daily outside God's plan for his life had caused calluses on his soul, but they were gone now, all of them. God, Himself, had removed them.

Nicole and Sean joined the conversation, asking more about the orphanage and the types of children who lived there. John reached over and linked fingers with Abby. "Maybe we should go, too."

Abby raised an eyebrow. "A footrace is one thing, John Reynolds. Building roofs in Mexico is another." She looked at Jo. "Ask us next year."

"Actually . . . it might be good therapy if—"

The door opened and Tim and Tara Daniels walked in. Jake was with them, a grin plastered across his face. He looked at John and the two swapped a knowing look. Abby knew immediately. The two of them were up to something.

"This a good time, Coach?" Jake moved in front of his parents and anchored himself near the foot of John's bed.

John did a quick survey of the room. "I believe it is."

"Hi, everyone." Jake waved at the others.

Abby could sense a slight hesitation on Nicole's part, but otherwise the group smiled and bid the boy hello.

"We won't be long. Just wanted to be here for a couple announcements." Jake nodded to his parents. "My folks can go first."

Tim took a step forward and looked from Abby to John. "Tara and I . . ." He reached back for her hand. "We wanted to thank you for praying for us. We've . . . we've talked it over and decided we never should've gotten divorced."

A quick giggle came from Tara's throat. "We wanted you to be the first to know."

"Other than me, of course." Jake stood between his parents and flung his arms over their shoulders.

"Of course." Tara smiled at Jake and then turned back to the rest of them. "Tim and I are getting married the first Saturday in June." She looked at Abby, tears welling in her eyes. "We want you and John to stand up for us. Be our best man and maid of honor."

"Right." Tim nodded. "Because it wouldn't have happened without you two."

"Isn't that awesome!" Jake gave a high-five to Kade and Sean, John and Matt. "My parents are getting married!"

"Oh, you guys." Abby moved around John's bed and hugged them, first Tim, then Tara, and finally Jake. "That's wonderful. Of course we'll be there."

Who would've ever thought a year ago—back when she and John were determined to divorce—that God would not only save their marriage and make their love stronger than ever, but that He'd use them to reach two people like Tim and Tara.

John's eyes danced and he pointed to the fish balloon. "In honor of your engagement, Tim, I think you deserve my balloon." He grinned at Tara. "I mean, what a catch!"

Everyone laughed and then Jake waved his hands. "Okay . . . quiet . . . it's Coach's turn."

A strange feeling bounced around in Abby's gut. Coach's turn? What was this about? And why hadn't John told her he had something to say?

"Dad?" Kade gave John a curious look. "You have an announcement?"

John shrugged as best he could with the brace in the way. His lopsided grin told Abby all she needed to know. Whatever he was about to say, he and Jake had this part planned out. "Yeah, I guess so."

"Go on, Coach. Tell 'em."

"Okay." John straightened himself once more. "Jake and I did a little talking the other day, and he told me next year'll be his best ever. I mean . . ." John angled his head, a grin playing on the corners of his mouth. "He'll be a senior and all."

"And for the first time I'll be really listening to Coach . . . you know, doing whatever he asks me to do . . ."

Abby held her breath. Could he be about to say—?

"So I decided to revoke my resignation." John lifted his hands and let them fall to his lap. "I'm going to coach next year, after all!"

The room erupted in a chorus of congratulations and hugs, high-fives and laughter. Jo slapped her leg. "That settles it. The Marion High athletic director—what's his name?"

"Herman Lutz." John grinned.

"Right, that's it. Lutz. Well, *he* gets the fish balloon. I'll take it into his office myself and hand it to him. 'What a catch, buddy!' I'll tell him, 'It's your lucky day because you just got John Reynolds back as coach!'"

Again everyone lit into conversation, guessing at the team's record next year and making predictions about how well Jake would do. Abby tuned most of it out and leaned against the hospital wall. Her eyes found John, and she saw that he wasn't listening either.

Instead they held a private conversation with their eyes. A dialogue where Abby told John how proud she was that he'd stood his ground and won, that he'd been willing to take a second look at the coaching job at Marion and realize it was where he belonged. And John silently thanked her for standing by him. Not just through the difficult days last season, or the horror of his accident, but during his wheelchair days and the anticipation over his surgery. And even now, when he was choosing to take time away from her once more to do the thing he loved.

"I can't wait." She mouthed the words, enjoying this private moment while the rest of the room celebrated loudly around them.

"Me, either." He held his hand toward her and she came, linking her fingers with his and feeling his love with every fiber of her being. "You know what, Abby?"

"What?" They were still whispering.

"It's going to be the best season ever."

Abby smiled and squeezed his hand. They had come so far, through so much. Yet now she was back where she'd started so many years ago. Looking forward to September and the warm glow of stadium lights on the face of the man she loved more than any in the world. Being caught up in a series of Friday night games, the way she'd been since she was a small girl.

The summer lay ahead of them, and with it no doubt dozens of small miracles. Haley would come home, and John would be up and walking again. But right then and there, Abby was consumed with one tantalizing thought.

John Reynolds was going to coach again.

Abby could hardly wait for the new season of their life together to begin. John was right . . . it was going to be the best ever.

Author's Note

PARALYSIS IS A DEVASTATING CONDITION. IN OUR COUNTRY today, the foremost cause of sudden paralysis in people is a gunshot wound to the neck or back. Car accidents follow as the second most common cause. The technology and treatment described in *A Time to Embrace* are futuristic and not yet in use. However, according to the American Association of Neurological Surgeons and the Congress of Neurological Surgeons, even at this very moment, the field of spinal surgery is enjoying an "explosion of new surgical techniques" designed to reduce or reverse spinal cord injuries.

In many cases these new surgical techniques are still in need of financial support and testing before they can be implemented. Some are years or decades away from working the way they worked on John Reynolds. I chose to allow Coach Reynolds to be an early benefactor of such new surgical techniques to demonstrate what I pray and hope will one day be a reality for anyone who has fallen victim to this devastating type of injury.

A Word to Readers

DEAR READER FRIENDS,

Thank you for traveling the pages of Abby and John's story . . . through their seasons of grief and gladness, joy and pain. This is my second book with these characters, and as such I have come to care for them a great deal. And to learn from the lessons they have taught me.

The most important may very well be this: life is made up of seasons. You don't have to be married to a coach to recognize the fact. Some months we're busy and distracted, others we can barely concentrate for the consuming thoughts of love that fill our hearts. Love for our spouse, our families, our Lord. There are seasons of joy and seasons of pain, seasons of grief and those of growth. Of heartache and hope.

If you ventured with John and Abby through the first part of their story—*A Time to Dance*—then you know the celebration they experienced at the end of that book. After very nearly giving in to their own separate desires, after making plans to divorce, they allowed God to rescue them.

I've talked with dozens of couples who have been through what John and Abby experienced in the first book. Couples who loved each other and intended to stay together a lifetime, only to find their marriage, their love, their oneness derailed somewhere along the road to forever.

God tells us in Scripture that He will never let us be tempted beyond what we can bear, but that when we're tempted, He will provide a way of escape.

That is always true, even when our marriages begin to crumble.

Of course, too often one or both spouses is not willing to look for that escape route, not willing to hear the voice of God above the voice of their own desires. But when both people will follow God's way of escape and put away their differences, the result is something more beautiful than you could dare to dream.

If you've read my other novels, you know that we have six children, the youngest of whom had heart troubles as an infant. Little Austin was born with a defective aorta, the main artery out of the heart.

In what was a very delicate surgery, doctors removed the bad sections of Austin's aorta and replaced it with a piece of artery from his left arm. The whole thing seemed unbelievable to me and my husband.

"What if the patch job doesn't take?" I asked the doctor after the operation.

"Oh, it'll take. In fact the area where there was trauma and healing will actually be stronger than the unaffected sections."

I thought about that for a long time and marveled at the truth there. Where there was trauma and healing, that section would be stronger than any other.

And so it is in our marriages.

Trauma will come to most relationships. Disagreements, differences, arguments. Even sometimes betrayal. God knew we'd stumble along the way, so He gave us His Word wrought with advice on how to handle it. How to make points of trauma, places of healing.

And come out stronger in the end because of it.

Forgive as the Lord forgave you.

Love is patient.

Love is kind. . . . It is not easily angered.

Be completely humble and gentle.

Love covers over a multitude of sins.

Bear with each other. Encourage on another.

Yes, God knows what it is to be wronged. Remember the first Good Friday? There He was with His closest friends, each of them making grand promises of loyalty and commitment, when suddenly a troop of soldiers appeared.

What did Jesus' most faithful followers do? They ran.

And that's the same thing we're tempted to do when our marriages don't go the way we expected, but we'd do well to follow Christ's example. Not only did He forgive His friends, He embraced them. When He appeared to them in the upper room after that glorious Resurrection Sunday, He comforted them with no thought of the wrongs they'd committed against Him.

When I finished *A Time to Dance*, many of you wrote to me wondering what happened to Abby and John . . . how they were able to work their reconciliation into an everyday life without falling prey to the problems that plagued them at first.

It was then that I realized the lesson of trauma and healing. The couples I know who have found glorious restoration in their marriages, almost always do so in a way that makes their relationship better, stronger, more loving than ever before.

The reason? A troubled marriage is a tested one. And when we look to God together as a way of passing the test, we will always be closer in the long run.

Please don't read into this a callousness toward those of you who've suffered through a divorce. It is the rare exception when two people determined to walk away from each other stop and look to God instead. Many of you would love to have a spouse willing to listen to God, willing to look for the escape route that would lead you away from divorce.

But far too often that spouse still leaves, completely hardened to God's voice.

For you, I pray God's tender mercy and healing upon your life.

That you would look to Him, the Author of life, for whatever your next step should be, and that you would believe He is the God of second chances. That He has good plans for you even now.

For those of you considering a divorce, mired in the throes of bitterness and betrayal, my prayer is that you stop attacking each other. Stop thinking it's your husband's fault or wishing you had a different wife. Realize, instead, that the enemy of our souls is the one who destroys what God has created. And the oneness of marriage is definitely a God-given gift.

Get counseling . . . pray together . . . pray for each other . . . look for ways to honor your spouse. And most of all search for the route of escape. Quite often that escape route is as simple as making an apology. Then allow God to heal your broken love. Let Him give you a time to laugh and love and live in peace.

A time to embrace.

And see if the bond you share isn't much stronger as a result.

On a personal note, we have had our adopted Haitian sons home for more than a year now and life couldn't be sweeter. Our biological children have embraced their new brothers in a way that can only be considered miraculous. Our entire family owes a debt of thanks to so many of you who have prayed for us along the journey.

We have had some hard times as well. After fourteen years of coaching basketball, my husband will be taking a few years off. Without getting into great detail, I can say this: some of the issues John Reynolds experienced the season before his injury were very, very close to home. We are, of course, glad to have Don home with us. The kids love it when he holds "mini-camp" in the backyard.

But still, there is loss.

If your son or daughter participates in organized sports, I have this challenge for you: thank the coach. If he or she is someone who cares for your child, someone who doesn't use foul language or abuse your kids for the sake of a victory, take time to be grateful. After every game, every practice, make it a habit to find those coaches who volunteer their time or who get paid only pennies for doing the job, and thank them. Coaches—*good* coaches—are hard to find. And when parents fail to see that, everyone loses.

As always, I pray this finds you and yours well, and feasting on our Lord's rich promises. We look forward with you to whatever adventures the Lord has around the corner. Keep praying that I write the books God places on my heart in a way that will leave a life-changing mark on yours.

In His love, and until next time . . .
Karen Kingsbury

P.S. As always, you can E-mail me at rtnbykk@aol.com, or contact me at my Web site: www.KarenKingsbury.com

Acknowledgments

AS ALWAYS, WHENEVER I PUT TOGETHER A NOVEL THERE are hosts of people working behind the scenes to make it possible. On that note, thanks must first go to my husband and kids, for understanding my need to hide away when deadline calls. There were reasons why this book was harder to finish than most. I couldn't have done it if you hadn't pulled together and allowed me the time to write. I love you all!

Also, thanks to my family support team, especially my mom and dad, and the rest of you who take time to read my books and offer valuable insight. A special thanks to my niece, Shannon, for always being the first with feedback. One day I expect to be reading your books, honey.

Prayer support is crucial when writing a novel—especially one with God-given truths woven throughout. I would be unable to write the stories God has given me if not for the prayers of my husband and kids, my family, and friends. I'm blessed to have not just those people praying, but also Sylvia and Walt Wallgren, Ann Hudson, and so many of you faithful reader friends who constantly lift me up in prayer. Thank you for your faithfulness. I pray you enjoy the fruits of partnering with me in this writing ministry.

Also, a special thanks to my assistant, Amber Santiago, for being everywhere I can't be as I set about the business of writing. Please know that your time with Austin and the hours you put in making my house livable are an amazing blessing to me. Thank you for your servant heart, Amber. I appreciate you more than you know.

In the writing of this book, I found myself desperately in need of quiet time. When that happened, I called up new friends of mine, Louise and Warren, and snuck off to their bed-and-breakfast for a few days of solid writing. Thank you for providing me with a quiet, phone-free environment in which to work. I am certain I'll spend many more hours at your hideaway.

Thanks also goes to those people who read galley proofs for me: Melinda Chapman, Joan Westphal, Kathy Santschi, and the Wallgrens. Your expert eyes have helped me turn out a novel I can smile about. Thank you!

On a business note, I'd like to thank Ami McConnell, Debbie Wickwire, and the good folks at Thomas Nelson for their commitment to excellence in women's fiction.

I had the privilege of working with my favorite editor, Karen Ball, in the course of this book. It was a difficult season for Karen, as she lost her dear mother, Paula Sapp, days before editing my manuscript. Karen, I ache with you at your loss and believe along with you that your mother is finally free. That even now she watches over you, praying for you, longing for the reunion that will take place one far-off day. Thank you for being willing to work with me even amid a season of heartache.

It is my belief that God teams writers up with agents for a good reason. As such, I am eternally grateful that the Lord brought Greg Johnson into my life. Greg is an author's dream-come-true agent, looking out for every aspect of my writing career. If you're reading this book, you can thank God for Greg's role in my life. I couldn't do this without him.

Also a special thanks to Kirk DouPonce of Uttley-DouPonce Designworks. Kirk and his amazing team of artists are quite simply the best cover designers in the business. If I had my way, every book I ever write would have their artwork gracing the front. Thank you for pulling off another amazing cover! You're the very best.

Reading Group Guide

1. Was the love between Abby and John stronger or weaker in light of the fact that they had so recently changed their minds about getting divorced? Explain.

2. Describe a time when you had a falling-out with someone you love. Was the love between you stronger or weaker afterward? Why?

3. Trust takes time to build again, especially in a relationship that has fallen victim to betrayal. How did this truth present itself in Abby and John's relationship?

4. Has trust ever been an issue between you and someone you love? Describe that situation.

5. How were you able to finally trust that person again?

6. The Reynoldses' son was involved in Internet pornography. What are your thoughts on whether this form of sexual sin is addictive? What examples from the book do you think would help in breaking that addiction for you or someone you love?

7. What role did Abby play in the family drama after John's injury? Why was this damaging to her?

8. Describe a time when you felt you had to fix everyone's problems.

How did this make you feel? How were you able to move past that season?

9. John's emotions varied quite a bit in the days after his injury. What event finally changed his attitude for the better? Why?

10. Nicole experienced a blow to her faith after her father was paralyzed. Why do you think this was? What finally helped her come back to a place of believing?

11. Have you ever suffered through a time that tore at your faith? What made believing in God so difficult during that time? How did you work through that time?

12. Jake's reaction to his role in Coach Reynolds's injury was one of horrendous guilt. What were Jake's feelings regarding his possible punishment? How did he grow during this season of sorrow and guilt?

13. Describe a time when you did something for which you couldn't forgive yourself. What brought about those feelings? How were you able to get past them and finally heal?

14. What were some of the ways the love between Abby and John grew during his wheelchair days? Describe your favorite moment between these two. Why was it special?

15. Love is not always easy. Describe a time when you were able to share love with someone through a difficult time. How did it strengthen your relationship? What did you learn in the process?

FOR A LIST OF OTHER TITLES
BY KAREN KINGSBURY,
GO TO

KarenKingsbury.com

Women of Faith Fiction

Women of Faith has shared the message of hope and grace with millions of women across the country through conferences and resources. When you see the words "Women of Faith Fiction" on a novel, you're guaranteed a reading experience that will capture your imagination and inspire your faith.

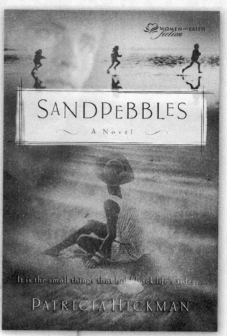

WOMEN OF FAITH fiction

SANDPEBBLES

~ A Novel ~

It is the small things that hold back life's tides...

PATRICIA HICKMAN

COVENANT CHILD

A Story of Promises Kept

TERRI BLACKSTOCK

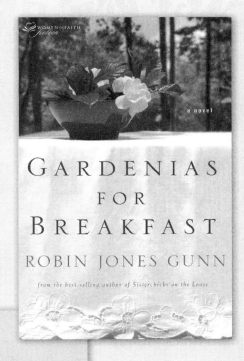

GARDENIAS
FOR
BREAKFAST

ROBIN JONES GUNN

from the best-selling author of Sisterchicks on the Loose

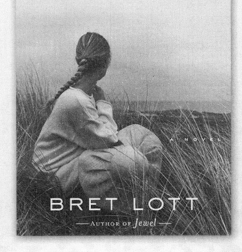

A Song I Knew *by* Heart

BRET LOTT

AUTHOR OF *Jewel*

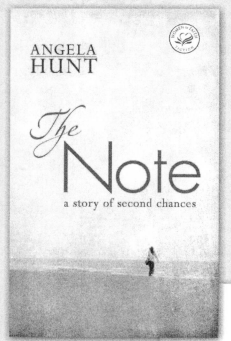

ANGELA
HUNT

The
Note

a story of second chances

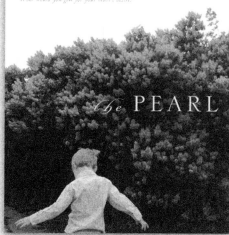

ANGELA HUNT

"What would you give for your heart's desire?"

he PEARL

THE STORY OF A PAST REDEEMED

THE DEBT

A Novel

ANGELA HUNT

A story of letting go

stranded in paradise

LORI COPELAND

WOMEN OF FAITH™
fiction

THOMAS NELSON
Since 1798

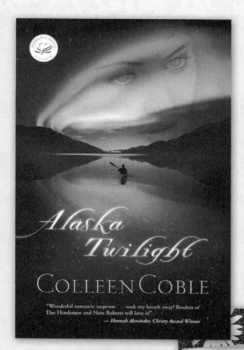

ALASKA
TWILIGHT

COLLEEN COBLE

"Wonderful romantic suspense . . . took my breath away! Readers of
Dee Henderson and Nora Roberts will love it!"
— Hannah Alexander, Christy Award Winner

WOMEN OF FAITH
fiction

Rene Gutteridge

My Life as
a Doormat

(IN THREE ACTS)

2006
NOVEL
OF THE
YEAR

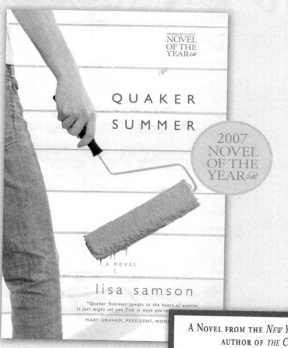

WOMEN OF FAITH
NOVEL
OF THE
YEAR

QUAKER
SUMMER

2007
NOVEL
OF THE
YEAR

A NOVEL

lisa samson

"Quaker Summer speaks to the heart of women.
It just might set you free in ways you've...
MARY GRAHAM, PRESIDENT, WOM...

A NOVEL FROM THE *NEW YORK TIMES* BESTSELLING
AUTHOR OF *THE CHRISTMAS SHOES*

the
Angels of
Morgan Hill

DONNA
VANLIERE

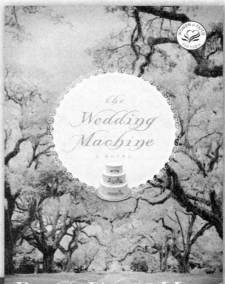

the
Wedding
Machine
A NOVEL

Beth Webb Hart
Author of Two of Booklist's Top Ten Fiction Picks for 2006

Colleen Coble is a master storyteller, whose heart-pounding plots
keep readers turning pages and coming back for more.
KAREN KINGSBURY, bestselling author of Even Now and Ever After

COLLEEN
COBLE

midnight sea

WOMEN OF FAITH
fiction

THOMAS NELSON
Since 1798

WOMEN OF FAITH *fiction*

THOMAS NELSON
Since 1798

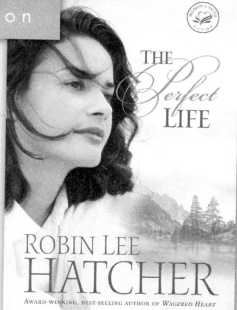